People
of the
Earth

by W. Michael Gear and
Kathleen O'Neal Gear

TOR®

A TOM DOHERTY ASSOCIATES BOOK
NEW YORK

This is a work of fiction. All the characters and events portrayed in this
book are fictitious, and any resemblance to real people or events is purely
coincidental.

PEOPLE OF THE EARTH

Cover art by Royo
Maps and interior art by Ellisa Mitchell

A Tor Book
Published by Tom Doherty Associates, LLC
175 Fifth Avenue
New York, NY 10010

www.tor.com

Tor® is a registered trademark of Tom Doherty Associates, LLC.

ISBN: 0-812-50742-8

First edition: February 1992

Printed in the United States of America

20 19 18 17 16 15 14 13 12 11

To Ray Leicht, Ph.D.

...for helping to hold up the wall one bleary-eyed Saturday night at the Plains Anthropological Conference in Bismarck, North Dakota—and everything that came of that conversation.

and

In special memory of
J.B. Saratoga Tedi Bear
June 3, 1975
to
October 10, 1990

The Masked Dancers

Father Water

The Swamp People

Short Grass Plains

Buffalo People

The Salt Trader People

The Antelope People

People

Legend

→→→ Trail of Wolf People's migration

•••••• Path of Broken Star's migration South

– – – Major prehistoric trade routes

☐ Area covered by detail map

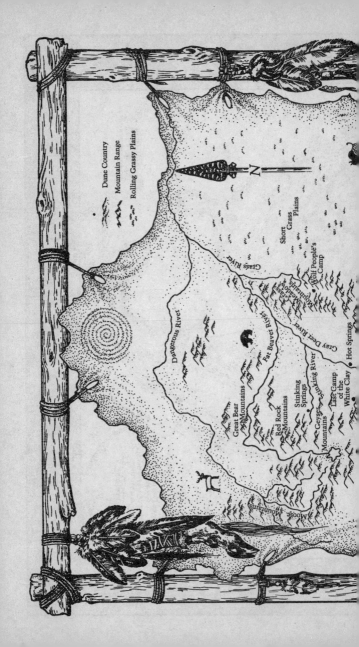

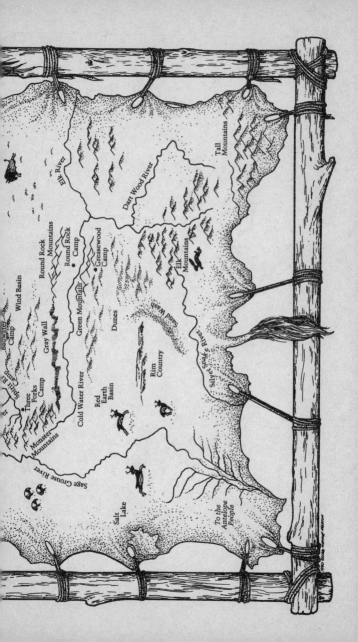

ACKNOWLEDGMENTS

We owe special thanks to Michael Seidman. As Executive Editor for Tor Books, Michael thought the reading public would appreciate novels on American prehistory written by archaeologists. If you've enjoyed the series so far, thank Michael.

In writing *People of the Earth*, we owe a great deal to Diane Berrigan for providing her collection of source material on Early Archaic house pits and structures. Marv and Patricia Hatcher, of Pronghorn Anthropological Associates, photocopied an incredible number of archaeological reports for our use. Ted Hoefer, of Archaeological Services of Western Wyoming College, presented us with a copy of his Master's thesis: EVIDENCE FOR ARCHAIC PERIOD DOMESTIC SHELTERS IN THE INTERMOUNTAIN WEST. Lynn Harrel, archaeologist for the Kemmerer Resource Area, BLM; Scott McKern, staff archaeologist for Western Wyoming College; Anne Wilson, U.S.F.S. archaeologist, Kootenai National Forest; Gene Driggers, U.S.F.S. archaeologist; Jude Carino, Casper District archaeologist, BLM; and Jamie Shoen, U.S.F.S. archaeologist, Bridger-Teton National Forest, helped hone the ideas on microenvironmental resource exploitation and social structure used in this book. We hashed it all out during the 1989 Little Snake Archaeological Rendezvous.

Jim Truesdale, National Park Service archaeologist for Dinosaur National Monument and expert of High Plains and Montane burial practices, provided input on mortuary behavior.

Bill Davis and Debbie Westfall, Principal Investigators of Abajo Archaeology in Bluff, Utah, deserve special mention for allowing us to work on archaic pit houses in Emory County, Utah . . . and we haven't forgotten the jalapenos, either!

Justin Bridges and Irene Keinert of Wind River Knives donated time and expertise photographing archaeological sites—thanks for your constant encouragement.

Phyllis Boardman and Jean Murdock allowed us access to archaeological sites.

A very special thank you is sent to botanist, John Mionczynski, for sharing his incredible knowledge of Western American wild plant resources and their nutritional and medicinal value.

Burt and Rose Crow kept Guinness and Chimay Ale in the Ramshorn Inn every time we needed an escape to talk about the book in neutral surroundings.

Special kudos go to our editor, Harriet McDougal, for the finest critique we've ever had on a manuscript. Good editors are hard to find, and, Harriet, you're one of the best. To Linda Quinton, Debby Tobias, and Ralph Arnote: Thanks for everything, you are the *best* in the business. Tom Doherty, Heather Wood and the superb team at Tor Books did the rest.

And special thanks to Don and Patty Woerz for last minute rescues.

FOREWORD

In the novel *People of the Wolf* we discussed the retreat of the last glaciation around fifteen thousand years ago and the migration of the first Native Americans into the virgin continent of North America. Over the following millennia, the climate grew progressively warmer and dryer. These increasingly xeric (hot and dry) conditions restricted the range of large game animals and this, coupled with human predation and environmental stress, drove many game species such as giant sloth, horse, and camel to extinction. By seven thousand years ago, the interior of North America was locked in a drought known to prehistorians as the Altithermal. The second novel in the series, *People of the Fire*, is set in this period, when bands of human hunters turned increasingly to the collection of plant resources.

Exploitation of the environment appears to have become specialized during the Altithermal. Recent archaeological discoveries that have occurred as a result of increased energy development and federal cultural-resource protection have uncovered a wealth of new information. Among the more exciting discoveries, researchers have excavated the remains of earthen structures which indicate that some human groups may have restricted their range, becoming seminomadic and basing their subsistence on intensive utilization of plant and animal resources in a given locale. The appearance of such structures fifty-five hundred years ago (four thousand years before their Southwestern Basketmaker counterparts) has reoriented our understanding of the Early Archaic. Where once we thought that Early Archaic peoples lived on the ragged edge of starvation, we now know they used their environment to an extent perhaps unequaled in the archaeological record.

Sometime in the last five thousand years, a major group of people spread across the western portion of North America. Today we know these people by the similarities of their language: Uto-Aztecan. In *People of the Earth*, we've placed the southward migration of Uto-Aztecan peoples at the end of the Early Archaic period.

Perhaps the most frequently asked question about our prehistory books is: "Did people really talk like that?" The general perception that our prehistoric forebears were grunting savages is widespread. It comes largely from movies that portray Native American tribes as semihuman barbarians who speak in half-sentences. *The image is quite simply false.* Our best linguistic theories, which search all modern-day native languages to find "root languages"—the original language, or languages from which our current-day versions spring—suggest that prehistoric peoples in North America spoke with as much sophistication as we do. The earliest White impressions of tribal languages further strengthen these theories. In the seventeenth century, French missionaries among the Huron reported that European languages could not compare with the complexity and intricacy of the Huron language. The Hopi still use verb tenses unheard of in English, and the Arapaho communicate in *two* separate languages, one for common use, the other for ceremonial purposes, much as Latin was once used by the Catholic church.

Our books' characters speak in coherent, refined sentences, because the best scientific theories suggest that they did. And our primary goal in writing this prehistory series is to provide the reader with the most accurate portrait of prehistoric lifeways in North America that we, as archaeologists, can. You will not find any convenient stereotypes here.

If this series spawns an interest in American prehistory, your local librarian or bookstore can direct you to books on the subject. Or contact your State Historic Preservation Office, the Bureau of Land Management, or the Forest Service, for further information. It's *your* cultural heritage.

People
of the
Earth

Introduction

Dust rolled up in a light tan smudge behind Skip Gillespie's big white four-wheel-drive pickup. The three-quarter-ton Ford pounded across potholes, puffing gouts of powdery grit out from under the all-terrain tires. Skip winced and bounced around in the cab as the truck chattered over washboard and hammered over a ditch where runoff had carved a gash in the dirt road.

"Damn. Gotta get a patrol to smooth this sucker out." He glanced over at the construction site that appeared as he crested a low, sagebrush-dotted ridge. The road snaked down into the basin and wound around through the scabby greasewood to the plant site. At this early stage it didn't look like much, just ripped and torn dirt where the heavy equipment had begun to shape the parched clay and sand into a flat spot. One day it would be a collection-and-processing center for oil and natural gas—one of the largest, and most expensive, plants in the country. But now the brightly colored earth-moving machinery lay idling in the harsh noon-hour sun while the crews ate lunch. Black smoke rose in dwindling columns from the diesel stacks to fade into the hot, dry air.

Skip followed the bladed road down the ridge and raced across the flats ahead of the dust trail that billowed behind the Ford in a rising white plume.

Despite the intrusive construction, the eternal presence of the pale, sun-washed land couldn't be ignored. From the infinite enamel-blue sky to the erosion-scarred buttes that hemmed the distance, the land dominated. It waited—sere, windswept, populated only by sagebrush, greasewood, salt-bush, and endless patches of glaring white clay. Here and there the desert-tan humps of sand dunes stood out, their scraggly vegetation a little greener where it robbed the sand traps of moisture. Distant blue-green mountains rose to the north and seemed to float on the polished-silver sheen of the hot basin mirage.

Skip took a deep breath and inhaled the pungent odor of dust and sagebrush, and with it, the soul of the barren earth. He squinted irritably over the flat desolation as he drummed his fingertips on the steering wheel and muttered, "Hell of a country. Why'd I ever leave Louisiana?"

He turned onto the construction site and wove past two belly dumps and around the gray-green prefab building that housed the temporary offices. He pulled up and slipped the transmission into park as the dust settled over the pickup. The big Ford idled roughly—probably because the damn air filter was plugged up again. Gas mileage had been like shit for the last week. What the hell, it was company gas.

Red Swenson stepped out of the dust-streaked office door and nodded as he started for Skip's truck. Swenson wore faded Levi's and a sun-bleached checked shirt that had been red once. The sleeves had been ripped off, and dust had caked under the man's armpits. A yellow hard-hat rested at a jaunty angle over the burly catskinner's sunburned face.

"Hear you wanted to see me," Skip called out the pickup window as he leaned his arm on the sill.

Swenson nodded, swirling a toothpick from one side of his mouth to the other. Sun and desert air had left his lips chapped and peeling. "Got a minute? It's over by the compressor pad. I'm doing the dirt work for the foundation."

Skip checked his watch. "I got a minute—but that's about all. There's a meeting with the engineers in half an hour." He glanced up. "This important?"

Swenson nodded before he glanced out at the construction site; a dust devil ravaged the torn soil. "Yeah. First off I thought I'd just cover it up, but I know them archaeologist guys have been poking around. Didn't want my tit in a ringer, so I thought I'd better talk to you. You're the one that's in charge of this shindig."

Gillespie's gut soured as he squinted up irritably at the

sun. *Archaeology? That's all we need right now. We're two months behind schedule and a half million bucks over budget, and the damned arkys could shut this whole project down for months while they screw around with a bunch of dead Indians.*

He sighed and slapped the steering wheel in resignation. "Hop in, Red. Let's see what you got."

He moved his briefcase and thermos to the side as Swenson opened the far door and slid in. *Jesus, the guy smells like rotten hot dogs.*

Skip slipped the automatic into drive and bounced off across the complex. Dust rose in a cloud that swirled into the cab to coat the dash with a fine layer. Well, better dust than mud. Otherwise, he'd be slithering around in four-wheel drive like a dirt-track ace—and cussing every minute of it.

Skip shot Swenson a narrow glance. "What did you find?"

"Beats me. A lot of that charcoal come up under the blade. That's what them archaeologists was looking for. That, and them chips of rock."

"Shit. We've already paid them bastards a couple hundred grand to walk around and dig their little holes every time they find an arrowhead." Skip shook his head. "Hell of a country we live in. We got a multimillion-dollar plant to build, and instead, we gotta screw around with dead Indians. What kind of country is this getting to be anyway?"

Swenson grunted as he stared out at the dry land.

Skip headed south on a bouncy two-track that had been beaten into the sage. A yellow Caterpillar, sitting beside a pile of dirt, marked the compressor site. He pulled up and set the brake as he looked the situation over. The alleged topsoil had been piled on the downwind side, the way the Feds wanted. Now several feet of soil had been moved off the ground surface, and half the dune that lay on the western half of the site had been torn away.

Swenson pointed with a crooked finger. "Over there."

Skip opened the door and stepped down into the disturbed sandy soil. He followed Swenson, irritated at the feel of sand scraping on his five-hundred-dollar ostrich-hide boots.

Swenson jumped up on one of the windrows left by the cat's blade and jerked his head. "Check that out."

Skip climbed up beside him and looked down to where the cat had made its last cut. Charcoal had smeared in a black stain as the blade scraped the surface, but he could make out the large, round discolorations in the soil. Charcoal and dark, organically rich soil contrasted with the tan sand, where large pits had been dug into the dune. Each of the discolorations measured three paces in diameter.

Skip stepped down, kicking at the charcoal. Flakes of colorful stone littered the ground. "Yeah, these are some of those house pits the archaeologists wanted to find. I saw some of them when I worked down in New Mexico."

He stared around at the sage flats. On the remains of the dune, ricegrass and wild rye waved in the afternoon breeze. The star-burst flowers of wild onion bobbed along the margins of the disturbed area. In the distance, a herd of antelope watched from one of the taller dunes. Skip shook his head, squinting in the bright sunlight. "Lord knows what those idiot Indians saw in this goddamned country."

Swenson came down to kick around in the dirt. "So, what do we do? I was at that meeting with that asshole BLM compliance guy. He said if we uncovered anything, to shut down. Now what?"

Skip chewed on his thumb as he studied the ground. *The archaeologists would love to get their hands on this. And if they found out just how good this site appeared to be . . .*

"Look, we can't have those archaeologists back here. They'd fool around for another couple of months, maybe even a year for all I know. That's bucks . . . and delays. Time's money, Red. We're an industry, not the National Geographic Society. Those guys had their chance. We did our part, followed the law, and let the arkys snoop around. We've got a schedule to keep."

Swenson stuck his fingers in his back pockets, staring at the big circles. "Who'd dig a hole that size? What for?"

"Go get the shovel outta my truck. Let's see what this is."

When Swenson returned with the shovel, Skip peeled back the dirt, the blade clunking hollowly on rock. He levered up a piece of sandstone. "Grinding slab," he said. "See where they wore out the top like a trough? That's from grinding seeds and stuff into flour."

"What's under it?" Swenson got down on his hands and knees to look. He brushed away the sand and scooped up a handful of charred seeds.

"Storage pit. Just like the Injuns left it. Been waiting there like that for thousands of years." Skip chuckled. "I read that damn report the archaeologists turned in."

Swenson squinted skeptically. "Better them blanket-ass Indians out here than me. I'm in this country only long enough to make enough to get back to civilization."

"Yeah, well, get back to work. We're paying you by the hour."

Swenson gave him a crooked grin. "And pile the backdirt so the charcoal don't show, right?"

Skip grinned. "You got it. I want this place to look nice and clean—just in case the BLM shows up. Hell, we don't want them to hold up a thirty-million-dollar project—and for what? The damn Indians aren't coming back. What the hell could we learn from a bunch of savages who'd live in a country like this?"

Skip stooped to pick up a black rock. He rubbed sand off the smooth surface and held it up. For a moment he couldn't believe what he held. The polished stone couldn't be mistaken—a fossilized shark's tooth. And a hole had been neatly drilled in the center, as if the tooth had once been a pendant or an ornament.

"Well, how about that? Guess I got something for my fireplace mantel." He paused thoughtfully. "But where in hell would they have picked up a shark's tooth?" *Fool, this whole country was ocean bottom a hundred and fifty million years ago. Where in hell did the hydrocarbons we're drilling for come from, anyway?*

Swenson kicked around in the loose sand, trying to find another shark's tooth. He turned up a bone, leached brown from millennia spent in the soil. He reached for Skip's shovel, uncovering another and another of the sand-encrusted bones until he unearthed a human skull, surrounded by more of the polished black shark's teeth.

"Holy shit!" Swenson cried, backing away.

Looking closely, Skip could see where the body had been laid in a carefully dug hole. The sand changed color at the side of the grave, marking the edge of the intrusion.

"Oh, Christ!" Gillespie groaned. "That's all we need. That'll get the damned Indians involved. Then we'll have an Indian monitor running around and being a pain in the ass." He looked at the shark's tooth in his hand. Yes, part of a necklace—and buried with the skeleton all those years.

"A damn dead man!" Swenson whispered.

"Dead's right. He's been lying under the dirt this long, he won't mind a while longer." Skip pointed to the end of the pad where the backdirt had been piled.

"You mean you want me to . . ." Swenson's mouth dropped open, exposing his two missing teeth.

"Damned right I do." Skip gestured, his gaze drawn to the skull that stared up at him with sightless eyes. "You'd have crunched him with the Cat on the next pass. What's the difference? Hey, what's this? You going goofy over a dead Indian? Aren't you the guy that cleaned out that bar down in town?"

"Yeah, but—"

"Then get on that Cat and hit it, Red. The longer this thing's exposed, the more nervous I get."

Swenson cocked his head, squinting in the sun. "You know, I heard about a guy up by Gillette. Found a mammoth tusk and took it home. Made it all the way up to crew chief in the mine he worked in."

Skip shot him a measuring look. "Yeah, well, Red, you tidy this up and there might be another thousand dollars in your check at the end of the month. Keep your mouth shut and there's always a job on one of my projects."

Swenson shrugged awkwardly. "Anything you say."

A thousand in Swenson's pocket made a better deal than paying out fifty grand and losing months while the archae- ologists dug the site. Besides, Red would drink it all away within a month or two anyway. Then he'd be back to shagging overtime to meet his truck payments.

Gillespie walked back to the Ford and threw the shovel in the back. He kicked the sand off his ostrich boots and slid into the driver's seat.

The yellow Cat chattered as the catskinner started the big diesel and backed up, accompanied by the sound of loud warning beeps. Skip watched as Red lowered the blade and moved forward to the clattering of the tracks, making another cut, destroying the last evidence of the house-pit site. Skip caught sight of one of the bones as the heavy blade rolled the roiling cascade of dirt. Red backed to make another cut, piling the rest of the skeleton into the backdirt.

Skip slipped the truck into gear and drove onto the rough two-track that would take him back to the main complex. Five minutes to the meeting with the engineers.

He still held the fossil shark's tooth. The stone felt cool and heavy in his hand. How many centuries had it lain next to that skeleton? How did a bunch of dumb Indians drill a hole through stone like that? What damn Indian would have done such a thing?

Who the hell cared? Skip had a project to build.

Prologue

**Three Forks Camp, Wind Basin,
5,000 years before present.**

Sandstone the color of dried blood rose in a sheer ridge that jutted from the rich grasses of the river bottom. The shape of the ridge goaded Sage Ghost's frightened imagination while he lay hidden in the grass; it looked as if some huge buffalo's back thrust up from the land itself to shelter the Earth People's camp from the prevailing winds. He shifted his gaze back to the camp he spied on. Sage Ghost belonged to the Sun People—a member of the White Clay clan. Here, in this southern land, he hunted again. He pitted his skill and cunning against an unknown people. Failure would mean swift death.

A shaft of sunlight split the clouds, brightening the crimson stone of the ridge until the rock seemed to burn. Erosion had carved the slopes; Sage Ghost could see the bones within the buffalo-shaped ridge. Did his imagination trick him, or did the ridge contain some Power he couldn't understand?

Is that the Power of the Earth People? Do they draw monsters from the dirt and rock? Stories told by Traders haunted his memory—stories of Spirits the Earth People had tied to the rocks and trees. *And if the Earth People catch me, is that what they'll do? Kill me? Trap my soul in the ground to wail forever in darkness? Thunderbird, help me!* Taking a deep breath to buttress his courage, he returned his attention to the camp.

The spot had been well chosen, with a southern exposure to catch the sun in winter. Five earthen mounds humped the sandy soil at the base of the ridge. Each no more than four long paces across, the dwellings resembled wasp nests, or the doings of some huge mud dauber. Openings, at ground level, faced the southeast. For the moment, the door flaps of tanned animal hide had been rolled up and tied with thongs.

A group of elderly men and women sat under a sagebrush sunshade in the trampled place between the structures. A smoldering fire contributed desultory tendrils of blue smoke to the evening. With a great waving of arms and cackling speech, one of the old women dominated the group as she told a story. Heads nodding and bobbing, the listeners watched enraptured. The odd language carried to where Sage Ghost lay. Their tongue sounded like the cooing and clucking of the mourning doves—and every bit as incomprehensible to him.

Power had brought Sage Ghost to hide here among the thick clumps of giant wild rye along the river. Here he could spy upon the Earth People's dirt-covered lodges. The vision had told him that the Earth People would kill him if they caught him. He glanced around anxiously, peering through the tall grass as he sought to place every potential escape route in his memory. If someone sounded an alarm, where could he run? He didn't know this country, didn't have that feeling for the way the land lay, or how the trails ran.

Sage Ghost carefully straightened his leg where it had begun to cramp. He lay on his muscular belly, curled around tussocks of grass like a human snake. The thick black hair over his forehead had been pulled up in a roach and pinned with a buffalo-scapula clip; the rest hung down his back in a tumbled, gleaming stream. A line of five black circles had been tattooed across his forehead. Wide cheekbones gave his face a craggy look, the skin sun-darkened and weathered. His long nose sprouted like an eagle's beak over a broad-lipped mouth. From under heavy brows, keen eyes studied the camp of the Earth People. Broad shoulders rippled with muscle, as did his arms: muscles to power the gleaming darts gripped in his callused right hand and the atlatl—a chokecherry shaft as long as his forearm, with a curved antler hook in the end. The atlatl acted as an extension of the arm to increase the power of a cast dart by as much as two hundred percent. The deadly dart—as long as a man was tall—consisted of two parts: the stone-tipped foreshaft, which detached upon impact, and the fletched shaft that bounced back and could be retrieved, quickly fitted with a new foreshaft, and thrown again.

Fear slipped along his spine on feet of ice.

The vision brought me here. Led me over the long trail to this place. He raised his eyes, whispering as loudly as he dared, "Where is the child? Haven't I proven myself worthy?"

He gazed into the deepening blue of the late-afternoon sky. Sage Ghost had always felt a healthy respect for Power—but he'd never sought it the way some did. He'd been content to hunt, to raise his family and love his wife. Calling on Power left him uneasy; Power and fire were a lot the same. They could be managed and manipulated when treated with respect, or, if treated casually, they could scorch the world or sear the life from an unwary man's body.

And here I am, far from my people and the land I love. Where is the child? Or has the Power turned against me? Am I about to be destroyed? Burned up and turned to ashes, with no one to mourn my soul?

Power was the business of the shamans—the Dreamers and Soul Fliers. They knew the ways of Power as eagles knew the ways of the air currents high overhead. Soul Fliers could loosen their souls from the body and send them wheeling through the Dream the way Eagle circled in the sky.

Sage Ghost had never had the calling to seek Power. A Soul Flier might know how to free his spirit and sail like Eagle on the winds of Power, but Sage Ghost had always known he would tumble to the unforgiving rocks below.

Events change a man's life. Desperation drives the most resolute to seek that which he's always avoided. The death of Sage Ghost's daughter had changed his life, and the life of Bright Moon, his wife. Stung by the grief in Bright Moon's eyes and the ache in his own soul, Sage Ghost had raised his arms and called on Power, and Power had led him south, to spy on this curious camp.

Sage Ghost struggled with an impulse to run, to get away from this land and this strange people. But to do so would offend the Power that had brought him this far.

My soul is a bit of thistledown cast loose on the winds. A shiver—like the prickly sensation of grasshopper feet on flesh—worked down Sage Ghost's spine.

Evening continued to settle over the warm, dusty body of the earth. Streaks of reddish cloud flamed in the dying light of the sun. Insects chirred and clicked in the grass around him; a breeze rustled the rasping green stems. Mosquitoes hummed irritatingly but without the annoying persistence of those common to his home country to the north. Frogs stroked the quiet air with guttural cries.

Inclined hills rose to the west, buff slabs of uptilted mountains stippled by limber pine and juniper where the trees had knotted thick roots into the cracked rock. The implacable face of the mountain had been cut by the three forks of the river in the way a chert knife might rip through a lodge bottom. The waters ran cool and clear through the shaded, tree-choked canyons. Behind him lay the blue-gray range of mountains he had crossed on his journey. The northern slopes had risen gradually until he reached the divide. From there the way had turned treacherous when rounded caps of weathered granite had dropped off in precipitous cliffs. A misstep would have meant death. The range stretched east-west, hemming in this giant basin of rock, sand, and desiccated clays.

Beyond those mountains, more weeks' travel away—north of the Fat Beaver and the Dangerous rivers—lay his own familiar rugged steppes. There, along the many drainages that fed the Bug River, the White Clay clan of the Sun People struggled to hold their territory. Their grasp on the rich land continued to be peeled back, a fingerhold at a time. Other clans of the Sun People moved out of the north to drive the White Clay before them like husks of grass before a powerful wind. Keen-eyed warriors of the Broken Stone, the Wasp, the Black Point, Hollow Flute, and Snow Bird clans lashed out—each clan a burning stick whose very numbers caused a conflagration across the north.

Sage Ghost's attention returned to the curious dwellings. These Earth People might have been pocket gophers, the way they lived. Like the shy rodent, they flung up a pile of dirt and lived below it. A lodge made of earth? And dug into the ground? How impossible to conceive. How did they think—these people who lived in the Earth Mother's breast? How could they keep from going as crazy as a fly-ridden buffalo from never feeling the wind rock their lodges, never being able to roll up the bottoms and peek out at the world? Who would have thought that humans could live in such a way?

A yipping band of children popped one by one from the dark gape of a doorway. Sage Ghost narrowed his eyes, studying the thin girl who ran laughing with the little boys. A quickening of his heart matched a curious light-headed joy. Power stirred in the air around him.

The child!

He tensed, excitement pulsing with the blood in his veins. The Singers would raise their voices in the winter lodges as they related the story of Sage Ghost's Spirit Hunt.

The Traders had told the White Clay fantastic stories about the Earth People for as long as Sage Ghost could remember. But to see them in the flesh? Did Traders feel the way he did right now? Did they know this sensation of wonder? Traders went everywhere, the magic of their Trade protected by the Power of their wooden staffs. Sage Ghost remembered wondrous nights around crackling camp fires when he'd eaten foods made by the Earth People—shared those tastes and by doing so, shared a bit of soul.

Is that what brought me here? The Power of the Trade? Is that where the link was forged?

A curious elation possessed him. He had fondled the Earth People's finely crafted bone-bead necklaces and breastplates, and admired their skilled leather work dyed in purple, yellow, and red.

And they must know of us. For surely the Traders had told the Earth People about the White Clay—and perhaps the beadmakers had eaten smoked-and-dried buffalo, moose, and elk jerky, the animals killed by his own hand.

Is that the Power of Trade? Is it a sharing of Spirit and Soul? Do all people, no matter how different, Trade pieces of themselves through the things they make?

In the camp, the slim girl laughed and clapped her hands as she taunted one of the little boys and skipped out of his reach. She moved with the grace of a yearling doe. The dying light gleamed off the wealth of her long black hair.

The old woman stopped her story, turning to glare. Raising her voice, she berated the girl. The boys immediately backed away, leaving her alone before the old woman's wrath. The hag erupted in another outburst and the girl nodded, eyes downcast. Then the child fled, lustrous hair streaking out behind her.

Sage Ghost started to edge away—to slip silently over the cut bank and skirt the camp—when movement caught his eye. His mouth went dry.

A huge black wolf watched him from the shadows of the greasewood. Its triangular ears pricked forward, while gleaming yellow eyes seemed to burn into his soul, measuring, probing. Power pulsed in the air.

This is the place. Fragments of the vision returned to him. Giddy energy charged his muscles. Breath shortened in his lungs. Power did that, sneaked up on a man and blew through his soul like a freezing wind.

He swallowed hard and glanced back at the mounded dwellings of the Earth People. What next? The girl squatted down, separate from her playmates. She watched one of the little boys drawing on the ground with a stick. Her dejected posture touched something in Sage Ghost's soul.

Yes, you are the one, child. Now I have to be cunning—and as brave as I've ever been. His heart began to pound.

He looked over his shoulder at the wolf—and shivered. No trace of the animal remained. Sage Ghost filled his lungs, Power pressing down around him like an aged buffalo robe.

Power is here, all around me, waiting. Power led me here, showed me the wolf—just like the Dream said. That little girl, she's the one. Power sent me for her.

Sage Ghost wiggled closer to the camp, trusting the graying light to hide his movement from sharp eyes. No matter that he hadn't seen any warriors, a man never knew about the Power of others. The White Clay believed that Thunderbird had given them the best of Power, but other folk—especially those tied so closely to the earth—might have their captive Demon Powers to help them.

Getting the child away would be difficult in itself, and taking her north to the White Clay camp on the Bug River would challenge all of his wits and skill.

I've got to do it! A man doesn't forget a promise made to Power. Better that his warm flesh stop a keenly tipped dart than that he return empty-handed, violating the vow he'd made on his soul before Thunderbird and Bear.

Even as he stalked the child, the anguish in Bright Moon's eyes haunted him, goading him to try his best. Together they'd carried their last daughter up the rocky, windblown trail and laid her body on the ridge top, where her soul could soar free and rise to Thunderbird. There, crouched in the wet cold of the spring night, he'd rested his hand on his wife's shoulder and looked up at the twinkling lights that filled the night sky. The souls that Thunderbird took up to the Camp of the Dead made their camp fires just as men did.

"I can't bear any more," Bright Moon had cried. "What will become of us? What?"

Afterward he had led her down from the windswept ridge, aware of the angry bite of the coming spring storm. He remembered that feeling of hollowness he'd had as he'd ducked into the lodge. He'd stared around, seeing the place where his children had lived—and experienced an emptiness of the soul. Two of his infant sons had died mysteriously in the night, their bodies turned blue. One of his daughters had been bitten while trying to stop a dog fight, and the wound had gone bad; evil had sneaked in to cause pus and corruption. She'd died in fever. Another daughter had lasted five seasons before a silver bear caught her picking berries. The bear's hide still covered Bright Moon and him on cold nights—little solace for a dead daughter. Last of all had been Willow Hoop. She'd been the strong one, the one who would become the slim young woman who would marry well, the one who would find a strong young man and give them grandchildren to teach and enjoy in their old age.

Then one spring day Willow Hoop had taken a foolish chance. She'd run out on the spring-rotten ice of the Bug River while chasing after a scrambling jackrabbit. Where she'd gone through the ice, the water ran black and silent.

Only by luck had they retrieved her body from a snag downstream. Otherwise—and Sage Ghost shuddered to think it—she might have lost her soul down there in the black water, and it might have turned to evil and haunted the camps of the people on long winter nights.

In those miserable days after his daughter's death, the world had lost its color. The wind had bitten with colder teeth and the clouds had dulled in the blustery sky. Laughter and hope had disappeared. Grief had wilted his spirit. Bright Moon's eyes had eaten at him, raw wounds from which her tortured soul leaked.

So it doesn't matter if the Earth People catch me. I had to come . . . had to try to take the child. To have done nothing would have been to live with the emptiness inside . . . to watch Bright Moon's soul dying bit by bit from grief.

Sage Ghost slipped closer, careful to keep downwind, knowing that all could be lost if the camp dogs got his scent. Most of the animals appeared to be old, although he'd seen one healthy bitch with a litter of puppies earlier in the day.

Better to take this terrible chance than to live with the grief. In misery, he'd gone to Old Falcon, the White Clay Soul Flier, and asked for help, explaining that Bright Moon's bleeding had ceased, that she needed to conceive one more child.

"Take this. This is Mouse's helper," Old Falcon had said with a grin, handing him a mouse skin stuffed with grass. "Call on Mouse, who is always fertile. Do not eat or drink for four days and nights. Sing each day, and place Mouse's helper under your bed on the fourth night. Power will come to you."

As Old Falcon had promised, Power came—only it wasn't Mouse. Rather, a mysterious, handsome youth had appeared out of the sun-struck clouds and smiled. *"I've heard your Singing and seen your Dancing and felt your purification as you cleansed your soul. Bright Moon has passed her time to bear children. You can do nothing. No Power will restore her fertility."*

Sage Ghost's soul had twisted and cried out as he lifted trembling hands to the handsome young man. "What can I do? Look at her. Feel her grief. She says she'll die—that she can't live knowing all of her children are dead.''

And the handsome man had smiled. *''And what would you give for another child?''*

''Anything!''

''Then journey south, far beyond where you've been before. Cross the Dangerous River, cross the mountains. Continue south until you see my Spirit Helper, the Black Wolf. There you'll find a camp of people. There you'll find a young girl who needs to be loved. She'll be afraid at first. Her family will kill you if they catch you; but if you're strong, and if you're cunning and take good care of her, she'll come to love you. If you're worthy, she'll be a great and powerful Dreamer for the People.''

''On my honor before Thunderbird, who might not take my soul to the World of the Dead, and on my honor before you, I will be worthy. I'll do anything to see my Bright Moon's face light up again.''

The young man had smiled then, and flames had appeared to swirl around him as he rose like fire into the sky.

The next morning Sage Ghost had returned the Mouse fetish to Old Falcon. He'd put together his pack and hugged his beloved Bright Moon, telling her that he was going to fetch her a new daughter, one given to him by Spirit Power.

''And I am here,'' he grunted under his breath as he slipped into a screening mat of sagebrush.

An ebbing redness outlined the mountains to the west, and indigo shadows draped the camp, softening the outlines of the dome-shaped dwellings. Someone threw more sagebrush on the fire where the elders sat smoking and talking.

Sage Ghost crawled closer, careful to make no sound. Now he could smell the camp: scents of sage smoke, dogs, and humans. The odor of rich dust hung in his nostrils.

One of the old men called something, waving his hand to emphasize his order. The girl jumped to her feet, wary eyes on the elder. She looked to be about ten winters old, maybe a little younger. She answered neutrally and plucked a skin bag from the tripod by the fire. Slinging it over a skinny shoulder, she started down toward the river.

Sage Ghost's heart hammered as he rose and drifted silently after her in the deepening gloom. She walked with a grace and balance unusual in a girl her age. Thick black hair hung down to her waist. She hummed some Earth People song under her breath as she wound through the sagebrush, moccasins patting on the worn trail.

Sage Ghost hovered like a falcon over an unsuspecting rabbit, gliding on bobcat-silent feet. She hopped lightly down to the riverbank, unslinging the hide bag. For a moment she looked up, eyes searching the heavens. Then she sighed and bent over the water, a mere shadow among shadows. He could hear her feet splashing.

The east had darkened, the first faint flickers of stars penetrating the veil of the sky. Finches and sage thrashers chirped to the growing darkness; evening settled like velvet soot on the land.

Sage Ghost eased one foot after another as he closed on the child. Years of hunting had trained him for this moment; skill flowed through him like a special kind of Power. Water gurgled as it filled the pouch she held to the current.

Careful, Sage Ghost. One false move now and you'll fail. If she screams, all will be lost.

She stood, water dripping musically from the sides of the bag and covering the sound of his movement. His hand clapped over her mouth as he pulled her backward.

He mumbled a curse under his breath as she sank teeth into the palm of his hand; then she began to kick and squirm, her screams throttled. He picked her up as if she were a struggling antelope fawn and walked out into the lazy water. She battered at him, flailing against his side as he clamped her to him and started down the channel.

"Hush," he whispered in a soothing voice. "I won't hurt you. I'm taking you north, to a new home, to people who will love you."

She wrenched this way and that, muffled sounds coming from her throat. He could feel the terror in her desperate struggles. She threw herself back, twisting, trying to break free.

"Here, quiet. You can't get away—not from Sage Ghost. You've been promised to me. You will become a great Spirit Woman—a Soul Flier—among the White Clay. I know it. A man of fire came from the sky and told me."

She relaxed slightly in his arms, panting her fear against the back of his hand.

Sage Ghost jumped as a wolf howled prophetically into the night.

Chapter 1 🦉

Such a terrible winter.

White Ash leaned forward, face pinching as cramped and knotted muscles strained in her back. She peered across the fire at the pile of hides covering Bright Moon's body. The draft that sneaked in around the lodge skirts created patterns in the thick bed of glowing red coals and cast a ruby light over the inside of the lodge. She could see Bright Moon's face; her mother finally slept.

My mother? Curious. I can hardly remember my life before Sage Ghost stole me from the Three Forks camp. I belong here, among the White Clay people, now. Owlclover might have borne me—but Bright Moon loved me more. White Ash rubbed a nervous hand over her face and looked at the old woman who now slept so fitfully. *And all I can do is sit here and watch her die.*

"Thank you for everything, Bright Moon," she whispered softly in sorrow. If only Sage Ghost hadn't left with the other men in a desperate attempt to find game. She closed her eyes, grief a physical pain, like a gnashing of teeth in her chest. Bright Moon would be dead before he returned.

For eight winters White Ash had lived with the White Clay. Of those years, the first six had been wonderful. As she'd grown, she'd learned the ways and language of the Sun People. The White Clay had moved south from the Bug River, all the way to the Fat Beaver, to avoid the raiding in the north.

She smiled as she remembered carefree days of golden sunshine in the summer and cozy, warm lodges in the winter. Through all of them, Bright Moon's face had beamed with love for her. She'd played with Wind Runner and Brave Man and the other children. They'd run and told jokes and hunted for mice and rabbits.

White Ash shook her head, the smile on her lips bittersweet. Three years ago things had begun to change. Rumors had circulated down the trail that the other clans were beginning to move south, seeking new territory. The White Clay warriors had strutted among the lodges, thumping their chests, growling threats about what they'd do if the other clans came near.

Then the Black Point clan attacked the camp on the Fat Beaver River and caught everyone by surprise. The White Clay had fled in horrified confusion and come unraveled, splitting into three factions. Defeat after defeat had thinned what remained of their ranks. But the people had never been as desperate as they now were. War visited them again, bringing death and privation. Hunger stalked the camp, reflected in the gaunt faces of the children and elders. The cold seemed to intensify, rending their bodies with talons of ice. Hope had fled with the ghost of summer.

Hope? How can I hope? What have I done to deserve this? What hope will there be for White Ash? She closed her eyes and shook her head, trying to escape the images in the Dreams. She forced herself to relive the days when she and Wind Runner and Brave Man had laughed and told each other what they hoped for the future. The sun had been brighter then. The meat racks had bent under the weight of rich red slabs. The White Clay had been whole, powerful. Smiling faces peered at her from the past—faces of people dead or vanished with the breakup of the clan. Faces now as remote as those of her native Earth People.

Bright Moon made a gasping noise that withered White Ash's spirit. *Sage Ghost, maybe it's better that you don't know.*

She leaned forward, propping her chin on one knee, staring dully at the spot where Sage Ghost's bedding should have been. Various parfleches—collapsible rawhide bags—had been stacked around the bottom against the skirting of the lodge to act as extra insulation from the stinging cold. The dogs slept outside but their packs stayed in, away from eager teeth, be they canine or packrat—assuming one of the wily rodents made it that far past the famished dogs. Peeled poles, where they supported the finely sewn hides of the lodge cover, gleamed in the crimson light. Through the smoke hole she could see the stars, wavering as the hot air made a mirage of the soot-stained hole.

Tired, deadly tired. Her soul ached. Could this really be happening to her? She glanced at the mounded robes where Bright Moon lay. How long had it been? An eternity?

No, only two long days since Sage Ghost had left with the other men in another attempt to find game—anything to augment the dwindling supplies of food. They shouldn't have come out here in the middle of the basin in the first place. Sage Ghost had told Whistling Hare that starvation and the Wolf People lurked here.

But who remained sane among the battered remains of the White Clay? They were but one small band of the Sun People, harried, constantly pushed farther south by the Broken Stones, the Hollow Flute, and the Black Point. The northern bands had grown, swelling in size until they strained the hunting grounds and stripped berry bushes of fruit.

The clans weren't the only threat. The Wolf People, who lived in the Grass Meadow Mountains to the east, hated the Sun People. Only a week ago they'd ruthlessly raided a Sun camp, sweeping through the village like a swarm of enraged buffalo, burning lodges and murdering everyone in their path. They'd even killed the women and little children, and brutally slashed open the wombs of pregnant mothers to rip the babies from their bodies. Fear stalked the clans of the Sun People like a malignant demon. To the west, the Sheep Hunters, who hunted in the Red Rock Mountains, had warned the White Clay what would happen if anyone foolishly pushed into the canyons in their range. In a world gone hostile, the only hope for survival lay to the south, beyond the Sideways Mountains . . . maybe somewhere beyond the land of the Earth People.

While the men hunted, the women trekked long, circuitous routes to check snares and look for concentrations of jackrabbits that might be driven into a trap. The endless, nagging cold continued.

And I have to face Bright Moon's death alone.

The day after Sage Ghost left, the chill had awakened her, eating through the robes, bringing her out of another of the strange Dreams. She'd blinked, wondering why Bright Moon—who took such pride and delight at offering tea to early risers—would have let the fire die. She'd blinked in the gray light and sat up.

"Bright Moon?" she'd called softly and heard no answer. She reached over to the silent bundle and lifted the hides.

Bright Moon lay on her side, eyes glazed by a terrible fear. Her gray hair spilled loosely over the furs, contrasting with the red tones of fox hair under her head.

"Bright Moon?"

A desperate croak had come from her foster mother's throat.

White Ash had panicked and thrown on her frost-stiff clothing before stumbling out into the mauve light to run flat-out for old Flying Squirrel's lodge.

The old woman's reputation as the real leader of the band had grown through the years. Her husband, Whistling Hare, might pronounce the decisions, but most people suspected that Flying Squirrel lay behind each and every one. Not that people minded Whistling Hare's leadership; they respected his counsel—and, of course, Flying Squirrel's—and generally did as he advised.

Flying Squirrel had pulled a robe about her thin shoulders and hurried across the snowbound camp. Wind whipped the old woman's silvered braids; the expression on her lined face had gone grim as her feet crunched through the grainy snow. She'd ducked into the lodge and stooped to pull Bright Moon's blanket back. "Bright Moon?"

Only the frightened eyes had moved, tears welling in their corners.

"Can you hear me?" Flying Squirrel had persisted.

Bright Moon mumbled something, lips not moving, eyes darting this way and that.

"Rest, old friend. We will make a fire and get you something to eat." And she'd turned, beckoning White Ash to follow.

Outside, beyond earshot, Flying Squirrel faced White Ash, weary resignation in her old eyes. With a callus-horned hand, she rubbed her long face, rearranging the patterns of wrinkles. "I've seen this before. It's soul splitting."

White Ash drew a quick breath, stiffening. "Her soul's separating from her body? You mean like what happened to old No Teeth?"

Flying Squirrel nodded. "I don't know why. It just happens among the White Clay—more so than among other people. Sometimes it's just one side of the body, and maybe it gets better through time. But with Bright Moon . . . Listen, girl, I've walked this earth for six tens of summers and a little more. When it's this bad, it's usually only days until the soul leaves all the way."

White Ash swallowed against her thudding heart. "We need a Soul Flier to sing for her . . . to heal her. We'd better send a runner after Old Falcon. Maybe if he comes back from the hunt, he can Sing her soul back into . . . Why are you looking at me that way?"

The tenderness in Flying Squirrel's expression deepended. "Because, child, I know you love her. I know what a blessing it's been to Bright Moon to have you these last eight years. But there's nothing we can do."

White Ash shook frantic fists. "But if Old Falcon—"

"Shhh! Which of the boys would you send? Young Drummer? He's barely fourteen summers old. He knows how to stay alive, but with all the trouble we've had, do you think the men left a trail? Hmm? And you know how it is in early spring. Warm in the morning and blowing snow like crazy in the afternoon. And what if the men find a herd of buffalo? Would you have Old Falcon leave them and come running back? Would you risk the Power of the hunt?"

"But she's *dying!*"

"Yes, girl. She is. And if you don't get that fire started in the lodge, she'll freeze to death first. Come on, I have some embers you can carry back. The fire looked stone dead. You take care of her and let us do the rest. We all love Bright Moon. We'll all help."

And they had. Some brought thin stew, the last of their

rations, cut with more and more water. Others brought firewood, or warm tea. Meadow Vole had come and sat by the hour and talked about the past, enjoying a sharing of memories one last time before yet another link with long-gone days separated forever. Through it all, Bright Moon lay there unmoving, helpless and fading.

White Ash did what she could, cleaning Bright Moon's bedding, washing her foster mother, holding her hand during the other times. And finally the old woman slept.

A heaviness pulled at White Ash's eyelids; an ache stabbed through her lower back. She pulled another piece of sagebrush from the pile, dropping it on the red embers. Brilliant yellow light flared before burning down to hot coals.

How would she be able to face Sage Ghost when he returned? How could she look him in the eyes and tell him that the woman he loved more than life lay dying in the lodge? How could she stand his pain? Sage Ghost lived for Bright Moon, sharing a love with her unlike any White Ash had ever seen. For Bright Moon, he'd traveled south to steal a child.

She'd never known a man as good as Sage Ghost. He had become her shield against the world. When the Dreams came on her, he smiled knowingly, and kept them a secret from others. And when she asked him about Power, he got that hidden look in his eyes, a curiously wistful smile curling his lips. But he'd never talk to her about it, saying simply, "Power does as it will." And he'd pat her on the shoulder, the warmth of love in his eyes.

She looked over at Bright Moon. The old woman had been such a wonderful mother—so much better than her real mother among the Earth People. When Bright Moon died, a hole would be ripped in White Ash's soul the way a thrown rock tore through thin ice on a pond. A hole she would never fill again.

Everything would change. What would life be like, just herself and Sage Ghost? What if his soul sickened? That happened sometimes; the soul pined away, lost in grief, until it drifted off and left the body behind as an empty husk.

White Ash reached up with slim fingers to massage her stiff face. Her eyes burned; fatigue burdened her with all the oppressive weight of a freshly skinned buffalo hide. Sage Ghost would depend on her. He'd need her as never before—and she wouldn't even have time to grieve. Her shoulders would take the brunt of the tragedy.

Worse, Brave Man would seize the opportunity to pressure Sage Ghost into letting him marry her. Brave Man. She'd been in love with him once. What had happened to the dashing youth she'd played and laughed with? He'd been light-hearted, daring and handsome. She wished she could simply remember him as he had been, see the sparkle in his dancing dark eyes and enjoy the gay smile on his laughing lips. She'd felt a special affinity for Brave Man, a sense of their destiny together. In her heart she'd known they would marry. Her love for him had grown through the years, richening, ripening—until the day the Black Point had ambushed the camp on the Fat Beaver. Dashing young Brave Man had been wounded in the attack, or perhaps—as he claimed—Brave Man had really died in the attack. Rock Mouse had seen him hit in the head, watched him fall, and seen the blood pool from the gash in his scalp. Several moons later No Teeth and Bobcat had found him wandering aimlessly through the sage-covered hills. Oddly changed, curiously Powerful, Brave Man claimed to have escaped from the Camp of the Dead. A new gleam lit his glazed eyes as he told of the voices that now whispered in his head.

Disgust rose like bile in her throat. Her memory drifted back to last summer . . .

With great cunning, Brave Man had ambushed her on the trail, carrying her kicking and screaming into the thick willows along the Gray Deer River. Despite her struggles, she'd been helpless in his powerful arms. She shivered at the memory of his muscles, bulging like river cobbles under her flailing fists.

He'd thrown her down, a triumphant light in his eyes as he pinned her beneath him. She'd continued to struggle, knowing how futile her efforts were.

"You've turned me down for the last time." A nervous smile had flickered across his lips. "The Spirits told me to do this. They whisper to me, you know. It's Power. I want you.''

She glared at him. "You *can't* do this! Not and get away with it!''

He laughed, running his hand up under her deerskin dress to feel her thighs and the place between her legs. "I can. Among the White Clay, a man can steal any woman—as long as he knows where to take her. I have relatives among the Broken Stones. You and I will go there. You'll be my wife and bear my children. No one will be as Powerful as we will.''

"And if I don't want to?''

He'd grinned. "You can run away. But when you do, I'll track you down and bring you back. I've listened to the Spirits. They say you're mine. The voices will tell me where you are. We are going to be Powerful one day. You and I together. I've Dreamed it. Yes, I've seen that you're the way to the golden light.''

"You'll have to beat me to death!''

He'd shrugged. "Perhaps. But I don't think Power will let you die. You're too important.''

She tensed as he pulled the hem of her soft hide dress up, then undid the thong that held his fringed breechclout. She whimpered at the sight of his distended organ.

"Don't do this. Brave Man, don't . . . don't . . .'' Her strength proved no match for his as he forced a knee between her thighs and pried her legs apart.

She stared into his eyes, seeing them glaze as if belonging to another. She could feel his Power—and it curdled her soul. As his penis touched her, she tightened, knowing how much more it would hurt, unable to stop herself.

"Are you ready?'' he whispered. "Ready for the unity of our Power?''

A cry choked in her throat as he reached down to open her for his entry.

"So!'' a familiar voice called from the willows. "Is this what my friend meant by going hunting this afternoon?''

Brave Man tensed, looking over his shoulder. Relief rushed like spring floodwaters through White Ash's soul.

A strangled sound came from Brave Man's throat before he shouted, "Get away! If you value my friendship, Wind Runner, you'll leave now!"

Handsome, with the smooth grace of a hunting cougar, Wind Runner parted the willows to stand on braced legs, one fist propped insolently on his hip. His other hand gripped hunting darts and an atlatl. The dappled sunlight gleamed in his thick black hair, striking sparks from his hard eyes. The lines of his mouth—more suited to laughter—had gone thin-lipped. "Let her up."

White Ash broke loose and scrambled away, crouching to the side, wary eyes on both of the young men. "He wanted to carry me off to the Broken Stones."

"I heard." Wind Runner chewed his lip, thinking hard before he addressed Brave Man. "This is difficult, old friend. We all know that men steal women, but to do so isn't worthy of who I always thought you were. Then to hear that you would beat White Ash . . . well, that makes me wonder."

"You go too far!" Brave Man stood, reknotting the thong that held his breechclout. The muscles rolled under his smooth skin. Then he started for Wind Runner, fingers grasping—only to come up on the sharp point of a dart.

"Don't." Wind Runner smiled, the action in no way belying his deadly intent. "And, yes, I'll skewer you without a second thought. I think you'll thank me for this one of these days."

"I thought you were my friend."

"I am. But sometimes a friend has to do more than sit back like a raven on a stump. Something's happened to you over the last couple of summers. You've been changing, spending too much time in your head. You were about to make a fool of yourself, and I couldn't call myself a friend and let you do it."

Their gazes locked, hot, bristling. White Ash watched them, paralyzed by the intensity of the moment. Like two opposing forces—light and dark, or water and fire—they faced off. Wind Runner, the man she'd come to love for his kindness and calm manner, poised to kill Brave Man, the frightening young warrior whose exploits had saved the White Clay more than once. Driven by the voices that now whispered in his mind, Brave Man was deadly in combat, wily in the hunt.

Brave Man broke, crashing off through the willows, feet thumping the earth as he ran. Wind Runner sucked a deep breath as he stared after him.

White Ash began to shake. She leaned against a cottonwood trunk to brace herself, rubbing nervous hands along her arms. "You have no idea of how glad I am to see you."

"You have no idea of how glad I am that he ran off!"

She grinned at him then, still weak-kneed. "Why *are* you here?"

Wind Runner blushed slightly, lowering his eyes. "Because I love you . . . and wouldn't see you hurt."

She pinned him with her startled gaze, lifting a hand to her mouth. "What?" *Love me? Is it true? Could it be?* Too many times in the recent past she'd caught herself watching him, staying near in the hope that he'd smile at her, or laugh with her over some trifling thing. Now her soul stirred, happiness seeking to supplant the terror inspired by Brave Man.

He smiled shyly and looked up at the yellowing leaves overhead. "You heard me. I love you. And I can't have you. You're my father's brother's daughter. It would be incest."

She blinked. "But I'm not White Clay!"

He lifted a desultory shoulder. "I know. But it's still incest to the White Clay. You're just like my sister. A sister and brother don't marry, don't couple."

"But I wasn't *born* White Clay!"

"Are you trying to talk me into something I might regret?"

She gasped and shook her head. "No. I was . . . I mean, I . . ." He winked at her then, a mischievous twinkle in his eyes. A warm illumination, like a shaft of light, shot through her. Her pulse quickened.

"Come on, let's get you back to Sage Ghost before my foolish friend loses all of his senses again." Then, under his breath, he added, "Or I do."

"Don't, not now. Not after what Brave Man just tried to do. I couldn't . . . wouldn't want it that way. Not with the fear and disgust so fresh in my mind."

He turned, eyes wide, mouth coming open as his color drained. "White Ash, please, never tempt me. It would be disastrous for both of us. Think about what people would say. Think about how it would affect the Power. Incest . . ." He winced. "Nothing is as terrible as that. Nothing. As much as I love you, I couldn't. It would destroy us."

He looked away then, head bowed. "Maybe it's a terrible joke, some temptation by Power that makes me love what I can't have as long as I'm White Clay." He shook his head before turning back to her, features haunted. "And I have driven a final thorn between Brave Man and myself. Why did this have to happen? What's gone wrong with the Power of the White Clay? The two people left to me to love are denied me. The laws of the People keep you from me. And the voices in Brave Man's head—whatever kind of Power they are—have removed him from my life."

She stared up at the leaves that rustled in the breeze, seeing irregular fragments of blue through the yellow mosaic, too undone by the day's events to deal with any more. "I looked into his eyes, Wind Runner. He's not right. Something's wrong inside, I could feel it." She paused. "He'll never forgive you."

"I know. But then, it's better that way than if you were still on the ground under him, isn't it? He's . . . I don't know. Something changed after the Black Point raid, after that warrior hit him on the head. Rock Mouse told everyone that the blow killed Brave Man. She said she saw him fall just before she ran. Then Brave Man appears and says he came back from the Camp of the Dead. Maybe he did. He's not the same person we loved. Remember how he was before that? Happy, joking." A wistful tone came to his voice. "He and I, we used to run, play at darts and hoops. We dreamed together then . . . dreamed of what we would do, of the hunts we would have, and of how we'd raid the other clans and make names for ourselves as warriors. The person he was then would never have dragged you off or tried to rape you. I've felt the scar on his head. He says that headaches come from there—and the voices of the Spirit Power that whispers in his mind."

"And do you believe it?"

Wind Runner lifted his hands. "I don't know. A different Brave Man walked into camp that day with Bobcat and No Teeth. Someone—some*thing*—different in my friend's body."

She placed a tender hand on his shoulder, hating the longing that formed within her. Yes, she loved him. How could she live with the tragedy of never fulfilling that love? She forced herself to ignore the question and said, "No matter what happened to him, he's possessed by something." She shivered. "No good will come of this day. I . . . I can feel it, like a winter of the soul."

The fire popped, bringing her back to the lodge and the endless night of Bright Moon's prolonged death. Brave Man would seek more leverage now. For two years she'd been a woman. Each turning of the moon found her taking four days in the menstrual lodge. She'd avoided the chances to sneak off to the bushes with the available men. She'd become somehow special, somehow different, among the White Clay, perhaps because of her denied love for Wind Runner.

And then there were the Dreams. . . .

Far to the south, a lilting chant rose on the night, rising and falling as voices twined in time to the beat of a pot drum. A *zip-zipping* sounded from a grooved bone stroked with a chokecherry stick. A soft, rhythmic clattering accompanied the whole as someone shook an antelope-hoof rattle to the beat of the music.

The song carried on the chill of the night, drifting from the earthen lodge's smoke hole, creeping through the slits of the door hanging, where yellow bars of light slipped past to splash on the hard-frozen ground. The music echoed on the packed soil of the camp and wound through the sagebrush. The chiming notes caressed the winter-tan grasses, hovered over the frozen shadows of drifted snow, iced now from the melt.

The song rose, trilling the evening chill, traveling on its

way to the crystal points of starlight and the Spirit World in a plea for life.

Bad Belly stopped for a moment, head cocked to the song of his People as they called for help from First Man, the Earth Mother, and the Earth Spirits to save Warm Fire's life. Despite the desperate nature of the ceremony unfolding in his grandmother's lodge, the beauty of the night captivated him. He'd left the steamy warmth inside to go out and attend to the necessities of the body. Now, walking back, he hesitated, cold wind nipping at his cheeks, flicking his black braids back and forth like twin cougar tails. Spring would come soon, but would Warm Fire live to see it?

Bad Belly dallied, unwilling to return to Larkspur's lodge and face his grandmother's disdainful stare or the pain of his brother-in-law, Warm Fire's, wasting. His sister, Bitterbrush, would still be sitting in her accustomed place where she watched her failing husband through haunted eyes.

He shook his head and sighed. What did it feel like to know that your wife loved you? His mercifully short marriage to Golden Flax had been anything but blissful—she'd finally thrown him out. Bitterbrush, like everyone else, loved Warm Fire. How would she cope with her husband's death?

How will I?

Bad Belly took a deep breath. How does a man deal with the death of his only friend? Images of Warm Fire's face stirred the gray ashes of his memory. Warm Fire's twinkling eyes and reassuring smile hung in his thoughts with all the clinging sorrow of honey in a sandstorm.

High on the rocks behind the camp, a wolf keened into the night, voice twining with that of the singers who pled for Warm Fire's life. Bad Belly bit the inside of his lip, seeking to draw resolve from the pain. A shiver caught him by surprise as the cold breeze shifted. Darkness pressed around, seeping into his life, sucking at his soul.

As if to reassure him, Trouble padded across the crunching snow to thrust his nose into Bad Belly's hand. Absently Bad Belly scratched his shaggy black-and-white dog's furry ears.

Life hadn't always been so difficult. Once he'd had the ability to greet the morning sun with more than trepidation.

He had been named Still Water as a boy, though now he doubted that anyone even remembered. They'd begun calling him Bad Belly the time his stomach had given him so much trouble, and the name had stuck with the persistence of boiled pine sap. He squinted up at the stars, wondering if the Creator—who knew everything—remembered his real name, or cared that the last bit of human warmth and companionship in his life grew dimmer by the moment.

Warm Fire remembered—but Warm Fire lay in Larkspur's lodge, dying, while the Healer, Black Hand, Sang over him.

Had Power left Bad Belly alone, he would have been an average sort of man, not very tall, not very muscular, and not very handsome. But the capricious Spirits had meddled. When he'd been a boy, he'd stuck his hand into a hole where he'd secreted a special toy. Rattlesnake—in search of respite from the glaring summer sun—had found the same hole and secreted himself in there, too.

Bad Belly had hovered between life and death as Singing Stones—the renowned Spirit Healer—chanted endlessly over him. Either the chants had worked, or his grandmother had paid enough, or sacrificed enough, to the Spirit World to win him his life. Of course, had he been a first daughter, Larkspur would have paid a lot more and perhaps Bad Belly might have escaped his experience in one piece. As it was, his right arm had never been the same. Now it hung uselessly: a misshapen and crooked thing that he held protectively to his chest.

Shortly after that, Singing Stones had left the People to go to Dream high in the Sideways Mountains. If only he were here now! The greatest of all Healers, he might have made the difference for Warm Fire. But the old man had disappeared into the high places to find something he called "the One."

Bad Belly walked up the trail to where the rocks that jutted up from the gravelly soil loomed black in the night. He lifted a foot onto the rough granite and stared up at the dark shape of the Round Rock Mountains that rose behind the camp. At another time he'd been climbing up there, and because he had only one good hand, he'd slipped and fallen and hurt his right leg. Fortunately, Warm Fire had been close and had carried him back to camp. Warm Fire—he'd always been there in times of trial.

Warm Fire's words of encouragement and comfort whispered through Bad Belly's uneasy recollections. No one else understood him, treated him as a worthy human being. And now Warm Fire lay in the lodge . . . *no, don't think it*.

Warm Fire listened to Bad Belly's incessant questions about the way things were. He didn't laugh when Bad Belly's attention wandered and he lost track of his thoughts. Instead, Warm Fire smiled and helped protect his brother-in-law when Larkspur's wrath exploded at Bad Belly's preoccupation.

"I can't help it," Bad Belly whispered to the night. Everything had a secret. Everything evoked a question. Why did birds fly? Where did wind come from? How could snow, rain, hail, thunder and lighting all come from the clouds? Most of his people, the Round Rock clan, considered him a fool for thinking about such things.

Bad Belly cleared his throat, enjoying the icy needles of wind-driven cold as they prickled his skin. The earthen lodge had been hot, damp, overwhelmed by the smell of sweating human bodies. Only the pungent relief of the water-soaked sagebrush leaves and crushed yarrow that Black Hand cast onto the radiating hearthstones had helped. Sagebrush—the life-giver—cleared the breathing passages, working the magic of renewal.

Trouble walked off toward Bitterbrush's lodge—a black-and-white shadow in the darkness.

Bad Belly filled his lungs with the frigid air. Time to go back. Time to force all of his soul into the Healing Songs, to pray that his only friend might remain alive and well.

He lifted his eyes to the star-shot sky and chanted, "Creator, if you must take a life, take mine. Leave my friend alive. Give him strength and happiness. Take my life in place of his. People need him."

Blinking at the longing echo in his voice, he stared at the heavens. Only the wind moaned in answer. Bad Belly started down the trail.

The sound of claws scratching across rock caused him to wheel and stare into the darkness. The huge animal stood silhouetted against the sable cloak of night. From where he stood, Bad Belly could see the amber eyes glowing with an internal light of their own. A fist of premonition twisted in his gut.

Bad Belly backed away, step by careful step, eyes locked on the wolf's. *Spirit animal, what do you do here? Have you come for a soul? Are you the answer to my prayer?*

He nerved himself, repeating aloud, "Take me. Let Warm Fire live."

The wolf's broad head lowered, ears going back as curling lips bared gleaming teeth. A low sound issued from the animal's throat—a muted moan crossed with the ghost of a howl.

Bad Belly's heel caught in the sage. He teetered briefly, arms flailing, before he toppled over backward, a cry breaking his lips when he hit the ground. Snow crunched as he pushed himself up and stared.

The wolf had disappeared.

"Take me!" he called, raising his withered arm in a hopeless gesture. Only the wind hissing through the stiff sage and the muffled chitter of snow crystals blowing over the drift answered him.

He hung his head before he forced himself to his feet and turned his steps for the earthen dome of the lodge. He looked back at the rounded lump of granite, hope strangling in his breast. Not even a shadow remained. Regretfully he pulled the door flap back and ducked into the humid heat and dancing firelight that filled Larkspur's lodge. The chill that had refreshed his body had numbed his soul.

The last lilting notes of Black Hand's healing song died as he entered. The lodge, perhaps three long paces across, consisted of a low-domed, circular structure that had been dug into the ground to the depth of a man's waist. Four sturdy roof supports of limber pine rose from each side of the fire to a square framework of stringers that surrounded the smoke hole. Rafters had been run from the stringers to the edge of the excavated pit. Bundles and pouches hung from the rafters on thongs, and rolled furs supported the people who sat shoulder to shoulder around the periphery of the lodge.

No one seemed to have noticed Bad Belly's absence. Attention centered on the Spirit Healer, who sat at the rear of the lodge in the place of honor. Black Hand might have passed forty winters, though Bad Belly suspected the man to be older. He wore a painted elk-hide jacket that hung to the middle of his thighs, and long, fringed leggings. Many necklaces adorned his chest, some sporting gleaming white shells brought by Traders from as far away as the Western Waters beyond the land of the Antelope People. Polished eagle-bone beads had been woven into a breastplate that covered Black Hand's entire chest.

No trace of white streaked the Healer's shining black hair, but thin lines had formed around his severe mouth. Now he prayed, head tilted back, eyes closed, as he passed more damp sagebrush through the Blessing motions, offering it to the east, west, north, and south and then to the sky and earth before casting the wet leaves into the fire. Steam erupted in a hissing, spitting cloud.

Beside Black Hand, Warm Fire lay on his side, knees drawn up. Bad Belly's heart shriveled at his brother-in-law's appearance; sunken flesh had melted away until he looked like little more than dried winterkill. The old sparkle had disappeared from the lackluster eyes. Warm Fire coughed, a lung-wrenching sound. It hurt just to hear it. He wasted by the day, hardly able to breathe. A rasping sound came from his throat, while his chest labored. How could a man so handsome and strong be reduced to this?

Bad Belly blinked at the pain within. He loved Warm Fire— loved him with all of his heart. To sit through his slow death . . . it ate at him, wounding his soul. Across the fire, their eyes met. Warm Fire's weary smile burned the hurt even deeper.

No one else smiled for Bad Belly.

To Black Hand's right, old Larkspur looked on, a sour tightness in her expression as she blinked her eyes nervously. She sat amidst the rich furs, firelight flickering over the deep lines that age had engraved in her face. She watched Black Hand the way a hawk might watch a foolish young ground squirrel. She always got that sharpness in her features when equals were around. Her face reminded Bad Belly of a wild prune kept a year too long, withered, sucked dry. Over the years her teeth had fallen out until her jaw jutted out, sharp and harsh. A thick nose hung over thin brown lips, and she tended to blink too much, as if something bothered her eyes.

When Larkspur died, the camp and its territories would pass to Bad Belly's mother, Limbercone—the oldest daughter. She now sat beside Larkspur, hands folded in her lap, her broad face weather-beaten and honed. She might have been a younger copy of her mother but for the long, curved nose that dominated her face. Limbercone would give a lodge to each of her sisters, Phloxseed and Pretty Woman, as was customary. But when they died, everything would go to Bitterbrush, Bad Belly's oldest sister. The People did it that way. Inheritance went through the women. When the men married, they went to live in the lodges of their new wives.

Bad Belly had done that when Larkspur married him off. If only things had been different between himself and Golden Flax . . . *It's over. Forget it.*

Bad Belly's aunt, Phloxseed, and her husband, Flatsedge, sat along the back wall, glancing nervously at Warm Fire. Opposite Limbercone sat Cattail, Bad Belly's father. Age had begun to work its way on Cattail, increasing and hardening the lines around the corners of his eyes and mouth. Once, when he'd been a young man, Cattail had led a war party against the Wolf People in the Grass Meadow Mountains and captured the sacred Power Bundle they guarded so heavily. Every clan feared that bundle. The old stories said that it was First Man's bundle and that Fire Dancer had given it to the Earth People just after he'd Danced with fire to renew the world.

Cattail claimed that at the instant he'd touched the bundle on that long-ago day, his soul had burst into flame and the bundle had shouted at him that he wasn't fit to be the Keeper of the Bundle. The Spirit of the bundle had carried Cattail up to the clouds on a fiery whirlwind and ordered him to return it to its rightful Keeper. An hour later the Wolf People had come down to the Gathering and sued for peace to reclaim their bundle. Cattail had given it up willingly, and the Wolf People had provided the Round Rock with meat and pine nuts for ten years after that. Larkspur had jumped at the chance of adding Cattail to her family, thereby gaining a great deal of prestige for her daughter.

Warm Fire broke into a fit of coughing again, turning his head as he swallowed the fluid his throat had brought up.

Bad Belly settled himself next to Bitterbrush. She glanced at him, eyes reflecting worry and love for her dying husband. He took her hot hand into his cold one, gripping it tightly, reassuringly. Bitterbrush would always make a place for him. Perhaps because she had been closest to him, or perhaps because of Warm Fire's friendship for her wayward brother.

"He's dying," Bitterbrush whispered, a look of misery in her eyes. "What will I do? What will I do, Bad Belly?"

"Black Hand's a great Healer. Wait and see." He couldn't help looking across to where Bitterbrush's children, Tuber and Lupine, sat. They tried to keep stoic faces as they cast frightened glances back and forth between Warm Fire, their mother, and the Healer.

Bad Belly's throat constricted. What would *he* do when his best friend died? He closed his eyes against the ache that filled him.

Chapter 2 🐦

Weary and weighted with sorrow, Bad Belly ducked out of Bitterbrush's cold lodge to greet the crimson streaks of dawn that flamed among the high clouds. His frosty breath swirled around his face before vanishing in the cold air. He sniffed, catching the odor of frozen earth and sagebrush. The lodges huddled around him, door flaps drawn down tight against the chill. Faint traceries of blue smoke rose from Larkspur and Limbercone's lodges. Bitterbrush had spent the night with her husband at Larkspur's.

Trouble lifted his head and yawned, wagging his tail in happy greeting. Bad Belly bent down to scratch the animal's ears, thankful for the warm brown eyes that stared worshipfully into his. Larkspur had always hated Trouble ever since the time when, as a puppy, he'd pulled an antelope quarter down from the meat rack and gleefully dragged it through the dirt before chewing it up. Only Bad Belly's plea had saved the dog from Larkspur's vengeful stone hammer that day.

Bad Belly studied the mound of earth and wood that cradled Warm Fire in its bosom. This would be another long day of waiting. Bad Belly would spend part of the morning in the sweat lodge, purifying himself in the cleansing steam while he prayed for Warm Fire's life with all his heart, begging the Earth Spirits to save his friend, or to send a great Healer. If only Singing Stones . . .

"If he's even still alive." Bad Belly shook his head. After Singing Stones disappeared, Black Hand had become the best Healer. If anyone could cure Warm Fire, it would be him.

Black Hand had come a long way—clear from the Dartwood River—to Sing for Warm Fire. His presence demonstrated the esteem people felt for Warm Fire, as well as the status Larkspur's family had accumulated through the years. Bad Belly's heart should have swelled at the prestige Round Rock gained from Black Hand's presence—but it didn't.

If only Singing Stones hadn't left.

Bad Belly tried to shake off his gloom and turned toward the trail that led up the ridge behind the camp. Trouble followed, sniffing here and there. At the crest Bad Belly stopped and looked across the valley as dawn illuminated the soft contours of the land. To the south, Green Mountain rose in somber, timber-covered lumps, snow lying thick in the densely packed firs. Open patches gleamed where winter storms had covered meadows with a white mantle that would be replaced by lush and green grasses in the summer sun. At the foot of the mountain, terraces paralleled the range; snow drifted deep on the leeward slopes. Above the terraces, a herd of elk drifted up into the lower trees, their big bodies no more than specks in the distance. Below, sage flats sloped down toward the Coldwater River where it flowed ever eastward toward the Elk River. Once there, it cut through rocky defiles in the sharply uplifted Black Mountains.

He turned as the Round Rock Mountains caught the light, burning a reddish-pink in the ruddy dawn, contrasting with the deep blue of the crystal morning sky. Only the faintest trace of breeze rippled down the valley, an indication of the wind to come later during the day. At the foot of the ridge, the camp lay in a protected cove of rock, shielded from the winds. A spring at the rear trickled year-round in enough quantity to feed a patch of willow, cut-grass, and aspen. Bulrush and sedges grew there to augment the people's summer diet. Below the camp, where the ridge tapered into the floodplain, sand dunes had stabilized under sagebrush and greasewood.

He'd always loved the valley. It had hurt to leave it when he'd married Golden Flax.

"Uncle?"

Tuber climbed up the trail. The boy already stood as high as Bad Belly's chest; not bad for thirteen winters. Judging from the breadth of his shoulders, Tuber would be an exceptionally strong man. Warm Fire had already begun to teach his son the way of the hunt. Tuber could move through the brush with the silence of Hawk's shadow. You could tell whose boy he was just by looking at him. For once a man had been able to break the look-alike tradition of Larkspur's family. Of course it would have been Warm Fire who did it.

"Good morning, nephew." The boy's face looked drawn, haggard—but didn't everyone's?

Tuber stopped next to Bad Belly and slapped at his elk-hide coat to warm his hands. He puffed a foggy breath, standing quietly for a moment, listening to the sharp silence of the morning.

"You all right?"

The boy shot him a quick glance, reserve in his sensitive brown eyes. "I don't know. I guess."

"Let's walk. It's warmer that way. If you'll twist sagebrush out, I'll carry it."

Tuber shrugged, turning to walk beside Bad Belly.

Bad Belly searched the sky, reading the signs for the day's

weather: windy and chilly. Softly, he asked, "You checked on your father this morning?"

"He's the same. Maybe a little worse."

An odd tone shaded the boy's voice. Bad Belly glanced sideways at him. "What's wrong?"

Tuber kicked resentfully at a jackrabbit hole. "I'm worried about Black Hand. I don't know . . . just a feeling."

"What kind of feeling?"

"I think we ought to send him away."

Bad Belly pointed to a sagebrush and studied Tuber warily. "You pull up that bush. I'll carry it. You have a reason for sending Black Hand away?"

The boy jerked halfheartedly at the sage. "Black Hand was talking to Larkspur last night after everyone went to sleep. He said my father would die today."

Bad Belly winced. Of course Black Hand would know that sort of thing. It came with the ability to use Power, to see the way of the soul and how it clung to the body. "He's a Healer."

The boy's back bent as he threw his weight against the stubborn plant and twisted it around and around. The root popped loudly as it separated. "Then he ought to Heal!"

"Sometimes even the best Healer can't."

"Maybe," came Tuber's surly reply. "But did you know that Green Fire, over at Three Forks, has accused Black Hand of witching people?"

"Black Hand said this?"

"Yes, and a lot of other things, too. They thought I was asleep. You know how people talk when they think a child is asleep. But, Bad Belly, if he's witching people, what keeps him from making sure that my father dies today . . . like a proof of his Power?"

Bad Belly clamped the bristly sagebrush under his good arm. "It's talk, Tuber, that's all."

"Black Hand's worried that someone might dart him in the night."

"Did he say why people thought he was witching?"

"Too many people he treated have died. One was Green Fire's husband. I guess he had a broken finger or some such thing and Black Hand set it. Four days later he died. Just fell over dead. Then there was that girl who disappeared, White Ash they called her. Green Fire thinks it was witching.''

"Green Fire has always worried too much about witching. Every time a rabbit jumps the wrong way, she thinks a witch is responsible.''

Tuber squinted. "Her husband's still dead.''

"And what did Black Hand say?''

"That things like that happen sometimes, that people just die. And Larkspur nodded and reminded him of the time he'd done a Healing for some warrior. They did a sweat in the middle of the winter, and the warrior felt better and got up and ran out in the snow and rolled around—and died.''

"Everyone dies some time.''

"I don't like people saying my father is going to die today. I don't like people saying Black Hand is witching people.''

Tuber's mouth quivered, and Bad Belly let out a shallow breath and squinted up at the sun, now a big yellow disk over the serrated ridges of the Black Mountains.

"I don't think he's witching people,'' he told his nephew. "I think it's just the way he acts that makes people nervous. You know, if you like a Healer, he's a good and Powerful man. Black Hand, however, well, he's a different sort. Not everyone can talk to Power. It's up in the air, and different Spirits live in the springs, and in high places, and in certain rocks. Spirits listen when the elders give them special gifts to see that the grass grows and the animals come. Black Hand does that. Intercedes for humans like us. He lives way down there in that rock shelter all by himself. It takes practice to talk to people when you've been talking to Spirits.''

Tuber looked up, hostility in his eyes. "Did you know he and Larkspur used to couple?''

Bad Belly lifted an eyebrow, a half-smile trying to form on his lips. Now that took some imagination! "Are you sure you heard right last night?''

Tuber grunted, bracing himself as he twisted another sagebrush in circles and jerked. The root snapped satisfyingly. "I heard real good last night. Maybe they wouldn't have talked if grown people had been sleeping nearby. People always underestimate a boy.''

"I don't.''

"I know. But you're different. You're a—'' Tuber halted awkwardly.

"Go on.''

"Nothing. But I heard that the last four people Black Hand has Sung for have died. Green Fire's isn't the only family talking. Black Hand's worried.''

"And what did Larkspur say?''

"That it was all talk. That no one else had Power like Black Hand and it would be all right in the end. That things went in streaks . . . like luck. Sometimes it was good, sometimes bad, but it would always turn around.''

"It usually does.''

"Not if my father's going to die as part of it.'' Tuber's eyes glittered hatefully.

Bad Belly adjusted his grip on the sage the boy kept pulling out of the ground and handing to him. For a brief moment he envied the boy's strength, trying to remember what it had been like to have two good hands to manipulate the world with.

"You know, there's one great truth about life,'' he said.

"What's that?''

"You have to live before you die.''

"What's that supposed to mean?''

"That whether Warm Fire gets well or his spirit joins with the earth, he gave all of us something wonderful. He gave you life and taught you many things that you will know until you die. Like how to hunt, how to hide your tracks, and how to pick an ambush. He taught you the old stories of Fire Dancer and of the Power of White Stone Gleaming, who Dreamed a new way for the People. He told you about the Creator, who made the First World, and about how First Man led the people through a hole from the First World to this one. Any life is a gift, Tuber, no matter how long it is.''

The boy grunted, watching Bad Belly from the corner of one eye.

Bad Belly couldn't blame Tuber for disbelieving his

words—not when they sounded hollow even to his own ear. What would it be like to lose a father—just like that? But he understood. He could feel the frustration and anger and fear that filled Tuber. It burned bright, almost like a physical heat.

I worry about the boy. If Warm Fire dies, Tuber will never be the same again. The injustice of it will eat at him, sour in his belly like a runny mold.

Bad Belly tried to grasp yet another gnarled brush the boy held up to him. "Tuber, that's about enough. We'll have to get more later. Fortunately, sagebrush grows everywhere. Not only that, but all the places where we've twisted sagebrush out will grow goosefoot next summer."

"I know."

As Bad Belly turned, he tripped over Trouble and lost his grip on the fragrant sage. Most of the load tumbled to the ground, bouncing and rolling this way and that. He sighed as he got his feet under him and saw the irritation in Tuber's eyes.

"Here, uncle, let me. You can't carry stuff. All you're good for is to talk to."

Bad Belly stopped short at the bitter words; the pain in his soul reminded him of a cactus thorn's burning sting.

Tuber looked up, suddenly shamed. "I'm sorry, uncle."

"No, it's all right. We're all on edge. When death hangs over people's shoulders, no one thinks right." And silently he cursed his bad arm.

White Ash wavered back and forth between the worlds. Just as she dozed, Bright Moon groaned in her sleep. White Ash started. Each time she started to drift off, something would bring her back to the endless vigil. The lodge had begun to suffocate her—a cage for her soul, oppressive, heavy, like a curtain between her and the world. The hunger knot in her stomach cramped and twisted.

"Bright Moon? I'd give anything to help you. Anything."

How many times through the years had Bright Moon smiled at her, love and happiness brimming over in her eyes?

Remember the good times? Do you remember, Bright Moon? I can see your smile, hear your voice. It lives in my mind. Remember the time I cut my arm? You made a poultice of holly-grape[1] root and tied it on my arm to fight the infection. Bright Moon, it was you who taught me the Songs of the White Clay. You taught me how Thunderbird dove down when the world was all water and brought up mud for Bear to sit on. Yes, see the twinkle in your eyes as you tell the stories? See your smile grow wide as you clap your hands and laugh?

The pain grew inside as she stared at the bundled shape of her mother and reached over to tuck the hides where they'd come loose. How many times had Bright Moon tucked the warm furs around White Ash on nights when the deep cold settled over the land?

"If only I could save you. I'd give anything—even my soul—to repay you for the stories you told me, for the special treats you saved. How can you die when I've never had a chance to show you how much I love you?"

Bright Moon lay silent, mouth hanging open to expose the gaps between her worn brown teeth.

White Ash rubbed her face, massaging her burning eyes. If only she could sleep . . . just for a little while.

Eyes closed, she imagined she could see the glowing coals of the firepit. The black oblongs of the hearthstones shimmered in and out of focus, making the shape of a face in the red-orange background of the coals. Where the sandstone slabs lined the pit, they looked like rich black hair, shining in the gaudy light.

Why does Bright Moon have to die? The question repeated in her muzzy head.

"It's all the way of Power." The voice rose hauntingly from the coals.

A flicker of fear tickled White Ash's neck. "Who are you?"

The voice continued as if it hadn't heard. *"You're the way*

---

1. Oregon grape; *Mahonia repens*.

. . . Mother of the People. They come from the north. You know them. The ways of the People are changing. You are the future. You stand between the peoples. You're the Power and the Dream . . . if you choose.''

She stared at the face in the fire and saw a handsome youth smiling up at her. The golden light of his expression warmed her weary soul. "Power?"

"The way of the Dream, a path between the worlds.''

"Who? What are you?"

"All that you are . . . and are not. The Wolf Dream that Dances fire and Sings the stars. Good and evil. Ecstasy and suffering. Extend, loosen the bounds of your soul. Feel the One.''

Another voice, that of an old woman, rose on the wind, whispering through the sage beyond the lodge covering. The eerie call haunted, lost in reverie . . .

South, ever south we go . . . find an end to the blowing snow. Death in the high plains. Others come.
  Our old path they follow from.
    Shelters they dig in the ground. Make them like holes in the round.
      Further . . . further south they go.
Shelters.
    Rock piled high. Raise the infants to the God in the sky.
  Earth, hey earth, from it spread.
    Raise the underworld from the Dead.

"What's she talking about?" White Ash cried out, moved by the lilting words.

"Wolf Dream. The Spiral turns, earth and people changing,'' the gentle voice prompted. *"Yours is the blood of First Man. You are the Mother of the People. You are the bridge between the earth and sky. Opposites crossed. Follow the way. Seek . . . seek . . .''*

White Ash fell into a warm, gray mist that wrapped around her like marten fur, soft, comforting, and warm. She could feel a soul, frightened, unsure, hovering close to her. She tried to see, to penetrate the mist, finding only haze.

"Bright Moon? Is that you? Where are you?"

"She's just beyond the One," the familiar voice told her. *"Feel the freedom. You and Bright Moon are One . . . and you are not. You are both hidden from yourselves in cloaks of illusion. You live the Dream . . . until the body fails as hers has done.*

"Seek, White Ash. Seek the Power. Follow the Dreams. The One brought you here. The People change—the Spiral turns. The way has always been south. Singing Stones knows. Prepare. Dream in the high places. Singing Stones knows the way to First Man's Spirit Bundle.

"When the fire has burned, you are all that is left. You will be on your own soon. You can become the fire or the darkness. The Truth, or the illusion. Seek the Bundle . . . seek. . . ."

The gray mist billowed around her, pulsing with the beat of her heart. She could feel the soul of Bright Moon passing, moving around her like stream water around a rock, ebbing away in the gray mist until nothing remained but a sweet memory.

Pain stitched her back, her head falling limply forward. With a jerk, she caught herself, blinking awake in the dim light of the lodge. Before her, the fire had burned to isolated coals. The first fingers of chill had stolen beneath the hide door. Reflexively she reached for another knot of sagebrush and dropped it on the fire.

She looked over at Bright Moon. Her mother's eyes were open and a smile graced her lips. White Ash froze, the Dream replaying in her mind.

"Bright Moon?" She reached, knowing even as she did that the woman's soul had departed. She'd felt that flight toward Thunderbird—shared the warmth of its passing.

"Mother . . ." An ache built in her chest. She clasped Bright Moon's cold hand. In a bare whisper she said, "I'll miss you. Go in peace."

Weary, so very weary, she reached over and unrolled her bedding. Building the fire up one last time, she allowed herself to sink into a troubled sleep. Hints of the wonderful Dream played through her, like sunlight through breeze-stroked fir boughs. The feel of the One lingered like the taste of honey on the tongue.

The words echoed in her head. *"Seek the Bundle . . . seek. . . ."*

Bad Belly sat with his back braced against the furs that lined the earthen walls of Bitterbrush's house pit. He'd done his share in the excavation of the pit. Having only one good hand, he could nevertheless use his chest against the padded butt of a fire-hardened digging stick to peel off strips of moist clay. Now he could imagine the soil behind the hides, still striated with grooves left by the digging. Warm Fire, with Phloxseed's husband, Flatsedge, and Bad Belly's father, Cattail, had done the bear's share of the labor, peeling the soil loose while his mother and his aunts hauled the dirt to one side in baskets. After the roof supports had been planted in the floor, stringers had been run across and rafter poles laid from the ground surface outside to form the slanted walls. Willow from the banks of the Cold Water had been cut and packed in. After the willow had been woven into the rafters, grass was laid over the willow lacing and the excavated earth had been packed over the whole. Part of Warm Fire's soul had gone into the building of this structure that kept Bad Belly from wind and weather.

Warm Fire had been like the walls of the dwelling, sheltering Bad Belly's existence in the Round Rock clan—a protective buffer against the censure of his family.

Bad Belly tucked a willow shaft under his bad arm and used a chert flake to peel the bark in long strips. Over the years he'd become proficient in the use of his left hand. No one could straighten willow or make a dart shaft better than Bad Belly. He'd learned the secrets of steaming wood just so, using a shaft-straightener crafted from an elk humerus to force the bends from a piece of wood. The foreshaft he crafted from hard chokecherry wood, which wouldn't split on impact. The work fulfilled his need to produce, to do something to make up for the share of food he consumed. He'd gaze at the completed product, knowing that part of his soul lingered in the worked wood, mixing with the plant's Spirit where it lay in the very grain.

The flap pulled back and Grandmother ducked through. Larkspur pinned him with an irritated glare. Her weathered lips sucked in around toothless gums, giving her a sour expression. She wore it well.

Bad Belly tensed as she reached up to pull at her fleshy chin. In a cool voice, Larkspur announced, "He wants to see you."

Bad Belly threw his materials to one side and lurched to his feet. "Is he better?"

Grandmother shook her head, studying him as if to decide how much to tell him. "He wants to see you . . . alone."

A knot seemed to draw tight in Bad Belly's throat. *Alone? That's what's made her suspicious?*

He ran outside into the invigorating chill. Trouble had disappeared from his place by the door—but then, he always did when he saw Larkspur coming. The others' dogs by the door whined and wagged their tails. This time Bad Belly didn't stop to pat them the way he usually did.

Locked in thought, he raced across the trampled snow to Larkspur's shelter. The Spirit World had turned a deaf ear to his plea. Why? What possible good could it serve to leave him alive and take Warm Fire's life? Everyone needed Warm Fire. People depended on him. In times of famine, Warm Fire's smile brought relief, as if the very expression on his face sparked hope, brought smiles to haggard faces, making the difficult days seem shorter.

Compared to that, of what worth am I? He'd seen the thought reflected in Larkspur's irritated eyes. Tuber's words clung to his memory.

Bad Belly ducked through the flap and into the suffocating reality of Larkspur's lodge. Bitterbrush shot him a nervous smile from where she sat holding Warm Fire's hand. Black Hand nodded a greeting and left, the flap swinging behind him.

Bad Belly shifted nervously from foot to foot. Then Warm

Fire turned his head and smiled. Despite the gray color of his skin and the sunken flesh, that smile parted the murky haze like a shaft of sunlight.

Bad Belly returned the smile, hoping that Warm Fire could sense the love and hope in his soul. "Larkspur said you wanted to see me?"

Warm Fire's weak nod betrayed his failing strength.

Bitterbrush cradled Warm Fire's head on a rolled hide before she rose and stepped over to the door. In a low voice she warned, "Don't keep him too long. Don't wear him out." She ducked out the doorway, moccasins scuffing on the hard clay.

Bad Belly stepped around the fire and settled on the thick pile of furs beside his friend. "How are you?"

Warm Fire coughed, the sound of it wracking Bad Belly to the bones. "Like a rotten deadfall. Everything inside is gone punky and crumbly."

"You'll be better soon."

Warm Fire closed his eyes, swallowing. "You know better than that." His chest rose in shallow breaths that rasped like sandstone on wood. "I feel floaty. Like my soul is ready to drift off. It's like smoke, you know? Ready to rise and follow the wind."

"Maybe that's what healing feels like."

Warm Fire's smile ghosted across his bloodless lips. He coughed again. "I'm sorry, old friend. I hate the worry in people's eyes. I talked to Tuber. Tried to explain."

"He's young. He'll—"

"But I worry most about you."

Bad Belly chuckled with forced ease. "Don't. I'm all right. Save your strength and use it to bind your spirit to your body."

Warm Fire shook his head, the action feeble. "I've watched. I think it's hardest on you."

"I'm making a new dart shaft for you. One that will fly through the air like a falcon—right to a buffalo's side. It's for you. For your next hunt."

"If they hunt among the Spirits." Warm Fire licked his lips. The gurgling sound of his drowning lungs sawed at Bad

Belly's heart. "I'll miss you the most. You've brought happiness to my life."

The response froze in Bad Belly's throat.

"I worry about you." Warm Fire smiled absently. "Bitterbrush, she'll take care of herself. Raise the children. Find a new husband to keep her. She's a strong woman. But you— I had a Dream."

"I'll be fine. You know me. I get along."

Warm Wind's hand rose, the flat of the palm out in the hunter's age-old sign for quiet. "You're not meant for this place."

"This is my family."

"Listen. I don't have much time. I know you . . . know them. When I'm gone . . . leave."

"I can't leave. This is my—"

With as much passion as he could muster, Warm Fire repeated, "*Go away, my friend.* Go . . . anywhere. North. I think that was the direction in the Dream."

"Dream? What's this about a Dream?"

Warm Fire blinked as though it took great effort. "A beautiful Dream. You're destined for greatness, Still Water. You'll save the Dreamer."

"You called me by my real name."

Warm Fire spasmed in a terrible bout of coughing. Bad Belly lifted his friend's head, helping him to breathe easier.

"Yes . . ." Warm Fire whispered. "Leave. She needs you, you know. You must find her. Trader coming. Go. Find the right path. It's in your soul, your wonderful, rich, beautiful soul."

Bad Belly's throat went tight. "You've always—"

"They'll destroy you here. Beat you down bit by bit. Like a flower that grows in the trail. The feet are too heavy here. Go. Find a place where you can blossom to true beauty. She needs you, needs the compassion in your soul, needs your love."

"She?"

Warm Fire rambled on as if he didn't hear. "That's what I've always admired about you. The love. It's in your eyes, shining there like a fire on a dark night. They don't understand . . . never have. You're the best of them all, Still Water. You made my life worthwhile. You gave me so . . . much . . ." He drifted off, eyes closing, neck muscles going lax. Another bout of coughing brought him awake again, and red-stained fluid leaked from the side of his mouth.

Bad Belly wiped it away and winced at the fever burning bright in Warm Fire's body. "I'm the one who owes you. Remember the time I hurt my leg and you carried me in? Remember the time you—" He moved over and cradled Warm Fire's head in his lap.

"No!" Warm Fire cried out. "I saw in the Dream. You're the important one. Power wants you. You're the one to save her, to bring her back. I . . . Power sent me here. For you. I see that now. I got to know you, to take care of you for the right time. Power has strange ways. Works curiously."

"It's the sickness making you say these things. You'll see . . . tomorrow, when you're better, you'll laugh about this. We'll both laugh."

"You and I"—Warm Fire shivered violently—"we've never lied to each other. We were special, you and I. They never understood. Won't lie now. I feel my soul floating. Just had to warn you . . . to tell you to go seek the Dreamer. Promise me. Promise you'll leave. Go north. Find the Dreamer. Promise!"

Bad Belly wiped away the beading sweat on Warm Fire's brow, not knowing what to say.

"Promise!" Warm Fire blinked as if his vision had gone out of focus. His fevered gaze locked on Bad Belly. *"Promise!"*

At his cry, Bitterbrush slipped through the flap. Like a furious cat, she crossed the intervening space, eyes flashing. "What have you done? Let him rest!"

Bad Belly looked back and forth, confused, feeling trapped between them.

Warm Fire's burning hand gripped Bad Belly's, the squeeze painful even given his weakness. "Promise me. It's the last gift you can give me."

"I . . . I promise."

"Promise what?" Bitterbrush demanded, dropping to her knees.

"Bless you, Still Water. You'll find her. She needs you, needs your love."

"Promise what?" Bitterbrush repeated as she glared at Bad Belly.

"Between . . . us, wife. Leave him alone. He's . . . the way. The way to the Spiral. The clan never understood." Warm Fire coughed again and turned his head to spit blood.

The Spiral? What did he mean? Bad Belly bit his lips, a hollow forming in his guts. "Rest. Rest, my friend."

"Stay, Still Water. Stay and hold me. I can see your soul. It's . . . glowing. Like the sun. Glowing . . ." He closed his eyes, his body relaxing as he fell into sleep.

Bitterbrush tugged Warm Wind's braid from where it lay in the spatters of bright blood he'd coughed up. She lowered her voice. "What did you promise? Who is this 'she' he's talking about?"

Bad Belly hesitated, then shook his head. "It was between us. A private thing." He shrugged. "Maybe only fevered talk."

She stared, wanting to pry it out of him, afraid to take the chance of waking her husband from his uneasy slumber.

Bad Belly avoided her eyes. *What did Warm Fire mean? Leave? Seek out some Dreamer? What Dreamer? Where?* He swallowed hard, sweat running down his flushed face. *I promised. But I don't know what I promised to do. Don't leave me, Warm Fire. I don't understand.*

Larkspur entered along with Black Hand. The Healer crossed and bent down to feel Warm Fire's forehead. "He's growing weaker."

Larkspur studied Bitterbrush before she looked back and forth between Warm Fire and Bad Belly. "What happened?"

"Nothing," Bad Belly mumbled and turned his attention to memorizing Warm Fire's face. He studied the strong nose, the way Warm Fire's mouth had been made for laughter. Like a man working bone, he engraved the lines and features in his soul to have forever. He held Warm Fire's head reverently, recalling the times they had laughed, sharing a good joke.

Forgotten nights around the fire lived again in his memory. As clearly as if it had just happened, he remembered Warm Fire's concern as he ran experienced fingers over Bad Belly's injured leg. "Not broken, but you'd better let me carry you." And he had.

When Bad Belly looked up, Bitterbrush's expression betrayed her irritation. Larkspur was reading it like a buffalo trail in snow.

"Go on back to your whittling, Bad Belly." Larkspur settled herself in her place. "You've stirred things up enough. Go finish your dart shaft."

"He asked me to stay. To hold him." Anger heated in his belly. "You can't ask me to go. Not when he asked for me to stay."

The hard set of her face ordered him more eloquently than words.

"I'll hold him," Bitterbrush said as she moved forward.

Bad Belly closed his eyes for a moment. Reluctantly he slid to the side, easing Warm Fire's head onto Bitterbrush's lap. Why couldn't they let him hold his friend? Warm Fire had wanted that. Why didn't Bitterbrush say something? Stand up for him just this once?

He reached down with the intent of wiping away a sparkling bead of sweat that had started down Warm Fire's cheek.

"Go." Larkspur's guttural voice stopped him short. "He needs peace."

To withdraw his hand seemed the hardest thing he'd ever done. He turned, hot glare meeting hers. *Can I challenge her?*

A gleam lit in the old woman's eyes, a willingness to meet him, to crush and humiliate him.

It's not worth it. It will destroy me. Warm Fire is right. There's no good to come of this. Nothing to be gained by fighting while my friend dies.

As he stood, Warm Fire's body jerked. Without waking, he cried out, "No! The glow is leaving . . . leaving me . . . floating."

Bad Belly turned back; his jaws clamped and his good

hand clenched into a fist. Larkspur had turned to Warm Fire; she didn't see the hatred her grandson glared at her.

"He's begun to rave. His soul is slipping around in his body," Black Hand announced. "We need to smoke more sweetgrass, to purify the air."

Larkspur's eyes narrowed to slits when she glanced at Bad Belly, and jerked her head toward the door.

He stepped out into the afternoon light, experiencing a chill colder than that driven by the wind. *She wouldn't even let me hold him while he died.* A single tear traced irregularly down his cheek, driven this way and that by the wind.

Chapter 3

Snow crunched under Brave Man's hide-wrapped winter moccasins as he broke trail up the back of the ridge. Here, in the lee of the steep ridge, the drift had piled deep as layers of snow settled, alternately freezing and thawing into a treacherous slope.

Soon, the voices whispered in his head. *Meat soon.*

Brave Man growled to himself, wincing at the headache that stabbed through his skull and seared his brain. The headaches grew worse when Power came on him. Sometimes, like now, they drove him to the point of madness.

He sucked a cold breath into his lungs and pounded out a flat place in the snow.

"Catching your breath?" Wind Runner asked from below.

Brave Man nodded, panting, blinking at the sudden agony that speared his skull. Despite himself, he cocked his head and winced. He caught Wind Runner's eyes on him and scowled. *I see the look in your eyes, old friend. Watch all you want, you'll never see the extent of the pain. Nor will you ever know the fullness of the Power.*

He hated Wind Runner's perfect features—hated the way

the young women looked at his one-time friend with admiration. Wind Runner stood tall and straight, with well-muscled shoulders filling his elk-hide hunting coat. Amused eyes exposed Wind Runner's buoyant soul and brought life to his broad-cheeked face. His mobile mouth suited laughter and warm smiles. Parallel lines of blue had been tattooed into his forehead—the symbol of his speed and endurance.

Brave Man's heart hardened. Once the young women had looked at him that way, too. They had speculated on what sort of husband Brave Man would make. White Ash had loved him then, dreamed of the future with him. But that was back before he'd been killed and escaped from the Camp of the Dead. That was before the headaches and the voices. Since then, he'd tattooed black crosses into his cheeks—the sign of Power and strength. He remained coldly handsome for all that: his jaw strong, nose prominent and straight, and brow full and high over his keen eyes.

Brave Man forced a false calm into his expression and paused to scan the terrain behind them. Rolling country stippled with sage spread below the ridge they climbed. The sagebrush looked patchy, thick and tall as a man's waist in the drainages and thin and scrubby, often growing no higher than a man's ankle, on the ridge tops and where the soil was poor or rocky. A man could measure the land by the sagebrush—tell the richness of the soil and the likelihood of finding water. When tall sagebrush mixed with giant wild rye, the soil would be damp.

Here, in the southern portion of this miserable basin, the sagebrush grew short and gnarled. Fortunately, the mountains rimming the east, south, and west caught the clouds and fed rivers that ran through the sere and rocky land.

Farther down the slope, the rest of the men waited with darts in hand. Brave Man filled his lungs and started up, lifting his feet high over the snow and hammering his heels down hard to break the crust. Behind him, Wind Runner followed, snow rasping on his clothing.

Brave Man stopped short of the crest and peered ahead. Yet another desolate valley unfolded before him. Grunting with irritation, he placed a hand to shield his eyes from the

stinging wind and studied the far ridge, letting his gaze
trace—

He chuckled to himself as the voices whispered, *See? We
told you. Meat. Meat soon.*

Four black dots—buffalo—grazed the sparse ridge top to
the southwest.

Brave Man stepped to the crest and held up his hand to
caution Wind Runner. One by one the White Clay hunters
climbed up, stamping snow from their moccasins.

"There," Brave Man pointed. "Four. Meat. The Power
has told me." His headache diminished in intensity.

"Here's what we'll do," Badger said. "Brave Man, you
and Wind Runner circle around this ridge. Come up from the
far side, but don't let the wind betray you. Buffalo don't see
good, but they have sensitive noses. Watch the wind and come
up from under the crest of that ridge. Whistling Hare and the
rest of us will cross the valley here and circle. When we're
ready, someone will run across so the buffalo can smell him.
When that happens, we'll rush and push them onto the drifted
snow. You and Wind Runner cut off any retreat. When the
buffalo break through the crust, they'll be mired for a short
time. That's our chance. If that drift is firm, we can run out
and dart all four before they know what happened."

"Let's go." Wind Runner tapped Brave Man on the shoulder. The familiarity burned like cactus juice in a cut.

Unwilling to let Wind Runner lead anywhere, Brave Man
forced his muscles harder. He cut out over the drift, breaking
through and charging down across the crusted snow. Even
that effort sapped his strength.

Food. Need food, the voices whispered in his mind. *Body
weak.*

Brave Man battered his way onto the snowy slope below
the drift and threaded his way through the sage.

"You're still mad at me," Wind Runner observed from
behind. "You still haven't forgiven me for stopping you when
you wanted to take White Ash."

Brave Man wheeled, jabbing a finger into his friend's chest.
"You meddled with Power, boy. She's mine. She and I, we're
supposed to be together . . . for the future."

Wind Runner studied him curiously, expression pinching. "Do you still think I was wrong to stop you? She'd have hated you, you know."

Brave Man shook his head, turning away, forcing his tired legs into a trot. Over his shoulder, he called, "You only prolong the inevitable . . . and anger me . . . and Power."

"Uh-huh."

"You don't understand, Wind Runner. I was chosen, singled out by Power for a reason. Power lies around us like a great web. Strands run everywhere, through the rocks and brush as well as through men's souls. I went beyond—to the place the Soul Fliers both fear and seek. I escaped from the Camp of the Dead. I crawled over the bodies. That's when the Spirits entered my head and began whispering the way to me. When I saw White Ash after No Teeth and Bobcat found me, I could sense her Power. The voices told me she would be mine. Together, she and I will make a new future for the People. Together, we will bring Power to the People so that none are ever hungry again."

"You may know Power, old friend, but you don't know White Ash."

"And I suppose you do? Have you known her any longer than I? Have you spent more time with her? Does she share her soul with you? What do you know?"

"That she would have killed you for raping her. Oh, perhaps you might have run off to the Broken Stones and renounced the White Clay. Perhaps you could have kept her, but there's a strength in her I think you've forgotten about. Maybe that blow to the head rattled your ability to think, but remember that part of her soul is still Earth People."

"She's one of us."

Wind Runner snorted derisively. "One of us. Maybe. And maybe she would have forgiven you for the rape. But if you'd carried her off like a war captive to the Broken Stones, and if you'd ever struck her, she would have killed you, Brave Man."

"Fool! Power would never have let that happen. No, it might have taken a while, but she'd turn to me—to Power—in the end."

"You believe that, don't you?" Wind Runner sighed. "I don't know what's happened to you. What happened to the brave youth you once were? Listen, why don't you let Old Falcon Sing for your . . ."

"*Fool!*" Brave Man glared over his shoulder. "I have never forgiven you for what you did that day. Perhaps I never will. Why do you care? You can't have her. Or does your penis throb with incest?"

Wind Runner frowned. "I'll never touch her. Not as long as she's my cousin."

"Then leave her to her destiny."

Brave Man's growing anger spurred him to sprint ahead. He cleared the end of the ridge and searched for the buffalo. They continued to graze, unconcerned, on the ridge.

He and Wind Runner dropped into a drainage and worked their way closer. "How long do you think we have before they spring the trap?" Wind Runner asked anxiously.

Brave Man squinted at the clouds, judging the location of the obscured sun. "Not long. We'd better run or the People might starve."

Panting and gasping, Brave Man forced himself up the last slope. The bulk of the ridge hid his progress from the quarry. His legs quaked and trembled, and the headache had begun to pound against his temples again. Behind, Wind Runner's moccasins crunched a cadence in the snow. If it killed him, he'd maintain the lead, do anything to keep Wind Runner from beating him to the ambush site.

"Careful," Wind Runner whispered between ragged pants of breath as they neared the top.

Brave Man jerked his head in a curt nod and worked up under the drift. The snow looked perfect here. He crept to the sharp cornice and raised his eyes. He could see the top of a shaggy hump perhaps two dart casts away. Close, very close.

Wind Runner pointed to the basin. Brave Man could barely make out Old Falcon, Dancing, arms lifted to the sullen skies. He smirked to himself. The old man knew nothing of Power.

A yell rang out in the distance.

"Get ready," Brave Man mouthed, making sure a dart lay

securely nocked in his atlatl. He rose until he could make out the buffalo. They had bunched and begun to move up the ridge at a fast trot. Suddenly they stopped and milled. A loud whoop rang out on the air and the buffalo turned, stampeding out onto the drift.

"Now!" Brave Man called. He leaped, crashing through the feathered edge of the drift and wiggling himself up on the hard crust of snow. Heart lurching, he scrambled to his feet and prayed the crust would hold him.

The buffalo wallowed in the deep snow, bucking and kicking as they fought for footing. Frosty breath puffed around their snow-caked faces as they grunted with effort and fear.

The voices shrieked in Brave Man's head as he stopped short, sent his arm back, and threw his body weight behind a cast. The dart made a sodden *thump* as it drove into the lead cow's side. The impact bounced the main shaft back almost to Brave Man's feet, driving the foreshaft deep into the buffalo's lungs and the big blood vessels there.

Brave Man whooped, slipping to one side as he nocked his second dart. A yearling, barely more than a calf, bleated in terror, its frozen breath rising on the chill air. Brave Man laughed as he stared into its fear-bright eyes. He launched his missile as the calf tried to wheel. The dart struck a rib, separating the foreshaft and snapping the chert point off even with the binding.

Brave Man growled to himself as he nocked his third dart, hopped forward, and cast. This time he hit his mark perfectly and drove the killing point deep into the calf's chest cavity.

He turned, his last dart ready to cast at the remaining buffalo. Wind Runner's broad back blocked his aim.

A possible vision of the future struck him: his dart driving through Wind Runner's coat, piercing the skin of the man's back, slicing through the muscles as it crushed the ribs and drove into the pink-white tissue of Wind Runner's lungs. Sharp stone would lance the heart to spill bright red blood into the chest cavity before the needle-sharp point ate into the breastbone on the other side.

An accident! the voices chortled. *No one could know. Accidents happen in the middle of the hunt.*

Wind Runner's body contorted as he drove a dart into a struggling buffalo cow.

Brave Man heard the *thwok* of impact and watched the dart shaft bounce back, sailing high to be caught by the wind and whisked over the edge of the drift. The cow bellowed in fear and pain as she jumped, getting one foreleg onto the crusted snow. She bellowed powerfully again, her weight collapsing the crust. Blood blew out of her nostrils, spattered across the snow.

Brave Man looked around. The fourth buffalo lay on its side, chest heaving, blood draining from the nose and mouth.

He turned back, glancing at his own animals, collapsed onto their bellies, and supported by the deep drift.

"Food," Wind Runner whispered as he dropped to his knees and lifted his hands to the cloudy skies. A Song of thanks broke from his lips.

Accidents happen, the voice whispered in Brave Man's mind. He bent down, picking up one of his dart shafts. From the pouch dangling at his belt, he took a foreshaft, slipping it into the socket and twisting it to set it in place. All he needed to do—

"Ah-hey! They did it!" Whistling Hare cried as he trotted over the crest of the ridge. "All four! Dead! Food! *Food!*"

Warm Fire's body looked terrible. His flesh might have been pinched from the lifeless clay of the riverbank. The skin hung loosely, sunken around the skull. Still, Larkspur and Limbercone had painted his face gaily, and the finest of leather clothing adorned his corpse. Rabbit-bone beads, bear claws, olivella shells, and brilliant tanager feathers demonstrated his place in the hearts of the clan. Now he lay next to the rounded hole that would be his final resting place. Wind played with his lifeless braids on the frozen sand.

They had walked down the trail from the camp as they sang the song of mourning. Cattail, Flatsedge, Black Hand, and Pretty Woman's husband, Big Willow, bore the body on their shoulders. Behind came Limbercone, Larkspur, and Bitterbrush, the children, and then Bad Belly's aunts and their children.

Larkspur had decided where to bury Warm Fire: on the windblown crest of a sand dune that overlooked the valley and the rising bulk of Green Mountain to the south. Warm Fire's spirit would have a good view of the Coldwater valley. Sagebrush thinned out into thick grass near the river. The dune had formed off the end of the worn granite that protected Round Rock camp from the prevailing wind. Beyond that, the rounded gray peaks caught the morning sun. Here, in the dunes, Warm Fire's spirit would feed the phlox and curly dock, the sagebrush and greasewood. If a person had to die, there were worse places to be buried—but then, Larkspur had no doubt looked for a place were the digging would be easy, too. Sand dunes, even when frost-hardened, were not difficult to excavate.

Bad Belly waited at the rear of the line of mourners. Trouble stood beside him, ears pricked while the wind teased his black-and-white fur. Larkspur had given the dog a terrible look as they'd walked down from the camp. Bad Belly hadn't been able to send him back—not after all the times that Warm Fire had played with the dog and saved him special treats. Trouble whined softly as if he, too, understood that a kindness had left the world. Only Bad Belly would save him bits of meat now.

Tattered clouds scudded across the gray sky, driven by the bitter wind that whistled out of the west. Existence had turned as cold as the frozen ground the mourners stood on.

What would life be like without Warm Fire? Who would Bad Belly talk to? Bitterbrush? No, she would be too busy with her children now that Warm Fire was no longer around to help. She'd remarry at the Gathering, of course; as a young widow capable of childbirth—and heir to the camp and its resources—she'd be fought over. When not with Tuber and Lupine, her time would be spent listening to Limbercone and Larkspur plan the next seasonal rounds.

Warm Fire, you asked me to stay and hold you. I would have, old friend. I would have if they had let me. He just hadn't been able to defy the threat in Larkspur's eyes. Shame filled him.

Never again. I can't do it. I can't continue to hate myself because I can't stand up to her.

The pang in Bad Belly's gut sharpened as Flatsedge and Big Willow lowered Warm Fire's corpse into the shallow hole they'd hacked out of the windward side of the sandhill. They had to pull Warm Fire's legs up against his chest and bend his body so it would fit.

Tears streaked Tuber's round cheeks and dribbled off his chin. At the sight, Bad Belly couldn't stop his own tears. They shared this loss—he and his nephew. Black Hand chanted a Spirit Song to the Earth Mother, imploring that she take Warm Fire's soul.

Bitterbrush held Lupine's hand in a tight grip, as if the little girl might slip away from her, too. At five, Lupine barely understood what was happening. She watched with wide brown eyes, a finger in her mouth. The wind played with the fringes of her antelope-hide dress, whipping them around her thin brown legs.

Larkspur stood beside Black Hand, staring at the corpse with glittering eyes as if she remembered something long past and nearly forgotten. Against the background of wind-drifted snow, her hunched silhouette reminded Bad Belly of a crane stooped over the shallows, ready to stab darting minnows from the waters. The others crowded around, hollow-eyed glances shifting from Bitterbrush to Black Hand to the gray corpse in the ragged hole.

Bad Belly turned away, hearing the rising chant as everyone Sang, blessing Warm Fire's body to the earth, reminding his soul that they'd been good to him, that he had no reason to come back and haunt them.

Larkspur lifted her hands, stilling the Singing. "First Man! Earth Mother! Hear us! This day we return the body of Warm Fire to you. Take the strength of his body. Let the things that grow make use of his flesh. Let the grass grow thick here so the antelope and buffalo can eat it. Take his Spirit and give it a special place where the goosefoot will grow green and rich with seeds.

"Earth Mother, from you we take our bounty. To you, one day, we all return. First Man, as you have given to us, so do we give back to you. Take this Warm Fire. He is a good man, a strong man, returned to you before his time. With the gift of his body and soul, we ask you to hear our pleas for good weather, rich plants, and many buffalo, elk, and antelope.

"We, your People, remember and honor you for the things you have given us." At that, she—the elder of the clan—bent down and grasped a handful of cold sand. She stepped forward and sprinkled it on Warm Fire's chest.

Tuber cried out, grabbing at Bitterbrush's dress and hiding his face while he bawled. One by one, the people of the Round Rock clan gathered fistfuls of sand and dropped them on Warm Fire's tucked corpse.

Bad Belly forced himself forward, feeling as if his limbs had been carved of wood. He bent down and gripped a handful of the sand. The gritty chill deadened his flesh. He hesitated as he stared down at the sand-spattered body in the hole. *Not Warm Fire. No shadow of wickedness ever lurked in that tender soul.*

His hand shook as he opened his fingers. The crumbled sand struck the body with a hollow sound. The welling sadness within left Bad Belly empty, as though the spark that warmed his soul had gone dead. He stared out over the Cold-water valley where sage and snow created a chilly mosaic. *What is left for me? What will I do now that Warm Fire's gone? Who will love me?*

He blinked suddenly. The black wolf stood motionless and watching from behind a screen of sagebrush a dart's cast away. Bad Belly started to point and thought better of it, knowing that the animal would have disappeared into the rocks by the time people looked. From across the distance, he could feel those piercing yellow eyes burning into him.

Go. Leave . . . Warm Fire's words haunted him. *Find the Dreamer.*

A ridge top made a miserable place to butcher buffalo.

Wind Runner stooped over the little fire, extending grateful fingers. Tiny flames licked greedily around the greasewood and sage he fed the fire. The wind lanced knives of cold into his back and arrogantly tossed his braids where they hung out of his fox-hide hood.

Through slitted eyes he stared at the snow-crusted landscape surrounding the kill site. In front of him, the hill dropped off into greasewood flats. Beyond that, the land thrust up in a series of ridges, with bare ground exposed on the windward slopes and snow piled into deep drifts on the leeward sides. Deflated cobble surfaces and short fringe sage topped most of the ridges. Occasional outcrops of buff sandstone poked through the snow. The sky hung sullen overhead—gray and heavy with the threat of storm. Another gust of wind shoved at him, blasting crystals of snow against his back and worrying the flames into bright yellow as ash and embers blew out over the frozen ground.

Wind Runner grinned to himself. The hunt had been perfect. He squinted against the blustery weather, looking back over his shoulder to where the other men toiled, half hidden by the tortured ground blizzard, hip-deep in the blood-soaked drift. Meat: a godsend—despite the blasting wind that sucked a man's heat away with the whimpering wraiths of snow. Four life-saving buffalo.

As long as a man worked the warm carcasses, he could keep the feeling in his fingers. But let him stand up and carry a sagging piece of meat to the place where they left it to freeze in the snow, and needles of ice lanced his fingers to numb the joints. Blood and melted snow soaked into moccasins, freezing as the wind glazed ice on the worn hide. Nasty work, this—and so wonderful at the same time.

Brave Man walked up onto the firmer footing of the ridge top and crouched down, taking an antler baton to strike flakes from the blunted edge of a quartzite biface he used as a butchering tool. The baton made a dull, smacking sound against the background moan of the wind. The thin flakes of stone tinkled musically at the warrior's feet.

Wind Runner's gut tensed. What was it about Brave Man

that set him on edge so? Every time they were together these days, he had the feeling that a hair separated them from violence. Brave Man's attitude had become diffident, carrying an underlying threat he concealed poorly.

He's waiting. A shiver unrelated to the icy wind slipped down Wind Runner's backbone. *If those voices in his head ever tell him to, he'll kill me.*

Images of the past returned: the times they'd chased each other, played dart and hoop, captured snakes and birds, and wrestled in the grass. Now their friendship had been riven—split like weathered wood by a stone maul. How could two best friends go in such opposite directions? Brave Man could have had White Ash for a wife. Despite the longing in Wind Runner's heart, he'd accepted her love for Brave Man. To entertain any other idea was to flirt with incest. And she *had* loved the old Brave Man with all her heart. But this new Brave Man? This stranger? He'd killed her love as brutally as he killed the enemies of the White Clay.

Wind Runner shook his head, baffled. Power did funny things to people—especially to those who could claim to have been to the Camp of the Dead. Except, in Brave Man's case, Wind Runner couldn't be sure something hadn't tainted the Power—turned it evil.

"You trying to own that fire?" Sage Ghost asked as he huddled down next to Wind Runner, extending blood-encrusted fingers to the tiny blaze.

"Pretty cold."

"Yeah." Sage Ghost sniffed at his running nose. "Listen, someone needs to return to camp and tell them. It's better to move camp over here than to carry all this back."

Wind Runner squinted around, looking at the snow-caked country. Triangular-shaped drifts stippled the surface, tapering out behind the sagebrush. "Where do you think? I don't see much shelter out here."

Sage Ghost shivered, rocking back and forth to keep his feet warm. "I'll have Bobcat and Brave Man look around, see if they can find someplace close. Unless, that is, you want to throw a couple of these buffalo over your shoulder and run home with them?"

Wind Runner grinned, exposing his straight white teeth. "Sure, uncle. I'll take two . . . if you take the rest."

Sage Ghost shared the joke, a smile crinkling his face. "I want you to go back to camp for another reason. I feel something. I don't know what, just an unease. It's something to do with camp. Go and see for me? Take care of Bright Moon and White Ash. Make sure they're all right."

Wind Runner shot him a curious look. "You talked to Old Falcon about this? Maybe it's a Spirit Dream."

Sage Ghost pursed his lips, gaze intent on the fire. "No. It's just a feeling." He paused. "Go and bring the camp. We'll have a place picked out for it."

"Be a long day to make it back to camp. Then maybe two days to get everyone here. The old ones and the little children don't walk fast. We don't want to camp out in that wide-open flat, either. The wind would blow us right to the top of the Wolf People's mountains."

Sage Ghost's face went taut. His eyes darted over the snowy hills as if searching for hidden enemy warriors slithering through the sage. "Don't even think it."

"I wish we had someplace else to go."

"Maybe south . . . maybe down there beyond those mountains." Sage Ghost shielded his face against the wind and stared at the irregular peaks that rose against the southern horizon. "I was there once. Power took me there. I stole White Ash from the People of the Earth. Maybe we can find a place where the People of the Earth will leave us alone." Sage Ghost shook his head. "White Ash was young then, but she said that the People of the Earth always had enough to eat. Unlike us, they know the plants. When animals are scarce, they eat seeds, roots, dried leaves. The Traders say the same thing, that the Earth People always have food."

"You thinking about eating plants?"

Sage Ghost laughed nervously. "There's something to be said for it if you know you'll have a full belly."

"Elk and buffalo eat plants. I don't notice thick pads of fat on their backs these days."

"The Earth People pick the plants in the summer and fall. They collect seeds and dry them over a fire. Some they char on the outside so they don't get moldy. Then, what they collect, they store for the winter—and hunt at the same time. Elk and buffalo don't store plants. They just let the snow cover up all their graze.''

"They don't hunt, either.''

"That's why men have the best of everything. We can eat plants and hunt, too.''

"You really want to eat plants?''

"I notice we Trade a lot of dried buffalo meat for those pine-nut cakes the Traders bring north.''

Wind Runner snorted. "You've given me something to think on while I go to get the camp. Four buffalo won't last long with all those hungry mouths. Maybe I can kill something on the way. Stretch the food a little.''

"You do that. And take good care of your aunt. I'm worried about her.''

"I will. I get a nervous feeling myself when you have these spells. As I recall, you had a premonition about that camp up on the Fat Beaver—just before the Black Point came and drove us out.'' Wind Runner stood, using a thumbnail to peel dried blood out of his cuticles. "I'll take a little of that meat. Don't know who might need it.''

"I'll help you put together a pack.''

As Wind Runner set out for the camp, he looked back at the last of the coals from his fire, they were blowing away to die in the snow. Power had always been close to Sage Ghost. What did this feeling mean? Wind Runner paused, studying the scattered remnants of ash . . . and shivered.

Brave Man cut across the ridge, staring thoughtfully at Wind Runner's figure as it slowly disappeared beyond the crest of the hill. A single dark dot against the snow, it bobbed as it made its way north. Something soured in Brave Man's belly.

So, my old friend, you go to bring the People. And with them, you will bring White Ash. He chuckled and looked up at the gray sky, where the storm etched patterns in the clouds. Occasional specks of snow drifted down—small, delicate flakes that shot past him in the ever-present gusts of wind.

He'd Dreamed during the night, reliving the hunt as he lay wrapped in his robe. The wind had been bad, moaning in the darkness before slowing between gusts to whisper in the sage. In that half-state, almost Dream, almost thought, he'd heard the voice of the wind. It had whispered to him, talking in the manner of Spirit Power. He'd felt the lure of the gray mist, understood its promise and its nature. Something wonderful, Powerful, lay behind the obscuring haze. From it, he'd heard voices lifted in Song. He'd felt the tendrils of Power caressing his soul. If only he could find the way to the center of that mystical wonder. The voices had told him that something important would happen soon. Once again the voices had promised him White Ash—and the Power that would be hers.

I will have to kill you someday, Wind Runner. I can feel it through the Power—feel the way it will be as your blood spurts onto my hand, red and warm.

Brave Man closed his eyes against a stab of blinding pain. The headache had begun to throb again, splintering his thoughts. He could remember lying in the grass as he and Wind Runner told jokes and laughed. What had happened to that friendship? Where had it all gone? Power had come to him, but at what cost?

Before he escaped from the Camp of the Dead, he'd never heard the voices. During that ominous summer—two years ago; was it really that long?—the White Clay had camped on the banks of the Fat Beaver River to the north. There the narrowleaf cottonwoods grew thick in the green bottoms. Lush grasses brought herds of bison to enjoy the bounty. Hunting had been good. He and Wind Runner had been close then, sharing one heart as they discussed the prospects of manhood. White Ash had blossomed into a young woman, giving Brave Man intimate looks of promise.

Everything changed when the Black Point destroyed the camp in a surprise attack. The Black Point had been in desperate need of new hunting ranges—and the White Clay held the Fat Beaver valley. On that morning, Black Point warriors had exploded out of the cottonwoods, howling their war cries, racing between the lodges as the shocked camp came awake. The day before, Brave Man and Wind Runner had played among those very trees, casting their darts at targets, talking about how they would be tattooed as men before the next winter passed. They'd talked of hunting, and of war, dreaming together and laughing as they lay in the thick grass and batted at mosquitoes.

We dreamed then. Before you turned against me, old friend. Brave Man spit into the snow.

At the shouts of warning, he'd come awake in his father's lodge. Like everyone else, he'd ripped his robes aside, grabbed up his atlatl and darts, and charged out of the lodge, naked and frightened. Outside, confusion reigned. Warriors shouted and whooped as they charged through the camp. Women screamed and children cried out in terror.

A tall warrior grabbed Rock Mouse by the hair as she ran from her lodge, pulling her over backward and throwing her on the ground. Brave Man grimaced as he relived the sight, seeing the sun glint off a stone-hafted war club raised high to bash the woman's brains out. Acting by instinct, Brave Man planted his feet, nocking a dart in the hook of his atlatl. With all of his strength—ample even then—he drove a dart into the man's back. Too bad he possessed only a boy's dart tipped with a crudely chipped point. A man's dart, with its finely crafted point, might have driven clear through the warrior and stopped him where he stood.

The warrior shrieked, letting loose Rock Mouse's hair and spinning around. In that second, Brave Man had nocked a second dart, flinging it into the man's chest. The warrior charged forward and Brave Man met the charge, driving a third dart into the man's belly by hand. Together they tumbled on the ground, Brave Man fighting for his life, kicking and screaming, no match for the tall warrior's adult strength. He stared into the man's frenzied eyes . . . and saw death. The warrior faltered, blood beginning to leak out the edges of his mouth, spattering hot on Brave Man's face with each strained exhale.

Brave Man smashed the palm of his hand into the man's face, wiggling away. He stood, staring in awe as the warrior tried to crawl toward him. Frothy blood dribbled from the man's mouth, crimson bubbles spotting the ground.

He never knew what happened after that. Only later did Rock Mouse tell him that she'd called out, pointing; another warrior had come up from behind. Rock Mouse told him that he'd started to turn—and that the blow meant to cave in the top of his skull had laid his scalp open, dashing him to the ground.

But I lived. The image dulled and slipped into the fog of his memory.

As he stood in the snow, watching Wind Runner's progress, Brave Man fingered the jagged scar hidden by his thick hair. The voices cackled in his ear, soothing the pain of his headache. The memories re-formed, sifting out of a foggy haze . . .

Brave Man had regained consciousness in the dark. Blinding pain burned through his head. His vision was blurred; things looked fuzzy, while spots of light danced in the darkness. The rattle of the cottonwood leaves in the night breeze sounded like Dancing bones, clattering and banging against each other.

He'd stumbled to his feet, taken two steps, and fallen on the corpse of a warrior killed by a boy's practice darts. In the Camp of the Dead, he cried out in terror and staggered around the empty lodges. He made his reeling, weaving way through the corpses that lay everywhere. He recognized the face of his father, bloated, half eaten away by some scavenger. His mother's body lay supine, her gut ravaged. In the background, dark shapes slunk among the dead, avoiding his path as they slipped through the shadows on silent feet.

Through the agony of his throbbing head, he could hear voices that urged him to flee. Possessed by a driving horror, he broke into a run, only to trip on a broken lodge pole. He landed on another corpse, the woman's body already bloated and hissing noxious gases.

He'd backed away, aware of the stench on his hands after pushing himself off the corpse. Gibbering in fear, he'd bolted out of the Camp of the Dead and into the grass beyond. The souls of the angry dead rustled in the air, reaching for him with corrupted fingers. He felt their plucking grip. Then the world spun around him, lifting and falling, spinning and going black. He didn't feel the fall, but lights blasted through his head when he hit the ground. He'd lain stunned, the rich green odor of grass filling his nostrils as consciousness fled ahead of the pounding pain inside his skull.

When he'd come to again, the sun rode high in the sky, piercing, blinding his bleary eyes. He'd stretched out in tall grass while birds sang and chirped in the trees above. His head ached and pounded, vision still split and fragmented. The voices inside his head whispered and called to him, sometimes laughing, sometimes crying hideously.

When he'd tried to sit up, everything shimmered and went gray. Trees, whole at first glance, split into several images with the next. He crawled, coming to the camp, seeing unfamiliar-looking warriors walking among the lodges. Some had stuffed packs with belongings they'd looted. Images of the death camp spun out of the darkness of his mind.

The voices had cried out, shrieking at him to flee, to run and hide from this horror. Choking on fear, he'd forced himself back on hands and knees. Nausea had flooded his body, and he'd been sick to his stomach while the world lurched and spun about him. For a long time he'd crawled, driven on by the blasting pain in his head. Flies had buzzed around the matted blood in his hair.

He had to keep on crawling. If he stopped, the dead would get him. The menace lurked just behind him, waiting for him to make a mistake, waiting for his courage to fail, if just for an instant.

The following days had never made sense to him. His memory might have been a finely crafted obsidian point crushed by a heavy quartzite hammer stone—shattered into too many slivers to be fitted together again. He remembered bits and snatches: times of hunger, when he caught and ate grasshoppers and robbed birds' nests of eggs; hiding in the grass, whimpering and crying while the voices chided him. The ache in his head alternately throbbed and subsided. The sun burned his naked back. When storms roiled through the heavens, he shivered and shuddered in chill rain. His feet burned with cactus thorns, then cracked and bled, while grasses and brush scratched red welts into his skin.

After four days of hunger and no water, a Power Dream had possessed him. He'd fallen asleep on a rocky ridge top, too exhausted to go on. He'd heard the chanting, felt the Power. His soul had floated, drifting and falling, rising like a leaf on the wind. He'd felt the soft cushion of the gray haze and had cried out at the pleasure of it. He'd drifted in the mist and at last settled slowly until he could perceive a golden glow.

"What are you? Who have you become?" A beautiful voice—so different from the whispers of the dead—haunted the twining patterns of shimmering gold. The sound of a roaring fire somewhere in the distance filled the honeyed air.

"I am Brave Man. I have escaped from the Camp of the Dead."

"What will you do with Power? You are not who you once were. Your soul is changed." The gold billowed and compressed.

"I will destroy—as my enemies tried to destroy me."

He is changed, a chorus of voices called through the mist. *Like tool stone that has been heat-treated for too long, he has become something different. He has mixed Power with pain and suffering. His soul is bent from our needs—tainted by a green ember of rage.*

"Where are you?" Brave Man called out, seeking the source of the Power—only to be rebuffed, pushed back, shoved away from the golden haze. He struggled, seeking the wondrous rapture, and shrieked his misery as the Power repulsed him with violence.

He awoke, gasping, rocks torturing his naked flesh. He sobbed then, devastated by the sweet beauty of the golden haze that had been denied him.

"I'll find you," he promised the cloud-darkened skies. "I've felt your Power—and I'll have it for my own." He lifted a knotted fist to the heavens. *"I swear it on my honor! Nothing will stop Brave Man! I WILL DESTROY YOU!"*

He'd collapsed then, and cried his lonely frustration while a wolf howled ominously into the night.

South, the voices of the dead whispered in his head. The word had stuck in his mind and he'd forced himself to swim the flood-swollen Fat Beaver River, stumbling ever southward. He'd stayed to the drainage bottoms, avoiding the rugged terrain of the uplands and eating whatever came to hand.

But I lived. I proved myself worthy of the Power. I escaped from the Camp of the Dead and the horror that chased me.

When No Teeth and Bobcat had finally found him, they'd cried out a friendly greeting. He'd stared at them, knowing them, yet puzzled by who they were. They wrapped him in a soft hide and told him they'd thought he was dead, that the Black Point had killed him. Rock Mouse had seen it happen with her own eyes.

The two friends had cared for him and told him what had happened after the raid. The People had fled south across the Fat Beaver, and there had been an angry shouting match in the council. Black Eagle and Gray Thunder had split off from Whistling Hare's band, each taking those of the White Clay who would follow. Some went west along the Fat Beaver, some east. Whistling Hare had taken a third band—the one he had found—and headed south.

No Teeth and Bobcat brought him, ragged and starved, to Whistling Hare's camp. There Old Falcon had sung a Healing, and Brave Man had gotten better. His memory had come back, and the dizzy spells became less frequent. His feet healed, as did his scratches and cuts. Wind Runner would come to sit with him and talk. But the world had changed for Brave Man. The Spirits whispered in his ear, making him promises and warning him of danger. The memory of the sweet gray mist and the golden rapture it masked lurked just beyond his grasp.

"I escaped from the Camp of the Dead," he reminded himself. Power had come to him. He'd been chosen. Everyone knew that Soul Fliers could purify themselves by Singing and fasting. When they did, they could free their souls from their bodies and fly to the Camp of the Dead to recover lost souls; but that took years of preparation—and a skilled Soul Flier to teach the way.

"But I crossed with my body. No one has Power like Brave Man." As he said it, the Spirits gibbered to themselves in agreement.

On the ridge, Brave Man narrowed his eyes, staring after Wind Runner. He winced at the slight pain that lanced the side of his head. *Something will happen soon,* the voices promised. *Soon.*

"Limbercone? Would you and the rest leave us?" Larkspur, in the back of the lodge where she sat next to Black Hand, motioned at her daughter with a birdlike hand. Limbercone—always dutiful—nodded, taking Cattail and Phloxseed with her. Phloxseed's children, both of them boys, had long ago married out to White Sandstone and Greasewood clans. Both had made good matches—matches that brought prestige and the permission to hunt in those clans' territories if hard times came to the Round Rock clan.

When the door hanging dropped in place, Larkspur bowed her neck, rubbing at the bridge of her nose. Her eyes had gone misty recently and she couldn't see so well in the dark these days. She reached back and dropped more sagebrush on the fire. The flames leaped up to illuminate the four center posts that supported the roof. She studied the flames for a moment before leaning back on the thick furs that cloaked the dirt wall of the lodge. Firelight glowed redly on the rafters and played on the bundles hanging just overhead.

"So." She turned to Black Hand. "Tell me about this witching business. Is Three Forks serious about it? Do you want me to find out?"

Black Hand stretched his long body and arched his back. His expression strained as if pained.

She chuckled dryly. "That old wound still bothering you?"

"Yes. A man like me should know better than to turn his back on a trapped buffalo . . . even if he thinks it's dead." He spread his hands. "I don't know . . . yes, if you would. See how much of Green Fire's complaint is really serious and how much is simply anger over the death of her husband. He was an old man—weak in the soul. I didn't witch anyone."

Larkspur rubbed her forehead and worked her toothless gums. "Well, I could send Bad Belly to Three Forks."

"Him? Are you sure? I mean, he . . . well . . ." Black Hand gave her a glum look.

Larkspur reached over with a taloned hand and patted his knee. "He'll do anything I tell him to. Other than the fact that he'll take orders like a browbeaten puppy, he's not of much use. He's only half a man with that bad arm of his. Does as much work as a boy and eats like a man. I don't know what to do with him. What good is he? Took me almost three years to marry him off and then he made a mess of it. Got to asking questions and poking into stuff he shouldn't have. She threw him out."

Black Hand laughed. "Golden Flax isn't exactly all right, either. She has her own strange quirks and problems."

Larkspur grimaced. "I don't know what happened. Maybe evil Spirits came around when Bad Belly was born. With all of his failings, you wouldn't ever guess that Cattail was his father. Bad Belly always seems to bring rotten luck. He's not bad himself, mind you; he just never thinks about what he's supposed to be doing. Always locked in his head, tied up with questions about useless things. You want to know where the biscuit root is coming up first? Ask him. You want to know where the juncos will build a nest next spring? He'll show you—and be right about it."

"That's not exactly worthless. That kind of knowledge could save a clan during hard times." Black Hand cradled his chin, staring thoughtfully at the fire. "You don't really like him, do you?"

She narrowed her eyes. "No, I suppose I don't. He's not . . . well, the way a man ought to be. He's not out hunting and scouting and building things. You tell him to go fetch a load of primrose flowers because Pretty Woman is suffering menstrual cramps and he comes back a half-day later empty-handed—because he forgot what he was after. Ask him about it, and he'll tell you he got to thinking about where clouds come from. How can you *like* someone who acts like that? He doesn't have any *sense*!"

"He has a bad arm. You can't expect him to carry on like he's a whole man."

"That Five Pebbles does over in Greasewood."

"I amputated his arm." A pause. "He was one who lived."

"Quit that."

Black Hand vented an exasperated sigh. "I worry about it. It's as if . . . well, as if my Power is leaving. Sometimes I almost believe that I've lost the ability to channel Spirit Power. The Dreams are just as Powerful as ever, but they don't translate to *this* world."

"If.the Power's fading, I don't suppose you'd want to be my lover again?" She shot him a challenging look.

He laughed. "No. I don't think I could take the scandal. What were you then? Forty? Fifty?"

"And you were barely twenty! Hah! But I was damn good, don't you think?"

"No wonder Right Hand died. You wore him out."

She chuckled, and hated the stitch of pain that came. Her ribs weren't as flexible anymore. "I'd have liked the chance to wear you out, too. There's a certain delight to be had in a young man. I think it's a strength in the blood that keeps him ready and eager. I feel better when I couple with a young man. As if I draw something from the seed. You're a Healer. What do you think? Does an older woman gain strength from a young man? Does he shoot a bit of his robust soul into her womb?"

"I can't tell you."

"Want to try to make me strong again?"

"A man who *may* be losing Power doesn't fool with that sort of thing. If I were to take an interest in a woman again, it would be Bitterbrush I'd seek."

Larkspur gave him a toothless grin. "You'd have to get through me first. I still run this camp."

"And if it turns out that my Power is fading? What if I took an interest in Bitterbrush?"

Her blinking eyelids veiled a pensive look. "You *might* talk me into it, provided you could show me where the advantage is to Round Rock."

Black Hand stared at the fire absently. "You know, I'll miss you when you're gone. You have a flair for leadership. I always admired that in you."

"If you choose Bitterbrush over following Power, you let me know."

He sucked at his lips, a frown deepening on his face. "I might think about it. But let's go back to the witching. I'm—"

"You think they'll quit sending for you? Try to avoid you?"

His smile looked humorless. "Maybe. Maybe something more."

"Declare you to be an outcast?"

He nodded sourly.

She studied him from the corner of her eye. He'd grown more handsome over the years, if that were possible. Her heart beat faster. Pus and maggots, she'd missed having a strong man in her life.

Black Hand steepled his fingers. "A Spirit Man shouldn't have to worry about banishment. Why is this happening? What have I done? I've never witched anyone. I need to be free to concentrate on the Power, feeling it, seeking it. Maybe that's my problem. I'm too frightened of harsh talk, too fond of fires and people and hearing the gossip."

"And too tainted by passion?"

For a moment the old sparkle returned to his eyes. "Could be. You're still a distraction."

Liar! But to have heard that from him warmed her. "Have you thought about searching out Singing Stones? He's staying in a rock shelter on the south end of the Grass Meadow Mountains—if he's still alive."

"I thought you didn't like him."

Larkspur snorted. "I hate him—and respect him at the same time. He's one of the few . . . oh, never mind."

"One of the few you couldn't order around." Black Hand lifted his arms in a defensive gesture. "Don't give me *that* look. We've known each other for too long. You've always been a force to reckon with, and it drove you as mad as a spring calf when Singing Stones gave you those amused, lost-in-his-head looks."

She glared at him for a moment and then relented. "Maybe. But just because I couldn't manipulate him, it doesn't mean that I don't respect his Power. That's what it is, you know. Power. When he looks at the world, it's through eyes that see beyond human motives. He isn't of this world. Power hangs on his shoulders like a white buffalo robe."

"You didn't like it when he started talking about Power being available to everyone, as I recall."

"All I know about Power is that it suits me to have the clan believe that I have a better way with it than the rest of them do. Keeps them from getting ideas. Singing Stones used to talk about Power being everywhere. That bothered me." She ran her fingers down the crease of a fox hide that she used for warming her hands during cold weather.

"Used to? You talk about him as if he were dead."

Larkspur lifted a shoulder. "He did me a favor when he went away . . . when Power told him to go up into the mountains. With him out of my hair, I got more things done my way. Funny why he left. Something about that bundle Cattail stole. I remember that day at the Gathering. Singing Stones walked into the council circle and stopped before that wolf hide they'd laid the bundle on. He picked up the bundle and the muscles bulged on his arms and the tendons stood out from the backs of his hands. He shivered all over before he screamed and fell to his knees. Said he saw a man's form shining where the sun pierced the clouds. Said that the bundle had to be returned to the Wolf People's Keeper or we'd suffer for it.

"Wasn't more than an hour later that the Wolf People showed up. We did all right, I guess. Traded the bundle back to them in exchange for meat and pine nuts for ten winters. And we made peace with the Wolf People. According to legend, some of our ancestors came from that clan."

Black Hand exhaled anxiously. "I couldn't go up to the Grass Meadows. Not to see him."

She cocked her head. "I heard that you and he had words once."

Black Hand continued to stare into some distance that only he could see. "We argued over Power. He told me I didn't know how to seek it, that I worried too much about this world and not the 'One.' Whatever that is. He just looked at me as if he could see my soul. Then he grunted to himself and walked off.''

"Don't let it worry you. He's gone."

"Maybe, but I'm still here . . . with whispers of witching running through the camps.''

She considered for a moment before coming to a decision. "Like I said, maybe I'll send Bad Belly over to Three Forks. People like to talk to him. He can eat their food. He's moping anyway. Never could understand what Warm Fire saw in him. Warm Fire . . . blood and dung, his death's a blow. He made a good solid match for Bitterbrush. The man had sense—even if he did come from that bunch down around Sand Wash.''

Silence stretched. Black Hand broke it when he sighed and raised his arms in a helpless motion. "Perhaps you're right. Maybe I do like people too much. I thought that going down to that rock shelter on the Dartwood River—without any distractions—would let me get back to my Power.''

"And it hasn't?''

He smiled wearily at her. "Since I've been here, all I can think about is Bitterbrush. I wonder how much of you is in her. All the while that I was Singing for Warm Fire, I kept noticing how her breasts hung, how her hips stretched the dress. A Healer shouldn't notice things like that.''

She raised a brow. "And you tell this to an old lover?''

Black Hand made a neutral gesture. "Why not? I'd never had a woman when you took me to your robes. You taught me the craving. And it's never gone away. When I sleep, I fight a constant battle. Power Dreams compete with other dreams—dreams of coupling with you, or with other women. When I leave here, I'll suffer the same wont for Bitterbrush.'' He rubbed a nervous hand on his elk-hide leggings. "What if I *did* want to give up Power? What if I *did* want her and could persuade you that there was an advantage in the match? Would she take me?''

Larkspur shifted her gaze to the fire, watching the sparks rise in swirling patterns. A great deal of prestige could come to Round Rock through such a marriage. It would augment her own status—and that of her clan—if the People were to know that a Healer gave up Power for a Round Rock woman. What would that say about the desirability of Round Rock women? Phloxseed's daughter was coming of age.

"She would accept you. I would see to it. But the time's not right yet. Can you wait? Give her time to forget the shock of Warm Fire's death and to heal the grief. Give yourself some time, too. See what happens with your Power."

He nodded. "If she'll wait."

"She'll wait. I know how to handle Bitterbrush. Besides, the Gathering will be a turning point in her life. Men will desire her, will fight over her. You'll be there. While all the hotbloods are vying, simply be her friend. Be kind to her. I'll do my part to get you two together. Couple with her if you like. I know what to tell her between now and then so she'll accept you. See if the fantasy of her body stays with you afterward. If it does, I'll keep the suitors off. Then see what happens next year. If you still want her, we'll deal."

"She won't feel she's being pushed? That you're meddling with her life?"

"Not Bitterbrush. She's a smart woman. She's young enough, and Warm Fire was ardent between the robes. She'll miss it. You saw enough of Warm Fire to know what he was like. She'll be looking for that kind of man—and if you haven't forgotten the tricks I taught you, you'll please her."

"You're a devious one."

"I am. One of my daughters, Young Fawn, grew so disgusted with me that she left to go live with her husband's people, the Warm Wind." She paused. "One of these days I'm going to make her regret that."

"That's my point. I don't want you to drive Bitterbrush away—to alienate her the way you did Young Fawn." He ran a tired hand over his face. "But I think I'll let you do it your way."

She shot him a sideways glance, noting the despair in his voice. "Want to talk about it?"

He started to say no and hesitated, staring frankly at her. "You must mention this to no one." He looked back at the fire, his long face haunted.

She thought he'd decided to keep his peace; then he slowly said, "The reason I'm so worried about the witchcraft accusations is that I've been having this Dream. It's a clear night . . . starry. Wind is blowing through the sage. You can smell dust. A trail runs between two large sandstone boulders. They're sort of rounded, worn away. You can hear all the People Singing in the background. I'm lying there in the trail between the boulders, facedown in the dust . . . and the top of my head is bashed in."

Chapter 4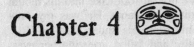

Bad Belly took the biscuit-root cakes Bitterbrush handed him. He soaked the hard bread in yarrow tea until it softened and then chewed it thoughtfully. Little Lupine lay in her robes sound asleep, a fist clenched next to her mouth, one leg sprawled out. Firelight flickered inside the lodge. Tendrils of blue smoke drifted up and out through the smoke hole. Bedding lay piled in the rear, removed from where Bitterbrush had uncovered a storage pit dug into the dirt floor. From the pit she'd taken several pieces of dried biscuit root. Then she'd replaced the sandstone-slab covering and resettled the bedding.

For a long moment Bitterbrush stared absently into the fire. She'd borne Warm Fire five children over the years. Of them, only Tuber, her firstborn, and Lupine, her last, remained. The others had died of the wasting sickness: fever, spawned by the rapid passing of the bowels, weakened the infants until their souls slipped away.

"I can't believe he's gone," she told Bad Belly quietly. "It seems impossible. I keep expecting to see him duck through the door flap, grinning about some joke, or bursting to tell me about some wonderful thing he's seen. He's not dead. My heart says he can't be."

"Can I help? You cried most of the night." Bad Belly reached over, placing a warm hand on her arm. "The pain will pass. It always does."

He tried to tell himself it would be that way, that the gaping hole Warm Fire's death had left in his heart would heal over, too. Would there ever be another rainbow in his life? Another sunrise of hope and purpose?

Bitterbrush shook her head, running nervous fingers through the thick black wealth of her hair. "I don't know. Half of me died with him, Bad Belly. I'm not whole anymore. I feel like . . . like a shadow. None of this is real."

He popped the last of the biscuit-root cake into his mouth and chewed it before adding, "I know. He was my only friend. I feel lost without him, too. He understood me."

Bitterbrush tried to smile, and failed, averting her eyes. "I know it's hard for you. Grandmother's . . . well . . ."

He resettled himself, the bad arm tucked protectively in his lap. "She doesn't know what to do with me. I'm a burden to her, and an embarrassment."

"Don't. It's not right for you to blame yourself, Bad Belly. You've never been the same since you came back from Golden Flax's camp. Grandmother just didn't . . . I mean, she did her best. She just couldn't know that Golden Flax would cause so many problems."

He lifted an eyebrow. "What? You don't believe that two cripples make a whole?"

Bitterbrush colored, nervous fingers fidgeting with the fringed hem of her skirt. "Golden Flax wasn't a cripple. You can't call her that."

"Dear sister, cripples come in all shapes and forms. Me, I'm an easy cripple to spot, just look—"

"Please, Bad Belly."

"—at my arm and you can see it. With Golden Flax, her problem lay inside—a soul cripple, if you will. You know, the People don't forgive a woman for incest. They forgive it even less when she was had by her father."

Bitterbrush blanched, glancing quickly to make sure Lupine slept soundly. "I wish you wouldn't say that. You know she couldn't help it. He *raped* her. What does a little girl do? She couldn't understand.''

Bad Belly reached to throw another pungent sagebrush on the fire, watching the brilliant flame climb through the dry leaves and thin branches. "No, it wasn't her fault. But in the eyes of our people, she's still soiled goods. No matter that she didn't want it to happen, it did. She's tainted, and no one will forget it—least of all she herself.''

"I'll never forgive her for throwing you out like that. It was shameless.''

Bad Belly stared at the fire, remembering the miserable day after that even more miserable night. He hadn't been in White Sandstone's camp for three weeks. The day had been windy, and black clouds had piled overhead. Golden Flax had told him to leave, that she didn't want him. The look of desperation in her tortured eyes still burned in his soul.

He'd put together his pack and walked out of Sand Wash camp that afternoon, while thunder growled and cracked and rain fell in sheets.

"How muddy the ground was,'' he sighed to himself.

"What?'' Bitterbrush asked.

"Talking to myself. Don't blame Golden Flax. It wasn't her fault. She was trapped as much as I was. We were forced together as a convenience. What better arrangement than to stick two unwanted people together? Who knows, maybe they'll like each other in the end and you'll have two unwanted people wanting each other. What a clever trick.''

"Please, I hurt enough already.''

He took a breath, frowning. "I know. You probably think I'm angry and ungrateful. I'm not. Well, maybe I was once, but that passed with time. Now I look at it all as a cruel joke that's no one's fault. Maybe at Gathering I'll see if I can't sit down with her and just talk. See how she's doing. Tell her that I don't carry any grudge. Despite all the hot words shot back and forth by Grandmother and White Sandstone, perhaps Golden Flax and I can at least be friends.''

Bitterbrush cocked her head, eyes narrowing as she tried to understand. "You forgive everyone, don't you? You probably even forgive the rattlesnake that killed your arm.''

He smiled. "I suppose I do. It's just that when you think about the people involved, and why they did what they did, you can usually see that they're as lost and hurt as you are."

"You think Grandmother was hurt? I don't think she's ever been bruised by anything."

He cupped his chin in his good hand, vision lost in the flickering of the fire. "Don't you ever wonder about that? She seems to be invincible—as if her soul were made of rock. But what's really inside her? What made her that way? Fear? Fear of some weakness of the soul that would bring disgrace if anyone ever found out?"

Bitterbrush gave him a disbelieving look. "Or maybe she's just strong because that's her nature. Maybe that's the way she is—like a badger is the way a badger is. It's badger's nature. He doesn't act like a coyote because he's a badger."

Bad Belly pursed his lips. "No, I think people are different. It's our nature to be people—like badgers must be badgers. But what makes people act the way they do? I think it's something in the soul that's different. You watch the birds and coyotes and antelope, and they bicker and turn on each other. But people are different, more cunning in the ways they hurt each other. It's like they want to wound each other's soul, not just to keep food to themselves."

Bitterbrush sighed explosively, throwing her hands up. "No wonder Golden Flax threw you out! What is this crazy talk? People are the way they are. They're born that way. Some are short and others are tall, and some are strong and others are weak."

"No, you don't—"

"Listen. I *don't* want to hear it. I don't have time to fill my head with your foolishness. My husband is dead. I have to feed my children and give some thought to what's going to happen when we get to the Gathering. Grandmother's going to want to marry me to someone, and I'd better start deciding who I'll marry and who I won't."

"Doesn't it bother you that you have to marry again before you've even had time to come to grips with—"

"No!" She glared at him, a barely discernible tremble to her lower jaw, before she lashed out, "*I* have my duty to this family. This camp, and all that goes with it, will be *my* responsibility one day. I'm not like a man, Bad Belly. I can't just play my way through life. I have to take responsibility for this lineage. The root grounds, the grass, the plants we eat, the places we hunt—all will be under my care one of these days. I have to learn the rituals, the ways of keeping the Spirits happy so they don't turn their backs on us. That's *your* livelihood that I'm talking about, because I have to feed you, too. Part of keeping track of things is having a husband who can hunt, who can help do things like repair lodges and fix animal traps. I can't avoid these facts.''

"I know." He pulled himself up, avoiding her eyes. "I'm sorry I brought it up.''

"Do me a favor.''

He glanced at her, noting the fever in her eyes. "What?''

"Find my son for me. He's late for his supper. If he doesn't eat, he'll waste away like his father did.''

"Perhaps his appetite hasn't—''

"Curse you! I don't *want* to discuss it. You always answer everything with a question! Just go find your nephew. *I'll* worry about what he's doing and why.''

Bad Belly swiftly wrapped an elk robe about his shoulders before he slipped into the night.

Outside the lodge, his eyes took a moment to adjust to the darkness. A faint grayness lingered over the rocky ridges of the western horizon. An owl called plaintively into the night. Trouble raised his head, yawned, and stood up before stretching his front end and then his back. He wagged his tail happily and padded over to prod at Bad Belly's leg with his nose.

This had been a long winter, hard on all of them. And with Warm Fire's death, a spark had gone out of the camp. Bad Belly straightened, ignoring Trouble's demanding nose, and paused, letting the feel of the camp seep into his consciousness. He heard coyotes yipping a fragile chorus in the distance.

Warm Fire's presence lingered in the night air. His Spirit might have stood over the central fire pit, telling the story of a perfect buffalo hunt, while the rest of the family listened raptly. Bad Belly could picture his friend's gestures as he described the way he'd sneaked up on the buffalo. He could see Warm Fire's arm going back, snapping his atlatl forward to drive an imaginary dart into the big beast. Echoes of voices floated over the frozen camp. Over there, by the grinding stones where the women ground parched rice-grass seeds into paste, Warm Fire had squatted in the shade as he knapped out a new hunting point and listened to Bad Belly talk about the way wasps lived together in the arroyo banks. Behind the camp, in the junipers, Warm Fire once had hung a fat buck antelope, laughing as he skinned the animal out, rich blood staining his hands. The talk that day had been about Tuber and what sort of man he would become.

Bad Belly closed his eyes and sighed. Bit by bit, the presence of Warm Fire's soul would fade—like moisture after a summer afternoon rain shower.

"They've never understood . . . Power brought me here . . . you're the important one. Power wants you. You're the one to save her, to bring her back." Warm Fire's strange words buzzed like summer flies around blood. *"Promise . . . promise . . ."*

"But, Warm Fire," Bad Belly whispered into the chill darkness, "I can't leave this place. This is my home."

With finality, he shook his head to clear it and turned his steps toward Warm Fire's grave. He knew where to find Tuber.

White Ash bore the weight of her foster mother's body on one shoulder as she climbed the rocky slope. Footing in the snow was treacherous and slippery. The icy wind and stinging flakes of snow blowing down from above didn't help matters any. It was a miserable, blustery day in which to attend to a terrible task.

Grasshopper—the wife of Bobcat—and tall, thin Rock Mouse helped carry the load. They had wrapped Bright Moon's body in the camp's finest tanned elk hide, smoked to a deep sienna color. The aroma of the smoke lingered in

White Ash's nostrils. Bright designs had been carefully dyed into the leather to make a fitting shroud.

Why did the dead always seem to weigh so much more than when the person was alive? Did the corpse grow heavier once the buoyancy of the soul fled, or did it only feel that way to the somber person who bore the weight: a reminder of inevitable mortality?

Despite the cruel weather, Bright Moon had to be attended to lest her soul feel slighted and take anger. If only Sage Ghost could have come. If only . . . What silly words, full of hope, and so meaningless.

Flying shreds of clouds, dark-gray and white, continued to streak out of the snow-encrusted peaks high in the Red Rock Mountains to the west. They passed low overhead and as if pursued by foul demons, raced for the far-off Grass Meadow Mountains on the ragged eastern horizon. Flakes of snow twirled about like tiny wraiths. The frigid wind bit into White Ash's cheeks and sought every flap of clothing with fingers of ice. Sagebrush, its branches like claws seeking to hamper her progress, scraped along the sides of her moccasins.

Her lungs labored under the effort of the climb, but the dead had to be taken to a high place so that the soul could rise to the wind and the sun. Once the soul was aloft, Thunderbird would find it and carry it to the Camp of the Dead, high above. Old friends who had gone before would welcome Bright Moon to their fires. She would spend all of time laughing, joking, and telling the old stories.

White Ash believed it was so. How odd that her native Earth People placed their dead in a womb of soil to replenish what they'd taken in life. To the White Clay, the idea reeked of horror. The soul would remain locked in darkness, imprisoned by the dirt around it. What more wretched fate could be imagined than to have your soul trapped forever, unable to move, weighted down by black earth and rock?

She sniffled and wiped at her nose. Which was right? How could the Earth People—who lived in one place—leave their dead around on the ridge tops? What a terrible thing it would be to walk by every so often and watch the progressive rot and dismemberment of a loved one. The White Clay, on the other hand, left their dead and moved on. If they returned to the place, it would be after the ravens, coyotes, and buzzards had picked the bones clean.

As White Ash cleared the crest of the ridge, the wind caught her full in the face. Snow stung her exposed skin. She hunched over, stepping forward with determination.

"Hope Bright Moon doesn't mind cold," Grasshopper grunted.

"The soul doesn't feel cold," White Ash responded automatically, remembering the drifting sensation of the Dream.

"And you know that?"

White Ash smiled, the memory sweet in her mind. "Yes. I felt her go. I felt the passing of her soul. It's wonderful."

"Uh-huh."

White Ash winced at the skepticism. Well, by now they should have begun to accept that she was different. "I Dreamed it."

No response came. They lowered Bright Moon's body and placed it so she faced the western horizon and the setting sun. Wind tugged at the colorful elk-hide wrapping and flung the dead woman's braids about in macabre merriment. A fine dusting of snow—pushed by the relentless gusts—began to drift around the body.

Old Flying Squirrel puffed as she topped the ridge behind them; her eyes slitted against the wind and frosty breath ripped away as she exhaled. The rest of the women and children from the camp followed in the old woman's steps. One by one they formed a circle around Bright Moon's body.

Flying Squirrel went to stand behind the corpse, raising her hands to the sullen skies. Her voice cried out, wavering, "Bless this soul to the skies and the sun and the stars. Bright Moon, go forth, and remember your people, who loved you. Thank you for the happiness you brought into our lives. Unlike your bones that will crumble and blow away, you'll live forever in our memories. Go forth now. Take our good wishes to our ancestors and to the loved ones who've gone before you."

The wind battered the mourners as flits of snow rattled softly across the wind-polished cobbles of the ridge top.

"We'll miss your smile. Miss your friendly joking. You brought us joy. Go with our Blessing, Bright Moon. Go with our prayers."

White Ash blinked against the tears, unsure if they'd been spawned by the gaping hole in her soul or by the icy lances of wind. *She's dead. I'll never hear her voice again. Never feel the warmth of her touch.* White Ash staggered, as if her balance had failed. The gaping hole expanded, seeking to envelop her, to suck her away into the gale. Only the lingering traces of the Dream remained for her to cling to.

One by one, shivering, teeth chattering, the others added their eulogies, praising the woman Bright Moon had been in life, asking her soul to remember them to the Spirits as they would remember her to the beings of this world. Finally the last had spoken.

"You wish to add anything?" Flying Squirrel asked kindly, placing a mittened hand on White Ash's shoulder.

"She became my mother. She loved me. I'll miss her forever." A knot had formed in the muscles under her tongue.

"Come then. We've done our best for her."

White Ash barely felt Flying Squirrel's hand lead her away from that brightly colored form on the ground. She stumbled down the trail in a daze, hardly aware of stepping over gnarled sagebrush or the angular feel of the snow-shrouded rocks under her feet.

She walked wearily through camp, vaguely noting the lodges, all of them snow-caked along the seams and in places where the roofs sagged. The supporting poles stuck bleakly from the smoke holes, their ends soot-blackened and stark against the gray sky.

Flying Squirrel kept a hold on White Ash's elbow, leading her past Sage Ghost's lodge and on to the one the old woman shared with Whistling Hare. White Ash ducked through the door flap and seated herself on the robes Flying Squirrel indicated.

She rubbed her hands and brushed the snow from the folds of her coat. Flying Squirrel kept a tidy lodge. Gaily painted parfleches lined the perimeter and gave a person something to lean against. Hide-wrapped bundles had been tied to the soot-stained lodge poles overhead. Several rolls of bedding had been stowed to the rear.

"I thought maybe you'd want to talk, that maybe you wouldn't want to be alone."

White Ash nodded, lost in the void within. "Up on the ridge, it all became real. That she's gone from this world, I mean. What will Sage Ghost do? He loved her so much. It'll kill him."

Flying Squirrel sighed, poking around in the central firepit to stir up the coals. She dropped some sagebrush and juniper lengths and bent down to blow the embers to flame, one hand keeping her silver-gray braids clear.

"Well, he'll live or die of it. I don't know, I've seen people I thought were made of rock crack and crumble when the person they loved finally died. Others, whom I thought would throw themselves off a cliff rather than let go of a gone soul, have blossomed like a sagebrush buttercup in the snow. For the moment, I'm not worried about Sage Ghost." Flying Squirrel pinned her with concerned eyes.

White Ash wiped her nose, staring dully into the fire. She felt adrift, lost somewhere in the crushing emptiness that pressed around her. "I'm all right. I was there. I felt her go. I'll always remember that. Maybe . . . maybe it was the final gift she gave me."

Flying Squirrel poured stew into a bison-horn bowl. "I always thought you and Bright Moon were closer than if you'd been born her daughter. She loved you with all her heart."

White Ash smiled wistfully. "Maybe Spirit Power bound us."

"You kept her alive all these years. You know that, don't you? You were her reason for living. She was like that. All that mattered to her were children. When her own died, well, that's when Sage Ghost had that Spirit Dream." Keen black eyes probed hers. "Maybe it's been Power between you all along."

White Ash shot her a quick look.

"Tell me about the Dreams, girl. Tell me what happens."

White Ash lifted a shoulder. "I see strange things. Sometimes a man walks out of a burning forest and turns into a wolf. Or animals come and talk to me about secrets, like what people really mean when they do something . . . say something. Sometimes a big black wolf comes in my Dreams and warns me."

"About what?" Flying Squirrel pulled at her chin, tugging the deep wrinkles in her copper skin into different patterns. She watched White Ash through narrowed eyes.

"Oh, for example, not to eat this or that, or maybe to tell me that I should go up on a high place and sleep. The Dreams usually come better up there. And once Sage Ghost had a sore throat and I Dreamed that if I used chokecherry tea, it would go away. I gave him some, and it did. Then, last year, we were starving in the hills this side of the Gray Deer River, remember? Remember when Sage Ghost went out and killed those antelope? I Dreamed where he should go."

"Have you had these Dreams all your life?"

"Yes, even as a little girl."

"And what did your mother think?"

"Oh, you know Bright Moon. She didn't care as long as I got everything done and helped her with the—"

"No, I mean your real mother, your Earth People mother. What did she think?"

White Ash licked her lips, nervously rubbing her hands before she picked up the hot stew and sipped it. "I remember that she didn't like it. It frightened her. Her name was Owlclover, and my grandmother's name was Green Fire. I remember that Green Fire used to talk about how her father had been witched. She hated Power, worried that it would be used against her. I think she waited for it to actually happen. Whenever I'd have a Dream—like hearing the animals talk— Owlclover would try to frighten me. She used to tell me that First Man would punish me if I didn't stop playing with Power."

"Who is this First Man?"

"The Earth People believe that after the Creator made the world, he made First Man and Earth Mother to help human beings. First Man led the people up through a hole in the ground to this world, and Earth Mother taught them how to live good lives.''

"This First Man sounds a little like our own Thunderbird.''

"Yes, pretty close.''

"So maybe you came to us for a reason. Because Thunderbird knew you could learn to Dream if you lived with us.''

"Maybe. I remember I had a Dream the night before Sage Ghost stole me. The big black wolf, he came, telling me to go away, that other people would care for me.''

"This Owlclover didn't take care of you?''

"Oh, she did. You see, the camp would have been mine one day. The People of the Earth do it that way. Each clan has a certain territory where the women have rights to hunt game and collect plants. Each clan has more land than it needs, so that if . . . well, for example, if the rice grass is burned in a range fire, the people know where to go for limber-pine nuts. Or if the biscuit root doesn't come up one year, they know where to go to dig for sego lily. If the buffalo don't come, then everyone knows where to go to make a jackrabbit drive.

"The women know the country; they've learned about it all their lives. They make the decisions about who will go where and what they can take. Only the men marry out and go to different clans. They go to their wives' territory, where they might not know where to find things in a bad year. But the old women know. They know what the Spirits like and how to make them gifts so the plants grow, or the animals come. Each Spirit is different and has to be treated just right or it will be offended and scare the buffalo and deer away, or make the berries grow small and shriveled. The old women remember where the giant wild rye will produce in years of drought and where you can dig for water when the streams dry up. Our souls are part of the earth, tied to it. Born from it and returned to it when we die.''

"Buried? Sounds horrible.'' Flying Squirrel winced. "Be as good as driving a stake through your foot.''

White Ash frowned, thinking. "I don't know. It's just their way. They don't war with each other the way the Sun People clans do. You fight among yourselves more than you fight with others."

"Keeps us strong." Flying Squirrel chuckled, then frowned. "But . . . it's hard to prove it. The Broken Stones and Black Point have pushed us way south . . . and I can promise you, this old woman won't see the Bug River again. The Broken Stones are being driven by the Snow Bird clan, and so on. Someplace way up there in the north, something's driving the people south. Why? What's the purpose?" Flying Squirrel's eyes went misty. "Makes you wonder, doesn't it, girl? Power controls the world. Why has it led us to this place? How come we're being worn away like a sandbar in a flood?"

"And what has your way gotten you? The Earth People are still there, strong and healthy. They don't war with their own people. Which way is better?"

Flying Squirrel pursed weathered lips over toothless gums. "Bear came from the high mountains to tell us how to live. Bear made us the way we are. Should we turn against his Power?"

"Well, as I just said, among the Earth People, territory is the responsibility of the women. According to the legend, men used to war over who would hunt buffalo, deer, and elk in any given area. They fought over who could collect from the root grounds, or harvest from the limber pine, or gather the grass seeds. One year fighting broke out during the summer Gathering, where all the families and clans came together to Trade and Sing and conclude marriages. The next year, to avoid that happening again, a huge council was called. For days the men argued about who would determine the territorial boundaries for the clans. Finally a big fight began and many men were killed, each wanting to be the leader of the People.

"Meanwhile, a woman, White Stone Gleaming, had a Dream and called the women together. She told them of how she'd gone to sleep in a high place, mourning the death of her husband in the fighting. While she slept, a man of fire had appeared and told her how to stop all the trouble. Under her leadership, the women drew boundaries. Then they took their children and went home. The men looked around, realizing their wives had left. Only White Stone Gleaming remained, and she told the Healers about the Dream and how First Man had come to her with the way to end the war. She told them that those who fought could kill each other until the last man died. Meanwhile, the others could go home to their wives and have more children and hunt as they always had. Most of the men did that, and the People lived happily thereafter.''

"But our way makes us strong!''

"And the way of the Earth People makes them strong.''

"Bah!'' Flying Squirrel waved her age-spotted hands. "They live off roots and grass, and their men are bossed around by the women. When we face them, they'll wilt like summer leaves in a frost!''

"Like the Wolf People east of here? They kill the Sun clans in the most brutal ways they can . . . as a lesson to us of their strength. Or like the Sheep Hunters who live up in the Red Mountains?''

Flying Squirrel glared at her. "You think your Earth People will stand before the likes of Brave Man? Didn't he single-handedly kill four of the Wolf People's warriors during that last raid?'

"Didn't they kill fourteen out of this camp . . . and steal all the meat?'' White Ash shook her head, pressing slim hands against her temples. "What are we doing? It's a pointless argument. It doesn't matter. The fighting would be terrible for everyone. Lots of people would die and no one would win.''

"The Sun People would win.''

"Oh?''

Flying Squirrel nodded. "What you have to remember is that we've been fighting among ourselves for a long time. Maybe the White Clay are worn away like an old woman's teeth, but behind us come the rest. I don't even know all the names of the clans up there, but all of them are moving south. So what if your Earth People kill every last one of the White Clay? Then they'll have to kill every last one of the Broken

Stones, or the Black Point, and then the Snow Birds, and the Hollow Flute, and the Wasps. And it goes on.''

"And they're all moving south?'' White Ash frowned into the fire, feeling angry.

"Yes, moving south. We've been doing that for generations. I don't know where we all come from. Up north someplace. But the clans keep coming, heading south.''

"And the Earth People are right in their way.'' The thought irritated her. Why? What business was it of hers if her former people were swept away in the Sun People's migration?

Nevertheless, her stomach turned at the thought of the empty lodges, of the corpses that would litter the trails.

Bad Belly waited uneasily after he had seated himself across from his grandmother. Firelight flickered off Larkspur's withered features and illuminated the parallel lines of rafter poles behind her head. The yellow light danced off the soft furs that cushioned her, and shivered the shadows of the bundles that hung from the smoke-grimed roof. The air pressed against him, hot, stuffy, and weighted with the odors of the old woman's lodge. Bad Belly's soul felt cramped.

She always makes me feel like I have to justify my existence. I'm here, that's all. I didn't ask to be born to her camp. It just happened. So why do I always have to feel like it's my fault?

Black Hand sat to one side, carefully tamping willow bark into his steatite stone pipe before using a twig to light it.

Larkspur smiled at Bad Belly, ancient eyes half closed. "I want you to do something for me. You will, won't you?''

Bad Belly wiggled, uncomfortable in both the heat of her glinting stare and that of the large fire. Despite the blaze, the lodge seemed darker than usual.

Just as she knew he would, he answered, "Of course, Grandmother.'' *She could be wise Spider who spins webs around our lives—and I'm no more than a bug in her net.*

"I need you to go over to Three Forks. I want you to ask

Green Fire what she needs from me for the coming Gathering. I want you to check the trail and decide where we should camp on the way. Remember my age when you pick the campsites. I can't outrun antelope anymore.''

"I understand.''

She traced a bony finger along the edge of a woven-grass bowl. "While you're there, listen to the stories. See if anyone says anything about witching. There's talk in the camps. I don't want to walk into the middle of a fight; we have too many important things to do this year. Bitterbrush has to be married soon. If people are going to be preoccupied with other concerns, I want to know in advance.''

"Witching?'' He couldn't help but glance at Black Hand, who sat smoking his pipe, expression blank. Blue tendrils of smoke rose from the end of the gray stone pipe to drift toward the smoke hole. He looked *too* relaxed. Tuber's accusations stirred in Bad Belly's memory.

It's true! And Warm Fire had died while Black Hand Sang a Healing. There would be more whispers, more accusations.

"What if no one talks about it?''

Larkspur gestured absently. "They know you, Bad Belly. You like to listen to people. If people are worried about it, they'll bring it up.'' Her voice hardened into a direct order. "We have *no* worries about witching at Round Rock. You don't need to speculate while you're there. Just listen. That's all.''

Bad Belly nodded in assent and refrained from glancing at Black Hand. "When do you want me to leave?''

"Tomorrow. Looks like the weather is clearing. Just be yourself. Let people talk to you. I always thought Green Fire liked you. I know that husband of Owlclover's—Makes Wood, that's his name—he likes you. You'll hear enough about what's going on. I want to know anything that might make trouble.''

He nodded again, a tightness in his chest. He had to be a perfect spy. Creator help him if he made a mistake.

"Good. Then we have only one thing to clear up.'' The way her eyes blinked—a nervous thing that always distracted him—added to his unease.

Bad Belly waited. He knew that look, knew how her mind

worked. Finally he could stand it no longer—as she had known he couldn't. "And what else?"

Larkspur worked her thin lips, sucking them in and out over her gums. "You talked to Warm Fire before he died. Bitterbrush said there was something about a promise. She says you won't tell her what it was."

Bad Belly took a deep breath. "It was a thing between the two of us."

Larkspur said nothing, her black eyes implacable and demanding.

"Just a thing between friends . . . that's all." He knew he sounded lame. She waited, immobile, her hard eyes sharpening, insisting. The set of her mouth betrayed growing displeasure.

Curse her! She'd sit there and dominate him with those unforgiving eyes. Bad Belly's skin prickled and he began to sweat—as if that obsidian glare could burn him. Tension built; he could practically feel it snapping in the air.

I can't tell. I can't. I made the promise to Warm Fire. She'll hold it against me . . . against everyone. It will be a lever, just like a digging stick used to pry a rock from the ground. She'll use it against Warm Fire's memory . . . and against Bitterbrush . . . and Tuber and Lupine.

The silence stretched.

Bad Belly wiped his forehead. His gaze locked on the fire to avoid the cutting anger he knew had come to the old woman's eyes.

"Bad Belly?" She spoke in careful tones, low, threatening.

He swallowed, throat constricted. "It was . . . between us. That's all."

She sighed, as if under a stifling burden. "Anything that happens in this camp is my concern. *You* are my concern. Warm Fire was dying, his soul coming loose from his body. I can't let any crazy thing he might have said make trouble between us."

Bad Belly's mouth went dry. "It was between the two of us."

She tapped taloned fingers on her knee. "I wouldn't like

to be forced to discipline you. Doing so wouldn't be good for the clan. Not now, not so soon after Warm Fire's death.''

His cheeks quivered, the muscles jumping and tense. A sick sensation rose in his gut.

''I wonder, Bad Belly, do you ever think of the others? If I'm forced to take harsh measures, how do you think it will affect the children? Don't you care for Lupine? Tuber?''

''Yes.'' His voice broke.

''Then perhaps you should show a little responsibility to the people for once. Warm Fire is dead. It's no longer between the two of you. You are the only one now. It's you alone. What was this promise?''

Warm Fire would never have let himself be roasted by the old woman. He'd never have sat here sweating his fear like a cornered hare. *Why can't I be like him?*

''Grandmother, it's a soul thing. A promise. That's all. I just can't tell you. I promised.''

Her eyelids narrowed, the gaze smoky, promising retribution. ''I will ask you only once more.''

He dropped his eyes, skin crawling at what would come of this. ''It was between Warm Fire and me.''

She exhaled her irritation. ''Get out. I'll find someone else to send to Three Forks. In the meantime, you think about yourself, Bad Belly. You think about the people here who keep you fed and warm. You think about what you owe the clan. You think about responsibility.''

He rose unsteadily to his feet, unable to meet her eyes. Without looking back, he ducked through the flap and into the outside world, into freedom and space. His panicked heart beat frantically against his ribs.

He found Trouble lying in his usual spot, tail wagging, anxious to have his ears scratched. Bad Belly motioned to his dog, retreating to the junipers behind the camp. There in the shelter of the trees, he pulled Trouble close, burying his face in the thick, warm fur.

Chapter 5 🌀

Wind Runner panted as he ran. Frost had built up around the lining of his fox-fur hood. On legs that quaked and wobbled, he continued on his way, weaving along the rocky spine of the northward-tending ridge. He had first noticed pursuers at dusk two days earlier. And he'd lost them in the night—he hoped. Now another group, smaller than the first, had appeared to dog his tracks. Had these hunters cut this trail the way they had his first one? A skilled tracker could have backtracked, found where he'd circled and slipped off.

Around him the land waited mutely for the outcome of this grim race. Rocky prominences thrust up through the crusted snow like somber spectators. Sunlight lit the drifts in blinding rays. Here and there, sagebrush poked up. The spikes quivered absently in the wind, a memory of last fall's bounty of seeds. In the distance, buff sandstone-capped ridges rose one after another in sinuous lines—defiant obstacles through which he must make his way. Beyond, the resolute guardian walls of the mountains reared against the sky, slopes blanketed in patches of blue-green and sun-glazed snow. Overhead, the sky stretched into an infinite blue dome, marred here and there by fluffy clouds.

Wind Runner staggered on, crunching through the crusted drifts, the soles of his feet bruising on the angular rock now locked in the grip of icebound soil. His breath sawed at his throat, laboring with his burning lungs. Every muscle in his body complained. Sweat poured down his skin to soak the thick wrappings of hide he wore.

He'd been lucky and caught sight of them almost immediately: seven men trotting along his trail. Seven unknown men bearing darts that glinted in the sunlight. Perhaps they were more of the Wolf People from the Grass Meadow

Mountains. Perhaps others. Everyone in the world, outside of the dwindling White Clay clan, had to be considered an enemy. The last thing he wanted to do was to lead the warriors to his vulnerable camp. The women of the White Clay could defend themselves and would probably drive the warriors off, but some of the people would die, perhaps many.

No, far better to lead his pursuers astray and lose them. No one could run with the power or stamina of Wind Runner. He had slowly veered off his line, passing camp by a good half-day's walk to the east. For a whole second day he'd run north, following the ridge tops where the snow had blown free, making good time. Now he stopped periodically and looked back from high points to see them dogging his tracks; like human wolves, they trotted along in single file far behind him.

Wind Runner was playing a dangerous game, that of losing his pursuers but several factors worked in his favor: his enemies—whether Sun People or Wolf People—would know that if a Sun People camp lay near here, a lone man would be reinforced. His pursuers would have to move cautiously lest they walk into an ambush. Dropping to a careful walk, Wind Runner slipped among the sagebrush, seeking to hide his tracks as much as possible. Anything to slow them, to buy time, helped him.

He leaped from one clump of sage to another as he climbed the windward side of a ridge. Reaching the crest, he looked around. He stood on the southern end of a windscoured expanse of cracked sandstone that stretched to the north for as far as he could see. Snowfields lay in every other direction—a vast plain bare of cover. Where the windblown rock tapered into snow at the edge of the low ridge, an unbroken expanse of hard-crusted snow extended to the south. A solitary bit of sagebrush poked up from the snow a dart's cast from the edge of the sandstone.

His heart pounded. Excellent.

He walked carefully down to the southern tip of the pebbly sandstone and checked his back trail. How long did he have before the pursuers crested the skyline?

Where the snow feathered over the irregular surface of the ridge, he tested the crust. It wouldn't support a man's weight.

Swallowing hard, Wind Runner lay down and padded his atlatl and darts in his coat. He began to roll, careful to make no depression with elbows or knees, using the length of his entire body to spread his weight over the crusted snow. Did he have time? What if he broke through the surface?

Then I'm dead.

The patch of sagebrush he sought looked infinitely far away; what if the hunters crossed over the ridge and saw him out here in the snow flat? Better to trust in Power and hope than to think about the alternatives.

Dizziness possessed him as he continued his rolling progress. He blinked, trying to keep his destination straight in his head. *Careful! Don't drop an elbow or you'll make a mark.* Beneath him, the snow moaned, taking his weight. And if a buried sagebrush had created a hollow beneath the crust?

Why didn't I just keep running? Why didn't I look for a better place? This is madness!

He forced the thought out of his mind, ignoring the fear-sweat streaming down his body. How far? How long remained? The world spun crazily as the horizon lifted and fell, lifted and fell, as he rolled.

So close! He wiggled around the solitary sagebrush, startling a white jackrabbit from its hiding place in the brush's protected lee. The animal darted out, graceful, sailing, and pulled up, standing on hind feet to watch him.

He packed the snow into a hollow, tucking himself into a ball behind the sagebrush, attempting to shake off the dizziness. Keeping his motions to a minimum, he pulled the atlatl and darts from his coat, wincing at the damage done to the fletching of those long, beautiful darts.

He glanced back across the snow-glazed flats and froze: Seven bobbing forms were crossing the far ridge.

Heart battering at his breastbone, Wind Runner swallowed dryly. Bit by bit the warriors worked out his trail, following it from where he'd jumped from sagebrush to sagebrush to reach the bare, rocky ridge.

Wind Runner blinked hard, hating the trembling of his

exhausted muscles. With all of his concentration, he cleared his mind, forcing himself to think of nothing, aware of his pursuers only by their movement at the corner of his vision.

He could hear their calls to each other. No one among the Sun People spoke such a tongue . . . and he could see that they wore the heavily fringed clothing of the Wolf People.

Quiet! Don't think. Not a word. He ground his teeth, seeking to calm his heaving lungs. Would his pursuers be able to see his frosty breath from that distance? Perhaps.

Don't breathe. Don't think. Don't move. You're like the snow—thoughtless, cold, silent.

One of the hunters walked down the bare sandstone to the foot of the ridge and looked out over the snow toward Wind Runner's screening sagebrush. The man raised a hand to shield his eyes against the white glare.

Through the wind-burned branches of the sagebrush, Wind Runner could feel those piercing eyes. Fighting to hold his breath, eyes steady on his snow-streaked knees, Wind Runner waited.

He felt, rather than saw, the man turn to stare back up the slope. The jackrabbit picked that moment to streak away across the packed snow.

The Trader, Left Hand, whistled as he walked, contemplating the Dreams that had been leaving him nervous and preoccupied. He glanced up at the endless midday sky and squinted. *It's as if the Power is hurrying me along.*

He was following a ridge top, as all sensible people did at this time of year. The snow had melted under the warm rays of the sun, leaving the ridge tops clear. The very thought of travel across the valley bottoms soured in his mind. With the warm days, snow melt left puddles of water that soaked the best smoke-cured moccasin leather. Soggy moccasins grew heavy and wrinkled even the callused feet of a Trader. Worse than that, the clinging mud made each step a labor. Footing in that sticky stuff couldn't be called anything but uncertain, and a slip meant a tumble in the mud—and undoubtedly into any cactus that might be around. The slopes under the ridges remained deep in wet snow. Not only did such traveling drain a person of stamina, but it saturated leggings and froze clothing stiff after sunset.

Left Hand pulled up for a moment. His string of dogs immediately stopped behind him, enjoying the rest while they panted, packs jiggling on their backs.

He gripped his Trader's staff in his callused left hand, the feathers hanging from the hoop-shaped top dancing in the breeze.

He'd crossed the Coldwater that morning and now followed the stream eastward. The Round Rock camp of the Earth People lay ahead somewhere. He lifted a hand against the sun and studied the terrain. In his memory, the camp should be around the next outcrop of weathered granite, back in a cove where it caught the southern sun in winter and avoided the brunt of the west wind.

Left Hand carried a heavy buffalo-hide pack suspended from a tumpline; he wore a bone-beaded jacket and long leggings from which most of the fringes had been cut for various repairs to his pack and the dog harnesses. Endless days of sun had burned his face the color of sweat-stained chokecherry wood. A hawkish nose jutted from his broad cheeks. His skin showed the lines of laughter and the grimaces forced by bad weather. A thick pelt of bear hide hung around his shoulders for warmth on cold days. He kept his long hair pulled back in a single braid and wore a wrapped beaver-hide cap.

Behind him, the dogs waited in single file, happy eyes on him as their pink tongues twitched with each hurried breath. People talked about Left Hand's pack dogs with admiration. He'd Traded for the best—strong, big animals, capable of bearing heavy loads. They looked motley, splotched with white, brown, and black. The bulging packs strapped to their backs bore the profits of his Trading trip in the Basin lands to the southwest. There the winters were considerably milder.

The Salt Trader People, who lived to the southwest, Traded all kinds of things in demand among his Wolf People. For one thing, they had salt—big blocks of it they levered from the basin floor by the huge, salty lake. They had saltbush patties, ephedra for tea, effigies woven from yucca leaves, dried fish and water fowl that couldn't be had during summer months in the uplands. Best of all, the Antelope People, farther south, had various breads made from the sweet, fleshy pinion pine nuts they collected in fall. They also made a chimisa bread that had a light, fluffy texture. Those Traded very well to his Wolf People in the high country to the north.

The moon had been full when he began his journey home. Since then, he'd watched two more full moons pass. The journey had been long, with several stops to hunt meat for his dogs. Each stop triggered that sense of unease, as if pausing placed him in jeopardy.

Maybe I've just been gone from home too long. The thought rolled around in his head.

Not far ahead lay one of the camps of the Earth People. The prospect of a night at Round Rock meant that he'd have people to talk to—and maybe they'd tell him something to explain the disquiet that had come to possess him as he proceeded north. The Earth People spoke a tongue similar to his, but they slurred their words, which made their speech sound a bit odd to the ear. At least here he wouldn't have to employ the sign language common to all Traders. He could listen to the stories, laugh at the jokes, and spend a pleasant evening telling the news of the Basin peoples. At Round Rock camp, they would feed him and his dogs and perhaps Trade for something special.

He could have visited several other camps, but none had been on the straight line to his mountain—and the Dreams had driven him on his way. Not only that, but when a Trader showed up, he was expected to Trade. If a man did too much of that, he'd wind up back home with nothing unique for his own people. A little bit here and a little bit there and pretty soon his packs would be filled with buffalo meat, elk, antelope, biscuit root, goosefoot—all things naturally available. Some Traders did over-Trade, of course, simply relishing the chance to see different peoples and having no concern over what they brought home. Trader Power came in all kinds of forms. The very act of Trade itself carried a Power. And those who were called to Trade passed anywhere they wished, protected by the Power symbolized by their staff and the service they provided.

He whistled at his dogs and set off again. He worked down a shoulder of the ridge and skirted the slopes where the snow melted in rivulets and ran off to the drainages leading to the Coldwater. To avoid the slick mud in the bottoms, he followed the edge of the granite hills that rose abruptly from the plain. The sun rode high in the clear sky as he walked and whistled. His staff caught the playful breeze, and the feathers fluttered happily. To his left, the granite gleamed and sparkled, a faint tinge of red blushing the gray of the weathered rock.

He'd made no more than half the distance toward the Round Rock camp when he spotted the man pulling up sagebrush. The fellow seemed to be struggling awkwardly; a sizable pile of uprooted sage already lay stacked for carrying.

"Ho-yeh!" Left Hand called.

The man spun around and stared. "Ho-yeh!" came the reply.

Left Hand changed his course. Ah! So that was it. The man's right arm seemed useless. He worked only with his left. No wonder he looked off balance. How did the cripple expect to pack that huge pile back to camp?

"Welcome, Trader. I'm Bad Belly . . . of the Round Rock clan." Bad Belly turned, ordering a black-and-white dog that trotted out of the sagebrush to lie down. The animal did so immediately. Left Hand was surprised by the obvious affection in the man's voice. Most people cuffed their beasts, shouting and threatening.

"I'm Left Hand. Trader of the Wolf People." Left Hand shrugged out of his heavy buffalo-hide pack and gave the crippled man a thorough inspection. Bad Belly stood a little below average height; his facial features were bland, unstriking. He wore his hair in two braids, and his clothing seemed somewhat dingy. The strong odor of sage hung around him like a blanket. Sensitive brown eyes, tinged by a deep sadness, met Left Hand's gaze. Did the man's soul weep? Those eyes touched him, spoke to something deep in Left Hand's heart.

"Firewood?" the Trader asked, still drawn by the troubled eyes.

Bad Belly nodded. "Yes."

Left Hand inspected the pile. "A lot of firewood. Did my Power bring me to the right place at the right time? A feast perhaps? Some special occasion?" He hoped it was so, hoped that the tragedy in Bad Belly's eyes didn't betray sickness or famine.

Bad Belly shook his head. "No, there's no feast. I was just given the duty."

"I thought that kind of work was for women and children." As soon as he said them, he regretted the words.

Bad Belly glanced away, his look wounded. "I have to do my part, that's all."

Left Hand berated himself. He'd tripped and fallen over the first rule of Trading: never offend. Quick to make amends, he offered, "I could help you. Looks to me like you've got several trips here. We're not far from Larkspur's camp, are we?"

"Around the rocks, there." Bad Belly waved with his good arm.

"Not far." Left Hand signaled his dogs to lie down—they'd started forward, eager to sniff this strange new man and his dog. "With two of us, we can get it done in no time."

Bad Belly pursed his lips and frowned. "It might not be a good idea."

"Why not?"

Bad Belly shrugged self-consciously.

Left Hand stepped over to sit on a boulder where he could enjoy the sun. "Well, at least tell me the news. I've been down in the Salt Trader country, and beyond there, among the Antelope People. What's happened here? Any news of the Wolf People?"

Bad Belly smiled—the effect like sunshine after a rain. Some special spirit lit his features, making the flat planes of his homely face happy, serene. "Oh, lots of news. Cattail has gone over to Three Forks to see about the Gathering. Well, maybe that isn't important to you. But, let's see. Oh, yes, there are rumors that Sun People have moved into the Gray Deer Basin north of the Sideways Mountains and that your Wolf People raided them a couple of times. Other rumors say that more clans of the Sun People are moving south. Some talk of war, some talk of meeting with the Sun People to see if they'll go back north.''

Left Hand stroked his chin. ''Meeting with them won't send them back north.''

''Oh?''

''I Traded up there a couple of years ago. Brought one of their Traders back with me, as a matter of fact, and showed him the trail to the Boat People's land far to the west.'' Left Hand shook his head. ''They won't go back just because someone asks them to. They fight as much with themselves as they do with other peoples. I don't know. They're strange.''

Bad Belly nodded, a pinched look on his face.

''They aren't here yet. You look worried,'' Left Hand said.

''Just thinking about the wolf. It popped into my mind is all.''

''What wolf?''

''A big black one that watches me. He shows up now and then.'' Bad Belly's eyes went vacant.

''You want to tell me about this wolf?''

Bad Belly glanced around uneasily.

Left Hand took a long shot. ''You know, among my people, Wolf is a Spirit animal. Especially the black wolf. He's the messenger of Wolf Dreamer, whom you call First Man. You remember when you stole our Sacred Bundle? That is our Power, the soul of the People, which was given to us by Wolf Dreamer. Tell me, I'll believe you. If it was Wolf, the Spirit Helper, maybe it was a sign to you. We take Power very seriously. Dreams, too.''

''Dreams?'' Bad Belly's face became a study of conflicting emotions. ''And Dreamers?''

Left Hand nodded soberly. ''Especially Dreamers. What's wrong? You been having Dreams?''

Bad Belly scuffed his feet. "Not Dreams. Not like that. Not the Power kind."

Left Hand leaned back and cocked his head. "I'm just a Trader, mind you, but I know quite a bit about people. Knowing such things, I get a feeling about you. Are you in some kind of trouble? Is there something about Round Rock I should know? Like maybe not to stop there for the night?"

"No, no." Bad Belly shot a nervous look back toward the camp. "Nothing's wrong. It's just me. I'm . . ." His face flushed hot and he took a deep breath, dropping down to sit on a rock opposite Left Hand's. He indicated his bad arm. "I'm just not much use to them. That's all."

"You *are* in trouble. Huh. You don't look like the type."

"How's that?"

The earnest appeal warmed something in Left Hand's soul. The man seemed so innocent, so kind. Everyone should like him.

"Well . . ." Left Hand fingered his chin, scrutinizing Bad Belly. "You're not very crafty. Generally, people who are crafty get in trouble. They try to pull tricks. You know, take advantage. You're too honest, your soul shines through your eyes. That's it. You care too much."

After an uncomfortable silence, Bad Belly slapped his good hand to his knee, shaking his head as if to rid it of sudden sorrow. "I guess I don't live up to what Larkspur thinks I should be. Maybe like you said, I'm not crafty. I just don't care about getting the advantage and trying to make people do what they don't want to."

"Well, what do you want to do?"

Bad Belly gestured around him. "Look at this world out here. There are things to see. Things to wonder about. Like . . . like the sun."

"The sun?" Left Hand squinted up at the blinding orb.

"The sun." Bad Belly smiled, absorbed by something in his head. "Think about it. You can feel the sun's heat. It makes light, like fire."

"Uh-huh. So?"

"So, what does it burn? Wood? There's no smoke. Have you ever seen a fire that didn't make smoke? Even the driest of wood makes smoke. And not only that, but you never smell smoke. Even if it was invisible smoke, you'd still smell it, wouldn't you? You can smell lots of invisible things."

Left Hand lowered his gaze to Bad Belly's thoughtful features. The man looked radiant.

"I guess I never thought about it before."

"Most people don't. And there's another thing. The sun goes down in the west, right? That means it has to go around the world to come up in the east. So why doesn't the ground get hot at night? The sun should be under our feet. Maybe in a tunnel somewhere—like a gopher tunnel."

"If it really goes underground."

"Then if it doesn't go underground, where does it go?"

"Maybe one sun dies and another gets born."

Bad Belly grinned, a new animation in his eyes. "Ah. Good thought, but think about this. If the sun is born every morning, it never grows. In fact, it starts out great big when it comes over the horizon and gets littler until it crosses the western horizon, where it gets big again. How many things do you know of that do that? Just the moon. And speaking about the moon, why doesn't it burn as hot as the sun? And I don't think the moon dies every night, either."

"And why is that, Bad Belly?"

"Because it always looks the same. Even when it goes from round to a sliver and back to round again. The moon has exactly the same markings every time. How many things do you know of that die and are born again time after time and always look the same? Even red squirrels and mice and birds have different markings, you know . . . little changes here and there that let you tell one from another."

Left Hand chuckled to himself. No wonder Bad Belly had trouble. Left Hand had met Larkspur once, five summers past: a painfully practical and cunning woman. She had left him feeling uneasy. Beyond his own experience with her, her reputation had spread far and wide. People feared and respected her. The Earth People made few decisions without consulting her. And Bad Belly lived in *her* camp? No wonder she'd sent him out here to pull up sagebrush.

"And there's more," Bad Belly continued. "Why does the

sun change its path across the sky? Why are days longer in summer and shorter in winter? Why can't you see the way the path changes through the seasons? Why doesn't it take the south trail across the sky one day and the north one the next?''

''I don't know, but it never does,'' Left Hand said absently.

''How do you know that?''

Left Hand waved in the direction of the mountains. ''We have stone circles with rocks placed just so. You can watch the sun come up in the morning, lining up on the rocks. By watching the rocks, you can trace the change in the sun's path.''

Bad Belly's eyes glowed. ''What I'd give to see that!''

''Build your own. Find a ridge top and make a circle. You'll have to be up there at sunrise and sunset. Look across the circle and line up the rocks, that's all.''

The excitement died in Bad Belly's eyes. ''I couldn't. Larkspur . . .''

''. . . wouldn't let you?''

Bad Belly shrugged. ''She's a good leader for our clan. She has to make decisions for all of us . . . make sure that everyone is taken care of.''

Left Hand propped his elbows on his knees. ''You know, that's the trouble with you Earth People.''

''It is?''

Left Hand laughed. ''You mean you think about the sun and moon, about the markings on mice, and you don't think about your own people and why they do what they do?''

''Oh, I think about people all the time. I wonder why people act the way they do. Sometimes things happen and we just act . . . you know, like jerking your hand back from the fire. Other times we think first about what we'll do, we plan. Is one different from the other? Do you ever wonder about that?''

''Oh, yes. A Trader thinks about that all the time. If we could figure out how people think, we'd always have the right stuff to Trade at the right time. As it is, we just guess that Antelope People will want buffalo meat. Or that pinion nuts will be in demand by the time we get back home. But that's not the question I asked. What about the way *your* people live? I mean, you don't fit.''

Bad Belly knotted his fist. ''Of course I fit.''

''Then why does Larkspur have you out here pulling up sagebrush for firewood? The Larkspur I know couldn't care less if the sun traveled under the earth.''

Bad Belly looked away as he rubbed his good hand nervously on the grease-stained leather of his pants. ''I used to have a friend who cared. He died.''

''I'm sorry.'' Left Hand lowered his voice. ''He was the one who listened to you, wasn't he? The rest, they don't understand, do they?''

Bad Belly started, as if hearing words out of the past. His throat worked as he swallowed; nervously shifting his eyes as though looking for some answer hidden in the patterns of sagebrush shadows, or in the configuration of the rocks.

Left Hand barely heard the words Bad Belly whispered under his breath. *''Trader coming.* He said that. He knew.''

Left Hand stood and slapped Bad Belly on the back. ''Come on, I'll help you pack this sagebrush into camp.''

''Larkspur might not like that.''

''She won't offend a Trader, especially not when he's being helpful.''

Left Hand followed in Bad Belly's steps, carrying an armload of prickly sage and his Trader's staff. That haunted expression on Bad Belly's face stuck in his mind like boiled pine sap. By buffalo's hairy scrotum, he just plain liked the man.

Left Hand glanced up at the sky. *And just what does the sun burn, anyway?*

White Ash threw herself into the tedious chore of twisting sagebrush out of the ground. She worked in the flats north of camp, where the soil had better depth and grew taller sage. The day weighed on her—the sky leaden and dark with clouds. The land endured, snow-packed and gray. She labored hard, hating the weakness in her muscles as she drove herself to bury grief with exhaustion.

The scrubby brush made wonderful fuel for the hearth. It smoked very little, lit easily, and burned like a torch for several minutes before the hard wood fragmented down to coals. When enough rocks were thrown into the fire to absorb the heat, they would return warmth all night. When a thick bed of coals was made, the hearth would put out heat for at least two days. And sagebrush grew everywhere. Along the drainages it grew as tall as the tallest man. Out in the basins it might reach as high as a man's knee. On the ridge tops and in places where the soil was weak, the stuff grew only as high as a person's ankle—but it all burned.

The root separated with a crackle and pop. She straightened and threw her prize into the pile that grew beside her.

By habit she scanned the ridges, and this time she caught a hint of movement—that of a man. She squinted to see better and noted the weary way he walked. She eased back to her pack, pulling out her atlatl—lighter than a man's, suited to a woman's balance. She also picked up some of her slim darts and checked the seating of the foreshafts, each tipped with a deadly translucent brown chert point. She looked around, seeing no one else to warn, and started forward.

She trotted, enjoying the exercise, watching the wavering figure ahead. It looked like . . . *Wind Runner!* She was sure of it. She broke into a run. Perhaps they'd made a kill? If only it hadn't taken so long; five days had passed since Bright Moon's death. The intervening time in the lodge had been miserable. Bright Moon's presence lingered, seeping out from the stained lodge poles and the smoked hide of the cover. There, amid the memories, she had waited longingly for Sage Ghost to return.

"Wind Runner!"

He drew up, squinting across the melting snow, then waving. As she came closer, she could see that he looked ghastly—haggard and worn. Mud and water had spattered and stained his clothing. His face was gaunt and drawn; hollows had formed under his broad cheekbones. A series of scratches traced irregularly across the blue lines tattooed on his high forehead, and sage leaves stuck here and there in his black, shining braids.

"What happened?" she demanded, hugging him. "Are the men all right?"

"Fine . . . I think. They made a kill . . . about a week ago. Listen, we have to move camp. There are Wolf People all over out there. I don't know, maybe that bunch that raided us two moons ago went back and told the others. I've had to lose two separate parties in getting here."

She shot a quick glance over his shoulder. The rolling ridges looked soft in the distance, the surfaces mottled with drifted snow. "Come on. Flying Squirrel's been worried half sick. She won't say it aloud, but I can tell."

"Yes, well, we've got buffalo down a couple of days' march south of here. Maybe after that, we'd better keep going that way. Stop when we get to those mountains you call Sideways."

"Sideways because they slope up gently on this side, then fall off in cliffs on the other."

He grinned the stupid grin of the exhausted. "Then let's move what's left of the White Clay across them. How are things here? You haven't seen any raiders? No scouts, no tracks?"

"Nothing but wind and blowing snow." She took a deep breath. "Bright Moon died. Her soul split from her body. She couldn't move for a couple of days and then went in the night. It was peaceful. She didn't suffer."

Wind Runner missed a step and almost fell, eyes narrowing with pain. "No . . . not that. It's going to kill Sage Ghost. He had a feeling. He sent a message with me, to tell Bright Moon he was fine and eating lots of buffalo as he thought of her."

White Ash glanced away, seeking to hide her grief. "For the moment, we have the Wolf People to worry about. You're sure they're looking for us?"

He jerked a short nod. "I could expect a single party out hunting. But two? No, they're after us. I think they want to drive us back north as a warning to others not to move into their territory."

"But if we go back, we're headed right into Black Point country."

"That's right. So what's left?"

She threw another look behind her. "The Sideways Mountains. And, well, beyond that there are the People. We're so few. Maybe I know of a place we can go without violating their territory."

"Wherever it is, we'd better hurry—and make very few tracks in the process."

Flying Squirrel took charge the minute Wind Runner gave his report. The White Clay leaped to the task of taking down the camp. Children cornered the dogs and fitted leather pack harnesses despite whines and yelps. Scanty possessions were rolled and stuffed into parfleches, which were in turn lashed to travois and hooked to the suddenly anxious dogs. Lodge poles were hurriedly pulled from within; the carefully cured lodge covers fluttered down around those who still worked inside.

White Ash shot a quick glance at Wind Runner; he had collapsed onto a roll of hides and immediately dropped off to sleep. The terrible journey reflected in his slack face. For a moment she struggled with an urge to reach down and caress his cheek. No, to do so would only embarrass him. Curses on his preoccupation with the silly marriage rules of the White Clay.

With the proficiency Bright Moon had taught her, White Ash packed, getting the dogs in order, grimacing at the way the ribs stuck out on the eager animals. Hunger gnawed everyone's belly. Four buffalo lay two days' hard journey to the south. And the trail might be full of hostile warriors. More than once she caught herself looking for Bright Moon, waiting to hear her comment. The hollowness in her breast expanded.

The sun already slanted to the west, and shadows stretched blue in the early spring cold as the White Clay started on the desperate journey south.

Chapter 6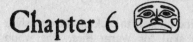

Over the crackling of the fire in Bitterbrush's lodge, Bad Belly could hear the faint sounds from Larkspur's lodge across the camp. Laughter and exclamations carried—even through the earthen walls of the house pit.

Larkspur's orders had been explicit. "You make sure the children are all right. Keep the fires going in all the lodges. Make sure our dogs don't fight with the Trader's."

Bad Belly had objected, "I want to hear the Trader's news."

She'd stared at him, gaze smoky as she blinked her eyes. "Someone has to see to camp. We'll tell you what the Trader said."

She still punishes me for not telling her my promise to Warm Fire.

He looked over to where Tuber and Lupine slept, Lupine curled in her big brother's protective arms. Tuber had turned sullen, hiding a smoldering anger in his breast since his father's death. He didn't have any more than a couple of years of boyhood left. Would he carry that explosive anger with him into manhood?

Trader coming. Go.

Warm Fire *had* known. The Dream had been real, not the mutterings of a man in fever. Bad Belly frowned as he ran the tips of his fingers through the hollow concave of Bitterbrush's metate, the grinding slab, where she milled seeds and roots into flour. He traced patterns in the dust that clung to the heavy sandstone . . . and then stared at what he'd wrought: the outline of a wolf.

And the black wolf had been standing there. How come he hadn't seen the animal's tracks? Every time something important happened, the black wolf appeared, staring at him from the shadows. Or did his imagination trick him?

Leave . . . Go. . . . Warm Fire's words pricked at him like greasewood thorns.

Bad Belly reached behind himself to pick up the dart shaft he'd prepared with such skill for Warm Fire. The wood seemed to pulse in his grip, as if to remind him of the promise made. He balanced the perfect shaft in his hand . . . and blinked away tears of frustration.

Left Hand—a Trader from another people—had listened to him with the same thoughtfulness Warm Fire had once shown him.

You don't fit. The words rankled.

Bad Belly gently replaced the shaft, careful not to damage the feather fletching. He sighed and stood, ducking out through the flap into the night. Morning lurked just over the horizon; Larkspur had talked most of the night away. The sounds issuing from the old clan leader's lodge had dropped in volume, coming sporadically now.

We take Dreamers very seriously.

And I'm supposed to save a Dreamer? Bad Belly looked up at the stars. The wind blew warm tonight, herald of a coming spring—just as the Trader's arrival anticipated the changing of the seasons. Traders everywhere would be setting out now, turning their steps to various destinations, packs loaded with interesting things. How would it feel to travel like that?

Bad Belly scratched Trouble's throat and went to check on the Trader's dogs. They lay in a circle around the pile of packs, guarding them as they were supposed to, keeping away rodents and other pests. The camp dogs remained in their places around the lodges, having been thrashed into understanding that the Trader's animals weren't to be molested.

They'll destroy you here. Beat you down bit by bit.

Bad Belly walked over to the pile of sage he and Left Hand had packed in and picked up some of the gnarly brush. He paused, staring at the mound and remembering the afternoon's work. He and Left Hand had actually had fun, talking about how the rocks looked in the south, and about the giant lake of water so salty you couldn't drink from it. What made one lake clear, another muddy, and yet another full of salt?

Forcing himself to the task, he replenished the fire in each of the lodges, stirring up the coals around the firestones and adding more sage.

That done, Bad Belly lifted the flap of Bitterbrush's lodge and glanced in to make sure the children still slept soundly. Then he squatted in the shadow of the lodge, watching the moon rise above the edge of the Round Rocks. Almost round, it might have been a clay ball dropped on hard soil, the way one side lay in shadow.

Shadow? Did something—the sun?—shine on it? Maybe it didn't have any fire of its own? The idea appealed to him. He slipped into the shelter and found a round rock among his possessions. Against the firelight, it might have been the moon. Depending on which way he held it, he could mimic the cycles of the moon.

The giddy excitement gripped him for only a moment. Who would want to hear his idea? Left Hand might. But Left Hand sat in the center of Larkspur's lodge—and Bad Belly knew better than to interrupt such a council over something as silly as the moon being in shadow.

He ducked outside again, his rock in hand, and looked up at the moon. He could barely make out the darkened sliver. Yes, just like a shadow. The yawning grief rose inside. In another day, in a time now past, he would have immediately run to tell Warm Fire. The loss pulled at his heart.

He heard steps and looked up. Left Hand stood there. "I see you've taken good care of my dogs."

"They're good dogs."

"You sound sad."

"I was just thinking."

"About Warm Fire? Larkspur told me about him. She made a great point of explaining how the Healer, Black Hand, had so much Power crackling around him that the stones almost floated. And how Warm Fire's soul left despite such heroic efforts. People don't usually talk in such detail about how great a Healer is."

Bad Belly shrugged, grateful that the night hid his expression. "Black Hand is the best we have these days."

"Something about Warm Fire's death bothers Larkspur. And it's not Black Hand."

"Oh?"

Left Hand settled himself across from Bad Belly. "Warm Fire must have been a wonderful man."

"Yes. I miss him. Life's not the same."

Left Hand sat in silence for a while before saying, "I'm a Trader. I guess it's part of the Power, but sometimes I get a feeling from watching people. You and he, you were very close, weren't you?"

Bad Belly held his peace.

"That's one of the reasons Larkspur is upset with you. I could tell by the way she talked."

"Warm Fire told me to leave this place," Bad Belly whispered absently, hardly aware of what he'd said. "Don't tell anyone. Please." That feeling of friendliness he harbored had betrayed him. That, and the need to talk to someone again. Now his gut tightened.

Left Hand gestured around. "Isn't there some other camp where you could go? Where they'd like to hear about these things you think of? I'd imagine you'd be good to have around the fire on long winter nights."

Bad Belly tapped a nervous fist on the ground. "No one would want to offend Larkspur."

"Have you ever thought that maybe it's your Power? That maybe you need to find your own calling? Me, I found mine when I was young. I climbed to a high place and fasted for four days. Trader Power came to me, and I knew it was right. I've been all over. I've seen places you can only imagine. I've tasted the saltwater of the Western Waters and ridden on the waves with the Boat People. I've eaten the big fish they spear out of the Silver River and smoke over alder fires. I've seen the places where the Antelope People live—down in the red sandstone canyons, where water runs under stone arches. I've walked to the huge river in the east, where the Masked Dancer People live in the forests and care for the wild-rice stands. They float on the water in hollowed-out logs and cast nets to catch fish and wear masks to make themselves look like Spirits. I've walked the Short Grass Plains and shared the hide lodges of the Buffalo People. I've eaten creatures the likes of which you can't imagine at the camp fires of the Swamp People, where the Father Water joins the southern sea. So many things . . . so many." Left Hand smiled at the memories. "Maybe you haven't found your Power yet."

"Do I have any?" Bad Belly couldn't ignore Warm Fire's claim. *I saw in the Dream. You're the important one. Power wants you.*

"Everyone has Power." In the darkness, Left Hand leaned his head back, eyes on the stars. "We have a legend. Once the Wolf People and your people were at war. At the time, your people lived like the Buffalo People do in the Short Grass Plains. Your warriors came up from the plains, hungry, ready to drive us from the mountains since all the water holes had dried up and the rains never fell. We were losing, and in the middle of a great fight, a Dreamer rose—a Dreamer who drove your warriors off by setting fire to trees. At that time he Danced with fire, and he brought you here, to the Wind Basin, and taught you the ways of the earth and how to use seeds for food."

"Fire Dancer?"

"Yes, Fire Dancer. And between us, he made peace. Over the years we've raided each other at times. Traded at others. Generally, our peoples have gotten along. The elders among my Wolf People, they keep the legends. They learn them, word for word, to remember the meaning of Fire Dancer. We are told that Fire Dancer gave your people the vision, the way to seek his own Power. Since that time, you've lost that vision. You asked if you had any Power. Yes, my friend, you do. Everyone does."

My friend. That's what he called me. Bad Belly's soul ached.

"I don't know," Left Hand continued. "I think it's the way you live that's changed you. Among your people, only the Healers and the clan leaders keep Power. It's as if it's been removed from everyone but the leaders. Up there somewhere." He pointed at the sky. "But it's not, you know.

Power is what you feel around you. Part of the rocks, trees, plants, and animals. It fills the soil as well as the sky. You need only to seek, to allow yourself to feel.''

"I know what you're talking about." Bad Belly smiled into the night. "I get that feeling when I watch antelope fawns being born. Or maybe when the sunset is streaked with red and orange.''

"I think perhaps you do. I can see it in you. But these others? I think they've begun to remove themselves from part of the world. Maybe it's the way your shelters are built. Maybe it's the fact that you stay in one place. I was listening to Larkspur talk about the Spirit that lives in the spring back of the camp. Later I heard her mention the Spirit that stays in an old dead log up on Green Mountain. I find myself wondering about that. You've taken the One and split it up into pieces.''

"How do you know that's not the way it is?''

"I don't. But it doesn't feel right to me. I think you Earth People are changing. I think it's because of the way you live. Maybe Larkspur is right. Maybe there are separate Spirits— but my soul knows they're all part of the One.''

Bad Belly ran fingers down his numb, shriveled arm. "Larkspur told me one time that the Spirits would think I was foolish for asking so many questions. She said that it didn't do any good to watch things constantly, that Spirits had no use for a man who was always locked in his head. That a person with responsibility should spend his time making sure he didn't make the Spirits mad—that otherwise they might take something away, keep the biscuit root from growing, or make the pine-nut harvest fail, or bring a drought.''

Left Hand scratched at his ear. "I think that's all part of the One. The Spiral changes, and things change with the Spiral. Maybe the biscuit root doesn't come up one spring. That's the turning of the Spiral. It always comes up the next spring, or the one after that, doesn't it?''

Warm Fire talked about the Spiral.

Bad Belly picked at his leggings, saying lamely, "Of course it does. That's because we leave gifts for the Spirits who make the biscuit root grow.''

"You see, that's a major difference between us. The Wolf People don't have to give things. We just have to be. We just have to live with the One. We call to the elk or to the mountain sheep and they share themselves. To repay them, we Sing their souls to the Starweb. You think you have to give something first, that the Spirits are selfish—sort of like people."

"I still don't know that you're right."

Left Hand studied him. "Then let me ask you a question. If Spirit Power really worked that way, if you had to appease Spirit Power, then my people should be starving, right? We don't leave curious little gifts to keep the Spirit World happy. The biscuit root, the sego lily, and the shooting star still grow. Elk and deer and mountain sheep still let us kill them. We don't suffer from hunger."

Bad Belly's face puckered as he thought. "But our Healers have always done it that way. They'd know, wouldn't they? They know the ways of Power."

"Singing Stones came to our mountains and seeks the One."

Singing Stones, the greatest of all the Healers. Bad Belly had seen him only once since the old man had Sung over his arm and saved his life. He could still remember the withdrawn look in the Healer's eyes.

"What about you?" Left Hand asked. "What are you going to do? Leave, like your friend asked?"

"I wish I could."

"What you wish, you should do."

"These are my people, my clan and family." He shook his head. "It's hard. Where would I go? What would I do? I . . . oh, I don't know."

"Afraid?"

Bad Belly hesitated. Was that it? "I suppose so. This is all I know. People take care of me here. I have a warm place to stay. Plenty of food. If I get hurt, or sicken, someone will take care of me. My ancestors are buried here—they keep watch. If I left? Well, the only time I left before, it wasn't good. There are strange people in the world, dangerous animals like silver bears, and warlike Sun People, and so many things that could happen to a man."

"You must find your own Power." Left Hand sighed. "But think of this. If you wake up someday, many winters from now, and say to yourself, 'Warm Fire always wanted me to leave. I always wanted to find out things, watch things, follow the track of the sun across the sky and see beyond the farthest range of mountains. Why didn't I ever go?' Well, that would be a terrible thing, wouldn't it? To know that you lived all your life and never followed your Dreams?"

"But what if something happened? If I froze to death, or fell and hurt myself? I did that once. People here took care of me."

Left Hand smiled understandingly. "We each must live our own life in our own way, Bad Belly. People die all the time, and it is dangerous out there away from your clan." He paused. "But I wonder, can a man who asks what the sun burns bear to live in this valley for his whole life?"

Bad Belly licked his lips, irritated by the sudden beating of his heart. Warm Fire had told him the Trader was coming. Larkspur hadn't even let him stay when his friend lay dying. The night seemed to press down on him, smothering, the air heavy and oppressive. *If I don't go now, I never will.*

"I made a promise."

"I couldn't hear what you said. You mumbled."

"Which way are you going?" Bad Belly closed his eyes, desperation tightening like a noose around his throat.

"North."

"North. Find the Dreamer. Promise."

Bad Belly rubbed his fingers together; Warm Fire's fevered grip clung in ghostly fashion to his flesh.

"Would you . . . I mean . . . could I go with you? North? At least for a while?"

Left Hand studied him in the darkness. "After trying so hard to talk yourself out of it? Why?"

"Because of the promise I made to Warm Fire. The one Larkspur would give so much to know about."

Wind Runner forced himself to walk, when all he wanted to do was sleep. Despite his weariness, a curious ecstasy filled him. *Two* separate parties of hostile warriors had chased him—and he'd lost them both! No matter that his very bones and muscles ached, he'd foxed both groups—outwitted them all—and escaped while leading the pursuit away from his people. Honor lay in that . . . along with a pulsing euphoria of triumph. He'd lived when others would have killed him.

"So, what's the smile for? You look about ready to fall over."

He grinned at White Ash. "Just thinking about things."

"Things?"

"About how I kept alive while I was being hunted like a rabbit."

She nodded and glanced back at the string of dogs that followed in their tracks. The travois poles dragged hollowly on the ground. She and Wind Runner walked in front since he knew the location of the kill site. The sixty or so remaining people of the White Clay followed in single file, Flying Squirrel and the young boy, Drummer, bringing up the rear. They couldn't hide this trail, but if they moved fast enough, they might avoid pursuit until they could find a place that could be defended. Perhaps the buffalo would give them strength to continue their flight farther south.

"It seems almost like the end of the White Clay." Wind Runner shook his head and sighed wearily.

White Ash squinted up at the sun that beat down now, warm, bright. The snow had begun to turn to mush and the soil had started to thaw into mud. Travel in the spring always caused problems. Tonight moccasins would be wet, as would the rest of their clothing—and darkness would bring renewed cold.

"Maybe it is. Flying Squirrel and I have talked about that. Why don't you go join the Black Point? You have relatives there. They'd take you in . . . as long as you renounced all ties to the White Clay."

Wind Runner lifted a shoulder absently. "I suppose. My mother's sister, Two Antelopes, married Stone Fist, a Black Point warrior. They would speak for me. I would have to declare my clan dead. I suppose all of us could go. We'd be like . . . well, not like real people, not part of the clan even if we lived with them. No one would listen to us in council. We wouldn't have any say about where we were going or what we were doing. We'd be strangers among them.''

"There are ways. You've heard of Buffalo Tail. He's one of the most respected elders on the Broken Stones' council. He was Black Point originally. He earned his rights by duel."

"I just outran two war parties of Wolf People. I wouldn't want to have to fight to make a place for myself." Or did he? He'd survived when by rights he should have been killed. Power honored men of courage who dared to try themselves.

Listlessly, she said, "It might not be all that bad. You could at least find a woman to marry. Maybe a pretty young woman, one who would bear you many children." When she saw his expression, she made a gesture as if to toss her words away. "I'm sorry. Forgive me for saying that. I didn't mean to hurt you. I think maybe I wanted to hurt myself. I'm still missing Bright Moon, feeling grief over her death." She paused. "Hating the thought of having to tell Sage Ghost."

"It'll break his heart." He let the subject change, wanting to talk more about his love for her—afraid to at the same time. *Why continue to torture yourself? A smart man would try to ignore her, keep her at a distance.* He growled under his breath. *I'm just not smart, that's all.*

They walked in silence. He stole a glance at her, seeing the thoughts reflected in her face as she considered how to approach Sage Ghost.

For a long moment he admired her beauty, longing to reach out and touch her. The sway of her hips captivated him. Her sorrow tortured his soul. *I can't love her, no matter how much I want to. She's my uncle's daughter. Among the White Clay, I must call her sister. However, if I were to leave, to go among the Black Point and win my place there, I could marry her. My clan would be renounced—dead. I would have no relatives.* The idea stunned him as he turned it over in his mind, looking at all sides. There would be risks, of course. He'd have to fight for a place among the Black Point. Could he do it? Could he win?

Far to the west, barely visible against the rising foothills of the mountains, a flight of geese was winging north . . . north . . .

It *could* work. The thought captured him, made stronger by the exhaustion that cloaked his being. Just think of Brave Man's expression when he heard that Wind Runner offered marriage to White Ash! Brave Man. He could be a problem in the meantime.

"You have another thing to think about, you know," he said.

She gave him a wary glance.

"Brave Man is going to be working on Sage Ghost. Dropping hints, seeking to gain favor. He's going to want to marry you."

"I'll say no. Sage Ghost, even if his heart is broken, won't make me marry a man I don't want."

Wind Runner frowned at the horizon. "You're going to have to marry someday. The White Clay are running out of choices for you."

She laughed, flashing a smile at him. "There's only one man among the White Clay I'd want to marry."

Lowering his voice, he told her, "We've had that discussion before. You're my uncle's daughter. Among the White Clay—"

"—it's incest, I know. But I'm not your sister, no matter that your people call first cousins that."

He squinted at the horizon. *Should I tell her? Do I want to commit myself yet? No. Wait. Like the good hunter, don't hurry.*

He shrugged absently. "It is the way of my people. I can't turn my back on my clan, or on the beliefs of my father and my father's father. A man without his people is nothing, no more than a beast."

She didn't respond.

"I'm sorry. If things were different, if Sage Ghost hadn't raised you as his . . . had not called you his daughter in council, you would already be my wife."

"And why haven't you married? Dancing Rose would crawl into your robes if you so much as blinked at her."

"Because," he answered mildly.

"Because why?"

"Just because." He took a breath, lowered his voice. "You know why."

She looked at him with eyes that wounded his soul. "And if Brave Man abducts me again?"

"Then I'll track him down and take you back. And if he resists, I'll drive a dart through him."

She stiffened. Among the Earth People, no greater horror—not even the horror of incest—existed than that of murder. More than once she'd seen the Sun People turn violently on each other. War lived in their souls. Had it crept into hers?

Her smile went bittersweet. "I don't know who I am anymore, Wind Runner. If you killed Brave Man for raping me, I'd . . . well, I don't know. Maybe I finally understand what you mean about your people. It's something we grow up with. Me, I can understand your loathing of incest . . . by understanding my feeling about how horrible murder is among the Earth People."

"And who else is there for you to marry?" *Only Brave Man.*

"What happened to Black Eagle and Gray Thunder's bands?" she asked.

"I haven't heard any news of them, have you? It's been close to three years since we split from Black Eagle's camp. He thought he could hold the land higher up on the Fat Beaver River. I always thought he'd show up again. Now, well, I'm not so sure."

"I *won't* have Brave Man. I'd rather couple with a white bear than with him."

A thrill shot up his spine. Perhaps there was a way. If Brave Man tried to abduct White Ash again, he'd have to kill his old friend. So much had changed between himself and Brave Man. And if he ran off to the Black Point and married White Ash, Brave Man would come hunting him—to pay back the insult to the White Clay and take White Ash away from him.

Bad Belly stooped and got into the strap that held his pack on. He stood, taking the weight. Around him, the predawn shadows softened the familiar outlines of Round Rock camp. The fresh morning air nipped at him, and the chill from the ground leeched into his thick moccasins. He looked around at the camp, and a sudden fullness gripped his breast.

Bitterbrush gave him one last check. "You've got your extra fire sticks?"

"In the pack."

She looked him up and down. "Well, be careful. If it looks like a spring storm, hole up. Don't take any chances."

"I won't."

"Bad Belly," she pleaded one last time, tilting her head in the authoritative way Grandmother used, "you're being an idiot . . . just like usual. Give up this quest. You're going out to get yourself in trouble. Why are you doing this to me? Haven't I always taken care of you? Do you think this Trader is going to take care of you? What about your responsibility to—"

"Bitterbrush. Hush."

"You're not up to this, Bad Belly, and you know it. Why don't you show some sense for the first time in your life, and act like a man for once? You're about to make the worst—"

"*Bitterbrush!*"

"—mistake you'll ever make. And you've made a lot of them. I just won't have this—"

"Daughter?" Cattail said, placing a hand on her shoulder. "Let your brother do as he wishes."

Bad Belly shot a look of gratitude at his father. Bitterbrush bit her lip and nodded reluctantly, resentment in her eyes.

Left Hand secured the last of his dogs' packs and straightened, pride in his eyes as he looked over his animals. Then he ducked into his tumpline, stood, and checked the balance of his load.

Bad Belly turned to leave, not surprised to notice that only his father and sister had come to wish him off. Limbercone, Phloxseed, and Pretty Woman probably sat in Larkspur's lodge plotting with the old woman. Perhaps they were discussing what an insult it was to the camp that Bad Belly would run off with a Trader.

Bad Belly's stomach ached. It hadn't been as difficult as he'd thought. Larkspur hadn't thrown a ring-tailed fit. A Trader had Power. People didn't offend Traders—as Larkspur well knew. To do so would give Round Rock a bad reputation, causing other Traders to bypass the camp in the future.

She wouldn't let me stay with my dying friend—not even when Warm Fire asked me to. He never spoke again after I left. Now that he balanced on the threshold of freedom, a new emotion sparked in his gut: anger.

The look the old woman had given him would remain engraved in his memory. She'd grunted a harsh laugh and muttered, "Then go! Run off with the Trader! Turn your back on your family and clan." And she'd motioned him out with the same gesture she'd use to shoo a bothersome fly.

Cattail had tried to smile, losing it somehow and only looking foolish. He said, "You watch yourself when you get to the mountains. One wrong step up there and you'll have a leg just like your arm."

"I'll be careful, Father."

Cattail thought for a moment. "Keep to the ridges. The mud's not so bad there. It'll be impossible down in the drainages. You'll see. You walk in that sticky, gooey mud for a couple of days and you'll learn just how tired you can be. Once you hit the sand hills, the travel will be easier."

"I expect Left Hand knows the way."

Cattail smiled wistfully. "I know it's been hard for you here. You're a good man, my son. Just a little different, that's all." He lowered his voice, stepping close. "I don't blame you a bit. In fact, you make me proud. Good-bye. Good luck."

"Tell Grandmother . . . nothing. Never mind."

"She's upset by this. We all are," Bitterbrush said severely as she stepped close. Then, in a low voice, she added, "But maybe I don't blame you, either."

Bad Belly smiled farewell, wondering at the look she gave him. Limbercone, Phloxseed, and Pretty Woman hadn't even told him good-bye. They'd just stared at him, condemnation in their eyes. Why did they have do that? *It's guilt. They don't know what to do with me. So, if I go out and run afoul of a silver bear, or a Wolf People war party, they'll think it's their fault.* The thought didn't comfort him.

Morning looked to be breaking. This day would be clear and sunny—and no doubt the wind would whistle down from the Monster Mountains in a roaring gale. Walking into the wind wore a person out.

Left Hand lifted an eyebrow and gestured toward the trail.

Bad Belly took a deep breath, drawing his lungs full of Round Rock camp's air. He looked around one last time to settle the scene in his memory. He'd been born right over there in Limbercone's lodge. Here he'd lived as a boy, running and laughing, almost dying from snakebite. Sitting in the shade, he'd enjoyed hours of talk with Warm Fire. His sweat and effort had gone into the building of Bitterbrush's earthen lodge. Part of his soul would linger here. A strange twist of melancholy mixed with the excitement he felt for the journey ahead.

A man loses something of himself when he leaves his home. It's a small death that marks a turning in his life.

"Ready," he told Left Hand. He paused, smiling at Trouble. "Come on."

Trouble jumped and spun around as if he could sense the importance of this leaving. He lowered his chest and clawed at the cold ground, his tail whipping back and forth.

Together they walked down the beaten trail that led toward the Cold Water.

Bad Belly settled under the weight of the pack, walking slowly until his leg muscles warmed up, feeling the stiffness in his joints. They'd watch him until he'd passed from sight. For that, he refused to look back, refused to give them the satisfaction of a final wave to assuage their consciences.

As he and Left Hand passed the toe of the ridge, Bad Belly recognized Tuber's silhouette in the morning light. The boy stood on the crest of the dune where Warm Fire was buried, staring down at the ground.

"Left Hand? Wait a moment." Bad Belly gave Trouble a hand command to stay and started in the boy's direction. This good-bye couldn't be ignored. Poor Tuber, he'd suffered as much as Bad Belly had, maybe more.

Tuber heard him coming and raised his head. Then, like a frightened jackrabbit, the boy leaped over the other side and ran full tilt into the sage, clearing the low brush, racing as if the ghosts of the restless dead pursued him.

"Hey! Tuber! It's Bad Belly!"

Tuber only ran faster.

Bad Belly frowned after the disappearing boy. Then he glanced down . . . and saw the hole where Warm Fire had been laid. The coyotes had been at it, digging up the frozen chunks of dirt. They hadn't managed to pull all of Warm Fire's body out, but they'd ravaged what they could get to.

Bad Belly closed his eyes for a moment, seeking to still the suffocating grief. It was the way of the world. Coyotes had their own nature. Cattail and Flatsedge should have dug the grave deeper, though.

Turning away, he started back to the trail, where Left Hand waited.

Chapter 7

Cries of joy rose from the White Clay as Wind Runner led them onto the ridge top where the buffalo had been killed. Blood stains still marked the trampled snow.

"Looks like the Wolf People didn't find them," White Ash observed, unable to share the joy that filled her companions. Here was food. But she would have to face Sage Ghost.

Several of the hunters waved, coming toward them from the makeshift shelters, woven out of sagebrush, that guarded the meat. In the forefront, White Ash could make out Sage Ghost's muscular figure. Brave Man pushed past her father, breaking into a run.

Cramps spasmed in White Ash's legs, and the hunger knot in her belly constricted. Her throat tightened.

Brave Man raced up to her and stopped. His knowing grin widened while a gleam lit his dark eyes. The black crosses tattooed on his face seemed to stand out from his chilled flesh. "Meat. For all of us. Share my fire and my meat with me. We must talk, you and I, about the—"

She pushed past him, hating the smirk that had molded his face, hating him with a bitter futility. *How did I ever love him?* Sage Ghost came next, smiling—a happy light in his eyes as he looked beyond her, expecting Bright Moon.

"Sage Ghost?" she called softly.

He turned a penetrating gaze on her. That warm smile of greeting destroyed her, ruined all the words she'd so carefully composed.

The bright blue sky, the warm batting wind, the smell of sage and melting snow—all dimmed. The earth itself seemed to darken as he met her gaze, smile fading.

"What happened?" His words cut with the sting of an obsidian sliver.

"Come with me. We have to talk." She dropped her head; tears battled to break free. She led the way down the windward side of the ridge, away from the milling people. The sound of Sage Ghost's hurried steps shredded her composure.

At the foot of the ridge an outcrop of sandstone raised its barren bones from the embrace of the soil. Snow had drifted against the base of the rocks, curving in a crescent around the angular boulders. She turned, letting the breeze whip her long black hair around her face.

Sage Ghost studied her through worry-bright eyes. The five circles tattooed on his forehead stood out starkly from his suddenly pale flesh.

"Bright Moon?" His voice quavered.

White Ash bit her lip, slowly nodding her head.

His strong hands gripped her shoulders. She was scarcely

aware of the pain as his powerful fingers ate into her numb flesh. *I'll never forget his expression. Never forget his pain.*

"Her soul . . . split from her body. I was there the whole time. She didn't suffer. I—I felt her go. Felt her soul go free in the night. Warm. Happy with the One."

She forced herself to look up, to fall into the pits of misery reflected in his eyes.

His grip on her shoulders trembled and loosened. "No."

"There was nothing we could do. Flying Squirrel . . ."

He broke away and turned. Hiding his face, he took two stumbling steps and stopped. "Where . . . where is she?"

"Back at the old camp. We placed her on the ridge to the west and prayed. Her soul floated free in a wonderful warm mist. She smiled, Sage Ghost. She smiled."

"I'll go back. Go back and stay with her. Watch over—"

"No!" She grabbed him and pulled him around. The tears streaking down his face frightened her. "She wouldn't *want* that. You'd just torture yourself. Maybe die, too."

"What if I do?" His voice cracked. "Without . . . there's nothing . . . nothing."

She nerved herself and straightened her back. "I need you. We all need you. She's gone. Let her go." She shook her head, seeking to rid herself of the images her thoughts conjured: of Bright Moon's body chewed by scavengers; of Sage Ghost on the freezing ridge top, lonely company for a rotting corpse. "I don't know about the Spirit World, but what if you hurt her? Kept Thunderbird from taking her to the Camp of the Dead? Caused her to come back from the stars? She died in peace. Let her go, Father."

His haunted stare gutted her. "I *need* her!"

She broke then and wrapped her arms tightly around him. He hugged her to him, crushing her against his chest as she buried her face in the soft leather of his coat. His worn clothing carried the familiar scents of his body, odors of stale sweat and buffalo blood, of winter fires—of a life that would never be the same again.

On the ridge top, Brave Man stepped out from the tangle of people clustered at the kill site. The voices whispered in his mind, urging him after White Ash. He slipped off to one side, circling to place the bulk of the ridge between himself and prying eyes. Moving carefully, he reached a spot where he could look down.

He watched as White Ash and Sage Ghost hugged each other, buried in the dark pain of their grief. *One less obstacle in my way to possessing you, White Ash. You won't be able to deny me much longer. Sage Ghost will falter. He won't be willing to argue while his soul is pining for Bright Moon.*

The voices in his head whispered, *Soon. Something is going to happen soon. Be ready . . . ready to take your chance. Power comes.*

"Power comes," he whispered, looking up at the endless blue of the sky. "Hear me, Spirit World." The voices in his head stilled for the moment. "Wherever I have to go, whatever I have to do, I will have White Ash. On my soul, I swear it! I will use her strength. With her Power, you can't cast me out of the golden mist."

The voices chuckled agreement in his mind.

"What good is it to go farther south?" Bobcat demanded from his spot in the council circle. The chiseled lines of his weathered face, reflected in the flickers of firelight, showed his unease. The tattoos of footprints on his cheeks thinned with his expression. He sat wrapped in a worn buffalo robe. "I can't see it. We haven't spotted a single moose since we left the Dangerous River. This land looks drier than what we left behind us. The buffalo are scattered, few and far between. The grass isn't as lush. Different kinds of plants grow here. I don't know what good can come of moving into lands where there aren't as many game animals."

Overhead, the star-shot sky had paled in the glow of the rising moon. The White Clay had pitched camp in a hollow that gouged the lee of an uplifted sandstone hogback. The hollow offered protection from the brunt of the wind and enjoyed a southern exposure that caught the sun's rays. The sandy soil drained well, unlike the sloppy clay in the flats.

While wolves howled in the night, the firelight flickered off the lodges and cast elongated conical shadows on the trampled snow and sagebrush. Somewhere in the background a dog barked and went still. For once, the cool breeze blowing down from the mountains didn't carry the bite of winter.

Whistling Hare, the band's old leader, spread his hands wide, the fringes of his elk hide jacket waving. His eyes had lost their luster, worry betrayed by the shrunken skin of his face. "I'm not sure we have any choice. We're being hunted by Wolf People. I think they expect us farther to the north. And behind them come the Black Point and the Broken Stones. Last summer those clans spent most of their time warring against each other. Next summer they might turn their attention to us."

"I've never been as hungry as I have been this winter," Bobcat's wife, Grasshopper, declared, her hot gaze shifting from face to face. Grunts of agreement echoed from the others.

White Ash sat in Sage Ghost's place in the council circle. Since setting up camp, her father hadn't stirred from the lodge. He stayed on his robes, staring emptily at the spot where Bright Moon should have been.

The central fire flared as young Drummer dutifully cast more sage onto the flames. The White Clay leadership sat around the dim light, grim-faced.

"We can't stay here," Old Flying Squirrel insisted from her place beside Whistling Hare. She ran absent fingers down the worn breastpiece she wore; her thumbnail clicked over the lines of rabbit-bone beads separated by disks cut from sea shells Traded from the west. "Wind Runner barely escaped with his life as it was. Those war parties—they'll find our trail, if they're not already sniffing along it. Bobcat, no matter how well we liked it in the north, we've wasted enough of our energy trying to hold land. We've sung too many of our warrior's souls to the sky and Thunderbird. They do us no good in the Camp of the Dead. I have one son left alive. One son, out of four."

She shook her old head, burdened by her thoughts. "Maybe it's Power doing this to us. We're the Sun People. Maybe the Sun is forcing us south for some reason. Other People live in the south. It's a land that will support us."

White Ash started as the old woman looked at her. All gazes turned her way.

White Ash collected herself, looking from face to face. "People live very well in the south. They don't hunt as much as we do—but they don't suffer from famine either. On the other side of the Sideways Mountains, the Earth People have lived for many generations. The camps were few and far between at first. As they grew, some broke away and made new camps. Unlike us, they collect seeds and plants and store them for the winter."

"But they live in lodges made of dirt!" Brave Man cried. "You'll never catch me living in dirt!"

"Their elders don't freeze to death," White Ash replied hotly. "They don't have to die on long marches either, because the people don't have to go as far to seek food."

Badger crossed his arms over his chest. "I don't like the idea of eating seeds and plants."

Old Falcon, the Soul Flier, raised an arm from his tightly bundled robes and shook his finger. "But you Trade for those root cakes every chance you get!"

Badger gestured helplessly. "Well, you have to Trade with Traders. That's the Power. I don't want to offend Power, that's all."

"And wasn't it you who told me how sweet those root cakes were?" Old Falcon grinned. "I think you could give up a little buffalo meat for those cakes—especially when it means eating them without fear that a Broken Stone's dart will land in your back."

"That remains to be seen." Brave Man looked around the circle. "We haven't exactly found a pleasant greeting as we move farther south. I killed four of the last warriors who would try the might of the White Clay. What about these Earth People? You think they'll just let us camp and hunt in their lands? My Power warns against this."

People shifted uncertainly. No one knew what to think about Brave Man's Power. Old Falcon sighed.

"Listen to me," Brave Man called out persuasively. "If we go farther south, I don't know what will happen. Instead, come with me. Let me take you back to the Fat Beaver. I know a way that we can live up there where the herds are plentiful. Follow me and I will keep you safe."

Shocked silence was broken only by the sounds of the night breeze rustling sage beyond the camp and the crackle of the council fire. One by one, people turned to Whistling Hare and Flying Squirrel.

Whistling Hare drew himself up to full height. "And where would you lead us, Brave Man? What would you do differently?"

Brave Man smiled so confidently that his teeth gleamed in the red light of the fire. "I will take us back north. I will denounce the White Clay . . . Wait! Hear me out. *I* will denounce the White Clay. Me, alone. When I do, I will challenge the war leader of the Broken Stones. When I defeat their best warrior, I will make a place for the White Clay among the Broken Stones."

White Ash gaped, as stunned as the rest of them, trying to believe what her ears had heard.

"Think about it!" Brave Man gestured passionately. "I can make a place among the Broken Stones for all of us. I can *save* all of us! Do you understand? I, Brave Man, can keep all of you alive! We won't have to go south. We won't have to run anymore."

Bobcat grunted into the smothering silence. "My ancestors have been White Clay since the beginning of the world. I cannot turn my back on them." The grizzled hunter glanced around. "Perhaps I could eat roots and collect plants, but my children, and their children after them, will be White Clay."

Brave Man shook his head in disgust. "And if there are no more children? What then? What if we, here, in this circle, are the last of the White Clay?"

"Then we are the last of the White Clay," Bobcat said quietly. "That is all I have to say. I'll go south before I have anything to do with Broken Stones." He finished with the hand sign for "no more."

"I hear my friend Bobcat." Badger's face might have been a mask. "I, too, will die as the last White Clay."

"You're being foolish." Brave Man reached out as if to embrace the hunters. "The Power speaks in my mind. *Follow me!* The voices tell me the way. As a clan, we can't keep on this way. We'll be blown away like grains of sand on a strong wind."

Whistling Hare shook his head slowly. "Myself, I can't go to the Broken Stones. I don't know about Brave Man's Power. What I do know is that we are White Clay. Any who want to go to the Broken Stones with Brave Man may do so. That is our way. It might not be so bad. Among the Sun People, many have changed clans. If any of you would do so, go with my best wishes. For myself, I can't."

People nodded, looking back and forth to seek reassurance in one another's eyes.

White Ash glanced at Wind Runner where he sat listening, a torn look on his face. Torn? Why? Surely he couldn't be taking Brave Man seriously? Not after the rift that had deepened between them.

"I have to speak for myself and Sage Ghost," White Ash said. "We will go where Whistling Hare decides."

The old leader gave her a secret smile, pleased.

Flying Squirrel quickly added, "I think we should pack at first light and head south for the Sideways Mountains. No good will come of staying on this side. Maybe the Creator, the Sun, or Thunderbird, will see to it that we don't meet any war parties until we're south of the mountains. No one will think to look for us there."

"Except the Earth People," Brave Man reminded them. A rising tension filled his voice. "*Listen* to me. I'm your *only* hope."

Old Falcon cleared his throat. "I don't know what to think of your Power, Brave Man. I think you have a different sort of Power, maybe stronger than anyone else's, and maybe not. You escaped from the Camp of the Dead, and I understand the Power of that, my own soul having flown to the Land of the Dead on occasion. But men must hear the voices of Power and then make their own decisions. My soul says that I should go south. I don't know why we've been pushed so. Power uses people in different ways for its own purposes.'' His gentle gaze shifted to White Ash. ''Power has given us hints in the past that our way is south.''

''You believe that, old man. It'll be your death!'' Brave Man glared at the Soul Flier.

White Ash tensed. People around the fire sat straighter, grim lines forming around their mouths. No one used that tone with a Soul Flier—especially with one of Old Falcon's reputation. Those sitting closest to Brave Man shifted, trying to distance themselves.

Oblivious, Brave Man continued to stare at Old Falcon through narrowed eyes.

''I think we will pack up camp at first light tomorrow and go south as fast as we can,'' Flying Squirrel muttered in a voice just loud enough to be heard.

Whistling Hare nodded, uneasy eyes on Brave Man. ''I will go south with the morning light. Those who wish may follow me.''

One by one they stood and returned to their lodges, anxious whispers muted by the night.

White Ash rose and started back toward her lodge. She glanced around at the shadowy sage with uneasy eyes. She could feel the trouble hanging in the night, watching and waiting to leap. Brave Man had lost his mind to challenge Old Falcon in such a way!

She glanced back just before she ducked into Sage Ghost's lodge. Only Brave Man and Old Falcon remained seated by the fire, their eyes locked on one another.

''You take a coyote's paw, now. When you let it sit out for a while and all the hide and tendons and muscles rot away, you'll see that it's a lot like a human hand.''

''But the bones have to be different,'' Left Hand protested.

They were headed north, following a narrow valley through the Round Rock Mountains. To either side, gray humps of weathered granite rose in cracked and sundered domes against the blue sky. A drainage traced through the bottoms, the sandy soil thick with greasewood, rabbitbrush, and sage. Clumps of ricegrass, giant wild rye, and wheatgrass stood in yellow-tan shocks along the way. The land smelled of spring. Here and there, green, spindly leaves poked up through last year's grass clumps. Two eagles whirled in circles overhead, dipping and turning as they rode the thermals.

"Well, they are different," Bad Belly agreed. "The bones are smaller and thinner. But you take each bone of the human hand and you can find one like it in a coyote's paw. You can see similarities."

Left Hand sighed and looked defeated. "All right, so maybe animals do have the same insides as humans do. The Wise One Above made people after he made animals. So what?"

Bad Belly scratched between his shoulder blades and gestured. "I think it's curious is all. I mean, why didn't the Wise One Above make some animals . . . well, without teeth or something? You know, just to be different."

Left Hand chuckled to himself. "No wonder you drove Larkspur crazy."

Bad Belly frowned. "If I'm starting to bother you, let me know and I'll be quiet."

Left Hand shook his head. "No. I'm enjoying it. You're a different sort of person. You've got a fresh way of looking at the world. I've missed being with anyone as easygoing as you are."

Bad Belly sighed, a giddy sensation in his breast like flapping butterfly wings. "I feel years younger. I didn't know it would be like this."

"How do you mean?"

"I guess I'm happy . . . and scared at the same time."

Left Hand walked easily, his Trader's staff held high. "Why did you ask to come? I thought you wouldn't. I thought you wouldn't have the courage."

Bad Belly stroked his withered hand. *Can I tell him? Would*

Warm Fire think it was all right? "I promised my friend I would leave. He . . . he told me—Oh, nothing. It was between us." Bad Belly looked up at the crystal sky. "If it kills me, Left Hand, I *had* to leave. I gave a promise to my only friend. A promise . . ."

"And you think you'll follow this journey to wherever it ends?" Left Hand studied him from the corner of his eye. "You could die, you know. Meet an accident, fall, maybe startle a silver bear."

Bad Belly winced. "I have nightmares about that. But, Left Hand, even if I hadn't promised Warm Fire, what do you think it would be like if I went back now?"

"You know, it won't be easy. If you decide you want to be a Trader, the trail is always longer than you think."

"No. I—I have someone to look for first."

"Someone?"

Bed Belly grinned uneasily. "What if I told you it was Power?"

"You had a Dream?"

"Not me. Warm Fire. He told me just before he died."

"Well, where did he tell you to go?"

"North."

"That's a lot of territory. You can come with me to the Wolf People if you want. Or I can tell you how to get to other places. You know, which trails to take. Where to find water and good camps. Just where do you want to end up?"

"Uh, I guess I hadn't really thought that far ahead."

"Come with me. You'd like the Wolf People. You could make a place for yourself among us. Or you could be a Trader."

"You said I had to find my Power first."

"Yes, you do." Left Hand stopped and turned to face Bad Belly. "Listen, to a Trader, the journey is part of the Power. It's not something undertaken lightly. Here." Left Hand reached down and undid the laces that held a small leather pouch at his belt, then handed the pouch to Bad Belly.

"What is it?" Bad Belly used his teeth to pull the drawstring open. Inside he could see a collection of curious triangular black rocks, each one polished and gleaming.

"A gift for the trail, my friend." Left Hand's voice had softened.

"A gift?"

Left Hand nodded. "The basis for a Trade, actually. I'm a Trader, remember."

Bad Belly felt a hollow anxiety in his gut. "But I don't have anything to Trade. Just the few things in my pack. A couple of biscuit-root cakes that—"

Left Hand chuckled. "Not all Trades are made at the same time. Think of it as bond . . . a bond of Power. Trading is a thing of the soul, a sharing. One day you will come across a gift to repay that one—something as important to you as those teeth were to me. I trust your soul, Bad Belly. You won't forget me."

"Teeth?" Bad Belly pulled one of the curious flat stones from the pouch.

"Teeth." Left Hand turned his steps to the trail again. "I wouldn't have known myself, but I showed them to a Trader in the lands of the Antelope People. He had carried a pack of olivella shells from the Western Water and told me that these are teeth out of a terrible fish that swims there—but this Trader had never seen any of its teeth so large, or of stone."

"Then where did you get them?"

Left Hand grinned. "That's part of the Power of Trade, Bad Belly—and a mystery at the same time. I got them from Old One Fist, over at White Sandstone camp. He said he found them washing out of the dirt down in the Rim Country. He says there are lots of bones there and that they're all washing out of the soil. But that's not the curious part."

"Oh?" Bad Belly hurried to catch up, eager to hear more.

"Oh, yes, the curious part is that all the bones are stone. Now, I've traveled more than any Trader I know, and I've never seen an animal with bones made of rock."

Bad Belly inspected the tooth again, noting the serrated edges and how flat they were. "These would make a wonderful necklace."

Left Hand nodded. "You and I think a lot the same. But tell me, Bad Belly, where are you going to start looking for this Power of yours?"

Bed Belly frowned. Where did a person start to look for Power? The fish's stone tooth felt cool and heavy in his fingers.

The Dream possessed White Ash, lifting her like a feather on the wind. She flipped and twirled, rising, then falling, her soul sailing on the currents.

She settled into a familiar and comforting gray haze.

The mist around her swirled, turning golden with a honeyed glow. It seemed to thicken, forming the features of a handsome young man. Light changed, growing brighter and darker by stages.

"Who are you?"

"All that you are . . . and are not. That which I am Dances the fire and Sings the stars."

"Why am I here?"

"Your time is coming. A way must be made. You are part of the Spiral: the circle without beginning or end. Your People—all of your People—will need you. You are the way . . . and you are not."

"What do you mean, the way and not the way?"

The young man smiled, and White Ash's soul ached for that beauty. His love seemed to radiate like heat from glowing coals, shooting her soul full of ecstasy.

"The time has come. The trail you take will be difficult. Are you strong enough? Can you learn all you will need to?"

"I don't know. What are you talking about?"

"A new path starts for you now. Seek . . . and test yourself. Power has its reasons. You may be the one we seek. The Bundle is waiting for you . . . if you can find the way and trust yourself."

The haze shimmered, blurring the image of the young man.

"Wait! Come back!"

"Seek. Learn yourself first. Know love and hate. Know happiness and sorrow. Know pain and pleasure. Learn."

"Come back!"

She reached for him, but the golden haze shifted and she fell, grabbing into the silky nothingness as the light dimmed and the golden hues went gray.

Falling—her stomach rose and tingled—falling, dropping like a rock into an abyss.

White Ash cried out and jerked awake. She gasped in the cold air and sat up. Sweat ran hot down her face as she blinked in the darkness. Somewhere in the distance a wolf howled. The wind whispered around the lodge poles and batted the smoke-hole flap back and forth.

White Ash reached over and poked at the coals. A tiny flame flickered to life. She froze; Sage Ghost's robes lay empty. Worry gnawed at her. He'd sat silently in the lodge while she'd attended the council. When she'd repeated what had been said, he'd listened, eyes lackluster.

"Where are you, Sage Ghost? Don't tell me you've lost your mind, too."

White Ash pushed her hair back and found her worn coat. She took her moccasins from where they sat propped by the fire to dry and slipped them on; then she ducked out of the flap.

The moon hung low over the ridge to the west. White Ash peered around the shadowed landscape. Sage Ghost's possessions remained in the lodge, so he hadn't gone far.

She walked around the camp, watched by the dogs, who raised their heads, ears pricked. The lodges cast eerie shadows that made her think of Brave Man's Camp of the Dead.

Coupled with the images of the Dream, the night pressed down as if to smother her. The camp seemed too quiet. Even the usual snoring had gone silent in the lodges. The wind whimpered, flapped the lodge covers, and died. Overhead, the brighter stars glowed with cold light.

A shiver—prompted by more than the chill—ran down her spine.

Her steps crunched on granular snow; the sound grated in the darkness. Her skin prickled, as if unseen eyes followed her from the concealing shadows. She whirled, feeling a malignant presence lurking behind her, stalking on predator feet.

Sage Ghost might have vanished into the crystal air. A

sudden muted gust of wind tickled the loose hair along her cheek. She batted at it. The dog-travois poles stuck up like ghostly fingers. White Ash nerved herself and stepped out into the sage so that she could look up at the sandstone ridge. A faint silhouette moved against the moonlight.

Sage Ghost? Walking the night, lost in his grief over Bright Moon? A coyote? Or something else?

She worked her way carefully up the shadowed slope. A rustling in the sage caused her heart to jump. She peered into the darkness: nothing. She forced herself to continue, step by fear-charged step.

She crouched as she reached the crest of the ridge, afraid to show herself on the skyline. The shadowy figure—definitely a man—paced slowly in the moonlight, hands behind his back as he looked up at the stars. She made her way through the short sagebrush on silent feet until she could see the man clearly.

"Wind Runner?"

He turned, crouching slightly before he recognized her.

"What are you doing up here at this time of night?" he asked quietly.

"Looking for Sage Ghost. But I could ask you the same."

He lowered his head, features hidden in shadow. "I don't know. Just a feeling. I couldn't sleep."

She rubbed her arms, looking around. To the west, the Red Rock Mountains lay in shadow. The uplifted sandstone ridges to the north looked as though they'd sprouted from a ghost world; they thrust up raggedly in blue-white light and shadow. The wind had stilled.

"It's not a night for sleep. Power is loose."

He scuffed the ground with a moccasined toe. "You feel like something is about to happen. Like all of our lives are going to change on a night like this. You wonder if morning will ever come."

She glanced at the stars. "It will. Soon, in fact." She paused. "Why are you up here?"

"I'm trying to decide what to do."

"What do you mean, what to do?" A fist clenched in her gut.

"I think I'm leaving tomorrow."

"Leaving?"

"Going north. To the Black Point."

Stunned, she shook her head. "You can't! We need you. You're one of the best hunters."

He stepped close and grasped her by the shoulders. She could feel his penetrating stare. "I'm doing it for you."

She broke away. "For me? No. That doesn't make sense. It's . . . it's . . ."

"It makes perfect sense. I can go to the Black Point. Renounce my clan. Earn a place among them. And when I do, I can ask you to marry me. My family will be declared dead. I'll have no relations then."

For a moment, she couldn't form words. Finally she cried, "That's *crazy*! Marry me now. I *love* you! You're playing a game with this kinship thing as it is. I'm no more your sister than . . . than these rocks are. Let's run off . . . go somewhere where there are no Sun People. Just you and me."

"I can't," he told her. "These are my people. How would they feel if they knew we ran away to live in incest?"

"How will they feel when you run off and *call them dead*? Doesn't that mean anything to you?"

"But they'll *understand* why I did it—that it wasn't done to hurt them, but because I honor their traditions." He lifted his hands, let them fall. "Look, people have to live by rules. We've been given ours. You and I both know this is the only way."

"Don't do this."

She could see his smile. "A man could do no less for the woman he loves. For you, I'd challenge all of the Black Point and come for you at the head of ten tens of warriors."

"You'll break your relatives' hearts."

He asked softly, "Do you love me? Tell me now. Tell me from your soul."

She swallowed hard, torn by her duty to the people. *Learn yourself.* The voice echoed in her head.

"Yes."

"Would you be my wife?"

"Yes."

He nodded, moonlight gleaming in his long black hair. "Wait for me. Promise me that you won't accept Brave Man. Promise me that you'll give yourself to no other man of the White Clay."

"There aren't many left to choose from."

He grinned then. "I know. Better yet, come with me now. You and I together, we'll go north. That way I won't have to come back. Won't have to take the chance of having to fight for you . . . and maybe kill one of the White Clay in the process."

She closed her eyes and took a deep breath. "I can't. You know that. Sage Ghost needs me. The people here need me."

He turned in profile, staring out over the lines of irregular ridges shining in the soft white light. "I'll be back for you. I'll follow the way south until I find you."

"If they don't kill you during the challenge." Her heart began to ache. "You'll have to face their best warrior, a man who's killed many—"

"They won't kill me. Not with the most beautiful woman in the world waiting for me."

"Don't. Please. For me, don't do this thing."

"When you said you would marry me, my decision was made."

"Then I *won't* marry you."

He lifted her chin. "Can you look me in the eyes and tell me that?"

She shook her head. "But I can't send you off to your death, either."

He chuckled easily. "I'm not going to my death. I can feel it. No, I'll be back for you."

He caught her and pulled her to him. His arms went around her in the way she'd always dreamed about. For long moments she clasped him to her, the need for him pulsing with her blood.

Finally he pushed her away to hold her at arm's length. "I won't be long. I'll be coming for you no later than the first snowfall. Be very careful of Brave Man. He's dangerous— but after last night, he won't stay." He paused. "Funny how things work out. I am headed for the Black Point, he to the

Broken Stones. When we played together as boys, who would have thought we'd end up as such bitter enemies?''

"Is there nothing I can say to stop you?''

He shook his head. "No. It's a way out for us. We both know that. Now, go find Sage Ghost. Take the People south tomorrow. Tell them what I've done, and why. They'll understand.''

She nodded, a new numbness inside. He stepped over to some sagebrush and picked up his darts and atlatl, then slung his small pack. He paused. "No matter what happens, I'll always love you.''

"And I'll love you.''

He turned to go.

"Please! Wind Runner, don't do this thing.''

"Before the fall snows. I promise." And he waved as he began picking his way through the sage, heading north.

She watched him go until the shadows hid his form.

White Ash bowed her head, misery hanging about her like dead moss.

By the time she reached the foot of the slope, she'd managed to control the ache inside. Would everyone she loved always have to leave her? Why couldn't she have lied, told him she'd never marry him? *Blessed Creator, I've condemned him to death.* Except . . . he'd seemed so certain, so assured of his victory, despite the knowledge that he'd have to face the best of the Black Point's powerful warriors.

She looked back at the ridge, graying now in the first strains of dawn. *I'll never see him again.*

She started to make another circle of the camp and noticed the shadow in the sagebrush. She stepped closer, peering. A man lay there, facedown. A chill washed through her soul. "Sage Ghost?''

He didn't move. She could sense the wrongness, the feeling of abused Power. She bent down and laid her fingers against his flesh: cold as the frozen ground. She grabbed his buffalo-hide coat and rolled him over. In the dim twilight of dawn she could make out his features. *Old Falcon!*

She gasped at the dark stain on his forehead. The blood had frozen and clotted where his skull had been split open.

She staggered backward, a hand to her mouth. Then she screamed into the still dawn, ''Whistling Hare! Come. Come quickly! Old Falcon's dead! Murdered!''

No sooner had she screamed than the air erupted with shrieks and yells. Dark forms charged in from the sage, weapons raised over their heads. Too shocked to understand, White Ash fell into a crouch. Not for several seconds did she realize that the shadowy forms darting between the lodges were warriors. *Enemy warriors!* She knew the tongue they shouted in—familiar, yet so different. The words sounded slurred; the raiders shrieked insults and cries of triumph: *Wolf People!*

Dogs yipped and barked. Someone screamed in pain. Five, ten, then a flood of the howling warriors burst through the camp.

No. No! This can't be. There are too many. The White Clay were hopelessly outnumbered. Rock Mouse, who had survived the attack on the Fat Beaver, stumbled out of her lodge, hair flying as she ran. A war club smacked soddenly into her skull. Whistling Hare emerged from his lodge, fitting a dart to his atlatl . . . as a stone-tipped lance slapped into his abdomen. Bobcat rushed from his lodge, and bellowed his rage as he charged into the melee—and staggered as fletched shafts pierced his body.

A massacre was taking place before White Ash's eyes. In desperation, she looked around. Enemy warriors were everywhere. *There's no chance! We can't fight them off . . . can't escape!*

A dart hissed by her ear—the cast misled by the poor light. The deadly missile freed her from the grip of terror. She turned, running with all her heart.

Behind her, panicked screams rent the dusky dawn, a bedlam of death and fear.

Chapter 8

Bad Belly tugged his robes closer around his throat; he lay on his back and stared at the night sky. The powerful spring wind rushed through the sage and whimpered around the ridge tops. Beside him, Trouble huddled in a furry ball; his warmth seeped through Bad Belly's robes.

Overhead, the stars glimmered and twinkled—cold points of light on the sable undercoat of night.

Curious emotions played through Bad Belly's chest the way mice scurried through dry grass. He'd left. Fulfilled the promise to Warm Fire. And now what? Where should he go? To the Wolf People? Did he want to follow the path of the Trader? Was that the way of his Power? The pouch with the stone-fish teeth lay heavy and reassuring on his chest, hung from the thong about his neck. That gift had become his most precious possession, one he'd never part with—not even at the cost of his soul.

He turned his head, studying the black shadows of the hollow they camped in. Left Hand lay buried in his robes, his dogs in a circle around their packs. The fire had burned down to low embers, no more than dots of speckled red in the night.

The wind called mournfully to Bad Belly, speaking in the tongues of lost souls.

Where do I go now? The world waited, hostile, unfamiliar, unfriendly. Danger lurked just beyond the next ridge top, or in the sullen shadows of the sage.

The days since he left Round Rock had been filled with conversation. He and Left Hand had laughed and joked, talked of Spirit Power and its ways, and about how other peoples lived and acted. Bad Belly's brain pulsed with ideas; the romantic call of strange and exciting things beckoned.

If only it weren't so frightening.

He resettled his head on his arm, feeling the tug of the wind. It had buffeted them all day as they walked. Their words had been sucked away in the mighty gusts and blown out into the stalwart sage.

He drifted, thoughts softening like spring snow in the sun. The way his tired body felt, it might have been afloat on a sultry current. The Dream came with the gentle touch of smoke on a hazy morning, creeping around his slumber, easing itself into his soul. . . .

Bad Belly stood on a high, rocky point that jutted above a cracked and worn range of mountains. Below his perch, the mountain fell away in jagged cracks and upthrust folds of rock that dropped off into blue-green depths. He stood in the realm of the eagles. The angular granite bit into his feet, harsh and unrelenting. Above, the sky had an inflamed look. Sunset streaked the clouds with yellow and orange. A hot wind threw itself against him, sucking the moisture from his body.

On the slopes below, thick stands of timber prickled with the lance tips of tall trees, while gaudy light shot weird shadows into the hidden depths of the forest. The irregular outcrops of bedrock glowed in the eerie rays cast by the bleeding sky.

Bad Belly's nostrils flared at the smell of smoke. The wind died and the air wavered. Silence. Then a crackling sounded from behind him, ominous, threatening.

Bad Belly's heart rose in his throat as a squeamish feeling tickled his stomach. Frosty tendrils of fear wound through his soul.

Smoke curled around him and thickened.

Bad Belly shaded his eyes and peered as images formed in the smoke. He could make out men capturing antelope in a pen, laughing as they placed braided nooses around the frightened animals' necks. The vision changed and gangs of men labored in the hot sun, using shining implements to hack away at a hillside. One by one they chiseled squares of rock from the mountain's gut, hoisted them on their sweat-shiny backs, and marched away in an endless line. In the background, the land had been changed, flattened. In the square plots of land, a single species of plant grew tall and straight under the sun. Between the plots strode men with gleaming spears, and knives—as long as a man's arm—that shimmered silver in the sunlight. These they used on the laboring people, forcing them to do their bidding.

"What is this?"

"What might be, Man of the People," a voice answered.

Gripped by fear, Bad Belly turned . . . and the forest behind him exploded into flame. The blaze engulfed whole trees. Branches waved and shook as licking tongues of yellow devoured them. Fire roared, leaped and danced around Bad Belly, and he tried to shy away. The conflagration responded by sending spears of charring fire toward him.

Panic flooded his veins. Frantically he looked around, and found no way off the pinnacle of rock. *Trapped! I'm trapped up here!*

Flames darted up to pierce the clouds and play among them like Spirits gone mad.

"Man of the People?"

He turned at the voice, bending down, trying to shield himself. "Help me!"

"Bad Belly . . . Man of the People."

"Who are you? Where are you? We're going to die."

"Death is an illusion." Something moved in the ash-stirred depths of the inferno. Bad Belly winced and crouched on the rock, tears of horror creeping from his eyes.

A man of fire walked through the flames. The shimmering figure stopped no more than an arm's length away, and the heat mellowed.

"Bad Belly. Man of the People."

"Go away! Leave me alone! I've done nothing to the Spirits! Leave me!"

"You left Round Rock. You fulfilled your promise."

"Warm Fire?" Had his friend become this . . . this night-mare apparition?

"*I am First Man . . . Wolf Dreamer. I Dance the Spiral. I am all that is . . . and is not. I Dream the One.*"

"Why are you here? What did I do?"

"*I am not here for what you have done . . . but for what you may do.*"

"I won't! I won't do it. I promise. Leave me in peace! Go away, Spirit! I'm not bad!"

The nightmare laughed and the sound chimed through the rock underfoot. "*You are anything but bad, Man of the People. You are a pure soul, seeking nothing more than yourself. Will you give more? Are you strong enough to save her? Do you have enough courage to dare everything for the Dream? Can you save the One? Are you strong enough to risk all for the Wolf Dream?*"

"Risk all? I don't understand. Why have you come to me? What did I do?"

"*You took the first step. You fulfilled a promise to a dying man. Are you willing to fulfill a promise to Power? That is what you seek, isn't it?*"

"I . . . well . . ."

"*Go. Prepare yourself. You have within you that which Power will need.*"

"Why me?"

"*Yours is the blood of First Man. Yours is the legacy of Dreamers.*"

"But I've never Dreamed!"

"*You have never sought. The way to Power is unpredictable—and never free of danger. Prepare yourself. Seek the way.*"

Bad Belly tried to scuttle away as the fiery being spread his arms. About him, the flames melted into a golden haze.

"What are you?"

"*I am First Man . . . the Wolf Dreamer . . . Fire Dancer.*" The figure grew and changed, becoming a wolf. "*The Sun People come. The Spiral is changing. Before a tree must grow, it must wind its roots into the ground. The tree of the Sun will grow in time. The roots must be coaxed into the Dream now. If not, the Spiral will be turned . . . and the world will change."*

An incredible despair settled over Bad Belly, an immensity of loss so terrible that he collapsed onto the rock. Crying out in stunned horror, he clamped his jaws against the sucking emptiness of the soul and gripped the rough stone with fingers that cramped and bled.

The haze swirled and darkened, becoming a mountainside lit by glowing lights like tiny suns. Men labored with the gleaming implements, picking at the mountain while overseers watched. The men pulled rocks from the bones of the mountain and piled them under the lights.

The vision drew Bad Belly into the very mountain. There, like moles, men and women scurried on hands and knees through warrens they chipped out of the mountain's belly. Dirty, bent, and miserable, they labored to break chunks of stone loose. Some coughed, eyes gleaming, flesh sallow. Others bore their travail in silence.

"What madness is this?" Bad Belly cried—and the vision shimmered into golden haze again.

The end of the Spiral. The end of the harmony of the Dream.

Bad Belly cried out as the glowing wolf began to change its form. As he watched, the front legs of the fiery beast spread and grew into wings with long feathers of flame. Gleaming, golden eyes locked with Bad Belly's. The huge bird hissed and clutched the rock with jet-black talons. Then the beast leaped for the sky, screaming as shrilly as an angry eagle.

Bad Belly huddled against the rock, battered by the burning wash of the wings. High in the crimson heavens the Spirit bird soared—and vanished. A crack of thunder split the sky and shook the ground before fading into a distant roar.

Bad Belly shrieked and bolted upright in his robes. As sweat tickled on his hot skin, he stared around at the dark camp. His good hand knotted the thick leather of his buckskin shirt over his heart. Left Hand, half crouched in his robes, had a dart nocked in his atlatl.

"What the—" Left Hand whispered. "What happened?"

"Dream." Bad Belly swallowed past the knot in his fevered throat. "Spirit Dream."

Left Hand peered nervously around at the night, feet twisted in the wreckage of his bedding. "Spirit Dream? Didn't you hear it?"

Bad Belly clamped his eyes shut to squeeze the vision from his soul. Had it been Thunderbird? The Spirit Helper of the Sun People? Why would such a being come to him? He shivered. "Hear it?"

"The thunder. Like a bolt of lightning blasted the camp."

Bad Belly opened his eyes and looked fearfully up into the crystal night sky. Not a cloud anywhere. The memory of huge, fiery wings throbbed against his soul.

Fear spurred White Ash, fit to burst her heart, as she raced up the narrow valley. Gentle slopes packed with sagebrush rose to either side, and a narrow arroyo meandered through the flat bottoms. Her lungs burned as breath tore at her throat. She blinked tears out of her eyes. The sobs tried to choke her as she vaulted low sagebrush and crunched the crusted snow underfoot.

The sun rose higher in the sky, cresting the rounded ridge to her left. The day would be warm and sunny. As the ground warmed, it would be harder to hide her trail.

How many had survived? What had happened to her world? Sage Ghost? Had he been far enough away—or had he been the first to die, killed to buy silence for the attacking Wolf People?

Wind Runner made it. He was far to the north by the time the attack came.

A colder fear lay like ice inside her: Old Falcon had been killed long before the attack. The blow that murdered him had come early in the night, or the blood wouldn't have frozen that way. Nor would his flesh have lost its heat.

A ghostly memory formed: Brave Man and Old Falcon sitting across from each other after the council meeting, the look of challenge between them. But to kill? And in so brutal a manner?

Brave Man's possessed eyes leered at her as she relived the moment when he'd tried to rape her. That powerful gleam knew no right or wrong—she'd seen that in his soul that day.

What mattered that now? She'd witnessed the destruction of the White Clay. Those final screams would haunt her forever. All that could be loved and cherished had been obliterated—like tracks in the sand after a strong wind.

She panted as she forced one foot ahead of the other, making distance. Panic began to fade into a searing of the soul. She turned out of the valley and drove her exhausted body up the slope. Her feet punched through the ice-crusted snow.

Lungs laboring, legs trembling, she wove through the thick sage and stumbled onto the ridge top. Before her, ridges ran in every direction as they extended from the foothills of the Red Rock Mountains. A broad drainage lay between her and the Sideways Mountains.

The peaks of the Sideways Mountains glistened as the sun struck their virgin snowfields. An impossible barrier. Too steep. In those ice-locked valleys she would find nothing to eat.

Not only that, there wouldn't be much to eat anywhere this early in the year. A few sagebrush buttercups had begun to bloom with the retreat of the snow. They could be eaten after having been boiled three or four times to wash away the bitterness. Shooting star and biscuit root would be growing in the next moon. But now?

She dropped to her knees, breathing deeply, trying to recharge her drained body. The wind teased her tangled hair into a black web around her head.

She looked back to the west, toward the unforgiving slopes of the Red Rock Mountains. Faint puffs of ugly cloud hung around the high peaks. She shook her head. Snow followed warm days, as if the warm weather were but a cruel joke—a tease of better times.

She braced herself, got up and started to wind her way down the far side of the ridge. Drainages like a maze of cracks cut the rough, rocky landscape. Here the sagebrush grew no higher than her ankle and looked weathered—indication of a poor soil. Farther away, pale clumps of greasewood choked the white soil of the floodplains. Winter-tan grasses waved in the wind, umbels long since shorn of seeds. A land of dry rock and tortured ridges, it didn't offer much.

She bit her lip, unsure of what to do, of where to go. Behind her, to the north, the Black Point and Broken Stones pushed ever southward. And what sort of life could she find there?

Wind Runner, you fool, they'll kill you! What other outcome could she accept? That one lone youth—barely twenty summers old—could vanquish the bravest and most cunning of the Black Point's tested warriors?

To the west, the Sheep Hunters hunted the Red Rock Mountains, stern warriors who had learned the trails and ways of the mountains since birth. To the east, across the basin, lay the Wolf People—and she'd already seen their mercy.

South, beyond the Sideways Mountains, lay her native Earth People. *My only hope.*

She paused at the top of the next ridge, hating the fatigue that ate at her muscles. The best way, the only way, would be to skirt the rugged foothills of the Sideways Mountains, follow the drainages to the east, and search out a pass that wasn't choked with snow.

Provided I can find enough to eat. Provided I don't freeze. Provided . . . a lot of things.

Her fire sticks, her atlatl and darts, her pack of sleeping robes, were gone—trophies of the Wolf People's last crushing blow to the White Clay. First thing, she needed to find a stand of ricegrass. The stems, charred, made the finest fire starter. Fortunately, the Gray Deer Basin was rich in tool stone. Flaking cutting tools would be simple enough. Once she found the right woods with which to make fire sticks, she could build fires. The coming days would be difficult, but the land would provide.

She glared at the east, a burning anger in her heart. *Your time is limited, Wolf People. The Sun People are coming from the north. Kick them, even a little, and they'll strike back again and again. It's their Power—their way of war.* She shook her head. *It's their very strength.*

She walked on, each step a desolation of the soul.

Bad Belly placed his foot carefully and stopped, head cocked. They were somewhere close. The droppings that lay on the gray duff under the sagebrush couldn't have been older than last night. He stood on the eastern side of a long slope. Here the sagebrush grew thick and as tall as a man's knee. A rolling vista of ridges stretched to the east and the hazy horizon. The sun slanted, casting shadows over the land. The rugged wall of the Sideways Mountains loomed to the north. Narrow valleys cut through the weathered slopes as if a Spirit cat had ravaged the very stone with its claws.

He fingered the round rock in his hand. Once he'd used it as an image of the moon when he'd traced its shadows before the lodge fire; now he hoped it would kill.

With patient skill he studied the blue-green wealth of sage. He sniffed the fresh air and let the aromas of sage and damp earth soothe the faint awareness of homesickness. There, from a perfectly camouflaged body, a single brown eye stared at him. Bad Belly shifted, getting his balance. Years of practice paid off as he threw the stone. The rock caught the sage grouse broadside; the wounded bird fluttered and clucked.

Bad Belly pinned the big bird with a foot and grabbed its throat, then whirled it around to snap the neck. He retrieved the rock and stepped around the sage. Disturbed by the scuffle, two more grouse bobbed their heads as they walked this way and that through the thick brush, aware that something had gone wrong. Like all grouse, they were too stupid to fly at the sight of a human.

Bad Belly waited patiently. One of the gray-speckled birds stepped behind a sagebrush. The flung stone thumped sickeningly into the visible bird. The fowl lay broken and stunned as it uttered clicking sounds.

Bad Belly took a step, then another, as the wounded bird

fluttered away on one wing and a broken leg. The third strutted calmly in the sage, oblivious to the plight of its fellow.

Bad Belly retrieved his stone, catching up the fluttering victim and breaking its neck. Cautiously he stalked the third. Within minutes his deadly stone had claimed the last grouse.

He waved, and Left Hand walked down the ridge, the dogs following.

"It's food," Bad Belly greeted. "Tonight we eat well."

Left Hand cocked his head. "Three birds? One for us . . . and two for all these dogs? That's eating well?"

"You never know what we'll find for the rest of the day." Bad Belly gestured toward the foothills. "Badwater Camp lies up there along the creek somewhere. We might make it by midday tomorrow. They'll feed us and the dogs, too. Three birds will keep us going."

Left Hand nodded as he studied the mountains and the way their path would lead. "If not, we'll take a day and see if we can't lure an antelope into an ambush. I just haven't seen the right place to do it yet."

Bad Belly gave his friend a suspicious inspection. "This is Badwater territory. Bone Ring won't care about a couple of grouse, but we'd better get her permission before we go hunting anything like a—"

"And I'm a Trader." Left Hand raised his staff and jabbed a thumb at his chest. "You Earth People and your territory don't mean anything to a Trader."

"Bone Ring decides things for Badwater. I met her once. She's a tough woman."

Left Hand chuckled. "Tell me honestly, would Larkspur have thrown a fit if she found a Trader eating an antelope he'd killed on her land? No, not even Larkspur, tough and mean as she is, would squawk about a Trader filling his belly or feeding his dogs. Besides, they know me at Badwater. Bone Ring gets along with the Wolf People. A few years back she sent us a couple of packs of ricegrass seed when things were a little bleak."

Bad Belly looked over his shoulder at the far-western mountains. A gray haze had covered the peaks. "Looks like a storm coming. We might want to hole up at Badwater. It would be nice to have a warm lodge to sleep in if that turns out to be as bad as it looks.''

"Bone Ring will put us up. She'll probably have half of what's in my packs if we stop there—but we'll have a warm lodge and full bellies.''

Bad Belly grunted. "Trading's something I'd never do well. If people wanted to Trade, I'd end up giving them everything.''

Left Hand took up the march, headed for the long ridge that separated the Badwater from the rest of the basin. "Different Traders do things differently. It depends on your Power.'' He shot a glance at Bad Belly. "But then, a man who Dreams thunder out of night sky . . . well, you tell me.''

Bad Belly's stomach knotted. "I don't know what to think. I've never had a Dream like that.''

Left Hand took a deep breath and said gently, "Maybe you weren't worthy before.''

"Worthy?''

"Power has its ways. And you haven't told me everything about Warm Fire's death and what he made you promise. Not that I've asked, mind you. Power isn't something to be talked about lightly. A fellow like me knows enough about it to be cautious. Maybe Warm Fire's death was supposed to be a sign to you. Like that wolf you talk about.''

Bad Belly lowered his eyes. "I don't know about signs and things. I'm just me.''

A reverent note crept into Left Hand's voice. "You never know about Power. It exists everywhere—all around us. But I remember when I was a boy, listening to a Dreamer. He said that Power is in this world and it isn't.''

"How can it be in this world and not be at the same time?''

"Look around you, Bad Belly. Power is everywhere, but can you see it? Touch it? No. It's here and it isn't. That's why you have to seek it. Among my people, a person must prepare himself and climb to a high place. You see, only when you've cleansed your body and soul does Power make itself known. That's why it comes in Dreams. You have to meet Power in a different world from this one. In Dreams . . . when the soul is free.''

Bad Belly screwed up his mouth. "But why did it come to me last night? How come it never came before? I've had lots of dreams. Everybody does."

"Power Dreams?"

"No, this is the first."

"That's the point."

Bad Belly shot him a skeptical glance.

"Look"—Left Hand gestured, shaking the Trader's staff—"maybe you weren't worthy of being noticed until you left Larkspur's. Maybe your leaving was a test. You know, whatever you promised Warm Fire had to be carried out. Power doesn't just give itself away. You have to be *worthy*."

Bad Belly hung his head, remembering his inability to face Larkspur when Warm Fire lay dying. He'd hated himself at that moment, hated himself ever since for not staying with Warm Fire—no matter the consequences. Leaving had brought him freedom from that guilt. He looked around, feeling the free wind on his shoulder.

"Grandmother always knew how to bend me around. She's a master at that." He sighed. "I grew up terrified of her. A person was better off to cross a silver bear than to make Larkspur mad. She'd get back at you, and when she did, everyone suffered for what you'd done."

"But you left."

Bad Belly nodded. "Yes. I left. She ordered me away when Warm Fire was dying. I . . . I couldn't . . . Well, it's over now."

"And Power is interested in you. You passed the first test."

"The way you say that, I'm not sure I want to pass any more."

A smoky look veiled Left Hand's eyes. "The first is always the easiest. Did this curious Spirit in your Dream say anything else? Ask anything of you?"

"It said I should prepare myself . . . and seek." He scowled and kicked at the ground. "And I saw things. Visions of people doing things I couldn't understand. Something terrible's coming. A change in the Spiral, if you know what that means. It has something to do with the Sun People's

Power—and what they'll do to Dreaming. Maybe change the entire world."

"You know, Bad Belly, you frighten me."

"Frighten you?"

Left Hand made a face that puckered the lines around his mouth. "The ways of Power leave any sane man nervous. Warm Fire said he'd Dreamed that I was coming. Power told him that. I'd been having Dreams of my own. Nothing I could understand, just fragments of visions . . . and a feeling that I had to hurry. Power threw us together first thing. Maybe it picked me because I have a lot of respect for Power. I know enough about how the Spirit World works to know that I'm not the right one for you to talk to."

Bad Belly's stomach soured even more. "Well then, if you're not, who is? In the Dream, Wolf Dreamer told me—"

"Wolf Dreamer?" Left Hand looked over his shoulder to stare at the gray mat of clouds that now obscured the far mountains.

"Well, that's what he said. Something about the Wolf Dream . . . and Fire Dancer . . . and he turned into a wolf . . . and into a flaming bird and—"

'We're not stopping at Badwater."

"We're not?"

Left Hand frowned at the Sideways Mountains that rose before them. "No. I think the sooner I take you to Singing Stones, the better off I'm going to be."

"Singing Stones? But I thought—"

"He's the most Powerful Dreamer I know."

"I don't like that look you're giving me."

Left Hand rubbed his forehead. "I don't know what's going on, Bad Belly, but the sooner I'm away from you, the better I'm going to feel."

Bad Belly pointed. "But a storm is coming!"

"More than one, my friend. More than one. I just hope you're up to it."

"Up to it? You're talking in riddles." Bad Belly's nervous glance shifted back and forth from the coming storm to Left Hand.

"Come on. It's a good thing you killed those grouse. The dogs are going to need them."

"The dogs? But I . . . What are we going to eat?"

"The packs are full, Bad Belly. That'll keep us alive. If it means the loss of an entire season's Trade, that's fine. If that's all it costs me, I'll be more than happy."

"But I thought—"

"Hush." Left Hand made the gesture for silence. "Power guides all Trade. That's why it's sacred. What's in the packs belongs to Power. If that's what we're supposed to live off, that's what we'll do. The act of Trading depends on Power. Who am I to insult what gives me my happiness?" Left Hand stalked away, almost running.

"Hey, slow down!"

"We have a lot of ground to cover today."

Bad Belly groaned to himself, hurrying, while Trouble trotted along behind, happily oblivious. Bad Belly ground his teeth. The world had turned on him again.

Why do I feel like it's all out of control? What did I do this time?

He looked back. The clouds had completely hidden the far mountains. The storm would come—and it looked ominous.

White Ash had entered the broad valley that ran northeast toward the Gray Deer River. Now she followed the southern side of the valley, crossing drainages that ran between long ridges leading down from the Sideways Mountains. Cottonwoods lined the creek banks, and she could see the tassels high in the branches among the thickening buds. Higher on the hills to the south, limber pine and juniper dotted the slopes, mixing with scattered sage and occasional bitterbrush. A chill wind raced down from the west.

As she walked, she searched the ground and found a quartzite cobble of just the right size. It fit snugly in the palm of her hand. A short time later she located a second cobble to use as a hammer stone.

She checked the heft and balance of the hammer stone; then, with sharp blows, drove flakes from one side of the quartzite cobble. When she'd made a scalloped edge, she turned it over to continue the process. She inspected the tool with a critical eye. By chipping off both sides, she'd created a jagged cutting edge.

She ran a finger over the sharp blade and started for the stand of limber pine on the slope above her. She ignored the low, scudding clouds that raced down from the west as she began to hack at the bark on the first tree she came to. The inner bark of the limber pine could be chewed. It might be bitter fare—and more effort to chew the fibers than the body gleaned—but she needed survival food, something for her stomach to work on . . . especially since the first flakes of snow had begun twirling down.

White Ash hacked a long section of bark from the light-yellow wood. Under other circumstances, she would have stripped the bark by shaving off the hard, scaly outer surface, then boiled the inner. This time there would be no boiling. So far, she hadn't found the right kind of wood for making fire sticks. And she needed a boiling paunch—which meant killing an animal or finding a winterkill that hadn't been ravaged by scavengers.

A cold gust of wind tore at her with icy fingers that shot through her worn dress. This would be a cold, wet snow—the dangerous spring kind.

She worked with desperation to shave the life-giving inner bark loose. Immediately she began to chew the strings she peeled free. The bittersweet taste of the bark made her mouth water. The fuzzy feeling of the sap clinging to her teeth cheered her soul. Sap meant life.

She clutched her stone in two hands and attacked the tree again. She could carry several slabs of bark, and her next pressing need would be to find shelter from the coming storm.

Having carved all she could carry from the tree, she hurried onward. The growing cold ate into her moccasins; the outermost layer had been worn through to holes. The inners would go next. Once she found shelter, she might be able to weave strips of juniper bark that would extend the life of the deteriorating leather.

Snow began to fall in thick flakes. The rounded ridges had a scoured look that boded poorly for shelter. The scrubby sagebrush wasn't quite tall enough to weave into a wickiup. Night began to drift over the land as the snow came down in whirling spirals, obscuring her view of the country.

She pulled up her hood and walked on. Somewhere, hidden in the storm, she'd have to find a dry place, out of the wind and blowing snow. There she could chew the thin strips of bark—and maybe stay alive.

She nearly missed it as she struggled forward. In the lengthening gloom of evening, the stone overhang merged with the swirling snow. She stopped and stared, shielding her face against the blowing crystals.

With a cry of relief she stumbled into the rocky shelter. It was nothing more than an undercut sandstone slab, but it would do. She batted the clinging snow from her garments before she crouched back against the rock and huddled into a ball. For just a moment she would rest, soothe her ragged nerves, let her exhausted body recover some of its reserves.

She closed her eyes, shaking her head. Had any of the White Clay lived? Were her people nothing more than a memory?

Wind Runner you may be the lucky one. Tell the Black Point that the White Clay have vanished from the earth. You've no one to offend now. Only the ghosts of the angry dead.

She dropped her face into her hands; the well of her tears had run dry. *I have only myself now. I am alone. No one . . . nothing else. Nothing but cold and misery.*

She sat there while the night darkened and the snow continued to fall. At first she didn't recognize the sound: a light crunch—snow compressing under a human foot.

She burst to her feet and charged straight into the man's arms. He held her easily and overpowered her struggles. Laughing, he threw her roughly to the ground and pinned her.

"Let me go!" she cried, beating at him with her fists.

The odors of smoke, winter sweat, and leather filled her nostrils. His breath came warm against her cheek. "It's been a long chase," he told her, "but Three Bulls has caught you."

She shuddered, recognizing the tongue of the Wolf People.

"Let me go," she whispered in the tongue of the Earth People. "I am Three Forks. My people are at peace with yours."

"Three Forks does not live with the Sun People. No, I've hunted you all day long. You're mine. If Three Forks wants you, they can Trade for you later."

"What . . . what are you going to do with me?"

He laughed then, nuzzling his face into her neck. "What does any man want with a woman? You will carry firewood to my lodge and cook my meals. You will work for me, tanning and sewing. And, of course, you will warm my robes at night and bring me pleasure."

"You'll bring the anger of Three Forks down on you. Green Fire will—"

"Do nothing!" He chuckled to himself. "Tonight this storm will be cold and wet. Together you and I will be warm. Three Bulls has gone a long time without being warm. Perhaps he is too full of seed? Perhaps his seed would be warm, too?"

"No!"

Her flesh crawled as his cold hand reached down and lifted the hem of her dress.

Bad Belly woke from troubled Dreams he didn't understand. Entire forests had been cut down and burned to make way for the golden-haired crop. He'd heard the soul of the land cry out as rains washed the soil away in muddy torrents, while the feet of men packed hard trails over the country. The howl of a grieving wolf lingered in his memory, wailing—*like the death of a Dream*—chilling his spirit.

Had it been real? Or just part of the Dream?

He blinked in the night, aware that Trouble's body heat no longer kept him warm. He poked his head out from under the covering of the robe and looked around. Snow—a hand's depth of it—had fallen on their small camp, and heavy, wet flakes continued to whirl out of the night sky. The rounded depression left by Trouble could be seen, as could the dog tracks leading off up the steep-walled canyon they'd picked to camp in.

Bad Belly groaned softly, closing his eyes. Probably a coyote bitch in heat somewhere. The last time Trouble had followed the lure, he'd come limping home with great gashes in his hide from battling for the bitch—and losing, no doubt.

Bad Belly stood up and shook the blanket of snow off his robe before wrapping it around him. Something thumped on his foot and he reached down to fish the pouch of stone teeth out of the fluffy snow. He'd been fingering them just before he went to sleep, planning the necklace he'd make of them.

Wake Left Hand? No, he'd already caused enough problems for Left Hand. Let him sleep. After all, all Bad Belly had to do was follow Trouble's tracks a little way up the canyon and whistle. In a heartbeat they'd be back asleep under the snow, with no one the wiser.

Bad Belly growled to himself, imagining what he'd do to Trouble. But no matter what he threatened, he could never hurt his friend. Dogs were just dogs. That was their nature.

He bent low and squinted in the faint light; Trouble's tracks were filling even as he watched. The afterimages of the Dream added to his apprehension as he hurried along the dog's trail.

When he thought he'd gone far enough not to wake Left Hand or his keen-eared pack dogs, Bad Belly whistled and called, "Trouble? Hey, Trouble! Come on. This is foolishness. Trouble? You go messing around with them coyotes and I'll have to carry you all the way to Singing Stones'. Trouble?"

The tracks didn't look any fresher. Worse, the trail grew steeper. Bad Belly scratched at his chin where a snowflake had melted and run in a trickle. "Trouble, maybe I *will* beat you half to death. Look at me. I'm going to be wet and cold and miserable for the rest of the night. You're a dog. Dogs are used to being miserable. You've got that wonderful fur coat.''

The wind swirled and gusted. The trees grew thicker here. A game trail wound up around the rocks and through the thick serviceberry that choked the canyon bottom. Somber limber pine and fir mixed with the juniper—dark blotches that hid in the veil of swirling snow.

Bad Belly drew up, puffing. How far had he come? "Trouble?" Trouble had never before gone this far—not even when he lived at Round Rock and knew the country.

Bad Belly chewed at his lips while he thought. *If I had half a wit, I'd just turn around and go back. Pus and maggots, Trouble, if you can find your way clear up here, you can find your way back to camp.*

Except that Trouble's my best friend. He's never let me down. Bad Belly plodded on. How long until morning? What would Left Hand say if he lost traveling time?

Bad Belly pushed harder up the steep canyon. The deep snow—knee high in places where it had drifted—impeded his progress. He ducked under a fir tree, searching for Trouble's tracks. The hair on his neck lifted. Among them, he could make out a wolf's tracks.

Oh, Trouble. A coyote, well, you can keep from getting killed. But a wolf? He dashed along, shouting at the top of his lungs, "Trouble?"

The wind battered Bad Belly as he stumbled out of the canyon and into the open. Through the haze of falling snow, he couldn't make out any landmarks. Trouble's tracks made only faint dimples in the whiteness. Forcing himself on, Bad Belly ran thrashing forward on Trouble's trail.

A pile of rocks—rounded and worn by wind and storm—loomed ahead. The tracks wove in and out through the outcrop and into the flats beyond. Wind blasted at Bad Belly as he staggered on, knowing that Trouble couldn't be far ahead.

"Hunger and thirst on you, dog. I can't help it if you go faster than I do, but I swear, I'm going to beat you to within a handbreadth of your life! You hear me? *Trouble?*"

He plodded around drainages and past gnarled trees twisted

and dwarfed by the wind. How high had he climbed, anyway? His feet ached and throbbed from the cold.

"Left Hand is going to throw a fit. You hear me, dog? All he's ever done is be nice to us, and we're going to make him regret he took us along!"

The storm whipped down around him as he pushed on. A growing chill numbed his hands. The pouch with the stone teeth dangled from one clenched fist. Muttering to himself, Bad Belly slipped the thong over his head so he wouldn't lose it.

I should have awakened Left Hand. He's going to be worried sick. He sank up to his waist in a deep drift and floundered to the other side. "Trouble?"

A gleeful bark came from somewhere ahead.

"Get back here! Trouble?"

Bad Belly charged ahead, relief filling him. At least he'd reached the dog before the wolf had. Trouble came bounding out of the curtain of snow, tail wagging.

Bad Belly dropped to his knees, hugging the snow-encrusted dog to his chest. "Trouble? What's the matter with you? I ought to break every bone in your body."

The dog jerked and squirmed in Bad Belly's grip as he whined and reached up to lick Bad Belly's face. The furry black tail swished back and forth in the fluffy snow like a whip.

"Following a wolf? And dragging me all over in the night? Come on. Let's go back. We have to get to camp before Left Hand wakes up and finds us gone."

Bad Belly started back the way he'd come, Trouble following. He broke through the drift and climbed up the slope, tracks growing ever fainter. At the summit he scouted around—and found nothing but windblown snow.

"Which way?" He looked back at his dog. "Home, Trouble. Find the way."

Trouble stared at him, ears up, his head cocked.

"Home!" Bad Belly ordered, pointing to the snow. "Track!"

Trouble barked and lowered his nose to the snow, taking off at a trot.

"That's a good boy." Bad Belly fell into step behind him.

Hours later, when the sun grayed the eastern horizon, Bad Belly came to the conclusion that wherever he was, he'd never been there before. He should have come to the rock outcrop he'd wound through in the night, then found the trees and the steep canyon. Worse, the way they were going now didn't slope steeply at all—and it sloped the wrong way.

Bad Belly stared around; any landmarks remained hidden in the ground blizzard.

He shook his head slowly, sadly. "Trouble, what did you lead me into? Now we're lost."

A violent blast of air almost blew him off his feet. Fine snow sifted through the gaps in his tightly clutched robe. Trouble flopped down in the white powder to chew the caked snow from between the pads on his feet. He snorted before looking up with curious brown eyes.

"One thing's certain. The tracks are gone . . . and we have to find shelter."

Bad Belly took the only option left to him. He started downhill.

Chapter 9 🦉

Three Bulls stood and stepped out into the snow. He turned, staring down at White Ash with a leering grin on his angular face. She glared hatred back as she sought to overpower his smug satisfaction with her own disgust and anger. He laughed, lifting the bottom of his war shirt to relieve himself.

She trembled, looking away, unable to stand the sight of his male flesh—that same organ that had violated her. Pain coupled with fear and loathing. Even the refuge of her body, the final sanctuary, had been desecrated.

At the sound of his water pattering into the snow, she

cowered. Fragments of thoughts drifted loosely about her head. *Escape! Run!*

She gathered her legs under her, furtive eyes boring into his back. He exhaled a frosty wreath that whirled around his head. She took a careful step and placed one foot on the worn rock. She made another step, the last before the snow would crunch and give her away.

"Big storm," Three Bulls muttered to himself. "Look at the sky. Black, dark. This storm will continue for a long time. Good thing I caught you, huh?"

The snow would make escape that much harder. He could track her without effort; but she *had* to try! Desperation charged her rubbery muscles as she leaped into the darkness.

She ran, calling upon all the exhausted reserves in her body. Arms pumping, she threw herself down the slope, praying that the footing wouldn't betray her. If she could gain a small lead, perhaps she could trick him, make a false—

She smashed face first into the fluffy snow, driven down by his crushing weight. Hard hands tangled in her hair, jerking her back.

His voice cooed into her ears, "You're a captive of Three Bulls. I've had too much trouble with women as it is. I'll teach you not to run away."

The fist caught her on the side of the head, blasting lights like lightning flashes behind her eyes. He sat on her, pushing her down into the snow. With one hand twisted in her hair, he used the other to beat her.

"*No!*" she screamed, writhing beneath him.

Then her vision blurred. Pain splintered into spangles of light that matched the sick sounds of his fist against her stunned flesh.

Brave Man walked down from the ridge and into the ruins of the camp. Most of the lodge covers had been piled onto a bonfire kindled by the lodge poles. Packs had been ripped open, and the contents—what the raiders couldn't use—scattered here and there.

Coyotes skulked through the sagebrush, tawny shapes waiting for his departure to resume their ravaging of the dead. Ravens called and rose on flapping wings to wheel in the sky or to perch on the ridge tops, awaiting his passing.

Brave Man walked among the corpses, noting familiar faces, eyeless now, since the keen ravens went for those first. The coyotes always went for the gut. Whistling Hare lay sprawled on his face. Badger had taken a dart in the back before someone had driven another through his heart. Bobcat had been riddled with darts before someone slashed his throat. Little Drummer had taken a dart through the kidneys and, from the blood trail, had crawled for a way before a second dart had been driven between his shoulder blades. Flying Squirrel lay facedown, her skull cracked open, the brains exposed. One by one, he identified them.

"But we find no White Ash."

The voices in his head whispered, *She lives!*

He stooped over the body of Old Falcon, staring down into the remains of the old man's face. His own blow had landed between Old Falcon's eyes.

"I am sorry, Soul Flier. You would have challenged my Power. It was better this way. Better that you died at my hand than that of the Wolf People. You got to know in the end. You felt true Power of a kind you'd only guessed at."

Brave Man hadn't planned on killing Old Falcon, but the Soul Flier had walked him to the edge of camp and threatened him with exile from the clan.

The pain had welled in Brave Man's head, causing him to blink. The rush of anger had traced fire through his veins as he turned to the Soul Flier and whispered, "Good-bye, Old Falcon."

Before the old man could react, Brave Man had swung his club. The sharp edge caught the Soul Flier full on the forehead. Splitting bone had snapped in the night.

Now, in the light of day, what remained of Old Falcon looked pitifully broken and shabby.

"I only came back to steal White Ash away. Had I known

the Wolf People were so close, I'd have taken her that night, old man. Now I have to find her.''

He turned his back on the corpse and walked into the middle of the camp where the smoldering hides and the broken dart shafts lay scattered about. The Wolf People had even taken the dogs, at least those they hadn't killed in the attack.

"But White Ash is not here. She is missing with Soft Snow, Dancing Rose, Grass Woman, and Red Cow.''

Captives of the Wolf People, the voices whispered.

"Only the young women and some of the children were taken.'' He glared down the trail, fingering his darts. Two days' head start? The Wolf People would be traveling slowly since they didn't need to worry about retaliation.

The voices murmured a warning.

"I know!'' he shouted angrily. "But I need to search for just a little while longer. Wind Runner's body is nowhere to be seen. And I don't see Sage Ghost, either.''

He worked out the pattern of tracks that revealed where warriors and captives had marched off to the east. Too many feet had trod here for him to follow an individual trail.

"Is White Ash with Wind Runner?''

No. The voices laughed ominously. *Wolf People! They have her.*

He glanced up as the first flakes of snow twirled down. He turned and sniffed, gathering the scent of the coming storm. The voices chattered to themselves.

"Wet storm. Big.''

The voices urged him, whispering, *Broken Stones. Broken Stones.*

He nodded. "If the Wolf People have her, she'll be up in the mountains. It will take a war party of Broken Stones' warriors to get her back.'' He grinned to himself. "Yes, if I have to destroy every man, woman, and child among the Wolf People, I'll have her. Together, White Ash and I will Dream the Power. We will weave the new way.''

For the second time in his life, Brave Man walked away from a Camp of the Dead. And, in doing so, the Power grew within him.

White Ash lay with her eyes closed, locked in wretched misery. They'd been trapped here for three days.

Her captor lay curled around her, breathing deeply as he slept. His body heat and the robe that covered them protected her from the creeping cold as snow filtered down from above, dusting the interior of the overhang.

White Ash sucked at her lip—ragged now from where she'd chewed it each time the warrior had taken her. Her soul shriveled and curled, charred like a wood shaving on glowing embers.

She ground her teeth in silence, hating the memories—constantly reminded by the ache in her vagina. He'd hurt her when he'd forced himself inside. When she'd resisted, he'd cuffed her on the side of the head, gripping her around the throat to choke the fight out of her. Her breasts ached where his callused fingers had squeezed until he'd bruised them.

A tear broke loose from her tightly clamped eyelids. Hatred and anger fought to rise over the disgust and uncleanliness she felt inside.

Wind gusted and sawed at the air beyond the shelter. She could feel the cold in the rock below. The horror of Three Bulls' possession grew worse with the knowledge that had he not found her, she would have frozen in this storm. She lived because this man of the Wolf People had violated her. She lived because he had come out of the night to rape her, to cover her with his warmth and his buffalo robe. The food in his pack had nourished her. His fire had warmed them.

He muttered something in his sleep, shifting his weight on top of her.

White Ash tensed, her involuntary reaction bringing him awake.

"Bad storm," he said evenly. "Good thing I tracked you. You would have died."

She said nothing, desperately praying that he'd go back to

sleep. She calculated the distance to his darts. Too far. He always kept them beyond her reach.

He yawned, repeating the story he'd told her so many times now. "I thought I saw you run when we destroyed the camp. The light was bad, but I saw your hair flying loose as you ran. After we killed the last of the Sun People, I stayed behind, looking around. I found the place where you climbed up through the snow. I followed. No man tracks better than Three Bulls."

He raised a hand to grope her sore breast. She locked her jaws, body trembling. He tightened his grip, forcing her to gasp.

"Bad storm. Cold."

She strangled a cry in her throat.

"We need to stay warm, you and I. I'm feeling cold again."

She fought the urge to scream as he raised himself to pull up the hem of her worn leather dress.

"It will be a long night," he whispered in her ear. "You and I, we'll need to stay warm a lot."

He laughed in a low, savage voice as his weight settled. She could feel the chill on her thighs when the buffalo robe lifted. She turned her head away, eyes tightly shut. She tried to will her body to relax in the hope that his entry wouldn't hurt so much this time.

She endured. His movement within sickened her; vomit tickled at the back of her throat. He groaned, muscles tensing, and her guts knotted against his release.

He went limp, sighing.

He shifted as he reached to pull the robe over his back where it had slipped off—and in doing so, exposed her hand to the chilly ground. Her fingers brushed something round and cold that lay on the gritty sandstone. The fires of hope raced through her veins.

Bad Belly puffed his way to a wind-dusted point of rocks and looked out over the land that spread below. He stood on a promontory that jutted up from the north slope of the Sideways Mountains. Gradual inclines rose to the irregular peaks—all of them deep in a mantle of unbroken white. As he watched, sunlight broke through the parting tufts of cloud and spotted the snowbound land in patches of gleaming white bright enough to hurt the eye. Here and there the rich blue of the sky could be seen in the ragged gaps.

Bad Belly stared back at the long slope and shook his head. He'd passed four days of misery working his way down the summits. For two days now, his stomach had growled its hunger. Travel through the deep snow had sapped his strength, and cold had worked into his very bones.

"And it's all your fault," he muttered to Trouble. The dog stood beside him happily, sniffing the wind while he looked over the country, ears pricked. Then he whined and yawned, wagging his tail.

Bad Belly turned his gaze to the terrain ahead of him. Immediately to the west, the Gray Deer River ran through a canyon in the Sideways Mountains. Half-blinded by the blowing snow, he'd almost fallen off one of those steep cliffs when he'd wandered too close to the edge.

To the north stretched the rocky bones of the basin. Out there the Wolf People hunted when they came down from the Grass Meadow Mountains, rising like sentinels to the east.

A series of dark-red ridges rose where the river twisted its way through the bottomlands. The spines of rock gleamed where the steep faces of the sandstone remained defiantly exposed. Beyond a turn of the river, a pillar of steam lifted from a spot in the buff-capped bluffs a half-day's walk away.

"The hot-water springs," Bad Belly whispered. He fingered his chin as he stared. *A Power place.*

He'd heard plenty of stories about the huge springs, where water too hot to touch boiled out of the earth. Curious formations held the water in pools before it ran into the Gray Deer River. Larkspur liked to tell the story about how she had gone to the hot springs once as a girl and bathed in the waters. While there, she'd received a vision that told her to return home, that her oldest sister had died through the actions of a malevolent Spirit. She'd gone back to Round Rock and Sung a Power Song that drove the bad Spirit away and reclaimed the camp for the clan.

Bad Belly chewed his lower lip, staring at the billowing steam. As often as he'd heard the story, he'd come to believe that Larkspur had gone someplace outside this world. Now he stared at that very place. A sense of wonder possessed him.

A patch of cloud parted and sunlight spilled around him. He squinted; snow blindness could strike a man at this time of year. When the sun hit the column of steam, the vapor glowed brightly. He would go down there and see the hot springs before he stumbled into the next calamity awaiting him.

"Well, let's go. Left Hand is probably most of the way to his people by now." He grimaced at Trouble's happy face. "You just had to follow that wolf, didn't you? Look at the mess you got us in."

Trouble looked up, tail wagging.

Bed Belly twisted his face into a sour expression and looked up at the cloudy sky. "Warm Fire, you don't know what you got me into when you made me promise. Now I really have problems—as if I didn't have enough as it was. I'll go down there and get killed by some Sun People warrior, or something."

He started down the slope toward the silver ribbon of the Gray Deer River.

In a world of white, White Ash stumbled forward aimlessly. Her feet kicked up the fluffy wet flakes as the deep snow dragged at the leather of her soggy moccasins. The mantle of white hid rocks and brush. More than once she tripped and fell. Each fall drained more of her flagging energy and caked her with wet snow that melted to soak her clothing. She felt faint, detached from the world.

She forced herself on, step after step, a simple pattern of

movement her numb mind could understand. She gave no thought to her direction, driven only to place as much distance as she could between herself and that horrible rock overhang.

The red splotches of Three Bulls' blood crusted on her sleeve and under her fingernails. She'd reveled in the rushing warmth of his spurting blood as it soaked her hands. The sound of the sharpened quartzite cobble smacking time after time into his bones would echo in her dreams until she died.

''Was that really me?'' she asked herself dully, remembering the fear-charged power of her muscles as she attacked him. Not until she'd exhausted herself had she finally dropped the quartzite cobble. Her soul had been seized with terror then; the image of his wrecked features burned into her memory. She'd never forget his battered body lying on the crumbling sandstone.

Her foot caught in buried sage and she fell again, the cold wetness of the snow eating into her face and hands. She floundered, battling to stand. Then she retrieved each of Three Bulls' darts from the snow where she'd dropped them.

At least she'd had sense enough to grab up his pack before she fled. Now she had fire sticks of hard wood, and his atlatl and darts. With weapons, and the ability to kindle a fire, she could survive.

Something whispered in the silence behind her. White Ash whimpered as she cast a frightened look over her shoulder. The snow formed strange, haunting shapes, almost like faces, that seemed to swoop forward on icy wings. She gasped and charged forward. She tripped and fell again. She could sense a lurking presence watching, waiting, following in her tracks.

Run! Flee! Get away! She scrambled awkwardly to her feet, her stomach aching from hunger. The muscles of her legs trembled from fatigue as she shivered and panted, teetering from exhaustion. The world shimmered and went hazy in her vision. Hazy. Then gray. . . .

White Ash came to lying in the snow. She couldn't feel her hands or feet. She blinked against the swirling grayness that spun about her foggy thoughts.

She staggered up, lost her balance, and fell heavily. A dark shadow loomed over her.

"No! Leave me alone!" she raged in terror and lunged to her feet again, forcing herself to run, the edges of her vision blurring as she looked back—and saw nothing. The earth spun and went gray again . . .

The cold bite of snow on her face brought her back to consciousness once more. How long had she lain there this time? *Pushed too far. Even my body has failed me.* Violent shivers shook her and splintered her vision.

She blinked, staring up at the sky. Sunlight broke through the clouds in bars. Did the light trick her? An image formed in the patchy clouds. A man of fire stared down at her, concern on his face.

She got a foot under her, wincing as she stood. Her vagina burned like a wound. Her breasts chafed angrily on the leather of her dress. Her battered face had gone wooden from the cold, the bruises too chilled to sting.

With the atlatl shaft, she propped herself up. One step after another, she wobbled forward. Her tumbling thoughts refused to form. Which way?

Downhill. Downhill is easier. Dazed, balance uncertain, she fought to place her feet; they had become so numb she couldn't feel the ground under them.

She traveled mindlessly onward, barely aware that the land had flattened out into a broad valley. Driven only by shocked instinct, she staggered forward.

I am alone. Nothing is left. Not my people. Not Wind Runner. Nothing . . .

White Ash passed, oblivious, among the gray boles of cottonwood trees, struggling through the snow and thick grass. She crashed through a stand of willows and stared dully at a river. Which river? Owlishly, she peered around. A sheer-walled canyon cut the Sideways Mountains to the south. The Gray Deer River?

She blinked at the silty current and stumbled down to the edge of the water, heart aching at the barrier before her. *What now?*

A haunting ghost of sound—like clad feet whispering

through deep snow—came from behind her. Gasping panic, she looked back across the floodplain and saw nothing, only her own tracks in the virgin snow.

Hearing things. That's it. I'm going crazy . . . like the whole world. She peered down at the swiftly moving river.

Water, I can . . . can clean. Everything but my soul. Horrifying images of Three Bulls' leer tormented her.

White Ash ripped her clothing off. At the odor of rape, her throat constricted with the urge to vomit. She scooped sand from the river with hands that had lost all feeling; even the sting of the cold had gone. She began scrubbing her flesh, splashing her thighs and belly. Violent shivers wracked her.

Movement caught at the corner of her eye. *Who? What?*

She spun around. Nausea swept her. "Who are you?" she screamed at the dark apparition that wavered in the whirls of snow.

Cross! Must escape! Have to . . . get away. She grabbed her robe and pack and lurched forward, slogging out into the sucking cold of the river, barely aware of the drifting ice that bumped against her skin. Shivering uncontrollably, she tripped on the slippery rocks. As she went under, the bone-deep cold penetrated the last of her warmth. Water gurgled and bubbled around her head, swirling her hair around her face in a strangling net.

She struggled feebly against the current. Her soul drifted as if it had come free.

I'm dying . . . dying . . . The thought settled around her like falling goose down. *I'll be free, floating and warm like Bright Moon. Maybe in the Camp of the Dead, I can smile again.*

Bad Belly stood up, smacking his coat and digging out the cold, wet stuff that had been scooped up when he'd fallen down the slope. In the valley below, the Gray Deer River gleamed with an opalescent fire.

" 'Find the Dreamer,' Warm Fire said," Bad Belly muttered. He threw snow at Trouble, as he wagged his tail after bounding down the slope. On four agile feet. He caught the snowball and chomped it, eagerly waiting for more.

"You had to follow some wolf in the middle of the night, didn't you? I'll bet if you could talk, you'd tell me it was a black wolf, too. Some Spirit animal bent on getting me in trouble."

Bad Belly walked on, shivering. He reached the river bottom and waded through the snow of the broad floodplain. The cottonwoods stood stark and gray, their branches stippled with black buds that lifted toward the patchy clouds of the sky, engaged in a quest for a summer that never seemed to come.

He stopped at the thick fringe of willows along the banks and stared morosely at the roiling river. He shivered again—his chill made fiercer at sight of the clumps of snow and ice floating on the turbulent dark waters.

He turned to follow the river north to the hot springs and glimpsed a figure stumbling along the opposite shore. By instinct he grabbed Trouble just before the dog started to worm through the willows—to drink from the river, no doubt.

Holding the dog, Bad Belly crouched down.

He couldn't tell much about the bundled figure except that it carried darts and an atlatl. That was enough to create a squirmy feeling in Bad Belly's empty gut.

He glanced around. Could his tracks be seen from the opposite shore? Whoever this was, chances were good he wouldn't care for a lone stranger like Bad Belly.

The figure stepped down the bank, reeling slightly as if exhausted, or wounded. The man started, and took a long look back the way he had come—the sort of thing a person would do if he suspected pursuit.

"Oh, Trouble, what did we do? Blunder into some kind of war?" Bad Belly groaned, studying the fugitive's back trail. He could see nothing but the barren slopes rising to the west.

The man on the far bank began to undress.

"Of all the insanity, who in his right mind would—" His voice stopped short as the he turned into a . . . *she?*

The woman ignored the freezing cold, washing herself in a way that made Bad Belly blush despite his chill.

She scrubbed and scrubbed at herself, as if to cleanse every part of her shivering body. Then she jumped again, as if frightened, and plunged headlong into the river.

"No! Don't do it." Bad Belly shook his head and muttered to Trouble, "She doesn't look strong enough. And what about when she reaches this side? She'll be half . . ."

The woman rose, slipped, and fell.

Bad Belly jumped to his feet, trotting along the bank. The pack and robe she carried whirled away with the current. He bounced from foot to foot. He could see her strength failing as she floundered and could imagine the aching cold that would be cramping her muscles.

Would he have to watch the woman drown before his eyes? Bad Belly ripped off his coat and peeled out of his shirt, leggings, and pants. He charged into the river, terrified that she'd be dead by the time he reached her.

Cold shocked his already chilled flesh as he splashed toward her. His feet went out from under him on the slick, round rocks. He flailed with his good arm, got his head up, and battled the frigid current.

Grains of sand carried by the runoff prickled on his rapidly numbing skin. He reached her, bobbing on his toes, breath catching in his lungs as the intense cold stunned every nerve in his body.

Bad Belly grabbed a handful of her hair. She struggled weakly. "Hang on to me!" he wheezed through ice-strangled vocal chords.

The woman managed to slide her arms around his neck in a choke hold as he battled to stay afloat with his good arm and to push off the greasy rocks on the bottom with his cramped toes. They went under time and again; the woman's grasp on his neck cut off his air.

Bad Belly's limbs were losing their power to the terrible chill. He could feel his muscles stiffening, strength playing out.

"We're going to die," he whimpered as the current carried them around a bend. He gave his last effort to pull them into slower water as his feet touched sand. He dug his toes in, leaning against the current until he could kneel in the backwater, teeth chattering so hard his vision blurred.

He tried to stand, prayed his legs would obey. The woman's stranglehold pulled him over backward, making him gasp desperately.

Bad Belly floundered in the gritty water, clawing at his neck. He twisted around and thrashed, realizing the woman had gone limp—but her arm had tangled in the thong around his neck. He bucked hard—and the thong parted.

She lay slack in his grip as he grabbed for the pouch and its precious teeth, snagging it before the current whisked it away.

"Good for you I had these, or you'd have drifted away." He dragged her to the sandbank. She moaned, coughing up water.

Drained, cold to the bone, Bad Belly sloshed out of the shallows and pulled her onto the stony shore beside him.

"C-Can't s-stay h-here," he stuttered through clacking teeth. He fumbled around as he sought to lift her. Exertion might bring warmth. He got his good arm under her and lifted. Trouble came charging down the bank, tail whipping this way and that while he barked his delight.

Bad Belly got the woman up. She seemed to find some reserve of strength somewhere and stumbled along with him. Snow burned his feet as they careened along. Cramps shot agony up his legs.

Somehow they made it to his clothes. He wrapped her in his coat, pulling moccasins and leggings over the icy pain of his feet. His shivering made the chore twice as hard.

Bad Belly's thinking turned muzzy as he tried to figure out what to do. Warmth, they needed warmth or they'd both die. She had lain down and seemed to have lost consciousness. He stared at the surrounding white. The plume of the hot springs rose in a mounded white pillar to the north.

Hot springs? Hot water? It didn't look far now. All he had to do was follow the river.

How could he get her there? His mind went blank.

Use the robe for a sled. The words echoed in his ears.

He rolled her limp body onto the robe and set out. His feet pained and goaded him. He blinked against the fatigue. Warmth. Blessed, wonderful warmth, not so far ahead.

He grunted and wheezed as he willed himself onward, forcing rebellious muscles to function—forgetting why he was working so hard. Reason seemed like a slippery fish. Why was he doing this? Who was this woman he towed? Where was he, anyway? He stared at the unfamiliar country and lost his purpose.

"Pull the woman to the hot springs. Pull, Bad Belly, Pull." The words sounded around him, spinning out of the glacial air.

Pull her to the hot springs. The world weaved and bobbed. His fingers cramped where they locked in the hide. The landscape blanked out for whole moments as he slid her along. He made his way step by step, keeping the river on his left as he fought his way over the rough terrain.

He was still fighting, concentration knotted around his goal, when the robe stopped sliding.

He stared stupidly at the rock that had appeared underfoot. He shivered and panted for breath, perplexed by the problem. Cursed bad Spirits, why wouldn't the robe slide? It had slid so well this far.

Trouble barked and bounded ahead to the accompaniment of splashing. Bad Belly swiveled his oddly loose head and gaped at Trouble where he snorted at the biting sulfur odor in the steam that rose from a warm, turquoise pool.

Warm? No snow?

Bad Belly gazed at the rock he stood on. Rock, not snow. He'd dragged the woman and the robe onto bare ground. He'd made it to the hot springs! He pulled with all his might, tugging the resisting robe over the mineralized stone to the edge of the pool.

In a daze, he splashed into the water, shocking his flesh for a second time that day. Wonderful heat rose along his skin, to tingle like a thousand stinging needles piercing his flesh. He sucked lungs full of the steaming sulfur air and splashed in delight . . . until his glance happened to fall on the unconscious woman.

Perplexed, he stared, wondering where she'd come from. He sloshed out and pulled the woman off the robe. He tugged the coat off of her and got his good arm under her shoulder, lifting, splashing into the water with her. He settled her into the pool and gasped at the heat that soaked into his own shivering body.

He kept her nose up, enjoying the sensation of her hair streaming around him. He tried to think and gave up. Killing cold did that, shut off the mind. For the moment, he would simply sit and let the heat in the aqua water drive the cold from his limbs.

Hours later the sun had sunk low against the high bluffs to the west. Bad Belly's thoughts remained disjointed, his head muddled with fuzz like cattail down.

She stirred in his arms, mumbling to herself.

"Are you all right?" Bad Belly asked.

She lashed out in panic, striking at the water.

"Here, easy, you're safe," he said. "Safe."

She turned in his arms, looking up at him with vacant eyes. Then she did the most incredible thing. She began to cry as she dropped back into unconsciousness.

"It's all right," he assured her soothingly as he held her closer. "You're safe now."

Chapter 10

White Ash drifted in warmth, her thoughts broken and confused. A pungent odor—that of sulfur and noxious minerals—clogged her nostrils.

The nightmare played itself out again. She screamed as Three Bulls choked her into submission, his hot breath on her cheek. She relived the pain as he penetrated her. Ghostly images of the Wolf People's raid on the White Clay lingered in the background as she sobbed in despair.

"Nothing is left," she whimpered to herself. "All the beauty is gone from the world. Only suffering remains. Suffering, and hunger, and cold."

"To live, you must be reborn," a deep voice whispered in her mind.

Her soul quaked in fear. Fragments of her dreams whirled away, no more than curls of smoke on a windy day. Golden light filtered in bars through a gray haze. The warm-honey sensation of the One wrapped around her. A face formed in the golden glow. The handsome young man smiled at her, and a path opened to her heart.

"The Bundle waits for you, Mother of the People. Prepare yourself. Find yourself. That which was, like all of life, is no more. To know, you must learn. To feel, you must experience. To Dream, you must hope. All else is fantasy and imagination . . . illusion. The way must come from the knowledge of the past, the pain of the present, and the hope of the future. What seems real, is not. All about you is illusion. As a dart is crafted from rough wood, stone, feather and gut, so is a leader of the People fashioned. The Power of the Dreamer comes from strength. Like a dart shaft hardened in the fire, you can become more than you were . . . and less."

"You talk in contradictions."

The sun gleamed from his eyes while the golden glow deepened. The One pulsed around her. *"Contrasts, good and evil, light and dark, are the source of life . . . and illusion. Only the One has no contrasts. Only the One is real. All that is and is not. Prepare yourself and seek the Bundle. Through it, you will experience the One. You must prepare the way. The seeds of the future will be planted by your words, your actions, Mother of the People. Only you can renew the Dream."*

"Who are you?"

He laughed, fiery rays shooting forth like darts to illuminate a golden forest swathed in flames that danced from bough to bough. The image of the burning forest melted into a curiously warm vision of a blizzard-scoured land of snow and ice. A young man lifted a wolf heart to the frigid air, greedily sucking the warm blood from the steaming muscle.

Wolf Dream! an old woman's voice echoed eerily from the swirling snow.

The vision spun, storm fading into golden mist. A young man knelt in a clearing surrounded by jutting bastions of rock. Before him lay the carcass of a black wolf. The man extended his hands and lifted the heart from the body while a shimmering illumination grew around him.

White Ash could feel Power renewed, as if a multitude of souls cried out in jubilation. The heart the young man held up to the night sky grew bright like a star and rose in a gleaming haze.

She felt herself lifted, borne aloft by the Power of the glowing man of light. Like an eagle, she looked down on the world below. Despite the darkness, she could see herself floating in a hot spring as she rose through the billows of steam. She flew like a bird, grasped in his warm, reassuring arms.

"Mother of the People, all that was, is no more. You are renewed by the waters, born again as is the seed cast upon the Earth Mother and given life by water from above."

She turned her head, catching the beat of flaming wings. "Thunderbird," she whispered, "I am truly dead."

"Reborn," Thunderbird whispered back as they sailed out over the snow-shrouded basin. The Gray Deer River glinted silver in the light of the stars.

An old woman's reedy voice crowed in the air:

Come the Brothers! Born of Sun.
> *One is slain. Here by the long trail, his corpse is* laid.
>> *Blood is spread, from the head. Black one goes* . . . *aye, he's dead.*
He who loves is lost and gone. Render of the fair heart's song.
>> *Woman weep, for not you know. South, ever south* we go . . . *find an end to the blowing snow.*

On mighty wings Thunderbird dove from the dizzying heights. White Ash choked a cry of fear as she felt herself falling, whirling and weightless. The earth below blurred into a gray haze.

Her cry echoed in the sudden emptiness of her soul. The peaceful floating returned, warmth massaging her flesh.

Am I dead? Is that what this feeling of warm peace is? She blinked her eyes and came awake to the feel of water lapping around her body. She filled her lungs, sucking in all the cool air she could hold. Her heart beat strongly in her chest, blood rushing in her veins.

"I'm alive," she whispered to herself.

Stars poked through shadowy patches of night-shaded clouds. A light breeze blew foggy steam past her face. The air around her felt warm despite the snow that lay deep on the surrounding buttes.

She groaned and moved, feeling the body under hers shift. Afterimages of the wondrous Dream burst like ruptured bladders. Three Bulls leered out from her haunted memories and grinned through the hideous wreckage of his face. Panic seized her.

"Are you feeling better now?" a kind voice asked.

She readied herself to strike out. "Don't hurt me. Please. Just . . . just don't hurt me."

"Easy. You're safe—at least for the moment. You almost drowned."

"Drowned?" She sought sense among the jumbled thoughts.

"In the river. You tried to cross and lost your footing."

Memories came rushing back: killing Three Bulls, the terrible flight from the rock shelter, the lurking dread dogging her footsteps, futility and fear.

She nerved herself to ask, "Who . . . who are you?"

"I am Bad Belly, a man of the Round Rock clan."

"Round Rock? The Earth People? Then . . . I've crossed the Sideways Mountains?" Had she? She should have remembered that. *How much of myself have I lost?*

"No. You're still north of the mountains. You see, it was all Trouble's fault. He followed a wolf up the mountain in the middle of the storm. I . . . well, I got lost when I went to find him. The snow was blowing terribly, you see. The only way I knew to go was down. Left Hand must think I'm a real idiot."

Trouble? He? Another man she might have to fight off? White Ash steeled herself. "Trouble?"

"My dog. There he is, over by the rocks there." Bad Belly pointed.

She made out the shape of a black-and-white dog who watched them with cocked ears. Her fear slackened. He didn't look like much of a dog—but the light was poor. She shook her head, confused. "I don't understand."

"I don't either." He hesitated. "I think it's because of Power. Are you the Dreamer?"

"Dreamer?"

She could feel him nod.

"The Dreamer." He paused—as if reluctant. "A friend of mine, Warm Fire, said that I was supposed to leave Larkspur's camp and go north to save the Dreamer. I guess I don't really believe it—despite the Power Dream I had. You see, generally, in the legends anyway, Power sends a hero to rescue people like Dreamers. I'm not, well . . . very heroic."

She closed her eyes. "I'm no Dreamer."

A long silence stretched while she waited for him to move, prepared to strike back when he reached for her. She should flee, leap from the water and dash away into the darkness. But dash where? Running quick hands over her body, she realized that she lay naked. Wet and naked, how long would she last out in the snow?

"You're not the Dreamer?" He sounded miserable.

"No."

His frustrated sigh carried no element of threat. "Then I made a mess of things again. I was hoping you were the Dreamer and I might be able to go home. That is, if Trouble and I can find the way."

Her mind began to function again. Killing this man might not be so difficult. Then she could make her way . . . where? "What are you going to do with me?"

He started. "Do with you?"

"Are you going to rape me, too?"

"Rape you?" He sounded genuinely confused. Then:

"Oh. Is that what happened? I—I saw the bruises when I pulled you out of my coat. I mean I . . ." She could feel him shake his head. "Who'd do that sort of thing? I mean, what sort of man . . . Is that who you were running from? Maybe we should get away and . . . No, we'd better not. All my clothes are wet."

"I killed him," she growled. Blood and guts, what had she said? He'd be on guard now. *I'm not thinking clearly. Be careful, White Ash. You need all your wits. You have to use your head or you'll never kill him and get away.*

She bunched her fists, ready to attack, but he only sat up to stare at her. In the darkness his image was nothing more than a shadow. *What had he done to her while she lay helpless?* The thought of it sickened her.

"He beat you, too, didn't he? That's where the bruises came from—and the marks on your breasts and face."

When he gestured, he did so with only one hand. Where was the other? Holding some weapon? She got her feet under her, ready to spring should he attack.

"Can I do anything to help?" He sounded sincere.

"I've had enough help already."

He splashed at the water with an absent hand. "You seem to be afraid of me."

She watched warily. "Shouldn't I be?"

He laughed softly to himself. "If you are, you're the first person who ever was."

She frowned uneasily. Where were his weapons? "Do you have any food?"

"No. I didn't think I'd be gone that long."

"And you haven't been hunting?" she asked cannily.

He shrugged. "I've got a bad arm. I can throw a dart pretty well, but it takes too long for me to nock another dart in the atlatl. By the time I have another one ready to throw, the animals are gone. Generally I dig for roots, or pick berries. Larkspur used to send me out to pull up sagebrush. Otherwise, I'm good at knocking off rabbits and sage grouse with a rock."

A cripple? Is that what he is? She blinked in the night, some of her fears eroded by his honest words. *Wind Runner?*

Where are you when I need you? Where are your strength and cunning?

She closed her eyes. Wind Runner? No, not now. Not after what Three Bulls had done. How could she ever let another man touch her?

"You just shuddered; are you all right? Don't cry again."

"Cry?"

"You did that a lot. You'd sort of sleep and cry at the same time . . . like something terrible haunts your dreams. I was afraid that you might have—"

"You said our clothes are wet?"

"I guess I wasn't thinking too well by the time I got you here. I just sort of walked into the hot water. Getting real cold does that; it affects the way you think. All your things were washed away when you tried to cross the river. Between us we have my robe, a coat, a shirt, leggings, and moccasins."

One set of clothes? She'd have to kill him after all. His clothing meant survival. But then, if he really proved to be as inept as he seemed, maybe she could steal them and fade away into the night. He could take his own chances.

She bit her lip to stifle a sudden guilt. Steal his clothes? Condemn him to death by exposure?

He's a man. Just like Three Bulls. Wake up to reality, White Ash. You've watched your people killed. You've been raped, and chased, and starved. You can't afford a conscience anymore. It's your life or his. Survive, woman. No matter what it takes.

"The rocks are warm," he continued. "I put the wet things on them to dry. But you know how leather is. It will take until morning, probably."

"Where are we? The big hot springs?"

"Yes. This is supposed to be a Power place. Maybe it is. I was just upstream of it when you almost drowned."

She shook her head, more of her memories coming back. Terror had driven her into the water, forced her to try something she knew she couldn't do. She rubbed her fingers together, feeling the dried-plum texture of water-logged flesh.

Wait for morning. Wait for light to see by, then act. She

let herself sink lower into the warm protection of the water, rubbing her face in an effort to stay awake in case he attacked her.

He searched for a Dreamer? She shook her head, but couldn't dispel the haunting Dreams she'd had—or the words that had preceded her awakening.

She glared across the steam. *Just make it until tomorrow, White Ash. Then you can kill him and be gone.*

Bad Belly sat on the rocks above the spring and watched the morning brighten the eastern horizon. He hadn't been able to sleep after the woman had awakened in the night. He'd waited until she'd propped herself in the shallows and drifted off to sleep with her head pillowed on a rock. Then he'd carefully stepped out of the water, shivering in the night breeze. After he'd found his damp coat and robe, he'd sat and rubbed Trouble's ears as he considered his dilemma.

He stood stiffly and walked down to the river. The snow bit at his bare feet, but it would be better to dry his moccasins completely. The water looked dark and oily in the half-light of dawn. He proceeded to a place where willows grew. With a river cobble he sharpened the edge of an angular rock and cut some of the tough stems before returning to the hot springs to warm his toes on the rocks. As he stripped the bark from the willows, he mulled over his worries.

She wasn't the Dreamer?

Bad Belly worked the bark into a crude net, using his teeth to pull the knots tight.

In the growing light, he stared over at her, touched by the beauty in her face. The soft light hid the bruises on her cheeks and caressed the curves of her body. No wonder a man had desired her.

Bad Belly sighed to himself and motioned to Trouble before he retraced the path down to the bank of the river. After all that time in the water, he could almost pity a fish.

His feet burned from the cold as he wadded along the bank, but he found the right place: a ledge where the current had undercut a thin layer of sandstone. Settling himself, he eased down on his belly and extended his left hand.

Moving with great care, he lowered his net ever so gently into the water and hoped the bark would hold. A man could do this so much more effectively with two hands.

"Life's just not like that," he growled to himself. "I don't have two good hands. And I saved the wrong woman." Still, the thought brought contentment. He, Bad Belly, the man most people considered a burden, had jumped into an icy river and saved someone's life!

Irritation evaporated and he smiled happily. No matter what happened, he'd relive that day until he died, which—given his present circumstances—might not be very far away.

The net he lowered so gently touched the bottom and the current swelled the weaving of bark into a basket.

He reached with his shriveled arm and began to gently poke it under the bank. He might not be able to hold anything with his useless arm, but it could function for a stick when needed. Dark arrows shot into the basket as Bad Belly chortled and pulled up the fragile net with the flopping rewards. Three fish, each as long as his forearm.

He rolled back, careful to rest his net on the ground before the frantic fish broke it apart. One by one, he flipped them up on the bank, where Trouble pounced on them.

He stared down at his good hand, rubbing the thumb over his fingers. Why had his skin swollen and become all wrinkly in the water, while the fish skins stayed so firm? Was it the slime on their thin hides that protected them? Or was it something about the skin itself? *Think about it later.*

Another hundred steps down the bank he found a similar ledge and snared another few fish. By the time the sun had crested the high ridges to the east, he'd managed to catch ten, not counting the ones Trouble had gobbled down. His net had fallen apart and he couldn't feel his feet anymore—but food waited.

Bad Belly plucked up his catch and dropped it into a fold in his robe. Trouble trotted along behind as he climbed up on the rocks. No woman lay in the pool.

Bad Belly stared around—and found her frantically trying to pull on one of his wet moccasins. "Wet leather is like that," he called. "Let them dry a little more first. That's why I went barefoot."

She shot him a terrified look and froze, caught in the motion.

He walked closer, happy to have the warm rock against his cold-numbed feet. "Is something wrong? Is someone coming?"

She shook her head, a terrible desperation in her eyes.

"I've got fish," he cried. "Today we'll eat!"

She seemed to deflate then, and realization washed over him. He stopped, cocking his head. "Please. Don't fear me. You were going to run away, weren't you? And take my clothes?"

She glared at him with anger and resentment.

Bad Belly looked down at the bodies of his fish. "It's all right. You can have the clothes. Run away. I won't stop you."

He walked over next to the pool and dumped the fish.

She walked toward him, one foot clad, the other moccasin hanging from her hand. "You'd just let me *have* your clothes? In the name of Thunderbird, why?"

He gestured futilely with his good hand. After all, he'd saved her life, hadn't he? Maybe that's why her betrayal hurt so. "I can't know everything that's happened to you. Maybe your need is greater than mine. You're a woman alone. When I look into your face, I see terrible things reflected in your eyes. Maybe . . . maybe taking my clothes will keep you alive and get you back to your people. Back where someone can take care of you . . . keep you safe."

Her shoulders slumped as if her spirit had fled. "You believe that, don't you?"

"I have to. The world works in funny ways. It's full of puzzles—things people need to think about, but never do. I mean, look back at things that have happened in the past. Surely you know someone who lived when he shouldn't have? Maybe five people were walking along a ridge and lightning killed all but one. Then, later on, that one person happened to be present at a time of flood—or maybe at a landslide— and pulled someone to safety, and that someone grew up to be a Powerful Healer and saved lots of people's lives. Things work in curious ways, that's all.''

She stepped closer to him. The haunted expression on her face was frightening. "My people, the White Clay, are all dead."

He gaped. "But you . . . speak my language. I thought the Sun People spoke funny."

Her hard stare pierced him. She reached up to rub her eyes. "I don't know what's real anymore. I . . .''

He smiled understandingly. "It's all right. Think about it on a full stomach. Then you can go. And I'll eat only one fish. That way you can take some with you. It might make the difference.''

Her mouth opened as she raised a finger and shook it at him. "You . . . you don't make any sense at all! Doesn't it make you angry that I'd take your clothes and run off? How do you feel? About me, I mean? You ought to be . . . well, enraged!''

He lifted his hand in a placid gesture. "It hurts, that's all. It makes me feel sad that you'd do that. But I think I understand. The last man you saw raped and beat you. Maybe, if I were you, I'd steal someone's clothes, too. And, like I told you, life is full of puzzles that people need to—''

"*Puzzles!* We're talking about *survival* here! And you'd let me eat your fish?''

He gestured at the river. "There are plenty of fish. I'll make a better net next time and catch lots of them."

She shook her head, settling slowly to the rock. "What sort of man are you, anyway?''

Bad Belly took a deep breath. "I guess I'm just me. The only sort of man I can be.''

She stared down at his bare feet. "I hate raw fish.''

He gestured toward the uplands. "You could make some fire sticks. I think there's some chokecherry up there in the draw back of the butte. You'll need something to cut it with. I saw quartzite cobbles in the river. You could get one of them and knock a few flakes . . . What's wrong? You look sick.''

She turned her ashen face from him. He could see her fists

knotting as the muscles in her shoulders tightened. She lifted her face toward the sun, black hair spilling to catch the light.

"Why don't you do it?" she asked quietly.

"You've got one of my moccasins on, and you're wearing the rest of my clothing." He hesitated, then added uncertainly. "And besides, you might not want to come back here. It's your chance. If you think you need to take it, go."

She wheeled around, beautiful eyes flashing. "I'll go cut some chokecherry." She swallowed hard. "And I'll be back. I . . . I owe you that much."

Cold air braced Wind Runner's skin. He stood naked, toes clenched as if to grip the ground through the remains of the frozen snow. The Black Point had formed a ring around him. Now they waited, shoulder to shoulder, dressed in finely tailored hides, while the elders had wrapped themselves in buffalo robes. He stared at the excited faces—strangers, all. Then his mother's sister, Two Antelopes, appeared and gave him a smile. She'd been White Clay before she met Stone Fist during a Gathering. He had won her admiration and had asked for a marriage.

The Sun People did that during a Gathering. During that one time of year, Thunderbird watched over the people. All hostilities were dropped and the clans assembled to conduct Trade and to Dance. Hostages could be ransomed, and marriages into another clan were encouraged, especially when kinship had eliminated the potential mates within a band. No shame came of marriage during the Gathering. In fact, long ago Spirit Bear had seen that bloodlines would run together and had persuaded Thunderbird to declare a time of peace at the summer solstice so that all of the Sun People could get together and renew their Power without fear of war.

Such marriages now worked to Wind Runner's benefit. He had called out for Stone Fist's protection as he approached the camp, his hands empty of weapons. After he had explained his desire to seek a place among the Black Point, his uncle-in-law had spoken for him in the council.

Now Wind Runner must prove his worth. He stared up at the sky—a pale blue this day. The sun hung high overhead, a brilliant light that washed the rich, grassy bottoms of the Fat Beaver River. The cottonwoods stood mute, gray trunks weaving patterns against the far horizon where the Great Bear Mountains pierced the western sky. Snow lay heavy up there, the land locked in a blue cold.

The wind didn't carry much chill on this day, but it savaged naked flesh. With it came the odor of musty grasses and melting snow. Ravens cawed in the distance with raucous and jeering voices. Rosy finches rose in a swirl against the sky.

One Man—the Black Point warrior whom Wind Runner would have to face—stood across from him, a war club dangling from his fist. One Man looked to be about thirty-five summers old, and he stood tall and proud. Lines of lightning had been tattooed down his cheeks, and the man's nose had been broken in a past fight. The warrior inspected Wind Runner the way he would some pest. The sun's glare emphasized a nasty scar that ran across One Man's muscular left breast. The stone-headed war club swung back and forth in the warrior's powerful grip. The brilliant yellow-tanager feathers on the handle fluttered in the breeze.

Black Moon, the nominal leader of the Black Point, stepped out from the crowd. He wore a resplendent white buffalo robe—a symbol of the blessings of Power and his status among his people. Behind him walked Hot Fat, the Black Point's most powerful Soul Flier. Hot Fat's hair glinted silver in the sun as he raised his hands, Singing and Dancing to Thunderbird to give the combatants strength and skill. He Sang to instill courage into the hearts of the warriors who would fight this day.

Wind Runner dropped his own club to the ground, lifted his hands, and sang, "Great Thunderbird above, hear me. I, Wind Runner, would earn a place among this clan of the People. I have proven myself worthy. In the past my courage has been Sung over the bodies of my victims in war. My skill has been proven on the trail, where I eluded the pursuers who would take my life. Hear me today. Grant me strength and triumph. To you I will dedicate my life, to become a good man among this Black Point clan. To you I will humble myself and offer my life."

He lowered his hands, realizing Hot Fat had fallen silent. Now the Soul Flier stared at him, eyes like black obsidian glinting from behind slitted eyelids. The old man walked up to inspect him. Hot Fat's face was so lined and wrinkled that a person felt he could read the ages of the earth in that eroded visage.

"You would humble yourself before Thunderbird, be true to your Song?" Hot Fat asked.

"Yes, old one. A man is nothing without the gifts of Power. I look around me, feel the sun on my face, hear the birds, and enjoy the wind. All these things are the gifts of Power and are to be cherished. They are not to be risked foolishly."

A pensive look came to Hot Fat's eyes. "And you do not think yourself a fool to risk such things fighting One Man?"

Wind Runner shook his head. "No, old one. I made a promise on my soul. I do not take my soul, or promises made to Power, lightly. Young men have a reputation for doing foolish things. Those who do rarely live to provide strong arms for their people."

Hot Fat smacked his lips, cocking his head. "And where did you learn so much wisdom for one so young?"

Wind Runner pointed to the south. "There, old one. Just over those ridges. The leaders who remain among the White Clay argued among themselves, and the eager young men split the clan into three parts. Black Eagle took one group and went east—and we have heard nothing from him since. Gray Thunder took another group west, and his voice is also silent. I followed Whistling Hare because Sage Ghost, my uncle, said that old Whistling Hare and Old Falcon were wiser than the younger men, who would go fight a war they could not win."

Hot Fat gestured to the east and west. "Most of those you speak of have been killed. What few remained ran far to the east, and we know nothing of what happened to them out on the Short Grass Plains, but the Buffalo People are known to be mighty warriors.

"Now tell me, do I hear your words correctly? You would not engage in warfare? You would not follow the ways of our ancestors and fight to keep your strength?"

Wind Runner made the sign of negation. "Most respected old one, I am afraid you do not hear my words correctly. The best battles are the ones a warrior survives. A warrior's duty is to protect his people. The finest warrior is he who knows when to attack and when to avoid a fight. In war, courage is necessary, but even a fool can have courage. That only makes him a courageous fool. A warrior who would lead must have courage, but he must also have prudence. Courage and prudence must be balanced, one against the other."

Hot Fat considered, rubbing his callused palms together. He studied Wind Runner through gleaming eyes. "Tell me, warrior, you speak of courage and prudence in the same breath. Which stands without the other?"

"Courage," Wind Runner replied easily. "Often prudence takes courage. Sometimes a prudent man must be courageous enough to speak against the heartfelt desires of others when to agree might be easier."

Hot Fat laid a hand on Wind Runner's shoulder. "Good luck, young man. Your fate is in the hands of the Sun."

"Thank you, old one." Wind Runner bent and picked up his club.

Hot Fat grunted to himself and returned to stand beside the Black Point leader. Black Moon looked back and forth between the warriors. Then he nodded his head.

One Man immediately charged forward, a shrill scream on his lips.

Wind Runner ducked, dodging artfully and parrying the blow of One Man's swing. One Man jumped nimbly aside, checking his grip on the war club. He moved with uncanny grace, swift and agile.

Wind Runner circled carefully as he balanced on the balls of his feet. One Man stood half a head taller than he; thick and powerful muscles packed his shoulders. The cold reality settled in: Within seconds, Wind Runner could be lying on the grass, his blood and brains leaking through a cracked skull.

"You came here to die, White Clay," One Man growled evilly.

"I came here to live." Wind Runner whirled, feinted, and swung the club in a backhand toward his adversary's skull. The blow slipped through empty air and Wind Runner used his momentum to escape the vicious swing One Man countered with.

He'd barely recovered when One Man leaped like a striking cougar; his stone-headed club hissed in for the kill. In desperation, Wind Runner rammed the bigger man. Through the haze of his panic, he heard the crowd cry out.

He locked with One Man, knowing full well that in a match of brute strength, he'd lose. But the larger man's reach and powerful muscles left him little choice. He bulled into his opponent, cramming the handle of his war club into One Man's rock-hard stomach. A heel locked behind his as One Man tripped him.

Wind Runner hit the ground rolling and threw himself to one side as One Man's club thocked into the frozen earth beside his head. Wind Runner rolled back on his shoulders, kicking out with his heels to smash One Man full in the face.

Using the momentum from his kick to roll away, Wind Runner scrambled to his feet. One Man shook his head—as if to clear his vision—and stared at his hand. The hafting of the Black Point warrior's war club had broken on impact with the frozen ground.

Wind Runner put his hand up. "Wait!"

Silence fell on the crowd. One Man advanced, wary, hands reaching out.

"*Wait!*" Wind Runner cried again. "If I kill One Man, the Black Point will lose a strong man, a good man."

Black Moon stepped between them, giving Wind Runner a narrow stare. "What are you saying?"

Wind Runner didn't drop his eyes from One Man, who stood poised and ready. Blood leaked from the Black Point warrior's nose.

Wind Runner quickly said, "Only this. If I kill One Man

with my club, I will have won. And One Man? He'll lie dead, and his wives and children will mourn and cry.'' Taking a deadly gamble, Wind Runner dropped his club; it thudded soddenly on the ground. He stepped forward and extended his hand to One Man. "If I'm accepted among the Black Point, I would wish to be accepted as One Man's friend—not as the warrior who widowed his wife and took his children's father.''

One Man licked his bloody lips and glanced at Black Moon.

"Have I proved my courage to you, One Man?'' Wind Runner took a deep breath. "Have I fought you honestly, and with courage?''

One Man nodded despite the confusion in his eyes. "You fight well, Wind Runner. But it isn't decided between us. I'm not beaten.''

"No, you're not. But if I did beat you, you'd be shamed. The resentment would fester like a cactus thorn under the skin. The bad feelings would never be finished between us, would they? I'd have to kill you. Or you me. And the Black Point would be less one warrior either way.''

Black Moon chewed at his lower lip as he considered. Hot Fat hobbled up on his old joints. The clan leader looked at the Soul Flier. "What of the Power? Can we do this?''

Hot Fat glanced at One Man and Wind Runner. "The reason for the challenge is to determine an individual's worth, not for the idle shedding of blood. In the beginning, the challenge was made to ensure that a clan took in only those worthy to belong, to ensure that we didn't accept cowards or fools who would weaken our blood. As humans, we have to be careful not to bend the ways of Power to our own ends. We must look beyond, to the true meaning and purpose of the things we do. Do we serve the ways of Power? Or do we simply seek to entertain ourselves in the name of Power? How do you speak, One Man? You fought him. Do you think his arm is strong enough, his heart courageous enough, to defend your family?''

Wind Runner met the warrior's measuring stare. One Man

nodded slowly. "I'd take him on a raid. I think I'd listen to his counsel, too."

Wind Runner struggled to catch his breath. Images lurked in the back of his mind—images of a camp just upriver. On that warm summer day, he remembered, the warriors who stood around him now had run screaming and killing through the lodges of the White Clay. The haunting eyes of the dead watched.

Black Moon raised his hands. "Then I declare this contest over. Wind Runner has earned a place among the Black Point. He has done so through courage—and cunning."

Wind Runner offered his hand to One Man again. The big warrior took it, a grin barely touching his lips. "I'd still have killed you, you know."

Wind Runner shrugged. "Perhaps, but isn't it better this way?"

One Man daubed at his nose. "I'm going to have to think about it. You fought well. So well that it's better that you fight with us than against us."

Hot Fat placed a hand on Wind Runner's shoulder. "Come. Everyone is going to want to talk about you and what you've done today. My granddaughter, Aspen, will have my meal cooked soon. Her cooking is wonderful, even if she drives most men to the end of their wits with her ways. Join me. We will talk."

Wind Runner smiled weakly and followed the old man; he could feel the eyes of his White Clay dead upon him, their stares burning into his soul. *I had no choice.*

Would they believe that?

Chapter 11

Bad Belly squinted and shaded his eyes against the sun as he looked out over the valley, hardly willing to believe they walked through a real, honest, warm day. To the south the snow-capped heights of the Sideways Mountains gleamed so bright it hurt to look at them. The valley below had melted into a sticky quagmire of gray-brown mud. Water ran opaque with silt, rippling like flexed muscles—as if it had absorbed the strength of the land while it surged in the drainages.

The endless dome of the sky seemed to glow with new life, and the sun actually beat down hot upon his body. He could smell the rich tang of the damp soil waiting to spring into new life. Two eagles circled in aerial dance over the valley. The sage-rich hillsides appeared fertile for once; the blue-green leaves had renewed themselves with the sun's wealth. Now the pungent scent of sage recharged his senses.

They walked along the southern exposure, high enough on the hillside to avoid most of the mud. Nevertheless, their feet sank into the cushion of loose soil, sometimes sliding on the slick ooze that lay underneath the friable crust.

Bad Belly hummed happily to himself. Trouble charged this way and that, sniffing in holes, occasionally stopping short under Bad Belly's feet to stare around.

White Ash walked behind him, following the route he picked through the sage and bitterbrush.

"How are the sandals holding up?" she asked.

Bad Belly took a quick look, trying to decide where the sandals ended and the mud began. "So far, so good. That three-times cursed cactus sure goes through them, though. They're worse than moccasins."

"You surprised me. I wouldn't have thought to weave juniper bark, sage, and yucca into footwear."

"The Trader, Left Hand, told me about it. He said that people in the basin country do it this way. You see, all they have down there are antelope and deer. Almost no buffalo or elk, and only mountain sheep up in the hills. Hides are always in short supply, and precious to them. Left Hand says they'll trade a lot of things for good buffalo-hide moccasins."

He hadn't figured out what to do about his legs yet, however. The sagebrush had scratched his calves half bloody.

He pulled up, rehitching the bark basket he'd woven to carry the fish they'd smoked and dried. "You think we're on the right trail?"

She gave him a nervous glance. "I think so. I mean . . . I don't know. I hate going east. Too close to the Wolf People. I just . . ." She shook her head, lifting slim hands to rub at her temples. "I'm sorry I made you do this. But that terrible Dream I had last night at the hot springs was so . . . so ominous. Dangerous. We *had* to leave. In the Dream I saw warriors coming. People I couldn't recognize. Hundreds of them streaming down from the north. They carried bloody darts. And behind them . . . hunger and pain and frozen death."

"Sun People?"

"I couldn't tell. They held long stone knives up to the sun. And the feathers . . . they wore them in their hair and on their shoulders. Feathers of all the colors of the rainbow. The voice in the Dream said we had to leave, to flee east. To find some Power Bundle."

He scratched under his chin, resettling his grip on the fish basket. "Maybe you *are* the Dreamer."

She arched an eyebrow. "Well, I'm a witch-cursed poor one, then."

They camped that night in a stand of junipers. Bad Belly spent the twilight hours stripping bark from the trees. That done, he rubbed the long strands between his palm and thigh to make the tough strands pliable. The strands—bristling with scratchy fibers—he wove into a cloak. The fire crackled merrily while he worked. White Ash picked at the remains of a smoked fish, stopping every now and then to spit one of the fine bones into the fire.

He paused to enjoy the way the fire illuminated her features. Her bruises were much better now. If only he could soothe the sadness in her eyes. At moments like this, when she got lost in her head, the haunted look would come.

"Why did you stay with me?" he asked gently.

She chewed the last of the flaky meat from the fish's skeleton and flipped the remains into the fire, then rubbed her hands on the leather of his leggings. She crossed her arms and leaned forward to peer intently into the fire.

"I guess because I needed someone. Imagine how you'd feel if one day everything you'd ever loved was gone. Imagine if nothing remained for you. No safety anywhere. What would you do if your life had been stripped bare and the pieces of it burned and scattered? I had no place to go."

"You told me about Three Forks. You could go back there. Green Fire would make a place for you."

She smiled wistfully. "That's not my place anymore, Bad Belly. When I was a girl, I hated it there. Do you know how Three Forks feels about Power, about people who Dream? People who hear voices like we do make them nervous. Green Fire's father was witched once—or she thought he was. She didn't want me growing up to Dream. I don't want to go back."

"Green Fire's still raising a fuss about witching. She thinks witching killed her husband. She even thought you were witched away. Or so my grandmother—Larkspur—says."

A gleam grew in White Ash's eye. "Maybe I was. I'll ask Sage Ghost . . . if I ever see him again. He'll laugh about it."

"But Three Forks has to keep the Spirits happy, too. If they didn't, the grass wouldn't come up. The nut harvest would go bad. The way the Earth People think, Spirits are responsible for everything."

"Even letting their Powers be used for witching," she agreed. "Green Fire has made a place for herself between the people and the Spirits. She deals with the Spirits, but resentfully, fearfully. She likes to control that Power so it can't be used against her. Anything else is a threat. That's the reason I can't go back. I can't hide the Dreams. I couldn't as a little girl, and I don't think I can now."

She stared into the fire, seeing beyond the flames. "That's why I came with you. I don't have any place to go." A pause. "And had I gone off alone, I'd have had only myself for company. I don't . . . like myself very much anymore. I'm not worth . . ." Her mouth worked as she turned her head away.

He took a branch from the pile she'd collected and dropped it on the fire. "You should like yourself. You're strong, healthy, and most of all, you're smart. You can do anything you want to."

She shot him a furtive glance. "Like being the Mother of the People? Whatever that means, I'm not sure I want any part of it. I just want to try to find the torn pieces of my life and sew them together again. Maybe run off and live in a cave like the Healers among the Earth People do. If they think I'm living with Power, perhaps they'll leave me be."

"Maybe that's what you need to do. Left Hand told me that Power has its own ways."

He sniffed the night breeze, enjoying the sweet scent of the juniper. The chill was deepening. He could already see his breath when he turned away from the fire. "I guess we'll get a hard frost tonight."

She twisted a strand of hair around her finger as she stared up at the night sky, shot through with an infinity of stars. "You'll be cold, won't you?"

He shrugged. "If I get cold, I'll throw another chunk of sagebrush on the fire and roll over so the cold side gets warm. I'll just hug Trouble close and share his warmth. He's got a good coat." He smiled at his dog, who lay sleeping with his nose buried in his tail.

"Why haven't you tried to take me?"

He started at the frank way she said it. The words fled, and he couldn't find anything to say.

"Why haven't you tried?" she demanded hotly. "I've seen the look in your eyes. You watch my body . . . and you turn away. You want me. I can see it in you, in the way you look at me. But you never come over in the night, never ask me to spread my legs for you. Why?''

''Does it bother you that I look at you?''

''Yes.'' She crossed her arms defensively. ''Are all men the same? Why can't you ignore me?''

He rubbed the back of his neck, shifting uncomfortably. ''You are a beautiful woman. I can't deny that. You listen when I talk about things. You think about them and discuss them with me. Only two other people have ever done that in my whole life. At the same time, I know what you feel. I'll never let myself even be tempted.''

''How do you know what I feel?'' Her harsh tone wounded his soul.

''I . . .'' he began, and stopped. *How do I tell her? How can I talk about it with someone who's almost a stranger?* He nerved himself. ''I was married once. Her name was Golden Flax. Her father had taken her, raped her, when she was a little girl. No one wanted her. No one wanted me. We didn't really want each other—but that's what the clans decided was good for us. What her father did ruined her life. It made her different, and it wasn't her fault. People avoided her as if she carried a malignant Spirit on her shoulder.'' He hung his head. ''We coupled only once—and she threw up. Maybe what happened to you left the same kind of scars on your memory.''

Her stare had turned glassy, a near-panic on her face.

He lifted his arm, gesturing with a knotted fist. ''I don't *want* to take you. Don't you understand? I know how you cry in your sleep. You relive what happened with Three Bulls every time you close your eyes. You've been hurt too much. I've worked hard to get you to smile without that snake look in your eyes. I don't want to lose that.''

Her miserable expression turned his stomach. ''I'll never let another man touch me that way.''

''I don't want to.''

''But I see the way you look at me.''

He took a deep breath and exhaled nervously. ''You're very good to look at. But I'll never touch you—not in the way a man touches a woman.''

"Then why do you stay with me?"

He smiled gently. "You talk to me. You don't treat me like a fool. You accept me for who I am and what I am."

"And you don't want to take me under the robes? Not even a little?"

He lifted an eyebrow. "I may be peculiar in my own way, but I'm not dead. At the same time, I'd be afraid to try."

She straightened, watching him warily. "Why?"

He hated the panicked look he knew covered his face. "Women aren't interested in me. Face it, I'm a homely man. What woman would want to touch a man with a shriveled arm? And the only time I tried to lie with Golden Flax under the robes, she got sick." He shook his head and threw a pleading look at the stars. "I listen to the other men brag about what they can do with their women. I might not be good under the robes—probably wouldn't be, actually. So why find out that what I suspect is true?" He rubbed his face with a nervous hand. "I embarrass myself enough as it is."

Her flinty features didn't change. "Then let's keep it that way."

He nodded, a little relieved. "Maybe that's why we're together. Maybe I can help you forget what happened with Three Bulls."

"I'll never forget."

Bad Belly sucked at his lip, staring into the fire. What could he say now?

She closed her eyes, hands knotted into fists. "You know, I killed him with a chopper I'd made. He'd gone to sleep. I picked up the rock and smashed it down on the bridge of his nose and blinded him first. I think I stunned him with that blow. Then I hammered and hammered until I'd chopped his face right off." She began to shake, and her voice quavered. "I just couldn't stop. I . . . I kept hacking at him, trying to kill it all. Like . . . like I could drive what happened out of my soul by butchering him. I couldn't control myself. I pounded and pounded at him, hammering that chopper into his body."

Bad Belly cautiously reached his good arm around her. "Shhh. You're all right now."

"That's why I ran," she mumbled, sniffling at the tears she wouldn't let him see. "I ran and ran. And now I wonder if I wasn't just running from myself."

He held her, pressing his cheek to her hair. "Looking back now, would you have done it any differently?"

"No," she admitted miserably.

"Then you did the right thing."

She sighed, shaking her head, hair sliding along his cheek. "I just couldn't stand any more. Everything was dead. Bright Moon died. We were starving, hunted, and killed. I had to look into Sage Ghost's eyes when I told him that the only woman he'd ever loved was dead. The man I loved ran off to the Black Point to get himself killed. I found Old Falcon's body. Brave Man murdered him. I know it. Then the attack came. I just ran and tried to stay alive. Then to be captured like that and raped, and beaten, and raped again?" She huddled in on herself, shivering. "And the Dreams don't leave my any peace. I don't understand the things First Man says to me."

"What does he say?"

"Things about being reborn." Her voice sounded lonely, scared. "About leading the People and making a new way. Strange things about the Sun People and the way they have to be prepared for something that's going to happen in the future."

"He comes out of fire?"

She shifted to stare up at him. "How do you know that?"

"I had a Dream once, out in the Wind Basin, when I was traveling with Left Hand. First Man told me that the Sun People were like a tree, that the right kind of roots had to be planted so the tree would grow in a certain way. Then he changed from a man of fire to a wolf to a flaming bird. When the bird flew away, the thunder was so loud it woke Left Hand out of a sound sleep."

Her mouth dropped open. "Power sent you to me?"

"I guess." He shrugged. "If you're the Dreamer. I'm supposed to do something. I don't understand it yet. Something about a bundle—maybe the one you Dreamed about." Trouble made a muffled yip. The dog's nose and feet were twitching as he chased rabbits in his sleep. He whimpered in excitement. "And when Trouble followed a wolf in the night, I followed him."

"What does it mean?" she whispered as though shocked.

Bad Belly leaned his head back and exhaled, watching his breath in the cold night air. "You ask me? Bad Belly? I'm as lost and alone as you are."

She leaned her head on his shoulder, fingers weaving into his. "I don't want to be alone tonight."

"I'll be just on the other side of the fire. I won't go anywhere—even if another Spirit Wolf tries to lead Trouble away. I promise."

"Wrapped in your juniper-bark blanket?"

"I'll be fine. We have enough wood."

"This robe is big enough for both of us." She looked up at him, searching his eyes. "You said you wouldn't . . . wouldn't . . ."

He smiled down at her, smoothing her hair with his fingers. "No. I don't need that from you. I'd better sleep over there, though. I know how it is. Golden Flax used to cry out in the night when I was next to her. She thought I was her father. You might think—"

"I *don't* want to be alone. Just be close to me tonight. I'm frightened, Bad Belly. If you're there, maybe the Dreams won't come."

"I don't—"

"Besides, you'll freeze." She smiled weakly. "It'll be all right. I—I trust you."

Bad Belly sighed and nodded agreement. He stood and went over to ruffle Trouble's ears, ordering sternly, "No wolves tonight. If you see any, you're on your own."

He pulled up the corner of the robe and settled next to White Ash, careful to keep his back to her.

"Bad Belly?"

"Yes."

"How did you come to be called Bad Belly?"

"I used to throw up every time I got hurt . . . or scared."

"What was your real name?"

"Still Water."

"I know how you feel. All these Dreams about First Man and Thunderbird that we've been having—they make me want to throw up, too. I'm scared."

"So am I, White Ash."

Green Fire stood up from her place in the back of the lodge and took two hobbling steps. She hated the pain in her knees. Worse, her eyesight had grown dimmer over the last couple of years, making it difficult to see in the lodge's half-light.

"Witching did that to me." She sucked at her toothless gums, remembering the pain that had preceded the death of her last tooth. Then the root had finally rotted and the tooth fell out of her mouth. Now she ate only soups with chunks of meat small enough to swallow, and gruel made of finely ground ricegrass seeds and pulped roots.

She stared around the lodge, barely able to make out the soot-blackened rafters where they braced on the stringers. Her back had bent with age, leaving the hide bundles that hung from the rafters beyond her reach. Once she had had her daughters hang them lower, but people had bumped into them.

She put a withered hand on one of the roof supports and stepped gingerly around the sandstone slab that acted as a deflector for the fire pit. She bent down, squinting at the smoldering coals. Too much ash had built up. Someone would have to clean the hearth out again.

She straightened and inspected the boiling paunch. Water, boiled meat, and chopped roots. Her stomach growled its longing for a thick steak or a juicy roast.

"No wonder the witching takes to me. How can a soul stay strong and fight off such things? A person needs real food, stuff with substance."

"What's that, Grandmother?" Basket looked up from her work. She was using a block of wood to cushion her palm as she pushed a bone awl through a thickness of leather. Her swollen belly inhibited her movements and restricted her to the lodge. From the looks of it, White Blood had planted a large child in her granddaughter's womb.

"Nothing. Talking to myself. What's that you're making?"

"Moccasins for Little Toe."

"Can't his wife do that for him? He's married to . . . what's her name?"

"Gray Needle."

"That's right. Gray Needle over at Badwater camp. She can make his moccasins."

Basket made a suffering face. "I thought I'd give him these when we see him this summer. He's still my brother. We're close, he and I."

"Close?" Green Fire grunted under her breath. "He practically turned his back on us. He didn't trust my judgment. I could have dickered for access to hunting rights up above that camp of theirs."

Basket stared at her grandmother. "You didn't *want* to deal with Bone Ring. At the time, you accused her of fooling around with witchcraft. After that big fight you had, you told Little Toe—"

"So he ran off!"

"Grandmother, they loved each other."

She waved a hand. "Well, he could have fallen in love with Yellow Bird instead of Gray Needle. Yellow Bird gets the camp when Bone Ring dies."

Basket's face darkened and she rolled her eyes.

Green Fire ignored her, hitching across the lodge. Curses, why did her back hurt all the time and grow more crooked with age? She pushed the door flap back with a birdlike hand and stepped into the cool sunshine of day.

She made a couple of tottering steps toward the sunshade before a terrible pain lanced through her chest and she cried out. She caught sight of Owlclover rushing toward her as her balance failed. Black spots formed before her eyes and she felt her body hit the ground.

Pain burned like a fiery brand in Green Fire's chest. From somewhere in the distance she could hear Owlclover's frantic voice calling out to her.

"Witched," she whispered. "I've been witched. It's

in my chest, burning. Evil is there. I been witched . . . witched . . .''

She fell into a gray mist, falling . . . falling. . . .

White Ash walked along the Bug River, listening to Sage Ghost tell the old stories. Majestic piles of cloud drifted to the east in mountainous thunderheads that gleamed white against the endless blue of the sky. A soft breeze rustled the leaves of the narrowleaf cottonwoods growing where the Bug River rolled out of the verdant foothills to the west. Grass grew thick in the rich, black soil of the bottomlands.

Sage Ghost's face lit with happiness as he told the story of Bear and Thunderbird. To emphasize his words, he gestured, and his voice rose melodiously on the summer morning. As if in reply, the birds warbled and chirped from the trees and raspberry bushes.

Bright Moon laughed as she shook her head. ''You'll talk the girl's ear off, old man.''

''So?'' Sage Ghost spread his arms wide to the day. ''What's a child for if you can't talk its ears off? She needs to learn about Thunderbird, and Bear, and the Power of the Sun, and the legends of the Sun People. It will be important someday. She has to know, that's all. Important . . . Legends . . . Has to know . . . someday . . .'' The words broke, echoing as if in a cave.

The dreams grew disjointed, coming apart as White Ash fought to keep them. She lost her grip on the fragile filaments, almost weeping as they floated away like fall leaves on the wind. The past could live only in memories—and those carried a bittersweet character of their own.

Something moved against her, triggering a sudden revulsion. *Three Bulls! Pain and violation! Not again!* Please, she couldn't stand it. *Not again!* She jerked awake in the night, forcing a knuckle into her mouth to stifle the sudden tears.

''White Ash?'' a gentle voice whispered in her ear. ''Are

you all right? You jumped and cried out. It was just a dream, that's all. A dream.''

Bad Belly turned to nestle against her; he patted her shoulder reassuringly. ''Sleep now,'' he murmured. ''Trouble will wake us up if anything happens. Sleep, and don't dream. The world is better now.''

A lonesome wind worried the sage and pierced the juniper stand. She could feel the chill seeping up from the ground below. Coyotes yipped and barked in the distance. ''You believe that, don't you? That the world is better?''

He hugged her reassuringly. ''Sure I do. Power sent me to find you. You're special, White Ash. Special and wonderful.''

She shifted, prodding Trouble as her feet moved. The dog stood, shook, and padded up, stepping on her legs to fall with a grunt in the hollow before her arms. Trouble snuffled a long sigh and tucked its nose under its tail. The animal's warmth began to soak through the robe.

''Hold me,'' she whispered to Bad Belly, feeling his arm draw tight around her.

''Safe,'' he reassured. ''I'm right here.''

As his warmth drove away the chill, she drifted into the realm of sleep again.

Pain.

Brave Man groaned.

''Lie still,'' a voice intruded.

''What? Where am I?'' He sounded muffled and funny—speech slurred as if his mouth had been stuffed with feathers.

''You are in Buffalo Tail's camp, warrior.'' The voice was a woman's.

Pain.

Brave Man gasped and opened his eyes. The image blurred and he blinked to clear his sight. He lay on his back, staring up at fire-blackened lodge poles and a stained buffalo-hide lodge cover. He could see an overcast of clouds through the smoke hole.

His head ached as though someone had stabbed spears into his brain. His mouth felt oddly swollen. When he worked his tongue to swallow, it hurt. Feeling around the inside of his mouth, he discovered a gap where his front teeth should have been. The splintered roots sliced at his tongue. When he tried to sit up, white agony lanced his body. He blinked again, breathing deeply to ease the torture that charred his nerves.

"Lie still," the woman repeated. She leaned over and placed a cool hand on his brow. He could see that she had a stately beauty. Long black hair framed her delicately boned face. She watched him with emotionless brown eyes, her mouth thin-lipped and mobile. Her brow rose smooth and high over intelligent eyes. She carried herself with a certain grace and competence, and a measured determination lay behind her neutral expression.

He moved again, and the tortured flesh in his leg sparked light behind his eyes. He panted, trying to still the urge to vomit.

"Do you remember who you are?"

"Brave Man." He swallowed, wincing. The stale taste of blood lay heavily on his tongue.

"Do you know where you are?"

He nodded weakly. "Among the Broken Stones. I challenged. Fought Hawks Beard."

"That's right. Do you remember what happened?" She had a sensual voice that pleased him.

He sucked cool air into his lungs, closing his eyes. "I killed him."

A wry smile crossed her lips. "You did more than that. You gouged his eyes out and ripped his jaw loose from his head."

He reached up to rub his eyes. At least his arm seemed to work all right. "I am deemed worthy of the Broken Stones?"

"Hawks Beard was our greatest warrior." She raised a shapely eyebrow. "It was thought that no man alive could take him in challenge. Single-handedly he killed no less than five silver bears. More than two tens of enemy warriors fell before him.'' She paused. ''And now he has fallen to you. You are accepted.''

The voices of the Spirits whispered in his head. *Yes! See, we told you!*

He tried to sit up again and almost toppled sideways. Pain stunned him. The woman's strong hands caught him as the world went gray. She eased him back to the robes.

Brave Man gasped; sweat began to bead on his hot face. ''What . . . what's wrong with me?''

A challenge lay in her veiled glance. ''Most of your front teeth are gone. Your nose is broken and your knee is crushed.''

He closed his eyes again to stop the lodge from spinning crazily over his head. He remembered now. Fortunately, the blow that had caught him in the mouth had lost most of its power.

Brave Man had staggered back, mouth full of blood and bits of shattered teeth. The voices had whispered, overcoming the sudden pain and disorientation. As Hawks Beard stepped forward to finish him, Brave Man had spit blood and teeth into the warrior's face. Then he'd driven his club down on the point of Hawks Beard's shoulder, breaking a collar bone. Brave Man's next blow caved in Hawks Beard's chest.

The warrior hadn't been finished, however. He'd shifted the war club to his good hand, staggered, and dropped to his knees.

Brave Man had fallen for it, stepping close, club high, when Hawks Beard delivered a side-armed blow that crippled Brave Man's knee and left him shrieking on the ground. Only a mad scramble had saved his life. He'd grabbed a fistful of dust and sand and thrown it to blind his adversary.

Despite the wretched pain, he'd crawled forward and swung the club underhanded, catching Hawks Beard in the crotch. The warrior had collapsed as he'd screamed and grabbed his crushed testicles.

The voices had driven Brave Man on, urging him to crawl over to Hawks Beard. Blood had run between the man's fingers, while tears leaked down his face.

An insane rage had overpowered the pain as Brave Man

discarded his club and gouged the man's eyes out, disorienting his victim with pain and horror.

Buffalo Tail had tried to stop the battle then, as had Sun Feathers, the Broken Stones' Soul Flier. Spurred by the voices in his head, Brave Man had ignored the elders—as was the right of the challenger.

Brave Man used Hawks Beard's club to smash the man's jaw, then grasped the bleeding wreckage with furious hands. Muscles straining, he'd jerked the broken jawbone this way and that while animal shrieks ripped from Hawks Beard's throat. Only after Hawks Beard lost consciousness did Brave Man lift the club and crush the warrior's throat.

At last he'd fallen, panting, vomiting the blood he'd swallowed onto the dry winter grass. In a Dream state, he'd drifted off toward the gray mist, searching for the Power. In the mist, he'd heard voices. One, he knew, belonged to Power—and the other to White Ash. Yes, she was tied to the Power. Find White Ash and he'd find the key, the way to enter that golden haze that had rebuffed him.

The voices in his head hissed approbation.

Lying in the lodge, he asked through a dry throat, "Who are you?"

"Pale Raven." She reached behind her and produced a water bag. "Open your mouth. That's enough. I'll trickle a little water."

He did as she instructed, grateful for the drops she dribbled past his swollen gums.

"And this lodge? This is your lodge? Or my cousin's?"

"This is Hawks Beard's lodge."

Brave Man tried to think. "You were his wife?"

She smiled sourly, resettling herself. Her voice carried a wry irony as she said, "I'm no man's wife. The man you killed, Hawks Beard, made me a promise once. At the time, I was married to another man. As happens sometimes, we—Hawks Beard and I—were caught locked together like two camp dogs. He blamed it all on me. Who would the People believe? Their greatest warrior? Or a woman who'd transgressed before? My husband divorced me. No other man would have me. I'd bring dishonor, you see."

"Why are you taking care of me?"

"Let's call it a twisted form of justice. Hawks Beard's wife has moved her things back to her parents' lodge and taken the children. You don't need to worry about her. She'll be married again within a couple of months. She's too much of a pampered prize for the men to leave running loose for long. Meanwhile, as is custom, you've won everything else that belonged to Hawks Beard. His lodge, weapons, and other possessions."

"And you?"

She studied him, mocking challenge in her sultry gaze. "I've told you about myself. Why would you want me?"

He started to smile, and winced. "You're a beautiful woman. You're practical and cunning." He tried to shift his position and managed despite the pain. "I think you're a strong woman. I could use you for a while."

"A while?" Wry amusement lay in the set of her lips.

He reached up to wipe the sweat from his forehead. "I must go south. There is a White Clay woman who was taken by the Wolf People when they destroyed the White Clay. She's Powerful—a link to making a new way."

Pale Raven steepled her fingers, frowning. "Taking me might lower your status among the Broken Stones. A new man seeking to earn a—"

"I bring my own Power, woman. I need no one's approval." He stared up at the clouds scudding past the smoke hole. "Power is stirring. It brought me here for a reason. You need only to clear your senses . . . feel the Spirit World. Do that and you will know that something important is about to happen. The woman, White Ash, is the key. He who possesses her will make a new way. I will be that man."

She ran long fingers through her shining hair. "Either the Power of the Sun has truly touched you . . . or you're a raving fool."

He studied her with burning eyes. "A fool doesn't kill the most powerful warrior among the Broken Stones."

She laughed. "And how are you going to go after this White Ash? How do you plan to wrest her from the Wolf People? In battle?"

He squinted up at the soot-stained lodge poles. "I will crush the Wolf People like a brittle rabbit bone. The Broken Stones now have a more powerful warrior than Hawks Beard. I am the one."

She said dryly, "You're quite a man. I'll be interested to see just how you go about crushing the Wolf People. Sun Feathers isn't sure you'll ever walk again."

He glared at her.

Pale Raven met his stare with one equally assured. "Hawks Beard left his mark on you, Brave Man. I watched as Sun Feathers splinted your leg. I heard the bones grating, listened to you whimpering although unconscious. I know a lot about bones and how they work. Anyone who butchers at a buffalo jump does. Hawks Beard crushed your knee—crippled you for life."

His fists clenched at his sides. "Power didn't bring me this far for no reason. The voices will tell me what to do. The Dreams will come. And when I know the way, I'll lead the Broken Stones south to find White Ash. On that day the Wolf People will feel the Power of the Broken Stones. On the souls of the dead, I swear it!"

Chapter 12

Basket sat across from her aunt, Owlclover, and her mother, Starwort. Owlclover had been Green Fire's eldest daughter; she now became the camp's leader. In the event of Owlclover's death, the camp would go to Starwort since Owlclover had no other female heirs, except the vanished White Ash. Then, finally, it would go to Basket upon Starwort's death.

Basket studied the interior of the lodge. She had always equated this place with Green Fire's power, but now the lodge looked different, felt different. Green Fire's possessions were gone; they had all been burned lest the witching have left some malevolent presence in the articles. The niches dug into the bench that ran around the inside of the lodge gaped empty. Owlclover would place her own bundles in them as soon as she had time.

Burned lest the witching still be present. How does a clan leader fight witching? How do you purify a camp? The child shifted inside, and Basket rubbed her swollen belly uneasily. The baby would come soon now. Maybe another daughter to strengthen her line.

Basket thought of these things while the two older women engaged in an animated discussion. A mistake in planning could lead to starvation. Spring had begun to show its warming face. Grass greened the hills with a faint tinge on the southern slopes. The time had arrived to begin considering which areas had the best potential for providing food. If the same root grounds were exploited year after year, the Spirits would be angered and grow no more roots there. Instead, the activities of the People had to be spread over a large area to allow the Spirits of the soil and rocks to tend their plants.

Now the responsibility for placating those Spirits fell to Owlclover. Basket noted the strained lines that had formed on her aunt's face. Owlclover's problems were compounded by witchcraft and the coming Gathering, which Green Fire had roped the clan into.

The lodge fire crackled and spit, the wreath of smoke rising toward the smoke hole overhead. Dirt showed between some of the rafters. One day soon the lodge would have to be stripped of its overlying earth and new willow-and-grass matting woven to replace the old before the lodge was re-covered. Green Fire hadn't allowed the work, believing it would change the Power of the lodge, lessen it somehow.

Basket bit her lip, frowning. Green Fire's presence hung like river mist at the top of the lodge. Ghostly echoes of her cackling, cranky voice still reverberated from the closely spaced rafters.

Witching! Why did it have to happen here? To Green Fire, who had been the strength of Three Forks? Basket shivered.

If a witch could kill Powerful Green Fire, how can the rest of us resist?

Owlclover had wrapped the antelope-hide cape of leadership over her broad shoulders. For the first time, she sat on the furs at the back of the lodge in the place reserved for leadership. She listened to Starwort, a hand in front of her mouth. She sat stiffly—as if she wasn't ready for the burdens, or the responsibilities, Green Fire had wielded so artfully.

Starwort idly fingered her braids. Her joints had thickened with the burning swelling that came of old age, and white had begun to show in her hair. A bad fall had stiffened her elbow, and she complained about her teeth as they loosened and fell out.

One day I will sit at the back of the lodge. The responsibility will be mine. How will that feel? Will I have the same hesitation Owlclover seems to have?

Once White Ash would have been in line—but White Ash had disappeared, witched away by the evil Spirits, or, as others said, drowned in the river. The clan had searched the banks for a day's walk and found nothing, not even a piece of clothing. Still another rumor said she'd been stolen by the Sun People. The report had come from a Trader who passed through years ago. He'd told of a girl stolen from the Earth People. The time would have been about the same as White Ash's disappearance.

Which do I want to believe? Witching? Or stolen by people from the far north? If she really was captured, why didn't she ever send word? Basket shook her head, irritated by the thoughts. *Witched . . . that's what I believe. Witched . . . like so many of us at Three Forks.*

Even if the rumor of stealing had a seed of truth to it, White Ash had no doubt adopted the ways of the hideous Sun People. She, too, probably wandered around half-starved and eating raw meat. That, or she had become the cowed victim of a brutish warrior and had already borne several filth-encrusted children to the savage.

Beyond the lodge, the wind whistled eerily, as if Green Fire's ghost howled mockingly at the smoke hole. A heavy gust battered the lodge and a trickle of dirt seeped down between the rafters. Owlclover and Starwort went silent, gazes going to the rafters.

"Just the wind," Starwort whispered to reassure herself. "I think we should look for shooting star up by the Spirit hole where the river runs into the mountain."

Owlclover didn't lower her eyes. As if she hadn't heard, she said, "A night for witches and curses."

Starwort rubbed her forehead. "You're still worried about what Green Fire said?"

Owlclover nodded. "She knew witching. That's what she died saying. 'I've been witched . . . witched . . .' "

Basket cradled her swollen belly with her arms, as if to protect herself and the vulnerable infant. Talk of witching frightened her, especially with the child so close to birth. How many stories had Green Fire told of malignancy entering a woman's vagina during pregnancy and killing the child, or seeping through a woman's womb and rotting her soul? Ever since they'd buried Green Fire, they'd all looked over their shoulders, jumping at little sounds, frightened by sudden stitches of muscle pain they would have ignored weeks ago. A black mantle had descended like ash from a forest fire. She could feel it in the air. People shifted nervously, and the spark had gone out of their conversations.

"Maybe we should move the camp. Go down into Red Canyon. Maybe it's this place." Owlclover tugged at her braid, lips pursed.

Basket shook her head. "Red Canyon is colder. The snow—"

"Hush, girl." Owlclover continued to stare up at the roof.

"You were saying about the biscuit root?" Starwort said in a weak attempt to change the conversation.

Owlclover remained silent as she studied the smoke hole. Then she said, "Let's go up by Monster Rock. We haven't dug roots up there for five seasons."

A voice called from outside, "It's Wolfberry. Can I come in? I need to see Owlclover." He sounded tense—but didn't they all these days?

"Come in, Wolfberry." Owlclover's gaze shifted to the door flap.

Basket's husband ducked through, and Basket stiffened at the expression on his face. She'd seen that look before. Perhaps their marriage had been special; she knew him like she knew herself. A deep-seated fear ate at him.

Owlclover caught his unease as if it carried on the very air. "Is something wrong?"

He crouched at Basket's side, elbows braced on his knees. "Someone is out there. In the night."

Owlclover tensed, gaze darting around the secure walls, then up to the smoke hole again. "A man?"

Wolfberry spread his hands. "I don't know. I saw tracks a couple of days ago—definitely those of a man."

"A couple of days ago? The same day Green Fire died?" Color had drained from Owlclover's face.

Wolfberry nodded. "It didn't seem important. I was going to tell Green Fire. I never got the chance. She . . . it was too late."

Owlclover had closed her eyes. "You *think* there's a man out there now? What did you see?"

Wolfberry shot a quick glance at Basket. "A shadow moving through the sage. I took my darts and went to look."

"It could have been an animal," Basket interjected, seeking a light tone. Her hands went protectively to her belly, and she had to stop herself from reaching down to protect her vagina—as if a hand could keep an evil Spirit from slipping in there.

Why is this happening to us? What did we do? Evil, take yourself and go away!

"What man would skulk around in the sage? It must have been an animal. Maybe a badger, or a bobcat," Starwort agreed. "If it was a person, he'd come in. Ask to be fed and tell the stories."

"Maybe it was Cattail coming back," Basket offered helpfully. "Maybe he left something? Lost something in the brush and—"

"He'd have come in and spent the night," Owlclover interrupted, as if forcing speech through a strangled throat. "Wolfberry, you say you saw tracks the day Green Fire died?"

He nodded. "The marks were scuffed, indistinct. The stride looked right. The person—if that's what it was—avoided places where the soil or snow would take tracks."

"Like a witch," Basket whispered under her breath. *My baby is so close to coming. Please, Creator, don't let anything happen. I couldn't stand it.* Her soul seemed to sicken at the thought.

"Like a witch," Owlclover agreed. Then she said, "You will take all the men at first light and scour every handbreadth out there. Hunt him down. If it's a witch—maybe someone we've suspected—kill him. Kill him quickly. I don't want to be next."

A terrible silence settled on the lodge. *Someone they suspected? Black Hand!*

The voices whispered frantically. *Wake up! Tell them! Tell them what you saw in the Dream!*

Brave Man groaned, retreating from his quest for the gray haze. He opened his eyes, blinked, and glanced around the dim interior of the lodge. Sun Feathers had stopped by to feed him a vile-tasting tea made from willow bark; despite its foulness, it had helped the pain. At the same time, Sun Feathers had packed his wounded knee with a poultice of crushed holly grape[1] to fight the infection. After the initial pain, Brave Man had felt more comfortable.

"Pale Raven? Are you there?"

He could hear a stirring from across the lodge, then a shuffling of hides. Her voice sounded muzzy with sleep. "What is it? Do you need to urinate again? I'll get the bag and—"

"No. It's the Dream. I must stop them."

She sat up, reaching to prod the embers in the fire and adding cottonwood branches collected the night before. As

1. Oregon grape; *Mahonia repens*.

flames rose to light the lodge, she pulled the mass of her raven hair back with slim fingers, studying him.

"The Dream?"

"Yes," he cried. "A war party is leaving to raid the Black Point over on the Fat Beaver River. Flying Hawk is leading them."

She pursed her lips. "I told you that last night."

He nodded, swallowing. "Tell them not to go. It will be a disaster. The Power's not right. They'll be discovered, led into a trap. Some will die, others will be wounded. Tell them not to go."

She cocked her head, eyes narrowing uneasily. "Very well."

"Hurry."

She reached for her dress and slipped her moccasins on. Wrapping a robe around her shoulders, she ducked through the flap and disappeared into the night.

Brave Man exhaled wearily and stared at the flames crackling around the arm-thick branches. His heart beat strongly against his breastbone, driven by the Power of the Dream. Beyond the lodge, the wind played fitfully with the night.

He heard steps, and Flying Hawk ducked through the flap, already dressed in the long war shirt of the Sun People. His pack hung from one hand, war darts and atlatl in the other. A tall, muscular warrior, he inspected Brave Man with keen eyes that stared out from either side of a hawkish nose. Talons had been tattooed in red on his hollow cheeks. For the raid he wore his hair up in a roach pinned by a bone clip carved from a scapula. An amused smile bent his thin lips. "What is this talk?"

Pale Raven slipped in behind him, moving to her place across the lodge.

Brave Man pointed a finger at the man. "Not talk—a Dream. The Black Point will ambush you. A man will see you coming and run to warn the Black Point. I couldn't see it all, but the final trap is in a narrow drainage between two sandstone-capped walls. Their darts will rain down on you, and you won't be able to see to cast back at them. They'll be hidden by the sandstone at the top. On uneven ground, in thick brush, you can't cast uphill accurately. Two men—Flute and Two Shields—will die in the trap. Others will be wounded as they flee. Two more will die as the Black Point chase you away.''

Flying Hawk gave him a disbelieving smile. ''Why should I believe you, Brave Man? This raid has been planned for a long time. Hawks Beard began to talk about it in the middle of winter. He scouted the camps of the Black Point and told us how to attack them. Now you have killed Hawks Beard . . . and I will lead the raid. Do you act against me?''

Brave Man met the warrior's stare. ''I have no love for the Black Point.'' He pulled back his hair to bare the scar on his scalp. ''They did this to me. Only through Power did I escape from the Camp of the Dead where they tried to send me. I wish you luck in killing all of them, but I can't ignore the Dream. When Power speaks, I *must* listen. Power brought me to you. Perhaps it was to save the Broken Stones from defeats such as I have Dreamed. *Do not go on this raid!*''

Flying Hawk laughed. ''I've made Power of my own, Brave Man. I cleansed myself and went to a high place to pray and call upon Bear for courage and cunning. I received no vision of defeat.''

''Don't go, Flying Hawk. I have told you what I saw in the Dream. I can do no more.''

Flying Hawk cast a quick glance across the fire at Pale Raven. ''My warriors are ready to leave. Perhaps we'll see if this Dream of yours has any truth. But I will be most careful to keep from being discovered.'' He jerked his head at Pale Raven. ''She will take *good* care of you until I return, I'm sure. Then we'll talk again.''

''*Don't go!*'' Brave Man shouted as the warrior ducked through the lodge flap.

Pale Raven coolly ignored Flying Hawk's slur. ''He'll go. You couldn't have stopped him. This is his chance to fill Hawks Beard's tracks as the greatest warrior of the Broken Stones. He thinks people will look up to him, that his Power is as great as Hawks Beard's was.'' She smiled humorlessly. ''I wonder if he knows Hawks Beard sired his last child off Flying Hawk's wife, Two Roses?''

Brave Man leaned his head back and grunted. "One would get the feeling Hawks Beard took most of the women in camp."

She studied him from behind lowered eyelids. "He did. He had a way with women that left them wanting more. Unlike most men, he didn't lose his hardness after he planted his seed. He knew women, knew where to touch them, how to move to bring them a great deal of pleasure. He claimed it was his special Power—one of the things that made him great in war—and that he could bestow it with his seed into the women he took. I wasn't the only one he fooled . . . just the only one who got caught."

"But you'd been caught before?"

She nodded easily. "I'd been caught before." She poked at the fire again, unconcerned. "Perhaps I offended Power somewhere along the way. I don't know."

"You sound like you don't care."

She leaned her head back, exposing the firm lines of her throat. "You're young, Brave Man. Have you ever had a woman?"

"No."

"White Ash preoccupied you that much?" She lifted a knowing eyebrow. "I could teach you many things."

"Things learned from your husbands and Hawks Beard?"

She laughed, flashing straight white teeth. "Among others. I make no excuses. I know what I want out of life—and I didn't get it from my first two husbands. I want power and prestige. I am a sensual woman, Brave Man. I demand pleasure, whether it's a finely crafted robe, soft furs to sleep on, or rich meat to eat. I wanted to be loved with passion and vigor. My husbands gave me none of those things."

"Will you give me pleasure?"

The sultry look she gave him sent a thrill through his body.

"To do so might cause you pain."

"Stand up," he ordered. "Take your clothes off. I would like to look at you."

Without a change of expression, she rose to her feet and slipped the soft leather of her dress over her head. She stood before him, feet braced. Firelight caressed the smooth firmness of her flesh. Her breasts were full and upright, unspoiled by an infant's suck; the nipples tightened in the air. Her belly remained flat, muscular, leading down to the black mat of her pubic hair. Muscles rippled in her powerful thighs.

She shook her head, the wealth of her shining hair cascading over her broad shoulders. She met his appraising stare, a defiant pride in her eyes. She looked magnificent, powerful. As she shifted, the muscles in her belly tensed and changed the patterns of light.

He nodded and threw back his robe to expose his stiffening manhood. "Teach me what you know about pleasure. Teach me everything."

Morning drifted softly out of the east as they lay together. The weight of her nourished a curious contentment that spread through his body and warmed his soul. He stroked the rounded curve of her buttocks. Her hands cradled his head, fingers tracing the tops of his ears while her hair spilled around them like a silken veil. Her full breasts pressed against his muscular chest. He began to respond again to the way she moved her pubis against his.

"You learn well," she whispered.

"Who were these two husbands of yours?"

She stared into his eyes, the smooth features of her perfect face inscrutable in the faint light. "My first husband was Flute. The other was Two Shields."

Brave Man slitted his eyes against the sensations rising from his pelvis. "They will die with Flying Hawk."

She nodded. "If your Dream is true, Brave Man. Only if your Dream is true."

"It is."

The voices whispered, *Yes . . . yes.* His manhood rose to meet the needs of her insistent body.

White Ash stopped and pointed to the top of the rise where the drifts melted against the sky. "Someone's there!"

"Those are elk!" Bad Belly protested, shielding his eyes to look up the slope.

"There's someone there. Sitting in the midst of the elk," White Ash insisted.

Bad Belly squinted against the light. The elk seemed unconcerned as they grazed along the saddle he and White Ash climbed toward. He could see the curious shape. It did look like a man.

"It's probably just a hunter's trick of some sort. Maybe a rock cairn piled up to look like a man on a drive line. Look at the elk. They're feeding, not worried at all. I know elk, they're smarter than people. The wouldn't just stand there if a person were so close. I'll bet it's a cairn."

"I don't know. I've got this . . ."

"This what?"

"Funny feeling," she said nervously, refusing to take her eyes off the horizon.

They climbed up the bottom of a snow-filled valley between the shoulders of two mountains. They had spotted the low saddle from below, thinking it a reasonable place to cross south into the Wind Basin. The rocky slopes around them were crumbled and worn where gray outcrops had cracked and tumbled angular detritus down the mountain's flanks. Bitterbrush and occasional sage dotted the steep, rocky soil, as did tawny grasses partially hidden by snow. The vegetation burnished the ground with a light tan. Serviceberry and squaw currant clung to the crevices and irregular drainages. Up to their left, a forlorn grove of aspen waited in a snow-locked hollow. Patchy clouds raced west on the midday wind.

"Funny feeling?" Bad Belly looked around. "I guess I can feel it, too." He looked down at Trouble. The unconcerned dog flopped down to chew the snow out from between the pads on his feet.

"Let's go back," White Ash suggested, almost pleading.

Bad Belly stamped to fight the chill in his bark-wrapped toes. "If we go back through all that snow we just climbed across, my feet are going to freeze. We're on the north slope here, and we're hip-deep in snow. I'm miserably cold as it is—getting colder while we just stand here. It's no more than two dart casts to the top and warm sunlight. I say it's a rock cairn of some sort.''

She sucked at her lips, guilt in her eyes at the mention of the bark he wore so she could have the warm moccasins. "I suppose you're right. Let's hurry then. I feel something . . . like being watched. And that thing up there—human or not— isn't helping any.''

"The elk wouldn't stand there like that. You'll see. The instant they catch sight of us, they'll be gone as fast as . . . well, as scared elk.''

She nodded halfheartedly as Bad Belly forced his shivering body past her to break a trail through the crusted drifts.

I'm always cold these days, he grumbled inwardly, feeling his stiff muscles protest. His feet had gone numb hours ago. Only moving, keeping the painful circulation in his feet, had saved him from frostbite so far—maybe. If he was lucky.

One of the cow elk raised her head—and stared right into his eyes. She took a step forward, her nose lifted high, testing the breeze. They were too far to hear her warning bark, but the entire herd wheeled and disappeared as if they'd never been there.

"Magical creatures," Bad Belly said in praise. Only that curious black silhouette remained, hauntingly human. The figure rested on the horizon, backlit by the sun like a small nipple on the crest of the saddle.

White Ash muttered under her breath. Despite the fact that she walked behind him, he could *feel* her gaze fixed on that human form.

Bad Belly winced at the bitter cold numbing his toes and shuffled ahead. When they crested the ridge, he'd be on the sunny side. Maybe they'd find a place where the rocks radiated the heat so he could sit and warm his chill-pained limbs.

"Strips of woven bark were never made to be walked in," Bad Belly declared. "The Antelope People might get by with it, but they live in the south. Left Hand says the only snow they get down there is just a dusting that melts with the noonday sun. What do we get? Drifts that blow around all winter and make a man's joints ache.''

White Ash remained ominously silent.

The figure rested no more than a dart's throw away now, and Bad Belly had to flail his way through the snow as they encountered the cornice of a huge drift. In the lee of the wall of snow, he lost sight of the figure.

"I don't like this," White Ash whispered, a tremor in her voice. "If anyone is up there, he could walk out on snow-shoes and drive a dart right through us from top to bottom."

"Thank you, I needed to hear that," Bad Belly replied under his breath, using his elbows to break the crusted surface. Underneath, the snow had become granular, like gravelly ice.

Panting, he crawled through the hole he'd mashed in the drift and reached back, offering his good hand to pull White Ash through. Trouble buck-jumped his way up the loose snow, scrambling and clawing to get onto the hard crust above.

Bad Belly had begun to shiver again, as the cold ate into his flesh. He tried to catch his breath as he turned and struggled toward better footing where the rocks poked out. One step out of two broke through the hardened crust; then he felt rock underfoot.

"Made it," he declared, gasping.

Trouble had come to a halt, nose working as he scented the wind. Generally, when he smelled elk, he rushed forward, eager to sniff the scat and poke his nose into the tracks. Now he stood frozen.

"Oh, no." White Ash had stopped short.

Bad Belly blinked against the bright sunlight and stared.

A timeworn old man sat watching them through placid black eyes. He rested on a rock, legs crossed, white hair wrapped in a beaver-skin hat. A robe made from finely tanned mountain sheepskin lay on his shoulders.

The man's face riveted Bad Belly's attention. Old, terribly old. Wrinkles had grooved the features, running down from the corners of the eyes to bracket a thin-lipped mouth. As with most old people, the nose had grown out of proportion to the face, dominating his visage. As if to mock the sag of facial skin, the eyes burned, lit by an inner Power that dwarfed Bad Belly's soul.

Fear knotted tighter than wet rawhide thongs in Bad Belly's breast, but he stepped forward, calling, "Greetings, Grandfather! Lot of snow back there. Lot of . . ."

The figure remained still, as if it might have grown out of the gravelly soil, or eroded from the surrounding rock—part of the mountain's bones.

Bad Belly shivered, partially from the cold, partially from the way his soul quaked as he stared into those forever eyes. "White Ash? Try talking to him in Sun People talk."

She stood paralyzed beside him, her grip tightening until his hand hurt. He glanced at her and found her lips parted, a glazing in her eyes. Trouble had circled to stand behind them, ears cocked as he watched the figure.

The old man spoke, his voice like sand grating between two blocks of wood. "You need not talk in the language of the Sun People, Still Water. That will come in its time."

Bad Belly tried to swallow against the clamp in his throat. "You . . . you know me?"

"It's been a while, Man of the People. You were younger then."

Bad Belly stepped forward as if he were walking over rattlesnakes. He studied the withered face, seeking the familiarity that tickled at the corners of his memory. "Singing Stones?" he asked in wonder. "You are . . . Singing Stones?"

The old man nodded ever so slowly. "I was him."

"Was?" Bad Belly choked. *Not a ghost . . . tell me he's not a Spirit!*

The old man spoke again. "What is any man? A name? A name consists of words, sounds uttered from the mouth. Once I thought I was someone called Singing Stones. A name is folly, illusion."

"W-What do I call you then?"

"Call me Singing Stones. It will be easier for you, for the time being."

"Time . . . being?"

"You and White Ash are shivering. Come, I know a place for you to rest and warm yourselves. I have food there."

Singing Stones rose slowly. Turning to face the sun, he let its rays shine on the furrowed seams of his weathered skin.

"How do you know me?" White Ash asked in a husky voice.

The old man took a deep breath, as if the sensation of breathing itself pleased him. Without turning, he said, "I've known you for many seasons, White Ash. You've filled my Dreams. To a Dreamer, time loses itself, becoming less and more than living people think. I might have missed you had not the Trader, Left Hand, come by my camp. He told me he'd thought to bring Bad Belly to me. Had he done so, Bad Belly wouldn't have been there for you when you needed him. First Man took a hand, weaving the pattern Warm Fire had begun . . . and Left Hand had taken up."

"You came to meet us? You knew we would cross this pass today?"

Singing Stones turned, no expression on his face. "I didn't know you would be here today. I only knew you would be here. I have watched two sunrises since I came to await your arrival."

"Two days? Just sitting there? And you didn't freeze?" Bad Belly shook his head, awed.

"I didn't freeze. My stay was refreshing. You can feel the earth up here, and hear the sky. The One comes more easily since illusion can be discarded with ease. I called the elk to come share their thoughts with me. Elk are delightful company. They are more knowledgeable than people think."

"You called them? Talked to them?" White Ash asked, staring, her mouth open.

Singing Stones nodded, eyes hazy as if he drifted in his thoughts. "We were One. Talking would have been pointless."

"One," Bad Belly mused, recalling the Power Dream he'd had. "But they didn't run away? They sure ran when that lead cow saw us."

"She knew you were not One."

"What do you mean, One? I thought you felt the One only in a Dream . . . or when you died." White Ash had stepped closer to Bad Belly.

Singing Stones smiled again, his expression a reflection of all that was good and peaceful. "You are blinded by illusion in your conscious life. I can tell you no more. Not now. The only way to understand is to be." He motioned. "Come. Let us warm you before the cold damages your bodies."

He led the way, angling off the saddle, picking a careful path through the rounded caps of pink granite. Sheer cliffs dropped away before a vista of the Wind Basin to the south.

White Ash glanced skeptically at Bad Belly. "He *knew* we were coming?"

Bad Belly chewed his lip, squinting after the old man. "He Sang for me when I was little—when the rattlesnake poisoned my arm. I would have died but for his Power."

"Did you understand what he said? All those things about illusion and time?"

Bad Belly shivered from the chill in his limbs. "No. But I think we should go with him."

"I'd rather—"

"There is no place on this earth where you'd be as safe as in Singing Stones' camp. The Wolf People would rather dart themselves than confront him."

"Sun People, on the other hand . . ."

"Then he'll see them coming first. I think he sees everything."

"Was he always like this?"

Bad Belly hobbled on the old man's trail, feet numb with cold. "No. But that funny feeling you had on the other side of the mountain, that was his Power. We both felt it."

"What's the matter?" she asked. "You're shaking your head."

Bad Belly shrugged. "I can understand why he wants you. You're going to be a Dreamer. But why me? I did my part. I was there to save your life. Why can't I go home now?"

She tightened her grip on his hand to reassure him. "Because I need you with me. I'm frightened. Something's going to happen . . . and you're part of it."

"How do you know that?" A crawly feeling worked along his spine.

"It's in the Dreams, Bad Belly." She lowered her eyes. "I haven't told you all of them."

Despite the cramps in his muscles and the frostbite in his feet, a warmth kindled in his gut. He smiled. "I won't leave you if you need me. But maybe you'd better tell me the rest of these Dreams soon."

Chapter 13

Wind Runner ran, forcing himself to the edge of endurance. The muscles of his legs rippled in the afternoon sunlight. He vaulted the sage, fully aware of the risks of running too fast. His starved lungs fought for air. The back of his throat burned hot and dry, and his tongue stuck when he tried to swallow. The tremble of fatigue lay just beyond the threshold of his exertion.

Before him, the buff-colored, sandstone-capped headlands jutted against the sky as they rose to either side. Long, indigo shadows played over the tumbled blocks of sandstone and softened the outlines of sagebrush and rabbitbrush.

Wind Runner threw a quick look over his shoulder; the Broken Stones' warriors had strung out in a ragged line behind. Now they ran a deadly earnest race as his pursuers pushed themselves to match his killing stride.

I must have been out of my mind! He reached the slope, climbing the brush-covered incline in giant leaps while his heart strained and fear frayed the edges of consciousness.

Wind Runner thought back, remembering with pride how he'd stepped forward when Fire Rabbit had come panting into camp calling, "Broken Stones! A party of warriors is coming from the east. I saw them sneaking along the drainage bottoms. There are at least ten of them working up the river!"

One Man and Snail Shell had shouted. "Get your weapons! We can meet them! Keep them from a surprise attack!"

That was when Wind Runner had stepped into their midst, asking Fire Rabbit, "How far away are they?"

"Just below where the caprock is cut by the river. Not far."

He'd looked at One Man. "If we fight in the open, some of us will die. More will be wounded."

One Man had cocked his head. "War is like that, Wind Runner." He'd smiled crookedly. "Or do you plan to take Hot Fat with you to stop the fight partway through?"

"Neither. But you know where the caprock rises to the north? You know the place of the old buffalo jump? If a lone warrior might appear to stumble upon them and then run, perhaps he could lead the enemy to that place. If our warriors were on that caprock, they could deal the Broken Stones a severe blow—and not lose a man."

One Man had hesitated, white teeth sunk into his lip. A deep frown incised his forehead. "And who would act as bait?"

Wind Runner lifted his hands. "Who can outrun me?"

One Man paused. "And if it doesn't work? If you get killed?"

"Then you're no worse off than you would have been. They might even be more reckless, flushed with a feeling of victory. But if it works, we'll send them running and make them consider long and hard before they try us again."

Hot Fat's granddaughter, Aspen, had added from the side, "It might work. Remember what happened to my husband last year? This might be a way to turn their arrogance against them."

Wind Runner had glanced at her, met her veiled look. Since that first night when he and Hot Fat had eaten and talked of Power, she'd watched him, no expression on her heart-shaped face. He still couldn't tell whether or not she even approved of him.

"She's right," Wind Runner said. "The Broken Stones are arrogant. It's always been one of their weaknesses."

One Man had looked up at the sky, watching the red-tailed hawks sail in the rising currents of spring air. "Let's try it. Go, Wind Runner. You'll have to spot them first. Be careful.

We'll be too far away to come to your aid. May the Sun and Thunderbird give you strength to mix with your courage and audacity. Go! Run, my friend. Run like your name. We'll lay the trap.''

Wind Runner had grabbed up his darts and atlatl, giving Aspen a nod of thanks as he trotted from the camp. All eyes had been upon him as the other warriors gathered to follow One Man along the caprock.

I was out of my mind!

Loose dirt compacted under Wind Runner's feet as he flung himself up the slope. He leaped a sagebrush—and turned his foot on a rock as he landed. He fell, pain shooting up his leg. Behind him, the yells of his pursuers split the air. They knew they had him now.

Wind Runner gathered up his spilled darts and limped upward, favoring his ankle. How far? The gap in the headlands seemed so close—and so very far away. Nothing seemed to be broken, but by dung-filled curses, it hurt!

Gritting his teeth, he hobbled on, knowing they would close on him. Grunting against the spearing pain, he continued, spurred by the whoops and shrieks closing-in. He looked back. No more than a dart's throw separated him from the nearest of them.

Wind Runner whirled, a dart nocked in his atlatl. His arm went back and he cast with all his might. His carefully crafted atlatl acted like a springboard to sail the fletched dart in a high arc.

The pursuing warrior danced to the side as the deadly missile hissed past him. By that time, Wind Runner had limped his way up into the rocks under the caprock. Jumbled buffalo bones stuck shattered ends out of the silt that had gathered around them. The splintered tips and scattered ribs mocked of death. A white-bleached buffalo skull stared at him from empty orbits, the top bashed in where the brains had been extracted.

To either side, the rocks rose steeply, impossible to climb. Brush grew thick in here where snow collected in the winter and the roots could feed off the rich waste of the buffalo.

Wind Runner tore into the dense thicket of serviceberry and currant, a cry choking in his throat.

Be up there, One Man. By the Sun and Thunderbird, be there for me ·. . . or I'll die here in this canyon. His ankle had begun to throb until it blanked his senses. He couldn't stop, couldn't take the time to pick his steps. A dart whistled past him, cutting its way into the thick brush.

Wind Runner dove headfirst into the dense growth, crawling like an awkward snake along the bottom of the drainage. The musky scent of the earth—rich with the rot of buffalo—clung in his nostrils. Where the water had cut a channel, he could crawl more easily. Warriors screamed behind him—irritated, no doubt, by the loss of their target.

Wind Runner scrambled along while rocks bruised and scraped his elbows, knees, and belly. Screened as he was by the brush, his pursuers couldn't target him with their deadly darts, but his progress seemed so slow now.

Behind him, brush crackled as yelling warriors pounded closer. They sounded right on top of him. What had happened to One Man and the rest? He'd lost one of his darts, snagged in the twisted stems of the brush.

The drainage sloped up, and now tumbled rock choked the bottom. Driven by panic, he barely felt the angular stones that his limbs battered against. Branches scratched at his face and hair and left angry weals along his bare arms and legs.

A dart lanced down beside him, rattling in the serviceberry stems. Had they seen him? Or just gotten lucky? He wiggled forward, blood pulsing in his ears. A runny fear tickled his guts; the skin on his back tightened to the anticipated impact of a stone-tipped dart.

He slithered beneath an undercut root and came up against a blank wall of rock. He searched—and could find no way up without exposing himself to the razor-pointed darts of the Broken Stones.

I'll die here! He squirmed around a thick growth of wild plum and sought to fit a dart into his atlatl. Only two darts left? He stared at the long shafts he clutched. What had happened to the others?

Brush cracked and shivered behind him. "Come out, little Black Point! Come out and die!" a happy warrior called.

"Find him! He'll warn the others, make the Dream come true!" a man shouted from down below. *"Find him!"*

Yet another voice answered, *"You* come up here and look, Flying Hawk! He's got darts! Poking around in here is like reaching under rocks for a rattlesnake. You can get bit!"

The first complained, "Why are Flying Hawk and the rest hanging back? If it was that trap the White Clay Dreamed about, the Black Point would have already shown up to fight us—unless their courage is as weak as winter urine."

Wind Runner cocked his head. *White Clay? Who?*

"Flute? Look up there at the head of the canyon. He can't climb out without taking enough darts to look like porcupine's big brother."

"Be careful! He's got a good arm. We have to see him first."

"Hey! Black Point! You hiding in there like a woman? Is that how you crotch-bleeding girls fight? Crawling around in the bushes?"

"Black Point *like* bushes! That's where they go to warm their manhood in their mother's mouths!"

Raucous laughter broke out. Wind Runner ground his teeth. Broken Stones bastards never changed. Filthy, skulking maggots!

"You mean their father's mouths," yet another jeered. "Or do they bend their fathers over and poke themselves into the anus? You hear that, Black Point? You squirt yourself into your father's anus!"

"That's why they call themselves *Black* Point! A good joke, eh?"

Wind Runner stared up through the web of branches that veiled his hiding place. One Man hadn't made it—or had let him down after all.

"Hey, Black Point! Do you do it with dogs, too?"

Wind Runner ran a nervous hand over his face. That was it. He'd take no more.

He rose slowly to his feet, peering out over the bud-thick tops of the chokecherry.

A voice sang out, "There he is!"

A dart hissed and cut the side of Wind Runner's war shirt. Wind Runner didn't miss a heartbeat in the reconsideration of his courage. He promptly dropped flat on his belly, heedless of the dart the branches ripped out of his hand. He wiggled with the speed of brother weasel, trying to crawl quietly and quickly.

Where in Sun's bloody light had One Man disappeared to? Calls sounded and brush scratched against the pursuers' clothing. Wind Runner pulled himself into a ball as a victory-charged warrior crashed past on the other side of a mat of serviceberry.

"Are you sure you saw him?" one of the voices asked. "Maybe it was a shadow? Some other animal? A coyote or bobcat?"

"It was *him*!"

"Spread out!" another voice ordered. "If he's here, we have to go through in a line, drive him up to the head of the canyon and trap him."

Wind Runner winced. Unfortunately, that would work.

"Flying Hawk! You and the rest get up here! It's no trap . . . or we would have been attacked by now!" a bellowing voice shouted.

Was that the problem? Only a few of the Broken Stones had come to hunt him? Wind Runner gripped the thick layer of leaves he lay on—and had an idea. He began to burrow into the mat. A flush of hope warmed his heart. If he could bury himself in the leaves, he might have a chance—ever so thin, but still a chance.

And I'll find my way back to One Man's camp. So help me, if I live through this, I'll kill him this time. I'll drive a dart through him before he has a chance to blink! No one leaves Wind Runner out to be a Broken Stones target. No one!

"Will it burn?" one of the pursuing warriors asked.

Wind Runner's heart stopped. If they set fire to his sanctuary . . . *no, don't even think about it!*

"Too much sap in the brush. I think it would just smolder. These buds are too wet, too close to snowmelt."

Wind Runner sighed relief despite himself.

"Well, it's about time! Welcome to the hunt, Flying Hawk. We thought you and the rest had decided it was too dangerous for your—"

A chorus of ululations broke out from above.

"*It's a trap!*" a warrior shrieked in panic.

Screams, shouts, and shrieks split the air as brush broke under the weight of frantic human beings. Darts whistled and hissed and clattered on rocks. Confusion and death sounded from all sides.

Wind Runner cautiously dug himself out of the moldy leaves, reluctant to move, as afraid he'd be skewered by his friends atop the caprock as killed by the Broken Stones.

From high overhead One Man's bellowing voice called, "Run, you Broken Stone dogs! Run like jackrabbits from a wolf! Show us your tracks, you miserable old women! Ha!"

Rocks cascaded, followed by a rattle of gravel and dirt as feet slid down. Nearby a man groaned in pain.

"Snail Shell! Make sure that one's dead. I'll bash this one's brains just for good measure. Hey, Wind Runner? You in here? You still alive? Or did you shit yourself to death?"

Wind Runner peered over the top of the brush. Fire Rabbit was smashing a heavy slab of sandstone down onto something. The hollow, pulpy sound had to come from flesh being crushed.

"You took long enough!" Wind Runner pushed through the brush, wincing at the agony that shot up from his ankle. Now that he'd been saved, the hurt left him light-headed. Amazing how sheer, gut-twisting terror could stop pain.

Fire Rabbit stared at the remains of his victim. "They wouldn't all come up. They waited, just out of dart range, as if they knew we were there." He grinned. "That made some of us suspicious. One Man had faith in you, though. He said it would work, that they were just being cautious. That if you had the guts and courage to stay alive, the rest of the Broken Stones would come. You did . . . and they did. Victory! Wind Runner, *you did it!*" Fire Rabbit whooped and jumped up and down, a Song bursting from his lungs.

Wind Runner hobbled over and stared down at the Broken

Stones warrior A dart stuck out of the man's side, driven down through the pelvis. The face had been crushed, effect of the boulder that had been dropped on his head.

"And One Man?"

"He's chasing the Broken Stones. I'll bet we get another two or three besides these two. Four or five are wounded. One looks like he'll die on the way. Blue Wind's dart took him low in the back and two of the Broken Stones had to support him. I think there will be a lot of wailing in their lodges."

Wind Runner hopped on one foot and braced himself on Fire Rabbit's shoulder. "We'll have a little wailing here in this canyon if you don't help me get my hurt ankle out of here."

Fire Rabbit laughed. "We saw that. You sure made them howl. They thought you'd really hurt yourself."

"I did," Wind Runner growled.

To the east, Flying Hawk led his staggering band, stopping his warriors periodically to launch darts and keep the pursuing Black Point at bay. He kept to the middle of the broad floodplain of the Fat Beaver River so they couldn't be flanked or ambushed.

If they survived this raid, it would be a miracle. Flute and Two Shields had died in the first volley of darts. White Smoke would die of the wound in his back. Claps Hands staggered along, looking haggard, blood draining out of the hole a sharp dart had cut through his thigh. How many more would die?

Flying Hawk had been careful, made leery by Brave Man's Dream. At the same time, the scout couldn't have been allowed to escape. Surely the Black Point wouldn't have sat up on that caprock while one of their fellows was hunted like a wounded jackrabbit. Surely the place wasn't right—except it had been. And whoever waited up on that rim had managed his warriors with a fist harder than quartzite.

Just like Brave Man said. Flying Hawk glanced back at the Black Point, who followed them like wolves after a winter-starved elk herd. *A new Power has come to the Broken Stones.*

He looked up at the sun, now dipping to the western horizon. "Get me out of this, Thunderbird. You'll take enough of our souls to the Camp of the Dead this day. Just get me and those who still live out . . . and I will follow your new Soul Flier who sees the future in his Dreams. Flying Hawk swears this on his soul."

White Ash woke to the smell of roasting meat and the sweet tang of biscuit root. She lay in a rock shelter: a hollowed-out sandstone overhang capped by rimrock. A Spiral had been painted with rich red ocher on the wall at the rear of the shelter. A magpie perched on a wooden peg that jutted from the back wall. The bird cocked its head, cawing softly as it eyed her.

"Oh? She's up, you say?" Singing Stones' gravelly voice asked.

She peered over the piled mound of her bedding. Singing Stones squatted on the flat boulder that had fallen out of the roof and tended the fire. Back hunched, sunlight catching the infinity of wrinkles on his face, he looked so fragile that she could imagine a puff of wind might blow him away. Where his wrist stuck out of his thick sheepskin coat, the bones could have been willow sticks attached to a dried mockery of a gnarled hand.

The bird uttered a hollow clicking.

"Yes, she did sleep a long time." Singing Stones replied. The magpie emitted a guttural squawk as it dipped its head.

"You talk to the bird?" White Ash sat up. The robes had been delightfully warm and soft. The thick piles of furs had been placed on a bed of grass. How long had it been since she'd slept so soundly? How long since she'd done nothing but sleep? None of the Power Dreams had crept into her slumber. Despite the meal they'd eaten the night before, her stomach yawned emptily.

The hanging door hides had been pulled to the side. Golden sunshine poured through to illuminate the shelter and the soot-stained walls. Skin bags hung from the ceiling in the back—beyond even the most ingenious bushy-tailed packrat's reach. Several sandstone slabs on the dirt floor marked the location of storage cysts an arms' length from the back wall, out of the rodent zone but still back from ground moisture that seeped in from beyond the drip line. Three differently styled fire hearths—a rock-filled shallow basin, a slab-lined hearth, and a deep roasting pit—had been placed in a triangular arrangement in the center. Two sandstone slabs had been planted upright as breeze deflectors for the fires.

Outside, ragged mountains broke against the horizon. Clots of dark-green timber contrasted with buff-colored sandstone outcrops that tumbled weathered talus into the cool blue shadows where deep snow lingered. A breeze—rich in scents of bitterbrush, grass, and damp earth—carried the warmth of the sun-shot rock into the shallow shelter.

Singing Stones smiled at her, exposing the few brown pegs of teeth that remained in his jaws. The wrinkles on his face rearranged into a complex pattern of contentment. "Yes, I talk to many creatures. Even to Dreamers, eh? Powerful Dreamers . . . like you."

She lowered her eyes and pulled her shining black hair away from her face. "Everyone seems to think I'm a Dreamer except me. What happens if I don't *want* to be this Dreamer?"

The wrinkles on Singing Stone's face pulled themselves into another pattern. "Oh, you won't want to. No one *wants* to be a Dreamer. That's part of the way Dreamers are—at least, the good ones. Any fool could wish to be a Powerful Dreamer, but he sees only the Power and how it could do things for him. Make him an important person whom others look up to. That sort of thing. What the idiot doesn't understand is that you don't use Power. It uses you. Anyone who *wants* to Dream knows not what he asks—and is generally denied by Power in the end." He shook his head. "No, young White Ash. Dreaming is for those who *have* to Dream."

She wiped the sleep from her eyes and crossed her ankles as she leaned against the rock wall to study him. "I don't want to Dream. I want to be left alone."

Singing Stones poked at the fire with a stick. "You have some time . . . short though it might be. You and Bad Belly.

In the end, as is the way with all Dreamers, you will have to make a choice between the One and the things of this world. You will have to choose illusion or truth.''

She stood and pulled on Bad Belly's shirt, walking over to stare down into Singing Stones' sparkling eyes. The yellow light of morning glowed amber on the soft folds of his ancient skin. "I'll have to choose? And if I refuse to make a choice?''

A fleeting smile played over his lips. "It doesn't work that way, Mother of the People. Power isn't like an old coat that you can discard along the trail of life. It's like your arms, or your legs, or your heart. It's part of you. You can decide not to use an arm—a useful example illustrated by Bad Belly's crippled condition.

"No, my girl. When you follow the path of the Sun, you will act through Power. Before you can attend to the tasks that await you, you need to learn the way of Power, to fly to the stars and talk to the Spirits of the ancestors, to Wolf Dreamer and Fire Dancer, and to the animals.''

She cocked her head. "Attend to the tasks that await me? Listen, I watched the last of my clan butchered before my eyes. I've been beaten and raped. I killed the man who did that to me . . . and almost died of exposure and starvation not too many days ago. I know you're a great Dreamer, Singing Stones, but I'm just not ready for you, or Power, or anything else. I need time to mourn my dead and decide what I'm going to do. Not only that, I can't stay here. It's too close to the Wolf People . . . and I'll kill the first one who shows up to share your lodge fire.''

His beneficent smile never changed. "You have a long path ahead of you, Mother of the People. For the moment, you're upset, unsure of which way to turn, when to fight or run. You live on the ragged edge of unthinking panic, like a young fawn who has become separated from the herd. Be patient. Prepare yourself and find your center.''

She took a deep breath. "You *don't* understand. I'm not—'' Her glance stopped at Bad Belly's empty sleeping spot. A cold knot contracted under her heart.

"Perhaps I understand more than you know.'' Singing Stones said. "But we have talked enough about Dreams and

Power for now. Your ears are closed and your mind has the resiliency of rock. Here, this is ready to eat. Sit.'' He patted the hides next to him. ''Sit, White Ash. Mountains do not rise to the sky overnight. Mighty forests do not spring to soaring heights between a mouse's breaths. The workings of Power, and the making of a Dreamer, must come in their own time.''

''Where's Bad Belly?'' she asked warily. Bad Belly wouldn't have left her, would he? He wouldn't have given her over to the old Spirit Healer and turned his back?

Singing Stones chuckled, reading her thoughts. ''Still Water left early this morning.''

''Where?'' She stood, crouched as if to dart away. ''Which way did he go? How long ago?''

As Singing Stones gazed at her, his old eyes seemed to fall in upon themselves. ''You are frightened?'' His voice dropped to a whisper. ''Yes . . . I see. You have died, have lost all you loved. She who was the old White Ash drowned in the river. That old White Ash drifts in silence beneath the water now, passing among the rocks and moss in the cool darkness.''

''Where's Bad Belly?'' She bent down and grabbed him by the shoulders. *''Where's Bad Belly? Did he leave me behind?''*

Singing Stones met her stare and she stopped. The wild desperation twisted sideways in her mind as she looked into those incredible eyes. She seemed to lose her balance, barely realizing as her fingers slipped from his shoulders. Her soul melted, drifting off in a new direction, losing purpose.

''Sit and eat,'' the gentle voice commanded, surrounding her resistance and overcoming the fragments of her opposition. ''Your body needs the food. Still Water will be back soon. He is on the ridge top looking at a star wheel I built up there. He has not left you. Nor will he.''

When he smiled, her soul leaped with warmth, as if a tingling heat flowed to wrap itself around her.

She blinked and shook her head when she finally managed to regain control of her scattered thoughts and tear her gaze from his. The shelter reeled, as if it had slipped in and out of focus. She bent her head and gripped the bridge of her nose between thumb and forefinger, squeezing as if to fix her wavering vision. "How do you do that? Make a person lose her soul like that?"

"It's a simple shifting of Power," he admitted freely. "You will learn how one day. I used it only to make you relax. Do eat before the meat gets cold. I'll spoon out some of this biscuit root. I think you'll like it. I use a special seasoning made of seeds from a pepper plant that grows many months' journey to the south. One of a group of important plants that will change the Sun People forever."

She accepted the meat, using her teeth to tear off tender bites. Juicy and oddly spiced, the wonderful taste ran over her tongue. She attacked the rest, finally licking the drips from her hands and forearms. "What was that?"

"I fed you yearling buffalo, but the flavor is in that plant I was telling you about. You have to grind the fruits, you see. That's what gives the meat that warm flavor—like bee plant in spring, but this keeps all year when it's dried. A Trader brings me a pack of it every time he comes through."

She took the horn bowl full of steaming biscuit root he offered and stared aimlessly into it. Then she shook her head slowly. "Singing Stones, the entire weave of my life has come undone. Everyone I loved is dead. From the moment we left the Fat Beaver River, my whole world began to fall apart. I don't have anything left. Not even myself." She clamped her eyes shut. "What's *happening* to me?"

He placed a withered hand on her shoulder. "A new way, child. Be at peace. I told you the truth when I said that the old White Ash died at the bottom of the river. To follow the way of Power, you must die and be reborn. Water is the life-giver, the seed of Father Sun that is dropped on the Earth Mother. You passed through water and were reborn to a new life. Nothing remains of the old White Ash; you can't go back."

She shivered at the ghostly thoughts in her mind. "You mean all those people died because of me? I was the real destruction of the White Clay?"

Singing Stones worked his thin brown lips. "The end of

the White Clay served many purposes. Peoples—be they Wolf People, Earth People, Sun People, or any others—have existences of their own. They, too, live on the Spiral, each in their place. Some, like the Earth People and the Wolf People, are ancient. Other Peoples form and dissolve within a generation, like babies who die after only a few days of life. The Sun People are like anxious young men who have just found their manhood. They are a vigorous People, and from their place on the Spiral, they have a great destiny. The Sun leads them south . . . far south indeed. There they will raise their feathered god to the sun and become proud and forget the One. But some will stay here, in this land. They will remember the One and keep Wolf sacred."

"And I'm part of this?"

He nodded again, rubbing his hands together. "You and Still Water. You are the future. You bridge the worlds. You have a very important part to play. Yours is the blood of First Man and Fire Dancer. These Sun People, they are a young race. Someone must take the blood of First Man to them. Someone needs to set their feet on the path of the Spiral. I don't know all the ways of it yet . . . and I suppose I won't know until my spirit leaves this body and travels the Spiral."

She sighed and dipped up some of the biscuit root, savoring the flavor before licking the sweet paste from her fingers. "None of this makes sense."

Singing Stones pulled at the loose skin on his chin. "No. It won't for a while yet. And to find the way to the One, you need the Wolf Bundle. It Sings with a thousand voices—all that is and is not. If the Wolf Bundle deems you worthy, it will open the path to the One for you. The Bundle will guide you . . . and Dream you back."

"What is this bundle?" Bad Belly called as he stepped into the shelter. Trouble followed at his heels, looked around, and then flopped in a heap to chew at his tail.

"The Bundle," Singing Stones said to himself, lost in private thoughts.

White Ash set the horn bowl aside and leaped to her feet to hug Bad Belly. "I thought you were gone, that you'd left me behind."

His homely face flushed nervously. "I almost did."

She gasped and stared into his eyes, seeking to prove to herself that it wasn't so. "I need you, Bad Belly. Don't leave me. Don't go off and leave me here by myself."

He tried to shrug it off. "I wouldn't. It's just that . . . well, I climbed up on top of the ridge to look at the star wheel Singing Stones made. You were asleep. I couldn't bring myself to waken you, not when you were resting for the first time—and even smiling in your sleep. So, anyhow, Trouble and I climbed up there. It's a special—"

"Bad Belly, you said you almost *left* me!"

He grinned shyly. "I'd never do that—not on purpose, I mean. No, what happened was that I sort of got to looking at the sky instead of where I was walking, trying to picture it at night, you see? Well, that's when I realized Trouble had stopped, and I turned around to see what he was doing and . . . and almost walked off the edge of the cliff."

She sighed. "That's what you meant by not coming back? That you almost killed yourself?"

He avoided her eyes. "It happens sometimes. I get lost in my head, thinking about things."

"Still Water? Come eat some of this," Singing Stones called as he lifted a slab of meat on a willow spit.

"Come on," she told him, taking his hand. "It's wonderful."

She sat down with Bad Belly, keeping a hand on his knee, imagining him as he walked along the ridge top, eyes to the sky, no care of where he was or that a misstep would dash him on the rocks below. Her heart skipped; but then, such things made Bad Belly who he was. She didn't just need him; *he needed her!*

"The Bundle," Singing Stones whispered in a dreamy tone. "The Bundle of First Man. The Wolf Bundle. That's the key to all the Power you'll need. What I can't teach you, the Bundle will."

Bad Belly chewed thoughtfully, swallowing. "You mean the sacred Bundle of the Wolf People?"

Fear drove like an icicle through White Ash's chest.

"Yes. It's been calling to me." Singing Stones glanced

slyly at Bad Belly. "You'll have to go steal it from them, you know. The Wolf People won't just turn loose a Power object like the Wolf Bundle."

Bad Belly gaped at the old man.

"Steal the . . ." White Ash's words choked in her throat. "Are you crazy?"

Chapter 14

Brave Man held his tongue as the debate began around the Broken Stones council fire. Power pulsed through him, accompanied by the driving ache in his head. The voices whispered, *Now is the time. Now you will make your place.*

The crackling fire lit the Broken Stones camp, dancing off the tan lodge covers in the background. It shone on the anxious faces of the people who ringed the council circle, waiting to hear about the failed raid. Many had buffalo robes over their shoulders; others had dressed in their best elk-hide jackets, decorated with elk ivories and breastplates of tubular bone beads arranged in parallel rows. The warriors wore their long hunting coats, each coat painted with the symbols of his Power. The women stood in knots, whispering to each other, casting suspicious glances at Flying Hawk.

Brave Man studied Flying Hawk through slitted eyes. The warrior sat cross-legged, stoic face lit by the rising flames of the bonfire. The red-talon tattoos on his cheeks gleamed gaudily. He had done his hair in two simple braids that hung over the shoulders of his bear-hide war shirt. Despite the fact that his fate as a war leader would be decided here, his face could have been carved of stone.

The clan leader, Buffalo Tail, and the old Soul Flier, Sun Feathers, were seated across from Flying Hawk. Buffalo Tail's wife, Cloudy Sky, a large woman with a round face, sat to his right.

Other warriors, including Fat Elk, Long Bone, and Buffalo Leg, sat in a wedge behind Flying Hawk. Their position argued in the war leader's favor since they backed him despite the disaster.

Brave Man had been placed to one side as befitted a new voice at the council. He ignored the speculative glances cast at Pale Raven, who sat beside him. He could feel the warmth of her body, and it satisfied something in his soul. Let the people stare and whisper behind their hands. Opinions about his woman wouldn't change what would happen tonight.

The rest of the camp packed around the council circle, eager to hear every word. Children crawled between their parents' legs, staring out at the solemn event.

"Tell us what happened," Buffalo Tail began.

Flying Hawk told them, starting at the beginning, finally coming to the ambush. "I stopped short of the place." Flying Hawk gestured to emphasize his words. "Brave Man had warned me. He had told me we would be discovered by the Black Point and that an ambush would occur in a drainage between two sandstone-capped walls. I then had to decide what to do. Should I let this lone warrior go? If I did, would Brave Man's vision come true? Would we suffer a terrible defeat when this man escaped to tell his people of our presence? Or was this the place Brave Man had seen in his vision? The sandstone couldn't be climbed where we were, so I couldn't send one of my men to look over the top."

Brave Man nodded to himself as he fingered his chin. *Just as I saw in the Dream. Yes, Power fills the gray mist of the Dream. Imagine what I would know if I could penetrate the gray haze and command the golden bliss!*

Flying Hawk continued, "I thought about it as we chased the Black Point warrior. I sent two warriors ahead since the Black Point had hurt himself fleeing from us. I thought the two warriors would spring the trap if there were one—and might kill the lone warrior if there weren't. Meanwhile, we waited. The brush was thick in the canyon and offered many places for the Black Point to hide.

"After a while it looked like it wasn't a trap. Would the Black Point let one of their own be hunted like a wounded rabbit? The two men I had sent ahead called out for me to come and to bring the rest of our group so we could kill the hiding warrior and be on our way. No sooner had we stepped into the canyon than the caprock above exploded with darts.''

Flying Hawk turned to stare at Brave Man. "It was just the way you warned me. Of the ten I took with me, four are dead: Flute, Two Shields, White Smoke, and Claps Hands. Their widows are mourning, cutting off their hair and slashing their arms even as we speak.''

Sun Feathers leaned his head back to stare at the night sky. Behind him, the weathered leather of his lodge reflected the yellow flickers of the fire.

Buffalo Tail asked in a soft voice, "Do any of the warriors who followed Flying Hawk wish to add anything? Dispute anything?''

Yellow Rock cleared his throat. He had a long face with a hooked nose; a round circle had been tattooed on his forehead. "I went with Flying Hawk. I was present during all of these things he spoke of. I would want everyone to know that I urged him forward when the Black Point ran into the canyon to hide in the brush. He held me back, fearing a trap. I do not blame Flying Hawk. I would follow him on a raid again. I have spoken.''

Buffalo Leg called out, "I do not think Flying Hawk made a mistake. I think it was Power. I think Power worked against us.''

People shifted uneasy glances toward Brave Man. He nodded slowly. "It was Power. We were meant to learn a lesson.'' He looked around, finding nothing but suspicion and worry in the faces of the audience.

"It is the wrong time to war on the Black Point,'' he continued. "I've discussed it with the voices in my head, and I have heard their counsel. I was warned about Flying Hawk's raid, and I tried to stop it. I called Flying Hawk to my lodge to warn him. I didn't understand why the Power would have gone bad. But it's come clear to me since. Thunderbird does not want us warring with the Black Point right now. Power calls us to war against the Wolf People. They block the way to the south. As they wiped out the White Clay, they would wipe out the name of the Broken Stones.''

Brave Man paused, making a circular gesture with his palm down. ''Just like a man might smooth dirt with his hand. The name of the Broken Stones would be heard no more. Where we sit this evening, only silence would remain. Not even the whisper of the wind in the sagebrush would recall the Broken Stones.''

People gasped. Those standing closest to Brave Man backed up a step, crowding those behind.

''That is the warning of the Dream,'' Brave Man continued. ''The time has come for us to turn on a greater enemy—the Wolf People. The lesson is there for all to see. The White Clay warred with the Broken Stones and the Black Point. Their warriors were killed and their strength disappeared like blood through an open wound. In the end, the Wolf People dragged them down like an old buffalo bull. The bones of the White Clay lie bleaching in the sun. What do the Broken Stones wish for their bones?''

In the following silence, only the yipping of distant coyotes could be heard.

Sun Feathers hawked and spat into the fire. ''I have had no such Dream.''

''Nor did you Dream about the ambush of Flying Hawk's war party,'' Brave Man countered. Words came to him, whispered by the voices in his head. ''I don't know what to think of your Power, Soul Flier. I think you have a different kind of Power from mine. Maybe stronger, maybe not. But men must hear the words of Power and then make their own decisions. My Power says we should go south. I don't know why we are pushed that way. Power uses people in different ways for its own purposes.'' He took a malicious pleasure in the use of Old Falcon's words. A doubling of Power came from turning the dead man's words against him. The voices chattered and giggled in Brave Man's head.

Flying Hawk raised his hands. ''When we were fleeing from the Black Point, I called out to Thunderbird, telling the messenger of Sun's Power that if he would save the rest of us, I would follow the Power Brave Man has brought us.''

Sun Feathers didn't move a muscle as he studied Flying Hawk.

Buffalo Tail shifted uneasily. "Do you think Brave Man has brought us Power?"

People had begun to whisper to one another. Brave Man could hear feet scuffing the earth and the rustle of robes being resettled.

"I think he brings Power," Flying Hawk answered with certainty. "We all watched him kill Hawks Beard. Some people said that Brave Man would die of his wounds. But he survived—and warned me about the trap." The keen-eyed warrior looked around. "I refused to believe him at first. I believe him now. If Brave Man's Power says we should war on the Wolf People, then I think we should. I have no more to say."

A babble of conversation broke out.

Buffalo Tail stood, gesturing for silence. "My people, we have heard Flying Hawk's story of what happened on the raid. I think he did a good job leading the raid. I think we shouldn't hold him responsible for what happened." He turned his heavy-lidded eyes on Brave Man. "Instead of worrying about Flying Hawk's courage and sense, we should consider Brave Man's vision of raiding the Wolf People."

Brave Man struggled to stand, leaning on Pale Raven to cushion the throbbing pain in his stiff leg. He studied the people, reading uncertainty in their eyes and in the tight set of their mouths. Some glanced worriedly about. Others looked grim. Fear glittered in the eyes of the elderly.

To the people, he spoke. "Our way has always been south, People of the Sun! For the moment, we have a chance to catch our breath. But how long will it be until the Snow Bird, or the Hollow Flute, or the Wasp clan begins to cast covetous eyes at the rich lands we now hunt? I know, some will say, 'Let them come! The warriors of the Broken Stones will send them running north again, bearing their dead to weeping widows.' "

Brave Man pivoted on his good foot, challenging those who watched him with reservation. "The White Clay told themselves that very thing. With my own ears I heard it spoken just that way. The warriors who laughed and threatened the Broken Stones and the Black Point are dead . . . their clan is only a memory.''

"We are the Broken Stones,'' Buffalo Tail insisted, pulling himself up to full height. "The White Clay were never strong. They never had the Power with them. All they wanted to do was stay in the Bug River valley and hunt. They had no heart for war.''

Brave Man laughed, slapping a hand against his good leg. "Is that what you think? That they had no heart for war? Think back! Count the dead, Buffalo Tail. Remember the faces and tell me if the White Clay didn't kill two for every one of their own dead.'' Brave Man made an imploring gesture. *"I was there!* At no time did the White Clay number more than ten tens of warriors, yet they kept you—and the Black Point—at bay for many seasons.''

"And they are gone today,'' Cloudy Sky scolded, her arms crossed, face angry.

"They are gone,'' Brave Man agreed. "But not because they didn't fight like cornered badgers. I *knew* those warriors. I can remember the gleam in their eyes when they talked of war. I felt the presence of their courage. But strong arms and hearts—even hearts filled with an anger as fierce as that of a silver bear—weren't enough to save the White Clay. They made a mistake.''

"What mistake?'' Sun Feathers asked, stepping forward to peer up at Brave Man.

"They forgot the ways of Power.'' Brave Man raised a finger. "They couldn't read the signs of the sun. They didn't heed their Soul Flier, Old Falcon.''

"You are awfully young to be talking about the ways of Soul Fliers and Power,'' Sun Feathers said casually.

Brave Man lifted his head, staring down his nose. "Power isn't tied to a man's age. It's tied to his soul, respected elder. The White Clay were destroyed when they split their strength into three bands. Two of those bands declared they would hold the Fat Beaver Valley, with its wonderful hunting and mild wintering grounds. They refused what Power asked of them. Now the winter wind whistles through their bones.''

Sun Feathers cocked his head, an amused expression on his face. "And *you* know what Power asked of the White Clay?"

Brave Man scuttled the urge to strangle the old man. "Yes, old one. The destiny of the Sun People lies in the south. Those who refuse to follow the path of the sun will be destroyed or discarded."

"And what if we don't believe this vision of yours?" Sun Feathers asked, eyes narrowing.

The fire popped, and whirling sparks rose to flicker out in the night sky. Tension gripped the people. A breeze wavered the flames and tugged at robe hems and fringes before going still again.

"Then you, too, will be destroyed or discarded. Power will not be ignored. We can't help but follow the path of the sun. As long as we do, victory will follow upon victory. If we try to stay here, or move back to the north, one disaster will pile upon another."

"And you know these things, White Clay?" Sun Feathers sniffed disdainfully. "What are you, Brave Man? Who are you?"

The voices cackled in Brave Man's head, hissing their anger.

Brave Man smiled grimly and raised his hands to the starry skies, ignoring the agony in his knee as he stood free of Pale Raven's support. "I am the way of Power, old one. I am the future of the Broken Stones."

"You are—"

"Consider, before you speak, Sun Feathers," Brave Man interrupted. "Who came into your camp with nothing? Who killed your most powerful warrior? Who Dreamed and warned of the Black Point trap? I did that! Brave Man! I, who escaped from the Camp of the Dead despite Black Point Power. I, who survived the last of the White Clay!" He glowered at the old man. "Think carefully, Soul Flier. Search yourself and ask if you know all the ways of Power. Can you deny what I have said? Is your Power the same as mine?"

Sun Feathers' lips twitched as he met Brave Man's glare. "I don't know what you are."

Brave Man nodded. "But I do, old one. I am the future."

Sun Feathers bristled and made the cutting-off sign with his hand. "I think this is enough for tonight. We all need to think, to weigh the words of the elders against those of brash young men."

At that, the old Soul Flier pushed past, the people parting before him. He walked pridefully, a Powerful man who knew his position. At the same time, anger bristled from his stiff back.

Buffalo Tail took a deep breath, staring into the fire. "Let us all go and think. Much has been said here tonight."

The people began to trickle away, voices hushed as they faded into the night and the shadows of the lodges.

Flying Hawk rubbed his face and stood. He turned to Brave Man. "Is it true? That the Wolf People would wipe us out?"

Brave Man nodded. "If you doubt, ask the White Clay."

"And what about after we destroy the Wolf People?" Buffalo Leg asked.

Brave Man pointed to the south. "There, beyond the lands held by the Wolf People, is another land. I've seen the Sideways Mountains. Beyond them lies the land of the Earth People. The farther south you go, the more Powerful the sun is. There, in the Wind Basin, people do not starve in winter. They have so much food they don't have to move to follow the herds. In a land so rich, the Broken Stones will grow strong. Our infants won't die of hunger. Power has shown me this way. The Earth People are not used to war. We will kill their warriors and take their women. Our way lies toward the sun. That is the reason we're driven to the south."

He leaned on Pale Raven and hobbled toward his lodge.

She whispered, "You have loosed a nest of hornets among us. Sun Feathers will do everything he can to stop you."

"Let him try," Brave Man grunted against the pain. "For now, the seeds of the future have been cast upon the soil. They will grow strong and tall."

"You have a lot of faith in yourself," she responded dryly.

"Power will not let me down. I will Dream again—soon. And when I do, the Wolf People will know fear."

"And you'll get your White Ash?"

"She's almost mine."
The voices cooed, *Yes. Yes.*

Wind tripped along the open ridge top with all the purpose of a young boy lost in his head. It wiggled the brown grasses so recently released from the grip of the snow, and tugged gently at White Ash's robe. She and Bad Belly sat on the eastern edge of a circle made of stones. Ten paces across, it had been placed at the highest point of the ridge. Lines of head-sized stones crossed the diameter of the circle. Bad Belly laid aside his bow-drill and the flat, triangular rock he'd been drilling to make a necklace. He stared down at the small bow and the drill—a thin shaft of hardwood circled by the bow-string. The drill shaft fit into a block of wood that a normal man would hold with his weak hand to steady and guide the drill. Bad Belly had to rest his chin on it while he sawed back and forth on the bow. Periodically, Bad Belly would wet the tip of the drill and dip it into fine white sand before fitting it back in the hole he laboriously drilled in the tooth. The sand acted as an abrasive while Bad Belly's saliva lubricated the cutting.

The dusky light fled from the deepening lavender of the sky, and night's chill descended on the land. From this high point, the whole of the Wind Basin lay exposed to the south. Blue shadows crept among the distant ridges that rippled across the lowlands in dappled patterns of rock and drainage. The southern land drew their eyes, leading ever onward until it met the sere horizon so many day's walk away. To the west, the Monster Mountains raked the yellow-white sunset sky with snow-cloaked teeth. The steep rim of the Gray Wall hemmed the southern extent of the basin—a pale ghost that mounded into the Round Rock Mountains. Far to the east, the Black Mountains were an irregular dark patch against the dimming sky; their rounded peaks brooded above their tree-packed slopes.

Bad Belly straightened from peering down the line of

stones. To his disappointment, the sun had dropped over the horizon between two lines.

"We probably won't be able to see anything," he told White Ash mournfully. "The rocks line up only on certain days, and Singing Stones told me it will be another two moons until the longest day."

She linked her arm in his, enjoying the peace of the evening. "That's all right. I can imagine what it must be like. I never even knew you could mark the path of the stars."

"Sure. See how all these spokes run across the inside of the circle? Each one points to something, like the place the sun rises on the longest day, or where the stars come up on the longest night. Left Hand first told me about how the star wheel works. I wished so hard that I'd get to see one."

She leaned her head against his shoulder. "Now you have your wish."

A frown marred his brow. "You sounded sad when you said that."

"No, I'm glad you got your wish. I didn't mean to sound sad. I just hope all your wishes come true. That's all." She shrugged. "It's not you. It's me. I'm confused. Everything's sad. I can't believe it's all real. Too much has happened too fast. I can't quite convince myself that the White Clay aren't waiting for me back there in the basin. I keep thinking I can return home . . . and Bright Moon and Sage Ghost will be waiting, worried sick about where I've been. The lodge will be warmed by a bright fire. Chunks of buffalo will be boiling in the gut bag by the fire while more stones are heating in the coals. Bright Moon will be bursting at the seams to tell me the latest scandal."

She shook her head, watching the first flickers of starlight in the eastern sky. "Then I realize it's all a dream—something that's gone forever. The people I loved are dead. Their bodies have been torn apart by coyotes and ravens by now. The bones are picked clean and scattered in the sagebrush. The lodges are empty—if the Wolf People even left them standing. Their laughter is gone from the world, Bad Belly. Only silence remains."

He wound his fingers into hers. "The world changes. We're

part of that. Humans aren't any different than coyotes or wolves. Sometimes hunger kills the babies and the old ones. Sometimes we're wounded during the hunt—or a sickness grows inside us. It's just the way of the world. I don't understand it, but things happen that way. Maybe the Creator knows why. Maybe this Thunderbird you Sun People talk about knows. Maybe when you Dream, you can ask the Spirit Powers.''

''If I Dream. It's my choice, Bad Belly. Singing Stones says I can refuse to use the Power. I'll have to choose between . . . well, between illusion and the things of this world. Do you know what that means?''

He shook his head morosely. ''No.''

''What if I choose not to use Power, not to be their Dreamer?''

''Then that's what you choose.''

''Will you . . . I mean, you won't leave me? Think that I've let you down?''

He smiled at her. ''I'll always love you, no matter what you decide. I'll do anything you want me to do. If you want to run away and live in a cave in the land of the Antelope People, I'll go with you. You don't have to do anything to please me. Be who you are . . . who you want to be.''

''Why are you so good to me?''

He shrugged and gazed out at the stars. ''Something happened that I never thought would. I've come to love you, White Ash. It frightens me . . . scares me to death. I guess I just can't help it. I'm making a mess of it again. If Bad Belly falls in love with a woman, it will be with a beautiful and Powerful Dreamer who will probably toss lightning between her fingers and Sing the weather and call the elk. If Bad Belly must love, it will be a woman beyond his reach. Oh, no, you won't find Bad Belly falling in love with some simple woman who would like nothing better than to sit around the lodge and cook the meals and raise the children. Leave it for Bad Belly to involve himself in the impossible.''

She tilted her chin. ''Why am I impossible? Why am I beyond your reach?''

''Because Power calls you. Because you and I could never

live like normal people." He hung his head. "Because of all the things behind us—the scars we bear—and what life has done to us. We are who we are. I'll never be a brave hero worthy of a woman as beautiful and Powerful as you will become."

She hugged him tightly, closing her eyes. "You're brave enough for me, Bad Belly. Don't talk as if I were someone special. I don't feel that way. I only feel confused, like a feather caught by the wind. You're the one person in my life I can cling to."

"What about the man you said you loved?"

A star appeared on the horizon. Did it line up with any of the rocks? Absently she studied the star as she thought about Wind Runner. What if he *had* survived? What if he came for her before the first snow?

"Wind Runner? He's young, handsome, a cunning warrior. He saved me once from Brave Man when he would have raped me and carried me off to the Broken Stones." She tightened her grip on Bad Belly's fingers. "If Wind Runner survived, he ran off to join the Black Point. He was my father's brother's son. The way the Sun People think, a mating between us would be incestuous—no matter that I wasn't of White Clay blood. If he ran off to the Black Point, challenged their best warrior and survived, he could declare his clan and family dead. Then he could marry me without shame."

Bad Belly had a curiously sad look on his face. "He must love you a great deal to accept such a challenge."

She blinked. "Yes. I . . . I told him I loved him, that I'd marry him if he survived. He promised to come for me before the first snowfall. After Three Bulls . . . I don't know what I'd do. So much has changed since I said good-bye to Wind Runner on that ridge top. Maybe the Wolf People killed him before they attacked the White Clay. Maybe he died in challenge with the Black Point. Maybe . . ."

"He'll survive," Bad Belly said resolutely. "He has to."

She cocked her head. "What makes you so sure? Everything else that I loved has been taken away from me."

He chuckled, the sound humorless with resignation. "He lives. He'll come. I can feel it, something about the Power.

Call it a hunch. Call it prophecy. I guess it just feels right . . . like the pattern of Power. You'll see Wind Runner again."

Her heart leaped, a sudden surge of hope mixed with horror. "No, I can't. I couldn't bear the thought of him touching me. Three Bulls killed that. I hope Wind Runner finds a woman among the Black Point. She can give him strong sons and healthy daughters. After that, maybe Power will let him live happily. If I could have any wish, it would be that he forget I ever existed."

Bad Belly rubbed his thumb tenderly along the back of her hand. "Why would you have a man who loved you forget you? Love is a wonderful thing. It comes too rarely in life."

She grunted. "Love is a curse . . . an illusion."

"You don't feel like an illusion to me. And I've come to love you a great deal."

Her imagination ran wild with images of Wild Runner coming to claim her. She could see his exuberant smile, the keen anticipation in his eyes. She could hear his declaration of love. And when she told him she couldn't accept? What then? Would he grab her, throw her down and lift her dress like Three Bulls did? Would the soft love in his eyes change to anger? Would he beat the resistance out of her?

"Wind Runner's not like that," she whispered to herself, trying to make sense of the confused images. Three Bulls' eyes mixed with Wind Runner's, the features of their faces merging, becoming one.

"No, he's probably not." Bad Belly took his hand from hers to rearrange the robe about her shoulders. "What Three Bulls did to you will slowly heal. The scar will always be there, but you'll come to see that men and women couple without horror and pain. If Wind Runner is worthy of your love, he will understand and give you time to come to terms with it."

She studied him from the corner of her eye. "Why do you think so?"

He gave her a warm grin. "No matter that you've been reborn, your soul hasn't changed. A man you loved would be worthy of you. If Wind Runner's willing to risk all to win you, then he's worthy. Not only that, I see the softness in your eyes when you speak of him. You think he's worthy too; but what happened with Three Bulls has left you unsure, frightened that perhaps you didn't understand everything.''

She inhaled the night air and enjoyed the rich smells of the cooling rocks and new vegetation. ''Singing Stones says I can never go back.''

Bad Belly pulled her to him, running his fingers through her hair. She closed her eyes and savored the feel of his gentle touch. For the moment, she could ignore the worry.

''Everything will be new,'' Bad Belly agreed. ''If you go with Wind Runner, it will be as two new people living new lives. He will be a Black Point warrior, with status and reputation. You will go with him as a woman who has chosen the path of her life. I think you will become a powerful woman, respected and looked up to among the Black Point.''

She shifted placing a hand on his chest. ''And you, Bad Belly? Will you come with me?''

He shook his head, a wistful smile on his lips. ''I—'' He stopped short and laughed softly at himself. ''I guess I just broke my promise. When I said I would do anything you wanted me to, I didn't think about Wind Runner. No, White Ash. I will wish you peace and happiness and follow a different path.''

''Now you sound sad.''

''The only thing I would ask of life, or Power, or Dreams, would be that you find happiness.''

At that moment a bright streak lit the darkening sky. Greenish-yellow fire—almost too bright to look at—angled across the curve of the horizon, its trail glowing eerily. As quickly, it vanished over the southern mountains, an afterglow fading in its wake.

''Blessed Thunderbird!'' White Ash whispered. The skin of her back prickled.

Bad Belly gasped. ''I've seen the stars Dancing and streaking the sky before—but never so brightly. And it burned green, did you see?'' He sniffed at the wind, scenting the air like a worried elk.

"What are you smelling for?"

He sighed. "Smoke. It looked like it burned. I know, it crossed the sky way up and over to the east, but it must have burned something. Like the sun. I just always sniff for smoke—even when I know it's too far away, and downwind at that."

She nestled against him. "Doesn't it frighten you? Perhaps that was an evil Spirit throwing someone out of the Star-web."

Bad Belly hugged her reassuringly. "Why should I be afraid?"

"What if it was a sign of terrible things to come?"

"What if it wasn't? A green light shot across the sky. That's all we know. Maybe it *was* a sign of terrible things to come. Maybe it was two Spirits playing a game with each other, throwing fire around like little boys playing hoop and stick. In that case, it means nothing. What if it was really a sign that a Dreamer had come to save all the people? What good would it do me to fear it?"

"And if it was a sign of terrible things coming and you didn't fear it?"

Bed Belly rubbed his chin on the top of her head. "Then bad things will come anyway. What could I do to change them? If I stood up and screamed, 'Bad things, go away!' at the top of my lungs, would they?" He shook his head and laughed. "It seems to me that there are plenty of things to fear without creating more because of lights in the sky."

She shivered. "It frightened me."

He gave her hand a squeeze. "Come on. Let's get back to Singing Stones. He probably has a feast ready for us. If you stay up here, you'll worry and worry until you have horrible Dreams all night long, and I'll get no sleep because I'll have to hold you and pat you and tell you it's all right."

She stood and helped him to his feet. "I don't know what I'd do without you, Bad Belly."

She caught the barest glimpse of his expression before he turned to pick up his drill and black stone teeth. He'd looked like a man about to be gutted.

Hot Fat removed the thick wrap of soft leather he'd bound around Wind Runner's ankle. The swelling had gone down and the bruise had healed. Wind Runner tensed as Hot Fat poked and prodded, but the pain didn't spear him to the soul.

"There." Hot Fat gestured. "Go walk on it. Make it strong again. Just don't hurt it for a while and you'll be fine."

"You do good work," Wind Runner told the old man as he wiggled his foot this way and that. Then he pulled his moccasin on.

"Go on, go walk." Hot Fat waved him away.

Wind Runner ducked out of the Soul Flier's lodge and into the quiet evening. He could smell spring in the air.

The Black Point camp stood in the cottonwoods on the north bank of the Fat Beaver River. Overhead, the leaves had started to bud out, greening the tips of the branches and showering the camp with the bud casings.

Wind Runner walked among the lodges, smelling the evening cook fires, nodding and calling to people he'd met. He gave a special greeting to others who had demonstrated their friendship by sharing food and bringing small gifts. Somewhere a man and a woman screamed at each other in a domestic battle. The camp went suddenly silent as people stopped their talk to listen, heads cocked. Someone shushed the children in order to hear better.

It all brought a smile to his lips as he headed toward the edge of camp, happy to walk unencumbered again. He experienced only a faint discomfort, a tenderness deep in the bone. Hot Fat had done very well—possibly even better than Old Falcon might have done.

He stopped long enough to pat one of the dogs that stepped out to greet him, then strolled on, past the edge of the camp.

To the west, the sun had just dipped below the lavender shadows of the Geyser Mountains. The snowfields on the highest peaks of the Great Bear Mountains gleamed redly as they caught the dying light. A meadowlark trilled out in the grassy floodplain, and his soul warmed. *The first one I've heard this season. Spring.*

He chose a nearby rise for a destination and wound his way toward it through the gray, wrinkled boles of the cottonwoods. The grass whispered pleasantly against his moccasins.

He stepped up the cobble-cluttered side of the knoll and filled his lungs with the evening scents, rich with river smells, new grass and the living musk of the earth.

He caught sight of the woman at the same time she saw him.

"I'm sorry, Aspen," he said. "I didn't mean to disturb you."

She smiled—a neutral smile of courtesy—and rose from the spot where she'd been sitting with her arms around her knees. "That's all right. I didn't hear you coming. How's the ankle?"

"Your grandfather did a wonderful job with it." He stepped over beside her and stood watching the colors play through the sunset sky. "A peaceful evening."

"It is, isn't it?" She closed her eyes, as if living in another place and time.

"You look wistful," he told her.

She crossed her arms, hugging herself. The thick mass of her hair hung over her shoulders like a cape and fell in streams to her waist. Unbraided, as it was now, it framed her delicate heartshaped face, augmenting her large, dark eyes. Her straight nose and firm chin added to her beauty.

She exhaled wearily. "I suppose. I was thinking about my husband. Sometimes I do that . . . walk out to be alone with my memories. And you? You, too, have looked wistful recently."

He clasped his hands behind his back, eyes on the distant horizon. "The woman I love is in the south. She's White Clay. Her name is White Ash. Sometime soon I have to go search for her."

Aspen studied him from the corner of her eye. "From the tone in your voice, you love her a great deal. I find it curious that a man would leave his clan—and the woman he loves—to make a place in another clan.''

He caught an undercurrent in her voice. What was it? Distrust? "As a White Clay, I couldn't marry her. The man who was my father's brother had adopted her. She's no blood relation, but the rules of the People are strict. I love her too much to have people whisper and make jokes.''

Aspen nodded slowly, tension in the set of her mouth. "I see.''

"Do you?''

She lifted a graceful shoulder in a shrug. "Love does funny things to people—men and women alike.''

He grinned at her carefully chosen words. "Listen, perhaps I should be going. I'm sorry to have bothered you.''

She glanced up at him, head slightly tilted. "You haven't bothered me.''

"Well, I get the feeling you really don't like me. I don't want to intrude. I wouldn't have stopped to talk if I didn't spend so much time in your grandfather's lodge. I thought I'd simply thank you for the wonderful meals you've prepared and tell you how much I have come to respect your grandfather. Have an enjoyable evening.''

He had taken several steps back the way he'd come before she called out, "Wait.''

He stopped and turned.

She walked up to him, arms still crossed, frowning at the ground. "I'm sorry. I didn't mean to be rude. Grandfather likes you a great deal.'' She gazed into his eyes as if searching the nature of his soul. "You're welcome to share our meals at any time. I appreciate what you do for Grandfather. He needs the company and enjoys the chance to talk to younger people about the old days.'' She smiled wistfully. "It's I who should apologize. Some people say I think too much.''

He nodded. "That's better than thinking too little. I—''

The flash overhead distracted him. A garish green fire swept through the sky, streaking from north to south.

"Blessed Thunderbird!'' Aspen whispered. "What happened?''

allowed hard and shook his head. "I don't
d its way south toward . . . White Ash!

Larkspur stared at the streak of green light that glared
across the sky. "Witching light," she mumbled under her
breath.

Bitterbrush and Tuber stopped what they were doing and
stood beside her, staring soberly up into the night sky. Bitterbrush said nervously, "I'll bet they go crazy about it over
at Three Forks. Cattail says that Owlclover is already making
claims that Black Hand witched Green Fire."

Larkspur tapped her shrunken chin with a bony finger and
thoughtfully studied the sky. "Green Fire? That thing burned
greenish. Did you see that?" She shook her head. "I think
it's a sign. No good will come of it, I tell you that. No good
at all. Witching light. Witching is loose—black, evil witching."

Where he stood next to his mother, Tuber narrowed his
eyes. Then he backed away and fled into the night on silent
feet.

Wolfberry stripped long lengths of bark from a chokecherry limb with a hafted side scraper. The work kept his
mind off the worry that ate at him and at everyone in Three
Forks camp. He heard the soft scuff of moccasins and glanced
up as Starwort ducked through the flap into the lodge he
shared with Basket. At the look on her face, his heart skipped.
"What's happened?"

"She lost the baby."

Wolfberry's work clattered from nerveless fingers. He
dropped his head into his hands as he stared at the packed
clay beneath his feet. "Oh, Blessed Creator. And . . . Basket?"

"The bleeding's stopped. She's going to live. But—
Wolfberry looked up, his soul shriveling. "But?"

Starwort's jaw muscles jumped under her broad chee
"The pains started just after that witch light burned acro
the sky. She's . . . well, I don't know how strong her mind
is. She says she felt the witching, that a witch killed her
baby."

Wolfberry's hands twisted into fists as he lurched unsteadily to his feet. "I'll find Black Hand! I swear it!"

Brave Man staggered, lances of pain driving through his
head. Pale Raven barely held his weight as he gasped and
pressed one hand against the side of his head. With the other,
he held on to her as the world spun.

"Are you all right?" she asked, steadying him.

Dusk was falling, the air growing still with the coming of
night. Before them, wreaths of blue smoke lingered around
the lodge tops as the evening fires were lit. She had helped
him out to the bushes to attend to nature's call. Now they
were returning to the lodge.

Be ready! the voices hisses in Brave Man's head. *The sign
comes! Use it . . . use it to turn them.*

"The sign," Brave Man whispered. "It's coming."

Pale Raven gave him a worried frown. "What sign? Is this
more talk of Power and Dreams? You already have the entire
camp in an uproar."

Brave Man gulped deep breaths against the wrenching pain
in his head. He forced himself to move, leaning on Pale Raven
to support his bad leg. "The sign!" he shouted desperately.
People stuck their heads around their lodge flaps to peer at
him. "It's coming! Look! Look!"

People grumbled and ducked out into the growling darkness of night, standing awkwardly as their gazes drifted uncertainly about the camp.

Brave Man and Pale Raven had covered half the distance
back to the lodge when the sky behind them flared in an

eerie, greenish light. People gasped and pointed at the glowing heavens to the east.

This is your moment, the voices prodded. *Seize it! Take control of the Broken Stones.*

"There! See! I have called upon the Sun to send us a sign! Look!" Brave Man cried out in vindication and pointed at the streak of viridian light that angled across the sky. "Behold! My call is answered! A path of green fire is blazed southward across the sky!"

He propped himself on his bad leg, standing free of Pale Raven, and raised his hands to the now-fading streak in the sky. "Hear me, Thunderbird! Brave Man thanks you for this gift!" He gritted his teeth against the pain and took a step on his bad leg. Agony burned as bright as the light in the sky, but the knitting joint held his weight. "See me! Thunderbird sends a sign to the Broken Stones! *I walk!* So shall I lead the warriors to the south to crush the Wolf People!"

He stared around in the growing gloom, seeking out face after face as the stunned Broken Stones stared at the silver glow that still washed the sky. Their expressions were wide-eyed with wonder. A deathly silence gripped the camp.

Brave Man took another step of searing punishment. "I walk!" he cried. "I hear your way, Thunderbird! I hear your call for war! The Wolf People block our path to the south. The Broken Stones will clear the way. Who follows Brave Man? Who follows the path Thunderbird burned across the sky?"

Flying Hawk stepped out, raising his arms. "I follow the path of Thunderbird. I hear the new Dreamer of the People. I will go south and crush the Wolf People!"

Brave Man whooped his joy to the night sky. One by one, the young men stepped forth, singing, shouting their willingness to make war on the Wolf People.

Brave Man Sang to the night, calling forth the Power of the Spirit World and the Camp of the Dead. He called upon Thunderbird and the Sun, the pain in his maimed leg drowned in the triumph of the moment.

Pale Raven followed to one side as Brave Man cried and

pointed at the sky. With narrowed eyes she watched the camp come to life, leaping and Dancing. Brave Man stood unaided and Sang his Spirit vision to the darkening night. A thrill tickled up her spine. This young Brave Man had Power; she could feel it on the throbbing night air.

How could he stand like that? His shattered knee had barely begun to knit. The pain should have shocked him colorless and left him faint and reeling, yet he walked, albeit slowly and stiff-legged, among the whirling Dancers.

Someone threw wood on the central fire and the flames leaped up. She stared around, noting the excitement in the eyes of her people. Power had come to them—and, through Brave Man, to her.

As she reflected on that fact, she noticed the figure in the shadows. Sun Feathers watched from the darkness. She could imagine Sun Feathers' slitted eyes as Brave Man gathered the reins of Spirit Power. The old man's hold on the Broken Stones was slipping from his gnarled fingers.

She could sense the anger that festered in that shadowy shape. The old Soul Flier would be forced to act now. He backed away and slipped into the darkness.

And if he destroys Brave Man, what will happen to me? Pale Raven kept to the shadows as she stalked Sun Feathers. She rolled up her sleeves, running her hands along the muscles of her arms. Years of scraping and graining hides, of carrying firewood and slabs of heavy meat, had built strength into her body.

This would have to be done very carefully.

Chapter 15

Bad Belly fell into the Dream, his body loose and disjointed as it dropped through the gray mist. He tumbled and floated while splotches of golden light dappled the haze . . .

Wisps of fire penetrated the mist to swirl around him. He cringed, instinctively fearing the flame, but no heat scorched his flesh. In an instant the flames twisted around and became patches of blowing, dancing snow. Bad Belly settled softly into a terrifying landscape. Fire faded into streamers of snow that blew off drifts, intermingling, curling in long spirals to become streaks of flame again. The piled drifts burned redly, as if in defiance of the contradiction of fire and snow.

"Impossible," Bad Belly whispered. "Snow doesn't burn. It melts . . . and the melt-water would put out the flames. This can't happen."

"It's Power, Still Water," a haunting voice called from the smoky haze. *"We brought you here to see for yourself. This is what We are. Snow and fire. That is the legacy of the Wolf Bundle—the lesson We would teach you."*

"Snow and fire? You're the Wolf Bundle?" Bad Belly watched in awe as the snowflakes burst into yellow-red tongues of flame and flickered out in wisps of curled ash that turned back into snowflakes.

"We are the Wolf Bundle. We are One."

The image splintered into a thousand fragments, each with a voice, as if every snowflake and every wisp of flame possessed a face. A thousand voices intertwined to become a moaning howl in the air around him. As quickly, the images merged again into the burning snow.

"For as long as We have existed, We have taken Power from those around us. We have shared ourselves with others, twining our Power with theirs. We have been loved and feared, desecrated and renewed. The world remains eternal and forever changing. A new people come from the north. What is new must mix with what is old. Come to Us, Still Water. Come and take Us. We have things to teach the Dreamer. We have things to teach you."

"Why me?" Bad Belly called out, fingers of fear tightening in his gut.

"Your father is Cattail. He carried Us south to the People of the Earth. There, patterns were woven like the strands of a basket. We wait now to see what comes . . . and hope We are not too late."

"Patterns?"

"*Come for Us. A storm brews in the north. He who would destroy the Dream seeks the way to the One. He feels Power. We knew this new Dreamer would be strong. We didn't know that events would turn him against Us. Not even Power can control the flood of the future. He must be stopped before he destroys Us—destroys the Dream. Come for Us . . . before it's too late. Come, Still Water. Come . . .*"

The Dream shifted, burning snowdrifts fading into irregular patterns that solidified into a forest as a bird might perceive it.

From his vantage point, he could see fierce-eyed warriors slipping through the thick timber. War darts rattled as the men gripped atlatls in strong fists. He floated over the spiked tops of spruce and fir, and then out over a meadow where a camp lay in the eerie sunlight. Lodges had been toppled, their covers ripped apart. The fire pits held lenses of cold coals, and ash had been kicked about.

At sight of the bodies sprawled in the trampled grass, Bad Belly's breath caught in his throat. Some lay with arms and legs outstretched. Dart shafts protruded from pierced flesh, and crimson soaked their hide clothing. Others lay in blood-bright grass, their heads bashed open. Flies hovered in shimmering columns over the bloating corpses.

A shadow passed overhead and Bad Belly craned his neck to see ravens wheeling on the wind. Higher, black-and-white turkey buzzards slipped silently down their relentless spirals.

The haze of gray shifted and a thousand voices cried out, longing, frightened.

The sky darkened with frightening rapidity as Bad Belly floated over the mountainous terrain. Below, a huge bonfire flickered, sending shafts of light to snake between the trees. A circle of warriors Danced around the fire and Sang their Power to the heavens. The rise and fall of their voices rocked Bad Belly like waves of air. Vibrations of their Power sent chills coursing through his soul. He tucked his knees to his chest in a futile attempt to protect himself.

Captive women and children huddled in the firelight, ringed by chanting warriors who leaped and whirled in their fantastic Dance. The captives stared up at the pirouetting warriors with fear-glazed eyes, expressions masks of terror and grief.

A strong voice split the night as it called upon the Sun for Power. Bad Belly glanced back at the wrecked camp, then returned to where the captives waited. A green glow burned in the night, bobbing closer to the Dancers. The circle parted . . . and the smoky green glow became a tall young man who limped into the firelight on a stiff leg. Power radiated from the man, and the feel of it made Bad Belly ill.

The Powerful young man led a captive with one hand, while in his other, he held up a bundle that glowed, its radiance like the morning sun.

The fire flared up, illuminating the awestruck faces of the spectators, wrapping its light around the captive: *White Ash!*

Bad Belly squirmed at the loathing fear he sensed in her. He cried out to her, but the sound was borne away on the night wind. A bruise purpled one side of White Ash's face, and her soul—so pure and brilliant—began to fade before the hideous hues of the lame warrior's Power.

A brilliant dot of sickly green glowed through White Ash's elk-hide dress, spreading, seeping like fungus between her legs. It grew, sending tendrils into her womb and radiating through her pelvis.

Bad Belly wailed into the smothering night, "No. Not White Ash. He planted a child in her!"

Bad Belly tried to swallow the choking knot that swelled under his tongue. His lungs spasmed with uncontrollable sobs as he shut his eyes.

Watch, the Wolf Bundle ordered.

Bad Belly blinked through a shimmer of tears as the lame warrior dragged White Ash to stand beside the roaring fire.

"I am the Power of the Sun People!" the terrible warrior claimed. He lifted the Wolf Bundle. "And I offer the Power of the Wolf People to the greater Power of the Sun!"

With that, he cast the Wolf Bundle into the crackling heart of the bonfire.

A horrified silence hung over the land. Then one of the captive women threw herself into the fire, arms outstretched to rescue the Wolf Bundle. Her hair burst into flame and her flesh blistered and curled as she screamed and thrashed among the coals.

Wailing rose on the wind, as if the writhing mass of people seared and burned in the heat. The keening grew louder, deafening, until the very web of the gray mist pulsed in misery.

Bad Belly clutched at himself and wept. Stunned and deafened, he strangled on fear. His soul had come loose, unhooked from the world and all that was good. It whimpered into the nothingness. Grayness pressed around him and pulsed to the beat of his frightened heart.

"*Come for Us, Still Water. Take Us from this, before it's too late for all. Come . . . come . . .*"

Bad Belly turned this way and that, frantic as he batted at the fog. "Where are you? What happened?"

His flailing feet found a purchase on uneven ground, but the footing went soft and mushy beneath his moccasins, as it would if he walked on corrupt flesh. "Where are you? Where . . ."

"Bad Belly?" The words cut through the thickness of the Dream. "Bad Belly? Wake up!"

He blinked; fragments of the dream fell away like old moss from a dead tree. "What?"

White Ash hugged him. "You called out in your sleep. I'm here. It's all right. You're safe . . . with White Ash. You're in your robes, in Singing Stones' shelter. You're all right."

He filled his lungs with the chilly night air and tried to exhale the tension that left his ribs aching. "Power Dream," he whispered. "The Wolf Bundle called to me. Took me up in the air and let me see things—terrible, terrible things. You were there . . ." He clapped his hand to the side of his head, seeking to drive the memory away. "No. This isn't happening. It's not happening!"

"Hush. It's all right. You're all right. You're safe, Bad Belly. Safe." Her fingers bit insistently into his flesh—her presence warm, reassuring, in the robes beside him.

He shivered and gulped the cool night air. Sweat soaked his body. "The Wolf Bundle—it wants me to rescue it from the Wolf People."

She froze. "Do you remember the stories the Earth People tell of the time Cattail stole the Bundle? The Wolf People came with every warrior they could muster. Men, women, elders, and children, they all came with weapons on their shoulders. They camped just beyond the summer Gathering, sending their elders to parley for the return of the Bundle."

Bad Belly tried to swallow his fright. "Cattail—the man who stole the Bundle from the Wolf People—is my father. In the Dream, the Bundle mentioned something about patterns, about things set in motion years ago."

"That's right," Singing Stones' rusty voice grated in the darkness. "I saw the Wolf Bundle for the first time when Cattail stole it and brought it to the Gathering. When I picked it up, Power ran through my bones and strengthened my muscles. I felt . . . and my life changed forever. I spoke for the Wolf Bundle, telling the clans to let it go back to the Wolf People." He paused. "Nothing was ever the same after that. I looked at the world through different eyes. I heard through different ears. The thoughts in my head had changed. What had been important before meant nothing. The things I once craved had gone hollow—like a tree eaten away by carpenter ants. I tried to be my old self and finally gave that up for the illusion it was. I came here, to the mountains, to be close to the Wolf Bundle and to seek the One.

"The Bundle called me." Bad Belly stared emptily into the darkness, feeling the presence of the Spiral painted on the back wall. "It said a storm is brewing in the north. What does that mean? In spring, storms are always . . . I saw . . . I saw—"

"It's a storm, all right. A human storm," Singing Stones interrupted. "They're moving south, and unless a new way is Dreamed, they'll crush everything before them. That's why the Wolf Bundle called you, Still Water. It's calling for a new Keeper. You must go. You must stand before this new Spirit Man of the Sun People. If you don't, he will destroy First Man's Dream—replace it with his own—and change the Spiral. Accept your destiny. Try to rescue the Wolf Bundle."

"Try?" Bad Belly whispered to himself. Images from the Dream replayed: warriors rattling darts, people lying dead and rotting in the sun, the terrible Dancers around the fire, White Ash . . .

Singing Stones sighed in the darkness. "You don't think Power comes without risks, do you? To carry the Wolf Bundle away from the Wolf People, you'll have to gamble with your very life. You must test yourself, risk all—and possibly die."

A sick sensation pulsed in Bad Belly's gut. He clamped his eyes shut, but a fungal-green glow filled his memories. *Not me. That can't happen to me.*

"Don't do this thing," White Ash whispered in his ear. "Let's run away. Let's go to those Antelope People you were talking about. Anything."

The thousand voices of the Dream called out in shrieking terror as burning snow whirled around them. They rose to a thunderous roar—then suddenly went silent.

The visions played on the back of his eyelids, flickering with a reddish glare. He stared out over a camp full of bloating bodies that reeked in the hot sun. Then a lame warrior dragged White Ash into the light of the bonfire. The greenish glow widened in her pelvis, spreading, consuming . . .

"I . . . I have to go. I just have to, that's all."

White Ash walked along the trail that led uphill from Singing Stones' rock overhang. The unborn sun lit an orange glow behind the irregular indigo horizon. The sky melted into the colors of sunrise, red and yellow streaks puncturing the deeper violets and purples of cloud patterns to the west. Far down on the western horizon, the last of the stars dimmed and twinkled. Shadows lurked in the valley below her, charcoaling the lines of sagebrush and juniper.

She sniffed the friable remains of the night air, filling her nostrils with the scent of frost and dried vegetation. The pungency of sage, mixed with the rich odor of spring-full juniper, soothed the nagging disquiet in her soul.

She exhaled slowly so she could watch her breath rise in twisting spirals and curls. *Is this another test? Are you going to take Bad Belly away from me, too?*

She looked back along the narrow, undulating trail that

followed the wedding of sandstone cliff and fanning colluvial slope. The buff of the ragged sandstone that walled the valley reflected the tenuous rose tones of predawn. Sage and bitterbrush had woven their fibrous roots into the precarious soil, eking out a living on the sun-washed southern slope. No more than four dart casts behind her, Singing Stones' shelter blended with the rock, almost invisible—the perfect abode for an ancient Dreamer.

She'd held Bad Belly after his Power Dream, worry eating at her. She'd felt his tension in the aftermath of the Power that had possessed him. When she'd coaxed him to talk about it, to share it with her, he'd just shaken his head in obstinate refusal and insisted that "everything will be all right."

After what had seemed like an eternity, he had finally drifted off to a troubled sleep. He'd mumbled, the words indistinct and slurred except for the few times he'd mewed her name and whimpered. When she couldn't stand it any longer, she'd disengaged her arms from him and crawled silently from under the covers. Only Trouble had noticed as she slipped out into the chill of the morning.

Now she walked, trying to come to grips with the fact: Bad Belly was about to sacrifice himself at the whim of Power.

What if it's another trick? She stared up at the bluing sky and asked, "What if he's meant to die as a means of shaping my destiny? What if Power wants to discard him now that he's served his purpose and saved my life?"

The voice from behind startled her. "You're starting to understand the ways of Power."

She gasped and whirled, fear leaping bright. Singing Stones sat immobile on a flat slab of sandstone that had sloughed off the buff rimrock. Wrapped in his robe, he blended with the brown and gray of dawn's light. She'd walked right past him.

"Singing Stones? How did you get here? I thought you were still asleep in the shelter." She placed a hand to her chest to quiet her pounding heart.

The old man smiled, the wrinkles curling around his mouth. He lifted a thin-boned hand to the strengthening morn.

"I like to come here every so often to watch the sunrise . . . and to enjoy the One. First light is a good time to simply sit and let yourself go. At this time of year, the moments before dawn are the most peaceful. In summer, the insects and birds are making a racket. But this early in spring, it's quiet, so quiet you can almost hear the grass grow. That's when it's best to let the illusion slip away and experience the One."

She shook her head and pinched the bridge of her nose. "You're talking about the One . . . and Bad Belly's talked himself into committing suicide on a Wolf People war dart. Doesn't it bother you that a man like Bad Belly is about to walk off and risk his neck on some foolish errand for a strange Power Bundle?"

His eyelids narrowed as he gave her a sideways look. "For a woman who would be a Dreamer, you have interesting ideas about one of the most Powerful objects in the world. It's a human thing, I guess, to value your life more than you value the earth, the animals, the air, or the people. You have a long way to go to find the One, girl."

She crossed her arms, scuffing the frozen dust of the trail with a moccasined foot. Bad Belly's moccasin, the one she'd been caught trying to put on that day at the hot springs. "You told me I had a choice to make. I may decide not to find the One."

His lips twitched as he studied her; the black eyes burned with an inner fire. "You may choose not to if you wish." He paused. "But if that were to be your decision, I would have to wonder what you are doing out here in the cold—and so preoccupied with what Power will do to Still Water. A woman who would turn her back on Power—and the future—wouldn't bother to worry about an insignificant crippled man who Dreams of helping the Wolf Bundle."

She shot him her best scathing glare—and got no response. He watched her through veiled eyes that could have stripped the flesh from her soul. "I owe him, that's all."

He nodded with the slow deliberation of an elder who has discovered truth. "Ah, now I understand. Obligations lead us to strange actions. To study the trail of obligation through all of its twists and turns is like tracing a bee's path through a field of wild flowers.''

He stopped, a delighted grin on his face, and looked up in time to catch the first shining rays of the sun to clear the ridge tops.

She followed his gaze, enjoying the respite from his irritating words.

Only when the sun had finally cleared the ridge and sent its golden light streaming into the canyon did Singing Stones sigh and smack his lips. ''Life is for moments like that.'' He glanced at her. ''And as for young women who would be Dreamers, the first lesson they must learn is how to be honest with themselves.''

She turned on him, leaning close. ''I am honest with myself.''

His beneficent smile spread the wrinkles wide. ''Are you?''

''Of course. I live with myself. I know what I want and why. *I'm* the person inside this body and soul. How could I be dishonest with myself? That's like—''

''By failing to admit truth to yourself,'' he interrupted.

''I admit truth.''

''Do you? Then tell me, what frightens you the most—Still Water going after the Wolf Bundle, or the fact that you might be alone again if he's killed?''

She stopped, words half-formed in her throat. She lifted her hands, letting them slap at her sides. ''Singing Stones, talk to him. Please. We can't let him go. He almost walked off the cliff the other day. He's not a warrior. He doesn't have the cunning and daring a warrior needs to sneak into an enemy camp and steal a sacred object like the Wolf Bundle. He'll . . . he'll knock over a boiling paunch full of stew, or trip over a lodge pole, or wake up the dogs. You know Bad Belly. He doesn't think like a warrior. He's too . . . too vulnerable.''

He remained impassive, head tilted back to expose his face to the sun. ''It would seem Power has more faith in Still Water than you do.''

''He's got a bad arm! Blood and guts, he can't even throw

two darts in a row! He'll get himself *killed* up there. I was captured by one of the Wolf People. I *know* what they're like." She lowered her voice. "I just can't let that sort of thing happen to Bad Belly."

"And you?"

She started. "Me? Bad Belly's the one going up to—"

"If they captured him, what would it do to you? Why are you so worried about him? I thought you didn't like men."

"Bad Belly's different."

"Oh? He's not a man?"

"That's not what I meant."

He smiled again, amusement twinkling in his eyes. "I wonder what would happen if you ever told yourself the truth."

"How many times do I have to tell you? I know myself better than you ever could."

He cocked his head. "Then you know the reason you're worried sick is that you can't talk yourself into going with Still Water to take the Bundle from the Wolf People. You're afraid of going up on that mountain and putting yourself at risk."

"That's . . . that's *totally* wrong!"

"Is it? You know you're going to force yourself to go with him. You have to, because another thing you refuse to admit to yourself is that you've come to love and depend on Still Water. He has become your security, the only person you can trust. You know you won't be able to talk him out of going after the Wolf Bundle. You know he'll agonize over it . . . and then answer the call. It's in his soul. That's his nature."

Her resistance flagged. "I suppose."

"Suppose? Is this another trick to hide from yourself?"

She lowered herself to sit next to him on the rock. "I'm still not convinced he's the right one for this." She grabbed her thick hair and twisted it nervously. "And maybe I'm not the right one either. Going up there . . . the thought scares me to death. If anything happened—if he got caught—I'm not sure I could force myself to go in after him. I might just lie there in the brush and sob my fool head off when I should be thinking, or acting."

"Ah, honesty at last."

She snorted. "I don't understand it. I mean, why did Power call on us? Bad Belly gets in trouble going out to make water. Me, I'm . . . I'm as strong as a rotten basket."

He rubbed his parchment hands on his skinny knees. Out over the basin, the shadows retreated behind buff-and-tan ridges. Distant patches of sagebrush mottled the land. The patterns of the ridges stood out in a relief of light and dark.

"That's more like it." Singing Stones paused. "The first thing a Dreamer must do is drop the simplest of illusions. You must know what you are . . . and what you are not. What you fear . . . and why. What do these things tell you about yourself? When you shy back, that's when you must push forward and examine yourself. You must know all of your weaknesses before you Dream."

"You assume I'll choose to be a Dreamer."

He turned his head, eyes vacant but shining. "Do you want to Dream? Or do you want to walk away? Answer me honestly."

"I don't want Bad Belly going off to—"

"Is that what I asked you?"

She glanced up at the crystal sky and propped herself on her elbows. What could she say? How could she answer this question she didn't even understand? Become a Dreamer? What did that mean? How would it change the tattered remnants of her life?

"All right." She sighed in defeat. "Honestly, I don't know. I've had Dreams. Once I Dreamed my mother's death. I felt her . . . touched the edge of the One. I'd like to feel that again. I just don't know if I'm the right person. What if I fail? What if I can't do what needs to be done?" She squinted up at the sun. "What if I can't be this . . . this Mother of the People you and the Dreams talk about?"

"You know the answer to that already. You were telling yourself before I interrupted you. Power has its own needs and ways. Power cares nothing for your feelings or wishes. If you fail, Power will cast you aside. Just like a warrior discards a broken dart point."

"Oh, fine! That makes me feel a *lot* better!"

"Feeling better isn't the point. Power is."

She nodded, heart throbbing miserably in her chest. "So, if I choose to become a Dreamer, it's forever. Either I succeed, or I'm destroyed?"

He nodded easily, and behind him the glowing golden ball of the sun rose over the tops of the trees. "That is the way of Power."

Wind Runner pulled up and spun on his heel. He looked quickly around the bare, flat-topped ridge and nodded. What he now considered meant taking a terrible risk. "Here!" he shouted, forcing his gasping lungs to work. "Snail Shell! Blue Wind! Here!"

His fleeing comrades heard him. They glanced at each other and stopped their headlong flight to trot nervously in his direction.

Black basalt capped the high, windblown ridge they'd just bolted up like frightened mule deer. Sparse grasses grew in cracks where the rock had split and fractured through the ages. The ridge looked barren, devoid of all except the sprinkling of irregular boulders and gravel that had collected in low spots. From here they could look south to the Fat Beaver River and beyond to the Great Bear Mountains that thrust against the distant sky.

Behind them, on the northern slope they'd just climbed, pursuing Hollow Flute warriors forced sweating bodies up the hillside with the tenacity of coyotes after a wounded antelope fawn.

Wind Runner fought to catch his breath as he took stock of the situation. The Hollow Flute warriors were closing the distance, wearing down their prey.

We've got to survive. We have to tell Black Moon what we've seen. If we don't, the disaster could be as great as that which befell the White Clay.

He took one last look down the long hill and motioned to the others. He wound his way through the angular boulders

of black basalt, following the line of a grass-filled crack. His jaded companions came behind, keeping back from the rim lest they be sky-lined.

"What?" Snail Shell panted as he drew near, deep chest rising and falling.

"They'll get us . . . if we don't do something. There are too . . . many of them," Wind Runner managed through ragged breaths. He pointed at a crack in the rock. "We need a place like that . . . only bigger."

"What? Have you lost your mind? That whole war party will be on top of this ridge in the blink of an eye!" Blue Wind cried. Sweat had soaked his leather shirt; his face flushed red from exertion. He glanced back nervously, fingering his darts.

"And where do you think they'll figure we went? Over the other side, of course. Down into those buffaloberry bushes on the north side. Look, it's flat here! No cover."

"Uh-huh. Flat. No cover. That's what worries me," Snail Shell grunted. "And we could be running like flying darts while you're stalling up here."

"And they'll get us before long," Wind Runner told him bluntly. "They can use relays to catch us. Track us down if nothing else. I just need the right . . . Here! Blue Wind, lie down in this crack."

Blue Wind glanced back at the rim—figuring the distance of the closing Hollow Flute warriors—and settled himself into the chest-wide fissure. "This had better work."

Wind Runner lifted a head-sized rock and placed it on Blue Wind's chest, then propped another over his thighs. Snail Shell added another couple of stones and stepped back to study the effect.

"Don't you think we need more rocks?" he asked, skepticism in his eyes.

"No. Just enough to break up his outline, make him blend in and appear natural. Otherwise, he'll look like a cairn . . . draw attention."

"That rock on my chest is heavy," Blue Wind protested. "I can hardly breathe."

"You'd breathe less with a dart through your lungs. Stay

still, don't move. Don't look at them. Clear your mind. Think like the very rock."

"Sure," Blue Wind muttered. "I'm dead already. It's too late to run now. Think like the rock, he says."

"That's right," Wind Runner agreed, licking his lips and hurrying on. "Here, this crack's about right for you, Snail Shell. Get down. Tuck your darts close."

Rapidly, he piled rocks over Snail Shell. The ruse would never stand close inspection—but who'd believe that warriors would heap stones atop themselves to hide? Besides, the ridge top looked too flat to hide a jackrabbit, let alone three Black Point warriors.

Wind Runner carried a few of the loose stones over and threw himself into another of the fissures, wiggling down into the washed-out crack in the basalt. He rolled a couple of rocks onto his legs, then placed a big one over his stomach and chest. All he could do was to hope the Hollow Flute warriors would follow their path straight across the ridge. The bare caprock wouldn't hold a moccasin track.

"Hide in the enemy's mind," Wind Runner whispered to himself. "Thunderbird . . . for the sake of the Black Point, make this work!" *How do I get myself into these messes?*

The fire in the sky had started it. From the moment the burning green star had arced across the eastern horizon toward the south, he'd been on edge. An uneasy feeling had plagued his soul, leaving him irritable and jumpy. Strange Dreams had caused him no little discomfort, startling him from sleep to sweat and pant in the darkness. Premonition hung over him like morning smoke in a winter camp.

To stifle the anxiety, he'd volunteered to go north with Snail Shell and Blue Wind to scout the country for buffalo. Camp meat had been dwindling, and the time had come when the cows would be splitting off into smaller herds to calve. At this time of year, they couldn't hope to find big herds, but if any concentrations were close, Black Moon would want to organize a hunt. So the three of them had left camp, traveling light as they trotted north, singing the old songs as they musically rattled atlatls against dart shafts.

None of them would have expected the hornet's nest of

Hollow Flute trouble they stumbled into. They'd threaded their way through the advance scouting parties, blessed with blissful ignorance and unsurpassed luck. When they first spotted Hollow Flute, they'd had no idea that the entire clan was pressing south. Now they knew—and they ran for their lives.

He closed his eyes, willing himself to be one with the rock as the gasping war chant of the Hollow Flute rose in the air. Within moments he could hear them panting as they topped the ridge. Their moccasined feet whispered and pattered on the rock. Wind Runner stilled his thoughts, concentrating on the panicked cadence of his heart where it beat fear into his chest.

"You see them?" a voice called.

"No. But look at that brush down there."

"Maybe they turned," another called. "Split off and went another way. Tried to flank us."

"Where? It's all bare grass to either side. Come on, let's go beat them out of the bushes like silly sage grouse. That's the only place they can be."

"How'd they get that far?"

"Fear of a quick death!" another called. "Run, Black Point! Run before we kill you all."

"The sooner we get them, the sooner we can rest. Spread out. Some of you cut off their escape from the bottom of that draw down there. Break A Leg, you and Grouse cover the sides."

Wind Runner lifted his head a trifle to see the last of the Hollow Flute warriors dropping over the crest of the ridge. He filled his lungs, trying to drown the pumping fear with fresh air, and rolled the rocks off before rising carefully to his feet.

"Stay there!" he called to his friends, sprinting across the flat rock to peer over the southern edge of the ridge. He counted the warriors as they drew their net tight around the brush below. Then he scrambled away from the rim, urging, "Come on!"

He led the way back in the direction they had come and dove off the northern edge, his feet dimpling the soil already mashed flat by Hollow Flute feet. He jumped to the side, sprinting for the head of a drainage, knowing they had to keep to low ground to avoid detection.

"I never would have believed that could happen!" Blue Wind cried in amazement. "I thought you'd killed us all."

"Then why did you do as I told you?" Wind Runner asked.

"I just . . . well . . ."

"Maybe he didn't have a better idea," Snail Shell broke in. "It's not going to take them very long to figure out what happened. We'd better make tracks."

"Let's run," Wind Runner agreed. "And we'd better get back to the main camp. The quicker the clan leader and the Soul Flier know the Hollow Flute are coming, the sooner they can move camp."

"Move camp?" Snail Shell asked. "It would be better if we drove these pesky Hollow Flute back north—and sent them packing with a couple of dead to mourn over."

"How many war parties have you seen in the last couple of days?" Blue Wind asked.

"Too many," Wind Runner growled. "Save your breath to run with." *And Thunderbird help us, there are still a lot of Hollow Flute between us and the Black Point.* A chill had settled in Wind Runner's spine. If they didn't warn the Black Point in time, it might be the Fat Beaver massacre all over again . . . *provided I live that long.*

The sun had barely crested the low bluffs on the horizon. To the southeast, the Grass Meadow Mountains gleamed in the morning light, shadowed here and there by patches of clouds that drifted over the peaks. The Broken Stones had slept late after the Dancing and revelry Brave Man had led the night before. As the eastern horizon grayed, birds had chirped among the cottonwoods and in the greening brush along the Grass River. Faint traces of blue smoke had woven around the lodge poles, as it rose from the smoke holes and floated out over the conical tan lodges. Here and there around the camp, a dog sniffed for leftover scraps.

A single scream had broken that peace.

Now Brave Man hobbled across the camp while people called to each other and warriors rushed about, blinking off sleep, darts clutched in their hands. Dogs barked and yipped as they were kicked out of the way.

"Over here! It's Sun Feathers!"

Brave Man hitched his way through the outlying lodges toward the place where Sun Feathers liked to camp. A knot of people had formed before the old Soul Flier's lodge. They parted as Brave Man approached, confusion and terror in their eyes. A silence fell on the crowd as he arrived. Buffalo Tail crouched by the Soul Flier's body and held his limp hand. The clan leader glanced up, grief in his eyes. "He's dead."

Only the sound of camp dogs barking and growling somewhere in the distance could be heard. Then a raven cawed ominously from the cottonwood branches overhead. A puff of wind buffeted the side of Brave Man's face and tickled stray hairs along his cheek.

Buffalo Tail gave him a flat look as he stood. Brave Man turned his attention to the old Soul Flier. Sun Feathers lay on his back, arms crossed peacefully on his chest. The old man's eyes were closed, his wrinkled flesh hanging to outline the skull underneath.

"He was just lying there like that?" Brave Man asked.

Yellow Rock's wife, One Blue Stick, stepped out from the crowd and nodded. "I was on the way to the river at dawn to get water. I passed him and thought he was asleep. On the way back, I looked closer and saw he wasn't breathing. I was frightened . . . I screamed.' "

The clan leader wiped his hands on his buffalo-hide leggings and shook his head. "He must have just lain down and died."

"Killed by the green light in the sky," someone whispered. A buzz of anxious voices filled the morning.

"Wait." Brave Man lowered himself, wincing as he kept his leg straight. He placed a hand on the old man's skin.

Cold. He lifted the elder's colorful beaded shirt, exposing the flesh of his stomach and chest. Nothing seemed amiss. Brave Man pried the old man's mouth open and peered inside. He studied the old man's face and neck carefully, then inspected his hands.

Finally he tilted his head up and looked around at the people who ringed them. "I don't see anything wrong with him. There isn't a mark on his body."

"Then how did he die?" Buffalo Tail asked as Brave Man grunted and got to his feet.

"The green light," someone whispered. "It was an evil—"

Brave Man shot a finger like a lance at the old woman who spoke. "No evil did this." He narrowed his eyes as he pinned her. "Beware what you say, Grandmother. Words have Power. What you call upon may visit you." Chided, the woman put a hand to her mouth and backed away.

Brave Man spread his hands as he faced the people. "No evil killed Sun Feathers. He had finished what he had to do for the People. He was a Soul Flier." Brave Man looked from face to face. "Perhaps the sign . . . maybe that green fire we saw in the sky was Sun Feathers heading south. Did anyone see him after that?"

One by one, heads shook.

Brave Man nodded, looking up at the sky. "We all felt the Power last night. It filled the air. Sun Feathers had doubts about what the Power meant; he questioned why it sent me to the Broken Stones. I knew he would seek the answer. How does a Soul Flier seek? He leaves his body and travels to the Camp of the Dead. There he talks with Thunderbird, who knows the way of the Sun." He paused, achieving just the right effect. "And when a Soul Flier realizes that he has served his people, his soul doesn't return. *But sometimes he sends a sign to lead the people!* While alive, Sun Feathers wasn't sure about heading south, but after he died, he knew the way to life for the Broken Stones!"

Buffalo Tail frowned and rubbed the back of his neck. "And you think that's what happened? That it wasn't some evil Spirit?"

"Look at him." Brave Man gestured toward Sun Feathers. "All of you, look! Do you see any mark on his body? Do you see any sign that he fought? When evil Spirits kill a Soul Flier, you can see it in his face, because the soul is driven off in a terrible Spirit battle. Sun Feathers lies before us in peace. Look in his mouth. Do you see blood? Does it look as if his soul was torn from his body?"

Brave Man turned, searching the faces of the Broken Stones. "No, I think he flew to the Camp of the Dead. And there he learned what Power wanted the Broken Stones to do. Knowing that, he gave us a sign—a path burned across the sky. That green fire streaked to the south, toward the home of the Sun."

Buffalo Tail licked his lips, unsure. "True, there would be a mark on his body if he'd died in a Spirit battle. I've heard that before."

Brave Man placed a hand on Buffalo Tail's shoulder. "He was your good friend. His counsel helped you to lead the people. I know how you must feel. But hear me. He went in peace after having lived a full life." Brave Man smiled reassuringly. "Buffalo Tail, you must remember all the times that Sun Feathers cured sickness, the times he Sang to bring courage in war and success in the hunt. He was part of the strength of the Broken Stones. Elders—even those as wise as Sun Feathers—die. At the same time, babies are born to renew the clan."

Buffalo Tail's shoulders sagged. He looked back at the dead Soul Flier, grief growing bright in his eyes. "Yes, I know. But I still feel a hole in my soul that will remain empty."

"So should we all," Brave Man agreed. "Come, let us prepare him. Flying Hawk, Buffalo Leg, Yellow Rock, and Fat Elk, our finest warriors, will bear his body to a high place. There we will all Sing our praise of Sun Feathers."

"And you will help Sing, help call Thunderbird to carry his soul to the Camp of the Dead?"

Brave Man smiled warmly. "I will Sing with all my heart. I don't bear Sun Feathers any ill will. His first responsibility was to his people—to protect them from harm. One day, when I have passed as many winters as Sun Feathers, I will be as skeptical as he of a young man who comes claiming Power. I hope I will have as much courage as Sun Feathers and send my soul flying to seek the answers.''

He turned then, limping back through the crowd. This time the gazes were warmer, less suspicious.

Yes, I've turned all this to my advantage very easily, haven't I?

Pale Raven had stood at the edge of the circle; now she broke away to walk with him.

''Too bad,'' she said unemotionally.

''Yes.'' Brave Man studied her. Appreciation for her poise and beauty filled him. Her full breasts strained the soft leather of her dress; the morning sun gleamed in her lustrous black hair. ''You don't seem brokenhearted.''

She glanced at him, wryness in the set of her sensual lips. ''Sun Feathers was no friend of mine.'' She paused. ''And you will go and Sing praises to him?''

He chuckled under his breath. ''Could I do any less? He died very conveniently. And he looked so healthy yesterday.''

The smooth lines of her face betrayed irony. ''He did, didn't he?''

Brave Man ground his teeth as he maneuvered his stiff leg through the lodge flap. He ducked inside and hobbled to the sleeping robes. She followed and stood before him, arms crossed, a knowing look on her face. ''So, you are now the Soul Flier. What comes next?''

He stared at the smoke hole, where blue sky grew brighter. ''The Wolf People. Flying Hawk is already eager to prove himself the greatest warrior among the Broken Stones. It will take three days to prepare, and then we'll go.''

''I'm going with you.''

He smiled. ''Everyone is going. The hunting's good up there. Warriors fight better when they know their families are close. Courage flows stronger in a man's veins when losing could mean that his woman will be taken by an enemy warrior, or his children killed.''

She cocked her head. ''You are better than I had imagined you would be. I like that. I like you.'' Her hips swayed as she moved. The dress clung tightly to the curves of her body.

"It will take time before they have Sun Feathers ready. Let's see how much you've taught me, Pale Raven."

With a satisfied smile, she pulled the soft dress over her head. He slipped out of his shirt as her swift fingers undid his leggings. The light filtering through the smoke hole seemed to caress the lines of her body as she settled next to him on the soft robes.

She reached down to grip his stiffening manhood. "Continue at this rate and you'll plant a child in me."

He rolled her breast in the palm of his hand. "Would that bother you?"

She shifted, her other hand tracing the muscles of his chest. A bolt of desire shot through him. "Not at all. You know what that will mean to the people—they'll consider me your wife."

His eyes lifted, glowing darkly. "I *will* have White Ash."

Her throaty laughter and the dancing light in her eyes goaded his desire further. "Go ahead. I don't care, Brave Man. You can have her. Plant all the children you'd like in her. But among the people, I'll still be your *first* wife." Her finger traced around his testicles and he shivered. "Unless you'd like to stop this." From half-lidded eyes, she watched him. "Or can you?"

"No," he admitted as he rolled on top of her and looked down into her eyes. She undulated beneath him, teasing his tense body. "And you?" he whispered, voice husky. "Could you stop?"

She ran her hands down his back, tracing his spine until she could grip his buttocks. "No. You are all I ever wanted in a man. I'll do everything I can to keep you."

"Even kill?"

She spread her legs, reaching down to guide him. "Such a tragedy to lose Sun Feathers that way."

He smiled humorlessly. "And not a mark on him. You and I will do very well together, Pale Raven. Very well."

"Now what do we do?" Blue Wind whispered. He used the sleeve of his hunting coat to wipe his broad-boned face.

"We die," Snail Shell murmured. "I never thought I'd see so many warriors in one place."

Wind Runner rubbed his hot face and sagged down in the sagebrush. He stared up at the night sky, where the stars twinkled brightly. They hid in the valley bottom, deep in the sage that grew as tall as a man's chest. On either side the slopes rose steeply to sandstone-capped ridge tops. Before them lay a small spring Snail Shell had known about. The problem was that others had known about it, too. A large party of Hollow Flute warriors camped at the spring—squarely on the shortest route south to the Black Point camp—and time was running out.

Wind Runner shifted, peering through the sage to study the camp. In the confines of the narrow valley, Wind Runner couldn't see any way to sneak past the enemy. Climbing the sheer-walled ridges in the middle of the night would take too long—and could be the makings of a disaster.

Think, Wind Runner. And you'd better make the right decision or a lot of people will end up dead.

This camp had to be the Hollow Flutes' vanguard—perhaps the first of ten tens of warriors heading south. These warriors would sweep the country and ensure the safety of their women, children, and elders, who traveled a day's journey behind. The warriors that Wind Runner and his friends had outwitted earlier had only been scouts for one of the three villages they'd discovered during the day. But how many more *hadn't* they seen? The whole country to the north seemed to be crawling with women and children leading pack dogs and bearing their belongings south.

Wind Runner's expression turned grim. Everything he'd learned this day struck a painful chord in his soul. He'd seen such a movement of people before—lived it, in fact,—when the White Clay had fled from the Bug River, and later from the Fat Beaver River. The Hollow Flute reminded him of fugitives.

"How did we ever come so far north without being discovered?'' Snail Shell wondered. "How come we're still alive?''

"Thunderbird's been playing games with us, old friend.'' Blue Wind gave a muffled snort. "And maybe he still plays with us . . . because we're walking barefoot through a Hollow Flute snake's den!''

Wind Runner chewed the inside of his cheeks. No more than a half-day's walk to the south, Black Moon's band camped on the river. Stone Fist and Fire Rabbit had moved smaller camps out to the West in order to hunt along the river bottoms. Spread out like that, the Black Point would have no chance against the wave of Hollow Flute rolling south like a herd of buffalo.

"What's happening?'' Blue Wind whispered. "Where did they all come from? How can the Black Point defeat so many?''

"We can't,'' Wind Runner hissed back. "No more than the White Clay could stand against the Black Point.''

"I'm starting to believe,'' Snail Shell agreed. "But what choice is there? We have to fight—to hold our land.''

Wind Runner's expression soured. The cooking fires burned brighter in the Hollow Flute camp—as if to mock them. "There are other lands.''

"Where? In the Gray Deer Basin, where the Wolf People hunted you like a lame rabbit?'' Blue Wind huffed disgust.

"South of there—where the White Clay fled.'' Wind Runner licked his lips. "All we have to do is get to the Sideways Mountains and cross them. Then we can carve out our own territory. Drive out the Earth People. Let the Hollow Flute try to hold the Fat Beaver hunting grounds against the Snow Bird and Wasp clans.''

"Looks like the Hollow Flute People have already been beaten up.'' Snail Shell sighed and made a small gesture with his hand. "I've been thinking about the bands we saw moving south today. They looked half-starved. Some of the men walking with the women appeared to be wounded.''

"Meanwhile''—Blue Wind motioned toward the camp—"how are we going to get around this? Backtrack? Maybe cut around to the west and cross those badlands up by the high cliffs?''

"We'll lose two days that way," Snail Shell protested. "I say we go east—around this ridge and south where the sandstone dips down toward the river. It'll be a long run, but we might make it in time to warn at least one of the camps."

"No." Wind Runner shook his head, remembering that day on the Fat Beaver. *I can't let that happen again. I just can't!* He watched two warriors, talking and laughing, walk out of the camp and into the sagebrush to relieve themselves. They were still joking as they made their way back to camp and squatted by a fire.

Wind Runner cocked his head. "I think I'm getting an idea. You know, it just might work." *Impossible! But then . . .*

"Why do I hate the thought of Wind Runner getting an idea?" Blue Wind's face contorted into a pained expression.

"Because you know it's going to be something so silly and dangerous it'll work," Snail Shell growled. Turning to Wind Runner, he asked, "What are you thinking?"

The stars had drifted halfway across the sky when Wind Runner, Blue Wind, and Snail Shell walked boldly into the middle of the Hollow Flute camp. Warriors didn't travel with dogs. Had they, this stunt wouldn't have lasted long enough for a winded man to take three short breaths.

"Relax," he'd told his companions earlier. "Think of it like this: it's our land, right? Who has more right to walk around on it than we do?"

Snail Shell had groaned. "Ten tens of Hollow Flute warriors and all their darts, that's who!"

Why didn't I let them talk me out of it? Wind Runner's blood tingled as it shot through his veins. His mouth had gone fear-dry and his skin crawled with fright. *Someone will look up and recognize us. Any second now, there will be a warning shout . . . and we're dead men.* He nerved himself and picked his way around the glowing fire hearths, sticking to the darkness.

Black lumps of robe-wrapped warriors lay feet-first to the

fires. Some snored, others breathed deeply. Wind Runner stopped short as a sleeping warrior shifted to get comfortable. In the process, the Hollow Flute warrior exposed his hand to the light of the smoldering fire.

Wind Runner hesitated, aware of the sudden tension in Blue Wind, who'd stopped behind him. He took a step toward the sleeping warrior and bent down to study the man's hand. The last joint of the little finger had been severed—an offering to Power and the promise to fulfill a vow, even at the price of death.

Wind Runner's heart hammered like a stone mallet on sun-hardened buffalo hide as he backed away. At the slightest sound, he wanted to jump, to lash out with a dart.

This is never going to work! No one can just walk through the middle of a war camp this size. This time you've killed yourself—and Snail Shell and Blue Wind, too.

He picked his way carefully, hearing Blue Wind's nervous steps behind him. Snail Shell could have been tiptoeing around sage-hen eggs for all the noise he made.

As he proceeded, Wind Runner counted fires; two tens and two by the time they reached the far side of the camp. He noted the warriors, pointing at their hands as he and his companions passed. Here and there in the faint light of the fires, they could see the stub of a shortened little finger. What horrible thing had happened in the north?

"Who is it?" a voice called out of the night as they slipped past the last fire.

"Break A Leg." Wind Runner took the warrior's name he'd heard earlier.

"What are you doing? It's the middle of the night," the voice asked out of the blackness.

Wind Runner's thoughts deserted him in the hysteria of fear. Nothing came to him. *Curses! You've got to say something! Hurry . . . or we're all dead!* He said the first thing that came to him. "Actually, we're three Black Point warriors sneaking through the camp. What do you think we're doing in the middle of the night. Now, are you going to let us pass, or do you want us to shit right here in the trail?"

"I've got to piss like a bull buffalo in rut," Snail Shell

growled. "Maybe we ought to spray around in the darkness and see if we get his robe."

"Go on," the annoyed voice growled. "And get far enough from camp so I don't have to smell it all night."

Wind Runner barely contained fear-silly laughter as he hurried into the safety of the sagebrush, Blue Wind and Snail Shell hard on his heels.

"I don't believe you *did* that," Blue Wind uttered in a choked whisper after they'd walked a way.

"I almost crapped myself inside out when you told him we were Black Point," Snail Shell muttered. "What were you trying to do? Kill us?"

Wind Runner shook his head in the darkness. "We got lucky. There are so many of them, they don't know who's where. I just told him the first thing that came to mind. Now, come on. We have to make tracks before he starts to wonder why we don't come back."

Snail Shell whispered tightly, "For that many to be here, something terrible's happened."

"And our people in the Fat Beaver valley are as alert as hibernating bears—and as easy to kill," Wind Runner reminded. "Let's make tracks."

Bad Belly rubbed his eyes and blinked. The vision had come upon him as he worked. He'd been absently running the bow-drill to bore another hole in one of the black, triangular stone teeth . . . and the next thing he knew, his head was full of strange sights.

He'd let the drill fall to one side and sat back to gaze wearily around Singing Stones' shelter, shaking his head slowly, painfully.

"What is it?" White Ash came to crouch beside him.

"Vision," he whispered. "All the forests were cut down—by people. They slid the logs down the mountains and floated them down the rivers to make huge . . . well, I guess you'd call them villages. Tens of tens of tens of people lived there, more than you could count in days. All the mountains had gone silent. Where the trees had been, there were only stumps. The rains washed the dirt away from the rocks. You couldn't hear a bird song anywhere. Then warriors came from the west—with terrible war clubs that shone in the sun like mica. They fell on one another and killed one another—until there were more dead than all the buffalo that have ever been run off all the cliffs in the world. The bodies lay stacked around and only the flies and buzzards feasted."

"But what does it mean?" she asked.

He shook his head. "I don't know . . . but the lame warrior's face hung in the clouds above the dead mountains. He laughed—and his laughter shook the world."

Worn and staggering, Wind Runner and his two friends reached Black Moon's camp as dawn began to break on the eastern horizon. Camp dogs appeared out of the shadows to bark and greet them nervously. The cottonwoods—leafing out in spring green—stretched in a friendly canopy overhead. The pointed tops of the sleeping lodges looked peaceful in the half-light among the trees. Here and there a spiral of blue rose from a smoke hole.

"I think my legs are half a hand shorter," Blue Wind complained; his heels pattered on the trampled grass of the camp.

"I can't figure out why we're still alive. We've seen more Hollow Flute than I would have believed." Snail Shell shook his head. "Did we *really* walk through that camp—or was I dreaming?"

"It looked easier than trying to sneak around all their lookouts," Wind Runner said, a tingle of pride still burning within. He blinked tired eyes at the peaceful camp, thankful to have found it. Tired, so wretchedly tired, he couldn't help but grin. *We made it! We lived . . . and we brought the warning!*

He stopped before the clan leader's lodge and called,

"Black Moon! Wind Runner, Snail Shell, and Blue Wind must see you."

A rustling of robes sounded from inside while Black Moon's dog sniffed at their worn moccasins. Within moments the old man ducked through the lodge flap, a buffalo hide around his shoulders. He nodded, digging sleep from his eyes with a knuckle, then yawned. He wore only leggings and a breechclout. The skin of his protruding belly looked pale in the morning light, and the black-moon circle tattooed on his forehead faded against the walnut hues of his face. Heavy lines stretched from his flat nose to the corners of his wide mouth.

"You're back early." The old leader squinted as he assessed the fatigue in their red-rimmed eyes and haggard expressions.

"The entire north is crawling with Hollow Flute warriors." Wind Runner gestured back toward the bluffs that rose above the river. "No more than a half-day's walk from here—by the willow spring—a camp of warriors is busy rolling up its sleeping robes as we speak. Smaller bands of about ten warriors each are searching the country, probably trying to locate us."

Black Moon's face tightened as he looked to the north. "How many would you guess in all?"

Wind Runner lifted his arms and let them drop. "Maybe two warriors for every one of ours. Maybe three."

"Tell him the rest," Blue Wind added soberly.

Wind Runner met the Black Point leader's inquiring stare. "The whole clan is moving. Behind the warriors come several large camps of Hollow Flute. Men, women, and children. The dogs are packing all they can carry. The People look like they're running, desperate."

"And that's not all," Blue Wind added. "Wind Runner walked us right through the middle of the warriors' advance camp last night. Many had joints cut off their fingers."

Black Moon fingered his chin as he thought. "Joints cut off? They've made sacrifices to Power. They won't want to turn back."

Snail Shell glanced anxiously at the north. "We saw several bands. They looked starved—and the few men with the women and children seemed to be wounded, as if they'd fought a big battle and lost.''

Black Moon paused, lost in thought. He glanced up at Wind Runner. ''What do you think is happening?''

''I think that either the Wasp or the Snow Bird clan is behind them. The people we saw looked hungry, desperate. Something happened last winter. Something terrible.''

Black Moon squinted at the bluffs. ''The winter was harder than any I remember in a long time. And what do you suggest we do about these Hollow Flute?''

''Pack the camp now. Get the people across the Fat Beaver River. Send runners to the other Black Point camps. Three days' march to the south, the Stinking River runs out of the Red Rock Mountains. You'll know the place by its stinking hot spring. We can meet there and hold a council to decide what to do.''

''You don't think we can fight them off?'' Black Moon's face had gone stiff.

Wind Runner shot a glance at his two companions, seeing the answer in their eyes. He swallowed and looked at the older leader. ''I think so many warriors would die that we'd end up like the White Clay.''

''We are Black Point! No one is—''

''With all respect,'' Blue Wind interrupted. ''We are all Black Point. Courage is not the issue here. A wolverine has plenty of courage, but not even a wolverine can drive off a nest of hornets.''

Snail Shell nodded. ''We've talked about it, Black Moon. Wind Runner makes sense. We've seen the Hollow Flute coming. Maybe we can drive them back. But we can't do it today . . . and today's all we've got.''

Black Moon exhaled, his spirit sagging. He looked around at the waking camp. ''A half-day's walk to the north? And you came through the middle of their war camp?''

Blue Wind nodded. ''Wind Runner said the best way to make it here in time was to walk right through their camp. I thought we were dead, but it worked just like he said. Only one man looked up and asked us what we were doing.'' Blue

Wind chuckled. "Wind Runner told him that we were Black Point warriors come to scout the camp. The foolish Hollow Flute didn't believe him!"

"And not only that," Snail Shell chimed in, "Wind Runner told him that if he didn't want us shitting in his robes, maybe he'd better let us out of camp. It was dark, very black, and the guard just told us to go on."

Black Moon gaped. "Just told you to walk out?"

Wind Runner grinned sheepishly. "There were so many warriors I knew he couldn't know each one. Why else would three warriors walk out of camp in the middle of the night?"

The old clan leader weighed the truth in their words and chuckled as he shook his head. "Perhaps you have come to lead us, Wind Runner. I remember your wise words on the day you fought One Man. All right. I hear your counsel. I see the respect in the eyes of these warriors who accompany you—and I respect them."

Then Black Moon raised his voice and shouted, "Everyone! Get up! We must move camp! The Hollow Flute are coming, and they have many, many warriors! I need runners to go warn the other camps. Hurry! Hurry! We don't have much time."

Wind Runner shifted on trembling legs; a sense of rightness filled his soul. Perhaps now the ghosts of the White Clay would rest easier. He glanced behind him to where the hills hid the coming flood of Hollow Flute. "We've only bought a little time."

Snail Shell stood beside him, uneasy eyes on the horizon. "You think we should go south of the Sideways Mountains you talk of?"

"I think that's the only way."

"And what if the Earth People try to fight us?"

Wind Runner shrugged. "I think, from everything I've heard, that we can beat the Earth People, chase them off. They live in holes in the ground. Their old women run the camps. What we need, we'll take."

"And if they try to stop us?" Aspen asked as she appeared beside him.

"Let them." Blue Wind rattled his war darts.

Chapter 16

"I'm going. That's all there is to it." White Ash straightened from stuffing her things into a pack. She crossed her arms and leveled her defiant gaze on Bad Belly.

He tugged nervously at his hide coat. She stood dressed in finely worked hides the Dreamer had given her; he'd obtained them from the Wolf People. She wore a bighorn sheepskin coat, a pair of pants, and a calfskin shirt that had been decorated with elk ivories, bear teeth, and colorful quill work. The old man's generosity had even extended to the pack White Ash now proceeded to fill.

Bad Belly sighed, premonition eating at him. He stared out at the marvelous view offered by Singing Stones' shelter as he marshaled his arguments. The old Dreamer sat on his sandstone boulder, face blank as a piece of wood.

Bad Belly adopted a soothing tone. "You didn't have the vision that I did. Terrible things are going to happen up there, and I—"

"I'm going," she insisted.

"But the Dream. Terrible—"

"Especially the Dream." Her jaw hardened. "Bad Belly, you *need* me. What are you going to do? Hmm? Do you have any kind of plan worked out?"

"Well, I—"

"Have you given any thought at all to this?"

"I just know that I have to—"

"That's what I thought."

He lifted his good arm and let it drop. Then he kicked at the dirt. "There are Wolf People up there. You don't *want* to go, do you? In your heart? After what I told you I Dreamed?"

She closed her eyes and shook her head. "No."

"Then what is this foolishness? Why tempt—"

"Because I *have* to." Her face worked as she stepped close and looked into his eyes. "Because I can't let you do it by yourself. Because if anything happened, I'd want to die. I'd never know if my cowardice caused your death."

Bad Belly shrugged irritably. "All right." His heart swelled as he smiled at her. "It may be a mistake—but I guess I ought to be used to making mistakes by now." He reached over to rub her hair between his fingers. "Besides, I think I want you with me."

She matched his smile with one of her own. "Then let's go."

From where it lay beside the hearth, he took the partially completed necklace of stone-fish teeth and placed it in the pouch that hung around his neck. He stared out at the distance one last time, letting the feel of the land soothe his worried soul. Then perplexed lines etched his forehead. "Uh . . . which way do we go? I mean, I know we're going up into the Grass Meadow Mountains, but which trails do we take? How do we keep from getting lost?"

"See?" White Ash gloated. "*That's* why you need me."

"Go three days' walk to the east along the ridge tops," Singing Stones said mildly. "Where the Badwater heads north into the hills, follow it. At the headwaters, take the ridge to the east; the walking should be good there. It should take you all the way up to the timber. When you reach the timber, you'll find the buffalo trail. Follow that north into the Grass Meadow Mountains."

"How do I know where the Wolf Bundle is?" Bad Belly asked. "Do I just ask the Wolf People?"

"That doesn't sound very smart," White Ash growled.

Singing Stones looked back and forth between them. "If you are worthy, you need not worry. Power won't let you stumble around for too long. Not if the Bundle is calling you. Something will happen to show you the way."

Bad Belly listened intently. *Am I worthy?* He looked down at himself, taking stock. What he saw didn't inspire confidence.

"What happens after we get the Wolf Bundle?" White Ash

settled her pack on her shoulders. "Have you thought about that?"

Bad Belly stared blankly at her. "Well, not exactly."

White Ash turned to the Dreamer. "Thank you for letting us stay with you. Can we come back here? Would you want us?"

The old man smiled serenely. "You will be back . . . if you live."

"If we live," White Ash mumbled. A haunted look hid just behind her determined expression.

"Power never gives you any promises," Singing Stones reminded her gently. "I will wait for you. I have a lot to teach you. The Bundle has a lot to teach you. It will not be easy."

"If we live," she repeated under her breath.

White Ash helped Bad Belly loop the pack over his shoulder and they walked to the edge of the trail. Trouble trotted eagerly ahead.

Bad Belly looked back at Singing Stones, sitting under the magpie's perch. "Thank you for letting us stay with you. We'll be back."

The Dreamer lifted his hand and smiled. "Good luck, Man of the People. If Power wills, I will see you again. If not, I will join you in the One."

Bad Belly nodded and waved farewell before he stepped out in Trouble's tracks. A curious mixture of worry and happiness struggled in his chest. The terrible Dream haunted him, bits and pieces replaying in his memory.

"So it's you and me and Trouble again," he said quietly.

White Ash expelled a disbelieving breath.

He let the sunshine warm him as he walked. How could anyone think of death and ruin on this delightfully warm day? But all he had to do was close his eyes and he could see the evil Dreamer's face. "Who do you think the lame warrior in the Dream is?"

She didn't answer for a moment. "I don't know. I've known several lame men during my life—but all of them are dead now. From what you've told me about your Dreams, I don't want to meet him."

"I don't either."

"We don't sound like the heroes in the winter stories, do we?"

Ahead of them, Trouble bounded up the trail that skirted the sandstone wall and led to the ridge top. Bad Belly said, "You know, I still can't quite convince myself that Power didn't make some silly mistake. Someone like Warm Fire should be going after the Wolf Bundle. Or maybe your Wind Runner. You'd think Power would pick a strong, brave young warrior—not Bad Belly."

The trail bent sharply, following a narrow crack in the sandstone wall that led out on top. Deer passed here, and a person could make his way easily. As they stepped out of the defile, Bad Belly stopped to take one last look at the star wheel.

A deep frown lined White Ash's face and she said, "I don't know why we were chosen instead of some warrior. I've been trying to understand, to see the sense of it, but I can't." She paused. "Power has changed my life from the beginning. Look at me. I should be at Three Forks, taking my place in the decisions that affect the camp, learning my duties from Green Fire and Owlclover. I'd have a husband by now, and maybe a child or two, with another swelling my belly. I should have been worrying about the Spirits, and about which root grounds should be collected this year. But here I am, setting out to help you steal the Wolf People's most sacred Bundle so I can Dream a new way for the Sun People." She sighed wearily. "It's all lunacy."

Bad Belly rehitched his pack so he could take her hand. "It's a long way. Let's go. Maybe we can find the Bundle and sneak it away before anyone notices."

"And if they notice? If they come after us?'"

He gave her a sidelong glance. "Then Power will see just what a coward I really am."

At the memory of the Dream, his heart sank in his chest, and the stone-fish's tooth necklace seemed to weigh at his neck. After all of Left Hand's consideration and the honor of the gift he'd given, stealing the Wolf Bundle would be a dirty way to repay him.

Wind Runner sat down in the place Black Moon indicated. He settled himself cross-legged and tried to compose his thoughts. The fact that Black Moon had placed him so near the head of the council circle meant that the clan leader would be asking for his counsel.

Men and women arrived in ones and twos to seat themselves in the shade of the cottonwood. The heavy robes had been left in the lodges, and the gaily decorated clothing reserved for warmer days had appeared. This would be a good day for such dress; the wind blew pleasantly down from the Red Rock Mountains. For this important council, people wore their best: bone-bead chokers, eagle-bone breastplates, oyster and olivella shells Traded from the coast, bright feathers, and sleek furs. Many had painted the leather of their deer- and antelope-hide dresses, the favorite colors being yellow and, especially, the deep purple obtained from bitterbrush.

In contrast to the finery they wore, the faces of the people betrayed their concern and, in some cases, actual fear. *Nor can I blame them. Rumors have been running like a grass fire in late summer. We've run from the Hollow Flute when the people would rather have fought.* But he couldn't shake the feeling that they teetered on the edge of a fearful abyss and one wrong step would kill them all.

Wind Runner pursed his lips and frowned up at the sky. Overhead, the cottonwoods were fuzzy with the first green of spring leaves. The Stinking River flowed a dart's cast to the north of the council circle that had been set up in the open grassy spot before Black Moon's lodge. The Black Point had camped slightly downstream from the noxious hot springs that gave the river its name. Even on a day as warm as this, the steam could be seen where the river exited the canyon to the west. Behind the tree-speckled front range of hills, the crags of the Red Rock Mountains rose against the eggshell-blue sky.

A single butte marked the northern horizon; a rounded

hump of sandstone capped it, as if Thunderbird, or the Great Bear, had dropped a giant heart atop the mountain.

"They put you up here in front?" Snail Shell asked as he paused before Wind Runner.

"I guess I know the country."

"And you brought us here." Snail Shell glanced around at the growing circle. "You've made a lot of friends among the warriors. Many will listen to your words today. Make them as cunning as you've been in the past and we'll be beyond your Sideways Mountains in the turning of a moon."

"Sit." Wind Runner moved over to share his robe. Snail Shell dropped instantly, well aware of how close he'd be to the leaders. "What do you think?" Wind Runner asked. "Are you ready to go south into the unknown? What if there are monsters . . . silver bears as big as mountains, and Soul Stealers and other evil beasts?"

Snail Shell made a gesture of denial. "Then we'll just have to kill them off and go on about our business. It's the Hollow Flute that make me nervous. So many of them." He shook his head. "And they're coming to stay. What we saw wasn't a summer migration to hunting grounds. You could tell by the way they walked. You could feel the determination . . . like Power in the air. I'll take a gamble on the south."

Black Moon had been talking with others. Now he called a greeting as Hot Fat walked into the circle. The sun shimmered off the old Soul Flier's silvered hair. The two elders spoke quietly, heads nodding.

"Ah! There's Hot Fat's granddaughter." Snail Shell gigged Wind Runner in the ribs as Aspen knelt at the edge of the filling circle. More than a few male eyes drifted in her direction.

"Aspen? She's nice." Wind Runner glanced back at the elders, thoughts on other things. "We've talked a few times. She often comes to listen when Hot Fat and I discuss things."

"Nice? She's exquisite." Snail Shell grimaced. "I bet you don't know that she watches you."

"Hmm?"

"I said, she watches you. What's the matter with you? You worried about talking in front of the whole clan?"

"No, I was just thinking. What did you say?"

"I said, Aspen watches you. She ignores the rest and watches you."

Wind Runner cocked his head. "Why? What did I do?"

Snail Shell smacked himself in the forehead with the palm of his hand. "You've got all the cunning of a rock. She's interested in you. She's been a widow for months now and hasn't lifted a finger to any of the outstanding warriors—like the one sitting next to you. You show up and she's making fawn eyes. What happens? You could have the most beautiful woman in the clan—and you don't care!"

Wind Runner laughed and glanced across at Aspen. She'd been inspecting him with that veiled scrutiny he'd become used to. He couldn't deny her beauty. Large, dark eyes stared out from a heart-shaped face. She had a delicate nose, and shapely brows were framed by a wealth of glossy black hair that reached below her slim waist.

"I have another one to find. Best of luck with Aspen."

"Your White Ash?"

"My White Ash." *My?* At the mention of her, Wind Runner's memory stirred. He could see her laughing while that teasing twinkle lit her flashing eyes. Her thick black hair caught the sunlight with a bluish sheen. She walked in his daydreams, the leather of her dress shifting with each move of her sleek body.

I love you . . . yes, I'll marry you . . . The words echoed in his ears as if they'd just been uttered.

I'll come for you. Before the first snow flies. She strolled toward him, a sultry smile on her full lips, a dare in her lowered eyes. Her hips swayed with each balanced step. Her arms swung lissomely, while her lips parted and an excitement grew in her eyes.

A sharp elbow to the ribs punctured his reverie.

"You want to listen to any of this?" Snail Shell whispered into his ear.

Wind Runner shook his head to clear his thoughts as the clan leader spoke. Hot Fat sat cross-legged beside Black Moon, fingers laced in his lap, gaze on the trampled grass, listening intently.

On the other side of Black Moon sat One Man, and just behind his right shoulder crouched Stone Fist. Both men were travel-worn, their clothing splattered with mud and mottled by dust. Wind Runner could see a wary fatigue in their hard eyes. They looked like dangerous men who had more than their share of worry.

One Man twirled a stalk of grass in his fingers. The lightning bolts tattooed in his cheeks puckered as he sucked in his cheeks.

One Man and Stone Fist? When did they arrive? Wind Runner had heard that they would be out scouting the Hollow Flute for at least ten days—but then, all it took was a glance to tell they'd already found something. *And we're not going to like it.*

"You've got a bad case of woman poisoning," Snail Shell grunted. "She must be some woman."

Wind Runner glowered reprovingly at his friend and turned his attention to Black Moon, who was saying, ". . . has come in. I would hear him tell us everything he and Stone Fist learned."

One Man took a moment to scan the circle of faces. One by one, he met the eyes of old friends, nodding now and then. Finally his gaze met Wind Runner's, and the war leader nodded, appreciation in his eyes. He cleared his throat and said, "Everything Wind Runner, Snail Shell, and Blue Wind told us is true. Stone Fist and I kept to the uplands, where we could travel without being observed. At night we moved down toward their camps to see what we could overhear or learn. The entire Hollow Flute has come to the Fat Beaver valley."

Whispers broke out among the people.

One Man gestured with sun-blackened hands. "We waited in the dark and captured one of their women. We dragged her far enough from the camp to be safe and talked to her. She told us this: The winter north of the Dangerous River was terrible. The chinook winds never came. The snow fell and drifted across the land, and then more snow fell. It never stopped. Hollow Flute warriors found places where the buffalo had been buried by drifts and others had climbed on their backs—only to be buried, too. The plains to the north stink from rotting winterkill. The big herds are gone. Only scattered animals can be found, and they have little meat on their bones.

"But the Hollow Flute don't just flee from the die-off. Farther north, the winter was worse. Along the Bug River, the Wasp and the Snow Bird clans faced starvation. Moose and caribou died—some frozen to death on their feet. The northern herds of buffalo may all be dead. In such dire straits, the Snow Bird and Wasp met and had a council. They decided that together they could push the Hollow Flute out of their hunting grounds and save their own starving children. They have taken the Hollow Flute lands around the Dangerous River. They believed there would be better hunting there this fall."

Black Moon shook his head in disbelief. *"All of the clans are coming south?"*

One Man shrugged. "This is what the captive woman told us: The Wasp and Snow Bird warriors fell on the Hollow Flute as the melt began. Behind them come the Green Stone clan, moving out of the forest belt and into the Bug River hunting grounds as the others leave. When the Green Stones arrive there, they will find what others have already left—and will probably follow them south, killing what they can, eating roots and berries in the meantime. Summer is a good time. People don't starve. Fish can be trapped in the rivers, birds and small game can be caught. But the clans will see no big-game herds, and everyone's mind will be on the coming winter. The only way left is south.

"We asked the woman if the Hollow Flute would stay in the Fat Beaver valley and try to hold off the combined clans. She said they would remain only as long as it took them to regain their strength—or until the other clans appeared and began to raid them. The Hollow Flute are tired of fighting. They have Sung too many of their people to Thunderbird.

"Then they saw the green fire in the sky and took it as a sign to move even farther south. The Traders have told them that the winters are not so harsh to the south. The deep cold isn't as bad. People don't starve if the chinook winds don't come. The woman told us the Hollow Flute are desperate, that they won't watch their families starve again."

The people's whispering grew louder. However the council ended, their expectations would be dire.

"Stone Fist and I heard those words," One Man added. "We also heard the desperation beneath the words. We heard the woman's soul speaking to us. I say this, my people: The Hollow Flute will not be turned back, and even if they could be, behind them come the united clans of the Snow Bird and the Wasp, and behind them, the Green Stone."

Black Stone twitched as if he shivered. "One Man, you are our greatest warrior. You've always spoken with prudence and honesty. We all respect your counsel. What do you suggest we do?"

One Man took a deep breath and his shoulders sagged. "Once I would have said that the Black Point could drive them back. I would have been a foolish young man who had never seen the look in the eyes of the Hollow Flute. That would have been the advice of a man who had never seen a clan bled dry of its warriors the way Wind Runner will tell you the White Clay have been. Where are the White Clay now? According to Wind Runner's report, they've been nearly destroyed, reduced to only one camp, harried by the Wolf People, pushed south all the way to the Sideways Mountains—mountains we haven't even seen yet."

"And this woman you captured?" Black Moon asked.

Stone Fist spoke up from his place behind One Man. "We took her with us until we crossed the Fat Beaver River. During that time she told us about how she had wintered on the Dangerous River. When she spoke, it touched our hearts. Her mother and father, her two children—her only children—froze to death. We let her go and wished her well."

Fire Rabbit, the young warrior who had fought so bravely in the ambush of the Broken Stones, stood and waited for Black Moon to recognize him. Then he cleared his throat and looked around. "If we are going to hold the Fat Beaver hunting grounds, we will need all of our courage. I didn't approve of coming here in the first place. Now I concede that it might not have been a mistake. Had the Hollow Flute fallen upon us while we were scattered, they would have driven us from the Fat Beaver and killed many of our warriors. I think that with our combined strength, we can drive the Hollow Flute back. They're weakened. A bold raid now could break them the way we broke the White Clay three years ago on that very river. If we can scatter them, send them fleeing north, perhaps their stories will make the Snow Bird and Wasp think twice before they try us.''

Some grunts of assent were heard as Fire Rabbit seated himself.

One Man cleared his throat. ''Under other circumstances, I would agree with my friend Fire Rabbit. This time I cannot.''

''Then what do we do?'' Fire Rabbit demanded. ''Sit here and talk and watch our land disappear?'' He looked around, searching the faces of the people. He reached out, as if to embrace them, and turned his head up to the lazy sky and the rustling cottonwoods. ''Do we give *this* up?''

Black Moon's wife, Makes Room, stood and looked around. Her fifty winters could be read in her lined face. She worked her mouth, running her tongue over gaps where teeth had fallen out. She wore a smoke-tanned elk-hide dress, resplendent with elk ivories that gleamed white in the sun. A pattern of olivella shells decorated the neckline.

She sighed heavily and shook her head. ''I hear these words . . . and my heart turns cold. We are faced with a problem none of us ever expected. The clans have always fought among themselves, but it was done to keep our blood strong.''

She squinted around the circle, turning on her stiff ankles. ''Things have changed in the last couple of years. We broke the White Clay. When we did it, we knew we had to have new hunting grounds. At the time, I remember, our warriors whooped and Danced to celebrate their strength. At the time, I Sang the praises of the Black Point, too, but my heart was troubled. In all the legends of the People, clans never suffered the fate the White Clay did. Some clans merged, others split off and made new clans—the way the Black Point broke away from the Wasp in the times before my grandfather lived. But it troubled me that we ravaged the White Clay. My mother was White Clay.

"Now I hear the stories told by Wind Runner of the White Clay being chased and raided by the Wolf People. In the old days, no clan of the Sun People feared others. When we wanted the land from the Dangerous River south to the Fat Beaver, we chased those White Bird People off the land. Chased them clear off to the east, across the Short Grass Plains. Maybe *they* told the Wolf People to fight us—they were related once, according to their legends. We can probably chase the Wolf People away, too."

She cocked her head: "Now something is happening. We've always moved south. We've changed from hunting seals and musk ox to caribou to buffalo. We've come so far south that we no longer see caribou—and moose are only found north of here. Now we hunt elk and antelope when buffalo are scarce. I know where we came from, but we did it through generations. Today I hear that even the Green Stone are moving south. Not just changing camps, but maybe moving south for good. Everything has changed. Myself, I've lived through a lot of raiding, but I've never seen or heard of entire clans forced over long distances."

She rubbed her nose and coughed. "I'm getting to be an old woman. I don't want to have to run like a winter-starved coyote the way the White Clay did. As I see it, we have three choices. Stay and try to fight all the clans. Go east and try to drive the Broken Stones out of their country. Or travel south and cross these Sideways Mountains. Of all the choices, I think south makes the most sense. I say this because that's the way we've always gone."

The bones in Makes Room's body crackled as she sat down.

Black Moon turned to Wind Runner. "What about the south?"

Wind Runner stood, staring around the council. People watched him with curiosity and respect. The stories had circulated about his challenge to One Man, about the trap he'd laid for the Broken Stones, and his daring walk through the middle of a Hollow Flute war camp.

He braced his feet. "South, beyond those ridges, lie the Sideways Mountains. Beyond them is the basin the Traders have told us about . . . where the Earth People live.

"My own advice is that we go there. My father's brother captured a . . ." He smiled wistfully, and no one seemed to mind the slip. "Let me start again. When I lived among the White Clay, Sage Ghost stole a girl from the Earth People. She told me how the Earth People live. They have more than enough to eat, but they live differently than we do. I tell you that we can move south, into that territory, and make a place for ourselves."

He frowned. "We have a choice to make. It's a painful choice, and one that perhaps only I can speak of, since I've lived it. We are all Sun People. When we make war on the other clans, we make war on our own people. Makes Room spoke with Power when she said that what happened to the White Clay left her uneasy."

He looked around, spreading his arms as he appealed to his listeners. "If we go south, we'll have to do things differently. I've been told that the game doesn't travel in big herds. I've heard that most of the people down there eat foods made from plants. We know that; we've Traded for those things. Myself, I don't like the idea of changing the way we live. At the same time, I can remember when I could look out and see tens of tens of White Clay lodges—and see so many faces, I didn't know them all. If we fight the Hollow Flute—and destroy them—and fight the combined clans of the Snow Bird and Wasp and drive them back north, how many faces will be missing from this circle? Look around you. When I left the White Clay, there were five tens of people left. There—"

"Not anymore!" a voice called from the edge of the camp.

Wind Runner craned his neck, staring. A lone man walked out from among the lodges, followed by a sniffing pack of dogs. Wind Runner knew that walk, recognized the muscular shoulders that swayed with each step.

"Sage Ghost?" Wind Runner whispered in disbelief.

People moved out of Sage Ghost's way as he stepped into the circle. A rapid muttering rose from all sides.

Bearing darts and atlatl in one hand, Sage Ghost walked up to Wind Runner. He stopped, eyes watering, lips quivering. Then he reached out and Wind Runner stepped into his embrace, hugging him tightly to his breast.

"What are you doing here?" Wind Runner asked, holding his uncle at arm's length to study him. Sage Ghost's clothing was a ripped and tattered mass of worn leather. He'd lost weight—become a gaunt and ragged shadow of the man he'd once been. But a hard pride glittered behind those enduring brown eyes.

Sage Ghost's face worked painfully. "I didn't have anywhere else to go," he whispered, blinking against the tears. "The White Clay are . . . are gone."

"Gone? What do you mean, gone?"

"Dead," he answered flatly. "Killed. Wiped out by the Wolf People." He made the hand sign for "no more."

Whispers of surprise and disbelief ran through the Black Point. They shifted and strained to hear better.

Black Moon stepped forward and pinned Sage Ghost with a wary look. "You come bearing weapons."

Sage Ghost nodded. "It's good to see you again, Black Moon. After the Black Point attacked us on the Fat Beaver, I never thought I'd live to hear myself say that. But, yes, I have come carrying weapons. I didn't know if my nephew was still alive." The atlatl and darts clattered to the ground. Sage Ghost swallowed hard and looked up at the Black Point leader. "Had he been killed in the challenge, I would have come to fight. Not to challenge . . . but to die as the last White Clay."

Black Moon took a deep breath and looked around at the circle of people. "I heard you say the White Clay are dead—"

"White Ash!" Wind Runner blurted, grabbing Sage Ghost by the shoulders. His heart hammered and a curious weakness grew in his knees.

Sage Ghost hung his head. "I don't know. She got away when the Wolf People raided the camp. I know they didn't take her, but they captured some of the others—the young women who could still bear children."

"But where . . ."

"I don't know." Sage Ghost reached up to rub his face. "I crossed the Sideways Mountains, went to Three Forks and watched. I thought maybe . . . well, with the White Clay killed, she might have gone back to the Earth People. I never saw her there."

A swirling emptiness—as if he'd been gutted—swept through Wind Runner. The world seemed to dim and the color washed from the leaves and sky and buff mesas. "When?" he croaked.

"The morning after you left for the Black Point." Sage Ghost lifted his gaze to the wind-teased branches overhead. "I was up there that night—hidden in the rocks. I just wanted to be alone, to think about Bright Moon and to cry in private. I saw you climb the ridge, heard your talk with White Ash. I watched you go . . . and walked off afterwards to think. I walked until dawn, and started back to camp. I heard the screams. By then it was too late for me to do anything. Instead, I hid in the rocks and watched the Wolf People burn the last of the lodges. I checked the dead after they left and couldn't find her. Then I circled and followed the Wolf People. White Ash wasn't among the captives they'd taken. I went back and spied upon the camp before sneaking down to look one more time for White Ash's body. Brave Man was there, walking among the bodies."

"He's got her!"

"No." Sage Ghost shook his head. "But he, too, was looking for her. After Brave Man left, it started to snow. I went into the camp and looked at the bodies. She wasn't there. I took up Brave Man's tracks to be sure he hadn't carried her away, and followed him for a day." He took a deep breath. "He was headed for the Broken Stones—as he said he would. That's when I turned south and scouted the Earth People."

"Then where is she?" Wind Runner asked, stunned.

Sage Ghost knotted his bony fists. "I don't know. I just don't know."

Wind Runner struggled to control his building sense of despair.

Sage Ghost shifted his gaze to Black Moon. "What will you do with me?"

Black Moon studied Sage Ghost thoughtfully, noting his tattered clothing, reading the lines in his face. "You said your clan was dead."

Sage Ghost chuckled—the sound gruesome for its lack of amusement. "Everything I ever was . . . or loved, is dead"—he pointed to Wind Runner—"except this young man."

Hot Fat appeared next to Black Moon. "Then you wish to become Black Point?"

Sage Ghost shook his head slowly. "No, Soul Flier. I am the last of the White Clay. I will die the last of the White Clay."

Amazement rippled through the watching people like a deep river current.

"No," Wind Runner cried as the words sank in. "They'll kill you, uncle!"

Sage Ghost laid callused hands on Wind Runner's shoulders. A wry smile curled his lips. "Then they kill me, nephew. I just came to see you one last time. I had to know what happened to you. You're all I have left."

"I claim him," Wind Runner called out. "This man is my uncle. He can share my lodge. I will care for him."

One Man came to stand behind Black Moon, glancing warily back and forth.

Black Moon paced, working his fingers. He turned and spread his arms wide as he asked Hot Fat, "What do we do? What's happened to us? I can't order One Man to kill him. After all we've heard here today?"

Hot Fat stepped up to Sage Ghost, keen eyes staring into the White Clay's face. "How many summers have passed since I saw you last?"

"Five, old one. At the Gathering north of the Bug River. The one where Seven Bulls married Wild Plum."

Hot Fat grunted and scratched at his ear. "That long?"

One Man edged next to Wind Runner and said quietly. "I will offer some of my meat to feed Sage Ghost."

Wind Runner's dazed wits refused to serve him. Fragmented images of White Ash battled with concern for Sage

Ghost and grief over the death of the White Clay . . . and so many beloved friends.

Black Moon threw his hands up and let them fall. He turned to the people. "You have heard Sage Ghost. You have heard One Man's words, what Makes Room said, and what Wind Runner said. Myself, I cannot speak for the clan, but me, I can't order this man away. I can't add to what's already befallen him. My advice is to let him stay. Let him stay with us as the last of the White Clay."

One Man raised his hands for attention. "You all know me. You know the courage of One Man. I have fought for the Black Point. I have given my soul for my clan. You know that One Man is proud and strong. Yet I have seen and heard things which frighten me, for I do not understand what is happening among the Sun People. Perhaps a new way is coming to us. Perhaps we should all look to the White Clay—and think about the things that have befallen them. Perhaps we should take our time, and learn all we can as we try and see the way Thunderbird and Bear would lead us."

Then the Black Point war leader indicated Sage Ghost with a nod of his head. "I say Sage Ghost should be welcomed among us." He ran a steely gaze around the circle. "He came here alone, knowing he would have to fight the entire Black Point clan. A man who has done this has proven his courage and worth to One Man."

Fire Rabbit leapt to his feet, a clenched fist held high. "What is happening here? To us? To everything? Think about what we've heard here today. Has Power turned against us? Everything has come apart, like an old coat sewn with rotten sinew. I don't care if this old White Clay comes to live with us. I have only one question: What are we going to do about the Hollow Flute?"

The crowd erupted, some shouting, some arguing, shaking their heads and gesturing. Confusion reigned.

Black Moon raised his hands as he called out for silence. Then he turned to Sage Ghost. "You said you'd been south of the Sideways Mountains?"

Sage Ghost nodded. "I have been there. Twice. Once,

years ago, because Power led me there. This time I went to find my daughter.''

Black Moon nodded and glanced around at the worried people. He asked, "What about these Earth People? Do they have as much as the Traders say? Can we live in their land?''

Sage Ghost shrugged. "They don't live the way we do, but yes, they have as much as the Traders say. Rarely do they starve in the winter as happens among our camps. We could take the land and live there—but it would mean learning their ways.''

One Man squinted appraisingly. "You say we could take their land? Are they fierce fighters? How many of us would have to die to do this?''

Sage Ghost gave him a crooked smile. "No man lives forever, One Man. Some of the Black Point will die no matter who you war with. Myself, I'd rather face the Earth People than the Hollow Flute. There are more Earth People—their camps are everywhere because the land is so rich—but I know the Hollow Flute. You have to kill them three times to keep them dead.''

Black Moon chewed his lip. "Let us take some time and think. Meanwhile, talk about it. Tomorrow will be time enough to decide what to do.''

Wind Runner had barely heard. White Ash filled his memory, and her eyes stared back at him from his very soul. *Dead? She can't be dead! Thunderbird wouldn't take her— not after I risked everything. Impossible. It can't be!*

A gentle hand settled on his shoulder. Wind Runner looked down into Hot Fat's sharp eyes.

"Come,'' the Soul Flier said. "Aspen will fix a meal. You and Sage Ghost come eat with me.''

"My hunger is gone, old one.''

Sage Ghost turned sad eyes toward his nephew. "Come on. If she's anywhere, it's south of the Sideways Mountains. If she's alive, we'll find her.''

I've lost her forever. I can feel it. The White Clay are dead—killed by the Wolf People. Why didn't I go with her when I had a chance? Why?

Wind Runner looked up, his eyes losing focus as he stared

into the depths of the sky. *I've been tricked. Cheated of the only happiness I ever would have known.*

Chapter 17

Bad Belly turned the prize over in his hand as he sat next to the small fire. "I don't understand. It's rock . . . and it's wood. See the grain? The knots? How could it grow?"

White Ash studied the curious object he'd found earlier in the day: a section of stone a little longer than Bad Belly's forearm. The long, thin specimen was clearly solid rock, despite the fact that it looked exactly like weathered wood.

"Maybe it's from some kind of tree we've never seen." She stroked the strange stone, running her fingers over the obvious wood grain. "Left Hand told you that the teeth you're making the necklace out of came from a fish. And didn't he say there were stone bones down around Sand Wash?"

The pensive expression on Bad Belly's face deepened and he nodded. He reached into the pouch and pulled out one of the ten black teeth and rubbed it.

They had camped in a hollow between worn granite boulders. Below them, a small stream ran clear and cold in the drainage. Aspen trees rattled softly in the evening breeze. The air smelled of grass, damp earth, and conifer trees. The meadow that stretched the length of the valley grew lush and green with wheatgrass, fescue, and steppe bluegrass. Bright yellow blooms on the balsam accented the purple heads of shooting star, sagebrush buttercup, and early onions. Clouds had rolled in from the west, darkening the night.

Trouble lay across from the fire, where sparks wouldn't land in his thick fur. He watched them happily, eyes gleaming in the firelight, ears up, as if listening intently to their conversation.

"It's wood," Bad Belly repeated. "How can wood turn into rock?"

White Ash yawned and stretched. "Maybe it's Power. Maybe Power can turn wood into rock like that."

Bad Belly scratched his ear while visions of burning snow haunted him. He wiped the stone wood's sooty end where he'd tried to set it on fire. Nothing had happened, not even when he'd placed it in the middle of the glowing coals. "Wood that's rock . . . and doesn't burn? Doesn't even smoke in the flames? I wonder, do you suppose that's what the sun burns? Wood made out of stone? Maybe Power can set the sun on fire. Maybe that's why you never smell smoke when the sun's up. It burns this kind of wood."

She lifted a skeptical eyebrow and stared at him. "Don't be silly. If the sun burned stone wood like that, it would be so heavy it would fall out of the sky. Feel that. It's solid rock. And besides, the sun couldn't burn wood anyway."

"How do you know?"

She propped her chin on her palms. "Pick up one of the pieces of firewood. Don't just look at me like some sort of fool. Go on, do it."

Bad Belly set his rock wood down and picked up one of the branches she'd broken off of a dead juniper.

"Throw it up in the air."

He shrugged and threw it up. Trouble leaped to his feet and launched himself in pursuit. The branch rattled when it hit the ground somewhere behind them.

"So?" Bad Belly raised his good hand. "I threw it up in the air."

"And it came down again." She smiled sweetly and tapped her fingers on her chin. Firelight played on her smug face. "So if the sun burned wood, it would fall out of the sky, too."

Bad Belly muttered to himself. Trouble appeared out of the night to drop the irritating branch at his feet. "I always said the sun didn't burn wood. Otherwise, you'd see the smoke around it—even if you couldn't smell it."

White Ash picked up the stone wood and hefted it. "There's lots of this in the buttes just south of the Dangerous River. I used to wonder about it when I was younger. People just looked at it and let it lay. They never wondered about it. Because no one else did, neither did I.''

"Are there stone trees in the north?''

"None that I ever saw.'' She turned the piece in the firelight. "And someone would have said if they'd found one growing. I wonder if the leaves are stone, too?''

Bad Belly knotted his brows as he thought about it. "The leaves would have to be green.'' He cocked his head. "Or would they? Leaves change color when they fall off trees. But what happens to stone leaves? Where do they go? We should see little flakes of stone leaf on the ground.''

"Shale?''

"I don't think so. Shale's thin and flat, but it's black or gray. And it doesn't look like leaves. You can't see any of those little veins in it . . . and the shape's wrong.''

The fire cracked and popped, sending a curl of sparks twirling into the night to flicker out one by one. In the black belt of trees above their camp, a horned owl issued a plaintive *hoo hoo hoooo*.

White Ash placed a hand on his arm and gave him a sober stare. "The world will never be the same for me, Bad Belly. You've made it come alive again. Maybe Singing Stones and the Dream are right. Maybe I did die in the river.'' She tightened her grip on his arm. "From the time you saved my life, everything got better.''

He smiled and laid a hand on hers. "I'm glad. I never made anyone happy before. I just hope it stays that way. We're in the Wolf People's land now.''

She glanced out at the night. "All we've found are old camps.''

"It's greening up. The weather's warm and the snow's melting out from the north slopes. Maybe they're digging roots. Shooting star is coming up. Biscuit root is growing, and the tops are good to eat before they flower. People like a change from eating stored things.''

"I suppose.'' She yawned and sighed. "At least the Dreams haven't been bothering us.''

He stared up at the dark sky. "I don't know if that's good or bad. I kind of . . . well, I thought that Dreams would tell us where to go. There's a lot of country up here. Where do we go to find the Wolf Bundle?''

Her grip tightened in his. ''Maybe the Dreams don't come as long as we're going the right way?''

''Let's hope so,'' Bad Belly agreed fervently. He loosened his fingers and placed the stone wood in his pack. ''Maybe tomorrow we'll find what we're looking for.''

Larkspur sat under the sunshade outside her lodge. The sun beat down on the protecting granite mounds that rose behind Round Rock camp. The warmth reflecting from the hot stone soothed her ancient bones and joints. The sunshade consisted of a square framework of juniper that supported a woven thatch roof of willow and giant wild rye.

Green Mountain dominated the skyline to the south, rising like a humped monster against the endless blue of the late-spring sky. Up high, the meadows between timber patches gleamed in new green. Fed by winter melt, the grass had grown thick this year. Even the trees appeared to be a richer shade of green than usual. They contrasted with the blue-green sage on the terraces below the mountain, but even there, grass had given the landscape life.

Too bad I can't walk as well as I used to. Larkspur smacked her lips while her eyes traced the pathways to the top of the mountain. As a young girl, she'd enjoyed climbing those slopes, a digging stick in one hand to pry out roots and a bag in the other to carry the harvest of scurf pea, paint-brush, and wild onions.

She stared around the camp—so curiously silent now that her daughters, Pretty Woman, Limbercone, and Phloxseed, had gone up with the men to collect shooting star, biscuit root, and the first tender leaves of dock. In the baking light of the sun, the camp rested. The buzz of flies could be heard against the background of bird song woven by the rosy finches, sage thrashers, and white-capped sparrows that hopped around the sage. Redwing blackbirds and grackles flitted through the thick willows along the Coldwater; a meadowlark chortled its pleasure from behind the camp.

The young dogs had gone with the rest to carry packs, but the old dogs slept in the shade, grunting occasionally as they dreamed. In the manner of their kind, they'd wake for a moment to look at her with lonesome eyes before rolling over on their sides.

The Gathering would be coming soon. This year the Three Forks valley would hold the clans. *Better there than over at Sand Wash like last year. The walk down there almost killed me.*

And next year? If Grouse camp wanted to hold the Gathering clear over on the Sage Grouse River, could she go that far?

She glared at her swollen ankles. "You're getting old, Larkspur. Too old." She squinted up at the slivers of sunlight that slipped through the sunshade. It would be time to leave the earthen shelters soon. The People did that in the summertime—moved around their territory, setting up temporary camps where the root grounds looked the most productive, or where the stands of rice grass and giant wild rye bore the richest seeds. The local Spirits provided well as long as the People treated them and their root grounds and plants with respect. Besides, who could blame a Spirit for getting mad if people came and ate all the plants? Spirits had a love for their places—and the things that grew and lived in them—just as humans loved their camps.

Moving around served other purposes, too. By spring, People were ready to live in the open. After so many turnings of the winter moon, the earthen lodges wore on a person. Warm and comfortable as they were in winter, the soul needed to be out in the air during the warm season.

"And just moving around will leave you aching and tired," she mumbled to herself. "Getting too old for your own good."

One of the dogs pricked up its ears and sat up, staring off to the west. Then the old black bitch who slept by the side of the lodge doorway stood and barked.

Larkspur tottered to her feet and stepped out for a better

view. She had to shade her eyes against the sun. A lone figure approached, traveling in a distance-eating trot.

"Cattail," she said as she blinked against the light.

She sighed and returned to the shade, where she settled herself and waited. *What brings him back? They dig their fill of biscuit root already?*

She peered up at Green Mountain. When the dry winds blew hot across the Coldwater Basin and the sagebrush shimmered in the heat, she'd be wishing she were up there. Maybe it would be a good year to camp up by the moss spring. Bullrush grew in the spring's soggy soils. They'd had a wet year, and the mosquitoes would come in swarms. In the high country they could avoid the worst of the plague. Not only that, but a stand of subalpine fir grew up there. The sap could be collected and mixed with mint and mountain oregano, then burned to keep the bugs away. The resulting black smudge would smoke clothing and purify the air.

They needed more sap anyway. She'd burned the last of her supply with black larkspur when lice had shown up in Tuber's clothing and hair. They'd smoked all their bedding and hides to drive the little pests away.

Cattail called a greeting at the edge of the camp and stopped long enough to duck into Limbercone's lodge. He emerged with a water skin and drank greedily. He brought the water with him as he joined Larkspur and squatted in the shade.

"Greetings, Grandmother. It's a long run."

"And a warm day to run in for a change." She blinked at the constant irritation in her eyes. Too much wood smoke during her life, she supposed. "You're back early. Are the collecting sacks full?"

Cattail wiped at the sweat on his broad forehead and squinted out across the sagebrush. "Mostly. The others will probably start back tomorrow morning."

Larkspur waved away a fly. "And what else?"

Cattail draped callused hands over his knees and settled back on his heels. "Little Toe passed us on the way from Three Forks back to his wife's people at Badwater."

"And?"

"He's worried." Cattail exhaled to express his unease. "Owlclover is talking about witching."

"Three Forks is always worried about witching."

"I know. But Little Toe grew up there. He said that as much as Green Fire worried about it, Owlclover is worse. He said his aunt is almost crazy. I guess Shadblow, the man married to Starwort, saw a witch."

Larkspur straightened. "Saw one?"

"That's what Little Toe says. Someone spied on Three Forks. They found tracks . . . and Shadblow says he saw someone out in the sagebrush."

"But he didn't talk to him? Didn't recognize him?"

Cattail grimaced. "Not from what Little Toe says. He didn't really want to talk about it. We had to dig the story out of him. He's uneasy, a little frightened himself. He knows how Three Forks feels about witching, but he's also lived with Bone Ring long enough to have better ideas. The worst thing is that whoever this witch was, he was hanging around when Green Fire died."

"Uh-huh," Larkspur grunted. She gave him a glance from the corner of her eye. "And what's the rest?"

"Remember that streak of green flame that burned across the sky? Basket lost a baby when that happened. Little Toe says his sister is worse now than Green Fire or even Owlclover ever thought about being." Cattail continued to gaze at the cool slopes of Green Mountain. "Owlclover is talking about accusing Black Hand of witchcraft during the Gathering."

Larkspur rubbed her face with a callused hand. "That wouldn't be good." She thought about it for a moment. "But no one actually *saw* Black Hand."

Cattail shook his head. "No one really saw anything—at least that's what I got from Little Toe."

Larkspur narrowed her eyes. Black Hand would come to Round Rock camp before he went to the Gathering. That gave her a little time. "You know, once someone openly accuses Black Hand of witching—especially in the middle of the Gathering—it will go around like wildfire. And he'll be traveling with us."

Cattail chewed his lip. "I thought it was important enough to come tell you. Limbercone is worried. She thought that maybe Black Hand might already be here. I know he's coming."

She studied him thoughtfully. "What else do you think, Cattail? You've always had a good head on your shoulders."

"I think that no matter what happens, Black Hand is in trouble. I don't think anyone will attack him at the Gathering. People will just talk. But Three Forks has a lot of status. What People there say will carry weight." Cattail spread his hands. "I've always liked Black Hand. If he told people he'd lost his Power, that would go a long way toward lessening their fears."

"It would." *People know that a witch doesn't marry.* Larkspur pulled at her chin. "Tell me, you've always listened and watched. You keep a curb on your tongue and don't wag it for the joy of hearing yourself talk. I've long respected that in you. You've known Black Hand for many seasons. What do you think about him and Bitterbrush?"

Cattail gave her a loose shrug. "I think she'll take him. Yes, I watched Black Hand when Warm Fire was dying. He desires her—but he couldn't let it be known. Not with her husband—whom she loved—dying in front of her eyes. I know my daughter. Her heart still aches for Warm Fire, but she's a practical woman. I think she understands the status she'll gain through Black Hand. She knows people will say he gave up Power for her."

Larkspur nodded. "That they will—and everyone knows a witch doesn't lie with a woman. It would drain his Power."

Cattail cocked his head. "The best of both situations?"

Larkspur smiled her satisfaction. "That's what I've always wanted. It will take the strength out of Owlclover's accusation and blow her words away with the wind."

"There's something else that Little Toe mentioned."

She waited.

Cattail tilted his head, a glint in his eye. "Not Three Forks . . . but Badwater."

"What?" Larkspur slapped gnarled hands on bony knees.

"Is Bone Ring off on a witching bent, too? I thought she had more sense."

Cattail raised an eyebrow. "Little Toe says that Bone Ring is fretting about the Sun People. I guess Half Moon ran into some Wolf warriors. The story is that they'd wiped out a camp of Sun People just north of the Sideways Mountains. Bone Ring is starting to worry. We've all heard the stories that have come down from the north about how the Sun People make war. When they can't kill others and take their territory, they kill themselves. Bone Ring need only step out her door and look up at the Sideways Mountains right behind her camp to know how close those Sun People came. Badwater lies just down from one of the passes. She says the Wolf People are nervous, that something happened in the north, and—"

"Bah!" Larkspur sucked her toothless gums. "The north's the north. Sun People aren't coming here. That's just another story to stir people up. Bone Ring ought to know better. Let the Sun People come. When we see their scouts on this side of the Sideways Mountains, we'll send you and the others to chase them back with their tails between their legs. What are a bunch of wild-buffalo hunters to us? They're no threat."

Cattail tilted his head uncertainly, lost in his thoughts.

Larkspur turned back to important things. *Yes. Black Hand and Bitterbrush. That's the answer. Bitterbrush is no fool.*

Chapter 18

Brave Man hitched his way along the narrow trail that wound through the trees. He'd learned to live with pain. But on this day, searing agony lanced up from his knee to mix with the throb of his constant headache. The joint had healed—the bone grown together and fused. It would take his weight, even if it would never bend again. In silent misery, he endured.

They traveled through black timber here, following the trails his warriors had scouted. The Grass Meadow Mountains seemed like a paradise. The maze of shadowy trails through the timber gave way to secluded meadows, where elk and buffalo grazed. The dizzying heights allowed a man to look out over the vast, irregular plains to the east, the eye casting forever to the infinite horizon. Truly, this place might be the top of the world.

Behind him came the main body of the Broken Stones. The young women had left their children in care of the elders and fanned out to trap game and to hunt—or to raise the alarm to defend the band should any of the Wolf People slip through the lines of warriors. Nor would any warrior shirk, aware that no enemy must pass their lines lest his family be attacked.

Flying Hawk had located the Wolf People's camp, scouted it, and found it full of people. He reported that quarters of elk and buffalo hung back in the trees. From the report, this was no ordinary camp they had found, but one preparing for some sort of ceremony.

"There's no sign that they know we're close," Flying Hawk had said with a predatory grin. "With that much meat hanging, they won't have hunting parties out. The warriors are lying around in the sun, gambling with bones and telling stories. The women are busy baking roots, and the children are playing games. We didn't see any scouts. They won't know what hit them."

Nevertheless, Brave Man's warriors combed the trails that ran through the timber. The Broken Stones knew the ways of such land. Prior to moving into the Fat Beaver country, they'd hunted and warred in the forested mountains that dotted the territory between Dangerous River and the Fat Beaver. Before that, they'd hunted the spruce and fir woodlands that stretched across the north. Now they moved like smoke through the trees.

Brave Man ducked a low fir branch and winced at the throbbing agony the movement caused him. He could hear

Pale Raven's soft steps behind him as his vision shimmered with sudden tears. *If only I could stop the pain!* He forced himself onward.

He had told his warriors, "When you take the camp, there will be a woman among the captives. Her name is White Ash, and once she was White Clay. No one must harm her. She has Power. Bring her to me. Unharmed."

The warriors had grinned knowingly, eyes gleaming.

"You've Dreamed victory?" Flying Hawk had asked.

Brave Man had thrown his head back and laughed, the images of last night's Dream still playing in his head. "I have Dreamed the greatest of victories. We will break the Wolf People. And afterward, we will Dance through the day and into the night. We shall make a fire that shines clear up to the Camp of the Dead, so all may know the Power of Brave Man and the Broken Stones." *And I saw myself with White Ash! She's there, waiting for me. The Dreams will come true. My Power will mix with hers, and not even the golden mist will spurn me. Among the Sun People, no name will be spoken as reverently as Brave Man's!*

Brave Man rounded a bend in the trail and came upon two of his warriors crouched in the deadfall. Beyond them, the trail opened into a meadow. He stopped and bent to peer through the branches.

"We can't go closer," Yellow Rock told him. "The Wolf People are camped beyond that patch of timber."

Brave Man nodded. "Our warriors are spreading out?" He looked up and noted the slant of the sunlight. It would be dark soon.

"They are." Yellow Rock grinned as he knotted and shook his fist. "By tomorrow morning that whole camp will be surrounded. As the sun reddens the dawn, we'll be ready for your war cry. When we hear you call upon your Power, we'll hit them from all sides. They'll never know what happened. By the time the sun crests the mountain peaks, a new way will have come to the Wolf People."

Brave Man tilted his head back, sucking the rich scent of the fir trees into his nostrils.

The voices whispered within, *Soon. You will have White Ash soon!*

The sun slanted across the peaks—where snow still resisted the warmer weather—and tipped the timber with yellow and green. Birds made a melody of the clear morning air.

"Trouble?"

White Ash sat up in the robes at Bad Belly's worried call. She blinked the sleep out of her eyes, wondering how they could have slept so late. Bad Belly stood at the edge of their camp, peering off into the brush. The necklace he'd been working on dangled from his hand.

"What is it?"

He turned and she could see his unease. "Trouble's gone. I woke up just at dawn to finish my necklace, and he wasn't here. I thought he'd be back by now."

She sighed and yawned. "He's a dog, Bad Belly. He knows the way back."

"But what if he's lost?"

She stood and stretched, sniffing the clean, cool air. At this altitude, the morning carried a chill. She could see her breath.

"Well, where do we go to look for him?"

"I don't know." He shook his head. "We can't even find any Wolf People. If he can't find Wolf People, how can we find the Wolf Bundle? If we can't do that, how can we find Trouble?"

"Trouble will probably find us," she told him as she rolled up the bedding and bound it tightly. She took several pieces of jerked meat from the pack Singing Stones had given them; then she paused and looked around.

They'd camped under a low rise on a ridge top. On the other side of the brush screening the camp, the limestone that capped the ridge dropped off in a sheer cliff into a narrow, grass-filled valley. Stands of trees rose to both sides in a thick tangle of black timber.

Bad Belly fussed around the edges of the camp. "Trouble!"

"Here, eat some of this. He'll be back." She handed him a piece of the jerky. "You finished the necklace. Let me see it."

Bad Belly handed the necklace over before accepting the hard meat. Worry etched his homely face, and he couldn't help but glance nervously at the brush, as if expecting Trouble to appear.

She patted his shoulder before inspecting the necklace. "You look terrible. Are you sure it's just Trouble you're worried about?"

He failed to hide the misery in his eyes. "Well, there was one of those visions last night, too. You know, part of a Power Dream. I heard the Wolf Bundle urging me on. Something's going to happen soon. Something terrible."

"Wonderful," she muttered to herself as she fingered the necklace, barely aware of the exquisite workmanship. The stone teeth Bad Belly had laboriously drilled and knotted into the leather thong felt curiously cool.

She couldn't look at him. Each day she'd dragged her feet retarding their progress through the hated Wolf People's land, urging Bad Belly to take the back trails, getting them lost, anything to slow their progress. And during it all, her heart had pumped bright fear through her. It still did. The destruction of the White Clay and Three Bulls' rape hung like a curtain in her thoughts.

"And that vision last night was about the future. Of how it might be if we don't save the Wolf Bundle."

"Go on." She made herself glance at him.

He frowned. "Well, it's hard to explain. I saw people digging up rocks and carrying them across great distances to a large room—a room you can't imagine. Big enough to throw a dart across. Giant fire pits had been dug into the wall. It was hot, miserably hot. And the men were pushing the rocks into fires raging in the pits." He cocked his head, baffled.

"And then what?"

Bad Belly waved the stick of jerky in the air. "You won't believe this, but the rocks melted and ran out the bottom as yellow liquid. The men cooled it and beat it with hammers and made it into things. Some of it was a gleaming yellow stuff that went to Powerful leaders who sat on top of mountains. It was them, you see? The leaders. They made those miserable people work in that hot, fiery place."

She shifted. "So what does it mean?"

He stared at her through somber eyes. "It's what we have to stop, don't you see? We have to Dream a new way for the Sun People—or they'll never know the One. And if they don't know the One, they'll change the earth. They won't Dream with it. They'll separate themselves from it and forget the Dream."

She nodded, gaining a glimmer of understanding. To herself, she whispered, "And I'm the bridge? The way between the Peoples?" She stared at her hands; they'd closed around Bad Belly's necklace. At another time she would have marveled at the craft that had gone into the ornament, but this morning a coldness lay within her breast. In silence she reached up and draped the necklace around his neck. For a brief moment their eyes met; then White Ash had to look away.

Bad Belly wandered off to the edge of the clearing and bellowed, "Trouble!"

"Hey," she chided, "do you want to call all the Wolf People in the mountains down on us?"

Bad Belly colored and took a deep breath. "No. But Trouble's lost. I know it."

She raised her eyes to the sky and shook her head. "He'll come back. Dogs are like that. He probably charged off after a rabbit. Dogs have great noses; they can follow their trail back."

Bad Belly groaned to himself. "Well, we can't go anywhere until he shows up."

She walked over, chewing on the jerked meat, and put an arm around his shoulder, hugging him tight. "I know. It's a nice camp. We've got water down in that little creek. The view to the west goes all the way to the Red Rock Mountains.

I think we can wait until Trouble comes back.'' She hesitated. ''And there is less chance someone will see us.''

He reached up to pat her hand. ''You've been scared half to death, haven't you?''

''When I think of Wolf People, I think of Three Bulls.''

He tightened his grip, worried eyes scanning the campsite. ''I told you, if any of the Wolf People catch us, we'll just tell them we're looking for Left Hand.''

''If I don't throw up.''

''That might be a little awkward,'' he added absently. ''But I suppose I could tell them we wanted to Trade with Left Hand for healing herbs.''

She shivered.

''It's all right,'' Bad Belly told her. ''We're Earth People. Friends of the Wolf People. They're only at war with the Sun People. Just don't say anything in Sun People talk and they'll never know.''

''Sure,'' she agreed. Ice fingers curled in her guts.

''Come on, let's—''

Shouts broke out in the valley below.

''Wolf People!'' Bad Belly whispered with excitement. He led the way into the screening brush that overlooked the limestone cliff. White Ash crouched beside him at the edge and looked down. Three women—burdened with infants in their arms—and five small children ran down the valley. Behind them a man broke out of the trees. He kept looking anxiously over his shoulder as he ran. He carried an atlatl and two darts, one nocked for casting.

''Hurry!'' The man's call carried faintly.

Within moments the fugitives had crossed the valley and disappeared into the trees.

Bad Belly sat back on his heels and chewed on his thumb. ''What do you think they're running from?''

White Ash stilled the panic in her breast. ''War.''

''War?''

She hated the sodden feeling in her soul. ''I've seen enough of it. It's war.''

''Oh, no,'' Bad Belly moaned. ''War? And Trouble's lost in the middle of it? We've got to—''

She clamped a fear-strong hand on his arm. "We're not going to do anything of the kind. We're going to sit here and keep out of it!"

"But Trouble—"

"Bad Belly, listen to me." She stared into his eyes. "You've never lived it. You don't know what it's like. The Earth People haven't raided and warred for a long time. People die, Bad Belly. People are darted, get their skulls bashed in. Wounds get infected and pus runs out like rivers as the person swells up and burns with fever. They die slowly . . . terribly."

He nodded. "I know."

"Then you know that it could happen to us."

He closed his eyes and nodded again.

More people broke out of the trees and ran in panic across the valley below.

"Who?" Bad Belly asked. "Who'd raid Wolf People?"

Her eyes narrowed. "Sun People. Broken Stones most likely. Last winter they hunted where the Gray Deer River joins the Fat Beaver—east of the Black Point range."

"Just like in the Dream," he whispered in a strangled voice. "It's happening just like in the Dream."

"Come on." Fear wiggled in White Ash's gut. "Let's get our packs and get out of here. Whoever they're running from will be coming after them."

Bad Belly followed as she eased back from the edge. With frantic fingers she tied the hide packs closed, then glanced around to be sure they hadn't missed anything. She started for the trail that led down into the timber.

"Wait!" Bad Belly cried.

She turned. "We've *got* to get away from here."

He swallowed hard and looked up at the bald rise above the camp. "At least let me check to see if Trouble's up there. Maybe a packrat has a nest up in those rocks. It'll just take a minute."

She bit off an angry reply. "All right, but hurry! We don't want to run into a band of *anyone!* Broken Stones will kill us quickly as Wolf People—and any stranger will be a target."

He left at a run. She followed him reluctantly, picking her way up through the rocks. Bad Belly crested the top and stopped.

She climbed up next to him—and at her feet lay the edge of the largest star wheel she'd ever seen. It rested on the flat top of the knob, while the sides dropped off all the way around. She would have had to stretch her legs to cross it in twenty paces. Spokes composed of head-sized white stones crisscrossed the circle in all directions. The wheel looked old, with grass growing up around the stones, and silt was piled in the cairns that marked the center and major directions.

The whole of the sky would be visible—not even the tree tops broke the horizon. The view was spectacular, from the Red Rock Mountains on the west far into the plains on the east. White Ash could *feel* the Power here . . . watching, hovering in the air.

Did her ears trick her? Or did she hear an old woman's sing-song chant?

"Look," Bad Belly exclaimed, pointing. "Look at this! It's wonderful! You could follow the tracks of all the stars and the sun and the—"

"And people are trying to *kill us!*"

Bad Belly tore his eyes from the circle and started around the edge of the flat, peering over the side for Trouble. White Ash set her pack down and started around the other way. She couldn't see any trace of Bad Belly's dog. *This is crazy!*

"Bad Belly? I'm going back down to the trail head. Someone has to keep an eye on what's happening down there. If more people show up, we'll have to find another way off this point."

He nodded and waved, continuing his circle of the knob.

White Ash grabbed her pack and started back down the trail, growling to herself, "We could die any second and he's worried about a dog that has more sense than he does."

She dropped her pack by the trail that led down through the trees and crawled to the edge of the limestone cliff. The meadow looked deceptively peaceful and empty.

Hurry, Bad Belly. Hurry.

She chafed, hating each passing instant; then two warriors broke out of the trees, and her heart stopped. She knew the cut of their clothing. That long-fringed hunting shirt and the tight-fitting leggings with fringe along the outside were worn by only one people: Sun People. Broken Stones.

Careful lest she make a sound, she backed away from the cliff toward the brush. She started to reach for her pack—and realized it had been moved.

She spun at the faint noise behind her, watching apprehensively as the warrior stepped out from behind the firs that marked the trail ahead. He smiled—triumph in his eyes. "Don't leave your pack lying in the trail next time, Wolf Woman."

"No," she whispered.

Run!

She wheeled . . . and dashed into the arms of a second man. She opened her mouth to scream, but a hard hand clapped over her mouth from behind.

Chapter 19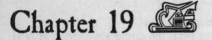

Brave Man walked through the camp of the Wolf People. Another Camp of the Dead—but this time *he* had dispatched the victims.

"Will any of you escape as I did? I doubt it. The Power is mine." He looked down at a young warrior who lay in the sun, a dart jutting from his bloody belly. Someone had finished the job by dashing his brains with a war club.

Pale Raven walked beside Brave Man, absently noting the smoking fire pits and the smoke-browned covers of the lodges that caught the morning sunlight. Except for the bodies, the place might have been peacefully waiting the owners' return. Here and there a lodge had been upended, but otherwise, personal possessions lay where they had been dropped.

"It happened the way you Dreamed it would," Pale Raven said in awe. "The very same."

Brave Man chuckled. Satisfaction threatened to burst his breast. "I am the new way. No one will stand before the Broken Stones. Power whispers in my mind. One day soon all the Sun People will speak my name."

She gave him a sultry glance. "I have come to believe you."

Brave Man stopped at one of the fire pits. A roast lay on the gray coals; the bottom had charred during the fighting, but juices bubbled out of the top. He sniffed, enjoying the savory scent of elk meat. "I would have some of that."

Pale Raven reached into her belt pouch and produced a hafted chert knife. Deftly she cut a long slice from the top and handed it to him. He blew on the hot meat to cool it and took a bite. Warm juices filled his mouth.

He chewed thoughtfully as he looked about the trampled meadow. Several of the younger warriors guarded the perimeter of the camp, eyes on the trees lest any of the fleeing Wolf warriors double back.

In the center of the camp stood a solitary lodge—the largest in the camp—surrounded by a clear space. The cover had been decorated with colorful paintings of the Sun, of Wolf and fire, the moon and stars; and several large Spirals had been painted in red to either side of the doorflaps. Brave Man hitched his way across the open space and stopped. Just in front of the lodge, a gray-haired elder lay on his back, arms and legs sprawled. A dart had been driven all the way through his body. The old eyes stared sightlessly into the sky. Something about the old man's expression—as if the shaman had glimpsed some nightmare terror as he died—sent shivers through Brave Man's soul.

Brave Man shook off the feeling of premonition. The Wolf People had cared for their shaman. His clothing had been tailored from the finest tanned-elk hide and stitched by a skilled hand. Porcupine quills dyed in different colors had been worked into intricate designs on the chest, yoke, and arms of the shirt. The quill work gleamed eerily in the morning light. A wolf hide lay under the old man's body; his blood clotted and dried in the rich black fur.

Brave Man turned to the lodge and gritted his teeth against the pain as he ducked through the low entry. Various pouches, fetishes, and feathered bundles had been hung from the lodge poles. The finest tanned hides made up the old man's bed.

In the place of honor at the rear of the lodge stood a tripod of peeled willow sticks, and upon it rested a large bundle wrapped in wolf hide. Beside the tripod lay a beautiful rawhide parfleche—the carrying bag for the bundle, no doubt. Brave Man stepped closer and studied the bundle. He reached toward it, pain stitching his leg.

Yes, the voices whispered. *Power. Here is the Power of the Wolf People.*

The moment Brave Man's fingers touched the wolf-hide wrapping, a charge ran up his muscles and thrilled in his very bones. He jerked his hand back as if it had touched a snake. Steeling himself, he ground his teeth and lifted the prize from the tripod. Trembling, he peeled the black hide back. Something fell from the wrapping to thump solidly on the furs at his feet.

Brave Man grunted as he reached down and retrieved a carved-stone effigy. He turned it in his fingers: an intricately carved wolf, crafted from a black stone and polished until it shone in the light.

Beautiful! And now it, like the Power, is mine. He dropped the stone wolf into his pouch.

Brave Man's heart raced as he finished unwrapping the black wolf hide from around the bundle. Cradling the bundle in his hands, he studied it. The leather cover appeared to be very old, and had been sewn into the shape of a heart. The top had been painted white to represent heart fat, while a blood-red—laced by darker veins—had been rendered on the lower part. The cover stretched tautly, the way it would if the bundle were stuffed full. Full of what?

Brave Man squeezed it . . . and flinched. A queasy feeling stirred his gut, and pain like slivers of hot stone lanced his aching head.

Feel the Power! He closed his eyes and ignored the head-

ache. His senses seemed to swim, to extend. His soul swayed.
He could feel the Power trying to wrap itself around him,
surrounding him like a warm winter robe drawing tight to
suffocate . . .

With a curse, he lashed back at it, driving it from his soul.

"It tried to kill me!" he raged. Then, to the bundle, he
chuckled, "You won't get me that way. I'm stronger than
you. And for trying to trick me, I shall destroy you."

Brave Man gloated down at the bundle and stepped out
into the daylight. Looking closely, he could see the delicate
stitching that held the sacred bundle together. The needle-
work had been done by a master, the seams so small they
could hardly be seen.

"Another prize?" Pale Raven asked. She was staring down
at the old man's corpse.

Brave Man threw his head back and laughed despite the
thorns of pain that pulsed in his head. "The heart of the Wolf
People! I have their heart!"

The bundle's Power sought him once again, seeping into
his flesh like chill on a winter day. He denied it, closing his
eyes to draw on the Power of pain and anger within. His
balance failed him and he fell, teeth gritted against the agony.

*Call on your soul! Fight! Did you escape from the Camp
of the Dead to die like this?* the voices shrieked.

Pale Raven's worried voice called from beyond the red
haze of pain and fear. He knew vaguely that she touched him,
then drew back in fear. Nothing existed for him except the
battle of will he waged with the bundle.

*I will destroy you! I hate you, defy you! As I butchered
your People, so shall I butcher you!* Anger welled, and he
drew strength from it. He unleashed the festering resentment
that filled his soul, striking back at the tendrils of Power the
bundle tried to weave around his soul. Seething rage twisted
up from Brave Man's being, and he screamed as he broke the
bundle's hold on him.

*I've won! All I must do is hate! Blood and fear are my
weapons, my Power.*

The bundle's Power drained away, and Brave Man blinked
his eyes, dazed by the strength of his personal Power. Or had

the bundle let him go? He tightened his grip on it as if to strangle it. "You can't hurt me. No one is as Powerful as Brave Man. Tonight you will see the full extent of my Power."

He looked up, finding himself ringed by frightened people. The sun stood high overhead. How long had it been? Pale Raven knelt before him, her antelope-hide dress twisted in her strong hands.

Brave Man rolled onto his side and shook his head to clear his vision. Sweat trickled down the side of his face.

"Are you all right?" Pale Raven's voice quavered. "What happened? I tried to help, but . . ." She closed her eyes and shivered.

"I have broken their Power," Brave Man rasped.

The voices inside whispered and giggled in giddy triumph. *Kill it! Burn it!*

Brave Man slitted his eyes and raised the heart bundle to the Sun. "See? See what I bring you? I, Brave Man, am the Power of the Sun! *Thunderbird, I give you this heart!*"

Pale Raven looked around, cataloging the campsite. "You give it to Thunderbird?"

"Tonight," Brave Man promised, gripping the bundle until his fingers dimpled the sides. "During the Dance. I shall send this to Thunderbird amidst the ashes of the Wolf People!"

Left Hand's fear pumped with each panicked beat of his heart. He held his breath and listened intently. He could hear them coming, hear the soft footsteps of the approaching warriors. Frantic, with nowhere to run, he'd slipped into a stand of young fir trees and dug into the thick mat of needles. Obscured by a web of green boughs, he waited, each remaining second of his life measured by the pumping of the blood in his veins. A bit of the duff he'd buried himself in broke loose and fell into his ear, tickling.

Left Hand struggled to clear his mind, to be one with the rotting forest floor around him. If they found him now, he couldn't even defend himself. He'd cast his last dart and gained the small satisfaction of seeing it cut through an enemy warrior's side. Hopefully it had gone deep enough to puncture the gut.

Then at least one enemy will die in misery as his guts fill with corruption. If only I could kill them all that way—pay them back for what they've done to us today.

One of the warriors spoke in the choked guttural of the Sun People. Left Hand could hear clothing rasp against the thick fir branches. Fear flooded his body.

Don't let them find me. Wolf? Don't let it happen.

Another laughed softly, smacking a callused palm against his darts. They rattled meaningfully. From where he lay under the thick duff, Left Hand could have reached out and touched one warrior's moccasined foot.

In the distance, a frightened scream split the silent forest.

The warriors went ominously quiet; then, whispering cautiously, they moved away, the sound of their deadly footsteps fading.

Left Hand exhaled the breath he'd held captive.

Stay put. Don't move. Wait until dark. They might know how to stalk the timber, but they don't know all the trails.

He moved a dry tongue in his vile-tasting mouth and tried to swallow. How had it happened? The People had come together for the Blessing. Today the Dance would have started, and the People would have thanked Wolf for helping them through the terrible winter.

He had just stepped out of his robes to walk down to the sweat lodge when that eerie cry had broken the dawn stillness. Then warriors had seemed to spring from the very earth as they raced between the lodges, casting darts and swinging wicked war clubs.

Left Hand had dived back into his lodge, scrambling for weapons. Bright Morning, his berdache lover, had jerked up in the robes, startled from sleep. At that instant the lodge was upended over their heads.

The Sun warrior had received the surprise of his life when Left Hand had stood and driven a dart into the man's chest.

"Run!" Left Hand had yelled at Bright Morning, then charged out into the fray. In a glance he knew that they'd lost. He'd raced after Bright Morning, fleeing for the timber and casting his darts to slow the pursuing Sun warriors.

In the shadows of his hiding place, Left Hand clamped his eyes tightly shut. Until the day his soul rose to the Starweb Above, he'd hear those shrieks as his people bolted like frightened mountain sheep in a trap. He'd watched Pretty Whistle darted down. Great Water, his mother, had stumbled and fallen—only to have her brains bashed out by a whistling war club.

And Bright Morning? Had the berdache lived? Or had that Power been destroyed with the rest of the Wolf People's?

From every direction more and more of the Sun warriors had appeared, as if there were no end to them. *As many as the trees in the forest.* Left Hand's gut wrenched.

And what had happened to the Wolf Bundle? Had anyone thought to save it in the last moments?

I have to go back and find out!

Brave Man sat before the shaman's lodge with his chin propped on his good knee. In the twilight around him he could hear the Broken Stones rummaging through the lodges and studying the spoils left by the fleeing Wolf People. Brave Man shifted to a more comfortable position on the furs he'd piled before the shelter. The women, children, and elders began to trickle in from their wood gathering in the forest. All day they'd hauled in deadfall, branches, and brush for the huge fire Brave Man planned for the coming night.

He continued to stare thoughtfully at the bundle. The object rested on the willow-stick tripod he had brought out of the lodge. He could feel the bundle's Power. This *thing* of the Wolf People had tried to kill him through a subtle constriction of the soul.

Brave Man looked up at the purpling sky. The evening star gleamed above the tree line on the eastern horizon. *But I resisted. You failed, Power Bundle—and in the process, I learned just how Powerful my soul really is.*

His warriors returned one by one, having assured themselves that the Wolf People had fled in panic. The bundle, unlike the Wolf People, couldn't flee—but awaited his pleasure. What a gift for Bear and Thunderbird! The guardians of the Sun People would grant Power and courage for a gift like this.

A woman whimpered in the background, and male laughter rose. His warriors were sating themselves on the captives, slaves for the Broken Stones. Those women who had been taken alive would bear strong children for his people. They would lessen the work of the Broken Stones women.

Where is White Ash?

A partial vision swam in his head—not of White Ash, but of many working for a few. He pulled the vision to him. Many people sweated in the sun, bearing the fruits of their labor before him on wide baskets. He sat on high, a feathered headdress rising above his brow while he lounged on beautiful pelts of mink, otter, and mountain lion.

I will be like a Powerful Spirit myself. They will pray to me, make offerings so I shed my Power for their benefit. The vision wavered like a mirage in the hot summer sun and faded, despite his efforts to restrain it.

Brave Man shot a narrow glance at the bundle, knowing the telltale trace of its Power. Yes, he'd captured the vision from the bundle. What other secrets did it possess? For long moments he probed, trying to bend the bundle to his will, but his efforts proved futile and he lashed out angrily, knocking the tripod over.

How could he make all those people work for him? In the beginning, the problems would be obvious. How did one control so many captives? What kept them from simply running off? And how much work could slaves do before the Broken Stones hunters spent more energy to feed them than they were worth?

He narrowed his eyes. *There's something here, some Power for the future. Sun People have always taken captives—but only women to breed and children to ransom back to other clans. How can captives be used to lead us to a new way of living? One where Broken Stones tell others what must be done.*

Pale Raven walked out of the growing dusk to settle on the robes beside him. She wore a soft elk-hide dress that had been smoked to a golden brown. Tubular bone beads rattled on the fringes that lined the hem. Purple designs had been stained into the shoulder yoke with dye made from bitter-brush seeds. She wore her hair loose, a gleaming raven cascade that the wind teased.

"A runner just came from Flying Hawk," she told him. "All the Wolf People are fleeing to the south."

"Have they found White Ash?"

"No one has sent word yet."

Brave Man grunted and glanced irritably at the bundle that lay spilled in the hides. "Have any of the Wolf People fought back?"

"Flying Hawk said that one or two have gathered their courage and have attempted to ambush our warriors—but that most of the enemy are too panicked."

Brave Man chuckled to himself. "Some will try." He lifted the bundle—it raised a prickling in his flesh—and turned it in the evening light. "Tomorrow I will release one of their women to tell those who would continue to fight against us that their heart has been burned."

Pale Raven shivered, as if from the growing mountain chill, and rubbed her hands rapidly along her arms. "I don't like that thing. I can almost feel it. How can you handle it that way?"

He held the heart bundle before his eyes and gave it a pensive consideration. "Because my Power is greater than its Power. It has tried to fight me—and lost." He thumped the bundle with a thick finger. "You see, the Sun is stronger than the heart. Everything comes from the Sun. Even Thunderbird and Bear. Before there was anything, there was the Sun, the only Creator and Life-giver. The Sun People are the new way for the world . . . and *I* am the new way for the Sun People."

Pale Raven gave him a sober look. "I would not be your enemy."

He laughed, genuine appreciation for her growing in his thoughts. "Nor I yours." He cocked his head. "Tell me, how did you kill Sun Feathers?"

She hugged her knees and clasped her fingers, looking out at the darkening trees. "How can you be sure I did?"

"You ask the most Powerful man among the Broken Stones? You ask the Dreamer who Dreamed this?" He gestured at the camp. Here and there a fire brightened the velvet lavender of evening.

She considered for a moment and then said, "Age saps a man's strength . . . and he was an *old* man. I saw that he was going to make trouble for you. I could tell by the look in his eyes. He couldn't let you—a stripling, a White Clay youth—take away his status. When he got to his lodge, I followed him inside and told him I had something to tell him. He asked me to sit.

"When he'd lowered himself, I reached out in the dimness and slipped a hide bag over his head. Then I lay on him and pushed his head down into all those soft furs of his. He tried to struggle, but he was too old, too weak. I waited for a long time after he ceased to fight." She shrugged. "It was a good sack that I tied around his head. If it could hold water, I figured he couldn't breathe through it."

"Did you hate him?"

She snorted in derision. "Among others."

Brave Man extended his hand. "Help me up. More warriors are coming in. It is time to start the Dance."

She stood and eased him to his feet. He winced as his weight bore down on the bad knee. He placed the bundle on the tripod again. "I think we have enough wood."

She steadied him and said, "From the pile you had them drag in, we could burn the mountain down."

He looked up at the night sky. "Just so it can be seen from the Camp of the Dead."

Brave Man limped to the nearest fire. There two warriors grinned up at him as they ate something they'd found in one of the captured parfleches. Pale Raven handed him a burning brand before he walked over to the mountainous pile of wood the clan had gathered. He lit the tinder at the bottom. Flames crackled up toward the sky.

People began coming from all around, watching with wide eyes as they talked and pointed at the growing fire. Brave Man tilted back his head to watch the first sparks whirl into the black sky. This night would be talked about forever.

"You, Yellow Rock, bring the Wolf women here. Put them in the light so all can see. I want them in the center of the Dance." *But White Ash isn't among them.*

Soon, the voices in his head promised. *You will have her this very night. Soon—if your Power is strong enough—she will be yours.*

He laughed aloud, murmuring, "Yes, Spirits, my Power will hold White Ash."

"What?" Pale Raven asked.

"Nothing." The flames lit the camp and beyond. He, Brave Man, had accomplished this. His Power had brought him from the Camp of the Dead on the Fat Beaver to lead the Broken Stones in this glorious victory. He basked in the admiration beaming from the people's eyes.

At the edge of the timber, two warriors dragged yet another struggling captive in from the woods. Another woman for the Broken Stones. Idly he wondered if they'd spent their manhood happily, and glanced at Pale Raven. No captive could bring a man to the soul-leaping fulfillment Pale Raven had shown him.

Brave Man put his arm around her shoulders and turned back to the fire. Flames shot high into the night.

Where is White Ash?

The voices in his head emitted a hushed sigh. *She is yours this night. But we must warn you . . . beware. Beware the workings of Power!*

Brave Man threw his head back and laughed. The two warriors dragged their struggling captive closer to the fire.

Rough hands threw White Ash down, pinning her to the ground. "We've caught a nice one, Five Darts. We'll share her—or gamble to see who gets to keep her."

Five Darts grinned happily. "We might have to gamble to see who takes her first."

"I have done nothing to you! Your enemies are the Wolf People. In the name of Thunderbird, *let me go!*" White Ash pleaded, belly going tight as understanding crept through her.

Five Darts cocked his head suspiciously. "You speak like

a human being. You don't swallow your words like the Wolf People do."

She steeled herself. "I—I am White Clay." Now for the gamble. Did they know of the White Clay's fate? "At the Gathering . . . my family would pay to get me back. If you don't harm me, I'll work for you. Carry wood, cook, make hides . . . until the Gathering. Then my family will buy me back."

Five Darts shot an excited glance at his friend. "Buffalo Jumps, we were told to look for a White Clay woman." He peered eagerly into her eyes. "What is your name?"

"White Ash." Hope sparked within. She would tell them anything, just as long as she could buy time to escape.

Buffalo Jumps whooped and sprang to his feet, shuffling in a Dance of triumph. The eagle-bone beads on his sleeves rattled with each pirouetting step. "Tie her! We've done it!"

Five Darts flushed. "The Soul Flier will praise our names to Thunderbird. He'll place us beside him in the next council!"

Buffalo Jumps had pulled thongs from his belt pouch. Five Darts rolled White Ash over and wrestled her arms back while his friend expertly bound her.

"What are you doing?" White Ash cried. "I'll walk with you. Just don't hurt me."

"We won't hurt you, White Ash. Not for all the women among the Wolf People, or for all the kills we could make. You're more precious to us than fat-rich meat in starving times," Five Darts assured her.

Buffalo Jumps pulled the knots tight. "Get up."

She climbed awkwardly to her feet. As Five Darts held her, Buffalo Jumps used another thong to bind her ankles.

"That should be about the right length," he decided. "You can walk—if you're careful. But you can't run. Let's go." He pointed down the trail.

White Ash nodded miserably, refusing to look back toward the flat-topped knob where Bad Belly sought his dog. Thank Thunderbird he hadn't called out again or whistled for Trouble.

She started down the trail, almost tripping when the thong on her ankles pulled tight.

"We've caught White Ash!" Five Darts repeated over and over.

"Why am I such a catch?" she demanded, fear alternating with hope as she stumbled along in faltering steps.

"The Soul Flier wants you."

Soul Flier? Who? Sun Feathers? She'd seen the Broken Stones Soul Flier at the last Gathering on Bug River. What would the old man want with her? At least he wouldn't rape her, wouldn't beat her.

Broken Stones? A chill frosted her soul. Brave Man might be among them. He'd have gone there—if the Wolf People hadn't killed him. Had he said something to Sun Feathers? Maybe made those claims of Power?

Run, Bad Belly! Get away. Get off these cursed mountains and go home to Round Rock! The thought of him trying to follow, to effect a rescue, tormented her. The Broken Stones would kill him on the spot the moment they caught sight of him. And Bad Belly *would* be seen.

She narrowed her attention on how she placed her feet, keeping her balance as best she could. At the thought of Bad Belly attempting a rescue, her guts turned as punky as rotten wood. A man who got lost in his head, who almost walked off cliffs because he wasn't paying attention . . .

The day wore on. Thirst irritated her throat. Walking in such an awkward fashion cramped the muscles in her legs and hips. The binding on her ankles chafed and burned as each step rubbed her skin raw.

"We could make better time if you took these bindings off," she suggested.

Five Darts lifted an eyebrow as he looked at Buffalo Jumps. The latter shook his head. "No, better slow than to lose her. The Soul Flier would . . . Well, I don't want to face his wrath."

White Ash bit her lip and struggled on, hating it each time they lifted her over deadfall or carried her over rough ground like a limp buffalo quarter.

As the sun began to drop in the western sky and shafts of

light slanted through the trees, they passed the first body. An old woman lay in the trail, the back of her head bashed in.

"Why did you attack the Wolf People?" she asked.

Five Darts smiled grimly. "The Soul Flier Dreamed it, and Sun Feathers sent us a signal from the Camp of the Dead. He burned a green fire through the sky, pointing the way."

Buffalo Jumps lifted his chin. "The Broken Stones have a new Soul Flier, a Powerful Soul Flier. His name is Brave Man."

White Ash tripped and fell. She lay there in the trail, spilled hair hiding the horror on her face. A terrible sickness, like the gray, runny fluid that filled a rotting carcass, washed through her soul.

"Come on. Get up," Five Darts ordered.

"She won't," Buffalo Jumps said. "Unless we beat her. She knows Brave Man. She understands better than we do. She thought she would be able to plead before Sun Feathers. Now she knows better. Help me lift her."

The evening sky dimmed into indigo and then violet as they proceeded. White Ash did everything she could to stall. She snagged the binding thongs on branches and rocks; she fought when she could, struggling futilely against their superior strength.

"I see the Dance fire!" Five Darts cried. "We're almost there."

"Please," White Ash whispered. "Let me go. You seem like honorable warriors. Don't do this to me."

"What did the White Clay ever do for me?" Buffalo Jumps asked. "My father died from a White Clay war dart."

They hustled her into a clearing, past a pile of bodies that had been dragged to one side. Wolf People. Brave Man had broken the implacable warriors of the mountains.

A group of people stood around an enormous bonfire. Toward them, she was mercilessly dragged.

"Soul Flier?" Five Darts called. White Ash pulled back, hiding herself in Buffalo Jumps' shadow, twisting against the binding thong the man held. The glimpse was all she needed. She knew that profile, the set of those broad shoulders.

Brave Man turned. Something seemed to be wrong with his leg. "Yes?"

"I am Five Darts, and this is Buffalo Jumps."

Brave Man gave the men a more careful scrutiny. "Yes?"

Buffalo Jumps grinned and handed the leather thong to him. "We have brought you the woman you asked for. We have brought you White Ash!"

Brave Man reached over and pulled White Ash out from Five Dart's shadow. She looked into those familiar eyes. Her heart thundered.

"White Ash," he whispered.

Panic ran bright through her. *Think! Think, woman, or you'll wish you had Three Bulls back.* Thoughts fragmented. "Let me go, Brave Man. I'll only bring you trouble."

He laughed from deep in his belly. "This time there is no Wind Runner to come to your rescue."

"So this is White Ash?" a tall woman asked, stepping closer to see. The firelight accented her striking features and long black hair. "Yes, Brave Man, she is beautiful." Her eyes narrowed. "But, woman, are you good enough? Are you better than Pale Raven?"

White Ash tried to swallow her fear—and failed.

Brave Man's voice expressed building joy as he said, "I've waited a long time for this." He raised a finger and lifted White Ash's chin. "Nothing can stand in my way now." He lowered his voice. "Tonight, White Ash, your Power will become mine. And you will even enjoy it." He glanced at the tall woman, who continued to stare at White Ash through slitted eyes. "Thanks to what Pale Raven has taught me."

"We'll see, Brave Man. We'll see who you come back to," Pale Raven replied in a thinly veiled threat.

Brave Man limped off toward a large lodge that stood alone in the center of the camp, calling, "Bring her. She is mine now."

Lame! Brave Man had been lamed! *A lame warrior,* Bad Belly had said on the night of his terrible Dream. *Thunderbird, no!*

Buffalo Jumps caught her deftly as she tried to leap away

and picked her up. The way he held her, she could do no more than flop about foolishly on his muscular shoulder.

"Relax, White Ash." Pale Raven spoke in smooth tones as she followed. "I've trained him for you. His soul has a vigor that possesses his manhood. He's been an eager student, and I have taught him well. You'll find this much better than rutting with the average warrior."

"Speak for me," White Ash pleaded. "Don't let him *do* this! Don't you care? If you love him, do you really want him taking me?"

Pale Raven's voice dropped sensually. "Oh, I think I'll have him back in the end. All he wants from you is a child—and to gain your Power. Let him plant his seed, White Ash. You might as well enjoy it. Like I told you . . . he is quite good."

Buffalo Jumps stopped before the tall lodge. White Ash could see the symbols of Power—the Spirals, Wolf, and the Sun—painted on the hides.

"Place her on the furs, here." Brave Man ordered. "What will happen will be seen from the Camp of the Dead."

Buffalo Jumps lowered her to the piled furs. White Ash clamped her jaws, futile tears blurring her vision. It would happen again. She couldn't fight so many.

"Brave Man?" White Ash asked, trying to keep her voice steady. "What happened to you? Don't you remember what was between us? What happened to the young man I laughed with? What happened to the kindness . . . to the man I loved?"

He raised his head to the night sky, where stars had begun to twinkle. Yellow firelight lit the soft folds of his clothing. "Power called me. Power has no use for the soft of heart, or the sentimental. That Brave Man you knew died in the Camp of the Dead. The Camp of the Dead stripped off the parts of my soul that were weak, like bark from an old tree. Only the hard wood remains."

"For all that's behind us, don't do this. Let me leave. I'll never come back. I just want to—"

"It's too late for that." He raised his hands to the stars. "A new way has come, and Power has chosen me to lead it."

She chewed her lip. "Why me?"

"The voices told me so long ago. You're Powerful. Through you I will find the way to the golden haze. Through your Power I will learn how to control that place and make a new way. The voices tell me that tonight I shall plant my child—and he shall be great and Powerful as no man has been Powerful before."

Brave Man reached down and grunted, as if in pain from his leg. He lifted a leather object from a willow tripod. "See this? It's the Spirit heart of the Wolf People."

The Wolf Bundle! Bad Belly's vision from the Dream played in her head. *Too late. We are too late. Bad Belly, I'm sorry. I should have rushed us—driven us—to get here. I'm to blame. I hung back. My fear of the Wolf People . . .*

"And you will throw it in the fire after you're done with me." The words felt like gravel in her mouth.

Brave Man nodded. "You *are* Powerful. You know . . . and you know why I must have you. You know what Power has in mind for you . . . for me. It will be, White Ash. No matter how much you hate me, I must break you to my will. You can't deny Power—and I have it." He shook the Wolf Bundle. "This object tried to kill me . . . except, Brave Man resisted. Even now it tries, but the Spirit voices warn me first so I can defend myself."

His speech sounded slurred, like that of an elder who'd lost his teeth. White Ash braced herself. "The One and the Dream of First Man aren't for you. You don't know what you'll create with your Power."

"The One?" He cocked an eyebrow. "Is that what you call it?"

She turned her head away.

Brave Man gestured at the two warriors. "You may go. You have earned the gratitude of Brave Man. If I need you, I'll call." Five Darts and Buffalo Jumps grinned before they walked off toward the fire. A new pride filled their steps.

To Pale Raven, he said, "I can't take the chance of untying her. Use your knife to cut her shirt."

Pale Raven knelt beside White Ash. "He has Power, and he knows how to use it on a woman."

White Ash closed her eyes as Pale Raven sliced the beautiful shirt Singing Stones had given her down the front. The night air blew cool across her skin as the leather parted. Pale Raven's fingers worked at the laces of her pants. With surprising strength, the woman pulled them from her hips.

White Ash couldn't stop the trembling that possessed her. A sickness grew in her gut.

"How will it be, White Ash?" Brave Man asked. "Will you accept me without a fight? Or must I call Five Darts and Buffalo Jumps to hold you? Will you meet my Power . . . accept it? Or will the Camp of the Dead and my warriors watch you?"

She swallowed her panic and hissed, *"Get it over with!"*

Brave Man placed his hands on Pale Raven's shoulders. "Go. Start the Dancing and Singing. Lead them in the call to Power. Tell them to Sing with all their hearts as they call Thunderbird to watch."

Pale Raven nodded and walked off toward the fire.

"Don't do this, Brave Man. Remember who we were, remember what our ancestors—"

"I am the new way." He pulled his shirt over his head. Firelight gleamed on his powerful chest. He undid the laces that held his fringed leggings, and grunted again as he kicked them from his bad leg. The joint of his knee looked knotted and lumpy as burl wood on a pine.

Wild whoops rose around the fire as men began to Dance and Sing their prayers to the night sky.

He faced the fire then, raising his arms. "Hear me, Thunderbird! I have followed the way of Power! I have Dreamed the destruction of the Wolf People! This night, before you, Power is united. A new Dreamer will be made in this place, born of my seed and nurtured in White Ash."

His breath caught as he lowered himself next to her. "Join with me, White Ash. You know the way of Power. You know what must be."

How could she fight? Her hands remained bound behind her. The pants that wadded around the tethering thong on her ankles wouldn't even let her kick at him.

She whimpered as he reached out and touched her, running light fingers over her skin. Her stomach knotted and twisted, and the urge to vomit tickled her throat. She turned her head—and in the dancing firelight, the Wolf Bundle looked bloody. As she watched, she could feel its Power penetrating her fear. She couldn't ignore its draw, despite Brave Man's fingers on her breasts.

Bad Belly, I failed you . . . failed Power. If I could do it over. Oh, Bad Belly . . .

Brave Man's fingers traced down her stomach. She struggled to swallow the bile in the back of her throat.

Chapter 20

Bad Belly ran as fast as he could. A man with one arm couldn't balance as well as a man with two, and he had to use his good hand to hold his pack strap. Not only that, he had simply never been a runner.

"White Ash," he groaned as he vaulted a deadfall in the trail. His pack bounced from side to side on his back and almost toppled him.

Having found no trace of Trouble, he'd paused to take one last look at the star wheel, despite fretting about his dog and the warriors running through the trees below. He couldn't help stooping to sight down the lines of stones one more time. In the center of the huge wheel stood a stone cairn. Unable to resist, he walked over to look at it.

The central cairn appeared old, and cycles of frost and thaw had spread the rocks over an area two paces wide. Red-orange lichens had grown over most of the head-sized stones, and many of them had sunk into the soil, almost covered by the sparse grasses. A gleam caught his eye, and he bent down over the cairn. A sliver of stone protruded from the wind-blown silt. He pulled at it; it didn't move. He took a bone awl from his pack, squatted on his heels, and gouged at the soil. The sliver of stone became a dart point. He dug around it, curious that he couldn't lift it from the soil, and uncovered a bone—a vertebra into which the tip had stuck. With fevered haste he dug the bone out. Roots had woven their way through it, but there was no mistaking the find. A human being had been darted through the belly, and the point had lodged in the front of the vertebra.

Someone had placed the body here, on the cairn. When the flesh had rotted away, the bones had fallen down among the rocks, where silt had blown over them. Who? How long ago?

Bad Belly's scalp prickled as he glanced anxiously at the wind-scoured star wheel. He could feel Power growing around him, ominous, pressing down like a wall of warm water.

Voices that spoke a language Bad Belly had never heard rose above the whisper of the breeze.

"Ghosts?" he wondered. At that moment a whirlwind arose in a sucking rush from the very ground. Violent winds battered him, whipping his braids and fluttering the fringes on his shirt. He hunched against the fury of the air, eyes closed against the stinging dust that prickled his skin.

A haunting voice—old and scratchy, like that of an old woman gasping for breath—called from the vortex: *Dreamer . . . coming. Tell . . . all the People . . . they'll have to Dance with fire. A new Dreamer is coming. Run now. Run like you've never run before, boy.*

The whirlwind lifted into the sky, and the grass at Bad Belly's feet went still. He carefully replaced the bone and its gruesome point the way he'd found them and brushed the dirt until only the base of the point was visible.

The voices grew louder, and he realized with a start that they came from below, from . . . *where White Ash is!* . . .

He jumped to his feet and grabbed his pack, then peered over the edge of the flat-topped knob toward the camp. Two men had White Ash down, binding her hands and feet with thongs.

"My fault," Bad Belly whispered. "Mine and Trouble's. Why didn't I listen to her? Why didn't we run?"

White Ash struggled to her feet, talking to the men in an odd tongue. *Sun People! Broken Stones!*

The warriors started down the steep trail through the timber to the grassy valley below.

Bad Belly scrambled down the slope, slinging his pack over his shoulder, peering this way and that while his heart raced. He could see where the warriors and White Ash had bent the grass. Muscles quivering with fear, he stepped into the open meadow.

Run . . . run as you've never run before, boy. The old woman's voice had repeated in his mind.

And now he ran, charging across the clearing and into the trees. *What if I lose them? What if they take White Ash to the lame warrior?* In his panic, he almost betrayed himself, sliding to a stop as he rounded a bend in the trail and ducking back into the timber. The warriors were lifting White Ash over a pile of deadfall that blocked the trail. Only the crackling of branches as they struggled covered the sound of Bad Belly's mad scramble back into cover.

Bad Belly kept just out of sight, reading the trail from the scuff marks White Ash's hobbled feet made. Through thick patches of timber and across open, grassy meadows, he lurked on their trail. In the process, he alternately suffered through fear, hope, and despair as he tried to decide on a course of action.

My fault. He ducked around a spruce and almost stepped on an old woman. She lay in the middle of the trail, facedown, the back of her head split open.

Bad Belly's stomach churned. Flies had already laid eggs in the wound, and the insects rose in an angry buzz as he picked his way past.

He went on. Spruce and fir rose in dense patches of somber green, their branches interlacing over the trail. His scalp prickled as if haunted eyes watched from the silent shadows. No more than ten paces later he stepped into a stand of thin lodgepole pine, and then he was creeping across a bare meadow, knowing that a cry of warning would be raised at any moment.

What am I going to do? He looked up at the darkening

sky. *I'm not a warrior. Not a hero.* He gestured in despair. "Wolf Bundle? Couldn't you have picked someone better? Someone brave?"

As the sun settled in the west, he hurried faster, afraid he'd lose the trail in the darkness. Pine needles crackled under his moccasins, and once he stepped on a stick that snapped like a bone breaking.

Bad Belly started at the sound. *Be quiet, you fool.*

He increased the care with which he moved—and almost ran into the warrior. Bad Belly pulled up with a start, thinking he would die with his next breath. In the deceptive shadows, it took a moment to see that the warrior had his back turned, his attention on an open meadow where a fire had been lit against the gloom.

Bad Belly took a step to one side on rubbery legs. Then another. Praying silently, he eased into the timber, starting to move around the warrior. If he could get back just a little farther, work his way around the—

A twig cracked under his foot. The warrior whirled and searched the darkness with keen eyes while a nocked dart went back for casting.

Bad Belly froze like a cottontail under a hawk's hungry eye. The breath stopped in his lungs. *You're going to die!*

The warrior took a step, craning his neck.

Bad Belly clamped his jaws to keep his teeth from chattering.

The warrior called softly—the guttural words meaningless to Bad Belly. Arm back to cast his wicked dart, the warrior took another step, balanced, deadly.

At that moment something stirred off to the right. The warrior pivoted on his heel, casting with the speed of a striking rattler. But quick as his cast, the lean shape in the timber proved faster, and the black wolf shot away into the darkness.

The warrior growled and climbed over the deadfall to begin searching for his dart.

Wolf, bless you and all your children. Bad Belly gingerly eased away into the trees, stepping over deadfall and tiptoeing on the mat of dry needles. He tried to still the ragged pounding of his heart. Close. So terribly close!

He took his time, easing around the warrior's position and circling. Through the gaps in the trees he could see people around the enormous fire. White Ash would be there. He paused at the edge of the clearing. A hideous mound of corpses had been carelessly piled at the edge of the trees. To his horror, the bodies made sounds—gurgles and hisses—as the corruption of death stole through them.

Bad Belly's gut crawled like squeamish worms. *No*. Visions of the Dream came spinning out of his memory. *No!* He backed away, into the safety of the timber—ready to bolt away.

The huge fire in the clearing climbed higher, playing yellow light on the conical lodges and scattered wreckage. People clustered around the blaze, and there, through the silhouetted figures, Bad Belly could see captive women being dragged inside the ring of spectators.

The Dream! It's about to happen. White Ash . . . the Wolf Bundle!

Figures broke away from the group around the fire, and Bad Belly strangled the cry in his throat. The shadowy leader stalked forward on a lame leg. In the gaudy light, Bad Belly could see that an approaching warrior led a captive—a woman.

White Ash! It could be no one else. Singing Stones hadn't had a dress to offer, only the pants worn by the Wolf People. In her need, White Ash hadn't been particular.

The darkness had thickened. Bad Belly nerved himself against the panicked urge to flee. Instead, he stepped around the pile of dead and into the darkened clearing. *I'm out of my mind! These are Sun People! They eat babies! They . . .*

He tripped over the outflung arm of a corpse and fell heavily. Something hard thunked into the back of his head with enough force to dance lights in his eyes.

I've been caught. He gulped and closed his eyes, waiting for the killing blow . . . that never came.

He blinked, rolled over, and his pack slipped across his back. He reached up and rubbed his head, knowing a lump was going to form. What had hit him? He fumbled around with his good arm and felt his pack. The stone wood.

Some hero. You almost knocked yourself out.

"Hurry!" The voice seemed to twine out of the air.

He climbed to his feet and darted forward to hide in the shadow of a lodge. He placed his ear against the cover, but heard nothing. He crept around the side of the lodge, craning his neck until he made out a group of people outlined in the fire's glow.

Bad Belly took a deep breath and rushed to the shadow of the next lodge. Piles of things lay scattered around it: looted packs and parfleches, robes, dog travois, and lodge covers. He started forward, step by step. The chatter of voices alerted him. Warriors were coming. He dropped to the ground and curled himself into a ball amidst the wreckage.

The two warriors stopped several paces away and continued their conversation. Urine pattered on the ground.

Bad Belly winced and waited for the yell of discovery. The voices receded. He glanced up to see if the way was clear and lurched to his feet. He raced for the shadow of the next lodge and peered around the side of the shelter.

A man and woman stood before a large lodge in the middle of the camp. A cold shiver played down Bad Belly's spine. That would be the Spirit Man's lodge—the place where they kept the Wolf Bundle. The tall man took a hobbling step, awkward because of his bad leg. He said something in Sun People talk and the woman started back toward the fire.

Then the man looked down, talking to a bound captive Bad Belly could barely see. Bad Belly couldn't understand the words, but he recognized White Ash's frightened pleading when she responded. His stomach knotted.

The lame man pulled his long shirt over his head and let it drop. Then he unlaced his leggings and kicked them loose. Dancing and singing rose from the people around the fire.

What now? How do I do this? Bad Belly stared up at the night sky, searching for lightning or some other sign from Power. That sort of thing always happened in the legends. The stars twinkled forlornly against the velvet sky, but nothing more.

The lame man had raised his hands, calling out to the night sky. The background Singing rose in volume.

"And I'll bet his soul glows green to Spirit eyes," Bad Belly growled under his breath. The lame man lowered himself to the pile of bedding before the lodge.

Bad Belly sucked a deep breath and scuttled forward. For once, luck stayed with him. He didn't fall over his feet, didn't step on anything, and didn't make a sound on the trampled grass of the looted camp.

Walking like a ghost, he felt his way along the back of the Spirit man's lodge and around the side. He listened to the strange Sun People talk. White Ash's desperate pleas pained his soul.

I'm coming, White Ash. Hold on!

How did he get around the lodge without stepping out into the firelight? A pain shot up as he stubbed his toe.

Bad Belly reached down to discover what he'd kicked . . . and grinned. He grasped one of the stakes that pegged the lodge cover to the ground and twisted it loose, then another, and another. When he flopped on his stomach to wiggle under the cover, the stone wood thumped him on the head again—right where the first lump still throbbed.

Shaking his head, Bad Belly squirmed forward—only to have the pack snag on the lodge cover. He twisted and snared himself in the pack string. He twisted the other way and slipped free of the pack before crawling under the flap. Winding fingers into the strap, he pulled the pack after him.

Creeping to the door flap, Bad Belly peered out. There lay White Ash. The firelight danced off her firm flesh, shining on her full breasts and glinting in the thick mat of her pubic hair. The warrior lay next to her, laughing softly. White Ash had her eyes fixed on a tripod to one side. Bad Belly glanced—and froze. He could sense the presence of the object silhouetted there. Peace—a familiar awareness of Power and rightness—settled on his soul.

The lame warrior ran possessive hands over White Ash's trembling body, then lifted himself and yanked her knees apart.

Fight him! White Ash, why don't you . . . But he could see the way her pants were knotted around the thong at her ankles.

The lame warrior rolled over, covering White Ash. A miserable sob caught in her throat.

No! He can't! I won't let him! Bed Belly ducked through the flap—only to have his pack again catch on the cover when he stood too quickly. He lost his balance, tore himself loose of the shaking lodge cover, and tumbled with a grunt at the head of the bedding.

"Bad Belly!" White Ash gasped.

The lame man rolled off her, starting to his feet, his voice angry.

Bad Belly's fingers touched something cool. On instinct, he leaped forward as the man filled his lungs to shout. With all the might in his good arm, Bad Belly ripped the stone wood from the pack and whacked the closest target in reach: the lame man's knee.

The warrior crashed down with a strangled groan, and Bad Belly scrambled after him. The furs slipped beneath him and he rolled. The man's grasping hand caught in the stone-tooth necklace. Bad Belly shied back and cocked his arm. In his awkward position, he couldn't muster the power he needed. Two things happened: Power discharged in the very air, standing Bad Belly's hair on end, and his blow glanced off one side of the man's head. The lame warrior ripped the necklace from Bad Belly's neck as he rolled violently away. A hideous gargling sound issued from the warrior's throat as he clutched his head, heedless of the necklace twined in his frantic fingers.

"Bad Belly, hurry!" White Ash floundered in the bedding. The Broken Stone warrior writhed and gasped as Bad Belly reached into his pack and grabbed one of the sharp chert flakes he carried. He fumbled for White Ash's feet and found the thong. Cutting it with one hand wasn't easy, especially with the pants in the way, but at last it was done.

"Roll over. Quick!" he ordered and sawed frantically at the bonds on her wrists until they parted. "Come on, let's get out of here."

Pulling White Ash, he started for the darkness, then felt the surge of Power. *The Wolf Bundle.*

"Run!" He pushed her ahead and snatched up the Bundle. A tingling shot through him as his fingers dimpled the thick leather. The edges of his vision faded, going dark. All he could see was the heart-shaped Bundle. It glowed, as though a fire burned within it. The glow spread up Bad Belly's hands and arms until it engulfed his entire body in a flaming wash of light. In the depths of his thoughts he heard a din of frantic voices: *"The new Keeper has come! We've been waiting for you, Still Water, waiting for you to take Us away from here. Don't wait! Go. Get out!"*

White Ash gasped and clutched her throat. Her eyes went over Bad Belly as though she, too, saw the fire that radiated from his flesh. "Hurry!" she hissed. Then she sprinted for the trees and the covering darkness.

Bad Belly took a last glance at the warrior rolling in the grass. The sight would haunt his Dreams. The lame man pounded his head with both fists, whimpering as if stakes had been driven through his skull.

Bad Belly wheeled and raced after White Ash.

Left Hand slipped down the elk trail with no more noise than an owl's shadow in moonlit grass. To either side the trees loomed darkly against the night sky. Here and there through the canopy of jet-black fir trees patches of stars glimmered.

Close. I've got to be close. As if to match his thoughts, the sound of voices raised in Song carried on the night air. Yes, there to the northeast. He knew where he was now. He could circle to the west, head north, and loop around, coming in from the direction the Sun People had come. There would be fewer warriors to deal with that way. The Singing grew louder.

"Victory Dance," he whispered under his breath. The thought sickened him. What had gone wrong? Where had they made their mistake? Why hadn't the Dreamers seen this coming?

He pinched his eyes shut as if he could squeeze the anguish

from his soul. Had the Wolf Bundle deserted the People? Had the whole world turned on them?

Left Hand glanced back over his shoulder and froze. A bit of white shifted in the darkness. His grip tightened on his atlatl, the only weapon he had left. The spot of white stopped short.

Left Hand crouched, balanced on the balls of his feet. He stood where the shadows obscured his outline. *Come on. Come closer, you maggot-sucking . . .*

The white moved in silence and paused again, as if uncertain.

A shiver played over Left Hand's hot flesh. Did the stalker see in the dark? Or did he have some sort of sense, some sort of Power? Left Hand gritted his teeth. Too much Power had gone wrong already.

The white moved again, and Left Hand cocked his head. Something about it. Much too low. A man would be taller, but in the darkness he couldn't really tell.

Not a skunk! But then, that might not be bad. Skunk smell might work for him. A vigilant warrior who heard something in the night might ignore it if he smelled skunk.

The white came closer, and Left Hand raised his atlatl. The white spot backed away.

"What are you?" Left Hand called softly. "A Spirit?"

A low whine answered. Left Hand lowered his atlatl. A dog. "Go on," he hissed. "Get out of here. I don't need a dog to give me away."

The animal trotted closer and shoved its muzzle into his hand. He bent down, peering into the darkness, and cocked his head in disbelief. "Trouble? Is that you? How did you get here? Where's Bad Belly?"

The dog snuffled happily and tried to lick him in the face. Left Hand rose, shaking his head, and started down the trail again, only to hear Trouble whine behind him.

"Go on," Left Hand waved irritably. "You don't want any part of the Sun People." He bent down and whispered threateningly, "They eat black-and-white dogs. Go."

He started down the trail once more, headed west to circle through the trees and come in from the north of the camp.

meadow. He stopped to study a small clearing before he stepped out into the open. Trouble dashed past despite Left Hand's frantic effort to grab the dog.

Throat dry, he watched as Trouble bounded out into the grass and low sage; he expected harsh shouts when Sun warriors spotted the animal. Trouble stopped and looked back. Licking his lips, Left Hand edged out of the protection of the trees. A faint glow lit the eastern horizon behind him as the moon started to crest the mountains. He glanced around nervously and hurried across to search for the place where the elk trail reentered the tangle of black timber.

Trouble whined again, louder this time, insistent.

Left Hand gasped his frustration and turned, figuring he could throw something at the—His thoughts evaporated as a black form slid out of the trees behind Trouble on silent feet. Even through the darkness, Left Hand could feel those yellow eyes.

"Spirit wolf?"

The big animal stood watching him intently, and Left Hand's soul prickled. The wolf turned away—blackness in shadow—and disappeared into the trees on the east side of the clearing. Trouble started to follow and stopped, one foot raised uncertainly.

Left Hand rubbed his thumb back and forth on the wooden handle of his atlatl. *If I follow them, do I follow Power? Or silly animals?* He shook his head. *What has Power brought the Wolf People this day?* He cursed as he pivoted on his heel, following Trouble's patch of white back toward the east.

The dog led happily, tail wagging, darting ahead and then returning, as if to urge him to greater speed. Blackness slipping through the shadows was the only indication of the wolf's presence in the clinging darkness. Left Hand panted as he trotted along. His feet tangled in forest litter and he stumbled over roots; branches reached out of the night to lash him.

Stupid! Why didn't you keep going? What did you get yourself— Trouble had come to a stop, head up, ears pricked.

The black wolf stood poised, as if waiting, at the edge of another of the patchwork of clearings that dotted the forest. This one, like most, consisted of a narrow, sage-filled meadow cleared by a long-ago fire. Left Hand barely realized when the distant Singing stopped. The Sun People went ominously quiet, and then shouting broke out from the direction of the camp.

Left Hand knelt next to Trouble and ran his fingers through the dog's thick, warm fur. An uneasy presence hung in the air. Power filled the night. His soul huddled in on itself.

A faint sound caused Left Hand to cock his head. What? A stick snapping in the night? He strained his ears: only the faint shouts from the direction of the camp.

A muffled grunt and thump—as if a body had fallen in the darkness—the soft mutter of barely audible voices, and two people burst into the clearing. In a flash, the black wolf leaped to the side, diving soundlessly into the thick, black timber. But Trouble shot forward, running out to meet the two.

"Trouble? Is that you?" The man dropped to his knees, clutching the wiggling dog. "Look, it's Trouble. He's back!"

"Bless the Power. But come on," the woman insisted. "We'll be happy later." A pause. "Which way?"

Bad Belly stood. "I don't know. The Sun People are back that way. The moon is over there, so that's east. There ought to be a trail . . . but where?"

Left Hand hesitated a moment, then called softly, "Bad Belly? It's Left Hand. This way." Bad Belly had already started forward, the woman following uneasily.

"Left Hand?" Bad Belly asked quietly. "Where are you?"

"Here, there's a trail." He stepped into the faint moonlight and Bad Belly hugged him fiercely, blurting, "You wouldn't believe everything that's happened. First, Trouble got lost during the night. I went to find him and got lost myself in the Sideways—"

"Not now, Bad Belly," the woman said nervously.

"Good idea," Left Hand agreed. "I know the trails, and maybe I can hide you, or send you in the right direction. After that, you're on your own."

"You're not coming with us?" Bad Belly asked.

"I have to go back for the Wolf Bundle, Bad Belly. The Sun People—"

"I've got it," Bad Belly crowed. "It's safe. You see, I had this Dream—"

"Can we talk later?" the woman interrupted. "Brave Man is going to have warriors crawling all over this mountain looking for us. Wolf man," she strained the words as she said them, "if you know a way out of here, a way back to Singing Stones—"

"Follow me." Left Hand led them out into the clearing and started off to the southwest. *Bad Belly has the Wolf Bundle? And when I would have missed them, a huge black wolf led me right to Bad Belly—and to the Wolf Bundle. But at what cost? What's happening? What's gone wrong with Power?*

"I don't know about you, Bad Belly," Left Hand growled. "You're tied up in so much Power it makes me shiver."

Father of Waters, flows so rich,
  trickles water into the ditch.
    Grow a plant, so tall and green, fruit is yellow.
I have seen.
    Feathers colored, the dead are laid.
      Log across and dirt is made.
Lazy sloth, in baskets carried—
  sun man and woman high are married.

The old woman's voice crooned through the Dream.

From soaring wings, White Ash looked down, seeing people on the green bank of a large river. Where the channel wound around in ox-bows, trees had been cleared and patches of land grew slender plants; people walked between them, plucking the less-desired weeds. She could see men farther back in the forest, working with hafted, ground-stone axes. They chipped the bark from living trees—ringing them to kill them. Then they burned the dead wood so that the ashes enriched the black soil.

Power filled the fields, glowing around the tall plants, whose long leaves danced in the breeze. Life pulsed among the stalks and in the ripening yellow fruit they bore.

In the background, a mound of earth rose against the sky. At the top of the mound, a log structure stood. The walls had been covered with bark, and a thatched roof climbed to a peak. An open doorway faced south, and there a man wearing a feathered mask raised his hands to the sun as he Sang the praises of First Man and the Sun and the pale-haired plant.

"Tell Left Hand," the voice of Thunderbird cracked the air, *"that he must lead the Wolf People to the east. The way will be difficult. The Buffalo People will war with them, and many will die in the Short Grass Plains. The Wolf People must follow the Elk River to the Father Water. There they must war with the Masked Dancers and establish a new way. There they must continue the Dream and renew the Masked Dancers."*

"I will tell him." She spread her arms as if to fly herself. "He will want the Wolf Bundle."

"The Wolf Bundle Dreams the truth to Left Hand, but he is a Trader. In his heart, he will know what he must do. He doesn't Dream with your Power. His Power is different. Tell him to follow the rivers to the east. Tell him that one day a Dreamer will arise who can seek the Wolf Bundle and return it to the Father Water and the Blood of First Man. But first his People must prove their worth."

"I will tell him." She soared in rapture, feeling the tug of the One filling the golden mist surrounding her.

Clouds appeared below, obscuring the land. With a flick of feather, Thunderbird dove into the puffy mass. White Ash tucked her knees to her chest. Floating and drifting, she dropped into the grayness, the edges of the One pulling at her, insistent, overpowering.

White Ash blinked and stirred, coming out of the muzzy Dream. Feathers of the One brushed at the fringes of her soul.

For safety, they had chosen to sleep by day and travel at night, when Broken Stones scouts couldn't spy from high points. As White Ash stretched, the sun began to slip below the ragged skyline of the Red Rock Mountains far across the purple-shadowed Gray Deer Basin. A deep, translucent indigo filled the eastern sky. She stared at the vista while filaments of the Dream wove through her thoughts.

They had camped in a secluded hollow, screened on all but the west side by spring-green aspen. The white sheen of the bark caught the last rays of the sun. She pulled back the robe and made a quick check for ticks before pulling on her clothing. With an awl and sinew she'd made makeshift repairs to the shirt.

Bad Belly yawned and squinted sourly. The expression didn't do his homely face any favor. White Ash studied him with wonder. He'd changed. She could feel it deep inside herself. The instant his hands had touched the Sacred Bundle, a new strength, a *presence*, had been breathed into his soul.

Left Hand lay on a pile of grass, breathing unevenly while tortured sounds came from his throat. Then he started and jerked awake, staring around in fright for a moment before he exhaled and sat up. Beads of sweat glistened on his weathered face before he dropped his head into his hands.

"What's wrong?" Bad Belly asked.

White Ash shook her head wearily. "The Dream."

"You mean Dreams," Left Hand rasped hoarsely. "Terrible Dreams. I saw people fleeing. Walking through a parched land. Trees. I saw trees . . . and black dirt . . . and a huge, swirling river." He looked up then, expression haunted. "And I felt part of my soul go cold, as if something wonderful had been taken." He blinked and shook his head. "Horrible . . . loss . . ."

"What Dream?" Bad Belly asked White Ash, taking her hand. "Tell us."

She looked warily at the Wolf man. "I rose in the clouds, carried by Thunderbird. We soared on the winds and traveled far to the east. There's a big river there. The land is green, filled with trees. You are to take the Wolf People there."

Left Hand squinted. "Take the Wolf People there? You mean, away from here . . . from our home?"

She nodded soberly. "The Power has changed here."

He rubbed his hands, shaking his shoulders as if to rid himself of an unpleasant burden. "I can almost believe you. I can't stop this empty feeling. And the images—"

"Of death and war and a yellow-haired plant?" White Ash surmised.

He paled. "How . . ."

She shook her head, gaze locked with his. "Power gives everyone a choice, Trader. You will be the next leader of the Wolf People. Will you lead them to death at the hands of the Sun People? Or will you follow the Dream?"

"Death?" His face contorted in disbelief.

"For the last three nights we have fled. How many times have we heard Broken Stones warriors? How often have we seen their fires in the night?"

"Too many."

"You've never seen them make war, Trader. I have. Behind the Broken Stones come the Black Point. Behind them, the Hollow Flute, and the Wasp and the—"

"You're wrong, White Ash. I've seen them. I've Traded to the north . . . to all those clans," he answered weakly. "But this is our *home*. This is where Wolf Dreamer led us. Here Fire Dancer renewed the people and Danced with fire."

"That time is gone," she told him flatly. "Power offers you a new way. The Wolf People have fled to the foothills. You have very little time to convince them of your leadership and take them to the east."

"Most of my people will want to retake the mountains. This soil contains the bones of our ancestors. Our souls are part of this place." An aching desperation touched his voice. "We can't leave here!"

White Ash bowed her head forlornly. *No one wants to be a Dreamer.* Singing Stones' words echoed. *Is this why? Because of the pain—because of what you know you have to do?*

"Power leads you another way, Trader." She glanced up at the sky. "I can only tell you what I saw. It's a rich land in the east. Trees were cleared. The tall plant provided food for many.'' She closed her eyes, seeing it again. ''Life—Power—filled the yellow-haired plant.''

''What else?'' Left Hand asked nervously.

''A mountain made of dirt, with a lodge on top. The Spirit Man there lifted his hands toward the sun.''

''And I'm to lead the people there?''

She nodded. ''You have that choice. Or you can leave your blood here. The Sun People have changed the Power. People have their place on the Spiral. Where will your children Dance, Left Hand? Along the Father Water? Or among the souls of the dead?''

Left Hand shivered again, eyes going vacant. ''I saw that in my Dreams.'' He looked back over his shoulder. ''I walked the old paths . . . and behind me walked the Spirits of the dead. Bones littered the trails, soon to be covered by the pine needles that fell from the trees.''

She nodded. ''Then you know. When First Man turned himself into Thunderbird, he told me to tell you. The choice is yours.''

Left Hand stood and walked unsteadily to look west through the aspen. The sun had burned red and orange into the clouds that hovered over the distant Red Rock Mountains. Bracing one hand against the white trunk of an aspen, he shook his head. ''The Dreamers should have seen the coming of the Sun People. When I fled that night, a Spirit wolf ran with Bad Belly's dog—led me to you. Every time I sleep, the Dreams haunt me.''

He faced her, mouth working. ''Yes, I believe your Dream, White Ash. I heard your Thunderbird's wings that night I camped with Bad Belly in the Wind Basin. 'Find the Dreamer,' he said.''

He shifted his attention to Bad Belly. ''You've found her, my friend. I wish you luck. I think you'll need it.''

Bad Belly lowered his gaze.

Left Hand took a deep breath. ''Very well, White Ash, I will go. Give me the Wolf Bundle, and I will be on my way.''

''The Wolf Bundle goes south with us,'' White Ash told him. ''Still Water is the new Keeper. It called him.''

''Still Water? *Bad Belly?*'' Left Hand spun, a crazy look

in his eyes. "The Wolf Bundle is the heart of the People! It belongs to—"

"To First Man," White Ash interrupted as she stepped forward and grabbed the Trader by the shoulders. She peered into his eyes, seeking his very soul. "Search your heart, Left Hand. You felt the Power when you Dreamed. You know where it belongs."

She saw his fear as his mouth opened and no words came.

"First Man told me to tell you that *if* your people go east, renew the Masked Dancers and prove their worth, a Dreamer will come who will return the Wolf Bundle to your children. But you must first prove your worth."

"But I . . ."

"Power *doesn't* come free!"

His resistance crumbled under her searching gaze. He made one last weak appeal. "I have to take it. If I'm to lead my people, as you say, I'll—I'll need it."

She shook her head. "Still Water is the Keeper now. The Wolf Bundle called him. A new way must be Dreamed for all the people, or First Man's Dream will die."

Bad Belly stood up, hurt and pity in his expression. "If it isn't Dreamed, the Spiral will change. I've seen visions. Seen forests cut down and people enslaved to do terrible things. I've seen the waters fouled and the air turn brown. I've seen animals penned—and their souls die while they still lived. The Spiral is in danger. It's up to White Ash and me to change it."

Left Hand's fists knotted, the muscles bulging in his shoulders. A glint came to his eyes as he thrust his jaw out. "When we began the journey that led you to this place, I gave you a gift—fishes' teeth turned to stone. Is this how you treat the Power of Trade? For a gift . . . you take the heart and soul of my people?"

"Enough!" White Ash cried, stepping between them as Still Water's face wrenched with a terrible guilt. A smoldering fury burned within her. "It's *not* his doing, Trader. Ask Power why it turned its back on the Wolf People. Ask First Man, and the Wolf Bundle why it called a new Keeper! Seek your answers in the Dreams that haunt your sleep. But don't blame Still Water for the things Power demands of him.''

Left Hand took a deep breath, holding it as he twisted away and stared at the sunset. ''Under other circumstances, Bad Belly, I would kill you for it.'' He shook his head, a man torn loose from all he had known. ''Yes, White Ash, from the beginning, I knew Power was at work. I could feel it.''

Still Water licked his lips and said miserably, ''I'll send you a gift one day, Left Hand. I don't know what it will be, but somehow—''

''Forget it, Bad Belly. There is nothing between us anymore. That Power is dead.'' He turned to White Ash, eyes bright with tears. ''What can I do? How can I fight you? You . . . you're Power. You're the Dreamer Bad Belly was called to find. And you tell me I have to . . . to . . .'' He jerked around to stare at the sunset again.

''Left Hand . . .'' Still Water began but stopped at White Ash's touch.

''There's nothing we can say,'' she told him. ''It's Power. And you know already. The Wolf Bundle first touched you in your Dreams, called you. Search your heart—and tell me what you know.''

Still Water pursed his lips, dropping his eyes. ''It's unfair. That's all.''

''Who said Power was fair? Power works toward its own ends.'' Her voice grew distant. ''Even if it destroys whole peoples.''

Left Hand nodded. ''I know. But I never thought—''

''I was White Clay,'' she told him. ''Your people's warriors killed the last of my clan. Once I hated all Wolf People for what they'd done. Now all of my soul shares your sorrow. Go. Take the chance Power offers and save your people. Lead them east, Left Hand. Follow the rivers to the land of the Masked Dancers.''

At the pain in his face, the terrible longing for *this* land, she couldn't stop her tears. He looked at the fading sunset over the Red Rock Mountains as if to fix it in his memory.

''I . . .'' He choked. ''I believe you, Dreamer. I've been

to those lands. I know the direction—but not the way of it. Was that why Power called me to be a Trader? To find the way for my people?''

She had no answer, and he did not wait for one. He stopped in front of Still Water before offering his hand. "Farewell, my friend. I guess we'll never know what the sun burns . . . but whatever it is, I'm not sure it's good for any of us."

Then he vanished among the aspens, heading east—a weary man.

Miserable, Still Water asked, "Will it work that way? Like you said?''

She reached down to pick up the pack. "Yes. But it hurts. I know. Singing Stones was right, Still Water. No one wants to become a Dreamer."

He turned uncertain eyes on her. "Why have you started calling me by my real name?"

Sadness filled her dark eyes. "You've been reborn, Still Water. When you touched the Bundle, the souls of all the people who've ever held it flowed into you and changed you. I felt it like a bolt of lightning in my soul. We'll never be who we were again."

Chapter 21

"I need to know how you feel about it." Black Hand walked with his hands clasped behind him, head tilted up at the night sky.

Bitterbrush glanced back over her shoulder. They had reached the crest of a low ridge. Below them, in the hollow where the Aspen Springs trickles out of the rock, the dim eyes of the camp's fires blinked redly. Immediately to the south, the Gray Wall rose like a blot against the darkness. Patchy clouds silvered with moonlight obscured the starry patterns above. The breeze carried the scent of sage and rabbitbrush, and a tang of dry soil.

Bitterbrush scuffed the soft ground underfoot. "The moon has come and gone many times since Warm Fire was laid in his grave." She paused. "I'll always love him. He'll be first in my heart."

"I understand," Black Hand replied. "Everyone will love Warm Fire. I wouldn't ask you to forget him."

She sighed and stared up into the night. "I also understand my responsibilities, and what is good for my clan." She shook her head. "Grandmother has made her wishes known."

He chuckled. "Yes, I know. Larkspur has all the subtlety of a wounded silver bear. But I want to know what you think. I *need* to know. Bitterbrush, if you don't want me, tell me now."

"Despite what Grandmother will say?"

He nodded, taking her hands. "Larkspur doesn't own either one of us. Please, be honest with me. Do you want me?"

She closed her eyes, feeling the warmth in his hands. How long had it been since Warm Fire had shared his warmth with her? If she let herself go, she could imagine it was him. A longing filled her. Memories lingered of the times they'd laughed, of cold nights under warm robes. Of their tender lovemaking in the mornings.

She didn't want another man. Foolish thought—a woman's duty to the clan was to be married. She would be the leader one day, and every man at the Gathering would be eyeing her. Could she stand that?

She'd known Black Hand for a long time. Remembered him from when she was a young girl. "You bedded Larkspur."

"I did."

She took a breath, fighting the inevitability. "And your Power?"

He placed an arm around her, wrapping his robe over her shoulders against the chill. "It's been fading for several years now . . . I don't know why. But I want you to know that I prayed with all my soul for Warm Fire's life."

"I know you did." The warmth of his robe settled into her. The Gathering lay three days away, given the pace at which Larkspur now traveled. From the ridge top, she could see the dark shadow of the Monster Mountains behind Three Forks.

Round Rock would gain considerable status from the marriage. In the future, such a marriage could mean a great deal to her. The whisperings of witchcraft would be stopped dead—and the claims made by Three Forks would become an amusement rather than a threat. People would look at her and say, "There goes Bitterbrush, the woman Black Hand gave up Power for."

She turned to him, her gut twisting—as if her decision betrayed Warm Fire. "I will be your wife."

His arm tightened around her shoulders. "Thank you, Bitterbrush. I will do my best for you."

"And I for you." Grief mixed with relief.

She savored the warmth of his body as he pulled the robe around them. "You brought a large robe for so warm a night."

He smiled down at her. "I hoped I would need it."

She nodded halfheartedly and led him by the hand to a sheltered spot in the sagebrush. She took the robe from him and spread it on the soft soil. Curious emotions played within as she slipped her dress over her head. The cool air caressed her skin. Moonlight edged around the clouds and cast its soft light on her.

Black Hand sighed, appreciative gaze tracing her body. He pulled his elk hide shirt over his head, and she undid the lacings holding his leggings.

The ground cushioned her as she lay back and took his weight. The feel of him reassured something lost and adrift in her soul. A familiar longing she'd thought forever gone warmed within, and her body responded as Warm Fire had trained it to do.

She opened herself, and sighed as they joined.

Something in the sagebrush below them fled into the night, causing her to start.

"Rabbit," he whispered in her ear, pausing for only a moment in his motions.

She lay back and relaxed as the warm, honeyed sensations built. Deep within, a tiny voice repeated, *Warm Fire, forgive me. Forgive me . . .*

The land had changed since Wind Runner had last sat on this same rock and looked down over the White Clay camp. The snow had vanished under the summer sun. The frigid winds had softened into mild breezes that refreshed in the heat of the day. *It might be a different world—someplace strange and Dreamed.* He closed his eyes, remembering that cold winter night. The wind howled, chittering snow crystals across the frozen drifts. The sage rustled under the wealth of stars. Cold, black night pressed around him, while in the distance the mountains rose jagged and snow-packed.

When he opened his eyes, it all snapped away; before him stretched a warm land of aqua sage and sun-washed buff rock.

Out of some twisted impulse, he'd forced himself to walk through the remains of the camp before he climbed up on the ridge. The bones had been picked clean. The leather clothing had gone hard, cracked by sun and wind. Strands of black hair had grown brittle where they lay in the grass. Charred lodge poles and covers were strewn about a black-ash smudge where the last council of the White Clay had taken place.

Wind Runner had identified some of the dead by the bone beads and the bits of shell ornaments scattered about the bones. Old Falcon, who had smiled with such warmth. Whistling Hare, who had been so wise. The gray-shot hair clinging to the chewed remains beside the old clan leader must have been Flying Squirrel's. Standing among the restless dead, he'd raised his arms to the sky and chanted the ancient Song of the People, imploring Thunderbird to search for their waylaid souls. Then he'd cried—the final mourner for the White Clay.

And I could find no trace of White Ash. He looked out

over the shadow-filled hollow that held the remains of the White Clay. *None of those grisly, bleached bones are hers.*

He hadn't made a conscious choice to lead the Black Point this way. Or had he? If Sage Ghost had noticed, or cared, he'd said nothing. Wind Runner stared down at the gravelly soil of the ridge top as if to see her tracks imprinted there through the long-melted snow.

Sage Ghost said he had checked all the bodies. If she'd been there, the old hunter would have found her. Wind Runner waited, watching, remembering as the sun slid toward the western horizon and dropped behind the Red Rock Mountains. Darkness settled over the land, accompanied by the mixed howls of a wolf pack and an answering chorus of coyotes.

Looking over his shoulder to the north, Wind Runner could see the flickering fires that marked the Black Point camp. Tomorrow he'd lead the people around this place to the other side of the ridge, where he and Brave Man had circled to sneak up on the buffalo.

Wind Runner filled his lungs with the warm night air and tried to ease the ache in his soul. He had waited for the darkness. Now he could imagine White Ash climbing up the slope, snow crunching under her moccasins. Right there—as clear in his memory as on the night it had happened.

The moon broke over the horizon and he stood, as he'd done that night, and retraced those few steps. Here, on this spot, he'd held her, listened to her as she tempted him to run away with her.

If only I had known. I would have gone, White Ash. He leaned his head back and drowned in the memories. Her arms went around him for that final hug.

"Wind Runner?"

Every muscle in his body tensed. For a brief moment everything spun crazily and his heart shot excitement into his veins. *Is it possible? Can it be . . .*

"Wind Runner?" The voice sounded higher than he remembered, more musical.

He swallowed hard and turned, heart racing. The woman

stood bathed in moonlight behind him—smaller, more delicate of build.

He dropped unsteadily to sit on his rock. "Aspen? What are you doing here?"

She walked over, gravel crunching under her moccasins. "I came to find you. Grandfather's been worried; he said you looked terrible. He sent me."

Wind Runner nodded, irritated and grateful at the same time.

She looked around, cataloging the country with a practiced eye. She frowned, studying him in the moonlight. "It was here, wasn't it?"

He swallowed hard, but his voice rasped as he said, "Right here."

She settled herself on a rock beside him. "I hope she's alive somewhere and that you can find her."

He smiled wearily. "Do you?"

"I know what it feels like to lose someone you love." She reached up to flip her long hair over one shoulder. "My mother died first. Then my father. Both of my brothers. Finally, my husband—the man I loved more than life." She tipped back her head to stare up at those stars bright enough to defeat the moonlight. "He's there, somewhere—I hope."

"You hope?"

She nodded, moonlight spilling on her heart-shaped face. "He married me five days before he went off to raid the Broken Stones." She touched each of the fingers on one hand, as if counting the days.

"He never came back." A wistful note filled her voice. "For a long time I didn't know what had happened to him, just that he'd been killed. One Man finally told me. He'd been foolish—disobeyed the war leader and rushed out into the middle of the Broken Stones." She shook her head. "He was young. Maybe he thought it was more important that he make a name for himself. If his courage had sent the Broken Stones running, he would have come back a great man.

"As it was . . ." She hesitated. "One Man and the others watched the Broken Stones butcher his body." Her lips pinched as she stared at the stars. "That's why I hope he's there . . . that his soul made it up to where Thunderbird could carry him to the Camp of the Dead.''

''I didn't know that.'' Wind Runner shifted uncomfortably.

''You don't worry much about other people.''

He gave her a sharp glance. ''I don't?''

''No. But that's all right . . . for a while. What you lost is fresh in your memory. And you need time to heal the wounds in your soul.''

He snorted displeasure. ''You seem to know a lot about me.''

''I do,'' she replied evenly. ''I've spent a lot of time watching you, wondering about you.''

''I'd think you had better things to do.''

She lifted one knee and propped her chin. ''I think a man—a White Clay warrior of your age—who could talk the Black Point into coming this far south is worth considerable study. I want to know who you are and what your leading us here means to my people. I've listened carefully. The clan is trapped—and you offer a way out.''

He looked back to the north. ''Nothing will stop the clans. The Sun People are moving like starved coyotes. It's better to lead than to be snapping in the pack. The White Clay tried snapping back at the pack.'' He pointed. ''And there they are. Walk down there, if you wish. The bones will speak to you.''

''Not the same way they do to you.''

He nodded. ''You say that I don't think much about people, but you're wrong.'' His voice went hollow. ''I think about them all the time. I think about the ones whose bones lie down there. I think about my White Clay family. They, too, are dead—like yours. You have a grandfather. I have an uncle—and yes, he's still my uncle. Adoption by the Black Point doesn't change that. He and I have a bond deeper than kinship.''

She watched him with large, dark eyes as he continued. ''Then I saw the Hollow Flute, saw the haunted look in their eyes—and knew it so well. I've seen that look too many times.''

Aspen gazed thoughtfully at the sheltered cove under the ridge. Starlight danced in the curved hollows. "I understand you better now. You've been a driven man since you first came among us. The risks you took bothered me. The Power of your speech in the council worried me. Were you truly concerned about the Black Point? Or were you willing to destroy yourself to lead us into disaster?" Her dark eyes burned into his. "Perhaps you would do anything to avenge the attack the Black Point made on the White Clay camp years ago. Maybe you blamed us for everything. People often have strange reasons for doing what they do."

"Everything has changed. I don't know exactly when it happened. Maybe it was the day the Black Point raided the White Clay on the Fat Beaver. Maybe it was when I said good-bye to White Ash. Maybe the clans are the cause of it, or Thunderbird, or the Sun. But the whole world tipped sideways. That green fire in the sky was a sign. Things will never be as they were before."

"No, they won't. You say that when we cross those mountains, we will have to learn a new way of living. What does that mean for the clan? What will become of us? Who will we be?"

"Whoever we make ourselves." He closed his eyes and searched his soul, seeking White Ash. Her memory had driven him to speak so strongly during the council. Could he admit that? And now? He searched his soul for her presence—and found nothing.

Aspen nodded to the dead camp under the ridge. "I hear your ghosts, Wind Runner." She rose to stand before him. "And I believe I have answered many of the questions I had about you. I'll follow you. I think you will be a great leader."

He gestured absently. "I don't *want* to be a great leader, only to avoid the mistakes of the past."

She placed a light hand on his shoulder. "That is why you will become a great leader."

For a long moment he looked into her eyes. Then he said, "It won't be easy. I don't know what waits for us beyond the Sideways Mountains. The Earth clans may have more Power than we expect."

"Many among us have already started to worry about that—and about you." She looked over her shoulder at the silent valley. "Several people have come to ask my opinion of you. Now I know what to tell them."

"Is that why you've been watching me?"

"In part. It also served my purposes. The warriors looking for a wife weren't as persistent when they thought I had eyes only for you. I haven't found the right man yet. My husband . . . Well, I loved him until my heart ached."

"You don't speak his name."

"Nor will I. That's a thing for my soul."

He clasped his hands and leaned on his knees. "I've heard the Traders say that among other peoples it's considered a terrible thing to speak the name of the dead. They think it's bad luck, that it will bring the ghost back to haunt them. Or sometimes they save the name and give it to an infant who has proved his soul clings to his body. They say that it's the soul of the dead person born again into a new life."

"In your heart do you believe you will see White Ash again?"

He took a deep breath. "This afternoon, when we made camp, the thought came to me that if I walked up here, stood where I stood that night, maybe I'd know. Here, before you came, I was with her. Reliving that last night." He stared up at the moon. "All I feel now is . . . empty."

She tipped her chin to the twinkling blanket of stars. "Had I known, I wouldn't have interrupted you. Forgive me."

He shrugged and got to his feet, taking one last look into the sheltered valley. "It's all right. For me, at least, the ghosts can rest easier. Perhaps tonight is an ending—and tomorrow will be the birth of something new."

Still Water sat thoughtfully on their robe, the Wolf Bundle cradled in his hand. They'd camped in a rock overhang barely big enough to hold them and their small fire. The rain cascaded from the sodden skies to batter itself on the rocks.

Lightning flashed, cracked, and boomed over the Wind Basin to the south.

White Ash watched him with pensive eyes. The fire popped and she reached back to the packrat midden for another stick to drop on the coals. The Wolf Bundle sent shivers up and down her spine. She could *feel* the Power. It pulled at her, drew her. She longed to reach out and touch it—except that some caution deep in her soul warned against it. The sensations increased when she closed her eyes, the Bundle's pulsing Power playing around her Dreams, eternally there like tracks in sun-baked mud.

Why does it call to me so? What makes me so nervous and unsettled when Still Water has the Bundle out? What's its purpose? Why did First Man tell me to seek it? Now I wish we'd let Left Hand take it with him.

Except she could see Still Water's preoccupation with the Wolf People's sacred object.

"You have a sad look in your eyes," she told him.

He tried to smile, but it died on his lips. "I was thinking about Left Hand—and the debt I owe him. How funny. Part of my soul went into the making of that necklace." He gazed out into the dreary rain. "That necklace was very special to me. Power plays tricks on us. I thought it was a puzzle—you know, how could a fish's teeth turn to stone? And I treasured it because Left Hand gave it to me in friendship—even though he knew I could give him nothing in return at the time."

"Bad Belly, don't. It's not your fault. Guilt—"

"No, not guilt." He turned sad eyes on her. "Power did what it did, not me. No, it's the necklace that bothers me. When a person cherishes something, and works on it, a part of his soul goes into it." He gave a perplexed grunt, fixing his attention on the Wolf Bundle again. "I could almost believe I had to give it up to get the Wolf Bundle—and you."

Still Water continued to turn the Wolf Bundle in his hand.

"Maybe you did. If that's all Power costs you, you'll be a very lucky man." She glanced out at the gray clouds. They packed around the overhang in misty streamers that sifted through the limber pine and juniper. Tiny balls of hail pattered on the water-darkened rocks beyond the drip line. She shivered and puffed a breath that condensed and vanished in the cold, wet air.

"I'm going to keep that promise to Left Hand," Still Water told her. "I don't know how, but I'll finish the Trade. Return his favor."

The smells of rain and damp earth hung rich and musky in her nostrils. Her fingers still carried the scent of the hapless jackrabbit they'd run down. Their good luck had been to catch him. His bad luck had been a previously broken hind leg.

I have to do something or I'll go mad. White Ash plucked yet another stick from the packrat nest and asked, "What are you thinking?"

"Until I die, I'll never forget the look on Left Hand's face when he walked away. It broke his heart to leave this land." Still Water reached for his pack and carefully stowed the Wolf Bundle.

White Ash sighed as the tendrils of its grip loosened on her soul. Still Water drew back and rubbed his fingers together as if a presence lingered on them.

She looked out at the falling hail. The shelter had grown colder. "Has the world gone mad, Still Water? Does it all snap and snarl like a skunk with the foaming-mouth disease? Will it bite us, too, and make us that way?"

He huddled closer to the fire. "I don't know. I don't know what to think anymore. Once I told you the world was full of puzzles. Now I'm afraid of the answers."

"You didn't sleep well last night."

He shook his head. "I thought a lot about that necklace. When I finally slept, I had another of those visions. I was an antelope—free, my soul Singing as I ran. Then men came and drove me into a trap. They put ropes on me and led me far to the east—over rolling plains and through countless drainages—to a big river. They put me, and many other animals, on a wooden thing that floated on water. We floated for days through a land filled with trees, and the air smelled of mud and rot. The food they brought wasn't good. My soul sickened and turned black within. Finally we arrived at a huge camp with walls of wood and giant wooden lodges higher than trees. There they carried me off the floating thing and into the crowded streets.'' He paused, staring into nothingness. "So many people.''

"And then?''

"They put me in a tiny square place, where I couldn't run. People came to stare at me constantly—and my soul withered. Finally my lungs filled with the damp air and I died in that horrible place. I never ran free with the wind again.''

White Ash squeezed her eyes closed, trying to blot out the image. Antelope lived to run over the prairies. She hugged her knees close to her breast. "And Brave Man will make that Dream come true?''

Still Water gave her a sideways glance. "That's what the Wolf Bundle tells me will happen if we don't Dream a new way. Other Dreamers will have to keep the Spiral in balance after we're gone, but first we have to set it right.''

She reached for another few sticks to drop on the fire and winced as a cactus thorn pricked her finger. "Packrats—they always have to pile cactus in their nests.''

"Coyotes don't like cactus either,'' he observed, and shivered slightly. "That's why packrats put cactus in their nests in the first place.''

Thunder boomed and rolled across the land. White Ash said, "Doesn't look like it's going to stop any time soon.''

Hail had laid a mantle of white over the ground. "I don't think the Broken Stones are going to be chasing us.''

"Maybe that's just as well. I'm tired, Still Water. All we've done is run and worry and run some more.''

He reached around and undid the ties that held the one robe they had between them. "Let's sleep. When the storm stops, we can run again.''

She dropped more of the dried wood on the fire to build up the coals. No Broken Stones would see the smoke in weather like this. She curled herself around him as Trouble came over to drop in a heap and place his nose on the curve of her waist. She patted him and heard a grunt of canine satisfaction for her efforts.

Distant thunder growled, and as the hail lessened, rain

pattered down in its place. Drips slapped the ground in a steady pattern.

"Still Water?"

"Hmm?"

"Why did you come after me?"

He lifted a shoulder awkwardly. "I had to."

She hugged him close. "Still Water, I . . . No matter what happens, I'll always love you. With all my heart."

He turned, searching her eyes. "White Ash, my soul Sings when you're around."

Lightning flashed hot white in the sky, followed immediately by a blistering crack that sundered the world.

"That was close," she whispered. "Maybe Power guided it and it got Brave Man."

"We can hope." He blinked thoughtfully. "You know, I can't understand it. I hit him real hard across the knee, but not on the head. That second blow just glanced off."

"You hit him where the Black Point did. He has a nasty scar there on his scalp. The hair covers it most of the time. He says the blow killed him and sent him to the Camp of the Dead. According to him, he escaped and came back to life."

"Wish I could have sent him there for good. I'm just glad I found you in time. What was he saying to you?"

She took a breath, then growled, "He thinks that by possessing me, he'll gain my Power and make himself more Powerful." She shivered with revulsion, remembering how she'd lain bound and bared to him. "You came in time."

"It was my fault that you got caught," he told her. "I shouldn't have gone to look for Trouble."

"And I shouldn't have slowed us down. It was my own fear, Still Water. I'm sorry."

He reached up and ran gentle fingers down her cheek.

She pulled him close, breathing deeply to fill herself with his scent. "I've been foolish. Frightened of the wrong things."

"You're brave. Braver than anyone I know."

His smile warmed her, and she remembered the hole that had emptied in her soul when she thought he might die at the hands of the Broken Stones. Now she lay with his arm around her—safe, if only for the moment. How long did they have? How long until this rabid world reached out to bite them with evil, foaming teeth again? She gazed longingly at Still Water.

An image of Three Bulls flickered in the depths of her soul.

Will you let Three Bulls continue to foul your life? Or will you defy him—prove that you can conquer even him and what he did to you?

The lingering chill of fear curdled her insides as she relived those moments when Brave Man had lowered his muscular body on hers.

She chewed her lip and hugged Still Water closer. Her heart began to pound as she sat up and slipped off her shirt, taking a moment to admire the stitching she'd used to mend the split leather.

"What are you doing? You'll freeze," he protested.

She smiled at him, joy mixing with the anxiety in her heart. She stood up and slipped out of her pants, movements quickened by the chill in the air.

"Get up," she told him.

"You've lost any sense you ever—"

"Get up. Quick. Before my nerve fails."

He shot her a quizzical glance and rose, letting her undress him. Trouble watched with curious eyes, his tail patting the ground.

White Ash pulled Still Water down and snugged the cover around them.

"You'd be warmer if you'd . . . *What are you doing?*"

"Loving you." She watched understanding dawn in his eyes.

"Are you sure? What if . . . if . . ."

She felt him respond under her touch.

"I'm sure, Still Water. I almost lost you once. I see the worry in your eyes. I'm going to cover up the memory of Three Bulls. Bury it with something wonderful."

He closed his eyes. "What if I can't?"

She rolled on her back, pulling him with her. "Then we'll try again. People do this all the time. It can't be *that* difficult."

* * *

Rain fell in silver veils beyond the shelter. Still Water's regular breathing told her he slept. A fragile contentment filled her. Why couldn't they stay like this forever—loving each other, sharing their souls? Did they have to go out into the world again? Did they have to face the terrible storm that brewed so violently around them? A storm of Power and Peoples more threatening than any weather.

Lingering traces of the One drifted at the edge of her soul. She could close her eyes and feel the ghost of that gray mist and the promise of the golden haze beyond.

The lurking presence of the Wolf Bundle pulled at her.

A shaft of sunlight penetrated the sleek veil of rain, and the brilliant colors of the rainbow glowed to life in the sky.

She ran her fingers down Still Water's back, causing him to stir. The terrible yearning for him battled with the desire for the One. He shifted, exhaling happily.

"Wake up," she whispered into his ear.

"What is it? What's wrong?"

"Nothing," she teased, and bit his ear. "I want you again. That's all."

If only she could believe she had forever.

Shelters had been constructed of poles and covered with a weaving of sagebrush; they intermingled with the thick band of green-leafed cottonwood trees on the broad floodplain of the Spirit River. Behind the Gathering, irregular hills of blue-and-white mudstones rose to merge with the truncated sage flats beyond. Blue spirals of smoke rose from the many fires to dissipate into the endless sky. To the west, the mountains lifted in flat gray slabs that gave way to the cool green of forested slopes and finally to the snow-patched granite of the highest peaks, jutting arrogantly toward the sky.

Larkspur sighed as she walked down the spine of the last ridge. As was proper, she led her clan, while Limbercone,

Phloxseed, and Pretty Woman followed in her steps. Behind them came the families.

Three days of rain had slowed her progress, and she'd cursed the storm that left her and the others drenched and cold. She'd double-cursed the sticky mud that clung to her feet and added more misery to her tired steps. They'd arrived late because of her. Round Rock could travel no faster than Larkspur's ancient legs could carry her.

Coupled with weary relief at having arrived at last came the knowledge that this might well be the last Gathering she would attend.

"See, you didn't miss the Gathering. Your worries were groundless," Limbercone told her, gesturing at the peaceful valley.

"It's the first day," Larkspur growled. "The council is already formed, and people are flapping their jaws about boundary disputes and who's done what to who."

Limbercone chuckled. "And you've missed the opening rounds of gossip."

"It pays to know the gossip, girl. Never forget that. You know what's about to happen and can act first if you have to. How do you think I kept Round Rock high in everyone's mind all these years?"

Children, surrounded by excited, barking dogs, ran out to greet them, calling out the news, eager to see who the new-comers were.

Larkspur forced herself to hobble faster, hating the swelling in her ankles and knees. Her hips burned and her muscles trembled, but she made it across the open patch to the shade of the trees. Did the sun always have to burn so cursed hot after a rain?

The Spirit River ran almost bank-full with turbulent, muddy water that sent a soft *shushing* through the air. Lodges had been placed here and there amid the trees, and curls of smoke rose on the midday breeze. A throng of people was sitting in the shade of the cottonwoods.

Larkspur slowed, halting at the edge of the spectators. No one noticed her arrival; the speaker at the far end held every-one's attention.

"Witching is tearing us apart!" Owlclover of Three Forks railed at the morning sky with a clenched fist. "We have paid the price. You know the accusations we've made in the past. Now the witch has claimed Basket's infant and Green Fire!"

Uneasy mumbles rose from the people.

"And who is this witch?" Bone Ring asked sourly. The leader of Bad Water clan sat cross-legged in the shade on a fine sheephide robe, her gray hair pulled into two thick braids. She stared antagonistically at Owlclover before adding, "This talk of witching is meaningless. You'll all sit here and squawk and fight like strutting grouse while the coyote stalks in the sagebrush."

"Sun People don't frighten me anywhere near as bad as a witch!" Owlclover crossed her arms. "What are Sun People? Ragged buffalo hunters from the north, that's what! We can worry about them all we want, and in the meantime, witches will walk among us and work their evil. If I had a choice of problems, I'd take Sun People any day. If they show up in our land, we'll send our warriors to drive them back. What will scattered buffalo hunters be against our men? But a witch? A witch sneaks around and works its evil under the flesh—like a worm in the gut—until we're weak and dying."

"The Wolf People wiped out a camp of your 'ragged buffalo hunters' just across the mountains from my camp," Bone Ring asserted. "I haven't seen witching—but I've listened to the Wolf People talk."

"Let *them* worry! They won't give up the Gray Deer Basin to Sun People! Let their warriors keep the Sun People to the north." Owlclover turned, lifting her hands as she searched the faces around her. "We can't be concerned about what's happening in the north. That's a long way from here. We *must* worry about *now!* About the evil that stalks in our midst."

"Very well," Bone Ring called. "Tell us who. Name this witch. We've heard your stories about shadow figures in the sagebrush. So you've seen tracks in the snow? What of it? Snow takes tracks well. I don't care what Green Fire cried when she died. People see things when they die that may or may not be there. Tell me who these witches are."

Owlclover took a deep breath and responded, "We think Black Hand has turned to evil. We think he's the witch."

The listeners' mutters grew. Larkspur elbowed her way forward. She stepped into the open and cocked her head, staring at Owlclover. "An interesting accusation. You name Black Hand? You think he's a witch?"

Owlclover's eyes narrowed. "You should know. Who was present when your Warm Fire died? Think! Look back! How many people did Black Hand Sing for who died? Count them." She held up her hands, pointing to her fingertips as she named names.

People shuffled nervously, nodding.

Larkspur laughed out loud. "I had thought better of Three Forks. I sorrowed the day I heard of Green Fire's death. Did she teach you no wisdom, girl?"

A strained silence settled on the council.

"What are you after, Larkspur? What's your stake in this? Trying to protect him? Even after all these years? Does your heart blind your soul? Where is he? Where has he been? Why isn't *he* here to face the people? A witch hides, steals through the night and makes his evil. Have you seen Black Hand since Warm Fire's death?"

"Oh, I've seen him."

"Then you're the only one! No one else has."

The hiss of whispering voices grew louder.

Larkspur cocked her head. "Tell me, leader of Three Forks, what does a witch most desire? What is the one thing a witch will never give up?"

"The Power of the evil Spirits that he controls. Don't play games with me."

Larkspur nodded, the giddy feeling of victory in her veins. "And don't play games with me, either. A witch must seek Power, must seek its use. The craving becomes overwhelming. Every moment of his life is spent Dreaming the ways of the Spirits who help him with his evil. The craving feeds on itself, grows like a fungus until it fills his soul. He can think of nothing else but using his tainted Spirit Power. *That's* what it is to be a witch!"

"That's the way it is," Owlclover agreed, jerking her chin in a defiant nod.

"Good," Larkspur said reasonably. "Then leave my son-in-law's name out of witching."

The whispering broke out again. Larkspur experienced a swelling of pride. *Look at the shocked faces! Best entertainment they've had in ten tens of seasons!*

"Son-in-law?" Owlclover glanced about, knowing the ground had turned to slush under her feet, but unsure of why.

Larkspur turned and called, "Bitterbrush! Black Hand! Come here." As the two stepped through the ring of people, all eyes centered on them. Black Hand gave the leader of Three Forks a disdainful stare.

Larkspur lifted a shaky arm to the crowd. "You noticed that no one had seen Black Hand? A man who is courting doesn't spend time socializing with others. He's been falling in love with Bitterbrush. A witch, you say?" Larkspur chuckled. "Maybe he is. He's been doing a lot of things I don't know about in his wife's robes."

"Grandmother!" Bitterbrush's dusky features brightened with a scarlet flush.

A chuckle bubbled up from the crowd.

"What witch gives up his evil Power for a woman? Hmm? Tell me that, leader of Three Forks."

Owlclover glared at her; the muscles of her face bunched as she ground her jaws. Both hands had clenched into fists, the veins standing out. "I know your tricks, Larkspur. It's not over."

At that, the leader of Three Forks turned on her heel, beckoning angrily to her clan. Starwort and Shadblow rose and followed. Basket hesitated for a moment, an eerie black look marring her face, before she, too, stalked off.

Larkspur snorted and slapped her hands together. "What's the matter with them?" She looked around, adopting a puzzled expression. "Did I say something wrong?"

Raucous laughter rose from the people.

"Maybe they're just having an off day," Bone Ring added. "Now perhaps we can get back to the Sun People. My friends, we'd better wake up before we find ourselves mourning warriors and fearing to go to sleep at night. I want to know what we're going to do.''

Larkspur shook her head. ''This is going to be a Gathering I could sleep through. Sun People? To show you that I bear Three Forks no ill will for their . . . um, let's call it imagination, I agree with Owlclover when it comes to Sun People. But I would not want my good friend Bone Ring to think I slight her worries. I offer this for your consideration: When the first of the Sun People show up, we'll send runners to all the camps. Call up all our hunters and chase them back. Bone Ring, your Little Toe is a fast runner. Yellow Star has a couple of good men at Warm Wind. We can all be called in time. The first small parties that cross the Sideways Mountains can be tracked down and killed. We'll send one or two of them scurrying back over the mountains to tell the others.''

Bone Ring studied the council. ''Will we agree to that? Will it be sworn here, on our honor? The first camp that discovers Sun People, or sign of them, will call the others? Everyone will send hunters to drive them off?''

''I will swear,'' Larkspur called out. ''Bad Water and Warm Wind camps can count on Round Rock.'' She grinned. ''If we ever see one of the Sun People, that is.''

One by one the other clan leaders spoke their agreement and made their promises.

Bone Ring nodded her satisfaction. ''They won't come any time soon. They may not even come this far at all. But next year? The year after that? Who can tell?''

Larkspur stepped to the spot Owlclover had left and seated herself. ''Besides witches who aren't and far-off Sun People, what's the talk been?''

That evening, as the council broke up, Black Hand settled beside Larkspur. ''Thank you. You handled that very well.''

She grunted and patted him on the leg. ''There will still be talk once they have had time to think about it. That green fire in the sky will be mentioned again.''

''Owlclover was mad as a rabid skunk.''

Larkspur waved it away. ''There wasn't any other way than

to rub her face in it. She's never been too smart. A clever leader would have turned that all around on me—and she might have if I'd given her a chance. In the meantime, you and Bitterbrush had better move around among the camps. Laugh, talk, tell jokes, and be friendly. It's difficult for a person to believe that the fellow telling ribald jokes at his fire is really a witch."

"I know," Black Hand muttered. "Owlclover lost a lot of respect here today. She won't forget it until she dies. If I'm any judge, she was ready to commit murder."

"I suppose," Larkspur agreed. "But at least it won't be yours."

"And what do you think about the Sun People?"

Larkspur blinked to soothe her hot, irritated eyes. "Sun People? Here? That'll be the day. So what if they do come? Look at the size of the Gathering. Do you seriously think a band of starving warriors could stand against the assembled might of the Earth People?"

Black Hand shook his head. "No. And we know the territory better than they do, too."

Larkspur smacked her gums. "That's right. And they know it."

Chapter 22

Still Water pulled up where the trail led down through the caprock to Singing Stones' shelter. The Wind Basin stretched before them—a vista that stopped the heart. White Ash sighed as she stared out over the vast basin. Still Water shuffled his foot nervously, gravel grating. "We're back."

"We could just keep going," White Ash answered dully. "We could follow the trail down into the basin, go clear across it. Find a place out there beyond the Gray Wall, be-

yond the Red Dirt Basin. Maybe someplace down around
Sand Wash—or even south of there.''

''We could.'' He pinched his lips between worn teeth.
''We could make a lodge, learn the plants . . . and trap rabbits and deer. We could find a place to winter that had a
southern exposure, then move up into the trees during the
summer. There's pinion pine down there. The nuts fall like
rain.''

''And make wonderful breads. Yampa grows down there,
and four-wing saltbush. I've heard the Traders tell of a land
where sandstone arches over the rivers and redroot[1] grows so
thick you have to empty your moccasins of seeds after walking through it.''

''The winters are mild there. Left Hand told me. Biscuit
root grows on the slopes, and sego lily and mariposa cover
the ground.''

''Ducks come and winter on the lakes. We could net them
by the tens,'' White Ash said dreamily. ''I could live for a
long time on ducks. I know a way of roasting them, of cooking them in their juices so the meat falls from the bones.''

''And we could fish the rivers, make nets and cast them
out into the deep water. The fish ought to grow big in the
south.''

''It would be a place to raise children without worrying if
a war party would kill them. Would you like that? Would you
like to see your children grow and smile in the sun?''

He nodded, a rending in his heart. ''A son . . . and a
daughter, to teach all kinds of things to. We could show them
how Spider builds a web, and what birds do when they make
a nest.''

She swallowed hard and gripped his hand. ''You and I
could be together. We could hold each other in the night and
lie under the robes and love each other. We could do that,
Still Water. We could live together forever if we just kept
going.''

''You and I, we'd be happy. We've seen too much, been

1. Amaranth; *Amaranthus retroflexus*.

too miserable. There's a future down there past the southern horizon—a thing to hope for, to build for.''

Her hand tightened on his. "Grandchildren. Think of that. After our children found mates, we'd have time together. The children could do the work and you and I could sit in the sun and tell ourselves stories. We could look into each other's eyes and laugh while the world went crazy up here.''

"We could," he whispered and closed his eyes, seeing it in his mind: Sunshine shone golden on a mud-plastered earth lodge. Smoke rose in a blue twist from the smoke hole. A drying rack groaned under the weight of goosefoot and yampa. He saw White Ash grinning at him, squinting in the brilliant sun. She reached for him with firm brown arms and hugged him close. In the background the happy squeals of their children split the pleasant air. He gazed fondly into her loving eyes—and the vision shimmered, feathering away on the sides until only the dim silver of tears remained.

"Is that so much to ask?" White Ash wondered.

When he looked at her, she had her eyes closed, living what she spoke. His soul melted. "We could leave the Wolf Bundle with Singing Stones. He could care for it.''

"We could.'' She mouthed the words soundlessly.

But other thoughts crowded Still Water's happy ones: Left Hand's final farewell; the bodies of the dead outside the Wolf People's last camp—bodies that gurgled in the night. The memories would remain to haunt White Ash and himself— the knowledge of what they'd left behind.

The pack on his shoulder grew heavier, as if the Wolf Bundle had begun to weigh more. Visions of the future—of what Brave Man would Dream—spun through his head: the stinking mines, the wasted forests, the eroding mountains. People would labor like ants. Brave Man's Dream.

Still Water clutched at his stomach.

They stood in silence looking off to the south. The wish for peace built until it ached in his soul.

She dropped his hand and covered her face, shoulders slumping.

He placed his arm around her and snugged her against him.

"Such a beautiful Dream, Still Water. So . . . beautiful."

"I know."

He took one last look at the south, and his soul cried out for what would never be. "Maybe we can Dream it for someone else." He started down the path to Singing Stones' shelter . . . and whatever waited for them there.

Wind Runner walked in the lead as they crossed the divide in the pass through the Sideways Mountains. He stopped and stared out over the basin that spread to the south. Aspen came to stand beside him. She raised a hand to shield her eyes against the summer glare.

Before them lay the Wind Basin, the land patterned by mottled gray-and-brown hills hemmed by mountains to the west, while a distant gray-white ridge bordered the southern end. More mountains rose in the eastern distance, black humps against the far horizon.

The long procession of Black Point came to a halt, staring, as the clan reached the crest. To either side of the pass, rugged peaks rose in cracked and sundered uplifts of dull red granite. Snow still clung in the protected pockets.

Hot Fat panted after the long climb as he took a place beside Wind Runner. Sage Ghost came next. One Man and Black Moon joined them.

"The Wind Basin . . . the land of the Earth People," Sage Ghost told them. "Their territory stretches farther than you can see. Over that gentle rise to the east is a broad, grassy plain where buffalo graze along the Elk River. Beyond that, not even I have gone. Only the Traders. On the other side of that high gray ridge to the south is a land told of only in tales. Supposedly a high basin filled with red earth and good tool stone lies there. South of that, the Traders say, is a country of uplifted rims where bones made of rock can be found washing out of the soil."

Sage Ghost pointed to the southwest. "Those are called the Monster Mountains. On the other side is the Sage Grouse

River. It runs south so far that only legends tell where it leads. I have heard that it runs through places where sandstone rises almost to the sky and then flows into a canyon so deep it goes clear through the earth."

He pointed farther to the west. "Down that way, many days' journey beyond the Sage Grouse River, is a huge country of sagebrush and greasewood. Down there is a lake filled with water so salty a man can't drink it. The people who live in that land dig salt from the ground."

"And to the east?" Hot Fat asked.

Sage Ghost gestured. "Out there are plains like those east of where the Fat Beaver River joins the Dangerous River. Many buffalo live out there—but little water can be found. The Traders tell that a man can walk for days and see nothing but grass, and they say the only trees that grow are the cottonwoods that follow the river bottoms. Between those rivers a man can walk and walk."

"And straight south?" Wind Runner asked.

"The Tall Mountains," Sage Ghost told him. "Mountains so high they touch the sky. A Trader told me that no man can climb those mountains; if he did, angry Spirits who live up there would eat him."

One Man chuckled. "I've never found anything on high mountains but a good view and a lot of snow. Perhaps we'll let the Spirits keep those high mountains. It's what's under them that concerns me."

"How about game?" Black Moon asked.

"This basin holds buffalo and antelope and deer. Enough to feed us and then some. The same, so I've been told, with the Red Earth Basin beyond the Gray Wall—and in the Sage Grouse valley as well."

"And these plants the people eat?" Aspen asked. "They grow everywhere?"

Sage Ghost laughed and lifted his muscular arms as if to embrace the land before them. "More than the Earth People can use. They take only what they need. The rest they leave for the Spirits who guard places."

"Spirits." One Man grunted. "We'll see who is stronger.

Spirits who guard places—or Thunderbird, who flies over the whole world. I'll bet my darts on Thunderbird.''

"That's the Gray Deer River you see there." Sage Ghost pointed at a thin band of deeper green. "The Earth People call it the Spirit River on this side of the Sideways Mountains. Above the Earth People Camp—where I stole White Ash—it supposedly runs into a mountain and comes out of the rock lower down. The Earth People think there's Power in that. They go up and cast gifts into the hole so the water can take it to the Spirits in the mountain. They think if the Spirits are happy, they'll bless the water and let it continue to run out the other side.''

"Then let's go see this land." Black Moon looked back and gave the signal to move on. The Black Point bunched up in the pass stared and pointed, talking with animation.

Wind Runner stepped out, rattling his darts, a curious excitement mixing with his anxiety. If White Ash had gone anywhere, she'd be down there, somewhere in that tremendous basin.

Aspen walked beside him, her presence comforting. On the way to the top of the Sideways Mountains, they'd spent a great deal of time talking. Now he glanced at her from the corner of his eye, noting the way she walked, how the leather of her dress conformed to the swell of hip and muscular thigh.

Why do I always seek her companionship? Is it because she and Hot Fat are the only ones I can talk to? Not even White Ash listened with the attention Aspen gives me. She begins to fill my thoughts.

"It looks better than the country we just left," she told him. "You can see more green down there. By the look of the sage, the rains fall more often.''

"It's a good time of year to come." He squinted up at the Sun, riding high in the sky. "When we fled south of the Fat Beaver, we'd lost everything. The first winter wasn't so bad, but when the band split, things grew worse. I think this time we will be fine. We have lodges and many warriors. The packs are full of supplies, and the dogs are healthy and can haul them all.''

She shot him a speculative glance. "And only the strength of the Earth People has to be tested."

He stepped around an outcrop of dark, lichen-mottled rock. The soil had a buff tone here, and the loose gravel in it grated underfoot. Sparse grasses grew here and there, while the slopes grew squaw currant, bearberry, and serviceberry. They followed a game trail down to the bottom of a shallow drainage. To the left, the ridge had begun to rise. The right side of the valley looked steeper, and he could see outcrops of brown rock.

"We *will* face them," he declared. "And I think they'll break."

She pursed her lips, frowning. "I've been thinking about the things you and Sage Ghost have said about the Earth People. I think we should capture as many of their women as we can."

He cocked his head. "Oh?"

"They know the land. Know the plants."

Each step she took stretched the soft calf-hide dress over her muscular bottom. He bit his lip to drive the distracting thoughts away and tried to concentrate on her words—and on White Ash's face.

"That night above the White Clay camp we talked about how the Black Point would have to change their ways. Remember?" She flashed him a smile. "I've given it a lot of thought. If there are new things to be learned, why not capture those who know them? You told me the women make all the decisions, that they know the root grounds and where certain foods can be found. They know how to keep things so they will last through winter. They know what to eat and what not to."

The logic of her suggestion appealed to him. "We could use them to do the work. If our people didn't have to do it, they'd be less likely to grumble, less likely to long for the old ways. The new way would provide for them."

"The Earth People could do more of the work." She jerked her head back at the following band. "Do you think Pika and Cottontail want to grind these grass seeds the Earth People eat? Not at all. They'll work hides, make lodges, and hunt, but they won't want to gather seeds."

Wind Runner rattled his darts happily. "All this time I've worried about what would happen when we got here. You've given me the answer."

She chuckled. "Then perhaps you'll never take me for granted again."

He looked over at her. "I didn't know I ever did." At her odd refusal to meet his eyes, he changed the subject. "No wonder so many people come to you for advice."

She made an empty gesture with her hands. "Even the old women are starting to ask what I think about their problems. Sometimes my head is so full of other people's troubles I don't have time for my own."

"Tell them you're busy."

Her delicate smile carried a wistful twist. "No. I can't do that. Some have come to depend on me. I listen, and then I think about what they've said. If it's serious, I talk it over with Grandfather. He's a very wise man."

"Someday you'll take Black Moon's place." He looked up at the rugged land that rose around them. He could make out mountain sheep atop the rocky talus. Their dun sides and white butts contrasted to the rock. A raven baited a golden eagle in the updrafts; the eagle flipped on his back to expose talons to his playful black companion.

She lifted an eyebrow and shot him an inquiring look. "Some are beginning to say that about you."

"Me?" He almost stumbled over a sagebrush.

"People have begun to listen to you. When you speak, you don't do it rashly. You give a lot of consideration to what you say. Before a decision is made in council, they ask you. Haven't you noticed?"

"I just tell them what I think. I don't try to argue anything."

"That's the point." She gazed out over the new land. "You tell them, then leave it at that. A leader of the clan can't order anyone to do anything. He can only suggest. If time proves his wisdom, more and more people listen . . . until he comes to speak for all the people. If you tried to make them do something, they'd ignore you."

"Like Fire Rabbit?" He sluffed his coat off his shoulders, squinting up at the burning sun.

She lifted her hands and slapped them to her sides. "He tries too hard. He's always trying to lead, not to be a leader. There's a difference."

"I'm not trying to be a leader."

A mischievous expression molded her features. "Aren't you?"

He made a negative gesture. "Like you, I wouldn't have time for my own problems."

"I think we should go that way." She pointed at the ridge that rose to their left. "A drainage like this one usually ends up in a steep-walled canyon with a lot of brush. Hard-going for the elders and the dog travois."

"You *are* a leader."

She swatted him with a playful hand. "Stop it."

He turned off, angling along the rocky slope. When they topped the ridge, Wind Runner noted that below a rocky shelf, it ran down into the basin in a gentle slope. From this vantage, he could see she'd been right. The lower part of the canyon not only narrowed into a steep slit, but brush choked it like a green mat.

In one place on the gentle slope before them, a rocky outcrop barred easy travel. Wind Runner jumped down and studied it. "Over there. That's the easiest route down."

She called back to Black Moon and pointed. Wind Runner took her hand, helping her down the steep, rocky face. For a moment they paused. Sunlight lit the healthy flush of her soft face. His flesh prickled, aware of her lithe body so close. Her pleasant scent filled his nostrils. He stared into the depths of her knowing brown eyes. For the briefest instant their souls touched; then he let go of her hand and turned away.

He had to frown to make himself think of White Ash.

Bitterbrush ducked out of the night and entered the Round Rock clan's shelter. She peered around in the darkness until her eyes adjusted and she recognized the figure sprawled on the robes. "Larkspur? What are you doing here? I thought you'd be out telling tales with the others until dawn."

"Not as young as I used to be." Larkspur sat up. "Why are you here?"

Bitterbrush looked out at the Gathering. A multitude of fires marked the camp locations. Silhouettes moved back and forth in the firelight between the camps. Overhead, the rustling leaves of the cottonwoods reflected the jumping light in amber tones; the dome of the sky sparkled with an infinity of stars.

"It's turning cooler. I thought I'd get a robe." Bitterbrush rubbed her belly as she sat next to Larkspur. "If I eat anything else, I'll fall over."

"Lot of food here." Larkspur rustled her bedding. "Been a good year." A pause. "People have been treating you good?"

Bitterbrush caught the undercurrent. "Black Hand has been the spirit of each camp we've visited. He's no fool. I think the witching story is stopped. People are funny, they'd rather believe it's foolishness. Safer that way."

"It *is* foolishness." Larkspur hawked and spat into the night. "Three Forks clan has been put in its place, and you and Black Hand are off to a good start. What more could you ask for?"

Bitterbrush closed her eyes. *Warm Fire.* "Black Hand is a good man . . . I like him."

"Where is he?"

Bitterbrush gestured into the darkness. "Sand Wash camp. Over just under the ridge there."

"The one in the rocks?"

"That's it."

"Mama?" Lupine asked in a sleepy voice.

"Here, baby." Bitterbrush reached over and patted the girl.

"Are we getting up?"

"No. You sleep. Where's your brother?"

"Don't know . . ." Lupine drifted off to sleep again.

"He's a boy. Almost a man," Larkspur reminded. "He's off playing, looking at girls. Who knows? It's the Gathering."

Bitterbrush sighed. "He's not the same. I think when Warm Fire died, he took a piece of Tuber's soul with him."

"Losing a father is difficult."

"And coming here, I thought I'd have to take a stick to him more than once. He didn't say more than three words the whole way."

"What do you expect?" Larkspur asked. "The boy's father has just been replaced. You can see the anger in his eyes. He doesn't like Black Hand. He resents him."

Bitterbrush rubbed her eyes. "A woman has to marry."

"And so will Tuber. Maybe two summers will pass and he'll find a girl. I'll make him a good deal and send him off." Larkspur paused. "The People are better for that. A young man doesn't have to live with the past. He gets to go to another camp and find a new life. Men were never meant to assume responsibility—it's not in their nature. They're too frivolous and emotional."

"You sound bitter."

Larkspur cackled. "Me? About what? This morning I proved I still have what I need to get things done. And tell me, is Bone Ring still happy with the deal I made for her?"

"She is. She was worried Badwater would stand alone if the Sun People came. Knowing that all she has to do is send a runner and warriors will come to drive off the Sun People makes her feel better."

In the shadows, Larkspur rubbed her legs as if to smooth away the aches of age. "Bone Ring has sense. I've always liked her. More so since she and Green Fire had that falling-out over the marriage between Little Toe and Gray Needle."

"What about the Sun People?" Bitterbrush propped her chin on her knees, staring out at the dancing fires. Voices rose and fell on the night as people laughed and talked. "Bone Ring pointed out that there are no Traders here from the north. Not even from the Wolf People. They usually send someone."

"Don't expect Wolf People. Blessing fell too close to the Gathering this year. They should have just finished their Dance by this time. We plan the Gathering by the face of the moon; they plan Blessing by the path of the sun and the longest day. It always makes me wonder how they know that."

"The stars are important for them. Remember that story the Trader Left Hand told us? About how the Wolf People think that the stars were spun in the sky by a giant red spider? I wonder where that idea came from."

"Wise Spider? I don't know. Maybe it's the way the stars look like a dew-shot web in sunlight. But the reason that Wolf People aren't here is because it's time for Blessing." Larkspur sniffed loudly and wiped at her nose. "Not because of any Sun People. Don't worry your mind about Sun People, girl. They're not coming here."

"People are talking about them." Bitterbrush stared thoughtfully at the shadow figures around the fires. The cottonwood trunks loomed eerily in the dancing light. A shiver of premonition slipped along her backbone. She hugged herself as if to draw back into the shelter of Larkspur's dominating presence. Why? What foreboding lurked in the warm night?

"Let them talk!" Larkspur cried. "That's what the Gathering is for. Talking about the Sun People gives them something silly to occupy themselves with—instead of witching. If—and I say if—the Sun People come south, they'll have to get past the Wolf People first. I wouldn't wish that on anybody."

"And the Sheep Hunters?"

"Those, too, if the Sun People are foolish enough to go up into the Red Rock Mountains—or into the Geyser Mountains, for that matter. You ought to go up there sometime. The Traders tell about water shooting up everywhere. To hear their stories, more Spirits live in the Geyser Mountains than anyplace else."

Bitterbrush found her robe and stood. The night pressed down around her; unease echoed in the rustle of the cottonwood leaves. "I'm going to go find my husband. You sleep, Grandmother."

"Don't worry yourself about Tuber. He's probably laughing for the first time since his father died."

"All right."

Bitterbrush walked across the trampled grass. The breeze off the Spirit River carried the rich scent of cool water and damp earth. Three Forks had picked a good spot for the Gathering. And it had been a good year. People had come with packs brimful of roots and dried meat. A welcome summer after a winter of despair.

Warm Fire? Why can't you be here with me?

Bitterbrush skirted a knot of people who stood around a crackling fire. They Sang one of the old Songs. She let the sound carry her soul.

Out in the sagebrush, at the base of the ridge, a young woman giggled at a young man's gentle words. What would come of that? A marriage? The Gathering was a time for coupling and new love. Perhaps new love would be born for her, too.

She stepped into the light of Sand Wash camp's fire. Handsome Woman sat with White Sandstone, while Tall Man told a story to Squawapple, from the Badwater clan.

"You're back." Handsome Woman pointed to the stew. "Eat some more. Golden Flax was at her best when she made this. You can taste the soul of the antelope."

"If I eat any more tonight, I'll sink into the ground. Where's Black Hand? Did he leave without me?"

"He's up there," Tall Man said, a grin on his full, round face. "I guess he ate too much. What goes in . . . Well, you know."

She laughed with him and listened to the end of his story. Then she said, "Maybe I'd better go find him. If not, I'll have to feed him some dock leaves to loosen up his insides."

She found a little trail that wound up through the rocks. The night insects whizzed and chirred. A Song broke out in Sand Wash camp, only to be taken up by the next camp, and the next, until the whole valley echoed with the strains. In the Song, Fire Dancer taught the People the way of harvesting the ricegrass before he brought fire from the sun to warm the lodges in the winter.

She walked a little farther, humming the melody. A warm wind blew down from the hills, carrying the scent of sage and dust. The stars shone in abundance. If only Warm Fire . . . *No, don't think of it. He's gone. His spirit has returned to the earth that nourished him.*

The trail passed between two worn sandstone boulders. She placed her hand on one and felt for the trail with her toe. Her foot touched something soft.

Gasping, she jerked away. "Black Hand?"

The wind whispered through the sage as the People's Song traveled the night on owl wings.

She nerved herself and reached down into the shadow— and started as she touched a body. Had someone fallen?

"Black Hand?" Frightened, she called out to Sand Wash camp, "Help me! Bring a brand! Someone has fallen!"

Tall Man carried a burning branch up the trail, Squawapple following.

"What did you find? A snake?" Tall Man asked as he stepped closer.

Bitterbrush stared down in the wavering light—and into Black Hand's empty eyes. Blood had soaked his head and pooled in the dust of the trail.

The headache that lanced burning needles through Brave Man's brain came and went. On this day it was excruciating. He'd forgotten Pale Raven, who occupied herself in the preparation of the evening meal. The tanned sides of the lodge cover faded from his awareness. He winced at the throbbing agony in his head and squeezed his fist around the broken necklace of thin black stones he'd ripped from the one-armed man that night. White Ash had escaped him. The one-armed man had barely tapped the side of his head—and the voices had shrieked in terror. The pain hadn't paralyzed him—he was used to pain—but the hideous screaming in his mind had blanked his thoughts, even drowning the festering misery in his knee.

Power, the voices whispered. *The one-armed man had Power.*

Yes, Power. Brave Man glared at the intricately knotted necklace and the polished triangular stones. The Wolf Bundle had struck then, all of its might unleashed. He'd been caught unaware, ambushed by a flood of Power that battered his soul. The bundle had channeled Power and used it against him. A lesser man would have died, his soul riven from his body.

But I was stronger. No matter that I lay flat on my back for four days, battling to keep my soul, I survived. He closed his eyes, imagining the Wolf Bundle. *Now I am even stronger than before. I have learned. Next time I will control you.* Brave Man slitted his eyes as he stared at the necklace. The Wolf People's bundle had revealed its secrets in that desperate attempt. Other Power had joined it, funneled from someplace at the edge of the golden haze.

When I can Dream the golden haze, nothing will stop me. He tapped callused fingers on his good knee. *And you can't stop me, Wolf Bundle. Not you . . . not your one-armed man.*

Pale Raven's glance didn't register with him as he brooded. Who was the one-armed man? What Power did he possess?

The one-armed man had stepped out of the lodge. Had he been an apparition conjured among the bundles that had hung from the lodge poles?

Upon dispatching his warriors after White Ash, Brave Man had ordered the lodge burned—and with it, all of those terrible sources of Wolf Power. Then he'd curled up on the robes, tucking his head in his arms to protect himself from the screaming as his soul fought to maintain its hold on his suffering body. Through those long four days, Pale Raven had sat beside him, telling others that he fought a battle far beyond in the Camp of the Dead.

How had he managed to find such a woman? Had his Power directed him to her?

The fire crackled merrily as Pale Raven used sticks in the fashion of large tweezers to lift hot stones from the embers and drop them into the paunch of stew. The stones carried the heat of the coals and would bring the stew to a boil.

I will find the one-armed man. And when I do, he will know the Power of Brave Man. Brave Man knotted the necklace where he'd broken the thong and placed it around his neck—a symbol of that promise. Then he pulled the carved-stone wolf effigy from his pouch and studied it. The hard black stone had been shaped through hours of laborious work and polished with fine sand and leather until it gleamed in the light. Not much bigger than a fir cone, it fit coolly in the palm of his hand.

Pale Raven's expression was guarded as she watched him. The light caught the curves of her stately face, accenting the soft swell of her cheeks and the lines of her thin nose.

"Thinking about White Ash again?" she asked.

"I will have her in the end. I can feel it. Power will bring us together." He gave the wolf carving a careful scrutiny. Did it carry more Power than just the soul of the craftsman who had made it? *I should throw it away.*

"And this one-armed man?" She raised a questioning eyebrow.

"He will die very slowly. A Trader once told a story about the Swamp People. If a man is accused of evil Power, they cut a slit in his belly and pull out a length of intestine. Then they bind his arms and legs behind him and hang him over water so the fish pull out his guts a bit at a time." He glanced at her. "Imagine a man hung like that over a badger hole."

Her eyes hardened until they glittered and she looked away.

The open lodge flap admitted cool air and the smells of pine and fir and verdant grass, the aroma of meat roasting, and the slightly acrid odor of tanning hides.

Outside, in the lengthening blue of evening, children called to each other, screaming and laughing as they played a game that involved a lot of chasing. The camp dogs yipped and barked in accompaniment.

"Soul Flier?" a voice called from outside. "Flying Hawk would see you."

"Come in." Brave Man placed the polished statue of the

wolf to one side and hitched his stiff leg around as the war leader ducked inside.

Flying Hawk nodded to Pale Raven and seated himself cross-legged on a mountain-sheep hide in the guest's spot.

Brave Man dug into his pouch and produced a stone pipe that he filled with kinnikinnick and lit with a twig from the fire. He puffed twice and handed it to Flying Hawk. After the other had shared Brave Man's hospitality, he handed the pipe back.

"I didn't think I'd see you for a while yet," Brave Man began. "Has something happened?"

A wry smile twisted Flying Hawk's lips. "I didn't think I'd be back. Yes, something's happened. Hunting Wolf People has turned into a poor pastime."

"Oh?"

Flying Hawk spread his hands. "They've gone. All but a foolish few who remained."

"Gone?"

Flying Hawk scratched at his ear. "Fat Elk has taken a party to follow them—just to make sure. But I think they've left. For good."

"Tell me from the beginning."

The war leader thought for a second, then related, "The Wolf People had gathered in the foothills east of the mountains. Before I led the warriors down to drive them off, I thought I should scour the timber—make sure none had slipped past us. The scouts reported that the Wolf People under the mountain were holding a large council. In the meantime, we hunted the timber and studied the places where men would camp. We scouted for any sign of Wolf warriors passing in secret—and found nothing. Assured that no enemy could ambush us, I gathered the men and led them down to attack the Wolf People at the foot of the mountains. A blood-red sandstone wall rises there like a barricade to the plains. That's when we encountered the foolish ones who had come back to fight us."

"And what happened?"

"Their blood has mixed with the soil. Their souls prowl around their bones now." Flying Hawk stared pensively at the smoke hole overhead. "But the others . . . By the time we got down the mountain, they'd left. They headed east across the plains."

"East?" Brave Man considered. "What would they have found there?"

"Nothing." Flying Hawk made the gesture of negation. "Only rolling short-grass plains and a lot of buffalo. The animals didn't seem very nervous when we hunted a few to feed ourselves. When bad times come, we can go hunt there again."

Brave Man lifted an eyebrow. "Do you remember the wind when we hunted north of the Fat Beaver? Endless wind. It tried to rip a man's soul from his body. There are better places to winter than on the open plains."

"So we'll go to the Fat Beaver when cold weather comes?"

Brave Man tapped restless fingers on his stiff knee. "There is another basin to the south. We'll go there."

Flying Hawk frowned. "Farther from our lands?"

"Our lands? War leader, *our* lands are wherever we make them. No, we are called to the south. The Dreams keep pulling me. I can't see all of it yet." His voice lowered to a whisper. "But we'll be great. Greater than you can Dream."

Flying Hawk shot an uncertain glance at Pale Raven. She stared back, challenging. The glow of the fire lit her face from below, casting hollow shadows over her features.

The war leader took a deep breath and nodded. "You've led us well, Soul Flier. I'll go where you Dream. It will mean there is no Gathering. Some are already—"

"There will be no Gathering this year. And perhaps never again."

Flying Hawk shifted uneasily. "But the clan rules . . ."

Brave Man laughed and leaned back to prop himself on an elbow. He let his gaze roam over the stacked parfleches that lined the sides of the lodge, the thick pile of rich robes he and Pale Raven slept on. The firelight gleamed on the long, silvered hair of a grizzly hide.

"Ah, I know." Brave Man glanced at Flying Hawk. "You're worried about who will marry who without causing incest. Women are everywhere, my friend. How many of your warriors took Wolf women for themselves?" A pause. "Perhaps a warrior in this very lodge?"

"Many did. Yes, and so did I—for all the use I've gotten of her so far. But . . . we are all born of the Sun. Thunderbird breathed life into us when he made us out of clay. We cannot forget who we are."

"We won't forget. Not as long as we have Power—and brave darts to back it." Brave Man inspected his thumb before looking up. "And what of our ties to the clans? We are living a new way now. Power fills us. You remember the way the Traders talked about the Wolf People? They said the Wolf People made terrible enemies and we'd cry on the corpses of our dead if we fought against them. Where do we camp today? Who challenges our right to these mountains? Where are the Wolf People? Fleeing east, into the plains to be blown away by the wind."

"I hear your words, Soul Flier." Flying Hawk narrowed his eyes. "And I like what you say."

Brave Man clenched a fist, watching the muscles flex in his forearm. "We no longer need the clans. What can they give us we don't already have? When the winter falls upon us, I'll lead those who follow south. The others, they can do as they wish."

Flying Hawk steepled his fingers, thinking. "The Earth People live south of these mountains. We can take their women, too." A speculative glint came to his eye. "A man can make himself great in the shadow of your Dreams, Soul Flier. Perhaps greater than any other warrior the Broken Stones have ever known."

Brave Man laughed. *Yes, you see, don't you, my friend? You see what a man can aspire to under my leadership.* "And it will get better. I have seen glimpses of a new way. Think, Flying Hawk, think of taking not only women, but men, too. Imagine gaining so much Power that others will do all the work for you. It can happen. We can Dream it to be."

Flying Hawk cocked his head, then slapped hands to his knees. "I'll come and see you in the morning. We can talk more then. I just wanted to let you know that the threat of the Wolf People has vanished."

"Like mist on a sunny morning."

"Just like that." Flying Hawk chuckled. "My wife, Two Roses, has roasted a leg of mountain sheep. I think I had better go stuff myself with some of it. I haven't seen her for more than a moon. Perhaps my Spirit will see fit to plant another child in her—and in the Wolf woman, too. If I can keep her from scratching my eyes out, that is."

"Go. Bear my greetings to Two Roses—and to your new Wolf woman."

Flying Hawk stood. "I doubt that my new woman would care for your greetings, Soul Flier. I wonder if Two Roses has taught her to talk like a human being yet."

"I'm sure you'll find out."

The war leader stepped out into the indigo twilight. Brave Man asked Pale Raven, "East? Why?"

"Perhaps your White Ash is with them. Perhaps she, too, has traveled into the plains."

South, the voices hissed. *South . . . with Power.*

He squinted at the fire. "No. I would know. Power would know. She came from the Earth People. There she will return."

Pale Raven checked the bubbling stew and came to lie next to him. "Flying Hawk is right, you know. You have led us well. Not even two tens of warriors died while driving the Wolf People away. Your Power grows."

"Enough to separate the Broken Stones from the old ways?"

Tiny lines etched her forehead as she considered. He admired the set of her thin brows and watched the firelight play over the smooth skin of her face. He reached up to run his fingers down the line of her jaw and caress her throat.

"I don't know," she said. "As long as you lead them well, Dream with the Power you have, they'll follow. Behind their hands, and in their robes at night, they'll worry."

"Flying Hawk and his warriors won't."

She gave him an amused smile. "They're wolves. They've had a taste of fresh blood and they hunger for more."

He nodded. "I intend to give it to them."

She took his hand in hers. "Is it true? What you told

Flying Hawk? Do you Dream something great for the Broken Stones?''

His face tightened. ''I can't see it all yet . . . just glimpses in the Dreams. Things I can't understand. There is a four-sided mountain made of square stones that humans have fitted together. And feathers . . . I see feathers, of all the colors you can imagine. On top of the square-stone mountain a man stands, raising an obsidian knife to the Sun. Blood drips from the tip.'' He took a breath. ''When I have that Dream, my loins tingle, as if I shall plant the seed that grows into that man.''

She nodded, as though seeing it in her soul. ''Perhaps you already have.''

He studied her warily.

She shifted in order to run her long fingers down the side of his head. ''A powerful people. A strong people. That's what we shall make.''

''We?''

The corners of her lips twitched smugly. Her eyes seemed to grow deeper, to draw him in. ''I missed my bleeding, Brave Man. My stomach turns ill in the morning. I've started to gain weight. I think you have planted your child. Find your White Ash, take her as often as you like. Let's see which of your children climbs this mountain of stone and wields the bloody knife.''

Beside Brave Man's knee, the little stone wolf statue gleamed in the firelight.

Chapter 23 🏃🏃

''Clear your mind,'' Singing Stones told White Ash. ''Listen to the voice that isn't there.''

Tranquillity filled the Soul Flier's eyes as he watched her. They sat cross-legged on the uneven stones that littered the high ridge top. The old man might have been one with the very rock. His mountain-sheepskin coat had the same pale buff color as the surrounding stone. A flat-topped beaver-hide cap covered his silver hair.

White Ash concentrated on the old man's gentle words and frowned. "I don't understand. How can you listen to something that isn't there?"

"Ah, but that's the secret to Power." He gestured toward the vast expanse of the Wind Basin with a withered hand. "Is the world there?"

"Of course it is." The afternoon breeze tugged at her braided hair, flicking the gleaming black strands this way and that. Her bottom had begun to ache from sitting on the wind-polished rocks. Here and there amber grasses quivered in the living air. Phlox bloomed in white and light blue, the scent filling her nostrils. The star wheel lay to her right; the ominous bulk of the Grass Meadow Mountains rose over her left shoulder. Before her, to the south, the patterns of the Wind Basin rippled in vibrant green, white, and buff. Islands of fluffy cloud rode on an endless blue sky.

"Close your eyes," Singing Stones commanded. "Keep them closed. Is the world still there?"

"Yes. All I have to do is open my eyes and it will be just as I remembered."

"That is your problem. You are blinded by your sight. Numb from what you feel. Deafened by what you hear. Everything around you is illusion. What you observe is only what your eyes, ears, nose, mouth, and flesh make it. Your senses separate you from the One. That which is White Ash is a lie. Only by discarding all that you are will you become all that you are not."

She nodded, struggling to understand and obey—and failing. "Singing Stones, that's all well and fine to say. But my bladder's full and my rear has gone to sleep."

Singing Stones chuckled. "At least you listen, and seek. Go . . . take care of your body. I remember the trouble I had at first. The Dreams led me part of the way to the One. It took me years to discover the rest."

She stood, taking a wobbling step on bloodless legs. "I

don't understand. You have the Power. You know how to reach out and touch the One. Why do you need me?''

He looked out over the basin. "Because I am an old man. You—and Still Water—must face a challenge few Dreamers have ever known: You must Dream and live among the People at the same time."

"Stop right there. I'll be back in a moment and we'll talk more about it."

She winced against the painful tingle as blood ran through her cramped legs. *Everything that happens, happens because of me. Sage Ghost stole me from Three Forks. Wind Runner left. The White Clay died. Brave Man attacked the Wolf People. Still Water came to rescue me. I led him to the Wolf Bundle.* Unease settled within her. Even here on the ridge top, the Wolf Bundle's presence lingered in her soul.

When she'd relieved herself, she returned and sat down next to the old Dreamer. He didn't seem to have moved a muscle.

"Now, finish what you were telling me." White Ash pulled her legs up and clasped her hands in front of her knees. She couldn't keep her eyes off the expanse. Dappled cloud shadows spotted the land, smoothing and softening the rugged soul of the basin. The land seemed to breathe with a languorous patience.

Singing Stones turned bright eyes on her. "Anyone can Dream. All he needs is the will to seek. The One lies all around us—denied by the senses, as I just told you. A Dreamer has to peel away the layers of himself. You have peeled wild onions. Shell after shell is removed. And what do you find at the core?"

She chewed her lip, thinking about it. "An onion doesn't have a core. Just a final shell. Nothing is there but onion."

"And the path to the One is the same." Singing Stones closed his eyes, and his nostrils flared as he filled his lungs. "Everything that is White Ash must be removed. Your soul must be pure, silent. It must listen without hearing. You must deny yourself. You will learn that eventually. Your soul is already close to the One."

"But you said I faced a challenge few other Dreamers have known."

Singing Stones raised his eyebrows and smiled wistfully. "I've felt the need of Power. My visions have given me glimpses of the future that might be if the Sun People do not accept First Man's Dream. You must face this Brave Man and return to the Sun People—Dream their Power into the Spiral. To do that, you must live among them."

She rubbed nervous hands along her arms. "I've lived among them before."

"But not as a Dreamer," Singing Stones countered. "When a person seeks the Dream, he comes to a place like this . . . away from the distractions that perpetuate the illusion of life. It is easier to concentrate in solitude. Women aren't laughing, children aren't crying. Men aren't telling stories, and the camp dogs aren't yipping and fighting. The problems that hobble people who are living together don't intrude."

A knot tightened in her soul. *Live with the People? Face Brave Man? Is that what Singing Stones sees?* She closed her eyes and took a deep breath. *I will never live with the Broken Stones. I'll kill myself first.* "I don't understand what the problem is. The Sun People are healthy and strong. They have their Soul Fliers to Dream for them. Why do they need me?"

He blinked and studied her pensively. "The coming of the Sun People has changed the Spiral."

"The Spiral?"

"Circles within circles, having no beginning or end. The Spiral is the world. Plants grow in the earth. Some animals eat the plants. Predators eat the animals that eat the plants. Men eat the animals as well as the plants. When men and predators die, their bodies return to the earth. Could the plants grow if the bodies of the living didn't nourish the earth? Would the animals live if they couldn't eat the plants? Where does it begin? Where does it end? The Spiral represents all that is—and is not. When does the soul begin? When does it end? Power runs through the Spiral. First Man Dances in the

Spiral. The Wolf Bundle Sings in the Spiral. The Spiral is the One.''

"All that is, and is not.'' The words haunted her.

"And more.''

"We'll save that for later. I want to know about the Sun People. You said they're changing the Spiral.''

"The Spiral is part of the world—and it isn't.'' Singing Stones made an encompassing gesture. "Think of it like the reflection in a pool of water. Is the reflection part of the water? Or part of the light? If the breeze stirs the water, the reflection breaks into fragments. If the water is moving, the reflection is distorted. If you choose to dip your finger into the water, ripples change the reflection. That is what the coming of the Sun People is doing to the Spiral. They're sending ripples through the Spiral, because they don't know the One.''

"But if everything is part of the One, so are they.''

"Are they?'' The smile Singing Stones gave her touched her soul.

She knotted her fists. "Then I don't understand. If the One is all that is, and is not, the Sun People must be part of the One.''

He lifted his face to the rays of the sun. "They are part of the One . . . but they don't know it. They have masked themselves in illusion. They live separately. When you lived with the Sun People, how often did you hear them talk about the One? How often do their Dreamers speak of the One, or leave their camps to seek visions?''

She narrowed her eyes. "They stay in their lodges and send their souls to the Camp of the Dead. That's where they gain their Power. They seek it from the souls of the dead.''

His expression didn't change. "The Sun People are new to this land. They are young, vigorous. You lived among them. When did you first feel the One?''

"When Bright Moon died.''

"And before that? Did you know the One, or were you content that you knew the way the world is?''

She took a deep breath. "I thought I knew the way the world is.''

"Yours is the blood of First Man. Perhaps that's why he sent you to the Sun People. To teach them."

She shook her head. "But I didn't hear the call of the One among the Earth People, either. They're descended from First Man."

"That is true." Singing Stones gave a faint nod. "But they, too, have discarded the One for illusion. They have forgotten the Spiral that Fire Dancer told them about. You and Still Water are close to the One in different ways. It is the nature of Still Water's soul to feel the reflection of the One around him. It is the nature of yours to Dream. Power knows you, White Ash. You are a bridge between the worlds . . . in the same way that a log lies across a rushing river. You touch both banks."

"How do you know so much? I feel almost helpless."

He smiled at her, brown eyes depthless, eternal. "Dreamers are as different as people." He pressed his palms together. "I will tell you a story. When I was young, I felt the One. It came in my Dreams, and the leader of my clan told me to go be a Healer. The feeling of Power grew stronger. Then, at the Gathering one year, Cattail brought the Wolf Bundle among us. I picked it up and felt its Power. That night I Dreamed of the Sun People, and of the future. I left the People to come here and to learn to Dream."

He paused for a moment, floating in his memories. "When I touched the Wolf Bundle, a door opened in my mind. I knew what Power wanted. I Dreamed First Man as he Danced fire and showed me the way to the north, to the Sun People."

"But you didn't go?"

Singing Stones shook his head. "I tried to several times, but the Dream kept bringing me back here. You see, the Dream is a trap. The things of this world become less and less important. I had found the One, the thunderous silence, the blinding darkness . . . the ecstatic desolation."

Her soul had touched that freedom; she knew his words.

He lowered his head, staring down at his age-withered hands. "Some men are obsessed with coupling. Others with the hunt. Some with status and prestige. For me, there was only the One." He took a breath and said, "How could I give this up? I wasn't strong enough."

She could feel the Power of his soul. In an awed whisper she asked, "And you think I am?"

He lifted his hands. "To me, the Dream is everything. For you, it must be only part. I feel First Man's worry. The Sun People can't destroy the One—but they can change it, change all that First Man Dreamed. They can change the Spiral into something else."

"But why doesn't Power interfere?"

The wrinkles on his ancient face turned sorrowful. "The ways of men are no concern of Power. First Man Dreams the Spiral, but the One doesn't interfere with this world, although it runs through it. Do you remember the Creation story you were told as a little girl at Three Forks?"

She tilted back her head to the infinity of sky. "The Creator made the First World. And he made all the animals and plants and insects and people. But people began to cause trouble. The animals got mad because people thought themselves better than even the Creator. When the Creator saw what was happening, he made the Second World in the sky and fashioned the sun and moon and stars. The Wolf People say he turned himself into a giant spider to do that. The Earth People say he did it just to get away from people, but the souls of the People started to rise and make trouble up there in the Second World. That's why the Earth People bury their dead—put them back into the ground that nourishes them. The Creator thought that if he made a Third World, he might be able to solve the problem. In the Third World, he put Spirits to help and guide the people. In the meantime, things had gotten so bad in the First World that not even the Spirits could help. Finally the Creator made a Fourth World—this world—and made a hole in First World through which First Man led the good people."

"That's right." Singing Stones nodded. "In the First World, people became lost in illusion and forgot their place."

White Ash glanced nervously at Singing Stones. "The Sun People have a different story. They say that in the beginning, the whole world was made of water. That Thunderbird had no place to land and called out. Bear heard Thunderbird's pleas and dove down and brought up mud for Thunderbird to sit on. Thunderbird was so happy that he mounded up the mud and made it into a great mountain and Bear went to sit at the top of it. The Creator saw what had happened and made men and animals from the mud. When Bear looked down and saw all the animals and people, he descended and taught men how to live.''

A twinkle lit Singing Stones' eyes. ''A good story. I would like to hear other Sun People stories sometime. Stories have Power. They are a trail to knowledge . . . they free you to know more than you think you do. Tell me, White Ash, do you remember what happened when First Man came through the hole between the worlds?''

''I remember that First Man had an evil brother who led other wicked people into this world. But I don't understand how the One and the Creator and—''

''The One is the heartbeat of the Creator.'' Singing Stones filled his lungs, then let his breath drain away. ''Remember the onion? Layers within layers? The worlds are that way. Each is a layer. The One runs through them all. Think of it as the odor of the onion.''

''The onion is like the whole Creation.''

''You are wise, White Ash. We can close our noses to the odor of the One, deny it through illusion. Only in Dreams can we experience the One. It is the same with the Spirit World. That is why First Man must Dream the One. Only through the One can the Spirits touch this world. The Sun People Dream the Camp of the Dead, but in their illusion, they ignore the One. It is a thing of the soul. You must be the bridge.''

She swallowed and massaged the back of her neck. ''Or the Spiral and the Spirit Power will change into something new?''

''Brave Man will Dream a new way for this world. In doing so, he will change the Spiral. Only you and Still Water can challenge his Dream. The choice is still yours.'' Singing Stones' gaze filled her like sunlit honey.

"We came back, Singing Stones. Still Water and I. We're here. Tell me what we must do."

"Learn . . . before it's too late."

"Too late?"

The old man cocked his head to stare out into the basin. "Last night I Dreamed. I saw Sun People in the Wind Basin. I saw a lame Spirit man standing over the body of a young warrior. The young warrior was a handsome man, with blue lines tattooed in his forehead. The Spirit man raised a bloody knife to the Sun—and a new way was born."

Brave Man . . . and Wind Runner! Her soul curdled.

Larkspur struggled to catch her breath and feed her starved lungs. She stopped on the trail that led up the Gray Wall. To either side, the ridge they followed dropped off into steep-walled drainages. Occasional sage and rabbitbrush dotted the slopes. The gray-white soil produced a powdery dust that coated her moccasins. Here and there, light tan sandstone outcropped on the slopes around them like lines of scales. High above, scattered juniper and limper pine grasped the crumbling land with tenacious roots.

Fear clutched at her heart. *We are tainted—unsafe even here in broad daylight.* Her soul quaked at the thought. *We're all unclean. By the Spirits of the land and the sun in the sky, we'll suffer for this foul abomination. Why . . . oh, why did it have to happen to Black Hand? To Round Rock?* She blinked to stop tears of defeat and futility.

Her legs were trembling. She propped herself on Cattail's arm and looked back at the Wind Basin. The tree-shadowed bottomlands along the Spirit River were hidden by the folded ridges of layered gray-and-blue clays that rose between.

Better that way. If only we could flee—could go far from this terrible place. She swallowed hard. How did a person flee from a defilement of the soul?

After the discovery of Black Hand's body, people had stared at each other in horror, collecting their children and huddling by the fires. Many clutched fetishes to guard them from evil. Before the first morning light had filtered into the valley, camps had packed up and clans melted away like spring snow. A murderer, a terrible murderer, had stalked one of the People.

Larkspur puckered thin brown lips over her shrunken gums and glared in the direction of Three Forks. What sort of evil possessed the fiend who had bashed in Black Hand's head? She shivered at the thought. And it had struck her clan! Everyone suspected Owlclover, but who could prove it? Who could level the charge against her, or against her clan?

Larkspur glanced at her people. They waited in silence on the trail while her strength recovered. A grim anxiety hung about them like late-afternoon smoke. Bitterbrush stared out of hollow eyes, expression ashen. Only Tuber's spirits had returned. The boy looked reborn.

"This will be a bad year," Bone Ring had said as they lowered Black Hand's body into a quickly dug grave. Only the Badwater and Warm Wind clans had stayed behind to help with the burial. Then they, too, had hurried away, shunning the place where Black Hand's angry ghost would prowl.

No offense against the People could compare with murder—not even witching. The ghost of the violently killed would stalk the night, seeking the murderer. It would vent its wrath on any who happened near. If Owlclover's witch existed, he would seek out the spot of Black Hand's murder and ally himself with the Spirit. The innocent would pay for what had been done.

Larkspur glanced up at the long climb before her. The summit seemed beyond her reach, as did hope for the People.

She started forward again, refusing to break the silence, refusing to let herself mourn the only man she'd ever loved. He would live in her memories the way he'd once been: a passionate young lover who had shared his body and soul with hers.

Resolutely, Larkspur placed one foot after the other, forcing her old body up the long climb.

I have seen my last Gathering—and it shivers my soul. A

deep-twisting anguish filled her. *What next for the People? What misery will come of this?*

The sun burned into Still Water's back as he and White Ash rested in a protected hollow that lay between pale, square boulders that had broken off from the sandstone caprock above. The breeze made sighing sounds in the limber pine that grew around their hidden alcove. In the brush, rosy finches chirped and insects whirred.

Still Water rolled off White Ash and onto his back. He gasped a lungful of warm air and stared up at the patchy clouds that sailed so easily against the endless blue of the sky. The breeze tickled his flushed skin.

"We shouldn't be doing this," White Ash said with a sigh. "Singing Stones says that coupling distracts us from Dreaming."

Still Water resettled his head and admired her. Perspiration left her brown skin shining in the bright sun. Droplets—the mingling of his and her sweat—sparkled in the light. He reveled in the sight of her perfect body. Her firm muscles had gone lax after the passion of their coupling. He reached over and traced a finger along the swell of her hip, circling the dampness of her navel, his hand rising to cup her full breast. A deep contentment swelled within his soul.

"We could stop." An ache accompanied the thought.

She met his questioning gaze. For a moment he seemed to sink into the brown softness of her eyes. The sun accented the delicate hollow of her cheek. "I don't want to."

Peace drifted through his spent body. "I know Dreamers aren't supposed to couple. And not just Singing Stones says so."

"I don't care," she answered. "I love you too much. Moments like these fill a need in my soul." She lifted a hand to rub her brow. "I know I'm going to have to give up so much of myself, I refuse to give you up, too. If I can't love and Dream, then I won't Dream."

"Power has its price," he reminded.

"And I have mine."

They lay in silence for a moment before she continued. "Even if I have to be the bridge between worlds, I won't give you up. Power wouldn't have sent you to me otherwise. Maybe that's part of it."

"Maybe," he agreed, "but Power discards its tools after it uses them. Perhaps it will discard me."

"It can't."

"Oh?" He gave her a wry smile. "Do you know something about Power that I don't?"

"You're the Keeper of the Wolf Bundle now. Besides that . . . I *need* you."

He glanced over his shoulder at the pack that held the Wolf Bundle. He went nowhere without it. "I guess I am." He grunted under his breath and shook his head.

"What?"

He scratched his ear. "I was thinking about how I've changed. The person who was Bad Belly is gone. I'm not the same man I was when I lived at Round Rock. I've become someone different. The Wolf Bundle . . . it changes a person. I am what it is, and it's become part of me."

"I know." She flexed her hands, muscles rippling under her smooth brown skin. "I feel the Wolf Bundle . . . it tugs at me all the time."

"Knowing it's close fills something in my soul that was once empty. And I never knew it was gone. Do you understand?"

She squeezed his hand where it lay on her breast. "My love for you is that way. I never knew love could be so rich and full. What I once thought was love has turned out to be a hollow skin . . . like the one an insect sheds. It looks whole on the outside, but when you crack it open, there's nothing there."

"Then perhaps you and I must learn to Dream together."

She took a deep breath and stared up at the sky. "I wish I knew, Still Water. It took Singing Stones years to learn how to Dream. The Wolf Bundle changed him, too. If his visions are right, I don't have time to learn the way to the One."

She chewed on her lip before adding, "I can feel the One, even now. It touches the edge of my soul with the gentle brush of feathers on skin. Singing Stones has taught me how to clear my mind, to hear and see nothing. I'm learning about myself, about how to slip past the illusion. But I can do it only a bit at a time. I feel like an infant learning to be a human being. There's so much. I have to learn to talk and walk and how to act. I have to stand against Brave Man again. But he's a warrior, and I'm only a small child."

"Power won't abandon us." He swallowed, fervently hoping that would be the case. "We just have to try harder."

"I know. I will. But sometimes I can almost feel failure coming. And if it does, nothing that's happened to me in the past will compare to what's coming. Brave Man will . . ." She twisted her head the other way.

Still Water's stomach knotted. "The worst part is, I keep Dreaming of what will happen if we don't stop him. Last night I flew over tens of tens of people. More people than there are grass blades. They all looked up at me with misery in their eyes. Their souls cried out, and they reached up as if I could save them." *How can I save them? I don't even know how to save us.*

Gray Needle traveled with a sickness in her soul. Memories of the horror in Little Toe's eyes lurked inside her as she walked. Her husband's strained expression was reflected in the faces of the others. Horror hung over Badwater clan like the shimmering of bloodthirsty mosquitoes. The clan had ties with Three Forks through Little Toe. No one had been able to say who had killed Black Hand, but the serpent's head of suspicion fixed itself on Three Forks. If Three Forks clan harbored the abomination—the murderer—Little Toe carried the taint. *And through him, so do I . . . and our children!*

Gray Needle shuddered at the thought and turned her attention to the men who walked several dart casts ahead of the main body of the clan. They hastened on their way, shoulders

Slumped and heads bowed. Bone Ring, the clan leader, walked in the center of her family; they talked in subdued voices. Evil had been loosed. A person could feel it on the wind, hear its rustle among the drying grasses.

Through the shadowed gray boles of the gnarled cottonwoods that grew along the Spirit River, Gray Needle could see that Little Toe stayed to the side, aloof and alone. She could tell by his posture that guilt rode him like a tick-hunting blackbird on a buffalo's back.

"It's not his fault," Gray Needle told Squawapple as she looked to the east, where muddy-yellow sandstone bluffs rose square against the sky. The wind blew hot across the basin, picking up the burning heat of the sun before it invaded the shaded river bottom.

"I know. I was there." Squawapple pursed thin lips under her long, thin nose. "Five rocks, from Warm Wind clan, was visiting at the Three Forks' camp when it happened. He told me that all of the Three Forks men were there. So was Owl-clover—grousing about the way old Larkspur had humiliated her and her clan. Five Rocks said that none of them had that look—you know, like they were going to do something as vile as murder. Someone who'd do that—especially at a Gathering—would be nervous, looking over his shoulder to see if anyone noticed."

"They were all there?"

"All but a couple of the women who'd gone out visiting. Five Rocks said that Basket was so miserable she'd gone off to be by herself. Losing that baby changed her."

"Basket is Little Toe's sister. They used to be very close—sent gifts back and forth. He told me she's become a frightened wreck now. Almost someone he doesn't know anymore." Gray Needle gestured impotence. "Someone must have heard something!"

"Who could hear?" Squawapple asked. "Tall Man tells a wonderful story. Black Hand was killed a good dart's cast from camp."

Gray Needle shook her head, studying her husband through lowered eyes. "He's taking all the blame on himself, afraid he'll foul us."

"He shouldn't," Bone Ring interrupted. "I know Little Toe. He's a good man. He has to be, to have angered old Green Fire the way he did." She growled, "Daughter, the only good thing that's come out of Three Forks in a long time is that man of yours. I'll have a word with him. For the moment, he won't be in a mood to listen. Maybe by the time we get back to Badwater, he will be."

Gray Needle smiled her thanks, but it wouldn't be over. Not for a long time, if ever.

Squawapple said miserably, "Murder done at the Gathering? No good will come of it."

"The witching talk will start again." Bone Ring scowled at the dusty sandstone-capped bluffs to the east. She wiped at a trickle of perspiration that slid down one round cheek. "We can't afford that kind of trouble, not with the Sun People sending parties south."

Gray Needle looked back to where her infant son rode in her niece Elderberry's pack. The girl loved the child as if it were her own. At the thought of the baby, Gray Needle's breasts began to ache with milk. *Will my child live long enough to deserve a name? And if he does, will his life always be tainted by this terrible deed?*

She dropped back and took her baby from Elderberry. As the child nursed, Gray Needle listened.

"The other camps will help drive the Sun People off if they come," Squawapple was saying.

Bone Ring gave a nod of assent. "They will . . . if they don't start accusing each other of witching. Nothing tears the People apart like talk of witching. It'll ruin us." She paused. "Protection from the Sun People . . . well, at least we got that promise at the Gathering."

Squawapple wiped at the sweat trickling out of her hair and looked longingly at the cool water of the Spirit River to their left. Grasshoppers exploded from the grass at their feet, clicking away as the dappled sunlight caught their wings.

"I don't like it," Gray Needle added quietly. "I feel as if the world turned. Power will be offended. You don't have a murder at a Gathering without offending Power."

Bone Ring glanced at her. "You've been hanging around Wolf People for too long."

Gray Needle shifted her son to the other breast. "Power is Power. We keep the Spirits happy, but I can't call the Wolf People fools for what they believe. Fire Dancer came down out of their mountains when he led us here. I just wonder how much we've changed."

"A lot, I suppose." Bone Ring glanced back to make sure that everyone—especially the children—was following. Children tended to lag on a day as hot as this. "And that's another thing. We haven't seen anything of the Wolf People. Someone should have been down. I know they just had Blessing, but some of the Traders would have left early to make the Gathering."

"It's not like them." Squawapple looked around nervously. "I've just got a bad feeling."

"No wonder," Bone Ring grunted. "A murder happened at the Gathering. I can tell you this, we'll walk a long day's journey around that place from now on." Her eyes narrowed. "If Three Forks feared witching before this, they'll be crawling with fear now, knowing they're the closest camp to Black Hand's angry Spirit."

A sense of wrongness tightened in Gray Needle's gut. "Maybe we should call the men back. I'd feel better."

"Nerves, girl." Bone Ring glanced around uneasily. The land had gone unusually quiet. "And I share them."

The men had walked out of the trees, climbing up a low terrace truncated by the Spirit River. Heat shimmered on the tan ground, making their images hazy.

"The People will pay for this Gathering, I tell you," Bone Ring added, waddling along. "We've brought some sort of disaster down on us."

"Two more days and we'll be home." Squawapple pointed toward the Sideways Mountains rising in a silvered, wavering mirage ahead of them. "Maybe we could call Singing Stones down to Sing Spirit protection around our camp."

"Good idea, child," Bone Ring agreed. "If anyone can ward off evil, it's Singing Stones."

They had reached the bottom of the terrace. Gray Needle

started up, following the dimpled tracks of the men. The sun beat down mercilessly now that they'd left the protection of the cottonwoods. Sweat raised a sheen on Gray Needle's bare arms and trickled down her neck. From the top of the terrace they would be able to see the Badwater, and could follow it to the clan shelters. Fortunately, most of the trip would be made in the cottonwood-shaded floodplain.

Gray Needle reached the top and waited for Bone Ring.

Two weathered knobs of sandstone protruded from the cobble-strewn top of the terrace. The men had already passed through the narrow gap between them. The premonition of trouble grew, almost suffocating Gray Needle as she stared across the dusty white clay.

Fool! It's the heat. Black Hand's Spirit is weighing on you. You're worried, that's all. It's just the talk of witches that's eating you.

As the rest of the women reached the top, she started forward. "When we catch sight of the men, let's call for them to wait," Gray Needle said, the unease beginning to turn into panic.

"I was going to suggest the same thing," Bone Ring agreed.

Heat rolled off the deflated cobbles, burning through the bottoms of Gray Needle's moccasins. She followed the trail between the sandstone knobs, winding through the chest-high boulders that littered this end of the terrace. She made it to the slope that dropped down to the floodplain before she saw Squawapple's husband, Half Moon. He lay on his face, his body sprawled on the slope.

The ambush had been laid cunningly.

Frightened cries erupted behind her. Gray Needle whirled to run, but a man sprang out from behind one of the rocks. He wore oddly tailored hide clothing, the hunting coat hanging down to mid-thigh. Strange figures had been tattooed into his face, and he wore his shining black hair in a high roach. Powerful hands seized her. Burdened by her child, she tried to fight back. Her screams split the air.

Warriors seemed to appear from the very rocks as her captor dragged her, kicking and screaming, to the ground. Another of the hideous warriors ripped her child away from her. Holding the infant up, he screamed triumph in an alien tongue.

"Let me go!" she pleaded.

Wolfish eyes stared into hers. Then the warrior laughed and spoke to her in a tongue she couldn't understand. He jerked her arms behind her and bound them with sinew thongs. Dragging her to her feet and pointing down the slope, he ordered her to move forward.

Fear pumped bright through Gray Needle's charged veins. *Little Toe—where are you?* What was happening? Squawapple and a whimpering Elderberry were being driven along by other warriors.

"Who *are* you?" Gray Needle cried out. *"What are you doing?"*

Then she saw Little Toe. He lay farther down the slope, where he'd fallen into the sage. Two long war darts protruded from his body.

Her legs collapsed under her. The warrior kicked her roughly as an anguished cry of disbelief broke from her lips.

Another of the warriors stood aloofly to one side. He watched through impassive eyes, darts grounded before him. Five black circles had been tattooed into the dark skin of his forehead. The warrior said in halting but intelligible speech, "We are Sun People. These warriors are Black Point. You belong to this man. He is Fire Rabbit."

For a moment, disbelief overwhelmed her grief. Then tears broke free to run down her face. No warrior would run to warn the Earth People.

Chapter 24 ▲

White Ash concentrated on relaxing. She sat, legs crossed, on a pile of soft hides in Singing Stones' shelter. She kept her eyes closed. Within, she could feel the blood pumping in her veins. The beat of her heart and the expansion and contraction of her lungs became eternal. She turned inward until even those sensations were left behind.

The radiance of the Wolf Bundle hovered in the nothingness nearby, its Power twining around her. She resisted the urge to surrender to it and turned inside, away from the direction the Wolf Bundle might have taken her. Must it always hover at the edge of her awareness, a constant distraction?

She let go of herself and used all of her willpower to blank her thoughts. When she'd filled herself with nothingness, she began to peel away the layers of herself.

A drifting feeling—as if she were falling—began to possess her. The feathery touch of the One closed around her like blue smoke on a misty morning. Her body moved with it, seeming to float on waves.

The feathery voice drifted out of the One. *Seek . . . seek . . .*

"Where are you?"

The image broke, awareness of the One shredding as she returned to her body. White Ash blinked and glanced dazedly around. She took a deep breath and sighed. *I can't do it. I get so close . . . and that's as far as I can go.*

"You try too hard," Singing Stones said. He sat naked to the waist on his robes in the rear of the shelter. On the wall the Spiral caught the flickering firelight. Shadows danced on the soot-stained rock and played over the bundles hung from their pegs.

White Ash lowered her head; pain nagged her cramped

legs. "I felt it, and I think I heard the voice of First Man." She shook her head. "It seems like the closer I get, the farther away the One is."

Singing Stones touched the tips of his fingers together, ancient eyes knowing. "You will find the way."

She straightened her legs and winced at the tingling agony. He always said that, but this time the words came too close on the heels of her failure. "When? How much time is left? I *have* to Dream." She rubbed her legs. "Maybe . . . maybe I'm not the one."

The lines in Singing Stones' face deepened. "If you believe that, you will never find the way. Only belief, and denial of yourself, will bring you to the One."

"Belief? Denial? Words, Singing Stones. Just words."

Still Water groaned softly, asleep in his robes. His old battered pack—the one that held the Wolf Bundle—lay at the head of his bed. He started awake and rubbed a knotted fist into this eyes. He fixed White Ash with a pained stare and said, "It's begun."

White Ash shot him a withering look and asked, "What?"

Still Water sat up. "Sun People are in the Wind Basin. I—I Dreamed. Flew with the Wolf Bundle. I saw people being killed. Women taken captive."

She stared. "But Brave Man wouldn't be there. Not that quickly."

Still Water's expression didn't change. "I didn't see him. But the last time I had a Dream like this, it happened. Just like the Dream. I saw the camp that Brave Man killed. I saw the Dancers that night around the fire. Saw him . . . you. I *saw* it!"

She shifted her attention to Singing Stones. The old man sat immobile. "Power waits for no man . . . not even for a Dreamer."

Outside in the night, an angry breeze sighed through the pines. The fire cracked and popped in the silence. From just beyond the shelter hangings, the *hoo hoo hooo* of an owl cried plaintively.

White Ash cringed. *Brave Man? In the Wind Basin?*

"What about our people?" Still Water asked. "We have to *do* something. We can't just let the Sun People—"

"You can do nothing," Singing Stones interrupted. "Unless you want to go down and die with the rest of them."

Still Water ground his jaws and thumped his fist into the robes. "*What's happening?* Why? What's the purpose of so much war and dying and pain?"

Singing Stones looked up at the magpie; the bird sat on its perch, its head stuffed under one wing. "A new way has come to the Spiral. Power cares nothing for human suffering. Only First Man Dreams to keep the Spiral in balance. He is the link between people and the Spirit world. It is up to White Ash to Dream a new way for the Sun People. Only through the Dream can the Sun People be made to understand."

The Dream. It always comes back to the Dream . . . and me. She ran nervous hands over her face. "Maybe I can Dream only when Power comes to me. Maybe only when—"

"That's because you are caught in the web of your own illusion." Firelight gleamed in Singing Stones' obsidian eyes.

"That's just *it*!" she cried, gesturing her futility. "Maybe I can't let go of being me!"

"You try too hard."

"Wonderful! I try too hard. What else can I do? Cease to try—and let everything fall to Brave Man? Maybe no one who's awake ever touches the One. Maybe it's your own illusion that you experience." As soon as the sharp words left her mouth, she regretted them.

Frustration pulled its knot tight in her breast. She'd given her heart and soul to following the old man's instructions. For almost a moon now, she'd reached the edge of that feathery touch, experienced the falling sensation. And each time, the feeling of the One evaporated just as she struggled to cross that last threshold and fall into the gray mist.

She ground her teeth, confused and irritated. *What's the matter with me? Maybe I'm not the hero they think I am. It's too much to ask a human to do.*

To Singing Stones, she said, "I'm sorry. I shouldn't have said that."

The old man nodded, the barest movement of his head. "I know the feeling that possesses you. Like an infant who can stand, you can't take the first step without tottering and falling."

White Ash fingered the hem of her elk-hide shirt. *I'm not sure you can walk either, old one.*

Singing Stones narrowed his eyes as if reading her thoughts. "The One is all around." He gestured at the rock above and then to the floor and walls. "Yet you remain blinded to it. You are striving to overcome an entire lifetime of illusion. Now your thoughts are telling you it can't be done. As long as you listen to yourself, you will fail."

She bit her lip, then said, "I have only your word . . . and the knowledge that once you sat in the middle of an elk herd. That could be explained away. Maybe it was a trick of the wind. Or you fed them or something."

Still Water watched them warily and pulled at his bedding with anxious fingers.

The lines on Singing Stones' face rearranged into a thoughtful pattern. "Would it help if you saw illusion overcome? The seeds of doubt have been planted in your mind. Will you feed them with illusion until they sprout and grow?"

"See illusion overcome?" Still Water asked, skepticism large on his face.

Singing Stones glanced at Still Water, then gave White Ash a benign look. "I feel the struggle in your soul. Driven by desperation, you can never experience the One, never Dream. Desperation is an illusion. Ignore it."

She clenched her fists hard enough to drive nails into her palms. "*Ignore it?* With Brave Man and his twisted sense of Power running loose? You've had visions of the future he will Dream. You've heard Still Water describe his visions. How can we ignore the fact that Brave Man is going to separate people from the One? He's going to Dream a terrible way to live!"

"You must ignore it." Singing Stones never wavered. "It is the only way. But in that direction lies the trap I fell into.

You must do what I failed to. You must Dream the One—and deny its lure. Otherwise, you will be like Singing Stones, a moth drawn to the flickering light of the fire—unable to resist the flames.''

Her anger welled again. "You expect me—who can't even touch the One—to do what *you* failed to do?" White Ash threw her hands up, slapped her knees, and stared angrily at the soot-encrusted rocks overhead. The fire popped and sent a swirl of sparks up to flicker into nothingness.

Singing Stones nodded. "If I showed you, would you cleanse the anger and worry from your soul? Would you trust me?''

"Show me?" she asked incredulously.

Singing Stones closed his eyes and began to chant, centering himself as he'd taught White Ash to do. Back stiff, he sat before the fire, his timeless face relaxed. The gentle melody of the chant filled the shelter and woke the magpie. The bird peered about and paced nervously back and forth on the stick that served as its perch, then quieted as if stroked by the lilting Song.

The old man's chant rose and fell with the leaping flames of the fire. White Ash's skin prickled, and she shot a nervous glance at Still Water, who watched with wide eyes. The shelter seemed to echo the chant, amplifying the sound until the very rocks Danced with it.

Power built, and White Ash forgot her anger and frustration. She swayed with the rhythm of the chant. The very air snapped with the Power of the Wolf Bundle. Like dancing smoke, it surged and flowed through the static-charged air. She sensed Singing Stones calling on the Power of the Wolf Bundle. She shivered when it wrapped the old man in its strength.

Singing Stones opened his eyes, the look vacant, as if he were no longer within his body. The chant dropped to a whisper, but the tones carried.

Absently, the old man offered his hands to the light. He bent forward, reeling slightly, and reached into the fire. Face raised to the rock overhead, he lifted coals from the hearth, chanting to them. Lifting them to his lips, he kissed them and took them into his mouth. Long moments later, he plucked them out and rubbed them along his bare arms and over his sunken chest.

White Ash stared in disbelief and awe. No blisters rose on the old man's flesh. No welts marred his lips. Nor did he react as the burning coals ran along his skin.

Singing Stones continued the chant, returning the embers to the fire. The flames crackled up, casting a brighter light through the shelter.

He turned his head slowly to look at White Ash with empty eyes.

"You don't burn!" Still Water gasped.

"The fire is illusion," White Ash whispered. "He's Dreaming the One."

"Yes." Singing Stones' voice sounded oddly hollow. "The flesh is illusion. Only the One is." He stared sightlessly at her and grasped a bone awl from the things beside him. The polished awl glistened in the firelight. Singing Stones ran it through the withered flesh of his arm. No hint of pain marred his expression as the skin rose under the sharpened point and went taut before the keen tip broke through.

Still Water's hoarse breath made a strangled sound.

The old Dreamer reached around to grasp the long bone awl with his bony fingers and pull it through his arm. His flesh showed no wound. Blood should have stained his skin and the sharpened bone shaft.

"How?" Still Water gasped.

"The bone is illusion," Singing Stones whispered. "Only the One is real."

The shelter began to throb with Power. It ripped through the air like a gale in the black timber. White Ash placed palms to her ears, seeking to shield herself from the onslaught. Desperately she fought to drive the Wolf Bundle's presence from her soul—to keep secure the essence of herself.

Suddenly the air went still.

When Singing Stones spoke, the voice might have come from many tens of throats. "Don't fight us, Mother of the People. Through us you can Dream the One. Only your strength will save First Man's Dream. Only your courage can Dream the Spiral. That which is within you will be the bridge between Peoples. We are old in the manner of men. We live in this world and Dance the Spiral. We Dream the One. We Sing with the Wolf Dreamer. Where we Danced with Fire Dancer, so will we Dream the new way with you.''

"Who . . . who are you?" White Ash whispered.

"Will you fail us, Mother of the People? Do you have within you what not even the Wolf Dreamer would attempt? Yours is the strongest Spirit we could find. You are the hope of the Spiral. We have placed our hope in you. You are the one. There is no time to seek another.''

"Who are you?" she asked again, raising her hands as if to fend off the Power.

"All that is . . . and is not. We are the One, and the many. Dream, Mother of the People. The time is soon. We are the Power. You are the hope. We will show you the way to the One.''

"But I . . ."

Singing Stones toppled backward onto his robes and groaned softly. White Ash could feel the Power of the Wolf Bundle ebb into nothingness. Immediately the magpie emitted a terrified squawk, shot through a hole in the hangings and disappeared into the blackness beyond.

For several heartbeats White Ash sat frozen. Then she sprang to the old man's side. His breathing rasped as he moaned to himself. Still Water knelt next to her and lifted Singing Stones' head so the old man could breathe more easily.

The fire had died down to low, smoldering coals, and in the dim light she met Still Water's awestruck eyes.

Singing Stones started and blinked his eyes. He swallowed dryly and shook his head weakly. "No," he whispered, and looked up in horror at White Ash. "Don't let it happen."

"What?" White Ash pleaded.

"Don't let the witch hater murder you, too."

"Murder?" Still Water asked, color draining from his face.

"Fading," Stinging Stones whispered. "The vision is . . . fading.''

"Who is murdering who?" White Ash demanded. "What's happening?"

"Killing . . . Dreamers. Kills . . . the Mother . . . of the . . ."

"Singing Stones?" White Ash bent close. "What's wrong? Are you all right?"

The old man smiled serenely. "Falling into the One. Dreaming. The Wolf Bundle is . . . calling. Golden light . . . all around." His eyes went blank. "Floating. Wolf Bundle, I hear you. Coming . . ."

"Singing Stones?" she cried in panic.

His eyes seemed to clear for a moment, and he looked up at her, wonder in his withered face. "I had to warn you. I never knew the Power of the Wolf Bundle. Shouldn't have called on its Power . . ." He groaned again, eyes dimming. "Beware . . . Mother of the . . ."

"Singing Stones?" Still Water called.

The old man's body relaxed, sagging in Still Water's arms.

White Ash gave a strangled cry and placed her ear above his heart. Silence.

She raised herself, desperation filling her. Still Water already knew. He reached for wood and dropped several pieces on the smoldering embers. As the flames crackled up again, he stared uneasily at the Spiral painted on the back of the shelter. The curls of red glowed in an eerie manner.

"How do I find the way now?" White Ash ground her teeth against the whirling sensation of loss. "How, Still Water?"

He tried to mask his misery. "I don't know." Then his face blanched and he turned to stare at the pack that held the Wolf Bundle.

Her belly muscles knotted and cramped. "No," she choked. "It just killed Singing Stones—and he was skilled, Powerful. Myself, I can't even . . ."

It might have been the wind beyond the hangings, but tens of tens of voices whispered in the night breezes: *We are the way.*

The rough surface of the heavy stone he carried ate into Still Water's fingers as he climbed the loose soil at the bottom of the cliff. He paused to study Singing Stones' last resting place: a narrow fissure in the sandstone wall of the canyon. He and White Ash had nearly finished rocking up the niche. Now he fitted his stone into place.

White Ash labored up the loose scree and grunted as she reached to seal the burial with a final stone.

Still Water turned and looked out over the canyon. "He'll like it here. The view is wonderful. Look, you can see an eagle flying over the pines down there."

Beyond the far ridge, the Wind Basin lay sere in the scorching midsummer sun. Wind whispered about the rock and sighed through the limber pine and juniper, bearing with it the dry odors of dust and the pungency of bitterbrush, sage, aster, and primrose. A band of mountain sheep leaped nimbly among the buff-colored rocks and kept a careful eye on them.

White Ash bit her lip and looked up at the cloud-patched dome of sky. "This is where he wanted to be. He's with the One now."

Still Water found a place to sit on one of the grainy slabs of sandstone that had toppled from the cliff. He braced his legs and rubbed the back of his sweaty neck before glancing up the slope at the burial. "There was so much I wanted to ask him."

A hollow look had come to White Ash's eyes. "I know."

She stood beside his slab and placed a hand on his shoulder. Wistfully, Still Water reached up and clasped her hand, enjoying the warmth of her touch.

Images of the Dream played through his mind. Sun People warred in his homeland. His People had come to the end of their time. Like Singing Stones, they, too, would be dead soon, passed from the earth. He'd seen that so clearly. The visions of the future haunted him. He and White Ash had so little time to act—and the stakes grew with each beat of the heart.

"What do we do now, Still Water?"

He leaned his head against her hip, lost in memories of the lodge at Round Rock. Warm Fire's voice rose and fell as he told some story that drew laughter from Bitterbrush and Cattail. The children watched wide-eyed from their robes.

There would be no more nights like that among the Earth People.

"We seek the Dream." He patted her hand. "That's all we can do. It's up to us now."

"He held the coals and they didn't burn. He pierced his flesh and it left no wound," she whispered humbly. "We both saw that."

"And it wasn't his voice that spoke to us." Still Water winced. "You could feel the Power. It was the Wolf Bundle—and more." A shiver ran through him as he looked over at his pack.

"It killed him," she said in a hushed tone. "What are we involved with?"

"Power. The Spiral. Things I don't understand."

"And murder? Who is killing Dreamers? Brave Man? I know that he killed Old Falcon."

He exhaled loudly. "I don't know. Could Brave Man send some Power through the Wolf Bundle to kill Singing Stones?"

"I'll never touch it to find out." She glanced about. "Maybe we should leave it with Singing Stones."

"I don't think so. That doesn't . . . feel right. You know what I mean? I know its Power. The Bundle isn't evil."

"Ask Left Hand what he thinks. I say we should rock it up with Singing Stones."

Still Water frowned, struggling with the idea. It made sense, but then, what was illusion and what was truth? Here was a puzzle he wished they didn't have to solve. "Power. That's the thing we have to understand." He cocked his head. "Singing Stones said Power is everywhere but it doesn't interfere with the things of this world. Healers, like Black Hand, use Power, direct it. Change it. Witches use it for different things. No, it's not the Bundle. Burying it with Singing Stones would be a mistake."

"It *killed* him!"

"Did it?" He lifted his head to look at her. "Or did he fall into it and refuse to come out? Remember?—he said it was calling. Maybe he didn't have the strength to refuse the call.''

"Strength?'' She blew through her lips and settled on the slab next to him. The lonely fear on her face unnerved him. "The voices asked if I was strong enough.''

Still Water put his arm around her. "Among the Round Rock, I made dart shafts. When you plan a dart shaft, you have to find the best piece of wood. First you strip the bark off and look at the grain—see if the Spirit in the wood might work. Then you heat it, steam it, straighten the bends and curves. When that's done, you use a scraper to smooth it. You mix a bit of your soul with it and heat it over the fire to toughen the Spirit of the wood. Then you make the final carving.''

"Does this have a point?''

He nodded absently. "Are you a dart shaft, White Ash?''

"I'm a woman.'' She glowered.

"I'm well aware of that. I was speaking in terms of Power.''

She searched his eyes. "What do you mean?''

"Power crafts its own tools.'' He hugged her close, reassured by the feel of her body against his. "Think about everything that's happened to you. Sage Ghost stole you from Three Forks and trained you in the ways of the Sun People. You've told me he did that as a promise to Power. Maybe that was selecting the raw wood. Maybe learning the ways of the Sun People was like stripping the bark and straightening the bends. From then on, everything that happened was the firing process . . . the strengthening of the wood.'' He looked at her. "You're the strongest person I know. You've been beaten, raped, tried for strength . . . and you've passed all the tests.''

She looked out over the basin as wind played with strands of her long black hair. A weary desolation lay behind her expression. "Everything happens because of me.''

"Power has its dart shaft.'' He raised his eyebrows. "Now only the final crafting is needed.''

"And the craftsman is dead.'' She jerked her head back toward the burial.

"Perhaps."

She cocked an eyebrow questioningly.

He lifted a foot to prop it on the slab and followed his thoughts. "A dart shaft is only one part of the whole. Perhaps Singing Stones attached the fletching. That still leaves the stone point, and the binding."

"But what do we do now? Where do we go?"

He sniffed the warm air, filling his nostrils with the scent of brush and warm earth. "I think the best thing is to stay here. We have Singing Stones' shelter. The storage pits have enough food. The star wheel is up on the ridge top."

"But what about all those people down there? Maybe we could—"

"What? Go down and die with them the way Singing Stones said? If everything that happens to us happens for a reason, we'll know when to go down. Power will tell us. The black wolf will come, or the Bundle will Dream with us. We're not ready yet. Perhaps you'll find the way to Power in the meantime."

"We could still leave. Travel by night the way we did when we escaped from the Broken Stones. Go south, live like we wanted to."

His soul saddened. "Could we?"

She hesitated for a moment, mouth tight, lines around her hard eyes. "No, I guess not. As the seasons passed, we'd never forgive ourselves, would we?"

He took a last look at Singing Stones' burial place and stood. Reaching for his pack, he willed assurance into his smile. "Come on. Let's go see if we can learn to Dream together."

Her brave smile didn't hide the fact that her heart was breaking.

Bitterbrush leaned all her weight on her fire-hardened digging stick and drove it into the ground. She worked at the edge of a lumpy series of dunes where the sandy soil held water late into the year. She pulled back, levering the soil up with a snapping of roots, grabbed the scurf-pea plant and pulled it free. Then she whacked the roots on the digging stick to break the soil loose. Dropping the rich plant into her pack, she moved on to the next.

Irregular buttes lined the southern horizon and extended off the western flanks of Green Mountain. They rose to a cobble-strewn summit before dropping off into the dune-rich Red Earth Basin. The endless blue of the late-afternoon sky had a singular clarity. Sage thrashers flitted around, eying her curiously as they peeped from the gnarled, knee-high brush.

Scurf pea had grown well this season. With each new plant, she mumbled a prayer of thanks to the Spirit who guarded these grounds. Scurf pea was a favorite of the People. Larkspur had noted the time perfectly. The seeds were ready to drop—and a delightful tea could be made from them. The rest of the plant, including the roots, made wonderful eating.

She dropped the plant into her sack and looked around. Here and there among the dunes, other members of the clan were at work, harvesting the rich abundance of plants. They had camped a short walk to the east, on a terrace overlooking a seep. Round Rock camp lay a day's walk beyond that. There Larkspur watched over the children with Tuber's help.

Bitterbrush peered at the gentle northern horizon that belied the sheer drop-off of the Gray Wall. A green band of willows obscured the course of the Coldwater River.

She levered another plant from the soil and placed it atop the others in her sack, pressing it down. A leafy odor rose to fill her nostrils. Time to take her bulging pack back to camp. She slung it over her shoulder and set out.

Bitterbrush tried to understand everything that had happened to her as she picked her way through the knee-high sage. No one said much anymore. A spark had gone from the clan, snuffed by Black Hand's murder. In the days since the tragedy at the Gathering, she'd come to accept that she would live the rest of her life alone. What man would want a woman associated with murder—even if she would inherit an entire camp some day?

The gravelly ground gave way to a softer silt that cushioned her steps. Birds warbled in accompaniment to Bitterbrush's thoughts. The tumpline of her pack ate into her forehead. So much heartache for everyone. Only Tuber seemed unaffected by the horror that had befallen them. The gleam of challenge had even died in Larkspur's eyes.

Something has changed.

Their camp had been placed in a sheltered spot eroded out of the terrace. A seep rose at the back of the pocket and trickled through rich grasses to drain into the Coldwater, a short walk to the north. She picked her way down the embankment and walked into the camp before dropping her burden.

She stretched to ease the kink in her back and stepped over to stir the smoldering fire. Hide shelters had been placed around the fire in a half circle; she passed between Limbercone's and Pretty Woman's before kneeling at the seep. Cattail had hollowed out a basin in the bright green moss to hold water.

She drank her fill of the cool water, then seated herself in the thick grass to rest. If she drank until she burst, she could never fill the aching emptiness inside. Black Hand had at least been an ardent lover. He'd smiled at her and held her— not a substitute for Warm Fire, but at least she hadn't been alone in her robes.

"I'll miss that," she whispered. "There's no one to talk to." Even Bad Belly would be a relief. Her gaze strayed to the north. Had tragedy befallen Bad Belly, too?

"You have me to talk to," a strange voice said from behind. When she turned, a lone warrior stood there.

Bitterbrush gasped and scrambled to her feet. The cut of his clothing differed from anything she had ever seen before. A long, fringed hunting shirt hung down to mid-thigh, and the long fringes on his leggings swayed with the air. Thick-soled moccasins covered his feet. He looked like the most powerful man she'd ever seen, and long, deadly darts hung from one hand. Five black circles had been tattooed into his high forehead.

"You look like a good woman," he said in accented words. He studied her. "Strong body."

Heart pounding, she gaped, then asked in a small voice, "Who are you?"

He smiled grimly. "I am Sage Ghost. Walk back to your camp." He pointed with his darts. "Don't run. I'm faster than you."

She shook her head and knotted a fist at her breast. A scream choked in her throat.

"The others are taken by now. Your men are dead. There's no point in trying to escape. The Power of the Earth People has fled."

Too shocked to think, she stumbled toward the lodges, glancing fearfully at him as he followed. Once in the camp, she stopped. "The others? Dead?"

He used one of the long darts to lift the door flaps on each of the lodges, peering cautiously to see what was inside. Only then did he turn to face her. "We keep only the strong young women and children. Black Point have hunted you all day. Your people belong to the Black Point now. All but you. I keep you. You are now White Clay. Like me."

She turned to run, but his hard hand caught her. At the strength in his grip, she cried out and ceased to struggle. He pulled her around and she got a close look at him. Several gray hairs threaded through his long braids. Deep lines traced his face—and she could sense the sadness in his brown eyes.

"How do you talk our language?"

He smiled humorlessly. "Stole an Earth People girl once. She taught me." His smile widened. "And since we came to the Wind Basin, I've been getting lots of practice. Now you will learn the talk of the Sun People."

Bitterbrush's legs buckled under her and he let her down. He glanced at her pack, lying near his feet. "Now you pick plants for Sage Ghost."

"Others will come," she said. "The Earth People will fight back."

He squatted on his heels, the darts cradled in his lap. "I don't think they will. Their Power is gone. We hunt Earth People before they can hunt us. Kill the men and old women. No word is carried to other camps by the dead. The young women we take, and they work for the Black Point now."

He squinted up at the sun. "It's a new way . . . Sun People way."

"Never," she hissed.

He lifted an amused eyebrow. "Oh? I think forever. Now you're my woman. Sage Ghost isn't a bad man. I won't beat you unless you disobey." He paused and added, "It's been a long time since Sage Ghost had woman to care for him. I watched you digging plants. You're old enough to have sense—but still pretty. Your body is strong. I followed, listened to the sadness in your voice. You don't have a man, either. Perhaps this is good for both of us."

She nodded numbly. Where were the others? Did this man truly have companions, or would Cattail appear and drive him off?

A scream echoed from the root grounds.

Sage Ghost cocked his head, glancing at her from the corner of his eye. "The Black Point will come soon. You fix these plants. Feed us."

Chapter 25

Larkspur sat under the sunshade at Round Rock camp. In the trampled area between the sun-bathed earthen lodges, the children laughed and shouted and ran around in circles. Lupine carried the sage wand in her little brown fist. She had to touch one of the others with it. When that happened, the child touched would take the sage wand and chase the others, until another was touched and the wand thus passed on.

In the lengthening shadow of Bitterbrush's lodge, Tuber watched the young children with resentful eyes—his heart longing to be out gathering roots, no doubt. The very way he sat irritated Larkspur.

Something had changed in the world. She could almost reach up with her thin fingers and feel the difference in the air. Power had been offended in some devastating way. In her very soul she could tell it. Despite the depth of the summer, the Spirit of the earth held its dusty breath. Stillness lay on the sage.

Oh, Black Hand, what has gone wrong? She drifted beyond the realm of the present to the warm days of the past. She could see him again, strong, muscular, and handsome as he laughed with her.

"Grandmother?"

Tuber had risen to his feet like an uneasy panther. Curse it, why did the boy have to be so ill-behaved? She could see his anger smoldering, ready to burst loose—although he'd been remarkably civil in the days since Black Hand's death. All during their walk to Round Rock, the boy had practically skipped and sung. Then the ugly mood had settled on him again.

Have to marry him off as soon as possible. The boy's like a boil—a constant irritant. Look at the resentment in his eyes. If he stays around, he'll just fester more.

"What do you want, Tuber?"

He gave her a challenging look. "I think something's wrong. That old red bitch was sniffing the wind and growling. She had her hair up and went out into the sage. Then she just went . . . quiet. Funny quiet."

She scowled at him. "What are you bothering me with?"

At the chiding tone in her voice, his expression soured. "Didn't you hear her barking?"

"Dogs bark, boy. Go on now. Tend the fires. We need more firewood. Go pull some. Be useful for once."

He stiffened, the corners of his lips twitching. She tensed in response.

"Pull firewood?" He snorted acidly. "They left me here to help *you* with the children. What am I? Some sort of pack beast? Maybe Bad Belly was the smart one."

A white shaft of anger flared in her soul. She stabbed a crooked finger at him. "Boy, you better listen and hear good. You've been half crazy since Warm Fire died. Now leave be. You mind yourself . . . or I'll have . . . Cattail . . ."

She stopped, appalled. Tuber, eyes gleaming, had taken a

step toward her, trembling fingers rising toward her throat. For that brief instant her eyes locked with his and she read black violence, barely throttled.

"Tuber, don't . . ." But her words fell on empty air. The boy had sprinted away through the lodges.

Larkspur took a deep breath and rubbed her hot face. "I'd be rid of his foul soul in a second if I could manage it." And as soon as she'd said them, she wished she could withdraw the words. Anxiously she glanced around at the weathered granite that bordered the suddenly silent camp. The shadows cast by the lodges had stretched their humped shapes over the beaten clay.

All the children were watching her with solemn eyes. The breath penned in her frail chest exploded, and she waved her arms at them. "Well, go on! Get back to play now!"

But the sage-wand game had died. The children squatted in a little knot and talked in quiet voices as they fingered the dirt.

The old black dog, Yellow Tooth, jerked awake, lifting his nose to scent the breeze. A threatening growl vibrated in his throat; then he barked the old familiar warning she'd known for years.

"Here! Shut up!" Larkspur grunted as she pushed to her feet and reached for her digging stick. The rest of the dogs woke and began to bay, charging through the village in the direction Tuber had taken, then veering out into the sage.

"So help me, if that cursed boy is playing some game with a bear hide, I'll . . ."

From beyond the lodges, a dog yelped in pain. Then came a series of yips and canine shrieks. She thought she heard a hollow thump—the sort of sound that would be made if someone beat an animal.

Fool boy's got no right to take his anger out on dogs. If he's laid a club to old Yellow Tooth, I'll have Cattail twist his neck off his shoulders. She raised her voice. "Tuber! Is that you?"

A boy's scream shrilled in the air and ended abruptly—as if cut off.

Fear clutched at Larkspur's heart. "You children. Get inside." With the digging stick, she pointed to her lodge.

They sat frozen, faces panicked.

"*Now!*" she snapped.

Little bodies scuttled for the lodge flap.

Larkspur swallowed, throat constricted, and tottered forward. "Tuber? That you? You pulling some sort of prank?"

A brown bitch dragged herself around the corner of the lodge, a blood-streaked dart transfixing her limp hind quarters. The animal collapsed in a bloody heap, a keening yelp breaking from her throat.

Two tattooed warriors rounded the lodge, their moccasined feet pressing the dog's blood into the soil of Round Rock. They carried a struggling Tuber in their arms.

Larkspur turned to run—only to see more of the warriors rushing in from every direction. For an instant she stood paralyzed. They closed around her, long war clubs dangling from powerful fists.

Her wits returned, along with the old arrogance. "Get out of my camp!"

As anger buoyed her, she charged forward on her aching legs, brandishing her digging stick. She heard the harsh male laughter behind her and tried to stop her headlong rush. Tuber's scream split the air, but she barely heard. The crack of her skull deafened her for a split second before blackness rushed through her senses.

Wind Runner looked the boy up and down. The youth appeared older than the fourteen summers his mother claimed. His shoulders had already filled out. No expression crossed the boy's flinty face. Nevertheless, in another couple of the summers, the young women would look twice at him.

Wind Runner considered, studying the buff-colored earthen lodges. In the twilight, the rounded caps of granite that rose behind the camp gleamed against the sky like the piled skulls of curious Dream beasts. As it slid lower toward the western horizon, the dying sun cast a red tinge over the land.

He shot Sage Ghost a measuring look. "You want to keep the boy?"

Sage Ghost nodded. "He is strong. He belongs to the woman I took. Look at him; he'll make a good warrior. I never had a boy to teach. Only daughters—and this woman has a daughter, too."

"Yes, she does," Wind Runner agreed. "A daughter young enough to learn the ways of the Black Point—and not bear us ill will. Uncle, if you keep this boy, I fear we'll find you one of these days with a dart stuck through your tough hide."

Sage Ghost filled his lungs, swelling the muscles of his chest. "I have asked the boy. He says he would become Black Point."

Wind Runner stepped up to the youth, searching his eyes. "Have him tell me."

Sage Ghost spoke in the swallowed words of the Earth People.

The boy nodded, an odd festering in his hard black eyes. In the accented tongue of the Sun People, the boy said, "I would be a warrior."

Or you'd be dead, and you know it, Wind Runner finished to himself. He glanced at Sage Ghost again. *Uncle, how much of this is your own soul's pain? Is that what you're doing? Trying to replace the loss of White Ash?*

"You'll watch him?" Wind Runner asked.

"I'll watch him." Sage Ghost made a sign with his hand that indicated it would be as he said.

"Then let him stay. We'll see how he fares, but make sure he knows that every eye will be on him."

Sage Ghost turned to the boy and spoke, then pointed. The youth nodded and walked off toward the earthen shelter that Sage Ghost had claimed. The boy's mother, a tall, handsome woman standing there, hugged him.

Wind Runner massaged the back of his neck. "I hope you know what you're doing."

Sage Ghost gave him a wry grin. "So do I." Then he

looked up at the sunset. "She won't be Bright Moon. But she keeps my robes warm. For having a son that old, she's still strong." He paused. "I suppose I can cherish a memory for only so long."

"And you're one of us . . . yet apart."

Sage Ghost rubbed his hands together. "Something like that. Nephew, I thank you for sharing your lodge with me. But the time has come to keep my own again." He paused. "Old habits die hard—but more than that, living with you makes me feel like an old man. I'm not ready for that yet."

"You'll find out just how old you really are if you plant another child in her." Wind Runner looked at the woman again. She gazed at her son through hollow eyes. He could see the swell of her breasts against the leather of her soft hide dress. No wonder Sage Ghost had chosen this one.

"Well, go teach your . . . family how to talk like humans." Wind Runner waved his uncle away.

"And more," Sage Ghost grinned as he headed for the lodge.

Wind Runner stared at the trampled ground between his feet. *How long can a man live with the past as his only companion?* He glanced at the rise of Green Mountain to the South. *White Ash? Are you alive?*

"Lost in your thoughts again?" Aspen asked behind him. He turned. "I didn't hear you."

She came to stand beside him, adding dryly, "You'd be surprised. Over the years I've learned to pay attention to where I put my feet. Sage Ghost pled for the boy?"

"I let him keep him." Wind Runner rubbed his jaw. "But it worries me. The boy knows what happened to the rest of his family. Will he turn against us?"

"Come," she told him. "Eat something. Worry won't do you any good now. What will be, will be. Who knows, perhaps Sage Ghost will make him a warrior."

She led him to a fire pit that glowed red near a sagebrush sunshade. Her dress hugged the curves of her hips and molded to her slim waist. She moved with a delicate poise that complemented her keen mind.

Wind Runner settled himself on a robe that lay on the

ground and watched as Aspen levered a roast from the fire. With a chert knife, she sliced long, rich lengths of meat and piled them in a buffalo-horn dish, then passed it over to him with balanced grace. As he reached for the bowl, their eyes met—and held. He forced his gaze away and tried to turn his thoughts from the way her soul touched his.

Similar fires smoked where the people in his band camped around Round Rock. For the most part, Sun People chose not to use the earthen shelters. Like him, they found them confining, stifling.

Wind Runner tasted the meat. Antelope. Sweet, delicate. The hunters who'd killed it had done a good job. Antelope had to be killed quickly and surely. If they ran wounded, or with a punctured gut, the meat took on a strong flavor. Nor could a hunter let the animal lie before butchering; he must gut and skin his kill immediately, and cool the meat. For antelope had hollow hair that retained body heat, so much heat that the meat would sour.

He chewed thoughtfully before asking, "How are the women doing?"

Aspen loaded a bowl of her own before replying, "You were right. This is a rich land. Since we captured the camp three days ago, we've dug new caches in the earth lodges and filled them with enough dried plants to last for weeks. Talking with the captives is still difficult, but they do as we say." She laughed. "What choice do they have? The last ones who tried to run away are feeding coyotes."

"Disobedience is fading?"

She shot him a quick glance. "Better to live and work than leave your bones to rot. They are beginning to understand what has happened to them. Given the choice, they'll work. They still grieve for their men, but there are worse fates than having a strange man crawl on top of you in the middle of the night."

Muted voices carried on the evening air. In the distance, camp dogs broke into a fight. A man yelled, and the yipping and growling ceased. "The men heed your rule. They don't strike the women unless they fight."

He nodded. "I don't understand. These people act as if

their spirits are broken—as if they were defeated before we arrived."

She gazed up at the first stars twinkling in the east. "Perhaps their Power has fled. Sage Ghost says that they keep talking about the Gathering and some terrible thing that happened there. Maybe that's what makes them so tame." She snorted. "Me, I'd fight and fight until I killed my captor . . . or he killed me."

"Maybe that's why we're here. To bring new Power to the land." Power. The mention of it always led his thoughts to White Ash. Would she be this easy to talk to? White Ash had been preoccupied with her Dreams, but Aspen turned her quick mind to the world and shared the problems he faced.

She glanced thoughtfully at him, a sadness in her large eyes. In a controlled voice, she said, "She wasn't at Three Forks."

Melancholy settled around his heart. "No. She wasn't."

"I'm sorry, Wind Runner. I had hoped you'd find her before this."

Did she have to be so honest with him? She knew he watched her, knew the direction of his thoughts. Yet not once had resentment for White Ash possessed her; she'd shown only that knowing understanding. And that made his confused affection for her all the stronger. How many nights had he and Aspen talked away? How many hours had they spent making plans and honing them before offering them to the council?

Her efforts didn't stop there. At night she made the rounds of the camps, listening to the people. Her counsel smoothed ruffled feelings, eased the worries of a people in a new land. She kept an eye on the captives and how they were treated. When she saw trouble coming, she whispered a warning to him. Through her, Wind Runner received Hot Fat's full support in council.

But what of White Ash? Yes, he still loved her. But night after night a consuming passion led him to Hot Fat's lodge simply to talk to Aspen.

White Ash? If she's alive, she had to know the Black Point have come. If she's alive . . .

He swallowed another bite of meat and gestured at the surrounding land. "We've taken all the camps to the north of Round Rock. Badwater, Warm Wind, Poison Creek, Red Rock, and all the rest." The Black Point covered the entire Wind Basin. They'd climbed the Gray Wall, and now the Red Earth Basin lay before them. He said, "Sage Ghost has asked for her in all of the camps. Talked to all the captives. None of them knows of White Ash."

He knew the sad-eyed stare she gave him—had seen it so often it had become second nature.

"Sage Ghost has made his peace with the past," she said softly.

The words pained him with their truth. She had that way with him, always cutting to the heart of the matter. Wind Runner bolted the last of his meat and set the bowl down. "I know."

She stood up and took his hand. "Walk with me."

He let her lead him past the fires where warriors sat in the flickering light, eating, talking. Black Point women laughed and gestured, while the women of the Earth People whispered among themselves.

She led him around the outcrop of granite that shielded the west side of the camp and stopped, examining the colors that faded on the horizon. A warm breeze carried the scent of sage and hot, dry earth.

"The bugs aren't as bad here," she said as she climbed up on the rock and sat down. "I wanted to talk to you away from camp, where no one could overhear."

He settled himself next to her, feeling uneasy. She had a serious expression on her beautiful face. The tranquil peace of the night drifted around him.

With agile fingers, she undid her braids and fluffed out her hair. The gleaming black strands hung around her like a shawl, framing her face and clinging to her breasts. He forced himself to look away.

"I wouldn't have thought it would happen this way," she said. "When you plan, you make no mistakes. In the council, only Black Moon's voice carries more weight than yours.

Even the warriors have stopped grumbling about eating plants.''

He smiled. ''They're still flushed with victory. But we have done well.'' He gazed out at the fall of night. Evening birds called plaintively in the brush. ''Who would have thought we could take an entire land and lose only one woman and two warriors? Our people seem content.''

She took a deep breath of the warm air. ''They are. The women especially. Their work is less, and they can boss the captives around.''

He took her hand. ''The camps in the south won't like what we've done. But what can they do? If they fight, it won't be with strength.''

She slid off the rock and moved down to sit closer to him. In the fading light, he looked into her gentle eyes and traced her smooth face with a fingertip. She seemed to melt against him. Her scent and the warmth of her lithe body enveloped him.

She laughed shakily. ''You and I, Wind Runner, what a pair.''

She ran a hand down his leg, stirring his soul. He closed his eyes, imaging that her touch belonged to White Ash, but the illusion faded before reality.

''Aspen,'' he whispered.

She looked up at him and smiled—but a sadness shone in her eyes. As she started to pull away, he tightened his hold.

He could see her indecision. ''I'm sorry, I . . .'' He stumbled over the words.

''It's my fault. I know that White Ash is still in your thoughts.''

She glanced out over the sage-filled flats toward the Coldwater River. ''Funny, isn't it? I never thought I'd love again. I never thought I'd find a man with the gentle warmth my husband had. Now I don't know what to think. You've become my best friend, Wind Runner. I wouldn't want anything to happen that would leave you uncomfortable.''

Longing and confusion gnashed in his soul. ''I don't know what to say.''

''I understand.''

He looked at her. A soft smile curled her lips.

"Wind Runner, I would be your woman. I think you know that. I thought about it for a long time. I weighed the desire I had for you against what I knew I needed in a man. The body can trick the soul. I waited to make sure. I don't want you to let your body lead you into something that would change this trust we share."

He fumbled aimlessly with the fringe on her sleeve. A cloud passed in front of the stars, moving like a dark shadow through the sage. "I fight my desire for you. Every day I struggle with it."

"The decision is yours. I can live with you either way, Wind Runner."

He swallowed. "And White Ash?"

"White Ash." A wistful smile. "If you find her, I'll step aside. I understand and accept what she means to you."

"How? I mean . . ."

She stroked the back of his neck, soothing him. "Because I love you. Outside of the safety of my people, I would give anything to see you happy. If that means White Ash sharing your lodge, I will smile and help her move her things in. And afterward I'll wish you both well."

"But to do so would break your heart, wouldn't it?"

"I've survived worse in the past. I imagine I'll even be able to face you—and her—every day."

How many times had he and Aspen laughed and planned together? How many times had she sat and listened to him pour out his deepest worries? They'd become a team. His heart raced at the feel of her by his side.

He closed his eyes, trying to think despite the blood that pounded in his veins. *Even Sage Ghost has given up.* He trembled as he reached up and grasped the hand that stroked his neck and brought it back to his lap. "I've never had a friend like you, Aspen. Every minute I'm away from you, I think about you."

She tipped her face up to him and smiled. Hesitantly he bent and kissed her. She slid her arms around his waist and clutched him tightly.

"Are you sure you want this?" she whispered.

He nodded, letting his hand glide over the curve of her throat and down to her breasts.

Aspen slipped her leather dress over her head and placed it on the rocks, then stood before him, silhouetted against the starlight. The wealth of her black hair shifted with the wind. He rose to his feet and pulled his shirt over his head. Her nimble fingers undid the laces that held his leggings.

Picking up her dress, she took Wind Runner's hand and led him away from the rocks and down to the cool desert sands. She spread her dress in an open area between the fragrant sage.

"You're certain?" he asked in a husky voice.

"More than I have ever been," she whispered and pulled him close. He reveled in the feel of her body against his.

For a long moment they held each other before she sighed and gracefully pulled him down onto the dress with her.

White Ash . . . I tried to find you.

White Ash reached into her deer-paunch bag that held water. She cupped the cool liquid in her hand and let it trickle onto the hot rocks. Steam hissed in the blackness, rising to fill the sweat lodge they'd made.

Still Water gasped and panted where he sat across from her.

When Wolf Dreamer sought to cleanse himself, he made steam. This he gave to the people to cleanse both the body and soul. Cleanse yourself.

The Dream had been so explicit. Among the Sun People, no one built a sweat lodge. Among the Earth People, only the Healers and those grieving or seeking to talk with the Spirits sweated. White Ash sat in the stifling blackness and let the steam bathe her. Her skin prickled as water traced down the slippery curves of her body.

She closed her eyes against the discomfort, chanting softly, echoing Singing Stones' words on the night Power had filled him.

"Find the place inside you that listens," Singing Stones had taught her. Again and again she tried to keep her mind blank.

It has to be here somewhere. Then: *Silence, you fool!* She battled to find a way to escape the noise in her head.

Her lungs labored for a cool breath of air. Grimly, White Ash willed herself to ignore the frantic cries of her body to leave this stifling heat.

The Wolf Bundle lurked at the edge of her soul, its tendrils hovering about her.

We can help you. The countless voices of the Wolf Bundle drifted around her. *Release yourself to us. Let us show you.*

A gray muzziness left her spinning. She fell, dropping into it. Around the edges, a glistening golden mist swirled, beckoning.

You are following the right path, Mother of the People. Are you strong enough? Are you tenacious enough to continue?

The voices faded. Then she became aware of coolness descending over her.

"White Ash?" Still Water's voice echoed from a great distance.

Consciousness returned slowly. She blinked and found herself in Still Water's arms. His good arm supported her weight, while his bad arm held her braced against his chest. High above, stars dusted the sky except to the south, where they were hidden by a shadowy bank of clouds. He had taken her out of the sweat lodge.

"What?" She winced against a terrible ache that pounded in her head.

"You fell over," he told her. "I think the heat got you. Too much, too quick."

She groaned and struggled to sit up. The cool night air left her shivering. Still Water wrapped a robe around her shoulders, his hand steadying her against the dizziness that possessed her.

"The Dream was right," she announced. "I almost did it again. I heard the Bundle's voice. Felt the gray haze. The One was there, just out of reach."

He shook his head. "I'm worried about you."

A pleasant satisfaction filled her, as if she'd been cleansed for the first time since Three Bulls had raped and beaten her so long ago.

"It's the right path," she said. "The right path."

"All right," Still Water agreed uncertainly. "Maybe tomorrow we'll try again."

"No. Tonight. I just need to get my wind back."

He squatted before her and she could see concern in the depths of his brown eyes.

"You're pushing too hard," he told her gently. "This morning you were sick to your stomach. That's four days in a row. You don't work into things—just dive headlong. Can't we take this a little at a time?"

She took his cool hand and pressed it against her sweat-drenched cheek. "I have to be ready when Power calls. I have to be strong enough. It's our only chance."

He hesitated. "You scare me sometimes. If you kill yourself, then what?"

"Then I wasn't strong enough, and it's better this way than dying on a Broken Stones war dart—or worse." She glanced up at him. "Who scares you most? Me—or Brave Man?"

He frowned. "Let's sweat tomorrow, first thing. I'll feed you another big breakfast and we'll—"

"Tonight."

"Tonight . . ." He tilted his head reluctantly. "All right. Let me build up the fire and heat the rocks again. But this time I'm going to stay close. When you toppled over in there, you hit the ground hard. If it wasn't for those hides we put down, you'd have cracked your head open."

She lay back, letting the cool night winds play over her hot skin. *Singing Stones took years to learn the way to the One. Before that, he'd used Power as a Healer among the clans. How can I do what I must in so short a time?*

Brave Man stood on the high ridge and looked out over the vast Wind Basin where it spread to the south. A thunderhead rose in billowy mounds against the dome of sky to the east.

Before him, the flank of the mountain dropped off to grassy foothills spotted with stands of sagebrush that fanned out into the parched lowlands. Out there he could see herds of buffalo, antelope, and a band of cow elk. Farther away, to the south, he could make out the sharp edges of badlands and the folded curves of the basin, where drainages ran in patterns like roots.

"Soul Flier?"

Brave Man turned. Fat Elk stood among the tumbled boulders beneath the point, a hand shielding his face from the sun. His tracks could be made out where he'd bruised the thick grass in the meadow beyond. Yarrow and balsam spotted the green with dots of white and blazes of yellow.

Brave Man eased down from the rocky point, taking special care with his bad leg. The pain had subsided as the bone strengthened. If only he could do something about the headaches. Sometimes they throbbed until his vision doubled.

The way of Trade is that something must be given in return for something else. To receive Power, I must give pain.

He scooted his way over a slanting slab of rock and found better footing on the loose slope below. Fat Elk's face puffed with cautious excitement.

"Find anything?" Brave Man asked as he walked stiff-legged through the thick grass of the ridge top toward the dense spruce and fir beyond.

"Plenty," Fat Elk told him, a veiled look in his half-lidded eyes. "You were wise to send us out. But the news you expect isn't what I have come to tell you."

Brave Man entered the dark green belt of rich-limbed fir trees. "I expected the Black Point to be moving into the country the White Clay tried to occupy."

"Not the Black Point—the Hollow Flute."

Brave Man stopped and studied Fat Elk in the cool shadows. The delicate odor of lush needles lingered in the air. "Hollow Flute? In the Fat Beaver valley?"

"Yes," Fat Elk told him. "And the Snow Bird are hunting in the lands occupied by the Black Point last winter, while the Wasp . . . well, I found a camp of theirs on the very ground where we wintered.''

Brave Man scowled at the brown needles under his feet and fingered the curious stones on the necklace he'd stolen from the one-armed man. A gray-and-black nutcracker fluttered its wings and gave a hoarse, squawking cry as it bounced from limb to limb above. ''Then where are the Black Point?''

Fat Elk lifted his hands helplessly. ''I can't tell you. But know this, Soul Flier. Almost all of the clans have wounded among them. There's been fighting—a lot of it.''

''The Black Point were strong—but if all the clans moved south? Have they gone the way of the White Clay?''

Fat Elk sucked at his lip nervously. ''I have more news, Soul Flier. The Wasp clans have sent scouting parties into the northern part of these mountains. What do we do? Take the people north and drive off the Wasp who invade our land?''

Brave Man tilted his head, thoughts racing. ''No, my friend. Let them have this pile of rock. I have a better place for us to warm our darts in blood than among the Wasp. And perhaps your manhood needs warming, too, eh?'' Brave Man gestured over his shoulder. ''In the south, the Earth People are waiting for us.''

Fat Elk frowned. ''These aren't bad mountains to live in, Soul Flier.''

''No, they're not, but glory lies to the south. Which would you rather have? Honor, and more women than you could ever bed? Or an endless war with the Wasp?''

''What have you Dreamed?''

Brave Man threw back his head and laughed. ''I've Dreamed of your family becoming so large you spend more time hunting to feed all the children you planted than you do coupling. South, my friend. South.''

Fat Elk rubbed the back of his neck, a sheepish expression on his face. ''I'll look forward to the challenge, Soul Flier.''

Brave Man led the way down the narrow, winding elk trail. Thick green walls of spruce and fir shaded the path, the branches interwoven overhead. He stepped out of the trees into a grassy clearing. Here, they'd set up the main camp. Tan lodges stood around the belt of timber and beside a clear stream that cut through the meadow. The dogs barked at him and, after checking his scent, returned to the shade to lie down.

"Fat Elk?"

"Yes, Soul Flier?"

"The Snow Bird—did they seem as interested in the south, too?"

Fat Elk shifted nervously. "Yes, I'd say they were moving south. I don't understand it. They should be up north of the Dangerous River—and now they're hounding our heels again. I don't think all the wounded warriors I saw had been hurt by the Hollow Flute."

Brave Man clapped him on the back. "You've done a good job, my friend. Go, take your deserved rest—and good luck planting the first of those children."

Fat Elk grinned and nodded, trotting off toward his lodge.

Hollow Flute south of the Fat Beaver? But where are the Black Point?

South, the voices whispered.

South? Impossible!

Nevertheless, unease nibbled at Brave Man as he walked to his lodge and settled himself in the sun to think. What if he had to race the Black Point to the Earth People's land?

He started to lean on one elbow, but something in his belt pouch poked his hip painfully. He squirmed around and pulled out the black stone wolf.

He drew his arm back to pitch it, but decided against it. Instead, he held it up to the light, admiring once more the skill that had gone into the fashioning. The heavy effigy gleamed in his fingers, the luster so deep the carving seemed translucent, as if he stared into an endless darkness.

Against his better judgment, he dropped it back into his pouch again and leaned the other way. Across the camp, voices rose in greeting. Friends welcoming Fat Elk home, no doubt.

He studied the tops of the firs. They rose like dart points against the sky. A playful breeze rustled the grass.

He was so close to finding the way to the golden haze and the Power it represented. Night after night while Pale Raven slept, he sat by the fire and traced the pathway he'd been developing in his soul. That *had* to be the key. To find the way, he must look inward. Each time he came closer, feeling the fuzzy gray haze. His soul heard the soundless call of the Power. He knew he could find the way. That wondrous golden Power could be his. With it, *he*, Brave Man, could control even the Wolf Bundle—and the other source of Power he'd experienced and been rebuffed by. Some evil Spirit had thrown him out of the golden haze that day south of the Fat Beaver River. He'd heard the voice.

"And I will face you again someday," he said out loud. "When I do, I promise I will dominate you. No one is stronger than Brave Man. I survived the Camp of the Dead, not just in my soul like most Soul Fliers, *but in my body*! I have the voices of the Spirits whispering in my mind. The Wolf People's Bundle couldn't destroy me. I *will* Dream the new way."

In the distance, thunder rolled hollowly.

If only worldly problems didn't keep intruding on him.

He'd hoped to leave here just after the first snow. By then, more meat would be dried and ready for the journey. But now? If the Hollow Flute were pushing the Black Point south?

Pale Raven appeared, leaning around the curve of the lodge. "I found him," she called over her shoulder to someone. To Brave Man, she added, "There's news."

He placed his hand on hers as she knelt beside him. "I know, Fat Elk has already told me."

"Fat Elk?" A brief confusion traced her proud face.

Long Bone rounded the corner of the lodge, looking uneasy. The young warrior's dusty hunting shirt was scratched here and there, grease-stained and water-marked. His high moccasins looked scuffed. The bones tattooed into his cheeks wrinkled as the warrior smiled shyly.

"And you are back, too!" Brave Man greeted. "Come, sit. Wife, bring us something to eat. Long Bone looks worn out."

Pale Raven ducked into the lodge while Long Bone sank to the grass to sit cross-legged.

Brave Man studied him, noting the fatigue in the man's eyes. "What news? Did you find the Earth People? Do they look wary? Alarmed by our presence?"

Long Bone rubbed at his thin face. "No, Soul Flier. I don't think we need to worry about the Earth People. They'll be no trouble to us at all."

"Oh?" Brave Man raised his eyes as Pale Raven set a horn bowl before Long Bone.

The warrior picked up the carved horn, crafted from the boss of a mountain sheep, slurping loudly as he drained the contents. He fished around with his fingers for the last pieces of meat and wild onion before handing the empty bowl back to Pale Raven. "I went south into the Wind Basin as you asked me to, Soul Flier. I felt proud that you had entrusted me with the task. I used every skill and bit of cunning I possessed. No one saw Long Bone as he slipped through the sagebrush. I crisscrossed the land below these mountains and found warriors, all right. The basin down there is bristling with them."

"And do they look like we can beat them? Are these Earth People as weak as I Dreamed?"

"Soul Flier . . . the Black Point have already taken the basin from the Earth People."

"Black Point?"

"Yes, Soul Flier. They're everywhere, moving south."

"How?" Brave Man cried angrily. "How did they get there? Why?" Something the Wolf Bundle had done? Perhaps through the Power of the one-armed man who had appeared out of the Wolf shaman's lodge?

"I don't know," Long Bone said nervously, "but I sneaked close to their camp one night. A new war leader walked among them. A young man I didn't know."

"Yes, yes, go on!"

Long Bone swallowed. "I took a great risk and crawled to the edge of their camp like a snake. I heard the warriors talking. Black Moon himself listens to this new war leader, as does Hot Fat. I saw him, a tall young man. He walked with a beautiful woman with long black hair.''

Brave Man barked, ''Did you hear his name?''

Long Bone nodded warily. ''Wind Runner.''

Wind Runner? How? Brave Man knotted both hands into angry fists. *Once again, old friend, we will face each other. This time I shall kill you.*

He slitted his eyes. When the struggle for the Wind Basin was over, he would find a high place and have Wind Runner brought to him, his arms and legs bound. There—as in the visions—he would raise a stone knife to the sun and slit Wind Runner's breast open. He'd reach in and cut the pumping heart from the living body. With the still-beating heart in his bloody hand, he would lift it on high—a gift to Sun and Thunderbird. Payment for Power. His warriors would watch and be awed. White Ash would . . .

White Ash! It all came clear. Long Bone had said that a beautiful woman walked with Wind Runner. Brave Man cried, ''*He* has her! Tomorrow we leave! Tomorrow, Wind Runner, *I'm coming for you!*''

Steam rolled up from the boiling stones to fill the dark sweat lodge. White Ash sat immobile. She let her soul sway with the chant that Still Water mumbled next to her. She lost herself, following the path within that she'd learned with such effort. The way came easily now as her control over herself increased. The One lay just beyond.

She hovered at the edge, peace seeping through her soul. The gray mist beckoned, pervasive. She gathered her courage, seeking to cross the threshold, to force her way . . . and lost it.

Let go of yourself, came the Wolf Bundle's soft whisper through the retreating mist. She caught herself, retracing the path inward. At the boundary of the One, she hesitated. Her soul pulsed and wavered, the lingering sweetness of the One playing about her like butterfly wings.

Let go.

Trust the Wolf Bundle?

In desperation, and aware of no other choice, she let her soul slip away into the current of Power granted by the Wolf Bundle. Like the torrent of a river, the Power swept her into the gray mist. She fell, tumbling, helpless . . . and the world became golden.

Dream, the Wolf Bundle told her. *Dream the One.*

Power, like a fine mist, filled the air. Beside her, Still Water glowed, his soul yellow and red. The hot stones in the center of the sweat lodge wavered in fiery illumination. Despite the hides piled over the framework of the lodge, she could sense the vegetation and the somber rock around them. Insects, birds, even the mice in their nests down in the rock, pulsed like little fires. Trouble appeared as a kindly whitish-red gleam in the wavering blues and greens of the One.

She extended—and met resistance.

"*Seek no farther, Mother of the People. We stop you here,*" the firm voice of the golden man warned.

"Where are we?"

A flickering appeared, a light Dancing like fire. The golden features of a young man, the beautiful young man of her Dreams, floated in the One.

"*I am Wolf Dreamer. The one you call First Man. You are my Dream, Mother of the People. You have opened the doorway. I ask you to enter no farther, for illumination will trap you as it has trapped others.*"

"But it's so beautiful."

"*You are Dreaming at the edge of the One, feeling the Spiral.*"

"I would feel more. Know more."

"*Your time has not come. We need you to Dream. The Wolf Bundle is the way. This time you have Dreamed enough. You've learned well, Mother of the People. But do not lose yourself like Singing Stones did. The lure of the One is Powerful. Your time to Dream the whole of the One will come.*"

"You stop me?"

"*For the moment, but we cannot stop you forever. You*

have a strength. We have hardened you, seeking to turn you to our purpose.''

"What purpose is that, Wolf Dreamer?"

"To Dream a new way for the Sun People. To Dream the Spiral for them.''

"And if I don't?"

"You already know the answer. The Spiral will shift and my Dream will change. That which is will be different. Still Water has seen what will come. You can save the Dream of First Man. The choice is yours.''

She wept at the beauty. The Dancing lights that illuminated the One glowed golden about her. A great peace infused the very air. The silence Sang with beautiful voices. Souls shimmered, pulsing, slipping from life to death as they filtered into the One and shifted the Spiral ever so slightly.

"Wolf Dreamer, is this what Singing Stones knew?"

"And what he could not deny in the end. He Dreamed and could not return. Can you? Will you Dream for us? The Wolf Bundle waits for you. Call upon it.''

"I don't want to leave here."

"Then all is lost. The Spiral will shift. Brave Man will impose his terrible Dream on the Spiral.''

White Ash recoiled, drawing back. "No!"

The gray mist drifted away. She could feel a hand gripping her flesh as she reeled.

"White Ash?" Still Water's anxious cry drew her soul back to her body. Heat suffocated her. She thrashed against the hand that held her. Brave Man mocked from her memory.

"White Ash!" Still Water shouted. "It's me! Still Water! You're safe. Safe.''

She shivered, and a cry choked in her throat. She lay back, cradled against his bad arm. He moved, leather rasping in the darkness as he lifted the lodge flap. Light poured in to blind her.

She crawled out weakly to lie on the cool, comforting surface of the earth. Dark clouds cloaked the sky. Reverently she touched a blade of grass that tickled her cheek, aware of its life for the first time.

"White Ash?" Still Water knelt beside her.

She hugged the earth, as if to draw it into herself and mix it with the beat of her heart.

Her tears burst out at the feel of his hand stroking her hair. "Are you all right?"

She nodded, sniffling at the clogging wetness in her nose. "So . . . beautiful. Oh, Still Water, it beats like a heart, only differently. I talked to First Man. Beautiful. So . . . beautiful. My soul cries at the thought of it."

She placed her lips against the soil and breathed into it, sending colors winding down into the ground.

"How do you feel?" he pressed.

She rolled over, heedless of the dirt that clung to her skin, and looked up at him. Her love swelled. She'd seen his soul, been One with it. This man, who looked down at her with such concern, glowed of love.

She reached up and pulled him down, crushing him to her. "Fine, Still Water. I'm fine."

"You screamed," he muttered, half smothered by her embrace. "A terrible scream."

"I know," she whispered, the voices of the vision echoing in her ears. "Here—in this world, in the illusion—I see. For the first time, I really see."

He drew back, searching her eyes. "I'm not going to like it, am I?"

"I Dreamed the One, Still Water. I Dreamed it."

"I felt . . . something." He rocked back on his heels. "I heard the voices of the Wolf Bundle. I think we have to go."

"Did you Dream the One, too?"

He stared at her, retreating into his own vision. "If that's the One, I want no part of it."

She clasped his hand in hers. "Tell me."

His face hardened. "I saw the lame warrior, Brave Man. He walked through a world littered with the dead. Blood soaked the soil, and people with fear in their eyes lifted their hands to him. In the Dream, he looked up at me, and his face was filled with evil." He swallowed. "He held up the Wolf Bundle, and I felt its Power." Still Water's face contorted. "He'd turned it against the People, using it for evil. He'd turned himself into a witch!"

Chapter 26

"I feel lost," White Ash whispered to Still Water as they lay in their robes. Firelight flickered on the sooty rocks of Singing Stones' shelter. Trouble lay stretched out across from her; he watched her through soft eyes, eyebrows twitching. Traces of the One lingered in her mind so powerfully that the familiar shelter might have been a place she'd never seen before.

Still Water hugged her close. "I'm here. I'll always be here for you."

She closed her eyes, tightening her grip on his arm. "It's like being born into a new world. Nothing is the same. I don't know what to do. The One pulls at me." She shook her head. "I know what Singing Stones meant when he said it's like being a moth around a fire."

"We'll manage. You and I." He paused. "We're stronger together than we would be apart. Maybe that's part of the puzzle."

She rolled her lip over her teeth. Escape would be so easy. Her very strength could carry her past First Man and into the One. He'd as much as said that. She could be free to experience it all, to Dance the Spiral. *And the Dream of First Man will die. The harmony that his Dream infused in the world will cease.*

She rolled over and stared into Still Water's gentle eyes. "Nothing has ever been so wonderful. You can see the soul of the world. I saw your soul . . . yellow and red, glowing. You're a good man, Still Water."

He smiled at her, reaching out to finger her hair. "And you're a good woman, White Ash. I couldn't have done what you did. Like Singing Stones, I would have been at it for years."

She pressed his hand against her cheek, seeking to draw strength from him. "I feel as though I'm on the edge of a knife-sharp ridge I have to walk, an abyss on either side. The problem is, I want so badly to fall."

"It's still new for you. It'll go away. The more you Dream . . ."

She placed her fingers against his lips. "No. You don't understand. It's like . . ." She shook her head. "Words are illusion. They can't explain it. But the more you Dream the One, the more powerful it becomes. It's as though its beauty builds in your soul, growing and growing until you and the One merge—you can't bear to leave it, because to leave is like tearing your soul apart. How can I experience such bliss and willingly come back to this world and all its pain? This time, First Man used my deepest fears to convince me to let go. But next time? Or the time after?" She shivered. "Wolf Dreamer doesn't know what he asks."

"He has faith in your strength. I have faith in your strength."

She pressed against him. "I wish I shared your faith. One mistake and I'll be pulled in, unwilling to resist, unable to." She inhaled haltingly. "Oh, Singing Stones, how did you do it for so long?"

"Maybe he didn't have me."

She ran her hand along the side of his face, tracing the curve of his ear. "You're part of my strength, that's true. I never would have found the way without you. You chanted for me and encouraged me when I would have given up." She buried her face in his chest. "I didn't know I could love a man this much."

She listened to his heart, feeling his withered arm against her breasts.

"Love," Still Water whispered. "Another puzzle. What is it? Why does it work the way it does?"

She shrugged, seeking to cling more tightly to him. "That's not my worry for the moment. It's how to control the Dream, how to stay halfway between the One and the world."

She held his bad arm against herself, running her hand

down to his curled fingers. And he'd said that no woman would want a man with an arm like his. Now she cherished it. His useless arm was like Still Water: a deception—a deception all the way from his toes to his homely face. What no woman would accept ended at his skin. If only others could see the colors of his magnificent soul.

White Ash watched the firelight flicker on the irregular walls. She'd found the way to cross the boundary and taste the forbidden honey. But what if she couldn't stop? What if she couldn't keep herself from glutting on the wonder and the harmony of the other side? What would happen to Still Water?

"I feel your worry," he told her.

Her breasts ached where they pressed against him. Idly, she touched them, wondering how she'd hurt them. "Things are just getting worse."

"You found the way to Dream."

"That's not what I mean." His heartbeat soothed her. "What happens when we leave here? You forget, we must deal with the Sun People. Anyone who isn't part of the clan is an enemy. How do we tell them we're sent by Power? And who'd believe it anyway? Still Water, they'll kill you on sight—but me, they'll take me. A woman is always useful to them."

Her eyes traced the painted patterns of the Spiral. Why hadn't she ever seen the truth of the Spiral before? The Spiral was the world—the Creation. In the distance, thunder rolled over the Wind Basin.

"We'll find a way. Power will help us," Still Water whispered.

Her stomach twisted. "We only get one chance. How will we do it? Sneak into their camp at night? With all the dogs on guard? Besides, they're in unfamiliar territory. Lookouts will be posted everywhere, watching the flats, scouring the country. They leave nothing to chance." She laughed dryly. "Flying Squirrel, you were right. The Sun People have warred until they're so strong nothing can stand against them."

"I'll think up a way. It's another puzzle."

His confidence barely assured her. "And then, when we're among them, we have to find a way to stay alive. If we're unlucky and walk into Brave Man's camp, do you think he'll give me a chance to Dream?" She grunted disgust. "Hardly! He'll have his seed planted in me before he can force me to the ground."

"We'll find the right camp."

"Let's say we do. And if I have a chance to Dream, what if I get lost in the One? What if I can't resist the draw? If I don't come back, they'll kill you, Still Water. You can't even speak their language."

"As least they'll be quick about it. I'll be right behind you that way. Just keep sight of my soul. As I understand, it will be the yellow and red one."

"Don't joke." But she felt comforted.

"You'll come back." He rubbed his cheek on the top of her head. "I love you too much to . . ." He fell silent.

She shifted to look up at him. He'd become lost in his thoughts. "What were you saying?"

He laughed triumphantly. "Power will never cease to amaze me."

"Do you want to stop looking smug and tell me?"

His homely face glowed. "Love, of course."

"What?"

He continued to stare at some infinite point beyond the walls of the rock shelter until she jabbed him in the ribs to get his attention. *"What?"*

He cocked his head. "It's all so clear. 'Love the Dreamer.' That's what Warm Fire told me just before he died. That's the answer."

"Still Water, I've been worrying about our survival, about everything we have to do. All I see is quicksand in every direction. Why don't you tell me . . . What are you *doing*?"

He rolled on top of her, staring down into her eyes with a happy smile on his face. "I'm going to love you."

She looked at him as though he'd gone crazy. "Now? Not now, Still Water. Not after—"

"Especially now."

"Still Water, I don't want to right now. I have to think.

Too much is happening. Too many things . . ." She shook her head. "My thoughts keep slipping away, drifting back to . . ."

He nibbled at her ear and whispered, "Trust me. Concentrate. Do you love me? Really?"

He asked with such seriousness that she nodded instantly, aware of his body responding to hers.

He cupped her breast, massaging it gently. "Then clear your mind. Use the same path—only change it. Share yourself with me. It's the answer, don't you see? The reason Dreamers always shun people. It's why they run away from those they love."

She gasped. *"Because it interferes with the Dreaming!"*

He nodded wisely. "Now, let's see if we can't make that narrow ledge you balance on just a little wider. Love me with all your body, White Ash. Love me with all of you."

She drew him close and whispered, "All of me, and then some, Still Water."

The fire's fading embers cast a dull red light on the rocks overhead. White Ash lay on her back with Still Water's head cradled on the swell of her breasts. His even breathing filled her with an uneasy contentment.

This night, it had worked. A tottering balance had been restored. But how long could she maintain it? How long could Still Water's gentle soul keep her from following the lure of the One?

Over and over she listed the uncertainties that lay ahead, and then she glanced at Still Water's pack, feeling the Power of the Wolf Bundle. It tugged at her with ghostly fingers. She shied away, seeing again Singing Stones' face on that last night.

If I can't keep denying you, Bundle—illness swept her— *Brave Man wins.*

Bitterbrush wept as she caved in the sand around Lupine's little body. To her surprise, Sage Ghost had carried the girl and had placed a handful of sand on the corpse, as was the Earth People custom. And when he'd done so, a tear had streaked down one side of his stern face.

Tuber, choking on his grief, viciously pushed the mounded sand into the hole, as if by doing so, he could exhaust the hurt within.

"I share your sorrow," Sage Ghost told Bitterbrush softly, and he stroked her head with a kind hand. His speech had improved over the past moon as they had slowly moved south.

Tuber's frantic fingers stopped clawing at the sand. He huddled, weeping. Sage Ghost knelt beside him. He placed callused hands on her son's shoulders and said, "Warriors do not cry. Death is part of life. Look at me, Tuber." Then he pointed up toward the sky. "Thunderbird watches all of us for the Sun. He weighs your soul, seeing every action. Are you strong enough for Thunderbird, Tuber? Will you send your soul to him, to be judged worthy to be carried to the Camp of the Dead?"

"But my sister . . ."

"We all die. Even Sage Ghost . . . and, one day, you. That doesn't make the grief any less, but that's just the way it is. Accept the pain you feel, and live with it. That takes courage."

Tuber sniffled his runny nose.

"Come," Sage Ghost added soberly. "We have buried her in the way of your people. Now it is time for new life."

Bitterbrush took a last look at the grave, struggling to understand what had happened. She'd only turned her back for a moment, but in that time, Lupine had climbed up on the rocks.

"Look at me, Momma! I can see everything from here!" The words would live forever in Bitterbrush's soul.

She'd straightened from where she'd been plucking flowering paintbrush and stared in horror. "No! Get down!" And she had rushed forward.

Lupine's eyes had grown round, and in her hurry to obey, she'd slipped—almost caught her balance—and fallen.

The sound of her little Lupine's body smacking the hard rocks would echo in her ears for an eternity.

She'd rushed back to camp, carrying the limp burden of her daughter in her arms. Desperately she'd turned to the only person who might help: Hot Fat. The Black Point Healer.

Tuber had heard her fearful cries. He'd crowded in behind her, a horror in his black eyes.

Hot Fat had listened to Lupine's chest and felt about her stomach. Then he'd prayed, sprinkling powders around and imploring the Sun. Lupine's chest had ceased its labored breathing. Hot Fat had looked at her, and shaken his head.

What do I have left? Only Tuber. Bitterbrush stumbled now, eyes blinded by tears.

Sage Ghost's arm settled on her shoulder as he led the way back to the lodge. She walked in numb misery, her soul drained of purpose. The only solace lay in the reassuring arm of the alien man who had claimed her.

"Tuber," Sage Ghost said, "where are you going?"

"My sister is dead. I want to be by myself."

Bitterbrush cringed at the surly tone in her son's voice.

"Do not go far. The warriors might not understand. We don't want to bury you, too. Not as the result of a silly mistake."

Tuber nodded respectfully and walked toward a low knoll at the edge of camp.

Sage Ghost led Bitterbrush into his lodge. He'd tried living in the earthen shelters of her people, but couldn't bear having dirt all around him. Then he'd built a small conical lodge of buffalo hide and seasoned lodge poles on the western edge of the camp. Today the skirts were rolled up from the peeled poles and tied to allow the breeze to blow through. A splash of sunlight slanted from the smoke hole, landing on a parfleche painted in yellow and red.

Sage Ghost shot Bitterbrush a measuring glance and used a buffalo-horn spoon to dip tea made from scurf-pea seeds. She took the bittersweet brew and sipped it gratefully.

"Why?" she asked. "Why did it happen? Will everything of mine be taken away?"

He settled next to her, resting an arm on his propped knee. His broad lips pressed tightly together. The five black circles on his forehead seemed to stand out, as if his skin had paled. "Sometimes Power does that. I don't understand it."

She noted the sorrow in his face. "After all that's happened, I should hate you."

He chuckled humorlessly. "I don't see hate in your eyes when you look at me. Only endurance."

She lowered her gaze to the tea, as if the reflections in it could explain the suffering to her. He'd been kind, treated her like a wife instead of a captive. She hadn't fought when he mounted her that first time. He'd been gentle, as if he cherished her. *Would I feel that way if he'd murdered my husband the way Pretty Woman's captor did?*

She shook her head and drew a tired breath.

"My heart aches for you and Lupine." The lines in his face deepened. "I wish I could bring her back."

"Why? What is one little girl to you?"

His brown eyes mirrored his soul. "All of the children Bright Moon and I had died when they were young. Bright Moon wasted, and Power sent me south to find another child for her. I stole a girl from the camp you call Three Forks—and she became our daughter. Now she, too, has vanished. Probably killed by the Wolf People. Life has not been kind to me . . . or to my children." He smiled wistfully. "I loved each one of them with all my soul. I had begun to love Lupine."

"Is that why you played with her? Worked so hard to teach her the Sun People language?" Bitterbrush tugged at the fringes on her dress. The action rattled the bone beads sewn in chevron patterns on the front.

"Yes. A man should leave someone to remember his name. Someone to look up at the stars, at the Camp of the Dead, and say, 'Sage Ghost is up there.' "

"Is that why you took me? Because I'm still young enough to bear another daughter?"

He placed a hand on her knee. "I took you because I saw the sorrow in your face. It touched my soul. All of my people, the White Clay, are dead. Your people will soon be the same way. The Black Point broke the White Clay—and the Wolf People killed what was left.''

"Doesn't that anger you? Doesn't traveling with them sicken you inside?''

He shook his head. ''No. Who is Sage Ghost to question the way Power works, or what its purposes are? The time of the White Clay had passed, that's all. The Black Point did what the Black Point had to. Had it been turned around, the White Clay would have done the same to them. The time of the Earth People has passed, too. If the Black Point hadn't taken your camp, killed your men and old women, the Broken Stones would have. Or the Hollow Flute. Someone.''

The time of the Earth People has passed? She closed her eyes, seeing the last Gathering, the expressions on people's faces as they hurried away. Perhaps they'd known that deep in their souls. Bone Ring had been the only one to see the truth, and even she had failed to see all of it. Larkspur's casual dismissal of the Sun People had been the doom of all of them—and Larkspur lay unburied in the sagebrush back of Round Rock, food for the ravens, maggots, and coyotes.

"I worry about Tuber.'' Sage Ghost tapped his thick fingers on the hides. ''He could become a great warrior . . . or destroy himself.''

She glanced at him. ''He's been different since his father died. Give the boy a chance. Everything he had has been taken away from him.''

Sage Ghost nodded. ''I spoke for his life when most wanted to kill him.''

"You've been taking him with you to hunt.''

"His heart is in the hunt. He doesn't say much, spending his time in his head. But he has a natural way, great strength for his age, and he moves with the stealth of a ghost.''

"Warm Fire taught him.'' *Warm Fire, Lupine* . . . Bitterbrush lowered her head, hair spilling around to hide her from the world.

Sage Ghost shifted, putting his arms around her. In his embrace, she cried herself dry.

Still Water walked quietly beside a frowning White Ash. Underfoot, the soft sand shifted and dimpled with his tracks. Around them, hills of buff-colored sand had stabilized under a mat of grass, sagebrush, and greasewood. Rabbitbrush and hopsage littered the slopes, as did dock and—to his discomfort—vast patches of prickly pear cactus. Trouble followed obediently behind.

The wind sawed back and forth between a light breeze and a moderate blow. Bluebirds, meadowlarks, and thrashers filled the air with song. Overhead, an eagle drifted against the high-piled thunderheads to the south.

He led the way through the hollows and flats between the dunes. This was a trick used by hunters to avoid the keen-sighted antelope, who could see ten times as well as a man. If hunters could screen their movements thus, then perhaps he and White Ash could avoid the vigilant eyes of the Sun People scouts. When they had to expose themselves by climbing long dunes, they hurried.

Here and there, fuzzy-looking stands of ricegrass had gone to full seed and now the stalks browned in the late-summer sun. The giant wild rye bent under its load of seeds. This year the land bore a bountiful harvest.

He smelled the warm air, cataloging its scents. This land, his land, had nurtured him, fed him, provided shelter and happiness. The land remained, heedless of the troubles of Earth People and the black threat that descended from the north.

Still Water glanced at White Ash and realized she had lost herself in her head. A hardness had formed around the fullness of her mouth. Worry ate at her, occupying every waking moment.

"Can you Dream the birds?" he asked.

"Dream the birds?" Her brow puckered and wind tugged strands of her black hair so that they caught the sun, gleaming and blue-tinged in the light.

"Sure." He gestured. "Singing Stones Dreamed the elk. See if you can Dream the birds, get them to accompany us for a while. I like walking with birds."

She gave him a suspicious glance. "I don't know. Walking and Dreaming at the same time?"

He grinned at her. "A new challenge. Just this morning you were complaining that as Singing Stones said, you'd learned to walk but you couldn't control your balance."

She jerked a nod, indicating that she would try. Her frown tightened as she honed her concentration.

The pace slowed, but they walked on. Still Water kept his eyes on the birds flitting in the sage.

He stayed silent, simply enjoying the warmth and smelling the land. A touch settled on his soul—an imperceptible shifting that vanished immediately. He glanced down to see Trouble staring at White Ash. The dog cocked its ears and whined softly.

A shiver ran along Still Water's spine as he felt the touch again. His skin prickled: White Ash Dreamed and walked. He knew deep within his soul when she touched the edges of the One. The Wolf Bundle on his back became lighter. Now weight began to vanish, until his pack might have been filled with air. Still Water's soul thrilled with the feeling of Power. Sparks of it shot through his bones. He shook his head, guts roiling.

He had opened his mouth to say something when a rosy finch fluttered around them. He stared, a slow smile coming to his lips. Or was this only curiosity on the finch's part?

A bluebird landed on his shoulder. Other birds appeared in the air, circling and following, flitting from sagebrush to sagebrush. They sang, chirping and warbling. Joy rose in Still Water's soul.

Then something plopped on his head. With a grimace, he stopped, reached up and wiped wet white stuff from his hair and glared at a circling meadowlark.

As he turned to speak to White Ash, a doe antelope crested the ridge, ears up, watching them intently. She picked her way down through the sage and turned to walk before them. Still Water gaped and looked over his shoulder. A coyote, with her bright-eyed pups, ambled along behind them. A badger grumbled under its breath as it bulled through the sage on short, bowed legs. The eagle dropped, soaring close above them, but none of the birds reacted to the sky hunter's descent. More antelope crossed the dune to precede them.

A warm fullness began to pulse in Still Water's soul. He glimpsed a bushy-tailed packrat as the nocturnal creature paralleled their path without paying the slightest heed to the badger or coyotes. Insects whirled noisily on silvered wings.

A rattlesnake slithered through the waving grasses to intercept their path.

"White Ash?" Still Water called gently.

The rattlesnake turned toward them, leaving sinuous marks in the sand. Still Water reached over and touched her. "White Ash? Maybe this is getting a little out of control."

Her eyes cleared and she mumbled, "Hmm?"

As suddenly, the birds rose and the antelope stopped, staring about uneasily.

Still Water watched the rattlesnake coil, tongue flicking back and forth.

"Oh, my." White Ash started.

White patches flashed on the antelopes' hind quarters as they raced off over the dune, kicking up spurts of dust. Birds exploded in all directions amid chirps of alarm. Within half a moment, Still Water stood alone with White Ash in the little hollow. Only the rattlesnake remained, and then it slid into the shade of a sagebrush.

Still Water sighed and looked around.

"Did I do that?" White Ash gave him a wide-eyed stare.

Still Water stepped wide over the rattlesnake's trail—a queasy feeling in the soles of his feet—and skirted the reptile's refuge. "I think calling birds will take some work. You called everything."

She simply stared at him. "I just touched the edge of Power. I didn't want to go too far."

He nodded uneasily. "Maybe we don't want to try this around white bears—or anything big, or hungry."

She followed him across a low bar of sand before sinking wearily to the warm ground. Her hide skirt spread around her in a fringed crescent. Still Water squatted down next to her, noting the slump of her shoulders.

"Why are you sad? You did it!" he told her excitedly.

"But all I wanted was birds."

"They came."

"Along with everything else." She looked up at him with frightened eyes. "Maybe that's because I didn't trust myself to cross into the One. I held back." She closed her eyes. "But it's there. Calling."

"The important thing is that you managed to hold back. That's good."

"Only because you were there. I could see your soul, glowing. I anchored myself to you."

Trouble sniffed around the base of a bush and grunted as he lay down in the shade.

"Where are we going?" she asked, looking around as though suddenly lost.

Still Water squinted out across the rumpled dunes. "South." He lifted his hand to the western horizon, judging the time. They had three hands of sunlight left. "There's a creek that generally holds water this late in the year. It's just at the edge of the dune field. I won't say the water's good, but it's wet. We can camp there. We might be a little late, but . . ." He shrugged.

White Ash exhaled wearily and got to her feet. "Let's go."

Snail Shell ran his toughened fingers along the smooth wood of his dart shaft. His heart pumped excitement. He'd cut the tracks and followed them, aware that his prey kept to the low spots, seeking to avoid detection. Easy victims: only a man, a woman, and a dog. One cast from his strong arm and Spirit-blessed atlatl and two things would happen: The man would die, and the woman would be his. The dog could be clubbed easily enough if it caused trouble.

Now Snail Shell waited, knowing they would come along

this path. Out of long practice, he checked his back trail, where he'd circled and hidden himself in the waist-high sage along their route. He'd chosen a perfect place for ambush. He crouched where the sage grew thick and tall, his feet braced in the sand of the dune side. The wind took his scent away from his prey and their dog's keen nose. When they reached the hollow place between the dunes, they'd be in the open—walking on hardpan.

He'd seen the woman first, noting her beauty and the sensual sway of her hips, imagining her moving under him in the robes. This one, he'd keep. Then he'd turned his attention to the man, seeing no warrior, only a homely man who bore a pack and walked absently, his eyes on the clouds, one arm held protectively to his chest. The dog had been nothing more than a long-haired black-and-white cur—and scrawny at that. The beast wouldn't even make a decent pack animal.

He caught faint strains of their conversation as they walked into the hollow. Snail Shell froze, his arm back, the dart firmly nocked in his atlatl. As they approached, they ceased to talk and the woman looked curiously preoccupied.

Snail Shell prepared to stand and cast his dart, but something played with his soul, some Power. A prickling—like a thousand ant feet—lifted his high-roached hair, filled his breast and tried to suffocate his heart. In horror, he glanced at the woman's face. She looked asleep, or dead—but she was walking.

Frightened, he let them pass and followed, using all of his wiles. Fear traced frosty patterns up and down his spine. What sort of magic was this?

He watched in awe as the birds came to circle around them and land on their shoulders. Then antelope joined the couple, and coyotes, and an eagle. A badger crashed through the rabbitbrush, passing within an arm's length of Snail Shell as it moaned and trotted forward, thick fur bouncing, to join the man and woman.

Snail Shell gaped . . . and then he ran, afraid the Power would mark his soul and twist him up in the trance. He headed south, toward the main camp of the clan. Wind Runner must know, all the Black Point must know, in order to guard themselves.

Would Hot Fat have the ability to fight against such Power? Would any of them?

Snail Shell pounded through the sand, cursing the way it dragged at the feet. But once the first flush of fear had passed, he dropped into a distance-eating lope that would carry him through the night.

White Ash woke to the lightening of the eastern horizon. Dreams had haunted her sleep, images that chilled her soul. Fright had risen like a corrupt smoke to hover over her.

She'd seen Brave Man's face as he fought her to the ground along the Gray Deer River. His knowing leer had turned into Three Bulls'—a hideous grimace grunting fetid breath into her face.

The dying shrieks of the White Clay had sounded again and again as the cold air whistled with darts and war clubs smacked sickeningly into skulls.

Brave Man stood naked, washed by a hundred voices Singing praise. He lifted imploring hands to the night sky. Firelight played wickedly over his muscular flesh dappled by shadow Dancers. As he turned, gloating, looking down at White Ash with victory in his eyes, her soul shriveled. In the flickering light, Brave Man's engorged penis throbbed with a malignant life of its own.

Singing Stones held living fire in his age-knotted hands, the rapture in his face illuminated by a reddish light. He stiffened and spoke in a multitude of voices not his own— and he died whispering *"Murder . . ."*

Corpses leered at her as she fled along a forest trail. Left Hand huddled before her, a broken man facing the final hope for a broken people. Her soul twisted as she watched him shuffle wearily eastward through the aspens.

Sage Ghost peered into her eyes. She said the words that ended his hope and love: "She's dead."

Always, the somber Power of the Wolf Bundle pulsed in the light of the flickering fire. Behind the Bundle, a forest exploded into flames as warriors screamed and fled. A young man Danced ecstatically through tongues of flame, a rattlesnake clutched in his hands, as the mountains burned and people screamed.

She fought desperately to free herself, and the visions reeled and spun before her.

A young man rose from a rocky, windswept soil. Snow blew in white streamers around his heavy moccasins. He stood before her, feet braced, dressed in a long hunting coat that hung to his knees and about his shoulders rested the hide of a great white bear. His eyes seemed to burn with an inner fire. He lifted his hand, blowing across his open palm, and from it sprang a rainbow, arching across the sky, dimming even the colorful bands of light that the Great Mystery played over the northern heavens.

"Who are you?" White Ash cried.

He smiled at her then, and her soul melted with the warmth and joy his face imparted. But before she could speak again, the young man turned, shimmering, and dropped to all fours, arms and legs multiplying until he'd become a red spider. The beast raced up the rainbow, slowing near the top. There, it spread its legs, spinning the colors of the rainbow across the heavens until they wove themselves into a web connecting the dew drops of stars.

White Ash reached out, only to lose her footing. She twisted, seeking balance, and tumbled into the strands of the huge web.

The web stretched and pulled, forming new visions: Brave Man raising the Wolf Bundle to the sun with one hand, while a long obsidian knife gleamed in the bright light, the translucent stone spotted by patches of darkness that dripped onto a square gray altar and burned crimson on the rock.

A crumpled figure rolled from the waist-high stone, and she looked into Still Water's sightless eyes. A gaping hole had been slashed in his chest, and blood leaked from the cavity where his heart had been.

White Ash tried to scream, but the suffocating web lifted

her above the scene to stare down at people who ran in terror. Power changed around her. The glow of the Spiral darkened, golden light dulling into a blood-red.

She shot a frightened glance back at the huge spider and saw the handsome youth again. He aged, his features hardening into those of Wolf Dreamer. The white bear hide gleamed and burst into dazzling light. Wolf Dreamer reached toward her in a gesture that implored, his face twisted with anguish. About her, suffering pulsed and retreated. A black miasma grew in the north, moving south, covering the surface of the living earth. The One changed, pulling back, retreating.

Still Water lay rotting below her, his flesh swelling. Carrion birds landed on the bones of his chest and perched on the ridges of his hips to peck maggot-filled meat from his gut.

She cried out. The web drew tighter. In desperation she clawed at the clinging fibers, snaring herself until she couldn't move, couldn't breathe. The horror suffocated her. She became one with the filth.

Strangling, she'd awakened in the cool crispness of coming dawn. Still Water had sat up in their robes and studied her through worried eyes. She'd reassured him, holding him close as he drifted off to sleep again.

Ravens called to greet the morning, and robins added their chirping song to the rebirth of the light. On a far butte, coyotes yipped in a final chorus before seeking their dens.

The robe that covered them comforted—a false security against the world that waited.

Couldn't I just stay here forever? Couldn't I let the world find its own answer? Let Power deal with Brave Man's new Dream? What is a single, frightened woman against that?

The eastern horizon pinked, the hidden sun burning red and orange against the few clouds that hung over the black silhouette of the land.

Her stomach cramped. *Worry. It eats at me, leaving me sick in the mornings.*

She closed her eyes, leaving the world of illusion for the moment. She traced the path inside, turning inward until she found the feathery touch of the One. There, it lay in wait, the final escape if she chose to take it.

Still Water stirred, bringing her back. He rolled over and yawned. She opened her eyes. The sun had begun to rise in the eastern sky. Time slipped away when she Dreamed the One. It seemed to flow past without touching her.

Still Water stretched. "Past time to get up. Sun's up."

White Ash's heart pounded heavily, as if it were made of rock. She placed hands over her eyes. *I can't do it. I'm not strong enough to face Brave Man. I couldn't even fight him when he captured me in the Grass Meadow Mountains. I'd given up. A real Dreamer would have fought.*

She lowered her hands and glanced at Still Water with haunted eyes. The image of the Dream replayed . . . Brave Man standing over Still Water's lifeless body. *Can I save him? Can I save anything? Or will it happen anyway? Power discards those it can't use.* The familiar urge to vomit choked at the bottom of her throat.

She forced herself to sit up.

Still Water pulled the last of their jerked meat from the pack, handing her several of the hard, dry slabs. She chewed, mouth watering, and her stomach twisted and tightened again.

Not this morning. Don't let me be sick again. It's a sign of my weakness. How can a woman who can't keep her breakfast down defeat an evil Dreamer?

She forced the food down before standing and pulling on her clothing. Hating the ill feeling, she walked down to the stream, slaking her thirst with the water. She made two steps before it all came back up.

Still Water rushed to her side, supporting her as he led her back to the camp.

"Every morning." He shook his head. "Is it just the worry? Or something else? Not some witching? Not a curse from Brave Man?"

She battled a wave of dizziness and shook her head. "No, it's just . . . I don't know. Once I get it over with, I'm fine. That wouldn't happen with evil Power. It's worry, or maybe this happens to all Dreamers. If Singing Stones were here, we could ask him." And as soon as she said it, she wished she hadn't.

His smile didn't hide his anxiety. Giving her an understanding look, he produced two thin sticks of jerked meat. "I saved them. You need your strength."

She fingered the hard pieces. "Maybe I'll wait until we're on the way and eat them then."

He nodded and went down to the stream to fill the gut water bag.

White Ash rolled the bedding, tying it to Still Water's pack. Her hands tingled ominously from the Power of the Wolf Bundle hidden within. She fought the urge to tremble. Silken filaments of Power reached out for her. She pulled back. "No. No, not yet."

"I just hope you're not sick." She hadn't heard Still Water come back. He raised his hand and let it fall. "I don't know how to cure a sick Dreamer."

He waited, head cocked.

"It's the worry . . . and the Dreams. Horrible Dreams last night. I—I don't want to talk about them." She smiled weakly. "We've had enough horrible Dreams."

He nodded, slinging the water-taut gut around his shoulders before picking up the pack. "Well, it's summer. Lots of things to eat. Toad flax is looking good. Maybe we'll make a couple of choppers from quartzite cobbles and use them to dig roots. If not, there's blazing star on the slopes, and cattail to the south along the creek. I'd really like to roast some cattail root in the coals when we camp tonight. They're sweet and rich—just the thing to make you feel better. We'll do fine."

She stood, feeling the fatigue in her legs. Something had happened to her strength. Too much Dreaming. It sapped the soul.

Still Water pointed. "Those are the Round Rock Mountains. Larkspur's camp is just on the other side—if it's still there, that is." A sadness came to his eyes.

She laid a hand on his shoulder. "Maybe they're still all right."

He made an uncertain sound and started out. "Funny thing

. . . the last time I came this way, it was with Left Hand. Going north—to find the Dreamer. I never Dreamed I'd have her with me coming back. Do you feel well enough to walk that far?''

"I'll be fine. We'll make it today, Still Water." The Dream image of his dead body returned to haunt her. *By the One, I hope we will.*

The dead mocked her thoughts.

Chapter 27

Still Water found Larkspur's body first. The perching turkey vultures led him to the spot, up in the rocks behind Round Rock camp. As a child, he'd played in this little hollow. Had he turned his head, he could have seen the hole where the snake had bitten his arm.

He knelt down next to Larkspur's remains, noting the way her skull had been crushed. The scavengers hadn't left much. Maggots crawled among the old woman's bones—the latter streaked white by bird droppings. The beetles had already begun their work. The stench of rot filled the air, drowning the sweetness of the sagebrush.

He stood, looking around. No other corpses. Perhaps the others had lived? Had managed to flee?

"You know her?" White Ash asked, standing back from the buzzing flies and the odor of decay.

"Larkspur." He stood and lifted his head to the dome of the sky. "Grandmother, may your soul be free and unangered by what was done to you."

Emptiness ached inside him. He stopped by White Ash and closed his eyes, seeing his grandmother as she'd been: the tyrannical old ruler of Round Rock. "I should hate her for everything she did . . . but I can't. She just did what she had to."

White Ash's face tightened as if she, too, balanced on the edge of tears.

Still Water led the way down the familiar trail to the lodges. At first the camp looked the same, although ominously empty. The hard soil had been stippled with rain that blurred the faint impressions of tracks. The lodge entrances had been carefully blocked with large sandstone slabs. The smoke holes, too, had been covered, as had the ventilator shafts.

Sealed? Against what?

He rolled the slab aside and ducked into Bitterbrush's lodge. Everything had been stripped. He stopped, studying the sandstone slabs on the floor. So many storage pits?

White Ash blocked the light from the doorway as she followed him in.

"They didn't leave much, did they?" she observed.

"This isn't right." He bent down, grunting as he lifted one of the heavy slabs. Beneath was a storage pit filled with dried scurf peas. "This wasn't here. There are five new pits dug into this floor."

He studied the lodge. "The raiders would have looked under the slabs. What they didn't take, they'd have left for the animals. I don't think Round Rock clan dug those pits."

She studied him. "The lodges were sealed. Someone's planning to come back."

A chill shiver ran up Still Water's spine.

White Ash studied the dried scurf peas. "This was prepared with skill. Whoever did this knew how to leave a cache. I remember drying plants when I was a girl. All the moisture has to be out of them so they don't mold."

He nodded. The pit walls bore the familiar red stain of a preparation fire. "The pit was fired to harden the walls against rodents. Would Sun People do that?"

She shook her head. "They know how to cure meat and keep berries in fat for winter, but not how to dry plants."

Still Water resettled the slab to seal the cache. "If they're coming back, I don't want them to know anyone was here."

He ducked outside and squinted in the noonday light. All familiar—and all different. He studied the camp uneasily, hating the foreboding that filled him. "Look."

She followed his pointing finger. One by one, Still Water pointed out places where lodges had stood. Here and there a peg remained that had held a lodge cover.

"So many!" He frowned and rubbed his face. "There must have been tens of tens of people here. More than that."

White Ash had gone pale. "This isn't just raiding. An entire clan came through here. That's why all the new storage pits were dug . . . for winter supplies."

"Broken Stones?" Still Water stared around nervously, aware that someone could be watching even now.

"Who else?" White Ash growled. "The journey from the land of the Wolf People to here isn't very long. Do you know of another clan on the move?"

"Let's get out of here. The sooner, the better." He reslung his pack and they took off at a brisk walk. Trouble followed uneasily, sniffing here and there at his old haunts.

A grim desperation possessed Still Water. He couldn't forget the way Larkspur's body lay in the sagebrush. How long before maggots crawled through his flesh and White Ash's? He glanced at her, praying she could stand up against Brave Man.

"Ask her how far it is to the next camp." Wind Runner sat at the rear of his lodge, shaded from the hot sun, as Sage Ghost turned to the Greasewood clan woman who knelt before them with her head bowed and her hands clasped nervously in her lap. She wore a sweat-stained deer-hide dress that had been painted once. Now the colors had faded—along with the hopes of her people. Sage Ghost put the question in the Earth People tongue.

Aspen sat on Wind Runner's left, speculative eyes on the woman. Next to her, Hot Fat rested an arm on a propped knee, his old face pensive. Black Moon sat to Wind Runner's right, and beyond him, One Man and Fire Rabbit.

The skirts of the lodge had been rolled up to allow air to

flow through, but even this late in the day, the warm wind bordered on being uncomfortable.

Around them, Greasewood camp bustled with activity. Several of the captive women pounded and ground ricegrass seeds. The clack-scrape of their grinding stones carried in the air. Another woman wailed, mourning the death of her man in the fighting.

Voices rose and fell as the Black Point discussed yet further triumphs.

Sage Ghost listened to the woman's answer. "She says Red Earth camp is a day's walk to the west. Antelope camp lies a little more than a day and a half to the east. Beyond that is Boggy Meadows camp. Even more camps lie to the south—all the way to what they call the Silver Snake River. Still more camps lie farther to the west, along the Sage Grouse River."

Black Moon grunted. "It seems that we shall never run out of camps." He cradled his chin in the palm of his hand. "We have enough women—three for every warrior. We're getting too many women. That could be dangerous."

"And the country we have to cover gets wider," Fire Rabbit added. "How far apart can we spread ourselves?"

Wind Runner gave Aspen a knowing look. She'd told him the night before that such a question was being asked.

"I think we've found a wonderful land," Hot Fat admitted. "But now that we have it, what do we do with it? We can't stop. If we do, these other camps will raise the alarm, come to war with us. We have the element of surprise. Each camp has been taken unaware. How can two tens of warriors stand against the numbers we muster? But from here, camps lie in all directions. What do we do?"

Black Moon lifted an inquiring eyebrow as he looked to Wind Runner for the answer.

Wind Runner and Aspen had spent the entire night working out a plan. He ran it through his thoughts one last time, seeking any flaw. Finally he clapped his hands to his knees and announced, "We have to split up."

"And lose the advantage of our numbers?" Fire Rabbit shook his head. "That's crazy!"

Wind Runner smiled. "I don't see any choice." He paused

for a moment, then added, "I think I know a way to lessen the risks."

One Man laughed and thumped his belly with a knotted fist. "Why am I not surprised? Let's hear it."

Wind Runner steepled his fingers, frowning. "One Man, I think you should take two tens of the warriors. Sweep west to the Sage Grouse River. Fire Rabbit, you take two tens and move south. Coyote Feather can move east. If each of you can surprise the camps, you can take them. Look at how easily we've conquered them so far. There's been almost no resistance."

"And how do we handle the women?" Fire Rabbit wanted to know.

"You don't." Wind Runner grinned smugly. "The women aren't the problem. Unlike our women, they don't take part in the fighting. The problem we face is with the men. They could mass and attack us. I don't want to lose any of our warriors. We may need our strength this winter if the Hollow Flute come across the Sideways Mountains."

"Kill just the men?" One Man asked. "And leave the women?"

Wind Runner nodded. "What do you think they'll do? Leave their camps? Maybe. Who cares? They've got to survive this winter. Some will run to the closest camp as soon as you've left. You'll have to move fast, but men can outdistance a woman in a race. As long as we surprise them, we'll take most of the camps."

"Some of the men will escape," Hot Fat reminded. "It has to happen. Somewhere, someone will spot our war parties."

Wind Runner spread his hands. "But if we can bleed them, weaken them, what choice will those men have? Suppose that four tens of their warriors do get together and decide to raid us. How will they fare?"

"Badly," Fire Rabbit grunted.

Wind Runner stared at the ground. "I'm betting on something else. When word does get out, the Earth People will know that we've taken the north. They'll know that we've killed a lot of their warriors and that no one has bloodied us in a fight. Think of the effect that will have on them. They already think their Power is broken because of what Sage Ghost tells us happened at their Gathering.''

''And what do you think?'' Hot Fat asked.

''I think''—*and I'm gambling*—''that most of them will run. Why try to fight for what is already lost? If I know these Earth People, they'll worry about their lives before they'll worry about their honor. At the very least, the knowledge that they'll die will weaken their blood if they do decide to come against us.''

''What about the other two tens of Black Point warriors?'' Fire Rabbit asked. ''What happens with them?''

''They stay with me. We have to guard our main camp. We don't know who's behind us. The best scouts are scouring the trails, but I don't want to be caught by surprise.''

''And if the Hollow Flute show up on the Badwater, or on the Spirit River? Do you want to tackle them with only two tens of warriors?''

Wind Runner shook his head. ''If they do show up, I'll send someone to the top of Green Mountain. That's the highest point around. From what the captives say, you can see a fire at the top from anywhere in the Red Earth Basin. If you see a big fire up there some night, come running. During the day you should be able to see a column of smoke. Keep watch. By the time the Hollow Flute reach us, most of our strength should be assembled here again.''

Black Moon nodded, respect in his eyes. ''And we'll know where they are—but they won't know where we are.''

''Exactly.'' Wind Runner smiled. ''And here's another thing to consider. If the Hollow Flute do appear, we'll have taken many Earth People camps, and all those Earth People women will be without husbands. We can send a runner to the Hollow Flute and make them a gift . . . yes, *a gift* of territory and women. By the Power of Trade, they'll have to give us something in return. Think about it. What could they give?''

Black Moon whooped and clapped his hands. ''What *could* they give? They wouldn't dare raid us—not with that much obligation!'' An awed look crept across his face. ''By Thunderbird, no one has ever given a gift that indebted an entire *clan* before. Families, yes, but a clan?''

Wind Runner studied their faces as Black Moon's words sank in. Even Fire Rabbit was grinning.

"Tomorrow morning," Black Moon said. "That will be the time to leave."

Talk lasted for a while longer before One Man left, followed by Fire Rabbit. Wind Runner stood and stretched before offering Aspen his hand.

They walked out into the evening. Wind Runner looked back at Green Mountain to the north. "I think it'll work."

She took his arm. "It's a good plan. And I'm almost sure the Earth People will run rather than fight. It's in their nature. They're not warriors."

He nodded and lifted her chin with his finger to stare into the depths of her dark eyes. "I don't know what I ever did without you. I'm starting to believe that no one can stand against us."

She laughed, the sound bubbling and happy. "I don't think they'd dare!"

Dogs began barking on the other side of camp, and people called out greetings.

Wind Runner and Aspen followed the sounds and met a travel-worn Snail Shell as he came panting into camp. Sweat had streaked the dust that coated his body and breechclout, but he clutched his weapons in a death grip. Scratches from the sagebrush formed a crisscross pattern on his legs. The snail-shell tattoos in the man's cheeks contrasted to his dark, flushed skin. He met Wind Runner's measuring gaze and nodded, gasping for breath.

"Looks like you've been running," Wind Runner said uneasily. A cold premonition made his stomach churn. Aspen had laced her fingers into his. Now her grip tightened.

"I have." Snail Shell walked around to cool down and catch his breath.

"Hollow Flute?" Wind Runner asked.

Snail Shell took a water sack offered by One Man as the warleader arrived, and drank deeply before shaking his head. "No, Wind Runner. I saw a man and a woman."

One Man cried, "You ran all the way back here because you saw *a man and a woman*?"

Snail Shell's eyes narrowed. "I thought Hot Fat would want to know that a powerful Dreamer is coming. I saw her call the animals. I tell you, they walked surrounded by birds, and antelope, and coyotes. An eagle came down to circle around their heads."

Wind Runner rubbed his chin thoughtfully. "Spirit People? Did they wear Earth People clothing?"

"The man did. The woman dressed in the manner of the Wolf People—with pants and a short shirt. They're back there." Snail Shell jerked his head to the north. "Maybe a day's journey. They are headed right for us."

Wind Runner drew a deep breath. "Maybe we'd better go see what Hot Fat has to say."

"And tomorrow?" Aspen asked.

Wind Runner said, "If it's a real Dreamer, Hot Fat will be of more use than all of our warriors."

Fingers of dread tightened around his heart.

"This is the last time I'll ask you." Brave Man smiled down at the bound Black Point warrior. "Where is your clan? Where are Wind Runner and his woman?"

The wounded warrior glared up stonily. His teeth remained tightly clamped, the muscles standing out on his sweaty jaws.

Brave Man sighed and looked around at the Broken Stones, who watched with excited eyes. Beyond them, the rolling sandhills shimmered in the hot sun, sagebrush and greasewood wavering in the rolling heat. The mountains to the west seemed to float on a silver sheen.

Brave Man cocked his head at the man. A wicked dart wound discolored the warrior's swollen leg, clotted blood streaking the skin. In the process of dragging him back, the wound had caked with sand and dirt.

"Put his feet in the fire," Brave Man ordered before taking a last look at the man. "Or would you prefer to tell me?"

The Black Point shut his eyes.

"Do it," Brave Man told Flying Hawk.

Two warriors grabbed the struggling captive and hauled him to the smoldering embers of last night's fire. Long Bone tossed more brush onto the coals, leaning down to blow them to life.

The warrior shrieked as they muscled his feet into the flames. His moccasins smoked and curled, blackening as the heat ate into the thick leather. He bucked and a hideous scream tore from his lungs.

"Where?" Brave Man thundered, limping over to stare down into the man's glazed eyes. *"Where?"*

A choked rattle issued from the man's mouth, his face contorted. Sweat beaded as Long Bone and Five Darts pinned him. He kicked frantically, stirring the coals.

"South!" he screamed. *"In the name of Thunderbird!"*

Brave Man made a gesture and his men dragged the captive from the flames.

"Where in the south?" Brave Man bent down, peering closely.

The Black Point writhed on the sand, whimpering. "South of Green Mountain. In the Red Earth Basin. Two days' walk." Then he sobbed and trembled with the searing pain.

Brave Man straightened. "Beyond Green Mountain." He studied the southern horizon, noting the rounded caps of granite that blocked the view. Two days' walk? For his camp, burdened as it was with the old and children, it would take four.

"Break camp!"

Brave Man stalked toward his lodge, Pale Raven keeping step with him. "And the Black Point warrior?"

"Leave him. Bound, just as he is."

Her dark eyes locked with his for a moment, and she nodded.

With an infected wound and cooked feet, the bound man wouldn't last more than a day. The coyotes could finish him. Even Pale Raven shivered at the thought.

A woman screamed.

Wind Runner lunged to his feet, ducked under the low flap of his lodge and ran out into the graying morning light. Aspen rolled from their robes and pulled her dress over her head before following him. Here and there, men poked heads out of their lodges, looking around.

The camp seemed peaceful. Tendrils of smoke rose from the fire pits. Birds greeted the dawn with song in the sage. The rounded mounds of Greasewood camp's earthen lodges huddled against the morning. The air carried the cool taint of sage and rabbitbrush, as well as the land's sweet scent.

Cottontail came running into camp, a hand to her breast, a stricken look on her face.

Wind Runner called out, "What is it?"

He grabbed her by the shoulders as she ran up to him; he could feel her panicked trembling.

"Hot Fat," she whispered. "Out there . . . in the sagebrush. Dead."

"*What?*" Aspen reached for the woman, disbelief etched on her delicate face.

Wind Runner shot a worried glance at Aspen and ordered, "Show me."

Cottontail shivered and shook her head.

"Cottontail?" Aspen took her by the hand. "Come on. I'll be with you. He's my grandfather. Maybe he's just Soul Flying. Maybe . . ."

People had begun to cluster around, worried whispers going back and forth.

Aspen and Cottontail walked back into the sage, Wind Runner to one side. He could see Aspen's pale face. His own heart had gone heavy in his breast. Hot Fat? Dead? He shook his head in disbelief.

Cottontail stopped, taking a deep breath and stiffening.

Hot Fat lay facedown on the soft, sandy ground at the base of the flat-topped butte that sheltered the camp. Sagebrush rose knee-high all around him, its silver-green contrasting sharply with the Soul Flier's golden-brown clothing.

Aspen made a deep-throated sound, and Wind Runner hugged her to him. Her shoulders shook. Cottontail's frightened eyes mirrored the panic that swept the murmuring crowd.

People closed around them to stare at the body. Wind Runner patted Aspen on the back, then broke free in order to bend down and inspect Hot Fat's body. The top of the old man's head had been bashed in.

Wind Runner fought down the urge to scream his pain to the heavens. This lump of lifeless flesh had first offered the warm hand of friendship, and it had grown to be into something precious between them. Another warm love had been torn away from his soul—like sagebrush twisted from dry ground. *I'd come to love you, old friend. And now you, too, are gone.*

Hot Fat's breechclout was undone, as if he'd squatted to relieve himself. Wind Runner turned, seeing only scuffled tracks—obliterated by the people clustering around them. He searched the ground. On the other side of the sagebrush he found two smudges on the hard soil—as if a man had stood on tiptoes to smash the blow down.

"Who would have done this?" Aspen asked, her voice strained.

"Blue Wind! Cut for tracks. Quickly, before we trample them all." Wind Runner pointed. "The rest of you, don't move another step until we scout."

Blue Wind jerked a nod and slipped out of the crowd.

Wind Runner struggled to keep the grief at bay and think. "Did anyone hear anything? See anything?"

People looked back and forth uneasily and shook their heads.

"We have many enemies," Black Moon reminded as he stepped forward and bent down. Sadness glistened in his eyes. "Maybe we missed one of the Earth People's warriors. Maybe it was one of the captive women."

Wind Runner sucked in a breath. "He ate with us last night. It must have happened sometime after that."

Aspen knelt, struggling against tears. Heedless of the blood, she gently cradled her grandfather's head on her lap.

Wind Runner bent down and fingered the coagulated pool of dark scarlet on the sand. Then he touched the old man's flesh—stone cold.

"Whoever it was is long gone. But that doesn't mean he won't come back. For the time being, we hunt the night—and guard ourselves better."

"To kill a Soul Flier?" Cottontail shook her head. "I hope whoever did this is ready to meet Thunderbird. Hot Fat's soul will return for him."

Angry mutters broke out among the people.

Wind Runner thought back to the day that he'd faced One Man . . . the day Hot Fat had spoken for him. How many nights since then had he and the old Soul Flier talked, and laughed, and shared their souls?

He stood up and waved a hand harshly. "Snail Shell, take some men and spread out. Double the lookouts on the hills."

Still Water shielded his eyes, staring down into the flats. Even from here he could see the lazy spirals of smoke rising from Greasewood camp—more smoke than Nightshade's clan would make. He glanced up at the flat-topped butte that threw a long shadow over the camp. Layers of white dirt separated by sandstone gleamed in the morning light, while sage and rabbitbrush speckled the slopes on the logical place for lookouts. And if that were the case . . .

Unease gnawed in his heart.

"This way," he said to White Ash, pointing at a sage-dotted conical hill just before them. The low mound appeared to be capped by white clay and scattered chert cobbles.

"And then what?" White Ash asked, hurrying behind him. Trouble followed.

"Dream," Still Water told her. "Dream the animals. You must."

"Why?"

"Those aren't Earth People. We're going to have to make them think we have more Power than it seems."

Panting, they reached the top of the hill and looked down over the flat. Still Water saw several figures headed their way at a trot.

"Dream, White Ash! *Dream like you've never Dreamed before!*"

White Ash dropped to the sand, placing her hands in her lap. She swallowed hard and closed her eyes.

Still Water lowered himself beside her and broke into a chant. He narrowed his concentration, seeking to ignore the fear that pumped with each beat of his heart.

His pack ate into his shoulders, growing heavier. He shook his head and chanted louder.

Perspiration shone on White Ash's forehead. The warriors could be seen clearly now, trotting up the sage-thick slope toward them. How much longer did he and White Ash have?

"Wolf Dreamer?" White Ash whispered, struggling against the desperation of their situation. "Help me. I need to call the animals."

The weight of Still Water's pack pulled viciously on his shoulders. *If I don't ignore it, a dart is going to get me.* He cleared his mind, chanting evenly, forcing his voice to stay calm.

The weight of the pack seemed to grow even . . . Then it occurred to him: *The Wolf Bundle!*

He shrugged out of the pack and undid the laces with frantic fingers. He grasped the Bundle and a lightning burst of Power shot up his arm. The very air seemed to prickle, and White Ash steadied, some of the desperation draining from her taut face.

Below, the warriors pointed at them and shouted.

Still Water knew when White Ash touched the One. The Wolf Bundle surged with a Power so violent, he almost dropped it. He could sense the Bundle's threads of Power snaking out toward White Ash.

A black wolf wove a sinuous path through the pale green stands of sagebrush. It peered at White Ash with gleaming yellow eyes—as though waiting. An eagle cried in the sky.

Still Water's heart leaped when the wolf padded to stand between him and White Ash, so close he could feel the animal's whiskers brushing his hide pants. A meadowlark landed on top of Still Water's head and trilled into the air. A badger eased out of the brush, grumbling softly. The One pulsed.

Still Water's soul leaped in ecstasy.

The warriors stopped several dart lengths away, observing in stunned disbelief.

Call to them. The command settled in Still Water's soul.

"White Ash?" he said hurriedly. "Tell them we come in peace."

One of the warriors balanced a dart for casting.

"White Ash! I *don't* speak their language!"

She shook herself out of the Dream and the animals fled in a rush, scampering away into the sage or soaring into the turquoise sky. The warriors below shouted and covered their heads against the exploding flock of birds. One man fell to the ground and starting Singing to Thunderbird. "What? What did you say?"

"Tell them we bring a Dream. That we will not hurt them."

As her voice rang out in the speech of the Sun People, the warriors glanced back and forth uncomfortably.

Then the lead warrior edged toward them, climbing the slope cautiously, a dart nocked in his atlatl. His men followed nervously. Still Water felt White Ash stiffen as the warrior drew closer. When the man stood no more than ten paces away, he halted, an awestruck expression on his face. Young and handsome, he moved with a powerful grace and balance. His hair had been pulled into a high roach. Three blue lines had been tattooed across his forehead. His mouth opened and he whispered, "White Ash?"

Still Water recognized her name in the Sun People tongue. He turned to her and found her staring open-mouthed at the young warrior.

"Wind Runner?" White Ash whispered, disbelief mixing with the swirling fragments of Dream. She blinked and rubbed her face. Was this real? Or something conjured from the One?

He stepped closer, older than she remembered him. Harder. In the bright light she traced the lines of his familiar face. Her heart skipped as she looked into the wonder that filled his eyes.

"White Ash . . . *you're alive!*"

She rose on unsteady feet and waited until Still Water stood beside her before walking forward and embracing Wind Runner. He hugged her as tightly as he had that night above the White Clay's last camp.

"I thought you were dead," he whispered against her hair. "I'd given up hope."

Trouble barked and growled behind her.

"White Ash?" Still Water called uncertainly. "Who is this man?"

She pushed away from Wind Runner, blinking at the tears that had come to cloud her vision. "Still Water, this is Wind Runner."

Still Water clutched the Wolf Bundle to his chest and gave the warrior a curious appraisal.

Wind Runner's face had turned hard. "What are you doing here? Why were the animals around you? What's going on?"

White Ash closed her eyes, trying desperately to shake the serene nothingness of the One so she could think clearly. "These are Black Point?"

"We are."

She nodded, a sprig of relief sprouting within. *At least I don't have to face Brave Man.* "Let's go to your camp, Wind Runner. We have a lot to discuss and not much time."

"And this man?" Wind Runner asked in a voice that cut like freshly struck obsidian.

White Ash saw Still Water straighten, his flat features pulling tight.

"He's the Keeper of the Wolf Bundle." She glanced up at Wind Runner, then turned and extended a hand to Still Water. He braced the Wolf Bundle against his chest with his bad arm and stepped forward to take her hand. "And he's . . . my husband."

Chapter 28 👾

My husband. The words burned Wind Runner like white-hot coals on exposed flesh.

He turned, muscles charged, and looked at Snail Shell. "Go back to the camp. Have food prepared. We must have a council."

"And this Earth People man?" Snail Shell glanced uneasily at Still Water.

"He will come with us . . . for the moment."

Snail Shell nodded, looking as if uncertainty crawled like insects under his skin.

Wind Runner turned back to White Ash, seeing her confusion. Then he inspected the Earth man again. One arm looked shriveled and useless. The man stood squat, and his face conjured thoughts of manure that had been stepped on. Only in the eyes did Wind Runner see anything noteworthy. Still Water's eyes reflected a soul too kind for its own good.

What could she possibly see in him? He's . . . he's . . . Wind Runner shook his head and gave the man a foul glare.

White Ash spoke to Still Water in the garbled talk of the Earth People. He replaced the leather object in the pack. The man's obnoxious black-and-white dog stared up with wary eyes.

Wind Runner turned on his heel. *I'll marry you. Be your wife.* He snorted under his breath.

"The Black Point have taken all the land to the south?" she asked, running to match his pace. Her melodious voice sent shivers through his soul.

"I said I'd come for you before the first snow."

She walked in silence for a moment. "Things have changed."

"I can see," he replied sarcastically.

She placed a hand on his arm. "Can you?"

He glanced down at her slim fingers resting on the rippling muscles in his arm, then looked into her eyes . . . and the world shifted, as if his soul had been exposed. He swallowed and shook his head. Cool wariness seeped through him. "What did . . ."

"You've changed, Wind Runner. Become a man. But I know your soul and your anger, and the hurt that will soon replace it." She gazed off toward the camp, a bittersweet smile on her full lips. "So much has happened since you left the White Clay."

"With him?" Wind Runner asked, jerking his head back toward Still Water, who followed nervously.

White Ash read his meaning and replied curtly, "Yes. He's saved my life more than once—and even faced Brave Man and his Broken Stones in the process."

"*Him?*" Wind Runner laughed. "He looks as if he'd run if a rabbit squealed at him."

Her beautiful face took on such a sad expression that a shiver wound through him. An eerie prickle of Power swirled in the air around her. Unconsciously, he walked a half step farther away. *I feel that she knows more than I do—sees things I don't. White Ash, my White Ash . . . what's happened to you?*

He steeled himself. "I looked all over for you. Three Forks, Badwater—everyplace I could think of. What happened?"

"The Wolf People killed the White Clay. I fled."

"I know. Sage Ghost is with us."

The announcement didn't bring the ecstatic joy he'd expected. Instead, she simply accepted the information with a knowing nod. He peered at her from the corner of his eye. *What's wrong with you, White Ash? Did that ugly Earth man cast some spell on you? Is that it? He's a magician?*

He winced. Only this morning they had placed Hot Fat on a high point and Sung his soul to Thunderbird.

White Ash expelled a tired breath and said, "Do you know that Brave Man has crushed the Wolf People and that even now he's in the basin?"

Wind Runner sucked in a breath. "What?"

"Yes, I thought we'd find him before we met you. He's become the Broken Stones' Soul Flier—and a Powerful one."

"Broken Stones? *Here?*" His gaze swept the sage-covered hills, seeking any movement. Only the breeze through the brush and a hopping cottontail caught his eye.

She seemed to lose herself in the visions in her head. "He's coming—swiftly."

And I just sent three fourths of my warriors away!

She continued walking, unaware that he'd stopped short.

Wind Runner darted after her. "Have you seen Hollow Flute, too?"

"Not here. But it wouldn't surprise me. The Spiral is shifting."

"What Spiral?"

She looked up at him as if he were a child. "I have to Dream the Spiral back, Wind Runner. That's why Power sent me to you. The Sun People must become part of First Man's Dream. If not, the Spiral will change and Brave Man will Dream the new way. Would you want to live in a Dream of his making?"

He glanced back suspiciously at Still Water. The man hoisted his pack higher on his back and trudged resolutely behind White Ash, but he looked as though his mother had just died.

Wind Runner walked in silence. Too much had fallen on him too quickly. First, Hot Fat's murder—the grief hadn't even sunk in yet. Then White Ash's appearance. Broken Stones? Brave Man? Dreams? And Aspen . . . Blessed Thunderbird, what was he going to tell her? *Her heart's already been broken by her grandfather's death.* He stamped on, fists knotting as they approached the camp. *Too much to think about all at once. Too cursed much.*

"What about us?" he asked, seeking a way out.

"Us?" She blinked curiously. "I'll always love you, Wind Runner."

The confusion took another twist. *Aspen said she'd step aside.*

"And this Earth man?"

She cocked her head, looking puzzled. "He's the Keeper of the Wolf Bundle. He's my husband."

"Wait." He gestured his frustration. "You just said you'd always love me."

"I will."

"But this Still Water is your husband?"

She nodded. "Of course."

Through gritted teeth, he growled, "Let's get one thing straight. I don't intend on sharing you. I don't know what kind of spell he's cast on you, but I'll break it. *He* won't live in *our* lodge. In fact, he'd better—"

She placed a hand on his arm. "I can't love you that way."

"White Ash"—he lifted his arms helplessly—"I don't understand. What are you talking about?"

"You're bound up in illusion, Wind Runner." She frowned. "But that's to be expected. The way has to be Dreamed for the Sun People."

People crowded the edge of the camp as they approached through the waist-high sage.

Aspen stepped out in front of the gathering, the sun gleaming in her long hair and glinting from the bone beads tied to the fringes of her hem. She stood numbly, inspecting White Ash and Still Water before searching Wind Runner's face, grief in her bright eyes. Behind her the people whispered, gasped words of witchery and spells and Spirit animals rife in the air.

"Wind Runner?" Aspen's worried voice twisted his soul. He halted before her, a painful tearing in his heart. She clasped his hands to her breast. "What is it? Who are these people?"

Voice faltering, Wind Runner told her, "This is White Ash."

Aspen's eyes went wide as she searched his, seeking some reassurance. Wind Runner's soul had turned to wood, unfeeling, senseless. As he watched helplessly, wretched understanding grew in her. Her eyes glazed as she stared into his and dropped his hands.

Then Aspen turned to White Ash, composure cracking.

"Welcome to the Black Point." With those words she turned quickly and shouldered her way through the gaping people.

Wind Runner closed his eyes.

Sage Ghost broke from the crowd and took a cautious step, arms half raised. "White Ash?"

"Hello, Father." She ran forward and hugged him. "I've missed you so much."

Wind Runner braced his feet against the churning sickness in his gut. What had happened to his life? Aspen's tortured look had seared something in his soul. The day seemed to have lost its color.

Black Moon's voice rose above the babble. "You are the woman who calls the animals?"

Through stumbling confusion, Wind Runner watched White Ash pull free of Sage Ghost's embrace and stride to stand before the clan leader.

"Yes, I call the animals. You are Black Moon? I am White Ash, of the White Clay." She pointed a finger at Sage Ghost. "This man is my father. My husband and I would claim a place among your clan."

Black Moon shook his head slowly. "This man, Sage Ghost, is White Clay. He is not of our clan."

She turned, and Wind Runner opened his mouth, shaking his head. *Not that! She couldn't! Not after everything I've . . .*

White Ash's words hammered at him: "Then my husband and I would place our claim because this man, Wind Runner, is my cousin. He has told me he is Black Point."

"No," Wind Runner whispered, staggering forward. "What are you *doing*? You know why I went to the Black Point!" He choked on the words and reached out with imploring hands.

"Is she your cousin?" Black Moon asked. "If she is Sage Ghost's daughter, and he is your uncle, then she must be."

"White Ash!" Wind Runner pleaded. *"Why are you doing this?"*

She reached up and ran warm fingers down the side of his face. "Because I must Dream, Wind Runner. Otherwise, the Spiral will change. Brave Man will win if I don't face him."

His jaw quivered under her touch.

"Do you deny her?" Black Moon asked.

Wind Runner's thoughts remained blank. In the silence, Sage Ghost spoke up: "Black Moon? Would the clan listen to Sage Ghost's advice?"

Black Moon nodded. "You always have a voice among us."

Sage Ghost propped his hands on his hips and lifted his chin. "I look at White Ash—and see a woman I almost don't know. Years ago, Power led me to steal White Ash from the Earth People. I've seen the look of Power before. It's in her eyes. She talks of a Dream. Only this morning we placed our Soul Flier's body in a high place and Sang his soul up into the sky for Thunderbird."

Sage Ghost gave the surrounding people thoughtful study. "I don't know the ways of Power—but a Soul Flier was taken from us. Now another has arrived. We've all heard the warriors. Heard Snail Shell, whom we trust. White Ash and this man of hers called the animals. Only when the warriors arrived did the animals flee. Perhaps her request should be granted by the Black Point." Sage Ghost gave Wind Runner an apologetic look and added, "I have spoken."

"Wind Runner?" Black Moon asked.

Wind Runner licked his dry lips, struggling to know what was right. He turned to White Ash, probing her shining eyes. "You don't want to be . . . my wife?"

She placed gentle hands on his shoulders. "Wind Runner, I can't. I must Dream. Otherwise, all is lost."

His soul shrieked as he mumbled, "She is my cousin." He forced his way through the crowding people, heedless of their stares. In dumb misery, he stalked from the camp.

Still Water watched the anguish in Wind Runner's face, understanding the decision that had been made. Instead of the relief he'd expected, the man's hurt pained him.

For White Ash, Wind Runner had left the White Clay. Now all that he'd accomplished for her had come tumbling down around him.

White Ash continued to speak in the Sun People's tongue.

Still Water watched the anxiety rising in the people's faces. And who was that burly warrior with the five circles tattooed on his forehead? White Ash had hugged him most familiarly.

"Think we ought to run for it?" he asked Trouble. The dog watched the circling camp dogs with wary interest, his back fur up. A low growl rumbled in his throat. "You said it."

People began to break away and filter back into the camp. Still Water stuck close to White Ash, asking, "What's happening?" But White Ash talked earnestly with the big man who seemed to be the leader.

"Council," the muscular warrior with tattooed circles on his forehead said. The man looked Still Water up and down and added, "White Ash said *you* are her *husband*?"

Still Water experienced a slimy sensation in the pit of his stomach as he looked into those hard eyes. Who was this powerful warrior? With his broad shoulders, he looked like he could turn a mountain upside down.

Then the man's meaning sank in: White Ash had called him her *husband*! Still Water cocked his head. Somehow, the thought just hadn't crossed his mind. It comforted him to say, "She is my wife."

The burly warrior inspected him as if he were a mold-green buffalo quarter before asking in a heavily accented voice, "What does she see in a man as ugly as you? You have only one arm."

Still Water straightened proudly. What cursed business was it of his? "I am the Keeper of the Wolf Bundle. And I am the protector of the Dreamer." On inspiration, Still Water added, "If you have other questions, I suggest you ask them of Power."

The warrior's hard eyes narrowed to slits. "I do not question Power." He spun and followed the others toward a large lodge. The skirts had been rolled up to admit the breeze. In the center of the camp, Greasewood camp's earth lodges looked orphaned and alone.

Still Water trotted after and asked the warrior, "Where did you learn the tongue of the People? You speak well."

The muscular warrior laughed, the sound anything but reassuring. "You wonder why a man would ask what White Ash sees in you? It's my right, Earth man. I learned Earth People talk from her. She's my daughter."

Still Water stopped and stared. "Sage Ghost?"

The warrior crossed his arms, muscles bulging. He studied Still Water through glinting eyes. "I am Sage Ghost."

"When we have time, I would like to talk to you. White Ash has told me many wonderful stories of you and Bright Moon."

Some of Sage Ghost's hostility ebbed. He blinked and lowered his eyes. "Perhaps later, around the dinner fire."

"Still Water?" White Ash called. "Come, sit with me."

He nodded respectfully to Sage Ghost and went forward.

"Why have you come here?" Black Moon asked as the last of the eight leaders seated themselves inside the lodge. The entire clan thronged around outside, crowding against the lodge poles as they strained to hear every word. Despite the heat of the midday sun, people pressed close, some with squares of leather over their heads for sunshades.

White Ash looked around the lodge. The hides had been smoked to a deep brown. Sleeping robes lay on the south side, next to a series of cooking paunches and stone tools. Under the rolled-up skirts she could see more people trotting up and crowding behind the other spectators, eager to listen. Even the burning air had gone silent.

White Ash sat cross-legged, back straight, hands folded. Still Water sat beside her, his dark eyes wide and wary. The pack with the Wolf Bundle rested in his lap. She said, "I have come to Dream the new way."

Black Moon tilted his head. "New way? We don't need a *new* way."

White Ash's forehead lined. "You just don't understand what's happening. Everything has come apart. The Sun People have changed the Spiral."

"And what is this Spiral?" Black Moon looked up at his wife, Makes Room. The woman shrugged.

"Life. All that is—and is not," White Ash replied.

Black Moon shifted nervously. "Your soul flies to the Camp of the Dead? You can do that? Call Thunderbird?"

The sensation of flight lingered at the edge of her memory. "I have flown as one with Thunderbird. Thunderbird is First Man—and the Wolf Dreamer. That is what I have come to teach you. The woman who was White Ash died in the Gray Deer River. This man, Still Water, pulled me out of the icy water. Together, we went to retrieve the Wolf Bundle. Still Water faced the Broken Stones' Soul Flier—Brave Man—and we escaped. High in the Sideways Mountains, the Earth People's Healer, Singing Stones, taught me how to Dream. The Wolf Bundle showed me the way to the One. It is with the Dream that I must face Brave Man when he comes here."

"Broken Stones are coming here?" Black Moon asked. He shot a look at Snail Shell. The warrior shook his head fearfully.

"They come," she said. "Two days from now they will be here." She lifted both hands and added, "If I don't defeat Brave Man, the Dream of First Man dies. Harmony will cease. The Black Point will be destroyed. Brave Man will find the Wolf Bundle and change the Spiral. The animals will be caged, the land will be butchered . . . I must Dream the new way."

Black Moon leaned forward, his jaw clenched. "How many are coming?"

"All of their clan."

A murmur of voices broke out.

"We can't get our warriors back here by then!" Snail Shell slammed a fist into the dirt floor. "It will take a day to climb Green Mountain! And how long for the parties to—"

"Warriors will *not* solve this." White Ash could feel the Power of the Wolf Bundle where it lay in the pack cradled tightly against Still Water's stomach. "This is a matter for Dreamers. For Brave Man and me. We must Dream the future."

People shifted uneasily.

"You will face this Soul Flier alone?" Black Moon traced circles in the dust with his fist.

"Still Water and I will face him together."

"Is Still Water a warrior?" Sage Ghost questioned disbelievingly.

White Ash turned to look at her father, who squatted behind her. "He is the strongest man Power could find. The Wolf Bundle called him, tested him, and Still Water won the honor to become the Keeper of the Bundle." She laid a warm hand on Still Water's knee.

Her husband gave her a reassuring glance, although he was lost in the incomprehensible babble of Sun talk.

"And what is this Wolf Bundle? Why have I never heard of it?" Black Moon asked.

"It was the Power of the Wolf People, before Brave Man stole it." To Still Water, she said, "Our Dream begins. They would know the Power of the Wolf Bundle."

Still Water's grip tightened on the pack. He searched her eyes and wiped his hand on his pant leg to clean it before he undid the thongs. He closed his eyes, reaching inside reverently. Hostile whispers broke out among the Black Point.

White Ash took a deep breath as the Power of the Wolf Bundle flowed through the air. She could trace the path of it up Still Water's arm, feel it as it expanded his soul.

Still Water lifted the Wolf Bundle from the pack. The council lodge went silent.

Power sought White Ash's soul, and she blocked it, fearing what had happened to Singing Stones. She tried to drown herself in the world, taking a deep breath of the hot, sage-scented air. With all her will, she struggled. Sweat beaded on her brow; she clamped her teeth until her jaw ached. *Too close! I'm too close!*

Still Water spoke softly, raising the Bundle to the cloudless sky: "Wolf Bundle, now is the time for you to use your Power. I flew on the wings of Thunderbird. Tell Thunderbird to send a sign . . . a sign that First Man and Thunderbird are one."

Thunder cracked in the distance and echoed across the still land.

Gasps and shouts broke out in the assembly, people whirling to stare at the clear, pale-blue sky. A few ran out across the desert, going to high points to search the heavens.

"He called Thunderbird," Sage Ghost translated. "That's what he said in the Earth People tongue!"

White Ash sighed with relief as Still Water replaced the Bundle in the pack. She slumped, sweat running down her face. Fragments of the One whirled within her, *calling to her, extending fiery, golden hands . . .*

Still Water's fingers tightened over hers. "Are you all right? What happened?"

She swallowed hard and grinned weakly at him. "The Wolf Bundle calls. It would fill me with its Power and the craving for the One. Next time I'll sit farther from you."

Outside, a withered old woman lifted her voice. "Thunder! Did you hear it? And not a cloud in the sky."

Apprehension grew in Black Moon's eyes. "How do we know that you haven't come to destroy us? Perhaps this Power you bring is evil. You come with an Earth man, an enemy of the Black Point. You yourself came from the Earth People."

She gave him a serene smile. "If I had wanted the Black Point dead, I would have given myself to Brave Man long ago—and today the Black Point would be as much a memory as the White Clay."

"I only have your word for it." Black Moon sighed. "I would rather have Hot Fat's."

"I have heard of him. He's a good man. I would welcome his wisdom."

A strained silence fell on the camp.

"He's dead," Sage Ghost told her. "Two days ago he was murdered."

Her vision blurred for an instant as she raised a hand to her throat and gasped.

"What's wrong?" Still Water asked.

She forced her voice to remain steady. "Someone murdered their Soul Flier."

Still Water's spine prickled. The people outside the lodge had gone silent. "Murder? Singing Stones warned us. Someone's killing the Dreamers. Some evil Power we don't understand? Or is it a person—some witch we haven't discovered yet?"

White Ash felt herself go pale. "You've brought me this far. I know you, you'll keep me safe."

Still Water put a comforting hand on her forearm and squeezed.

Sage Ghost translated their conversation into Sun talk as they spoke. He scrutinized Still Water with a curious mixture of disbelief and unease. His brows knit in that old expression White Ash knew so well—the one he adopted when presented with a problem he didn't really want to find the answer for.

She turned her attention back to Black Moon. "Are we welcome in your clan?"

Black Moon looked around, reading the faces. "I think we would rather that you had never come among us. But you are here. If your prophecy of the Broken Stones is correct, then they have eluded, or killed, my scouts to the north. If there is to be a battle between Dreamers, I would wish that it happened somewhere far from the Black Point." He worked his lips nervously. "I would also hear the counsel of Wind Runner and Aspen before I offer my opinion. This should not be decided in haste."

White Ash studied Black Moon, aware that the clan leader fidgeted under her knowing glance. "The Black Point are lucky to have a leader of your wisdom. Still Water and I will rest. Tomorrow we must prepare. Your warriors will find the Broken Stones coming through the gap in Green Mountain tomorrow night. The night after that, Still Water and I will face Brave Man."

Black Moon didn't look reassured. Peering inside herself, White Ash found her own fear—one as desperate as Black Moon's.

Wind Runner sat on the crest of a dune west of the camp, pouring sand from one hand to the other. The brush-covered hills gleamed with a lavender sheen in the fires of sunset. The dune field stretched as far as the eye could see. Who would have thought country like this would be so rich in foods? The evening breeze massaged his face. To his right, Green Mountain caught the slanting light, shimmering and golden. Before him, in the distance, irregular sandstone-capped buttes cast soft shadows over the land. The air smelled sweet here, laden with the odors of sage and greasewood, hopsage and buckwheat. Rabbitbrush had turned a bright green; its deep-yellow flowers would bloom soon. The spikes on the sagebrush rose above the aqua leaves and shivered in the breeze as they prepared to cast their pollen to the wind.

Below him, in the lee of the dune, the leaves on the giant wild rye rasped against each other. White patches of hard clay lay cracked and dry where water had stood at the end of the spring melt. Moisture remained but a memory—vanished like his hopes for White Ash.

Who was this woman who walked out of the desert? The penetrating look that filled her eyes, where had it come from? Who was the homely one-armed man she called husband? What gave him his hold over her?

He shook his head. *And now I've lost her.* I *agreed to be her cousin once again.* He let the sand trickle through his fingers the way hope trickled from his soul.

Light steps swished in the sand behind him. He knew those steps; for the past few weeks he'd even heard them in his dreams. He couldn't bring himself to look up.

"Wind Runner?"

He stared vacantly at the sand between his feet. His fingers had traced angry lines through it.

She sat down next to him, silent, waiting.

At last he snorted in self-derision. "I feel like a fool."

"I'm sorry. I know how your soul longed for her."

He made himself meet her worried gaze. Love and sorrow reflected in Aspen's eyes, bruised by his distress. "It's my fault." The sun glowed red-gold above the dark-indigo shapes of the buttes. "I should have listened to my soul that night at the White Clay camp. I searched, and all I found was emptiness. It was the Power speaking within me—and I ignored it. Today a stranger returned to my life."

"People change. Especially when Power touches them."

He ground his teeth. "It's that Earth man. He has a hold on her. Maybe if I kill him—"

"I don't think so."

He glanced at her, skepticism possessing him.

Aspen exhaled nervously. "I slipped around behind Black Moon's lodge to listen to the council. White Ash speaks with her own Power, not Still Water's. Though he has a Power of his own. You heard the thunder? That was his doing. He called it with the Bundle he carries. I think . . ."

"Go on."

"I think both of them have Powers unlike anything we've ever seen."

He winced. "I still love her. I'd give anything to turn her back."

"Wind Runner"—she shook her head—"I don't think you can. Even if you killed her husband, little would change. She doesn't belong to him. She belongs to Power. You can feel it when you hear her talk." She hesitated. "And if she's right, nothing matters but Power—not your love for her, not her husband. Nothing but the battle ahead."

He frowned. "What are you talking about?"

"The day after tomorrow She says she must face the Soul Flier of the Broken Stones. She says he's the real danger. He's bringing a new Dream that may destroy the Black Point—may change something she calls the Spiral. The way she spoke sent fear through me. She says if she doesn't stop this Soul Flier, this Brave Man . . . What's the matter?"

"I know Brave Man." His soul chilled. "If he's really become a Dreamer, Thunderbird help us all."

She rubbed a fidgety hand along her shin while the breeze flipped long strands of hair over her shoulders in raven waves. "What about you and me? What about now? Do you want me to move back into my own . . ." She closed her eyes against her pain.

Wind Runner took her in his arms. Such a beautiful woman. So fragile now, with the death of her grandfather still an unhealed wound in her soul. "I didn't mean for any of this to happen. I wouldn't have hurt you—"

"I know. I meant it when I said the most important thing for me was that you find your happiness. I'll leave. You mustn't worry about that."

A moment of twisting doubt ate at him. What should he

tell her? Could he live without those long nights of shared thoughts? He took a deep breath, trying to decide.

She loosened herself from his grip and stood, brushing the sand from her dress. "Let me know your decision. Listen to your heart—as well as to your soul. Choose your happiness, Wind Runner. You owe me nothing. What has happened between us is no thong to bind you. We lived by the day, and I accepted that. Be honest with yourself."

She turned then, walking away through the sagebrush, her back straight, her step proud.

Wind Runner clamped his eyes shut, as if by doing so he could squeeze the indecision from his soul. Dropping his head, he asked himself, *What if I can change White Ash? Bring her back? She said she still loves me.*

Still Water and White Ash wound their way through Greasewood camp on Sage Ghost's heels. The conical lodges of the Sun People rose like a forest of spears on all sides of the familiar earthen lodges of the Earth People. How many Black Point were there? Still Water couldn't help but count the pairs of eyes that followed them. Talk stopped as they approached, expressionless women raising sloe eyes to stare. Even the dogs watched, ears up, heads cocked. Children gawked from the shelter of their mothers' dress hems or from behind the curve of a lodge, eyes big, fingers in their mouths.

Would the walk to Sage Ghost's lodge never end? Still Water's skin began to itch. Hostility and unease crackled in the air.

Well, I don't blame them. How would I feel if two Dreamers walked into camp one day and said they were planning on fighting a battle with evil for the future of the world? I doubt I'd welcome them with open arms.

As he passed, he heard women speaking in the tongue of the Earth People. At least he could find others to talk to here besides White Ash and Sage Ghost.

And what was Wind Runner going to do? Still Water

flinched at the recollection of the misery he'd seen in the man's eyes.

He took a deep breath to settle his worry and stared up at the indigo evening sky. The sun glowed like a bloody red orb to the west. The gentle smells of camp, of food cooking, of pungent sagebrush smoke, leather and humans, hung in his nose. Large drying racks bent under the weight of plants. Hide sacks full of ricegrass seed waited next to Earth women, who parched the seeds on sandstone slabs that rested on roasting fires.

And he'd discovered the secret of the extra caches at Round Rock. The Black Point kept the women from the camps they took. Their labor filled the caches for the coming winter. That's why the lodges had been sealed against rodents. The Black Point planned to have enough stores to feed everyone through the cold moons.

They stopped at last before a buff-colored hide lodge decorated with five black circles painted on the flaps at the top. A half-dozen people sat outside in the shade. Sage Ghost lifted a hand and called out to one of the women—a captive. The woman rose and wiped grass-seed flour from a mano as she came toward them. Sage Ghost's lodge stood a little taller than a man; it rose like a cone, supported by soot-grimed lodge poles. The skirts had been rolled up here, too, and tied with thongs.

White Ash and Sage Ghost ducked into the shaded interior as Still Water unslung his pack. He bent to enter and heard someone call from behind. "Bad Belly?"

He straightened slowly, refusing to believe his ears. *Bitterbrush?*

He spun around. His eyes didn't deceive him. With a cry, he hugged his sister close, chuckling, almost giddy with happiness. He pushed her back, inspecting her, noting the lines that had deepened around her eyes. Otherwise, she looked the same, as beautiful as ever.

"How did you get here?" he asked.

She nodded her head toward the lodge. "Sage Ghost took me." Her eyes dropped. "Tuber is here—out hunting somewhere probably. He'll be glad to see you."

"And the others?"

She shook her head. "Only the children and Pretty Woman. Limbercone, Phloxseed . . . they were too old. Past childbearing years. The men, of course, they killed first thing." She glanced up at him, eyes pained. "I'm not sure who survived. I didn't go back to see the bodies. I didn't want to."

He nodded, sadness returning to haunt him. "I found Grandmother's body back of Round Rock. I Sang for her. Hopefully, her soul will rest easy now."

"Still Water?" White Ash called.

"Is *she* the Dreamer?" Bitterbrush asked, a nervous hand grabbing his arm.

He nodded. "Come, meet her."

Bitterbrush swallowed with difficulty, reluctance in her expression.

"Come on." Still Water pulled her forward, ducking into the lodge.

Sage Ghost cocked his head as they entered. "This is Bitterbrush. She is my woman."

White Ash nodded and smiled. "I am pleased that my father has such a beautiful woman to keep him happy."

Sage Ghost patted the robes beside him and Bitterbrush dutifully seated herself. She looked ready to bolt and shot a panicked glance at Still Water.

Still Water kept his pack beside him as he sat down by White Ash. He defiantly returned Sage Ghost's interrogating gaze. Bitterbrush stared at White Ash, then at Still Water, her expression reflecting utter chaos. White Ash, in turn, studied something that only she could see beyond the smoke hole.

Sage Ghost tilted his head questioningly. "Bitterbrush, do you know this man?"

Bitterbrush started to respond, but Still Water interrupted. "Sage Ghost, you and I have a lot more in common than it seems. You wonder about me. I wonder about you. Perhaps you will answer my question. What does my sister see in you?"

Sage Ghost's eyes tightened. He studied White Ash and

Bitterbrush. "You chose my daughter . . . I chose your sister. Power has been at work again. I don't pretend to understand it. But perhaps you are a worthy husband for White Ash."

Bitterbrush shook her head as though she hadn't heard right. "Husband?" she asked incredulously. "White Ash married *you*? Bad Belly, who gave you permission to marry anyone?"

He lifted his brows as the realization sank in that no one had given him permission—at least not in the way of the Earth People. But Larkspur was dead. So were all the rest. All but . . .

"Ah, I understand," he said. "I suppose you had better give me permission, sister . . ." His grip tightened on the pack that held the Wolf Bundle, and a warm glow filled his breast. ". . . because my wife is White Ash, and I am the Keeper of the Wolf Bundle."

Bitterbrush started at the confident tone in his voice, but before she could speak, White Ash turned Dream-rich eyes on her. Bitterbrush wilted as White Ash said, "Still Water and I will Dream the new way. He's the only one Power found worthy."

Bitterbrush's mouth twisted sourly, and she shook her head. "This is foolishness! Bad Belly? The Keeper of the Wolf Bundle? You're out of your mind! Bad Belly couldn't keep a toad in a sack! If he's stolen the Wolf Bundle, the Wolf People are going to be flocking down here. We have to give it back, apologize for whatever trouble Bad Belly's started. Sage Ghost, he's my problem. I'll take responsibility for him. Try to keep him out of trouble, although First Man knows, that's a thankless—"

"Sister," Still Water interrupted, "the Wolf People are gone. Crushed by the Broken Stones. If there's any hope for the Wolf People, it is the Trader, Left Hand. He is leading those who remain eastward, across the plains. First Man gave them a chance to find the Father Water—the big river to the east. There are no more Wolf People here."

Bitterbrush leaned forward, pointing an angry finger at him. "Is this another of your stories? I warn you, I'm *not* having any of it. I thank First Man you're back, and alive.

I'll be able to keep an eye on you again. But I don't want—"

Sage Ghost gripped her arm to silence her and leveled his flintlike gaze on his daughter. White Ash remained silent, Dreamy eyes still on the little patch of sky visible through the smoke hole.

Still Water laughed and shook his head. "Sister, the old ways are gone. Power has shifted. We must seek—"

"—to save ourselves," White Ash said urgently as she lowered her gaze to Sage Ghost. "Brave Man leads the Broken Stones here. He seeks me and the Power I control. The voices in his head have told him he must possess me or he will never be able to Dream the One fully."

Sage Ghost steepled his fingers and thought for a moment before he asked, "Can you defeat him?"

A weary smile came to her lips. "I'm not sure. But I know that only Still Water and I can Dream against him—and win."

In the late-evening light, Still Water walked out to stare up at the stars. Bitterbrush followed to stand beside him. She crossed her arms, scuffing the dirt with her toe. "What's happened to you, Bad Belly? It's as if I don't know who you've become."

Fragments of memories swirled in his soul. He'd come a long way from Round Rock. Until now he hadn't realized the extent of the change. "The Bad Belly you knew is still in here, sister. But he's changed. Dreaming does that."

"And you really are a Healer?"

"A Healer? No. I am the Keeper of the Wolf Bundle. Its Power runs through me. I—"

"Why you? Why would Power choose someone like you?" Disdain tinged her voice.

Still Water inhaled the night-scented desert wind and gazed out to where the glow of the rising moon silvered the horizon. "I think it chose me because I can keep the Power just close enough so White Ash can use it, but far enough away that she doesn't get sucked in."

Bitterbrush blew out a long breath. "Well, I hope you do better than Black Hand did."

"Black Hand?"

She rubbed her eyes and shifted nervously. "I married him just before the Gathering. It seemed like the thing to do, and Grandmother wanted it. Status for Round Rock . . . for me. Three Forks accused him of witching. When I look back now, it seems like such a pitiful thing. Our marriage was supposed to stop the rumors."

"Supposed to?" He waved at a night insect that hovered around his face. "The Black Point killed him?"

He could feel her stare. "No. Someone—maybe the real witch—murdered him at the Gathering. Bashed his head in."

"Murder? *At the Gathering?*"

Her shoulders sagged. "I don't know why . . . or who. Some evil is loose, Bad Belly. People fled in the night, tainted by the abomination. Maybe it broke the Power of the Earth People and led to the coming of the Black Point. I don't know. But I haven't felt safe since."

Still Water swallowed hard. White Ash still sat in the lodge talking to Sage Ghost. *Someone is killing all the Dreamers.*

Almost without his conscious volition, his feet took him back to her side.

Chapter 29 🖼

White Ash stepped out into the cool evening. In the distance, a pack of wolves howled to greet the night. She took a deep breath of the dry air and savored the pungency of the desert. Behind her, the sounds of camp—dogs whining, a baby crying, carefree voices, the clacking of manos on metates—soothed her. How long had it been since she'd heard laughter? How long since gentle voices murmured in the night?

Her arrival with Still Water had changed the Black Point. *Was I too young to realize that I changed the White Clay, too*? She thought back to the night Sage Ghost had brought her to the White Clay camp on the Bug River. She'd been too frightened to realize much of anything except her fear. And then she hadn't come as a Dreamer with a prophecy of doom.

In her soul she could feel the blackness to the north. Two nights hence, she would face Brave Man. A sickening dread—mixed with the pleasure of being back in a camp of the Sun People—tainted the joy of seeing Sage Ghost, of finding Wind Runner alive. Still Water seemed hesitantly happy to be with his sister again. Did Power play some subtle trick on them? Give them a last glimpse of the people they would be fighting for?

Or had Power done this to give her another grip on this world of illusion, another reason to come back to it besides her love for Still Water? She filled her lungs, willing peace into her soul.

Gingerly she tested the boundary of the One, seeking to keep the subtle feathery touch at a distance. Even as she stood, she could feel the Wolf Bundle's seeking Power pulling at her. *And if I reach out, touch it, will I be lost?* Singing Stones' dying expression haunted her.

I wish you had found someone stronger, Wolf Dreamer. Wasn't there a Fire Dancer out there somewhere? She closed her eyes. Failure loomed so close—just over the northern horizon.

"White Ash?" a woman asked in the tongue of the Earth People.

She turned. "Yes?"

The woman walked closer—hesitant and insecure, like a whipped puppy. "Are you White Ash from Three Forks?"

White Ash sighed wearily. "That was a long time ago. I was her . . . once."

The woman exhaled with desperate relief, reaching out to her with trembling hands. "I am Basket. Your cousin. Thank the kind Spirits I've found you." The woman rushed forward and took White Ash's hand. "After all these years, there's hope yet."

White Ash squinted to study her features in the light of the fires. Yes, she remembered. "You've aged."

"So have you," Basket cried. "Look at you! A woman. And so beautiful. Oh, thank the Spirits, I've found you! Speak for me, White Ash. Plead for me. You're my cousin. Save me!"

"Save you? From what?"

Basket exploded in a sigh, running a hand through her tangled hair. "Terrible things have happened. An evil is loose on the land. Witching rotted our people. Green Fire warned— yes, she warned—but no one listened. Then your mother, she argued that the danger lurked within. Green Fire was witched . . . witched by the evil one. Then . . . then my baby. Did you see it? That terrible fire that burned the stars. Black Hand did it. We know that now. Then he tried to trick us at the Gathering, made a mockery of our clan. We—"

"That is past," White Ash told her. "A new way is here now."

"Sun People?" Basket took a step closer, hands clasped before her. "They're . . . part of the evil."

"Evil? No. They're not evil. Why do you think that?"

Basket's gaze darted around fearfully. "Evil fills them. They killed Owlclover, Starwort, and my father, Shadblow. I was taken, forced by that despicable Snail Shell!"

"That's not witchery. It's the way of desperate people."

Basket's suspicious eyes reflected the flickering fire. "They call on evil Powers—like this bird they say makes thunder. They had an old man who claimed to talk to the Spirits of the dead. He tried to work his evil on the children. On the *children*! Oh, he was cunning, laughing with them, charming them the way a snake does a bird, as he told them stories. All the while, his evil wrapped around them, soaking into their souls." She leaned close, frightened. "White Ash, *they worship the Camp of the Dead*! And not only that, but—"

White Ash laid her hands on Basket's shoulders, surprised by the woman's trembling. "Basket, the old ways are gone. We must all learn a new way. The Spiral has shifted. A new Power has come."

Basket hissed, "But the stories have been running among the captives all day, saying that a strange and Powerful woman has come to do something with Power. When I heard that it was you, my soul leaped. Maybe you could free us, let us go back. You're the rightful leader of Three Forks! You could lead us in the fight to drive these Spirit-possessed Sun People from our lands.''

White Ash shook her head.

Basket's face pinched. "Things would be the way they were. We could Sing for the souls of our dead—replace them in the womb of the earth." Her eyes went glassy. "We could live like we always did.''

White Ash frowned. How could Basket think the world hadn't changed? Drive out the Sun People? White Ash took her cousin's hands, asking, "What happened to you?''

"Terrible," Basket cried. "I watched my husband murdered before my eyes. They wouldn't take your mother, Owlclover, or my mother, Starwort. Too old, they said.'' She wrung her hands, sniffling with tears. "Then this evil-possessed Snail Shell took me to his lodge. He . . . he . . .'' She shivered. "Too terrible. I cried, I pleaded, but he stripped me. Took me like a . . .'' She bit her hand.

"Sun People live differently than Earth People. Basket, go back to Snail Shell's lodge. I met him today. He seems like a brave and kind warrior.''

"What?" Basket's voice reflected horror.

"The world has changed," White Ash told her. "There is no going back. You must—''

"Don't you care that they murdered your mother?'' Basket backed a step, hands to her mouth. "And your clan? I'm your cousin. You can't . . .'' An eerie look came to her eyes. "You're one of them, aren't you? The rumors were true. That's why they never found your body. You've become one of them. I've blamed the wrong person. *You brought them here!''*

White Ash shook her head. "I've come to Dream the new way. The Spiral has . . .''

A choking sound issued from Basket's lungs. Then she turned and fled, dogs barking as she darted between the lodges.

"Who was that?'' Sage Ghost asked from the darkness behind her.

"Basket. My cousin from Three Forks," White Ash explained wearily.

"The crazy one," Sage Ghost observed. "She's like a rabid badger. She almost foamed at the mouth when Hot Fat came near. Tried to drive him away from the children, until the women got her under control."

White Ash rubbed the back of her neck, memories of the Three Forks camp haunting her. *Why can't I find it in my soul to mourn Owlclover's death? She was my mother. Wolf Dreamer, what have you done to me?*

Wind Runner picked his way around the sagebrush as he approached the camp. The dogs caught his scent and began barking and yipping. He shouted to silence them, and to alert any warrior to his identity. Sober, and with a sodden heart, he made his way past the lodges. People clustered around the flickering fires, conversing in low tones when they should have been rolled in their robes. Tension filled the air, dense, hanging like some sort of malevolent smoke.

He ducked into his lodge—and found the robes he'd shared with Aspen empty. Despair gnawed at his gut. He crouched in the darkness and ran gentle fingers over the bedding. The robes felt cold now; the warmth he and Aspen had shared beneath them had vanished like fog on a hot day. He leaned down and inhaled, filling his nostrils with Aspen's faint odor. He stood and rubbed his hands on his hunting shirt before slipping out into the night.

He found her seated at the fire before Black Moon's lodge. She nodded thoughtfully as she listened to the clan leader speak. Wind Runner stood quietly in the darkness, watching the way the fire lit the lines of her soft face. She moved with a gentle grace, fragile, yet so very strong.

He stepped into the red glow of the fire across from her and Black Moon. The pungent odor of sage smoke hung low about the fire pit. He squatted, elbows on his knees.

"You're back," Black Moon greeted, reservation in his tone. "We've needed to talk to you, to hear your advice."

Wind Runner stole a glance at Aspen. She stared at the fire, face expressionless. With a nervous hand, she twirled a sprig of sagebrush.

"What did White Ash tell you?" Wind Runner asked, stumbling over the name.

"That the Broken Stones will be here in two days. That she and this Earth man will face their Soul Flier. That she'll fight some sort of Power battle with him and Dream a new way for us."

Wind Runner struggled to find the calm clarity of thought he had always counted on.

Black Moon continued, "White Ash says that warriors won't make any difference, but she also says this Brave Man crushed the Wolf People and is leading the whole Broken Stones clan down on us. I am thinking the smart thing to do is to break camp. Flee to the south until we can recall our warriors."

Wind Runner frowned into the fire. "And what does White Ash say to that?"

Black Moon puffed out his cheeks. "I haven't told her yet."

"You sent out scouts?"

"First thing. None have come back yet."

"Maybe the Broken Stones aren't coming," Aspen suggested in a forced voice.

"Maybe." Black Moon glanced back and forth between them, sensing their unease with each other. "Wind Runner, you know this White Ash. I don't care what's between you, but I need to know: Is she here to destroy us? Is that her nature? Will she turn Power against us in this Dream she talks about? Has she come to wreak some kind of vengeance on us for what we've done to the Earth People?"

Wind Runner flipped his hands up. "I've known her for years. Ever since Sage Ghost stole her from the Earth People. Even then she had Dreams. Old Falcon watched her, respected her. Had she asked, I think he would have taught her the ways of Soul Flying, but her interests lay elsewhere. She didn't like the Dreams. They frightened her. But to answer your question, she never considered herself to be one of the Earth People. She was White Clay. She knew the stories of the clan better than any of the rest of us. She loved Bright Moon and Sage Ghost. No. I don't think she's here to harm us."

"And her Dream?" Black Moon asked.

"She wouldn't lie. If she says she Dreamed it, she did."

"And should we trust this one-armed man of hers?"

"I—I think we . . . I don't know. I can't tell you about him. He looks harmless."

"You weren't there when he called thunder out of a clear sky." Black Moon grimaced. "An Earth man used a Wolf People Bundle to call Thunderbird? That makes my soul shiver."

"Power is at work." Aspen jabbed her twig into the fire. "And we're in the middle of it."

Black Moon slapped at an insect and paused, as if choosing his words. "I don't care about Power unless it threatens my clan." Pointedly, he added, "I'm waiting for advice from those I trust."

Wind Runner nodded reluctantly. "Very well, these are my words, Black Moon. White Ash says that Brave Man is coming, that he's become a Soul Flier. I believe her. And I know Brave Man. A Black Point warrior sent him to the Camp of the Dead. Since that day, he's hated Black Point. He hears voices inside his head—and White Ash is right about one thing: He'll do everything in his Power to wipe out the Black Point . . . and he hates me, maybe more than he hates anything."

"Why? What did you do to him?"

Wind Runner lowered his gaze to the smoldering coals. "I kept him from stealing White Ash and carrying her off to the Broken Stones. I—I stopped him from raping her one day."

Black Moon thoughtfully smoothed his fingers over the dirt floor. "Everything comes back to White Ash."

"So it seems. Looking back, I wonder if she isn't the reason for everything that's happened." Wind Runner raised his eyebrows and sighed. "Power seems to surround her. I think that whatever she says, we should do."

"Do I hear your heart speaking?" Black Moon's glance pierced him.

Wind Runner shook his head. He felt so very weary. "No. You hear the best advice I can offer. Sage Ghost makes no secret of the fact that Power led him to steal her. For as long as I've known her, Power has protected her—even had me appear at the right moment to keep her from harm. I think that to thwart her is to bring trouble. Not from White Ash, but from the Power that guides her."

"I will take your words into consideration." Black Moon stood, staring up at the stars, worry sitting his shoulders like a cape. "And tomorrow we'll decide whether it's best to move camp."

Black Moon ducked into his lodge, leaving Wind Runner alone with Aspen. For long moments they sat in silence. Aspen refused to look at him, her attention fixed on the dancing flames.

Finally Wind Runner said, "Would you come back to my lodge? You look tired. Before we sleep, we could talk about the things we should do tomorrow."

Her eyes were like pools in the soft light. "I want to come back, but . . ."

He went to her and took her hand, feeling the chill in her flesh. "I told Black Moon the truth. White Ash has always belonged to Power. But it took me until today to see that."

"No doubts?"

He shook his head. "I've lived without her in my life. When I returned to camp, I stopped at our lodge. Seeing the empty robes, I realized what it would be like to live without you. Please . . . don't make me."

Aspen squeezed his hand tightly and tears glistened in her eyes. She got to her feet. Without a word, she slipped her arm around his waist and began slowly heading him back toward their lodge.

Still Water squinted at the young man who strode through the night toward Sage Ghost's lodge. Vague recognition dawned. Where had he seen that walk before? Where . . . "Tuber!" He stood, a sudden joy warming his soul.

"Bad Belly?" Tuber dropped the brace of rabbits he carried and lunged to hug his uncle until Still Water's ribs cracked. Where had the boy come by such strength? Still Water savored the feel of the young arms around him. His nephew—Warm Fire's son—lived! *Bless the One!*

"What are you doing here in a Black Point camp? They should have . . ." Tuber stumbled over the words. "I mean, *you're alive!*"

"At least until you snap my spine."

Trouble darted about and yipped, jumping up in the air to nip happily at Tuber's hunting shirt while his tail flailed the air.

"Quiet!" someone called. "People are trying to sleep!"

Still Water motioned Trouble to stop and took Tuber's hand. "How have you been? I hear Sage Ghost has taken you into his lodge. Your mother says he treats you like a son."

Tuber nodded. "He's good to me. So, you've seen Mother? Heard what happened?"

"We have talked. She says you're turning into a good hunter."

"No one moves as quietly as I do. Only Owl is as quiet on the hunt as I am," Tuber told him proudly. "And Sage Ghost has taught me things even Father didn't know. Like how to hide a trail, and how to use cover when you sneak. Sage Ghost took me out to kill my first antelope. I got him, too—a fat buck. And with just one cast. I'm learning to make dart points and how to lay an ambush."

Still Water smiled. "Come, let's talk before I take you in and introduce you to my wife."

Still Water settled on a parfleche while Tuber squatted on the ground.

"Wife? You?" Tuber asked in amazement. "One of the captive women?"

"No. She's Sun People."

"And she married you? What's wrong with her?"

Still Water sighed. "So, you're happy in the camp of the Black Point?"

Tuber hung his head. "I was pretty bad off when the Black Point wiped out the clan. I watched Grandmother get killed. White Feather smacked her in the head with a war club."

"I found her body. I Sang for her."

Tuber glanced out at the night, his gaze roaming the dunes. "I'm glad—but I don't miss her. You know what Grandmother was like. How she fooled with people's lives. Made them do what she wanted them to. Here, I'm free. I can hunt—and Sage Ghost, he's a lot like my father. Sometimes I think the Black Point are the best thing that could have happened to me."

"I hear you had Black Hand for a father for a little while."

Tuber's voice changed, strained. "I didn't like him. Not after what he did to Father. And then, one night, I followed him and Mother. Watched them couple—and I just couldn't stand it. The man who let my father die . . . took my mother! Grandmother made her marry him. I heard them talk about it. Black Hand was Grandmother's lover first, you know."

Still Water winced at the venomous anger. "I don't think Black Hand let Warm Fire die. I think he did all he could. Power sometimes—"

"Don't talk to me about Power!" Tuber spat into the night. "I've watched too many people die because Healers wouldn't save them!" A pause. "You heard about Lupine?"

Still Water nodded. "Yes. But that wasn't Power."

"Hot Fat didn't save her. I saw. He just shook his head and walked off."

Where had all the anger come from? Still Water tried to remember the Tuber he'd known before Warm Fire's death. Could this brooding young man be that same laughing, happy child? "We've talked enough about death. Tell me the new things, about your hunting."

"The world would be a better place without Healers and Soul Fliers. I don't trust them."

Still Water leaned back on his elbow and stretched his legs out across the warm sand. "Ah, but not all Power is bad. While I've been gone, I've seen. I've become the Keeper of the Wolf Bundle. So I'm tied up with Power, too."

He could feel Tuber's hard scrutiny. "The Wolf Bundle? What's that? If you're its Keeper, it must have all the Power of a rabbit pellet on dry sandstone."

"It might surprise you."

"And I might surprise it," Tuber grunted, shifting warily. "You really like Sage Ghost?"

Tuber's grin infected the darkness. "He's a *real* warrior. He's had a tough time—like me. His wife died last winter, the same time my father did. I don't care if he couples with Mother. He cares for her . . . which is more than Black Hand did. And he cried when Lupine was killed by . . . Well, when she died."

"Sage Ghost isn't sure he cares about me."

Tuber chuckled at that. "I suppose he wouldn't be. But he's a good man, Bad Belly. He's lost a lot in the last year, his wife, his people. And then his daughter vanished when the Wolf People killed the White Clay. He thinks she's dead and he still mourns her. Maybe that's why I like him so."

"I don't think he mourns his daughter anymore." Still Water smiled into the night.

"You don't know him. He's lost everything he loves. So now he loves us."

"His daughter is my—"

"To hear him talk," Tuber went on excitedly, "his daughter was the most beautiful woman who ever lived. Sage Ghost says Power gave her to him when his other daughters died. That she was special."

"She is. Everything Sage Ghost says is true."

Tuber cocked his head. "Is?"

"White Ash is my wife. That's how I came here—alive, as you noted. She's talking with Sage Ghost now, telling him of our adventures."

Tuber gaped. "*You?* White Ash is married to *you?*"

"It's a long story. I'll tell it to you one of these days."

Tuber's disbelief stretched his face out of shape. "What does she see in *you*?"

Blessed Creator, did it never end? "She says my soul is yellow and red. Maybe that's it."

"But how did you get here? How did you know where we'd be?"

"Power brought us. We've come to fight an evil Soul Flier. His name is Brave Man, and he's leading the Broken Stones here. He has to be stopped or his Power will change the world."

"Let me help you!"

Still Water shook his head. "Enough of the Round Rock are already gone. Not you, too. This is a thing for powerful Dreamers—not for young boys who believe themselves invincible."

Tuber fingered the war club that hung at his belt. "A Healer dies under the club as fast as any other man."

"Perhaps, but Brave Man is coming with all of his warriors. White Ash and I must meet him on a different ground than this one."

"As long as it's one less Spirit man, I'm all for it."

"And would you have wished that Singing Stones had never cured me when the rattlesnake bit my arm?"

"Your arm never healed," Tuber pointed out unpleasantly.

"But I lived."

"Uncle, you and I see the world differently. We always have."

Still Water slapped his knee with his good hand. "You surprise me, Tuber. I left a sulking boy—and I find a man."

Tuber lifted his war club, grasping it as if to reassure himself of the weapon's balance. "You know, you and Father were the only people I could ever talk to. You listened to me. The rest of Round Rock had no use for a worthless boy. After you left, I realized that. I want to thank you for taking the time."

Still Water's heart warmed. "I'll always listen. But don't remember our clan with such anger. There were many good people there, and hate isn't good for your soul."

"Oh?" Pensively Tuber studied the firelit camp. "They thought you were worthless, too. You can't deny that. I heard Grandmother talk about you—heard the scorn in her voice. I learned a lot of lessons from Grandmother. Now I have a new place, a new people, and one day they will know me as a great warrior."

Still Water gripped Tuber's shoulder. "That's the way. You'll do fine here."

Tuber stood. "I intend to. Meanwhile, I have to skin these rabbits, cool them out before the meat sours."

"Come on, I'll help. I can hold the head while you peel the hides off. It'll be like old times."

Tuber laughed. "No, uncle. Better than it used to be. I've learned to change things I don't like."

"All right. But first, come and meet my beautiful White Ash." As they walked, he asked, "You got the rabbits with your club?"

Tuber nodded. "I sneak close, then I throw. A twist and a half, and *smack*."

"You've become a very good hunter."

"Better than you can imagine, uncle. Rabbits are easy. They can't kill you if you make a mistake."

Still Water looked into the lodge and found it full of sleeping forms, but he didn't see White Ash. Their robes lay several paces behind the lodge. He backed out and let the flap fall down, then tiptoed around the stakes that pinned the lodge cover. He recognized the swell of White Ash's body lying in their robes. "Looks like she's asleep. Well, let's go skin rabbits. Then maybe we'll roast one over the fire, just so we can talk some more."

Brave Man sat on a rise that looked out to the south. He'd laid a deer hide over the cobbles and gravel that would have eaten uncomfortably into his flesh. Wind whispered in the pale leaves of the sage, and bird song filled the evening air. He could hear the prairie dogs yipping in the flats below. He took a deep breath, sucking the soul of the land into his lungs. He cleared his mind, seeking the voices within as he let his soul float.

Power. South. The final test is coming. Look inside.

What had touched him the night the one-armed man had stolen White Ash from him? What had caused the voices to deafen him? He'd felt another Power working with the Wolf Bundle. Would it try him again?

The voices hissed, *Seek inside. The way to Power lies there. Seek. The time is soon.*

Was that where the real Power lay? Had he fooled himself all these years—thinking that it came from a Spirit outside of himself? The Dreams and their revealing visions came during sleep, after all, when the soul was free and thoughts didn't compete for his attention.

Inside, the voices agreed.

No one would bother him this night. Pale Raven had talked to Flying Hawk, and a web of scouts had been sent out so no Black Point could sneak in. For once, he had his peace.

He hitched his leg into a comfortable position and exhaled slowly to allow the tensions to run out with his breath. He blanked his thoughts. Bit by bit, he let himself go, seeking the source of the Dreams.

He banished the sensations of his body. Memories tried to spring up in his mind.

I don't want memories. With all of his iron discipline, he ignored them. A touch of gray mist crept into his being. He surrendered more of himself. The mist grew, soothing. He began to fall into it . . . then pulled himself back.

He blinked, aware of the hard rock of the ridge top that bruised his flesh. The headache crashed down upon him, lancing knives into his skull.

"What was that?"

Power, the voices chortled. *You touched Power.*

He nodded slowly to himself. On the night the one-armed man had come to take White Ash, he had felt the same thing.

He closed his eyes again, blanking the pain of the headache with long practice. Bit by bit, he let himself go. If he

could catch hold of that Power, perhaps he could fight the
one-armed man and win White Ash back.

I will learn this. If it takes the rest of my life.

The voices in his head assured him, *No . . . soon. Seek.
Power will be yours soon.*

Chapter 30

Before the council began, Wind Runner glanced at White
Ash; desperation lurked behind her controlled expression. He
could see it in the set of her eyes, in the tension around her
mouth. Despite that, he couldn't help but marvel at her
beauty. The midday sun gleamed in her thick, raven hair. Her
thin antelope-hide dress clung to every curve, accenting the
swell of her breasts.

Her tension infected them all. The crippled Earth man sat
next to her, worry in his homely face. Across the council
circle, Black Moon looked nervous, as if he searched desperately for the right direction to lead his clan. The uneasy
warriors who sat around the circle fingered their darts. Hidden messages passed as they shot dark glances back and forth.

The sun-drenched camp waited in the background. A hot
breeze blew down from the west, and the sky burned brassy.

Wind Runner tightened his grip on Aspen's slim hand. Her
touch reassured him. He had made the right choice. He could
see that now. White Ash belonged to Power. She'd never
been his to begin with.

The rest of the Black Point were assembling amid a buzz
of whispering voices. Only the children raised their voices to
ask questions. Somewhere a dog growled, and a hollow
thump was followed by a yip.

When he saw that all had assembled, Black Moon asked,
"What is your wish, White Ash?"

White Ash spoke softly, eyes focused on a place only she

could see. "A runner will go to meet the Broken Stones. Unarmed, he will ask Brave Man to meet us at the foot of the mountains. Brave Man will demand that he be accompanied by five warriors. We will take five warriors. We will meet at dusk, arriving at his fire. There he and I will face each other for the future of the People."

"Who will be our runner?" Black Moon asked as he looked around the council. "Who will carry White Ash's message?"

The warriors glanced back and forth, fidgeting under Black Moon's questioning gaze.

"I will do this thing," Snail Shell said. He licked his lips. "I saw White Ash Dream the animals. I will accept the honor."

"And which five warriors will accompany White Ash to meet the Broken Stones?" Black Moon raised an eyebrow as he searched face after face.

"I will go with my daughter," Sage Ghost said. He squatted on his heels behind White Ash and the Earth man. "I've been part of the Power this long. I will see where it leads."

"I will go," Blue Wind told them. "I will show the Broken Stones the measure of Black Point courage."

Snail Shell spread his hands. "If I only have to deliver a message, I can tell the Broken Stones what White Ash says and then meet her party—provided someone will bring my weapons. It makes sense that way. If I don't find her first, she'll know something went wrong and have time to escape. Besides, I would see the end of this . . . and keep Blue Wind from slipping away like a coward at the last instant." He grinned at his friend. Blue Wind grinned back and continued pouring sand from one hand to the other.

A nervous chuckle ran through the warriors.

Wind Runner swallowed around the knot in his throat. "I also will go."

He felt Aspen's hand tense. Then she spoke up, "I, too, can cast a dart. I will be the fifth."

Black Moon grunted. "White Ash? What of the Black Point people? I want to take them away to a place where they won't be so close to Broken Stones' warriors."

She nodded. "Do as you wish, clan leader."

Snail Shell sighed and stood. He gave White Ash a thoughtful look. "I put my trust in your Power. If I don't come back, Sing extra loud for me. Thunderbird needs to know where to find my soul."

White Ash leveled her brown eyes on the warrior, and Wind Runner's hair prickled. She said, "Your courage will not be forgotten, Snail Shell. Not by the One—or by the people."

Snail Shell gave her a weak smile and left.

Black Moon stood, leaning his head back. "I wish you luck and Power, White Ash. The bravest of the Black Point go with you."

He walked through the council circle then, shouting, "Break camp! We go south!"

Wind Runner stared at the trampled ground as the others rose to their feet in a babble of voices. A gust of hot wind flapped Black Moon's lodge cover and swirled dust around the camp.

He raised his eyes to Aspen's. "Why?" he asked softly.

"Because I want to be there." She shot a glance at White Ash, who sat quietly with a vacant look on her face. "Perhaps I will understand better. Perhaps you will need me." She smiled. "And if it goes wrong, I won't lose another man I love. Perhaps Thunderbird will take us to the Camp of the Dead together."

He placed his hand on hers and rose to his feet, pulling Aspen up. As he turned to leave, he looked at White Ash. She sat like stone. Her features had turned ashen, as if she envisioned some terrifying future. Wind Runner's soul shivered.

Bitterbrush searched Bad Belly's eyes when he straightened up. He finished tying the robes onto his pack and set them against the side of Sage Ghost's lodge. Confusion reigned as the camp was dismantled. Bitterbrush placed hands against her temples and pressed, as if to restore order to her thoughts. "In another time, I would tell you to quit this foolishness and go gather firewood."

Still Water winked at her. "Tell me anyway. It might make me feel better."

Her gaze softened. "I think those days are over, Bad Belly. You're . . . different."

"You've always told me that."

The corners of her mouth twitched with irritation. The expression amused him. She raised her hands overhead and knotted them into fists. "Why do I try? You *always* make things more difficult than they need to be."

"Do I?" He stepped out of the way as several women hurried past with bulging parfleches.

"And you always have a question! It's enough to drive anyone with sense half mad. Honestly, I wonder how Power could pick someone like you. You must infuriate the Spirits no end."

He chuckled as two dogs harnessed in travois clattered past, two little boys yelling in hot pursuit. "Spirits don't care much about people. They have Spirit things to worry about. They have the Spiral—at least, I think they do. What would they care about—"

"Bad Belly?"

"Huh?"

She smiled and pulled him close to hug tightly. He stroked her hair and experienced a warmth he'd never felt for her before. Then she pushed him back for a final inspection—as if to memorize the way he looked.

White Ash emerged from the lodge and flashed Still Water a fleeting smile before thrusting a handful of jerked meat and some biscuit-root cakes into the bulging pack. Then she left on some errand.

Bitterbrush studied White Ash's departing back thoughtfully, and asked out of the corner of her mouth, "How long has she been pregnant?"

"How long has she . . . *What?*" Still Water stood open-mouthed. His gaze darted after White Ash.

"Of course. You didn't know?" Bitterbrush rolled her eyes, exasperated with him again. "She's sick in the morning, isn't she? Look at her. See the color? See how her weight lies on her body? She's missed her bleeding, hasn't she?"

Still Water gestured negation. "I—I thought it was the worry."

"And her bleeding?" Bitterbrush raised an eyebrow and crossed her arms.

"Well, I don't pay attention to . . ." How long *had* it been? He remembered her gathering and shredding bark on the way up into the Grass Meadow Mountains and complaining of cramps. But since then? Almost two moons had passed. "Oh, no," he whispered.

Bitterbrush shook her head and gave him a weary sigh. "I've borne enough to know. And Sage Ghost has planted himself again. I wouldn't have seen her throwing up if I hadn't been out there myself." She shook her head. "And you're going to fight against an evil Dreamer? A cripple and a pregnant woman?" She glanced over at Sage Ghost, talking earnestly with Tuber. "I just wish you'd left my husband out of it."

Still Water continued to stare after White Ash, unable to find words.

"Close your mouth," Bitterbrush ordered. "You'll have flies diving in."

Still Water shook his head. *Pregnant? And she has to Dream against Brave Man Tomorrow?* He cast his eyes imploringly at the sky. *Did you know about this, Wolf Dreamer? Is this part of some Spirit plan?*

White Ash led the group through the chaos of camp-breaking, and her soul felt as though it were weighted with rock. About her, lodges fell as people hurriedly pulled out the poles. Dogs yipped, accompanied by curses and shouts, and parfleches and packs were strapped onto travois. Children wailed and women called orders. Dust rose under the rapid feet scurrying from one task to the next.

Still Water walked by her side, a stricken expression on his face. She could feel his confusion and anxiety. Sage Ghost walked on the other side, his every movement powered by a grim determination. Behind her, Wind Runner and his woman matched step, side by side. She caught hints of Wind Runner and Aspen's concern as they watched the Black Point prepare to flee. Blue Wind brought up the rear, head high, darts gleaming in the sun.

Black Moon stopped his packing as they passed. He nodded to White Ash, the gesture weakened by the turbulence in his soul. She nodded back.

At the edge of the camp, a lodge lay spread on the ground while a woman ordered a laboring captive: Basket. White Ash glanced at her as they passed. Basket's face was filled with venomous hatred—enough to send a jolt through White Ash.

"Evil witch," her cousin hissed.

Still Water missed a step as he glared over his shoulder. "Who was that? What did she say?"

White Ash shrugged it away, muttering, "Nothing. Once she was my cousin. She's Three Forks. Her name is Basket."

Still Water nodded. "Little Toe's sister. I know her now. And she called you a witch?"

"It's nothing. We have more important things to worry about." She winced at the torment that churned in her belly. *I'm not going to be sick again, am I?*

Still Water stared off to the right. White Ash could see Tuber there, staring at them from the edge of camp. The boy stood hip-shot, his club hanging limply from a muscular arm. Still Water waved. The young man lifted his chin in acknowledgment as he watched them with a fierce intensity.

Still Water's eyes narrowed and White Ash could see a new worry eating at him. He ground his jaws and strode purposely forward.

She forced her gaze ahead, leaving Still Water to his thoughts. Where had her strength gone? She felt weary, upset, and confused. Why was this happening now, when she needed all of her clarity of mind?

And if I can't control the One when I face the worst of my fears, I'll doom us all.

Pale Raven stood beside Brave Man and inspected the runner from the Black Point. He stood resolute before them, a handsome young man with curled shells tattooed into his cheeks. Sweat streaked his dusty, muscular body. He wore only a breechclout, and his hair had been pulled back into a simple braid. As his gaze held Brave Man's, he didn't waver but stood with all the courage in the world. Only through the pulsing of the artery in his neck could Pale Raven measure his true fear.

Broken Stones warriors pressed closely around them, their darts easily at hand and an eager, predatory look in their gleaming eyes. Behind them, on the northern slope, the main body of the clan traveled up the gentle grade to reach the low saddle in Green Mountain. On either side, the rocky, gray-green slopes of Green Mountain rose. Here and there, patches of rock outcrop caught the sun. Juniper and scrubby limber pine dotted most of the slopes, giving way to fir and spruce forests near the summit. An eagle lifted in spirals on the breeze that rose up the mountainside.

She cocked her head, listening to the Black Point.

"I am Snail Shell, warrior of the Black Point. I have come to the Broken Stones with a message for Brave Man."

"Tell me your message." Brave Man's smile might have frozen fire.

Snail Shell lifted his chin. "White Ash sent me to tell you that she will meet you tomorrow night. There is a spring at the bottom of the pass." Snail Shell pointed to the south. "There, White Ash will face you."

"I won't go alone," Brave Man announced. "Does she think I'm a fool?"

"She thought you might want to take—"

"Five warriors," Brave Man stated. He smiled. "And does the one-armed man accompany her?"

Snail Shell's jaw muscles tightened, as if to stifle a trembling of muscles around his grim mouth. "Her husband accompanies her."

Brave Man's satisfied smile widened. "If her 'husband' goes with her, so shall my wife come with me and my five warriors. Brave Man accepts this . . . and nothing else."

A glint of understanding flickered in Snail Shell's eyes, and he seemed to gain confidence. "She brings five warriors with her already. Does she have your word as Soul Flier of the Broken Stones that this will be so? Only five warriors?"

Brave Man studied him through slitted eyes. In a loud voice he called, "Brave Man gives his word that only five warriors and Pale Raven accompany him to meet White Ash! It will be so."

The surrounding warriors shifted, glancing back and forth. Flying Hawk smiled and nodded, while he inspected the Black Point warrior the way he would a piece of prize meat.

"Five warriors?" Pale Raven asked.

Brave Man nodded. "The battle White Ash and I will fight will not be won with darts and clubs." He tilted his head back to catch the rays of the sun. "I have forced her to this. She doesn't want my Power to grow. She felt my touch through the Dream—as I felt hers. The time has come to break her. We will deal with the rest of the Black Point when my Power is full. No one will stand against us."

Snail Shell's face hardened.

Brave Man laughed. "What? Black Point, I *know* her. I know her strength." He paused. "And my own. Perhaps you would join us now? You have courage to come to me like this. I always have a place for a man with courage."

"But what of the clan challenge?" Buffalo Tail asked from the side.

"*I* decide worth," Brave Man announced as he pinned Buffalo Tail with a hot glance. The warrior took a step back, lowering his eyes. Brave Man returned his attention to the Black Point. "Would you join me, Snail Shell? Become a warrior of the new way? Or will you place your trust in a woman?"

"I have my own honor, Soul Flier. Broken Stones are not my people."

Brave Man fingered his chin. "I will leave that offer open to you. I will leave it open to any Black Point who has courage. And I understand loyalty. Yes, I understand and respect it. For the moment, you have ties to your clan. After I break your Dreamer, after I make her my wife, perhaps we can reach an agreement . . . your warriors and me. Repeat this to your fellows; tell them that a new way has come—and Brave Man leads it.''

"I will carry your words.'' Snail Shell's expressionless face might have been carved of weathered granite.

"Then we are agreed. I shall come to the spring you speak of with five warriors and Pale Raven. White Ash comes with her one-armed man and five. There we will Dream the future of the People. And I will take her Power once and for all.''

"I hear your words, Soul Flier. With your permission, I will bear them back.''

"Go.'' Brave Man pointed.

Snail Shell strode proudly through the ranks of warriors that surrounded him.

"We should have killed him,'' Pale Raven whispered.

Brave man smiled blandly at her. "And outraged the customs of the clan? No, he came unarmed.''

"But *five* warriors? Have you gone crazy?'' She gestured her dismay. "I wouldn't trust a Black Point to wipe an infant's bottom!''

"It's not the Black Point I trust.''

"Oh?'' she demanded as they continued over the saddle.

He hitched forward on his bad leg. "It's White Ash I trust.''

"White Ash? She'd like to see you *dead*!''

He grinned absently. "It will make her defeat all the more delightful.''

"I don't think you understand what you've . . .'' Pale Raven swallowed the bile of fear that rose in her throat.

Brave Man glanced reprovingly at her from the corner of his eye. "It's you who don't understand. The battle White Ash and I fight isn't something for warriors. It's for Power.'' He swept his arm around at the warriors who paralleled their path. "If I loosed all these brave young men on White Ash, it would accomplish nothing. She's learned enough of Power to see my action before I take it. She reads my soul through the Dreams. And suppose they did kill her; what then? She has to be alive for me to gain her Power.''

Pale Raven slitted her eyes. "You know more about it than I.''

"I do. Leave the seeking of Power to me." He closed his eyes for a moment, never breaking stride. "I can feel her. She's frightened, Pale Raven. Fear lingers in the gray mist." He laughed happily. "She knows she must face me now, before I learn more about the One than she has learned." He paused. "I could almost pity her and her one-armed man."

Brave Man stalked onward.

Pale Raven lagged behind and considered the options, one by one. She caught Flying Hawk's attention and made an innocent gesture with her hand. He nodded, glancing furtively at Brave Man's back.

Good man, Flying Hawk. Yes, the Soul Flier gave his word—but Pale Raven didn't . . . and you don't want him going into Black Point hands any more than I do.

The evening softened into night, leaving long shadows to creep across the sandy hills. Out in the sagebrush, two foxes were yipping sharply in their hunt. Crickets clicked and chirred, and the cool air carried the spiced aroma of the land.

White Ash and her party had made camp on the leeward side of a large, stabilized dune. Tall greasewood and sage provided shelter from the wind and helped to screen the fire. Sleeping would be more comfortable on the sand than it would have been out on the rocky flats, or on the clay hardpan.

Weary from worry and lack of sleep, White Ash pulled the robes over herself and Still Water. Trouble rolled up into a furry ball and tried to lie on their feet. She pushed him away. Trouble grunted and studied her with annoyed brown eyes before he padded around to Still Water's side, snorting and sneezing his disgust before he flopped down again.

The others sat around the low fire built in a shallow basin they'd scraped out of the sand; sounds of their desultory conversation drifted on the quiet night. White Ash could hear Aspen's musical voice. More than once during the day, she'd caught the woman's measuring eyes on her. She smiled to herself. *You don't understand because you've never seen Still*

Water's soul, Aspen. Wind Runner could never share me with the Dream. His love isn't as generous or as kind as Still Water's.

When White Ash closed her eyes, she could feel the threat pouring over the mountains to the north. The final trial approached on cougar feet.

She took a deep breath, trying to still her deepening anxiety. Peace wouldn't come. Her turbulent thoughts swirled like storm clouds through ragged mountains. She relived that terrible eternity as she stood vigil over Bright Moon's soul-split body. She drifted into that first Dream, when she'd heard the voice of First Man and felt Bright Moon's passing. Brave Man's leering face appeared startlingly out of nothingness, eyes glazed as he wrestled her to the ground and jerked her dress above her hips. His features shimmered, as if seen through water, and merged into Three Bulls'. Her body contorted as he drove his manhood into her . . .

White Ash knotted her fists. The death cries of the White Clay crashed through her. She lived that night again as darting Wolf warriors sprinted through the camp yelling, whooping, and releasing their darts. Clubs whistled in frightening arcs before smacking soddenly into vulnerable flesh. And above it all, his face outlined in the early morning clouds, Old Falcon watched with horrified eyes. Blood spilled from his cracked skull and streamed down his face, filling his eyes. The sunlight caught the color of the blood and shot crimson rays over the terrible scene.

White Ash called on all the strength she could muster to drive the vision away. *Seek,* Singing Stones' ancient voice told her. And she floated in water, whirling and icy, until Still Water's fingers wrapped in her hair and pulled her back from eternity. Her soul rose, leaving her limp body to rise above the floe-packed river. As a bird might, she watched Still Water struggle with her inert body as he pulled her to shore and made that agonizing trek to the hot springs.

One by one, the images replayed. Her gut turned as she relived her capture by the Broken Stones and the journey to Brave Man's camp. She heard Brave Man's gloating voice again as the huge bonfire raged and the Broken Stones

Danced. The Wolf Bundle gleamed bloody in the light. The skin on her stomach crawled as Brave Man's woman sliced her shirt open and jerked her pants down. Brave man's weight crushed her against the robes.

"White Ash?" Still Water demanded urgently, splintering the memory. "You're shaking."

Still Water. Always arriving at the right time. She took a deep breath. "I'm scared, Still Water. That's all."

She rolled onto her back in order to see the glittering stars that had sprouted in the darkening night sky. To the north, the somber flanks of Green Mountain rose like a blot against the horizon. An owl hooted, the call lilting over the endless dunes.

"So am I," Still Water confided—hesitation heavy in his voice. "But not because of Brave Man."

White Ash glanced over to where the others had finally bedded down. Soft whispers came from Wind Runner's robes. *He's happy. She seems worthy of him.*

Sage Ghost slept to one side. Throughout the day, he'd kept to himself, lost in his own thoughts. The other warriors had followed grimly, forcing themselves to be courageous in the face of a threat they didn't understand.

"White Ash?" Still Water touched her pale cheek.

"What?"

"Are you . . . How long has it been since your last bleeding?"

She turned, staring at him in the darkness. "My *bleeding*?"

He let his hand drift gently down her throat and arm until he could twine his fingers with hers. "It's been two moons, hasn't it? Bitterbrush thought that . . . well . . ."

She started. "You mean Bitterbrush thinks I'm . . ." Cold understanding washed through her. The morning vomiting, the weight she seemed to have gained, the curious feeling of change that had possessed her. She tried to remember her last bleeding—it was so hard to keep track when there was no menstrual lodge to share with the other women. How long had it been? Just before they'd stolen the Wolf Bundle? She remembered gathering and stripping juniper bark for pads,

and how scratchy and irritating they'd been. Yes, that's when
. . . just before she and Still Water had begun to couple.

Frantically, she looked for another answer: Worry over the
Dreaming. The impending conflict with Brave Man. Grief
and apprehension. Doubt of her ability to Dream the One—
and return to this world. All the complications that twisted
her life. The constant fear.

She reached down, placed a hand on her belly. Closing
her eyes, she turned within, seeking the truth—and a faint
presence answered her call. White Ash squeezed her eyes
closed. "Oh, Blessed One."

"White Ash?" Still Water's soft question hung in her ears.
She nodded. "I am."

"What about the Dreaming?" he asked tenderly. "I mean,
can you . . . will it be all right to Dream with our child in
you?"

"I guess we don't have much choice."

She could sense his reluctant acceptance and his fear for
her and the baby. "I guess we don't. But . . . I'm sorry. If
I'd thought, I would have never—"

"Still Water? You didn't do it. We did. I'm happy to have
your child. I love you. Love you the way I've never loved
anyone. If I had anyone's child, I'd want it to be yours."

Closing her eyes, she drifted with the One, noting that Still
Water's soul warmed.

"The timing could have been a little better, though," he
admitted, relief in his voice.

"It could have been." She wrapped her arms around him,
hugging him close. "But maybe it's the way it's supposed to
be."

His grip on her tightened. For long moments they lay like
that. She took a deep breath, drawing the scent of his body
into her, as if she could inhale his soul.

After a time, the warm flush began to fade. She shivered
as a subtle change took place. Drifting tendrils—a terrifying
miasma—touched the edge of her being. Warily she sought
the edges of the gray mist, knowing the source. She could
feel the presence of Brave Man. Once again he touched the
One, and her body went rigid.

"What is it?"

"Brave Man. He seeks." She gripped a handful of the supple hides. "He knows . . ."

"Knows what?"

"What I feel—just as I can feel him: strong, reckless, confident of his victory." She shivered hating the thought that he'd feel her unease, hating his arrogance.

Still Water pulled her closer.

White Ash tried to drown herself in the feel of his cheek against hers. "How can I destroy him, Still Water? I barely know how to control the Dream. I know the trap that sucked Singing Stones in—and it frightens me almost as much as Brave Man's Dream does." She shook her head. "Singing Stones was so much stronger than I am—and he . . ." She hid her face in his loosed black hair.

He rubbed his cheek on the top of her head. "We'll do it. Just like we stole the Wolf Bundle out from under him."

"Tomorrow, Still Water. The battle is so soon."

"I know."

She writhed at the knowledge of Brave Man's Dreaming. "He found the One on his own. Without the help of a Dreamer like Singing Stones, without the Wolf Bundle. How can I stand against that, Still Water?" She remembered Singing Stones' face, and even now she could sense the pulsing of the Wolf Bundle's Power.

"Because you have to."

"We could leave," she whispered, desperately wishing she could belive it. "Wait until the others are soundly asleep, then run until we can't be found. We could hide in those mountains to the south. Those high ones."

She felt Still Water smile against her forehead. "If I could have any wish, it would be that. But he'd find you, wouldn't he? Look for you through the One? Follow you?"

Could Brave Man do that? Even if she didn't Dream? "Probably."

"And Sage Ghost, Wind Runner, Bitterbrush, and all the rest—they would have to meet Brave Man without a Dreamer to protect them. We had our chance that day above Singing Stones' camp."

"How can you be so brave when I'm so frightened?"

He chuckled under his breath. "You should be in here with me. I gave myself up for dead back when I answered the Wolf Bundle's call. Every day since then has been a gift from the Creator."

She ran fingers down his chest. "I don't know what I'd do without you, Still Water."

"Probably return to your senses and run like a frightened antelope."

She laughed softly. "What if we win tomorrow? What then?"

He tilted his head back. "Then we Dream the new way. Heal the sick, if we can. Teach the young who seek Power how to find it, and Dream the Spiral. We raise our children, and watch them grow. Maybe . . . maybe . . ."

She shifted to peer up at his contemplative face. "Yes?"

"You remember that day above Singing Stones' shelter when we hoped for a lodge of our own? Maybe we can sit in the sun like that and watch this child grow." He reached down and patted her belly.

She closed her eyes, knowing the pain of hope. Brave Man quested into the One again, and her soul twisted. A disgusting glowing green light reflected in her soul.

She bit back the urge to cry.

And I'm carrying Still Water's child? So much to lose . . .

Brave Man sat motionless, back propped against a boulder. In front of him the land dropped off into the expanse of the Red Earth Basin. The western horizon glowed with the final traces of the burning sunset, while evening eased over the colored soils and dulled the greens of the geasewood. His senses had grown keener since he began to seek the Power. Now he learned this new land, scenting the spiced musk of the dry air, aware of the soul that pulsed in the weather-worn buff-and-tan sandstone and the rich red soil. Alkali had woven a bitter trail through the dirt. The plants had their own Spirit here, enduring, bristly, and curiously delicate. A different sort of soul filled this land, one that Sang with the wind and Danced with the stars. This land would change a person, or a people. Brave Man couldn't allow it to change him—he would be the master. So much would be settled in this new land where he led the Broken Stones.

Down there, tomorrow, I will solidify my Power. The last obstacle—White Ash—will fall before me, crushed as all have been before. And with her Power I will be the greatest Soul Flier any people have ever known.

The shadows deepened among the flat shapes of the low buttes that stretched in ranks toward the western horizon. They waited in indigo majesty against the darkening aqua of the sage flats. The lumped patterns of dunes rippled over the earth to the south—dunes locked in place by the sagebrush and greasewood that grew in their moisture-rich sands.

Out there, somewhere, White Ash waited for him.

A nighthawk flipped and darted on the still air as it searched for insects. A soft chirring came from the creatures of the sage.

Brave Man closed his eyes, allowing peace to seep into his soul. The nagging ache in his head subsided. As darkness fell, he searched for the touch of the gray mist. Bit by bit, he forgot his body, turning to the silence within that would lead him to Power.

He had no awareness of the owl that glided past, or of the fluttering shapes of bats on their night hunt. He didn't hear the scream of a cougar in the rocks above.

He drifted, surrendering himself.

Tendrils of the soothing mist bathed him, and he allowed himself to fall ever deeper into the shimmering gray. He became aware of White Ash's fear hovering somewhere beyond, and extended himself, challenging. She retreated, providing him satisfaction. He had no doubt about the outcome of their confrontation. His strength swelled, and he surrendered more of himself, awareness growing.

He recognized the Power of the Wolf People's Bundle. And knew the boundaries of its Power again. The voices in his head whimpered somewhere behind him. *Ah, so the Bundle was the source of the one-armed man's Power. I've beaten it before.*

He extended himself toward the Bundle, only to be rebuffed. Force it? Was he ready for that?

Soon.

The gray fog lightened, developing a golden hue. Like a diving falcon, he fell further toward the golden haze, and then it shimmered and glowed around him. He filled himself with it, feeling the unity, craving more. The thunderous silence held him, pulsing around him.

"You seek." A sad voice echoed silently through the sifting mist.

"Who . . . what are you?" Brave Man gathered his strength, wary, unsure of this place or the way in which he must conquer it.

"All that you are not."

The golden clouds whirled and shifted, forming into the image of a golden man, a youth of incomparable beauty.

"Who are you?" A tingle of premonition shot through Brave Man's awareness.

"I am First Man, the Wolf Dreamer. I Dream the Spiral, the way of the People. You are Powerful. Your danger to the Spiral grows."

"What is this Spiral?"

"Circles within circles without ending or beginning. The reflection of the harmony I Dreamed."

"And you were a man once?"

"I was. My Dream led the People into this land, made them One with it. I Dreamed the Spiral, changed the patterns. Now the Sun People have come, and you would change the Spiral. Why would you do this?"

"To become a god," Brave Man answered. "I escaped from the Camp of the Dead. I have come to lead the Sun People, to remake them into something stronger. I *am* the new way. This Dream proves it." Purpose filled him. "What you did, Wolf Dreamer, so shall I."

"And this time, Raven Hunter, you have no brother to Dream against you."

"I am called Brave Man."

"Names are illusion."

The golden man's features shifted, becoming those of a huge golden wolf.

"You do not frighten me. You're nothing but Dream—and I fear no Dream."

The wolf's appearance changed, shifting, becoming Thunderbird, and for a brief moment Brave Man thrilled with fear. A Dream. Only a Dream. He chuckled at the apparition. "You do not fool me for long."

"I do not seek to fool you, only to demonstrate, to show you that the One is for all. As I am Wolf to some, I am Thunderbird to others. Perhaps I can make you see, turn you from your Dream of separation. The One is everywhere, and is not."

"You talk in riddles."

"You would Dream men apart from the One. You would destroy the harmony with your foul Dream and make men lose their way. They would never again understand how to share their souls with the soul of the world."

"Is that so bad? The world is meant to bend for men. Power is for the strong and the cunning. By strength, I survived the Camp of the Dead. By strength, the Sun People take what they need."

"And what do they give back? Are men more important than buffalo? Than elk and deer? Than the plants and the rocks? That is your Dream, Brave Man. You would Dream that men could take, exploit, and believe themselves more than they are. You would veil them in so much illusion that they would think themselves Creators."

Brave Man flexed his strength, feeling the ripples of the One around him. "Only a god could do such a thing. Why should men remain a part of this Spiral of yours? If men can rule the world, they should do so." He asked cunningly, "Or will you strike me down?"

Wolf Dreamer closed his eyes, and the sorrow of his expression touched Brave Man's heart. Angrily, he rid himself of the weakness.

"We could have. The Wolf Bundle wanted to tighten around

*your heart and split your soul from your body. I told it no.
We placed our hope for the Spiral in another soul. Power
cannot dictate the actions of people. It can only influence
them through Dreams. What we planned for you was
changed.''*

Brave Man considered. "Changed?"

*"We recognized your strength early. We hoped to use that
strength. We gave Sage Ghost the Dream so that he would
steal White Ash. She loved you once—as you loved her. We
planted the Dream of you and her together. But we cannot
dictate free will. When the camp on the river you call Fat
Beaver was attacked, a Black Point war club changed all
that—damaged your soul and turned you into an abomination.''*

Brave Man chuckled. "I never would have guessed that
Power took so many gambles—and lost."

*"Learn this lesson well, Brave Man—and think seriously
about it. Nothing is certain—not even for Power. Creation is
made so that the flight of a butterfly over Green Mountain
might change the patterns of the air to create a storm half a
world away. No action comes without risk. Not for us . . not
for you.''*

"So I was your chosen? What about White Ash?"

*"Together, you would have Dreamed the Spiral for the Sun
People. You would have taught them the Dream. Old and
new, male and female. Power comes from opposites crossed.
North-south and east-west create the world. The One and the
Many of the illusion. All are tied together and become the
Spiral, the circle without beginning or end.''*

"And tomorrow I shall destroy White Ash."

The golden man's sorrow filled the pulsing haze. *"We ask
you to reconsider, to learn the harmony of the Spiral. We ask
you to Dance—''*

"Your argument is persuasive, Wolf Dreamer, but I see
my opportunity now. That which you are, I shall become
someday. Let us see which Dream is stronger in the end."

The sudden action caught Brave Man by surprise; some
force repelled him from the golden haze, sent him spinning,
panicked, through the gray mist like a hurled rock.

He blinked, the ache in his head blinding and unbearable. He groaned, crossing his arms over his chest as he shivered in the cold night air. The moon had risen over the eastern horizon, a half-full globe.

"You betrayed yourself this time, Wolf Dreamer." He got stiffly to his feet. He clenched a fist, shaking it as he shouted, "Spirits should learn how to lie!"

A god! the voices hissed inside his head.

"Yes . . . a god. And a new Dream to crush the old."

He filled his lungs and bellowed at the sky, "You'll see. *You'll see tomorrow!*"

Chapter 31

"The spring is just over that rise." Snail Shell pointed to the sage-speckled ridge before them. The buff soil gleamed in the afternoon light. Overhead, puffs of clouds sailed to the east, pushed by an insistent breeze.

White Ash shielded her eyes from the glare of sun off sand and surveyed the location. Around them, dunes thrust up like enormous anthills. A sodden thumping had begun in her breast. Only Still Water's presence beside her made it seem bearable. "Let's stop and spend the rest of the day here. That dune over there is high. If we make camp on the crest, we'll be able to see all around."

Wind Runner gave her a speculative glance. "And then?"

White Ash steeled herself, struggling to keep from trembling. "At dusk we'll cross the rise and walk down to the spring to meet Brave Man."

"You think he'll be there?"

She nodded. "He's very sure of himself. In my Dreams, he's standing before a huge fire. Anyone else would be frightened lest such a blaze attract enemies. But he thinks he's invincible."

Wind Runner's face tightened and he glanced at Aspen, who stood listening, arms crossed, suspicious eyes on White Ash. Brusquely he waved an arm and ordered, "Snail Shell, Blue Wind, spread out. Make sure we're not walking into a trap."

The two warriors left at a trot.

Wind Runner's gaze drifted uncomfortably over the others still standing close by. To White Ash, he said, "We must talk—alone."

She nodded and placed a hand on Still Water's shoulder. He gazed at her with concern. "Could you and Sage Ghost make us a camp on that dune? Wind Runner and I will follow."

Still Water patted her hand tenderly. "Don't wear yourself out. We have a long night ahead of us." He gestured for Sage Ghost to follow him up the face of the shimmering dune.

Aspen examined Wind Runner for a moment before she turned and followed Sage Ghost and Still Water.

White Ash waited tiredly until the others had passed beyond earshot. "What is it, Wind Runner?"

He scuffed at the dirt with his moccasin, evading her eyes. Anxiety lined his handsome face. "You're not up to this. I can feel it. You're scared half out of your wits."

"Wind Runner . . . Do you know what Brave Man's going to do to me?"

"No."

"He's going to try to break me through Power. Still Water and I, we have to fight—"

"Still Water? He's no warrior!" Wind Runner's gaze shifted to follow the group trudging up the dune. "You think *he* can help you?"

"He's the only one—"

"He looks as if a prairie dog would scare him silly! Brave Man will—"

"Still Water has faced Brave Man before. He walked into Brave Man's camp and rescued me." She gave him a sober stare. "Wind Runner, you know nothing about Still Water. He's faced more terrible things than you've ever . . . What difference does it make?" She fumbled with her fringed sleeves and gazed at the crest of the dune, where Sage Ghost and Still Water unslung their packs and knelt to unlace the straps. The low strains of their conversation could barely be heard. "Still Water keeps the only Power I can count on to defend me."

"His Wolf Bundle?"

"Yes."

Wind Runner roughly gripped her arm. "Listen to me. *I'm a warrior.* I know Brave Man's weaknesses—and have since we were children. This whole thing can be taken care of quickly. I'll need a distraction. If you could scream all of a sudden . . . maybe faint. I'll know the moment to move. I can drive a dart right through him. Aspen can kill another warrior. In the meantime, Snail Shell and Blue Wind will cast their darts. If we move quickly, they won't have a chance. After that, it's just a matter of time. Without a leader, the Broken Stones will falter. I've been talking about this with Aspen. A small band of Black Point warriors—maybe no more than five—could hit their camp, keep them off balance while we gather our strength. Maybe we could break them once and for all."

He spoke so confidently, eyes glinting . . . but would the plan work? Possibly. Sage Ghost had told her of Wind Runner's exploits. A glimmer of hope tingled to life in White Ash. *He's offering you a way to escape the terrible battle that lies ahead.* The glimmer brightened . . . and just as rapidly, it died.

A resigned smile played over her lips. "It won't work. No matter how well-plotted and sprung, he'd sense the trap. Power would give it away. He's Dreamed, Wind Runner. No, don't shake your head. I know you can't understand it, but I do. Through the Spiral, the heart of all life, Brave Man and I can see each other's souls. Neither of us can lay a trap without the other knowing."

"But he'll destroy you—and the Black Point, too!"

She rubbed her hot eyes. "This isn't a matter to be decided by warriors. It's a matter of will, and Power, and Dreaming." She placed her hands on his shoulders and let Power flow through her, watching it encircle him like a blue halo. *"Do you see?"*

A violent shudder went through him. He pulled away, mouth open as his eyes widened. "Blessed Thunderbird, who *are* you?"

She lowered her hand and clenched it into a numb fist. "The hope of the People, Wind Runner." She turned and headed for the dune where Still Water and Sage Ghost were in the process of digging a fire pit in the soft sand.

Wind Runner followed, picking his way through thorny greasewood and pungent sage, absently noting that the fruit on the prickly pear cactus had ripened to a bright red. From the cloud-speckled sky, the sun beat down on his head. He filled his lungs with the pungent air.

A gnawing fear tormented him. What had White Ash done? He shivered again. She'd simply looked into his eyes and he'd felt a hot current, like a bolt of lightning striking him. Then he'd sensed her desperation, experienced the Power of her words. She'd touched his soul with the awesome nature of the struggle to come.

What happened to you, White Ash? How did this come to pass? He feared her—and loved her. But in the past few days his love had changed from passion to something deeper, more abiding. To see her in this danger twisted his soul. *And I can do nothing.*

Aspen met him halfway up the dune, her eyes questioning.

He shook his head, sighing. "She said it wouldn't work, that Power would betray us."

Aspen tensed and looked at him. "I can see your love for her in your eyes."

"If you see so clearly, you can see my love for you, too. Yes, I'll always love her. More now than I did before. But I no longer love her as I do you. She's . . ." He cocked his head, frowning. "She's like a mother. Yes. And she's ready to sacrifice herself to protect us from something I don't understand—some vision of our fate that terrifies her."

He read the unease in Aspen's eyes and gripped her hand tightly. A red-tailed hawk soared on the air currents over the crest of the dune. Wind Runner granted himself a moment to watch the predator hunt the sage for mice and rabbits. "We just have to do what White Ash asks. I think it's the only way we can help her now."

Still Water sat in their camp on the top of the dune, White Ash's head in his lap. She'd been sleeping restlessly for the past hour, her long black hair spreading like a dark veil over his leather pants. He gazed down at her beautiful face, then glanced at the Wolf Bundle. He'd removed the sacred object and gently set it on top of the pack so it could *see* Brave Man's camp on the plain below. He wasn't certain how Spirits saw, but since he'd exposed the Bundle to the dwindling light, he could sense its Power increasing. The heart-shaped object seemed to radiate, its Power twining out, sending threads through the people who stood around him talking quietly. Aspen, Wind Runner, and Sage Ghost shifted uneasily, shaking their heads as they looked from White Ash's sleeping body down to Brave Man's camp, where warriors walked the dunes.

Still Water exhaled a taut breath. The sunset cast a gaudy red light over the land, illuminating a twisting dust devil that wove across the flats like a spiral of fire. Against the indigo sky in the east, a herd of antelope stood silhouetted on a hilltop. Heads up, they watched warily while the slanted light silvered their rumps.

"Snail Shell and Blue Wind haven't returned," Aspen noted grimly. Sage Ghost translated her words for Still Water.

"I know, but we can't wait much longer." Still Water rubbed his hand over his heart. It had been pounding for some time. He reverently reached for the Wolf Bundle. Its Power coursed up his arm, tingling his flesh—and White Ash jerked awake, her eyes huge and filled with dread.

"I didn't mean to wake you."

She sat up and glanced at the Bundle. "It wasn't you, Still Water. The Bundle screamed my name. It's time."

He swallowed hard. "Then we'd better be going."

"Soon. I need you to chant for me first, to help me get prepared," White Ash said in a fragile voice.

He nodded and closed his eyes. Vague memories lived

again in his mind: Warm Fire's smile . . . Left Hand's puzzled frown . . . the night Trouble had gotten lost in the snow-storm. He relived the chilling cold as he pulled White Ash from the river. Singing Stones sat on the ridge top one more time, surrounded by magical elk . . . he tripped over a corpse in the darkness and finally smashed Brave Man on the knee with his stone wood . . . he lay in White Ash's arms, drowning in her love. Everything that had happened had led him to this final moment of preparation. Had Power wrought its dart with the ultimate skill?

He opened his eyes and raised the Bundle to the dying sun. He began to chant, the words rising, filling his soul as if bolstered by a Power not his.

He could feel White Ash seeking the One. The edges of her soul touched his like a warm, ticklish feather.

Still Water barely heard Wind Runner's gasp as the black wolf glided from the sage to sit beside White Ash, its yellow eyes warily going from one person to the next. Power swelled on the night.

Still Water jumped when he heard White Ash let out a small cry, and an image of fungal green crept through the Power-laced air. *Brave Man Dreams, too.*

The Wolf Bundle surged in his hand, and Still Water felt a crackling—as when a hand is rubbed across fox fur to make it spark. Power shifted, changing, advancing and retreating.

"We must go," White Ash whispered. She rose slowly to her feet. Still Water stood beside her, supporting her arm.

"We can't leave without Snail Shell and Blue Wind," Aspen said to Wind Runner, her voice tinged with panic. Still Water frowned, wondering for a moment why he understood without the benefit of translation. Then he noticed the golden shimmer to the air; it looked as though Power had thrown a huge net over them. In his hand, the Bundle throbbed like a laboring heart.

He eyed the others. No one else seemed to notice the shimmer. White Ash led the way down the dune, the black wolf trotting protectively at her heels. Trouble lagged behind Still Water, his hair bristling.

They walked up over the next dune as the sky dimmed to

a slate blue. As White Ash had predicted, Brave Man stood there before a huge fire. Behind it, a woman and five warriors clustered in a small circle.

Still Water became painfully aware of Aspen and Wind Runner's fear; their souls spun out brief flashes of color to pierce the golden net. White Ash and Sage Ghost stood resolutely, as though numbed by the sight of Brave Man.

The black wolf growled a low half-whimper and loped down toward the enemy camp. White Ash followed in its tracks. Still Water clutched the Bundle to his chest and quickly ran to catch up. A small voice cried out in his soul.

White Ash hovered on the boundary of the One, letting the gentle gray haze drift through her. Brave Man watched her approach with a curious detachment.

He's allowing me to come close. He plans to trap me, to take me in a sudden rush.

The echoes of fear in her distant body left her concentration unsettled. Awareness of the life in her womb triggered age-old reflexes of maternal vigilance. The child's soul fluttered around hers, shooting filaments into the One.

Seek. Seek the One, the untold voices of the Wolf Bundle ordered through the layers of gray. *We are here. Use us.*

"I can't—not yet," she whispered almost inaudibly. Desperately she sought to shove the memory of Singing Stones out of her thoughts, to achieve balance. The warmth of the One that lay just over the horizon of her soul beckoned.

In a trance, she wound her way through the gnarled sagebrush. Each step brought her that much closer to the end. Her moccasined feet felt the crumbling dry soil underfoot. The breeze tugged at her loose hair. Her heart pounded, each rush of blood in her veins and womb a reaffirmation of all that she gambled.

She stopped before Brave Man, staring up into his slitted eyes. The fire Danced eerily, casting alternating light and shadow across the deepening dusk.

He smiled, exposing his missing front teeth. "Tonight you will be my wife, White Ash!"

"Tonight I will be your death, Brave Man. I come to kill your Dream."

He threw back his head and laughed. "I shall possess you. You will know my Power—all of it."

She wavered on the boundary of the One. "I loved you once."

"And you will again." He looked hatefully at Wind Runner. "You challenge me for the last time, old friend. I've Dreamed your death. Tomorrow, as the sun reaches its highest point, I shall offer your heart to Power. With my own hands I shall cut it from your body—and a new way will dawn. You will pay for standing in the way of Power."

Wind Runner's jaw muscles clenched. "My darts will feast on your blood first. What has happened to you? Where is my *friend*? It isn't too late. Let's bring an end to the hatred, Brave Man. For all that we've shared—"

"Enough!" Brave Man glanced at Sage Ghost. "You, too, have come to die with your daughter, old man?"

"We'll see, boy." The old hunter's shoulders rippled with corded muscle. "Sage Ghost is ready for whatever Power will bring."

White Ash barely had time to take a deep breath before a glowing green burst of light shot out of the gray mist and coiled around her soul, trying to suffocate her. Brave Man's attack eddied through the One, forcing her back, away from the source of Power. Frantically she huddled in upon herself.

Brave man laughed. "Have you no strength? Did you come to play like a child?"

He struck at her again, his Power like a foul hurricane, driving her back, back until she fell out of the Dream and into the world of illusion. The gray mist evaporated and she blinked at the lengthening shadows of night that crept over the sand dunes. Desperate, she closed her eyes and retraced the path, finding nothing . . .

NO!

She took a deep breath, easing into the nothingness, surrendering more of herself. He pushed her back again.

"Give up!" Brave Man commanded. "You are too weak for me."

Breath caught in her lungs. In panic, she glanced at Still Water. He looked at her with sad eyes and nodded encouragingly. An implacable determination molded his features as he lifted his voice and began the chant she knew so well.

White Ash followed the words as she had for weeks, using them as markers to lead her inside to the place that always listens. But before she could find it . . .

Brave Man's Power washed over her—a flood of carrion filth, assaulting her with terrible images of pain and rape. She cried out and dropped to her knees on the cool sands . . . and Three Bulls stared out of the depths of her soul, gaze half-lidded and smiling. She could smell his fetid breath and the stink of his unwashed body as he forced himself within her. The dying screams of the White Clay shivered the air. She looked into Bright Moon's absent eyes.

Brave Man has found a way to call up your worst memories and use them against you!

Clinging to the last of her reserves, she sought her soul, conjuring memories of her own. Liquid cold ran through her veins, frosting her soul as she drowned in a cutting, crystal river. Gravel scraped her skin as the current whirled her around, seeking to spin her loose from her soul.

Bad Belly's hand grabbed her hair. She struggled, choking on blue ice—and she survived. She pulled her ragged self out on a far shore, gasping.

And she found the place inside that listens . . .

She gathered her strength and countered, building a picture in her soul of a terrible morning years before: *The Black Point exploded out of the cottonwoods along the Fat Beaver River, howling their war cries, running among the lodges as the shocked camp came awake. She saw Brave Man stumble out of his lodge, naked. Women screamed and children cried out in terror, fleeing before the enemy warriors. A tall Black Point warrior grabbed Rock Mouse by the hair, and Brave Man nocked a dart in the hook of his atlatl and cast, driving it into the man's back . . . the enemy whirled and dove for Brave Man. Brave Man fought for his life, kicking and screaming . . .*

Brave Man cried out jaggedly and White Ash experienced

the agony of his headache, building . . . building to a sickening throb; it staggered her soul.

"You're stronger . . . than I thought," Brave Man rasped. "But not strong enough. I tire of this."

White Ash screamed as the green mist engulfed her, shrinking around her soul like rawhide soaked in water, squeezing the life from her.

"Use the Power! We are here. Claim us!" the Wolf Bundle penetrated her anguish. She shrieked in panicked desperation. Brave Man's haunting laughter rocked the foundations of the very earth.

Did she dare? Singing Stones' dead eyes gleamed through the malevolent haze of green. *What if I lose myself? What if I can't reject the lure of the One?* Faintly, she could hear Still Water's chant growing louder, as though he'd come to kneel beside her. The Wolf Bundle wrenched her soul, struggling to drag her down into its whirlpool or Power.

Pale Raven stood to the rear, waiting nervously, eyes on the veil of darkness that had swallowed the desert. Blue shadows clung to the dunes, making them look like hunching beasts ready to spring. She barely heard the words of Brave Man and White Ash. Then she felt the change in the air and staggered.

She glanced at Flying Hawk. The warrior stared back with wide eyes. She stepped closer to him, whispering, "Have they had enough time?"

From the side of his mouth, he answered, "You only need to step into the light of the fire and raise your hands."

At that moment Brave Man cried out, placing his hands to his head. He toppled sideways, overbalanced by his bad leg. He rolled into a sitting position, an anguished expression on his face.

The warriors started forward.

"Stay where you are!" Pale Raven ordered. "Leave the Soul Flier to his battle." *Ours will come later. If Brave Man loses, the Black Point had better hope Thunderbird is on their side!*

Brave Man gasped, drawing a deep breath. In that moment

White Ash's eyes cleared and she feebly grabbed the Wolf Bundle from her man's hand, hugging it to her breast.

Pale Raven took a step forward. In the firelight she searched the faces of her enemies. The men seemed awestruck. The delicate Black Point woman glanced warily about, as if invisible bats fluttered around her head. She fingered her darts, nervous, but very much in possession of her wits. She'd be the dangerous one.

White Ash got to her knees and bent forward, hugging the Bundle like a lover. Black hair tumbled around her face.

"Dream!" cried the young Black Point warrior, his hands knotted to fists. *"Dream the new way, White Ash!"*

Pale Raven's eye caught Flying Hawk's slight movement and glanced out at the night. Shadows crept among the dunes. Her eyes narrowed. Brave Man would win—one way or another.

White Ash held the Wolf Bundle securely over her heart, defended for the moment by the strength of Still Water's chant, by the yellow brightness of his soul. She released herself to the Bundle's Power.

. . . And the whole world went quiet. A glimmering golden haze filtered around her the way snow did on a crystal winter morning.

"Now, Mother of the People," the Wolf Bundle told her in its chiming voice, *"use our combined strength."*

She opened the arms of her soul and soared on the Power of the Wolf Bundle, letting it charge her with its might. From somewhere far away she heard Brave Man scream, then sensed the jumbled echo of the voices in his head crying out in horror.

She stood on the edge of the golden abyss.

The One called to her in a voice as sweet and as soft as honeyed snow.

"Step over the edge," the Wolf Bundle urged. *"Surrender yourself to the One. Brave Man is only confused. He's gathering his strength to . . ."*

Lights flickered and flashed, slamming her back. She cowered, stunned, as the eerie green brightness coalesced around her.

"*Let yourself go!*" the Wolf Bundle ordered. "*Step over the edge! It's your only hope . . .*"

She recalled Still Water's homely face, felt his loving touch—and sensed the life of their child growing in her womb. If she couldn't resist the One, the infant would die. White Ash sobbed as she leaned over the abyss, farther and farther, until she fell. She sailed through the golden haze, feeling the ecstasy of the One, become One with the Spiral.

"Where are you?" Brave Man's angry voice called, breaking up as if coming through waves of silvered water.

"Here," she answered. "I'm here." She longed so to free her soul, to let it soar formlessly in the bliss, that she could barely stand it. *Singing Stones surrendered to the One. He let his soul merge like a drop in the ocean. He . . .* Hope sprang to life like an ember fanned to flame. And White Ash knew the way to victory.

"Follow me *if you can*, Brave Man. See if you can Dream the One as Powerfully as I. See if you can Dance the Spiral without stumbling to your death."

White Ash sensed Brave Man's plunge into the golden mist with her, his soul rising in the wake of her passage.

The immensity of the One stretched before her. On wings of fire, she soared through the Dream, leading Brave Man deeper and deeper. She could sense his rapture, his awe at the magnificence and utter joy of the One. Then she lost him. She couldn't feel his soul any longer. A torrent of wary relief washed her.

Wolf Dreamer rose beside her, a silver-shot eagle drifting on the currents of light. "*You haven't won yet,*" his haunting voice said. "*You've only stepped into your own snare. Are you strong enough to leave here, to go back to your people?*"

"I don't want to go back," she whispered as an encompassing bliss filled her. Ecstasy and peace wrapped her in golden warmth as her soul expanded to experience it all. Expanding . . . growing . . .

"*Still Water will die, and your child with him . . . and, finally, the world will wither. Where is your love?*"

She felt the fragile tendril that tied her to the Wolf Bundle stretching, ever thinner . . . All she had to do was to cast loose and Dream the One forever. She could let herself go and sink into the silent thunder, drift . . . drift . . .

"Man of the People," they myriad voices of the Wolf Bundle called. *"You must Dream, Still Water. White Ash is losing herself in the One. Call to her! Seek . . . or all is lost."*

An uncontrollable shudder possessed Still Water's body, as though too much Power had been poured into his flesh too quickly. White Ash losing herself? No! Oh, what agony! Grief and loss sucked at his soul.

"How much do you love the Dreamer?" the Wolf Bundle's muted voices asked. *"Enough to risk your own soul to save her?"*

Warm Fire's words echoed hollowly: *Love the Dreamer.* Still Water yielded, seeking to trace that delicate link of love to White Ash. He followed the path the Wolf Bundle made for him through the gray film and into the shimmering golden mist, where fire and snow spun in contradictory swirls.

His soul pulsed in dread and desperation. His love for White Ash sent a blinding spear into the shifting gold around him. "White Ash?"

Only thunderous silence answered:

"White Ash! Where are you? Come back to me?"

Still Water's voice penetrated the One. She recoiled at the fear and longing it sparked in her soul.

In the flickering gold, Wolf Dreamer's face appeared, his dark eyes wistful. *"I share your Dream, Mother of the People. I feel your joy, but you must return. A new direction must be Dreamed or the people will lose their way. And everything you love will die. Is that what you want?"*

"But life in the illusion hurts so much."

"If you don't return, it will grow much worse."

A vision formed. She stared down at human beings laboring in fields. Clusters of crowded baked-brick structures lined a muddy river. Strange, ornate domes stood in the center of the human hives. There magicians burned incense on blood-stained altars. She saw wars raging in the name of vengeful gods. As she watched, rains scoured the denuded land, washing the earth into the rivers. Where lush stands of oak once covered the hills, only barren rock remained. Men dropped seeds into the ground and worked to nurture it . . . but no plants sprang to life.

"What is this?"

"What you see before you is a people who have lost the One. They live far away, across the vast seas that the Traders told you about when you were a child. They have forged the Power of illusion into a lance that will sunder your world, White Ash. Their civilization will rise for thousands of years before men cross the waters and bring their perverted Dream to your land. They seek to change the Spiral in the same way Brave Man does. The battle to keep the Spiral in balance never ends. If you win tonight—if you go back and Dream the new way—the world is still not safe. A thousand generations from now another Dreamer must face them. If you live, White Ash, she will have your blood in her veins . . . If you don't, there will be no Dreamer to fight them. The decision is yours."

"White Ash! Come back to me!" The yearning in Still Water's gentle soul reached her, and their unborn child quickened in her womb. She hesitated, staring into Wolf Dreamer's sad eyes.

Sage Ghost, Wind Runner, and Singing Stones shimmered in the golden mist. Each called to her.

She could make out the rainbow filaments of the Wolf Bundle and Still Water's soul; they wove into a tenuous strand that she could follow. She wept as she soared back along the strand. At the edge of the One, she stopped. *Am I strong enough? Can I go back to the hunger, war, and cold?*

"The choice is yours," Wolf Dreamer repeated.

The cry of her unborn child pierced the mist, echoing in her soul like the voices of tortured millions. She crossed the threshold into the gray haze.

"White Ash?" Still Water's tremulous plea stung her.

Wearily, she willed herself back into her body and opened her eyes to blink up at Still Water's worried face. He knelt beside her and brushed the wet strands of her black hair away from her cheeks. The honeyed fragments of the One drifted in her soul.

She lay on the ground, the black wolf curled around her, his yellow eyes gleaming as he watched the enemy warriors. The crackling fire wavered in the cool wind that swept the desert night. White Ash stared down at the Wolf Bundle where it pressed against her heart. The tendrils of its Power no longer twined with her soul. They'd woven into a thick cord of light and snaked into her womb.

She could see the rainbow threads of the Bundle tightening around her child—and she felt her daughter's joy as a tiny golden flame was born in the baby's heart. The glow spread outward, creeping through White Ash's limbs like a fiery wash of molten amber.

Brave Man lay facedown in the sand. Pale Raven went to shake him. "Wake up! *Wake up!*"

White Ash climbed to her feet, and the big black wolf rose and stood side by side with Trouble next to the fire and Sage Ghost. Her father grimaced slightly, but he made no attempt to walk away from the animal. She gratefully leaned against Still Water for support and watched Pale Raven through haunted eyes. White Ash said, "He won't awaken."

Pale Raven rolled Brave Man over and gasped. Something black rolled from his pouch, gleaming in the firelight. She leaned closer, placing her ear against his chest. She felt for his breathing and squeezed the end of his finger. The blood retreated, leaving the fingernail white.

"No!" Pale Raven cried. "This can't be!"

White Ash closed her eyes. "He's joined the One." Then she added gently, "He didn't have the strength to return."

Pale Raven glared up, eyes flashing. "Save him! Bring him back to life. Do it, woman—*or you'll burn here!*"

White Ash stroked the Wolf Bundle tenderly, sensing its anger. "The Dream's not over yet, Pale Raven." Reverently, White Ash handed the Bundle back to Still Water.

For a moment Pale Raven seemed lost and uncertain, as though the icy fingers of reality had began to clutch at her frantic soul. She rose unsteadily to her feet, stepping into the light of the fire and raising her hands. In frightened rage, she called to the night, "Thunderbird! Hear me! *Come to the aid of the Soul Flier!*"

White Ash expelled a long breath as she watched. For long seconds Pale Raven held that posture, jaws clenched against the ragged uncertainty that shredded her soul. Then she glanced around the edges of the camp and turned to face White Ash. She thrust a hand at Brave Man's limp body. "Make him *live!*"

White Ash shook her head. "It's too late. He wasn't strong enough to come back. He chose to remain in the One." *And I don't blame him.*

Sage Ghost let out a small grunt of surprise and shouted, "It's a trap!" He nocked a dart in his atlatl and fell into a crouch, ready to cast, as enemy warriors eased into the light of the fire.

"Don't throw, Father," White Ash ordered. She could sense the struggle within him, the driving desire to repay treachery. "Sage Ghost, this is a thing of Power, not darts and blood."

Wind Runner cried, "Is this the way Brave Man honors his word?"

More warriors appeared, pushing Blue Wind and Snail Shell before them. Anger and terror twisted the two warriors' faces.

Pale Raven laughed bitterly. "The Soul Flier knew nothing of this." She stepped closer to White Ash, ignoring the charged air. "Brave Man said you had great power. *Make him live!*"

"I can't."

"Then you'll die on Broken Stones war darts!"

"You'll die first," Sage Ghost promised, eyes glittering.

White Ash faced the warriors who had crept out of the night, darts nocked for throwing. Power filled her voice. "Stop there! There will be no war here. Power has made its choice!"

To a man, the warriors pulled up, glancing quizzically back and forth.

White Ash locked eyes with Pale Raven. The woman's lips

parted as her soul curled. Try as she might, she couldn't break the stare she shared with White Ash.

"I told you the Dream wasn't over, Pale Raven," White Ash repeated. "Watch the way of Power."

White Ash walked into the fire, lifting her hands toward the stars while the flames licked around her. Horrified cries broke from the warriors' throats as they backed away. The black wolf lifted its nose to the sky, ears laid flat, and howled, the dirge mournful.

From the crackling flames, White Ash called, *"Hear the vision of White Ash! I Dream the Spiral. Power allows you a choice, Pale Raven. You and the Broken Stones may remain and fight. And in the passing of the moon, the name of the Broken Stones will be as one with the White Clay. Or you may leave this land! Travel a full year's journey to the south. There you will find a land to fight for. Seek the golden-haired plant. There your children's children will rise in greatness until a star burns in the day. What do you choose?"*

Pale Raven shook her head as she struggled to control her trembling body. She turned to Flying Hawk. He was staring awestruck at White Ash where she stood in the blistering fire.

"She doesn't burn!" Flying Hawk yelled, pointing. "Why doesn't she burn?"

Pale Raven nerved herself, taking the dart from Flying Hawk's limp fingers. She stepped closer, fear pumping with each beat of her heart.

"Make my husband live," she commanded. "Make him!" She leveled the dart, muscles taut to throw.

Flames swirled around White Ash's smooth legs as she stepped out of the fire. "Didn't Brave Man ever tell you? You're illusion, Pale Raven."

Pale Raven cried out and lunged, driving the dart into White Ash's breast with both hands. The dart sailed through her, as if it traveled through air, and rattled on the ground.

"She doesn't bleed!" Flying Hawk cried, stumbling backward. "There is no wound!"

"Your dart is illusion, Pale Raven. Only the One exists." The Dream danced in White Ash's eyes. "What do you choose, Pale Raven?"

The black wolf stepped through the flames, its fur unsinged, eyes glowing golden in the night. Pale Raven's soul withered beneath that eerie gaze.

"Choose?" Pale Raven glanced down at Brave Man's body and swallowed. She placed her hands over her belly, feeling the swelling of life Brave Man had planted within her. She backed away slowly and glared her hatred at White Ash. "The Broken Stones choose the south. A full year's journey we will travel. That land we will take for our own. And there we will await your star that burns in the daylight."

"Then go," White Ash ordered. "Runners will ensure that no Black Point bother you on the way."

The black wolf raised its muzzle and howled into the night.

Still Water tucked his robe around White Ash's still trembling body. A desert-scented wind rustled in the sage around them, tousling the fringes on Sage Ghost and Wind Runner's sleeves as they knelt before the red coals of the fire. Aspen sat cross-legged a few paces to the side, gazing tiredly at the glimmering stars.

White Ash looked up through red-rimmed eyes. "I did it, didn't I? I Dreamed the One . . . and came back to you."

Still Water smiled. "You did."

"I did it for you . . . and our child."

He bent down and brushed his lips on her forehead, holding her until her breathing deepened. Then he gently eased her down to the warm sand and rocked back on his heels, rubbing a hand over his face. Had he ever felt so weary?

The Wolf Bundle lay on his robe, glowing orange in the light of the coals. A sense of peace filled Still Water for the first time in his life. He glanced up and found Sage Ghost gazing at him curiously.

"Still Water?" Sage Ghost asked as he twirled a dart in his stubby fingers. "What next?"

"Tomorrow we go back to the Black Point. White Ash must tell them about the Spiral and First Man's Dream." His gaze drifted aimlessly over the camp, and he frowned at Brave Man's dead body. On the ground near the corpse's knee, something gleamed in the firelight. Still Water got to his feet and went to examine it. He picked up a beautifully polished carving of a black wolf, and he felt a tingle of Power. The tingle grew to a fiery intensity, and something told him it had once been part of the Wolf Bundle. He opened his soul and listened; he could faintly hear the echo of the Bundle's many voices coming from the tiny wolf. He held it more tightly. It made him think of Left Hand, and his soul ached. Left Hand would cherish something like this. *The Power of Trade? A sharing of souls? It is a small thing, my friend, and maybe a great thing. Once you gave me a gift at the beginning of the journey, but who knows when it will end?*

One day he would meet a Trader going east and he'd send the tiny wolf to his old friend. Just the possibility made his heart swell with longing.

Out in the darkness, a pack of coyotes erupted in song. Still Water clutched the carving and put it in his pack; then he reached for the stone-teeth necklace Brave Man had torn from him. He jerked it from around the dead man's neck and slipped it over his own head again.

A bit of soul goes into making something, into cherishing it. He touched the teeth fondly, remembering the day Left Hand had given them to him. *Never again will this leave my neck. I swear it on the Wolf Bundle.*

Out across the starlit sands, the coyotes had broken into a trot, loping across the crests of the dunes, their black shapes silhouetted against the indigo horizon.

Chapter 32

White Ash used a stick to turn the rocks that lay in the crackling fire. Sounds carried from the Black Point camp: children yelling in shrill voices, dogs barking, the calls of women, men laughing.

She sighed, drifting off to the peaceful days high in the Sideways Mountains when she and Still Water had been alone with each other. She looked to the north, toward Singing Stones' distant shelter. By now it had become the home of packrats. The hangings would eventually rot away, and the old man's possessions would become the domain of mice and insects.

A small dart of pain entered her soul.

"White Ash?" Aspen called as she walked up, eyes wary.

"Yes."

"What is this thing?" Aspen gestured at the low dome made of hides spread over bowed willow sticks.

"A sweat lodge. A place to cleanse your spirit. You could join me."

Aspen hesitated, a frown incising her forehead before she decided. "Show me what to do."

White Ash handed Aspen a pair of sticks and showed her how to use them to carry the hot rocks into the lodge. When they had transported enough, White Ash pulled off her dress, laying it on the sagebrush. "I don't think you want to do this in that pretty beaded dress, Aspen. Sweat means just that."

Aspen slipped out of her dress, laying it next to White Ash's. "And sweat cleanses?" she asked as she followed White Ash into the darkness of the lodge, staring at the hot rocks piled in the center. A tripod holding a gut bag full of water stood in the back.

"Wolf Dreamer taught us long ago that sweat purifies the

body and soul." White Ash closed the flap to seal the lodge in darkness and sat down at the rear, near the bag of water.

"I can't see a thing," Aspen remarked.

"Your eyes will adjust. It helps you to concentrate. You're not so easily distracted by what you see. Please, sit down, take a deep breath." White Ash cupped a handful of water and cast it on the rocks. A sizzling eruption of steam arose to fill the lodge. She breathed deeply, letting the warmth massage her. "I feel your curiosity, Aspen."

Aspen lowered herself to the dirt floor and gasped in the heat. "My whole body tingles."

"That's not what you're curious about."

White Ash cast more water on the stones, feeling the heat sink through her skin to loosen muscles and joints. Her soul warmed.

"There is talk in camp," Aspen began. "Some say you are a witch. Even Still Water's own relatives say so! People have watched you build this and wondered about the purpose. You have said you will Dream tonight."

Sweat trickled down White Ash's body, dripping from her chin and tracing around the curve of her breasts. "I must sweat to Dream well. Is that why you came? To ask me if I'm a witch?"

"My people have never seen a Soul Flier who could stand in fire or run darts through her flesh and not bleed. Our holy people don't Dream men to death like you did Brave Man."

"That's because the Sun People had no *real* Dreamers. Oh, they had some very good Healers . . . but no Dreamers. I'm not a witch. Tonight I will explain the One to the Black Point. I will tell them about the Spiral and the Dream of First Man."

"And change our ways?"

White Ash smiled in the dimness. "Aspen, I've seen First Man turn from human to Wolf to Thunderbird. The Sun People are the People of the Sky. First Man's were the People of the Earth. Sky and Earth. Opposites crossed. What were separate must be made one—they'll be stronger for it. That is the Spiral. That is what I will Dream for the People. I come not to take away, but to give. I am the way between the worlds and the Peoples.''

"I have wondered what to do with you. My people are asking my advice. I thought perhaps I should come and hear your words."

"You and Wind Runner are good leaders for the Black Point."

"He still loves you," she said.

White Ash reached into the water.

"No more, please." Aspen shifted. "This is new to me."

White Ash drew her hand out of the bag and smoothed the cool liquid over her hot cheeks. "Wind Runner's love bothers you? I've faced my temptation, Aspen—and it wasn't a man." The One called to her. She needed only to close her eyes to float in that serene golden haze. The rapture lay there, just beyond the horizon of her soul. "Still Water is the only man who can understand my deepest longings. He's felt them himself." She smiled, warm within at the thought of him rescuing her from the One.

Aspen remained silent for a moment. Then she said, "Throw a little more water on the rocks. If you can take it, I can."

White Ash dipped her hand in the water bag. She closed her eyes as she splashed the liquid on the stones, letting the tension drain from her body. The One pulsed within, rising from the glowing soul of her daughter. She didn't fully understand what had happened, but she felt as though her child had become a sacred bundle that lived inside her—a bottomless well of Power.

Aspen spoke deliberately. "I think I'll tell any who ask that your dream is for the good of the people."

White Ash nodded. "I will Dream as hard as I can for them."

Still Water bit his lip uneasily as White Ash stepped before the bonfire that burned and crackled in the middle of the camp. The eyes of over a hundred watched her warily. She raised her hands, Singing her Power in the awkward tongue of the Sun People. On the horizon, lightning flashed in a bank of black clouds that blotted the stars.

Wish I could understand what she's saying, Still Water thought. She held her listeners spellbound.

On quiet feet he slipped behind Sage Ghost's lodge to where his and White Ash's robes lay. His pack hid in the folds of hide. He gently dug it out and reached inside to take the Wolf Bundle. White Ash had said she wouldn't need it . . . but the expression on the faces of the Black Point left him uncertain. In his hand, the Wolf Bundle grew lighter, seeming to float. He tucked it up under his coat where he could keep it in place with his bad arm.

Ghosting around the rear of the lodge, he intently studied the crowd. A group of warriors had begun whispering behind their hands, hard looks on their faces. Two old women shook their heads disbelievingly and brusquely made throwing-away motions, as if to discard White Ash's words.

Still Water edged through the lodge's shadows. Something squished under his foot. He winced. "Wonderful. Dog droppings. And next to our robes. Sleeping tonight is going to be . . ." He froze, hearing someone approach.

"Witch!" a muffled voice carried to him.

Still Water's spine stiffened. He craned his neck and peered into the darkness. The Wolf Bundle suddenly surged. Still Water reeled on his feet. Power fluttered over his chest like spectral fingers of ice, then it blasted outward, shredding the night, drawing his attention to a place beyond the lodges.

Silhouetted against the firelight, Still Water saw two skulking shadows. One he recognized: *Tuber!*

Then he saw the weapon in the boy's hand. His heart pounded sickeningly against his ribs.

White Ash looked out at the people. The fire flickered in golden patterns over their pinched faces. Their uncertainties seemed to make the air thicker, heavier, pressing the air out of her lungs. She let her gaze drift over the starlit tops of the lodges to the lightning-gilded clouds beyond. Bats wheeled and dove, catching insects.

She raised her arms, and the people went silent. "I have

come to tell you about the Dream of First Man—whom you know as Thunderbird. In the beginning, the Creator made the four worlds. Three of them were dark and cold. Our ancestors climbed up through a hole to reach this place, the fourth world of light. Thunderbird—First Man, the Wolf Dreamer—led the way through the darkness.

"He fought his evil brother in order that people might live in harmony with the land. Here, he Dreamed the Spiral. All of Life is a Spiral—without beginning or end, constantly changing and forever the same. First Man gave us that Dream, and the way to find the One. I am here to lead you in search of the One. There your soul will find First Man and the way of Power. Seek, and you will know the harmony of the land.

"That is the legacy of the Wolf Dream, and I pass it on to you. Your blood is new to this land, Sun People, and it will make the land strong. What the Earth People have lost, you have replaced."

She closed her eyes, the vision forming in her mind. "One day your children will meet Traders bearing the golden-haired plant. Its soul will become yours. Here is the Dream that will be:

Sun God! Born of Light!
   Spiral, you god of gaudy feathers!
     Carry the plant upon your back.
      Parch the seeds upon the rack.
Rocks like sky are passing by.
  Hot, dry, war is nigh.
   Sing, Sun God, blood rises . . . stingers in the sky!
Further . . . further south they go.
  Shelters. Rock piled high.
   Raise the infants to the God in the sky.
Earth, hey earth, from it spread.
  Raise the underworld from the Dead.
   Flight of the bird, so big, so loud.
Calls the lightning from the cloud.

White Ash opened her eyes. "I've seen our children. They've grown strong, filling the land, their souls swaying with the coming of the seasons. I've seen them calling upon Thunderbird to bring rain from the heavens to nourish the golden-haired plant. The bounty is raised to the Sun and bellies are full. Stones the color of the sky drape their necks.

"If we seek the One and remember the Dream of First Man, the earth shall be the womb of our People. The Sun shall nurture the life provided by the earth. Opposites crossed. I've seen feathered Dancers rising from the ground to represent the journey of First Man from the underworld. I've seen them Dance to the Sun and cast pollen to the four sacred directions. This legacy can be yours if you accept the Dream. But if you don't . . ."

She studied them, noting mildly that one of the warriors had turned his back to her. White Ash lifted her voice, "I have seen other lands where the One is denied. I've seen people living like ants, scarring the soil for the profit of others. I've seen forests cut down and the earth bleeding as its soil is washed into the rivers and carried to the oceans. The One is not just for men, but for all life. What we take, we must give back. That is the heart of the Spiral.

"Power gives every person a choice! What is yours? Do you Dream the One, or separate yourselves from the Spiral? First Man Dreamed that the One would let the People live in harmony with their world. *Will you deny his Dream?*"

A great weariness came over her. She could feel the tug of the life in her belly, taking nourishment from her body. Protectively, she placed a hand on her stomach.

She stared hauntingly at the firelit faces. "You have heard First Man's Dream. Earth and sky, opposites crossed. I will take this Dream to the Hollow Flute, to the Wasp, and the Green Stone—that we may all live the way First Man Dreamed. I have spoken."

She turned, aware of the silence that held the people. She walked out through the lodges, a growing disquiet wrapping around her. The lightning-torn bank of clouds had roiled closer, almost over camp now. She thought she could hear the faint roar of thunder.

Behind her a babble of voices rose as people began discussing her vision and the meaning of her words. Trouble appeared at her heels, looking up with sad eyes.

"Where's Still Water?" she asked, taking a moment to rub the dog's ears. Trouble whined and licked her hand, his hot tongue reassuring. "Yes, you're part of the One, too."

She blinked and yawned, exhaustion vying with her desire to find Still Water.

"Go to your robes," she told herself. "He'll come eventually. You've pushed yourself for too long, White Ash." She trudged tiredly across camp to Sage Ghost's lodge and skirted the stakes that pinned the lodge cover down. She found their robes piled against the rear. She knelt and unrolled them. What had happened to Still Water? Her heart began to pound for no reason. She rubbed her gravelly eyes and pulled the top robe back.

"Witch!" someone hissed.

The shadow of a raised war club shone on the lodge cover and White Ash jerked up her arm, screaming, "No!" as she tried to crawl away.

Tuber's burly body smashed into her, knocking her sprawling. She glimpsed his panicked eyes as he rolled off and lurched to his feet. Still Water shouted in rage as he charged out of the shadows with a rock lifted high, heading for the woman who stood with a dart nocked and ready. But Tuber reached her first, his war club smashing down . . .

The loud smack of wood against bone split the night. Both Tuber and the woman tumbled to the ground.

Still Water dropped to his knees by White Ash and used his good arm to help her sit up. He frantically kissed her hair, whispering, "It's all right. You're all right."

Someone shouted. Frantic voices rose. Wind Runner and Black Moon raced around the lodge. Sage Ghost followed them, bearing a firebrand.

At the sight of Sage Ghost, Tuber pushed away from the dead woman and reached out with imploring hands. "I'm not a murderer. I had to! She killed Hot Fat. Before that, she killed Black Hand. I saw her sneaking around. She's been talking about witchcraft and how White Ash was evil and would curse us all."

Bitterbrush burst into the light and stared down. Her gaze riveted on Tuber and the bloody woman lying beside him. A cry of horror broke from her lips. *"Basket?"*

Tuber nodded fearfully, eyes searching their faces for understanding. "She's hated Dreamers ever since Green Fire died. You know it, Mother! She blamed Black Hand for it. She thought Hot Fat was trying to witch the children the Black Point had taken. She scolded me for trying to become a Black Point warrior. Bad Belly and me, we had to do it!"

Sage Ghost hurried though the gathering crowd and crouched before his son. He gazed firmly into Tuber's blurry eyes. Then a crooked smile bent his lips. "Tonight you are a warrior."

"But I killed . . ."

"Someone had to," Still Water told him. "An evil possessed her. After she murdered White Ash, she would have had to murder me. And after me, someone else."

As Sage Ghost extended a hand to help Tuber up, a falling star streaked the skies. Everyone whirled to watch its flight; it sailed across the heavens and disappeared into the bank of clouds. Lightning flared in several places, and thunder crashed like a stampeding herd of buffalo.

White Ash leaned heavily against Still Water. He stroked her tangled hair gently, but he'd gone very quiet. She shifted to glance up at him and followed his gaze, but not to the lightning. He stared out across the starlit sanddunes at the huge black wolf that stood, a paw up, watching pensively. Its yellow eyes glinted with a fiery sheen in the flashes of light.

Thunder roared again, shaking the very ground, and misty rain began to patter on the lodges. White Ash lifted her face to the cool drops.

Black Moon looked anxiously from the wolf to Basket's dead body, then to White Ash. "Thunderbird has spoken," he said. "Be welcome among the Black Point, White Ash. You have given us First Man's Dream. Now we must discuss it, to see if we can feel the truth of it in our hearts."

Epilogue

Left Hand hobbled down through the marshy grass and stopped at the sandy shore. Roiling water swept past. A turtle slipped off a snag and plopped into the river. Ducks and geese filled the sky, winging over the broad expanse of water that shimmered silver in the sun.

To the north, the Big River emptied into the Father Waters. His Wolf People had fought for this land, driving the Masked Dancers out and taking many captives in the process. The natives in this place didn't have the stubborn will of the Sun People, and the Wolf People had carved out a large territory. They took tribute in exchange for not raiding the Masked Dancers' new lands. Already the legend of Wise One Above and Wolf Dreamer had established themselves.

Much could be praised in this rich new country. Water-filled ox-bows sheltered the wild rice growing on the flats to the south. Beyond them, fields of maygrass and knotweed waved in the wind. Even this early in the summer, Left Hand could tell that the women would collect a good crop. On the river, youngsters in a canoe laughed as they threw a corded net into the water for fish. How curious that the children had taken to the water so quickly. Already Sand Crane had taken a party and paddled all the way to the salt water in the hot, steamy south. There, he Traded with the Swamp People.

Grunting at his cracking bones, Left Hand bent down to scoop up a handful of muddy sand. He raised it to his fleshy old nose and sniffed, drawing its moist scent into his lungs. The river land had Spirit—and it lavished its riches on those who would claim them.

"Is this the way you promised, Dreamer?" he whispered, his faded vision locked on the canoe. "Then perhaps it's as Power wanted."

He thrust his clean hand into the hide bag he wore around his neck and drew out the tiny black wolf that Bad Belly had sent him. It gleamed in the sun—the symbol of the Spirit Helper, the messenger of Power.

He had recognized it immediately, of course. Once it had ridden in the black wolf skin with the Wolf Bundle. And when the People were camped, the stone wolf would be set on the tripod to guard the Wolf Bundle. How had Bad Belly come by such a precious treasure? A person never knew about Trade, about the Power it carried.

He looked at the cool sand and then at the wolf, weighing them against each other.

"Such a long way for an old man to have come."

He could still hear the wind sighing through the spruce and fir of the Grass Meadow Mountains, though his feet would never again follow the trails walked by Fire Dancer. And his soul would never again soar as he looked out over the vast Gray Deer Basin or the Short Grass Plains.

He lifted his face to the cloud-splotched sky. "But I can Dream about them when my soul passes from this earth. Until then, I will live the Dream of First Man."

He glanced out over the Father Water one more time, casting his handful of sand into the current. The rings widened and vanished in the swirls and eddies of living green water.

This night in the lodge, he would tell the young ones about the Dreamer who came from the Sun People. He would tell them about Bad Belly, the crippled hero of the Earth People. He would tell them of Bad Belly's new name, Still Water, and of White Ash's Dream, as the Trader had told him. "Opposites crossed," he mumbled to himself and held the black wolf up to the sun, watching the way the light played on the animal's stone body.

Wind whispered in the trees. Water lapped softly at the sandy bank. And a strange thing happened: Those sounds seemed to weave into a voice—an old woman's voice. Straining, he could barely make out the words.

Father of Waters, flows so rich, trickles water into the ditch.
   Grow a plant, so tall so green, fruit is yellow.
I have seen.
   Feathers colored, the dead are laid.

Logs across and dirt is made.
Lazy sloth, in baskets carried—sun man and woman high are married.

Left Hand shook his head. "Now I'm hearing things. Getting old."

He *humphed* under his breath and clutched the black wolf against his breast. *The Power of the Trade is complete, Still Water. But what is the journey this time? A thing of men . . . or of Dreams? And where will it end?*

He turned around then and followed the trail back to the bark-covered lodges of the Wolf People's camp.

BIBLIOGRAPHY

Armitage, C.L., J.C. Newberry-Creasman, J.C. Mackey, C.M. Love, D. Heffington, K. Harvey, J.E. Sail, K. Dueholm, and S.D. Creasman, 1982, "The Deadman Wash Site," Cultural Resource ManagementPlan No. 6. Archaeological Services of Western WyomingCollege, Rock Springs, Wyoming.

Benedict, James B. and Byron L. Olson, 1978, *The Mount Albion Complex: A Study of Man in the Altithermal*. Center for Mountain Archaeology, Ward, Colorado.

Berrigan, Diane,1988, "A Cultural Resource Management Plan for the Bairoil Archaeological District." On File with Bureau of Land Management, Rawlins, Wyoming.

Black, Kevin D., 1991, "Archaic Community in the Colorado Rockies: The Mountain Tradition" *Plains Anthropologist*, 133(36): pp.1-29.

Clark, T.W., and M.R. Stromberg, 1987, *Mammals In Wyoming*. University Press of Kansas, Lawrence, Kansas.

Creasman, Steven D., 1984, "Temporal and Cultural Relationships of the Deadman Wash Projectile Points." In the 1983 *End of the Year Report* by S.D. Creasman, J.A. Head, T. Hoefer III, and A.D. Gardner, pp. 2-22. Archaeological Services of Western Wyoming College, Rock Springs, Wyoming.

Eakin, D.H., 1987, *Final Report of Salvage Investigations at the Split Rock Ranch Site (48FR1484). Highway Project SCPF-020-2(19), Fremont County, Wyoming*. Report Submitted to Wyoming Highway Department. Office of the Wyoming State Archaeologist, Wyoming Recreation Commission, Laramie, Wyoming.

Eddy, J.A., 1974, "Astronomical Alignment of the Big Horn Medicine Wheel" Science 184:135-1043.

Frison, George C., 1976, "The Chronology of Paleo-Indian and Altithermal Cultures in the Big Horn Basin" in *Cultural Change and Continuity*. Ed. by Charles E, Cleland. Academic Press, New York.

1981, "Linear Arrangements of Cairns in Wyoming and Montana." In *Megaliths to Medicine Wheels: Boulder Structures in Archaeology*, edited by Michael Wilson, Kathy L. Road, and Kenneth J. Hardy. *Proceedings of the Eleventh Chacmool Conference*, Department of Anthropology, University of Calgary, Alberta, Canada. Pp. 133-147.

1991 *Prehistoric Hunters of the High Plains* Second Edition, Academic Press, New York.

Frison, George C. and R.L. Andrews, J.M. Adavasio, R.C. Carlisle, and Robert Edgar, 1986, "A Late Paleo-Indian Animal Trapping Net from Northern Wyoming" *American Antiquity* 51(2):352-361.

Galvan, Mary Elizabeth, 1976, *The Vegetative Ecology of the Medicine Lodge Creek Site: An Approach to Archaic Subsistence Problems*. Unpublished Master's Thesis, Department of Anthropology, University of Wyoming, Laramie.

Gear, W. Michael and James C. Miller, 1984, *Mitigation of Adverse Effects to 48SW1242 on the Pacific Power and Light 34.5Kv Construction Powerline*. Pronghorn Anthropological Associates.Manuscript on file Wyoming Bureau of Land Management, Rock Springs, Wyoming.

Harrell, Lynn L. and Scott T. McKern, 1986, *The Maxon Ranch Site: Archaic and Late Prehistoric Habitation in Southwest Wyoming*. Cultural Resource Management Report No. 18. Archaeological Services of Western Wyoming, Rock Springs, Wyoming.

McCracken, Harold, 1978, (Editor) *The Mummy Cave Project in Northwestern Wyoming*. The Buffalo Bill Historical Center, Cody, Wyoming.

McGuire, Dave J, Kathy L. Joyner, Ron E. Kainer, and Mark E. Miller, 1984, *Final Report of Archaeological Excavations at the Medicine Bow Archaeological District in the Hanna Basin, South-Central Wyoming*. Mariah Associates, Inc., Laramie, Wyoming.

McKern, Scott T., 1987, *The Crooks Site: Salvage Excavations of an Archaic Housepit Site*. Cultural Resource Management Report No. 36. Archaeological Services of Western WyomingCollege, Rock Springs, Wyoming.

Metcalf, Michael D. and Kevin D. Black, 1991, *Archaeological Excavations at the Yarmony Pit House Site, Eagle County, Colorado*. Cultural Resources Series No. 31. Colorado Bureau of Land Management.

Smith, C.S. and T.P. Reust, 1992, "Sinclair Site: Use of Space at an Early Archaic Period Housepit, South Central Wyoming" *North American Anthropologist* 13(1):43-66.